SHINING THREADS

When beautiful Tessa Harrison and her twin cousins take over the lucrative Lancashire mill from their parents, they are plunged into responsibilities for which their luxurious upbringing has ill-prepared them. For Tessa, there is an added but forbidden attraction at the mill. The foreman, Will Broadbent, with his genuine understanding of the business and its workers could not be more different from the dashing cousins. Yet, like the twins, he is hopelessly in love with this untameable girl. Their love for Tessa will lead one to death, one to the arms of another women, a third too faint-hearted to take up his rightful inheritance. And Tessa, the girl who could choose any man she wanted, is forced into more commitments than she could have imagined, before she can be united with the one man she truly needs.

SHINING THREADS

Audrey Howard

CHIVERS PRESS
BATH

First published 1990
by
Hodder and Stoughton
This Large Print edition published by
Chivers Press
by arrangement with
Hodder and Stoughton
1999

ISBN 0 7540 1325 1

British Library Cataloguing in Publication Data available

Printed and bound in Great Britain by
REDWOOD BOOKS, Trowbridge, Wiltshire

Again,
for Howard and Janet,
with my love.

CHAPTER ONE

She was like a young queen in her hauteur. The warm honey of her skin, the pale, cat-like grey of her eyes, the sweeping burnished darkness of her hair which flowed unconfined down the length of her straight back promised a stunning beauty to come. She had on a white cambric shirt, frilled down its front, with full sleeves which were caught in a narrow band at the wrist, and, amazingly, pale buff riding breeches of the finest doeskin. Her knee-high boots were brown and of the very best leather, polished until they gleamed, and she wore brown kid gloves and carried a riding crop.

Had it not been for her hair and the knot of scarlet ribbon with which it was carelessly tied back she might have been taken for a boy. She sat astride her small chestnut mare with the regal grace which spoke of generations of majesty, of the divine right to rule stretching back into eternity, and yet her grandfather had been no more than a humble handloom weaver.

Her two companions were as attractive as she, with the same magnificent seat in the saddle. Dark as gypsies with eyes as blue as a cornflower with a touch of violet in them, they possessed the wide, laughing mouth which was so eternally female in her, but which in them was firmed into masculine arrogance. Their hair was thick and curling, tumbling in boyish disorder above fiercely swooping black brows. They were dressed just as she was but where her breeches were buff theirs were dove grey, clinging to their strong young

1

thighs and buttocks.

It was a bright and pretty day. The sky was a high, placid blue and the sun fell in a brimming haze on the three young riders. They were laughing. Their heads were thrown back, their brown throats arched and smooth and the noise they made disturbed a scatter of magpies. The birds scuttled about a stretch of tussocky grass for a moment before lifting above the bracken and into the air, drifting away on almost motionless wings.

The slight breeze was warm and soaked in the fragrance of heather and gorse. It moved the shadows cast along the track by the shoulder-high bracken and rippled through the hair of the riders. A curlew took flight in alarm, its liquid, bubbling song rising into the clear air, and the high-stepping, mettlesome mounts rolled their eyes and tossed their fine heads. Around their feet quarrelled a pack of dogs, tall and black with brown markings and no tail to speak of, glossy and well muscled and as healthy and vigorous as the youngsters and the horses they rode.

'Do you think my mother believed you?' the girl said. Her voice still quivered with laughter as she spoke. She lifted her gloved hand to push back the heavy weight of hair from her forehead, an impatient gesture implying she would dearly love to be free of it, as she was free at this precise moment of every other female constraint which hampered girls of her age and obvious station in life.

'Lord, I don't know, but what could she do about it? It's not the first time we've made that excuse to Aunt Jenny but short of sending a message to old Wilding to check that he had actually summoned us to the schoolroom she was forced to accept our

2

story. Anyway, what does it matter? We're out now and it will be worth the flogging we're bound to get from Charlie when they discover where we've been. And we did ride into the schoolyard and out again so we're not lying when we say we've been there, are we?' The boy who spoke grinned impishly. 'And, by God, I would submit to half a dozen beatings to get away from that damned mill for an hour. We'll be there soon enough one day, I suppose, when we have done with lessons. But now we are on holiday and I fail to see why we should be forced into the weaving shed, don't you agree, brother?'

He turned to laugh in the direction of the second boy and he might have been looking at his own reflection in a mirror: the same arrow-straight back and broadening young shoulders, the same eyes and smiling mouth, firm white teeth and tenacious jaw, the same look of sleek and graceful high spirits, and it was plain there was no more than a minute or two between them in age.

'But what did she say?' the girl demanded to know.

'Oh, the usual stuff. She could quite believe our school-master was not satisfied with our performance as scholars and that we needed to do extra schoolwork to help keep up with the rest but that in her opinion we were wasting our time and his.'

Drew Greenwood grinned broadly and his boyish face glowed. 'Aunt Jenny's not taken in by us, you know. She realises that if we can manage it we'll not go into the mill with her and Charlie. She understands too, whereas our mother doesn't. Mother believes that anyone with the blood of

3

Chapmans and Greenwoods in their veins could not fail to be intoxicated with the idea of being a millmaster, as she was, but Aunt Jenny's a good sort and she'll not press us yet.'

The girl sighed. 'I wish she was the same with me. I had to slip out of the side door while Laurel's back was turned. Then Walter refused to saddle my mare saying he'd been given orders not to and that if I showed my face in the stables he was to send for Miss Copeland at once.'

Tessa Harrison's face was indignant. Her clear skin flamed to poppy at her cheekbones, the reminder of the stable boy's outrageous behaviour so incensing her she moved her mare to a faster gait as though to escape it.

'What did you do?'

'I had to saddle her myself.'

'Did Walter try to stop you?'

She turned to grin lazily, lifting an amused eyebrow.

'Oh, come now, Drew Greenwood, would he dare lay a hand on *me*?'

'No, I don't suppose he would. Silly question, really.'

The three young riders had reached the summit of Badger's Edge where, it was said, a 'badger' or travelling salesman had fallen to his death in a snowstorm many years ago. With fluid grace both boys sprang from their saddles and with a word to their horses, two tall bays with impeccable bloodlines, to stand, they sauntered across the uneven spiky grass to stare, shoulder to shoulder, over the sprawling town which lay far below in the valley. The girl dismounted more slowly, speaking softly to her mare, rubbing its nose affectionately

4

with a strong, slender hand before moving to join the others.

All three were tall. The girl was a bare six inches shorter than her companions who were exactly the same in height and size and colouring and so compellingly identical it was impossible to tell them apart. Pearce and Drew Greenwood then, twin sons of Joss and Katherine Greenwood, and beside them their cousin, Tessa Harrison, only daughter of Jenny Harrison, their father's sister, and all three of them would inherit a share in the fortune, the great estate, the mills, the railway stock and every other asset which made up the wealth of one of the most influential and affluent families in south Lancashire. Endowed from birth with not only the shining good looks of the superior beings they so obviously thought themselves to be, they possessed too the glorious belief that they were unique in their world, and in every other come to that, and had the financial provision which made other, lesser mortals reluctant to disagree.

'They should have let us go away to public school at Arnmoor with Nicky Longworth and Johnny Taylor instead of to that damned grammar school in Crossfold.' Pearce said moodily, flicking his riding crop against his leg. 'We might have been taught something other than two and two makes four and how much profit a successful manufacturer may realise before breakfast, which, as far as I can make out, must be at least double what *other* manufacturers are capable of. Mother can't see it, of course, nor Father, as we are to spend our lives in the mills, they say. What use would the education the *Squire's* son receives be to us, she asks, for we are to be industrialists and not landed gentry as Nick is. Our grandfather and *his* father before him did not slave to make money merely for Drew and I to spend. I nearly said "why not?" I'll tell you this, if we *are* to be cotton manufacturers as she says, I'll not do it without a fight.'

Pearce Greenwood shaded his eyes from the sun, looking towards the west and the thick pall of smoke which lay like a sour blanket over the town below. A great sweep of wildly rolling moorland stretched between, rough and uneven, patched with wide folds of growing bracken, gorse and heather which, in a few weeks' time, would be thick and verdant with colour, yellow, green and purple, as summer reached towards its peak.

Tessa stood between the two boys, all three with their backs against a grey-veined rock. A skylark sang high above them and they turned to stare upwards into the great vault of the blue sky until their sharp eyes detected the black speck which was the bird. She sighed gustily then lowered her gaze to scan the familiar landscape which lay at her feet and stretched as far as the eye could see on either side of her and high at her back where the south Pennine heights rose up and away towards Yorkshire. She had roamed these hills with her cousins ever since she had been able to sit a horse, trailing far behind them at first since she was younger and had not the strength nor expertise to keep up. But it had not taken her long to be as swift and as skilful as they in guiding her mount across streams with dangerously unstable wooden footbridges, following narrow lanes winding in long curves up steep slopes and on into the misty distances of the packhorse routes which had once

6

carried goods to outlying hamlets and isolated farmhouses. She learned to go over stony paths which led nowhere but to huge outcroppings of rock, stretches of moorland which were steep and identical to a dozen others and in which a man could lose himself for days, or forever! It was damp for the most part, with grey-topped hills reaching into the clouds, peopled by none but the starving, itinerant families who moved from town to town looking for work, or mischief, and often not caring which they found, ruffians some of them who would knock a man senseless on the chance of a farthing.

'What *will* you do then?' she questioned her cousins. Her eyes were half-closed against the brightness of the sun. 'Aunt Kit has set her heart on at least one of you going into the mill. She doesn't much care which as long as there is someone to carry on the dynasty as she did.'

'Like hell she did! She got married and passed it over most conveniently to your mother and Charlie and followed Father up to Westminster as fast as the coach would take her. She doesn't really give a damn about any of the mills as long as there is enough money to support him as a politician. I can scarcely believe the stories we are told about her when she was a girl. Obsessed with the mills and as determined to do with them as a son would, they say. Learning to be a manufacturer just as though she was a man, and making more of a success of it than any other millmaster in the valley, we're told. Can you imagine anyone, man or woman, being consumed with the tedious task of spinning and weaving cotton when one could be far more enjoyably employed elsewhere? And yet Mother

7

did it until she was twenty-five or six and married father. Can you believe it?'

Tessa found she couldn't, really. Joss and Katherine Greenwood were notorious in the Penfold Valley for their absolute devotion to one another, to the exclusion of everyone, even their own sons. Some would have it that there had never been a more mis-matched pair: Joss Greenwood, a radical, a revolutionary in his younger days, it was rumoured, much concerned with strikes and machine breaking; and Kit Chapman the daughter of the very mill-owner whose machines he had wrecked.

Pearce Greenwood lowered himself to sprawl on the springing turf, his back resting against the grey-pitted rock and the other two did the same, stretching out their legs and crossing them at the ankle.

From behind them there was a sudden snapping of dogs quarrelling amongst themselves. They were only half-trained and excitable, curiously like their young owners, ready enough, it seemed, to be amiable providing no one interfered with them but with a snarl of temper just beneath the surface. They lay down, lowering their splendid heads until their muzzles rested on their paws, but their eyes were never still as they kept watch against anything they might not greatly approve.

They all lounged indolently in the early summer sunshine: healthy, thoughtless young animals, sleek, graceful, high-spirited, dangerous when crossed, with very little difference, it seemed, between the well-bred horses, the magnificent dogs and the handsome young people. They were arrogant in their complete belief in themselves and their place in life, which was privileged and secure. They were defiant of fetters which might attempt to bind them to a life which was safe and tedious. They cared only for freedom, the freedom to go where they pleased, to do as they pleased, a desire which was, as yet, sufficiently met up here on the high moorland.

They did not speak for several minutes. Drew held his face up to the sun, his eyes closed and the luxuriously thick fan of his eyelashes forming a shadow on his brown cheek. Pearce chewed a blade of grass as he gazed reflectively at the slender ribbon of the river which could just be made out through the thickening foliage of the trees in the valley bottom. The dogs moved restlessly: one stood and lifted its leg against a rock, while the others sauntered across to sniff where he had left his mark, then lay down again waiting for the signal which would herald the wild race across the tops in which all such days ended. Minutes passed and still nothing was said. They all dozed in the soft spring sunshine, the dogs' eyes opening and closing in that half-sleep into which animals fall, the youngsters graceful and lounging, even the horses, heads drooping, seeming to nap a little in the peaceful warmth.

'I wonder if the millhands are to have a day off next week when the branch line from Oldham to Crossfold is opened?' Pearce's voice was lazy, quite unconcerned, really: *he* was to see the celebrations so what did it matter if the lower orders did not? In fact he, his father and brother were to ride on the railway train from Crossfold to Oldham and even on to Rochdale, if they had the fancy for it, since Joss Greenwood, as Member of Parliament for

9

Crossfold and a man of substance in Lancashire, was to be one of its most important guests on the occasion of the opening. There was to be champagne, Pearce had been told, bunting and bands playing, the train filled with the town's leading industrialists, those who were to make even *more* profit with this marvellously rapid method of speeding their cloth and their piece goods to the Exchange in Manchester. It was 1853 and the age of 'railway mania', it was called. Each week new railroad schemes were announced in the Press. So far there had been 357 of them, inviting subscriptions from 332 million pounds' worth of stock. Many of them were entirely bona fide, and astute men of business such as the Greenwoods had made themselves even wealthier: but some who had invested in companies which had been floated merely for the purpose of extracting money from the gullible, had subsequently gone under in their eventual collapse.

But none of this concerned the Greenwood sons. What was it to do with them, they asked each other, since they cared nought for the slightly distasteful business of making money?

'Why should they?' Drew grunted, settling his back more comfortably against the rough rock. 'They can't afford the price of a railway ticket so what difference will it ever make to them?'

'Oh, I don't know. They are saying there will be track laid all over Lancashire and even over the Pennines into Yorkshire. Many believe that railway travel will become cheaper and that eventually everyone, even the poorer classes will be in on it.'

Both boys sat up and their young faces glowed with interest. They had been to London once, by

10

coach on the rutted, bone-shaking turnpike roads. Though the onset of the journey had been of great excitement to them as young boys, twenty-four hours later it had become so tedious to their restless minds and bodies they had decided it was of no interest, nor the several days they had spent in their father's company being shown the 'sights' of London. Give them the open moorland, the excitement of being part of a walking line of guns every autumn, shooting the grouse, the pheasant, the young birds hand-reared expressly for the purpose of a gentleman's sport. The thrill of Squire Longworth's hunt was what they enjoyed, leaping hedges and ditches, wild gallops across open fields, the fox no more than a breath away, the hounds giving voice on a frost-bitten winter's morning. They wished to be gentlemen, in the company of other gentlemen, following the fine and gentlemanly pursuits their pedigreed friends followed.

But the railway train! Would that not make a difference? The idea of moving at great speed, to Liverpool where no doubt there would be fascinations dear to the hearts of the young men they almost were; to Manchester, now that Oldham and Crossfold were *connected*, and whatever heady temptations lay there, and even, as the men of steam predicted, through the tunnel they were to dig beneath the Pennine chain and on to the 'other side' where God alone knew what delights might await them.

'It might be worth seeing, brother, what d'you think? When Father said we were to go I was not particularly concerned but it might be fun, you know. We've never been to Rochdale.'

'Yes, we have. We went with Mother once to see some dreary Chapman relative, don't you remember?'

'No, I can't say I do.'

'Of course you do. My God, Pearce, your memory is as bad as some old woman's.'

'And who are you calling an old woman?'

'If the cap fits . . .'

'Would you like to stand up and say that?'

'With the greatest of pleasure. A bloody nose would look well on you next Wednesday.'

'And a black eye for you, brother.'

The quick, snarling Greenwood anger slipped its leash and lifted both boys to their feet, their eyes flinty blue, their black brows dipping furiously as they clenched strong brown hands into fists, ready, each one, should it be needed to kill the other to prove himself right. But Tessa sprang up, stepping between them as she had done a hundred times—when it suited her—before a blow was struck.

'And what about me?' she snapped. 'Why can't I go with you on the train? Who declared it should be you two and not me? I'm just as interested in the railway train *and* in travel and would dearly love to go to Rochdale. Miss Copeland told me it is situated in the most beautiful valley and that the manor of Rochdale was once owned by Lord Byron.'

Both boys looked confused, not perfectly certain who Lord Byron was though they had an idea he might be some sort of literary person and as such surely of no interest to their cousin who held books in as much contempt as they did. But she was merely clouding the issue and well she knew it.

'You can't be serious.' Pearce lowered his fists as

12

Drew did.

'Why not? Why can't I go if you can?'

'There are to be no ladies included, that's why.'

'And why not?' Her eyes snapped furiously.

Drew shrugged. 'I suppose because the gentlemen imagine they will not be interested.'

'Mother is, and Aunt Kit and they haven't been invited either, have they? Oh, they can go and stand on the platform and watch the gentlemen have all the fun but they are not to ride on the train. It simply isn't fair,' Tessa declared as she did at least once a day. 'They are both concerned in the business world, just as Mr Abbott and Mr Jenkinson are, so why shouldn't they go? Tell me that.'

Drew scratched his head wonderingly then looked at his brother for really they had given it no thought. Indeed, they had given little thought to their *own* inclusion in the great event. Their father would no doubt officiate at the splendid moment when the engine had got up steam and was ready to head off on its journey. They themselves would certainly share in the excitement, watched and admired by the ladies who would come to see them off, but, as usual, this cousin of theirs was not satisfied with her own *female* part in it.

She had begun to whirl about in her indignation and the dogs milled at her feet, moving excitedly as her fierceness communicated itself to them. She turned to face her cousins, hands on her hips, legs apart, chest heaving and her expression was bright and furious. Her eyes snapped, the pale grey velvet shaded, like a stormy sky, to the tints of slate and charcoal, deep and threatening. She could scarcely contain herself, not, as they thought, in her rage, but in fear.

Tessa Harrison by, in her opinion, a fluke of nature, was born a girl and for as long as she could remember, though she defied authority and her own femininity, she had resented it. Whenever she could throw off the reins her governess slipped about her, the bridle which convention and her mother put on her as the gently reared daughter of a wealthy middle-class family, she had escaped from them, riding about with her male cousins and their friends wherever they went. She would put on a pair of their outgrown breeches and riding boots, leap on to the mare's back and gallop away exultantly, as they did, knowing that she would be punished later for it, not caring, for that would be *later* and this freedom and excitement was *now*. But lately, as they had begun to move away from boyhood, she had sensed that her cousins were ready to leave her behind, that her participation was accepted somewhat reluctantly, that they were a trifle *irritated* by her female presence as they went off on their completely masculine jaunts with Nicky Longworth and Johnny Taylor. They wouldn't tell her where they were going sometimes, which was worse, saying carelessly that she was not at all likely to enjoy it, eluding her grasp and her furious demands to know what they were up to, and she had become increasingly alarmed. She had not accepted it, naturally, begging them to wait for her, declaring that she was not going to be left out of it, whatever it was, but they had gone off nevertheless, and she had become even more afraid. She could ride and even shoot as well as they, for they had taught her. She had been given permission by her mother to ride to hounds with the Squire's hunt, for were they not gentry and therefore, in her mother's eyes, responsible and understanding of the need to protect a young, unmarried girl's reputation? But that was not enough for Tessa Harrison. She wanted to go wherever her cousins went, illogical and absurd as that might seem, and she would tell them so. What else was she to do with her life if she could not be with *them*, she asked herself, do as they did, laugh with them over the foolishness of those who were fettered to rules, risk herself in the hazards they were to know? What would her life be without them in it?

'I'm going with you next week. I want to ride on the train just as much as you do and I shall ask Mother and Uncle Joss to let me go. Why should you go and not me? I can do anything you do, cousins. I can ride, yes, *outride* the pair of you and you know it. I could race you both from here to Greenacres and be home five minutes before you. Don't you dare simper at me, Drew Greenwood, or I'll take my crop to you. I could open your cheek to the bone and then that cheeky little dairymaid . . . oh, yes, I've seen you hanging about, both of you, outside the dairy. Well, she won't smile so sweetly at you then, will she? I can do anything *you* do and I don't mean to sit at home next week and sew on my sampler whilst you enjoy yourselves . . .'

'*Sew! A sampler! You!* Now that *would* be a sight worth seeing, don't you agree, brother?' Pearce stretched his growing body, throwing back his head in a shout of laughter.

'I would have to see it before I'd believe it.' They were both laughing now, taunting her, for there was no finer sight than Tessa in a rage. They all had hot tempers, they were the first to agree, especially

15

themselves, snarling, knife-edged tempers which could flare in a minute from mere irritability to a rage from which the servants fled in alarm. Their Aunt Jenny, who had them in her charge whilst their father was at Westminster, refused to become involved with what she called their childish squabbles.

'Let them fight it out between them, preferably in the stable yard,' she would say wearily, eyeing their bloody noses with distaste, her attitude perhaps the result of the accidents, some of them leading to death, and the floggings she herself had witnessed as a young spinner in the mill she now managed. It had not been unknown for an overlooker to break a child's arm with his leather thong, and her nephews' bruises inflicted on one another seemed petty indeed when compared to the suffering, the real suffering which had once prevailed. Her own brother Charlie had taken such a beating when younger than they. It had almost killed him and he bore the scars on his back and face to this day.

'I can do anything I have to, Pearce Greenwood,' Tessa remarked loftily, '*anything*, and that includes sewing a sampler if I put my mind to it, though I must admit I'd rather fight a game-cock.'

'Perhaps, little cousin, but you cannot beat me or Drew in a race to Greenacres. That little mare of yours is game but no match for my bay, or Drew's.'

'Fiddlesticks! I'm not talking about keeping to the tracks, you know. I mean whichever way any of us cares to take and if that frightens you then you have only to say so and we will forget the whole thing.'

'Now hold on, Tess. You cannot mean to gallop

16

across the moorland. It's as rough as hell out there and if one of the animals should put a foot in a rabbit hole or be faced with rocks which . . .'

'Well, of course, if you are not up to it . . .'

'Of course we are, but . . .'

'Then what are we waiting for?'

Pearce shrugged, then turned to grin at Drew who leaned indolently against the rock, his eyes half-shut against the sun, seemingly oblivious to the wrangling between his brother and cousin. He was well used to this throwing down of the gauntlet by one or the other of them—a challenge which must be taken up if the scorn of the others was not to be endured. They loved the friction which set the blood tingling, the dare which must be accepted. Wild as young colts, all three of them, daring and reckless, they gave no thought to danger, to risk, beyond a care for their nervous, high-stepping mounts, to anything which might smack of caution. The brothers, young as they were, defied all comers at school, fighting back to back for the sheer joy of risking their handsome faces, their fine young bodies against boys older and heavier than they, often over nothing more serious than the sorry cut of a fellow's jacket.

'What d'you say, Drew? Will we take her on? I know it's a shame to risk her mare against our bays, but if she's mad enough to do it who are we to deny her?'

The stretch of moorland from Badger's Edge to Greenacres lay to the east of Crossfold and Edgeclough. It was rough terrain and uneven, about three miles mainly downhill and inhabited on the 'tops' only by rabbit and stoat, curlew and magpie and wheatear. It was fit only for small

17

animals and birds but within ten seconds of the signal, which was the dropping of Tessa's scarlet ribbon, they were all three soaring away from the sun which was beginning to lower itself towards the hills on the far side of the Penfold Valley.

Tessa could feel her mare start to take charge and she let her go, trusting her instincts, guiding her only generally in the direction of Greenacres. She could feel the intense excitement vibrate through her own body and she knew she communicated it to her mount for the mare surged on as madly, as blindly as she herself did, not caring what came up before her, not seeing it, only sensing the rapid approach of the scattered rocks, the dips and folds and hollows which must be traversed before she and the mare clattered into the stable yard. At no time did she even consider that she might not get there, nor be the first home.

The mare nearly pulled her arms from their sockets and she flew like a wild bird, a bird knowing it should be alarmed at its own height and speed, and yet unwilling to return to earth and safety. On and on, and at her back she could hear the frenzied yelping of the dogs, the thunder of her cousins' mounts as they dashed over the stretch of grey rock. For a moment, as the mare turned instinctively to avoid an outcrop of tumbled rocks higher than a man's head, the sun was in her eyes and she was blinded but she let the animal take her round the rocks.

They came to a dry-stone wall, then another as they reached the lower ground for it was here that enclosures had made inroads upon the edge of the moors, and the mare rose lightly over each one, her hooves not even clipping the crumbling stones.

18

There was a cottage or two clustered in a hollow, sheltered from the cruel Pennine winds, and women and children stopped to stare in amazement, then shook their heads and turned away since it was only the wild Greenwoods trying to kill themselves as usual.

Drew and Pearce raced a scant yard behind her, watching her back with fond pride for, really, was there another girl like her in the whole world? Her hair streamed out three feet behind her, a banner of dark, burnished chestnut in the late afternoon sunshine. They were so close they could see the sweat stain the back of her shirt and hear her breath, ragged and urgent in her throat. She was fearless, leaping shoulder-high rocks and wide, quite appalling chasms cut in the rough ground in her determination to be first home. She did not even look back so convinced was she that they had been forced to drop behind, unable to keep up with her.

'Shall we let her do it, brother?' Pearce shouted, for really she deserved to win, but she heard him and her outrage exploded in her, flowing madly to every part of her body. With a fierce shout she urged her mount on until the animal's legs were no more than a dark blur against the grey and green of the moorland. The smell of gorse was everywhere and she thought she had never been happier in her life. The wind created by her own speed and momentum slashed at her face and plastered her shirt against her chest. She could feel the animal beneath her strain harder and harder. She could sense the heartbeat, like a rapid tattoo on a drum matching her own, and she threw back her head in joy, catching for a moment a glimpse of the tiny

19

speck in the sky which was the skylark wheeling in perfect grace above her. It was free, as she would be free, always. It flew high and wide allowing no man's hand to capture it, filling its days with no employment other than the ecstasy of living, being, breathing, its existence tied to nothing other than the next moment, and she would do the same.

She could hear the explosion of hoofbeats at her back and the sound of Drew's voice, breathless and frantic as he realised that she might win, not by his allowing it but by her own efforts, and a great shout of triumph erupted from between her lips. She could see the chimneys of Greenacres ahead of her among the magnificent trees which clustered about the house. Then she was in them, galloping, moving as precisely as the bird in the sky as she guided her mare expertly between their enormous trunks. For a moment she had been sightless, coming from the brilliance of sunlight into the dim and dappled softness of the trees, then she was through and beyond them was the gate into the stable yard at the back of the house. Walter, the stable lad, had heard her shout and was running across the yard to open the gate but she could see he would not get there before she did. Not for a second did she hesitate. Up she went, she and her mare, up and up, high as a man's head. She was over with no more than an inch to spare, landing on the other side as lightly as drifting thistledown. There was the smell of steaming horseflesh and the sound of the animal's laboured breathing, the ring of its hooves on the cobbles, and for a timeless moment she was alone in the magic world she and the mare had just shared. Then they were there, Drew and Pearce, crashing about the yard, their faces red and sweating, their eyes admiring, bestowing on her the accolade of acknowledging she was as good a horseman as any they knew, including themselves.

Walter hovered on the fringe of the mêlée caused by the three overstrung horses, joined by Thomas and Jack, ready to lead the animals away when they were told. On the faces of all three grooms was an expression of resigned acceptance which said quite clearly they were of the opinion that none of the young people would make old bones! They strode off laughing, arm in arm, and though Drew and Pearce were taller than she was, and six months older, they looked considerably younger. They were boyish, their faces almost formed in that curious way of males who are not quite men. Tessa, on the other hand, though only sixteen, was completely a woman, even if her appearance at the moment belied it.

*   *   *

Charlie Greenwood glanced about the dinner table at his family. They were all there this evening. His brother Joss, down from Westminster, splendidly handsome in his evening black and white, his hair still thick and curling about his head but where it had once been dark as a gypsy's, now it was threaded generously with white. Commanding of eye and well used to moving amongst all classes of men from the operatives in the mill to the Prime Minister, the great Lord Aberdeen himself, Joss was as usual no more than an arm's length from his serenely smiling wife, Katherine, their hands, or so it appeared to Charlie, to be forever hovering, each ready, should it be needed, to give loving support

21

to the other. Their devotion had once been the talk of the Penfold Valley; anyone in their company was immediately conscious of their apparent inability to be more than a yard or two apart and of the secret and sometimes disconcerting smiles they constantly exchanged, but now, after twenty years of a marriage which most had said would not last, their passion for one another was unabated.

Kit Greenwood turned to her husband, her own glossy hair slipping from the intricate chignon her maid had devised, as it had done for as long as Charlie could remember, and his brother put out a tender hand to tuck the straying tendril behind her ear. Her eyes, the same violet-blue as her two sons', softened as they looked at Joss, as they did for no one else, and her silken gown, simple, stylish and extremely expensive, Charlie knew, matched their colour exactly. She had amethysts in her ears and at her throat and looked ten years younger than her actual age which Charlie knew to be forty-eight. Indeed, her own daughter, Laurel, who was Charlie's wife and in her twenty-ninth year, they calculated, looked scarcely younger. Of course, she was still grieving the loss of their fifth child and could not be expected to be as sleek and glowing as her mother, who was not really her mother for Laurel had been adopted, as had his own sister, Jenny, as a child of four or five.

Poor Laurel, though a stranger looking at Laurel Greenwood would be hard pressed to understand why Charlie should think that about his wife. She wore a gown which was fashionable and obviously expensive. There were pearls at her throat and in her ears, lustrous and costly, and in the room about her were the luxurious trappings bought by the wealth of which she was a part. But she was a part only by adoption, which was where the trouble lay. Until she was five years old or thereabouts she had laboured in the Chapman mills, abused and starved, and indelibly printed in her mind was the memory of those years though she did not consciously recognise it. She had longed all her life, from the day she had been old enough to shape the thought, to be as *they* were, to be *them*, if you like. She yearned to be as carelessly confident of the security which was theirs as were her brothers and cousin, to have a *proper* place in the order of things, not by gift but by *right*. She felt she had not and it had eaten into her so that she was tense and insecure, afflicted with the deadly and completely irrational fear of a return to the terror she had known as a child. It made her sour, envious and uncomfortable to live with. Charlie loved her, made allowances for her and wished his niece and nephews could do the same.

What a labyrinth of relationships his family was, Charlie thought, as he watched his sister, who was not really his sister, lean forward into the candlelight, emphasising a point she was making with the flat of her hand on the polished table-top. Joss and himself were true brothers, but Jenny was a foundling and, like her daughter Tessa, whom he and Joss called niece, and Laurel, his wife, was no blood relation at all.

But Drew and Pearce Greenwood were. They were true Greenwoods for all to see. Not quite seventeen years old and from the moment they were born they had been thorns in the flesh of everyone—as they had been today, he had been told—from the lowest scullery maid who had the

23

continual scrubbing of the muddy tracks they made wherever they marched their imperious boots, to their own father who was as determined to make businessmen of them as they were to avoid it. Lusty, brawling babies they had been, terrifying their nursery maids with their devilment from the moment they had been able to get up on their sturdy, well-fed legs and strut like young lordlings doing whatever *they* wanted to do. Laurel had been eleven or so at the time, a quiet child as he remembered, made that way by her beginnings in life, at peace in the schoolroom with Miss Copeland and in the nursery with Flora who had once been her nurse. It had been as though a whirlwind had descended, since Tessa Harrison was born only a scant six months behind them. New nursery maids and a full-time nanny had been engaged to order them about, and Flora too, who had not cared for it after seven years with the placid Laurel, nor for the constant demands, arrogant and made with the utter certainty that they would be immediately attended to, of one wilful girl child and two rowdy boys who were as alike as two leaves on a branch. The noise and complete devastation had driven Laurel and Miss Copeland to shut themselves up, to *lock* themselves up in the schoolroom, but even there, a year or two later, her brothers and cousin were knocking on the door demanding to be let in, saying this was *their* schoolroom, *their* house, *their* pencil and ruler and book. What a trial they had been, the three of them, and still were to her, Charlie knew, as she did her best to run the household with the same precision he and Jenny ran the business.

His sister, Jenny Harrison, was a widow now

24

though to look at her one would not have thought so. Years ago when she was a spinner she had cut her hair short and it still swirled in loose curls about her head, dark and glossy and springing. A brazen girl, it had been said of her, who cared nought for convention, which perhaps explained her carelessness with her own daughter's upbringing. She had ignored the observance of the standards of her own class, flaunting her beliefs that all men were equal in the radical cause.

Charlie believed that the only reason Jenny married the man she did was that he was as weak as she was strong. Joseph Harrison was not a man who had it in him to command his wife to stay at home where she belonged, to mind his hearth and the girl child he gave her, and it was precisely this quality in him which made Jenny choose him. The son of a weaver the same age as herself, he was the shadow who followed her footsteps wherever they led but without the spirit to challenge her will, let alone the congestion in his chest which carried him to his death. It was as though he had never existed, Charlie considered, if it were not for the vital daughter he left behind and who was cast, thankfully, in her mother's image.

Tessa Harrison. She wore the simple white tulle which was considered suitable for a young unmarried lady, chosen for her by Laurel, no doubt, since Tessa herself showed no concern for the gowns and ribbons, the embroidered fans and shawls, the frilled parasols and flowered bonnets which were considered to be the sole interest of young ladies. She was heiress to her mother's fortune, made in service to the mills, a girl who, when it suited her, could be as docile as a kitten, as

25

sweet as a gillyflower, but who, as everyone from the maidservants to Joss Greenwood himself knew, had the wildest temper, the most self-willed and obstinate disposition of any of them. The trouble was, of course, that her own mother was seldom at home and whilst she was absent, Miss Tessa Harrison, determined to follow the path along which her male cousins walked or ran shouting with high-spirited laughter, simply ran with them.

The house in which they all lived was named Greenacres for obvious reasons. It stood in a splendid twenty acres of land some miles north-east of Oldham. When it was built almost eighty years ago by Kit Greenwood's grandfather it had been surrounded by woodlands and, at its back, the magnificent hills of the South Pennine chain. Since then the industrial factories and chimney stacks, the dwellings built to house the millworkers had fanned out from the centre of Crossfold which had then been nothing but a cottage or two, a church, a forge and an ale house, until they reached almost to the high stone wall which surrounded the Greenwood estate.

Greenacres was built of stone, mellowed now to a soft shade of silvered grey. The windows at ground level rose from floor to ceiling allowing in the luminous northern light. Some were flat to the wall, others had deep bays, the rooms they illuminated richly panelled and high. The roof was steeply sloped with two dozen tall chimneys and on the south-facing wall was a conservatory, burgeoning from glass wall to glass wall with gardenias, orchids, magnolias, camellias, all mixed with cascades of trailing ivy and tall ferns. There were hanging baskets of verbena, fragrant all year

26

round, singing birds in cages and wicker chairs stuffed with fat cushions in which to sit and enjoy it all.

The house was square and solid, with a look of permanence and steadfast reliability, but though it lacked the elegant lines of houses built in Georgian and Regency times, it had a pleasing symmetry overall. James Chapman had liked what he called a bit of 'style' about him and had commissioned delicate rosewood for his hallway and staircase, soft, glowing. Yet in comparison the fireplace was enormous, burning great logs on most days of the year for he also liked warmth and comfort. The drawing-room had not been changed since the day he and his son, Barker, had filled it with comfortable velvet sofas and chairs, rich, deep carpets of Axminster, oil paintings and water colours, porcelain of Sèvres and Meissen, Wedgwood and Spode, Chinese screens and grandfather clocks in lacquerwork cases. There was silk damask upon the walls and crystal chandeliers, and in every room in the house lovely furniture by Chippendale, Sheraton and Hepplewhite. There was a dining-room, a morning room, a 'back' parlour, a study and a library containing thousands of books. The bedrooms were large, airy, most warmed by fires in winter and summer for the northern climate was not known for its hospitality. On the first floor there was a gallery which ran round three sides of the house, filled with paintings of lovely women, handsome men and splendid horses, with sofas and armchairs, and flowers everywhere. Beyond it and entered from one end, seldom used now, was a 'large salon', furnished with spindle-legged chairs in blue velvet, inlaid rosewood tables and screens of delicate Chinese lacquer, all of which could be moved out so that the room could be used for a concert or a dance.

The house was set in what had once been nothing but woodland. Removing only enough trees to clear a space for it, and an acre or two of undulating lawn, the oak, the ash, sycamore, pine and yew stood all about the grounds, and flower beds, planted with dahlia, chrysanthemum, rose and fuchsia, glowed like jewels amongst them. Rhododendron and hydrangea grew, not formally but arranged to harmonise with the splendid backdrop of the hills and moorland. There was a driveway lined with plane trees, winding from the gateway to the entrance porch and then round the back of the house to the extensive yard and stables. There was a small lake on which swans glided and crocus, hyacinth, snowdrop and wild daffodils clustered thickly about it and starred the lawns in spring, and a heath garden lay at the base of the walls of the house. It had a quiet and informal beauty, which, at the back of the house, spread out into paddocks filled with splendid thoroughbreds, an orchard or two, vegetable gardens, until it reached the high wall which enclosed it.

'Well, I'm for a stroll round the garden,' Charlie declared suddenly. 'It's a lovely night and I reckon a bit of fresh air would be very welcome before we turn in. Will you take my arm, my love?' he said to his wife.

Instantly, like three lamps which have just had their wicks turned up, Drew, Pearce and Tessa came alive, and when Charlie and Laurel walked down the worn stone steps of the terrace and on to the dewed grass, his niece and nephews were already running like wild colts down the slope of the lawn, Tessa with her skirts bunched up high above her knees.

CHAPTER TWO

Charlie Greenwood walked between the rows of well-spaced machines which filled the enormous room, stopping every now and then to speak to a spinner or to watch the smooth movement of the spindles on the mules. Kit Chapman had installed 'self-actors' almost twenty-five years ago, the mechanised spinning frame replacing the old manual machine where the spinner had to move the carriage by turning a driving wheel. It had been a heavy and exhausting task, usually done by a man. Now the operative, without touching the fly, just turned a guide, a movement needing no more than the lightest pressure which instantly set in motion the spindles and took in the heavy carriage. It was so easy and light to use that a woman with the help of one 'piecer' could manage not one machine, but two.

It was twenty years since the first effective Factory Act had come into force, with an Inspectorate which was legally empowered to enter any factory it so desired. Children under the age of nine were not to be employed, it stated, and those under the age of thirteen were to be at their machines for no more than twelve hours a day. Of course, these same children and young people had no way of proving their age, should they have wanted to, since the compulsory registration of

29

births was not enforced until 1837. It was doubtful their own mothers, who bore a child regularly every year, knew the exact age of each of her offspring, having neither the strength nor inclination to be concerned. The employers had one yardstick: if the children were the right *size* they were considered fit to be employed in the mill, and one did not ask for sight of a birth certificate.

The Act also declared that regular meal-times were required for the children who worked at their mules and looms and provision must be made for two hours' schooling each day but when a 'hand', which is all they were to unscrupulous millowners, was at its desk and not 'minding' its machine, little profit is made, and besides, what does a man who is to spin or weave for the rest of his days want with reading and writing?

Of course, Charlie Greenwood's sister-in-law had attended to all these matters twenty years ago at the Chapman Spinning and Weaving Concerns, her new mill at Chapmanstown, and, as far as possible, at her four older mills which her grandfather had built in Crossfold. She had begun her enlightened, some said lunatic improvements in the conditions of her operatives' lives with the renovation of her factories and the building of new houses on the land she purchased on the outskirts of the town. They were sturdy little dwellings with a parlour and a scullery, two or three bedrooms, a bit of yard at the back and a privy for each family. There was piped water from the clean, fast-flowing river and allotments, one to each man, so that he might grow his own vegetables. A church, an ale house, a school, a library were also built and a Mechanics Institute where sturdy young lads, eager

30

deaths, and she'll not live then. D'you not think I don't want to run like a madman up on the moors shouting her name? Jesus . . .' His face worked and in his eyes was an expression of suffering such as Walter had never seen before. He himself was right fond of a certain laundrymaid and he supposed he would lay down his life for her if asked but this chap looked . . . well, wild . . . maddened with some savage emotion which consumed him and lit his eyes to deep brown pits of fire. He'd heard rumours about him and Miss Tessa, hadn't they all, years ago but he'd laughed at them. Now it seems there was something in them after all, looking at this chap's face.

'Now give me that list,' the man said and his voice was choked.

'Right, sir, a cup o' tea wouldn't go amiss whilst tha gets tha coat, like.'

*   *   *

The pain in her shoulder awoke her, that and the sound of someone crying. It was a child weeping its heart out in the most desolate fashion, and a child in pain by the sound of it. God, but she was cold, and wet too, and there was a strange softness, like butterflies' wings, falling on to her face.

'Aunt Tess, Aunt Tess, please come and get me,' the child wept and in an appalling moment of terror it all came back to her. She tried to sit up but the tearing agony in her shoulder pinned her down to wherever she was. Joel . . . oh, dear Father, who art in heaven . . . take care of Joel . . . hallowed be Thy name . . . and she tried to raise her voice to tell him she was near but nothing seemed to come out

693

of her mouth and Joel continued to weep.

There was a deep silence when next she regained her senses, soft and gentle and strangely enough she no longer felt cold. In fact, she was most comfortable and didn't mind a bit waiting. What was she waiting for? Who? ... Someone ... she knew she was waiting for someone. She remembered Joel drowsily, wondering if he was as cosy and warm under his white blanket as she was. She hoped so. She called his name softly, up into the veil of snow which fell endlessly out of the sky and knew a small pang of misgiving when he did not answer. Perhaps he had already left? Perhaps he had climbed the rock face and got on his pony and ridden off to Greenacres? A good boy, Joel, and sensible and he'd bring him ... Who? ... Who would he bring? ... Where ... Where was she? ... And how ... ?

*   *   *

The dogs snarled ferociously, a close-packed, snow-covered, almost invisible shape crouched on her cloak and would allow none to approach them as they guarded her, and what was hers.

'Call them off, for God's sake,' the man shouted above the howling of the demented wind.

'Nay.' Walter's voice could scarcely be heard. 'They'll not shift fer anyone only 'er.'

'Then bloody well shoot them.'

'I've no gun, sir.' What did he want with a gun on a night like this?

They watched, the circle of tired men as the big man strode fearlessly through the drifting snow towards the group of savage animals and when they

694

parted for him one or two attempting to lick his hand as though they knew him, the men surged forward to watch in amazement and a legend was born that night.

'She'll be down there. Get ropes.' He wasted no words.

' 'Ow does tha know, sir?' Walter shouted, his face gaunt in the light from the flickering lamp.

'That's her cloak, isn't it? And those are her dogs guarding it.'

She felt his arms go round her and though her shoulder shrieked in agony she gave a great contented sigh of relief as she moved thankfully into their shelter at last. Where had he been for so long, she wanted to ask him but when she looked up into his dear face she merely smiled for she knew he had come as quickly as he could.

'Will,' she said, laying her head against his chest.

'Aye, who else?'

They were there when she awoke, two anxious faces which both cleared, ready to smile as her eyes opened. The boy had his right arm splinted to his body and there was a swelling above his ear which gave him a somewhat lopsided look but he leaned forward, putting his face close to hers. She could feel his breath fan her cheek and smell its childlike sweetness and knew he was safe, whole and sound. Slightly damaged perhaps, but in the way of children whose recuperative powers are quite amazing, he was ready to engage in whatever she herself was capable of.

'Oh, there you are, Aunt Tess,' he said, just as though she had been out to tea and him waiting impatiently for her return. 'We got you back just as soon as we could but the doctor said we were not to wake you.' He raised his wounded arm a fraction, important and proud of himself for surviving what had, naturally, been an event of great magnitude. 'I've been up all day,' he continued accusingly, 'and waiting here with Mr Broadbent for you to wake. None of the others could come in, of course, though Jane wept and begged to be allowed to look after you but the doctor said you were to sleep.'

Her eyes moved beyond his still pale but excited face to the one which had waited enduringly for as long as she could remember. But there was a hint of impatience in it now which its owner made no attempt to conceal.

'Darling,' she murmured drowsily and both the boy and the man knew the endearment was meant for him.

'How long has it been?'

'Too bloody long.'

The boy stared at Mr Broadbent, evidently much impressed with this sign of his superiority, then turned back to the bed.

'Is your shoulder better now, Aunt Tess?' he continued anxiously, for she was dear to him but a dislocated shoulder could not compare with a broken arm.

The man fidgeted and began to scowl.

'Yes, darling, now give me a kiss and . . . well, I have a word or two to say to Mr Broadbent so perhaps, now that you are satisfied yourself that I am recovered, you could go and tell the others.'

The door had barely closed behind him when Will drew her carefully into his arms but she had done with care and steadiness, with self-control and sobriety.

'Kiss me properly, for God's sake,' she

696

demanded huskily against his mouth, which strove to be gentle, and when he did they were both unsteady with the joy of it.

'Damnation, woman, I don't want to hurt you.' He was ready, should she show signs of weakness to place her, reluctantly, back amongst her nest of pillows, but, his expression said, he was even more ready to join her there.

'Hurt me, Will, I beg you, since I have felt nothing, nothing, for years.' And but for the sound of the household beyond the bedroom door he was ready to make love to her right then and there.

'Soon, dear God, soon . . .'

'When we are married, you are saying?' she laughed breathlessly against the hollow of his strong throat.

'And before that, my lass, for I'll not wait. I'll make sure of you this time.'

Again they fell into the sweetness both had denied themselves so often in the decade since they had first met, their flesh melting into that ecstasy which they had found only with one another. Then:

'You will not object to a ready-made family, Will?' She felt a moment of wariness since surely . . . ?

'I mean to add to it,' he said gruffly.

'And the . . . ?'

'Aye, Tessa Harrison, the bloody mills an' all.'

'You would have no objection to . . . ?'

'We'll work side by side, lass, you know that.'

The words put the last mending stitch in the torn fabric of their love, returning it to its durable and everlasting strength, a strength which both of them knew could never be damaged again.

sake tell me . . .'

'Miss Beale ses yer ter come at once.' Walter's tired face was pale in the lamplight which spilled from the open doorway and across the steps, and the snow was like a shimmering curtain about him. Drew Greenwood's bay drooped behind him. He had been ridden hard and long this night and Walter knew he would go no further but *he* would once he had passed on Miss Beale's message to this big chap. He'd got the list in the pocket of his greatcoat and he was to ask him to pick a place. *The place.* He'd know, Miss Beale had said, and he was to go straight there with Walter and as many men as he could find. There'd only be one chance—though others would naturally search for as long as they could elsewhere—and if he made the wrong choice they'd not find her, not this night and not on any other until the snows thawed. Blankets and ropes and lamps they'd take and whatever this man said was needed, and if he didn't make the right choice Walter would personally choke the bloody life out of him, aye, and swing for it an' all. For a moment a picture came into his mind of a lovely young girl, excited and wild, daring her cousin to cut her long glossy hair. When he had done so, it had lain all over the stable floor like a carpet. After they had gone he had tenderly taken a shining length of it and he had it to this day in a bit of paper in a drawer in his room above the stable.

'Come inside, man, and get warm while . . .'

'*Get warm!* I've no time fer that, beggin' yer pardon, sir. Here's t'list. Tell me where ter go an' I'll be off.'

'Don't be daft, man. We need things. We can't go off half-cocked or we'll be floundering to our

692

She shivered uncontrollably, her own shirt wet and freezing to her back, her hair wearing a cap of snow which melted and dripped on to Joel's still face. She knew his arm was beneath him, probably injured in the fall but with a little care and a great deal of good luck she might . . .

With a small cry, whether of pain or fear, the boy lurched suddenly into a sitting position, a cry spiralling up into the darkness and completely knocking her from the delicate balance she only just preserved on the ledge. She grabbed at the rock face, at the tufty grass beneath her, at anything which came to her desperate hands in her hopeless struggle to remain on the ledge. Yet even in her fight for what she was well aware could be her own life she was careful not to grab at him. She must not hold on to him for as she fell, and she knew she was about to fall, she must not take him with her.

She made no sound as she went. She had some jumbled idea in her head that she must not frighten him any more than could be helped and her last conscious thought as she slid over the edge into the snow-dancing emptiness of air was that the only man who could save them no longer loved her.

*   *   *

'Tell me, quickly, damn your soul to hell! For God's sake, speak up, man, or I swear I'll strangle you where you stand.' The big hands grabbed Walter by the shoulders and shook him savagely.

'I'm tryin' to, sir. Please, I can't say 'owt with thi 'oldin' me up like I was a bloody sack of . . .'

'I'm sorry . . . please . . . I'm sorry. For Christ's

on Joel, keep him alive, warm until help came. Having come down the escarpment she knew finally, now that she was here, that she would never get up again, with or without this child she loved.

She had pulled off her gloves, throwing them unthinkingly behind her, not knowing or caring where they landed, and with her bare hands she gently lifted the boy's head, supporting it with one as she searched for injuries with the other. She could feel a large bump to the side, just above his ear but there appeared to be no blood. Her hands crept beneath his chin and to her incredulous joy she felt a pulse throb against her fingers. Oh, thank you, God, thank you, and she lifted her weeping eyes to the blinding snow for a moment.

But he was so cold and so was she now that she had been still for several minutes. If only she had her cloak? It was made of wool and lined with fur but she knew that she could not have climbed down here with it draped across her shoulders. She brushed as much snow as she could reach from the boy, then carefully eased her jacket off and placed it across his chest. She tucked it under his chin, leaning across him to protect him from the steadily falling blanket which was an inch deep all over him, wondering if she might ease him slowly, slowly towards her. If she could lift his small frame . . . so slender, so light-boned . . . up against her where she knelt, might she not keep him warmer, transmit some of her own body heat to him?

She realised then that she was kneeling on his cape which was spread behind him. If she could get it from about his neck, lift it and place it over his uncovered legs it would at least keep the heavy, wet snow from the lower half of his unprotected body.

someone I want thi ter fetch. But first of all give me a list o't places she an' the lad go to. Every damn one, Walter Hobson, an' look sharp or there won't be a soul stirrin' wi' this damn snow comin' down.'

* * *

She reached him as the first fine blanket of snow had covered his crumpled figure completely. She could not get past him to reach his legs for she dared not step on his bit of ledge for fear she would tumble him into the depths of the darkness which yawned below him. She laid a trembling, terrified hand on his face, brushing away the snow from it, appalled at its coldness and smallness.

'Joel,' she whispered, scarcely daring to breathe now that she had reached him, desperately needing to find a heartbeat or pulse which would tell her he still lived. Where? His throat, his temple, where, dear God, where? She wanted to pull him into her arms, to cradle him, shelter him, warm him but their position was so precarious might she not dislodge the pair of them if she moved him in any way? Best be slow and cautious, examine him as well as she could with careful hands, since she could hardly see him in the snow-filled darkness. She began with his face and head, amazed at the fragility of his childish neck, the small bones of his head and face, the soft flexibility of his boy's ears.

'Oh, Joel, I love you so much,' she mumbled and for a moment she was cast back into another place, another time, with another male figure in her arms. He had been unconscious too, needing her and her strength and she had given it to him, brought him back with her love. But now she must concentrate to 'get on', were learning things which would surely lead to revolution among the lower orders. What would it be next, the stunned inhabitants of Crossfold and Edgeclough, and indeed the whole of the Penfold Valley had asked, and more to the point, where was the profit in it? But twenty years after the Act in many of the mills it was *still* the practice to employ children under the legal age, many of whom were worked until they fell asleep at their machines. Only last week, Charlie had heard, a little lass who swore she was nine years old but who could have been no more than six or seven was half-scalped at Jonathan Abbott's mill when her long hair—which should have been tied up in any case—became entangled in the machine, still moving, which she was cleaning. She had been dragged clear by her demented mother for whom she was 'piecing' and taken to the infirmary in Edgeclough to be stitched up. It seemed it was of no concern to her employer when she had turned up for work the next day at the customary time of five thirty for her twelve-hour shift—in need of her wage one presumed—the bandage on her head already grey and stained with the filth with which she and her family were in daily contact.

Despite the open windows, the long room with its rows of clattering machinery was fearfully hot. Scores of women and older children attended the mules whilst others ran from machine to machine piecing the broken yarns, sweeping up the cotton waste, the smallest clambering beneath dangerously moving straps and pulleys, chains and wheels, all fenced off, to get at the oil-coated waste which collected there. Some carried empty roving bobbins, taking them to the machines and bringing

31

away the full bobbins of spun yarn which were placed in a huge basket and dragged away by a sturdy and cheerfully whistling lad. The air was thick with 'fly', specks of cotton fibre and dust which, despite all efforts to dispel it, still hung in a mist about the workers' heads.

Charlie did not expect to find anything amiss in his spinning room. Nevertheless, it did no harm to let the overlooker see that he was on the alert for any infringement of those rules made to protect, not exploit the operatives. This was part of his daily round and though today's took place as usual it was at a quicker pace than he would normally proceed. As soon as he had finished his inspection he was off to Crossfold's new railway station to join his brother and nephews, ready to take his seat on Crossfold's first train, by invitation only, and ride the exciting ten or so miles from Crossfold to Rochdale. His carriage was even now waiting in the mill yard, the horses' hooves striking sparks on the cobbles in their eagerness to be off.

A young boy of ten or eleven drowsed over a snarling machine, his head drooping since it was almost the end of his twelve-hour shift, and Charlie tapped him lightly on the shoulder. The overlooker, who walked at Charlie's heels, snapped his malacca cane angrily against his own leg, his expression revealing that left to himself he would have used it on the boy. He regretted the loss of the customary 'tackler's' thong, several straps of leather six inches long, but which Mr Greenwood, as daft as his sister and the rest of the Greenwood family, would not allow in his mill. Edwards was a good overlooker with many years' experience as a spinner until he had been 'made up', and knew as

32

much about the machines as the engineer in whose charge they were. He could get more yarn out of his 'girls' than any other tackler in the factory but he did regret the reducing of his own authority by the . . . well, he could only call it the *softness* of the Greenwood family with their refusal to allow him to discipline his young charges. Children were beaten in factories. They were beaten on farms, in mines and indeed everywhere they were employed, but the floggings, the dousing in cold water and all the other necessary punishments which kept children up to the mark were frowned upon here.

Mr Greenwood stopped at the end of the row of machines, smiling at a cheeky-faced young boy who had just emerged from his 'scavenging' chores beneath a machine. The child was far from plump but his bones were straight, his flesh firm and his eyes were bright. He was dressed in the usual fine cotton drawers and sleeveless shirt with no shoes on his dirty feet but his grin was impudent and carefree.

' 'Ow do, Mr Greenwood,' he said.

'How do, lad.' Charlie grinned down at him.

'Grand day, Mr Greenwood.'

'It is that.'

'Sorry about that, sir,' the overlooker said through gritted teeth, feeling in some way that his authority had been again undermined by the child's cheek in addressing one of the managers of the mill, but Charlie shook his head smilingly.

'It's all right, Edwards. I like to see a child with a bit of spirit.' He took out his wrap-reel and began to study the 'wrapping' of the yarn as the carriage on the machine was drawn out. At his back the overlooker fumed silently. It was like this every day when Mr Greenwood inspected the spinning room and but for the splendid wage he earned and, as an overlooker, the neat little villa he rented so cheaply from his employer, he wouldn't take it. Interfering in what he considered to be *his* duties. The supervision of the spinners, the piecers and scavengers, *and* their chastisement if he felt they needed it, was *his* job. Of course, he had heard of the family's squeamishness before he took up employment with them but sometimes when he saw the, to his mind, *free* way in which their workers were allowed to approach them if they considered they had a grievance, it was almost more than he could take. What was the world coming to when a lad could address the owner's *brother*, for God's sake, and get no more than a friendly greeting in return? Naturally, when Mr Greenwood or Mrs Harrison weren't about he'd fetch a lad, or a lass if it came to that, a clout or two, not hard like, for it would be more than his job was worth, since it had been known for a 'rough' overlooker to be dismissed on the spot.

Charlie looked about him and sighed in satisfaction. He was pleased with the general air of cheerfulness which lay over the room, the smiles the women and children gave him as he passed and the sound of a man whistling nearby. Years ago a man could be fined for whistling at his work though Charlie often wondered what any man had found to whistle about in those days. The greatest boon, in his opinion, of the 1833 Factory Act had been to open a window to the rest of the world on the industrial conditions which existed in the mills, though it seemed to him that not a lot of good had come out of it in many of them, despite the reports of the Factory Inspectorate. Tales of abuses had shocked the world and there had been outcries from a great number of people on how conditions should be changed. But poor building materials had produced unsafe buildings, bad ventilation, suffocatingly high temperatures in which the hands worked. Very few millowners were prepared, as Mrs Jenny Harrison and Mrs Joss Greenwood were, to spend money on renovating factories which quite satisfactorily produced the required yardage each week. Long hours and the increasing speeds at which the machines went exhausted the operative, but she turned up for work each day so what was the millowner to do but allow her to do it? Disease thrived in the overworked and undernourished bodies and adults who burned themselves out were easily replaced by others. More, not fewer children were employed since the new machine did not need the brute force of a man to run it, and besides, was not a child's wage a quarter of that paid to a man?

Nine years ago a further Factory Act had reduced children's working hours to six and a half each day with a half day's compulsory schooling. However, what was known as a 'relay' system was introduced by unscrupulous millowners, the factory day stretching over fifteen hours, from five thirty in the morning until eight thirty at night, making it almost impossible to detect whether the new law was being observed. The Act, passed to protect the overworked and underpaid labourer, mainly children, not only in the textile trade but in all forms of employment, was once more obstructed by the unprincipled employer. Children continued to work for fourteen hours a day, and profit, the god, the duty, the right of the master, grew a hundredfold.

John Fielden, supported by Joss Greenwood, continued to press for the 'Ten-Hour' Bill, a ten-and-a-half hour day from six in the morning until six at night with one and a half hours for meals, and in 1847 the Act had been carried for young women and children. This further incensed the millowner since, if he was to turn off his engine for two-thirds and more of his workers, it was scarcely profitable to keep it running for the remaining third. But again, with a series of shifts and overtime, which could be checked by no one, the Bill was got round and women and children laboured, just as they had always done.

'Mr Greenwood'. A light touch on his arm made Charlie turn but before he could speak the overlooker at his back, his face thunderous, began to bluster, attempting, without appearing to, to hustle away the girl who stood there. She wore only the briefest of skirts and a scanty, sleeveless bodice. Her feet were bare but she was sturdy enough, with the wiry look of a young greyhound.

'Get back to thy machine, my lass,' the overlooker hissed, 'an' don't thee be mitherin' Mr Greenwood. Can thi not see 'e's busy? If there's 'owt wrong I'll see to it mesen directly.'

'No, let her speak, Edwards. What is it, lass?' The overlooker was forced to stand back, his face red, his eyes snapping with vexation, his expression conveying to the unfortunate girl that she'd be sorry for this, really she would. Charlie frowned, a feeling of unease evaporating his former sense of satisfaction.

'What is it?'

'Oh sir ...' Though she seemed somewhat overcome at her own daring now that she had his attention since he was *manager* of this mill in which she was nought but a humble spinner, her chin lifted stubbornly and there was a resolute gleam in her almost colourless eyes. She had never spoken to Mr Greenwood before, indeed it was not her place to address anyone higher than the tackler who was over her, but this was an extreme circumstance and extreme circumstances made for extreme measures.

'Yes?' he said kindly and she took heart, despite the tackler's steely expression, looking directly, bravely into Mr Greenwood's eyes. They were a greeny-brown, she noticed, surprised that she should observe such a thing, the state she was in, but they were smiling encouragingly at her and he bent his head a little the better to hear her in the clangour around them. He was not a tall man. In his early childhood there had been poverty in the textile towns of Lancashire. His diet had not encouraged the building of sturdy limbs and firm flesh, but later, when his family's circumstances had improved, so had his physique. He was not handsome really, but with a nice face even though the scars on it, one across his mouth and the other above his left eye, gave him quite a rakish air. She had heard, though perhaps it was just a rumour, that he had been a 'piecer' himself once and had been beaten within an inch of his life by a bullying overlooker for defending a little girl who was the butt of the overlooker's ill-temper. It was hard to believe when you looked at the smooth, beautifully tailored cut of his coat and trousers, the immaculately ruffled white of his shirt front, the gold tie-pin and cuff-links and the impression of superb good health which glowed about him. And even harder to believe was that the lady who was his wife, Mrs Laurel Greenwood, was that very same small girl he had rescued. It sounded very romantic, if you believed in such things, which *she* didn't, and anyroad she was not here to speculate on the past of this man who was in charge of the whole of the spinning side of Chapman Manufacturing. Really, how she had got up the courage to speak to him at all, she didn't know, but speak she must, choose how.

She drew in a deep breath.

'It's new under-tackler what's bin took on, sir. 'Im as come from Abbotts.'

'What about him?'

She bared her teeth for a moment as though she would like nothing better than to sink them into the new tackler's neck. Mr Greenwood was waiting patiently and though she was well aware that the overlooker at his back was warning her with narrowed eyes that she had best know exactly what she was doing since she was going over *his* head, she continued courageously.

' 'E's got our Nelly in't tackler's room, Mr Greenwood.' Her voice held a note of apology as though she was sorry to be bothering him over such a trifling matter and him so important, but there was defiance in her since it was her *right*, her eyes said, to speak up when an injustice was being done. And there was fear too, for though such things were rare in the Chapman mills one did hear of such terrible happenings, especially to young girls, in other mills in the valley. 'She's bin in theer ower 'alf an 'our an' . . . well, tis a long time, sir. 'E said

38

as 'ow she were cheeky an' needed a talkin' to but that be a long while talkin' to a little lass, an' anyroad ... well ...' She squared her thin shoulders obstinately and her pugnacious little chin lifted, 'I reckon someone ought ter fetch 'er out.'

Charlie Greenwood straightened up and looked beyond her in the direction of the tiny office at the end of the room, the door of which was closed, and the overlooker behind him stirred uneasily. He too had heard, aye, even witnessed some of the ... well, to give it a *kind* word ... the mistreatment of little lasses in the industrial areas of the country. Though he himself was not slow to give a child, *for its own good*, a lick or two with his overlooker's cane, since many a time it could save that child's life by preventing it from falling asleep and into the moving parts of a machine, he didn't hold with interfering with young girls.

'Lead on, lass,' Mr Greenwood said ominously and the overlooker added 'aye' just for good measure.

The girl turned thankfully, light as thistledown in her relief, running on bare and filthy feet between the neat rows of machines all set in pairs and at each pair a woman and child. It was very hot, not a dry heat, but humid like some tropical jungle, and every man, woman and child in the room was dewed with perspiration. The heat brought out a variety of smells from the cotton itself, from the oil-soaked pinewood floor and from the mahogany carriages and creels. Above it all was the whirr of spinning spindles, the shriek of tortured leather straps and the thump of carriages 'letting-in'. At the door to what was known as the 'little cabin' the girl stopped, with Mr Greenwood and the

39

overlooker directly behind her. It was a small room opening off the main spinning room, used as an office, and in it the overlooker kept his equipment, usually no more than a simple balance and wrap-reel, a quadrant-type yarn tester and a ready reckoner. With these he checked the yarn from each mule at regular intervals and ordered gear changes to be made whenever his 'wrappings' indicated a departure from the required count.

It was somewhat quieter here away from the vicinity of the clattering machinery and Charlie could hear the echo of his own and the overlooker's boots on the floor of the main passage along which they had just hurried. This part of the flooring had been overlaid with maple to withstand the relatively heavy traffic of shod feet. Only the overlookers, of the work force, wore boots. Everyone else was barefoot and it was common practice among the operatives to pick up waste with their toes which became, in a sense, a third 'hand'.

From the office came no sound at all.

'Oh, Mr Greenwood, tell 'im to give ower. Tell 'im ter let our Nelly out.' The girl, whose protective instincts were savagely alert put her hand to her mouth, her eyes huge and desperate in her chalk-white face. She was afraid now, not of the sound of anger, or even the dreaded overlooker's strap, but by the absence of any sound at all.

'Out of me way then, lass,' Mr Greenwood said menacingly, putting his hand on the door-knob, turning it, ready to thrust himself into the room, surprised when he met resistance since there was no lock to the door. It was unnecessary as there was nothing of value worth stealing. His face

40

darkened as his frown drove down his fierce eyebrows and the girl edged up to his back, as eager as he to get inside, willing, it seemed, to lend a hand in the breaking down of the door if it should be needed.

'What the hell's going on?' Mr Greenwood roared and the sound of his voice lifted every head in the lofty room, turning each one avidly towards him. They had all been aware, of course, that Annie Beale had accosted their employer; most had been keeping half an eye on the small drama but they could afford no more than that since each operative spinner was paid a sum directly and precisely related to the amount of yarn she had spun in the preceding week. Besides, if a thread should break in the fraction of time it took to glance away and the yarn end be lost in the machinery, it would take valuable time they could ill afford to find and repair it.

'Open this bloody door.' Charlie Greenwood's voice was dangerous now and even Annie was alarmed since she'd never seen such a killing rage in anyone's face. His eyes were slitted and gleaming, the whites suffused with blood, and his big hands had formed into fists which threatened to smash through the door-panels, indeed through *anything* which stood in his way. But the door remained shut though on the other side could now be heard small scuffling sounds and a child whimpered.

'Nelly ...' Annie Beale whispered and before the name had sighed from her anguished throat Charlie Greenwood's sturdy frame had smashed against the door taking it from its hinges as though it was made of cardboard, sweeping it into the

41

cabin. The chair which had been placed beneath the door-knob went with it.

The man was still fumbling with his trouser buttons when Charlie fell on him. He was a thin, sallow-hued, round-shouldered little man with a hank of dusty hair who, if something was not done to stop it, would be snapped in two like a bit of dry stick in Charlie Greenwood's maddened grasp.

'You rotten bastard . . . you filth . . . you stinking piece of filth . . . I'll kill you, kill you for this, d'you hear?' Charlie was yelling, out of his mind, it appeared, his face white and sweating, his eyes staring at something which surely, thought the overlooker who had followed him in, had really nothing to do with what had been done to the frightened child. He seemed to be looking at and acting upon images of such horror and obscenity, awakened by the scene in this room, that Edwards knew that if he himself did not act quickly, Charlie Greenwood would commit murder.

Nelly Beale stood against the wall, her eyes wide and shocked. She was fully clothed but down the inside of her bare, grubby leg ran a dribble of blood. She was nine years old and almost at the end of her own six-and-a-half hour shift as her older sister's 'piecer'. When it was finished, when she had washed herself in the women's washroom Kit Chapman had installed twenty-five years ago, when she had eaten her 'baggin' in the dining-room provided for the workers, she would spend the afternoon doing her sums, reading her book from which over the weekend she had learned by heart a whole passage to 'say' to the teacher. She would be a little girl in a normal little girl's world, singing, playing a tambourine, giggling as little girls do with

42

others. But now, in a moment of animal lust, her young innocence had been cruelly taken from her.

Her sister ran to her wordlessly, swift in her need to remove her from the violent destruction which threatened. She put her arms about her and led her from the room where, it seemed to her, not only rape but murder was to be done today.

'Mr Greenwood, sir . . . Dear God in 'eaven . . . Mr Greenwood . . . leave 'im be . . . Christ man, thee'll do fer 'im . . .' Edwards was grunting, his own considerable strength unable to control Charlie Greenwood's killing rage. The molester of the child was screaming like a pig with a butcher's knife to its throat and in the spinning room women began to cry out, their machines coming to a standstill, threads snapping and children running this way and that for want of direction.

There was a cracking of bone and the sallow-faced undertackler went as limp as an old dish-rag in Charlie Greenwood's grasp and as he slid, like water which can be held in no man's hand, to the floor, Charlie regained his senses. Edwards, who had grasped him fiercely from behind about the arms and chest, slowly, carefully, stepped away from him, hardly daring to look at the crumpled heap on the floor, though it was nowt to him if the man lived or died. The heap stirred and groaned, then was violently sick and Mr Greenwood inched away from him looking as though he could quite easily be sick himself. The man fumbled his way to his feet holding the arm which Edwards had heard snap, shivering and sweating at the same time, and when Mr Greenwood lifted a hand to wipe his own sweating face, recoiled away from him.

'Nay, I'll not touch you again, man,' Mr

Greenwood croaked. 'I'm only sorry I soiled me hands on you in't first place. I thought never to see the likes o' this again, not in *my* mill, anyroad, but it seems I was wrong. But you'll not satisfy your perversions again in this town, no, nor in bloody Lancashire, if I've 'owt to do wi' it.' In his distress Charlie Greenwood had begun to revert to the broad northern vowels of his youth. 'If I could have you clapped in gaol or flogged at the cart-tail, by God I would, but I know the magistrates in these parts, aye, an' the rest o't country an' all.' His voice was bitter. 'Throw up their hands they would if it were one o' their own but some poor workin' lass'd be nowt to them. So get yer gone before I have yer thrashed in't yard fer all to see. An' don't go lookin' fer work in south Lancashire fer I'll make sure you find none.'

The man had gone and Charlie and Edwards stood uneasily side by side in the cabin.

'I can't abide that sort o' thing, Edwards,' Charlie Greenwood said at last.

'Nay, sir, tha don't 'ave ter say 'owt ter me.' Edwards protested. 'I can't say as 'ow, if I'm 'onest, I agree wi' all tha methods in't mill but I don't like ter see a lass taken down, especially as young as that 'un.'

Charlie looked surprised at Edwards words. 'What is it you don't agree with then?' He was calmer now, glad it seemed, to talk of normal, everyday things.

'I don't reckon it 'arms some o' them bigger lads to 'ave a bit o' discipline now an' again.' Edwards stuck his chin out. 'I 'ad a few thrashin's in me life an' it did me no arm.'

'Happen not, but I'll not have it in my mill, think

44

on. And you're not the only one, lad, to have been given a beating. Where d'you think I got this face of mine? Not in the prize-fighting ring, I can tell you.'

'Aye . . . well . . .' Edwards cleared his throat and moved towards the smashed doorway. He'd said his piece though much good it would do him. 'If that'll be all, sir, I'll get back ter me work. Them women out theer are runnin' about like 'eadless chickens and the machines all tangled up. It'll tekk the best part of an hour ter sort 'em out. Oh, an' I'll 'ave to 'ave another chap ter take place o't . . .'

'Right, Edwards . . . and thanks for stopping me from killing that . . . bastard. He deserved it but I wouldn't like to swing for him, just the same.'

'No, sir.'

He was still brooding, lounging against the cabin wall, his narrowed eyes staring at where the child had stood but seeing pictures which seemed to grieve him when Annie Beale slipped across the threshold, pale as wood-ash and just as insubstantial.

'Thanks, Mr Greenwood,' she said quietly.

'Nay, lass. I'm only sorry that it happened in my mill and that we didn't get to her in time to . . .' He struggled awkwardly with the words since he was a man and ashamed of his own masculinity at that moment. 'Why didn't you report him to Mr Edwards as soon as the bugger took her into the cabin?'

'It's not my place ter tell one tackler what t'other's up to, sir, you know that.' She looked quite shocked and he was saddened that even now, after all these years of enlightened treatment, this girl was still afraid of a system which might lose her

45

her job if she 'spoke out'.

'But . . .'

'Anyroad, sir . . .' she interrupted smoothly, seeing no need to dwell on something which could not be undone. 'I've cleaned 'er up an' she's back in't jennygate . . .'

'Good God!'

'Aye, well there's bread 'as ter be found an' only way ter pay fer it is wi' brass what we both earn.'

Charlie sprang away from the wall and almost lifting her from her feet led her from the office. His face was contorted with anger, not at her but at the circumstances which forced this girl, scarcely more than a child herself by the size of her, to accept not only what had been done to her sister but that she must be prepared to 'clean her up' and return her to her work as though nothing untoward had happened. And this was *his* mill, known throughout Lancashire as a *model* mill; a model mill built on the spot where once had stood row upon row of mean hovels thrown up by Kit Greenwood's grandfather to house his own operatives. She had razed them to the ground and in their place had erected the factory which had become the talk of the textile industry. Six storeys high, the site covered several acres. The rooms in which the work was done were high and spacious with windows which opened—as the old ones had not—in order to allow in what fresh air there was, and blinds were put on those which faced south to keep out the heat of the sun. The machines were set, in pairs, at a decent distance from one another, most of the moving parts well guarded. At the back of the building was a separate room with tables and chairs where the workers could eat their 'carrying-out' in peace instead of beside their machines as they did in other factories. There was piped water, brought from the river, clean and cool, and separate privies for the men and women. Insanity, those millowners with whom Katherine Chapman had done business called it, sheer madness and where the hell would it lead? Might not *their* workers want the same thing, indeed were they not already grumbling about better conditions and higher wages?

Charlie Greenwood looked down at the girl who was apologising to him for causing a disturbance, assuring him, *him* who had defended girls just like her, and children too, all his life, that she and the child would soon have the machine going again. She was anxious to let him know, just as though he was as unrelenting as any other millowner, that he would lose no profit over this little commotion. Did she not know that his own scarred face had been given him by an overlooker in circumstances very similar to those in which her sister had been involved? Had she not heard of Joss Greenwood, his own brother, now up to Westminster as radical Member of Parliament for Crossfold, who had caused such trouble and aggravation on behalf of the working class in his younger days he had been put in prison for it? Was she not aware that his father, Joshua Greenwood, had died for his belief, aye, given his life at St Peter's Field in the massacre which took place there?

'Nay, lass ... what's your name? ... Annie Beale. Well, Annie, thi shall have thy bread and a bit more besides,' he went on, deeply moved, 'if I've 'owt to do with it, and as I'm bloody maister I reckon thee can count on it. Now get thissen home,

47

you and the child an' when *she* feels up to it, you an' her come back, d'you hear? Send someone to collect thy wages an' you shall be paid. Now, don't you argue wi' me, Annie Beale, for I'll not 'ave it. Dear Lord in heaven, what next . . . no, please . . . I want no thanks . . .'

He could do no more, he told himself; it wasn't much but still a damn sight better than she could have expected in any other mill in the Penfold Valley, for despite his family's efforts to improve the lot of the workers in the textile industry there were still tens of thousands in the land who suffered under the tyranny of profit-mad millowners.

He shook his head sadly as he walked out of the spinning room and into the bright, sunlit yard, since their dream of equality was as far off as it had been over thirty years ago when his father had died for it.

CHAPTER THREE

'Mr Greenwood's not here just now. He had some business to attend to up at the Cloth Hall later on so happen he's gone straight there. Unless it's some family thing which has held him up, as is more than likely. There's always something with them Greenwoods. If it's not them wild lads who should be here in this very room right now as ordered by their father—and the Lord only knows where they've got to—it's the lass. She's as bad as them, let me tell you. Why, only last week we heard she'd been seen over at . . .' The man who spoke turned

48

his head to look back at the long passage which led into a room where a dozen clerks employed in the main counting house of Chapman Manufacturing had their heads bent industriously over their tall desks. Satisfied that he could not be overheard he beckoned to the large man who blocked the doorway and automatically the man bent his head to listen.

'She'll not be told, you know, and her no more than sixteen,' he continued importantly, implying that he was privy to the Greenwood's most private family business, indeed, his manner seemed to say, had been asked on more than one occasion for his advice. Will Broadbent straightened up distastefully, unwilling to listen to gossip.

'Have you no idea when Mr Greenwood will be here?' he asked curtly, letting the clerk know he was not concerned with tittle-tattle about the girl of whom, he had heard, the whole valley gossiped, nor indeed of the family who owned the mill. He was aware, as who was not, of the tales of the wild Greenwoods: the woman who had begun the legend over thirty years ago, the man she had married and whose involvement with the outlawed radicals, as they had been then, was still spoken of with some awe by those he had fought for, and now their sons who were if anything, it was rumoured, more rebellious than both of their parents put together.

'No, and if you ask me . . .'

'Yes, yes,' Will interrupted him brusquely, then looked about him as though searching for someone to tell him what to do next.

'You had an appointment with Mr Greenwood then?'

49

'Aye, at eight thirty sharp.'

'Well, I can't help you and if that will be all I'll get back to me work,' the clerk said, implying that if this chap had nothing better to do with his time than hang about gossiping, he had.

'Thanks.'

Will turned away and walked down the steep flight of steps, hesitating on the bottom tread to gaze out into the yard. It was bustling with activity. There were enormous waggons pulled by enormous horses, all loaded with Chapman goods ready to be taken to the new railway station in Crossfold. Men grunted as they shifted huge sacking—wrapped bales of the finest fustians, velveteens, sateens and muslins, all to be despatched to the warehouses of Piccadilly and Portland Street in Manchester where they would be stored awaiting shipment to every corner of the known world.

Against a building at the far side of the yard other men unloaded bales of raw cotton each weighing 500 pounds, just come from the southern states of America by way of Liverpool. The Chapman enterprises were situated in five mills in different parts of the town, two concerned only with spinning, two with weaving and this one which combined the two processes and all the other processes connected with the manufacture of cotton cloth. It was huge, six storeys high and covering many acres. On the ground floor, where the humidity was the highest, were power looms since the weaving process must be done in a damp atmosphere to prevent breakage of thread, and the heavy beams on which the warp thread was wound were of too great a weight for the upper floors. Here also, and on the first floor, were carding, drawing and roving rooms and above them spinning was done on the top four floors.

The men were hot and sweating from their exertions and their brawny muscled arms rippled in the smoke-hazed sunshine. There was a clatter of horse's hooves on the cobbles and a chestnut mare galloped dashingly into the yard, scattering the men and boys who were about to address themselves to the task of moving the bales of cotton to the blow room where they would be opened and the raw cotton cleaned and blended.

The men might have been a pack of dogs for all the notice the rider took of them. They were useful, naturally, for the work they did, but not to be spoken to, nor any particular care taken to avoid them since they were expected to get out of *his* way. He threw his leg over the horse's back and leaped lightly from the stirrup to the ground and with a shock Will realised that this was no arrogant lad, but a girl, a girl like none he had seen before. He could do no more than stand and stare, mouth slack and eyes wide with astonishment, since she was wearing a shirt and breeches more suitable to a male than a female.

'Where's that boy?' she shouted, her clear voice carrying above the crash of hooves on the cobblestones, the cries of the men and the creak of the pulley which was being used to winch some machinery to the first floor of the mill.

From across the yard a young lad darted amongst the activity, avoiding men and carts and horses until he reached the girl, catching the reins as she threw them at him, pulling the peak of his cap as he did so.

'Give her a good rub down, Sam. I shall be here

for about half an hour and she's hot. We've been out since dawn up to Longworth Moor.'

'Yes, Miss Tessa.'

Miss Tessa! Miss Tessa Harrison! He should have known, of course, for who else could it be? This was the girl about whom the manufacturing class of the whole of the Penfold Valley whispered and, by God, he could see why. He stared quite openly, unable to do anything else since she was undeniably the most magnificent young woman he had ever seen. Any female so dressed would be bound to attract attention but it was not just her clothing which drew every male eye in the yard to her, though that was indecent enough. It was the way she tossed her imperious head, the defiant stare which did not really *see* the low-born beings about her, the square and challenging set to her shoulders and the graceful way she strode across the yard towards him, masculine in its arrogance and yet eternally female in its fluid movement. There was insolence written in every line of her taut young body but its symmetry was spellbinding to these men whose own wives revealed little of their bodies to them, and then more than likely only when the candle had been blown out. Her young breasts, unbound beneath the silk of her shirt, bounced joyously as she walked and Will felt his breath catch in his throat.

Bloody hell! How did she get away with it? She must be no more than sixteen—that was what the clerk in the counting house had told him—the daughter of a well-known and well-regarded woman, the niece of one of the wealthiest men in south Lancashire. A female of her class could lose not only her reputation but with it the chance of a

52

good marriage which was her destiny in life, so he had heard, if she were to be seen talking, unchaperoned, to a man who was not a close relative. Not a whisper of gossip, even of the most innocent, must touch her. She would be guarded like a precious jewel, always accompanied by another lady and never, never allowed to be alone with a gentleman, not even the one she would marry. Dressed like schoolgirls in modest gowns were the ones *he* had seen in their carriages, usually in white, bonneted, gloved, every inch of flesh which might be considered indecent hidden from sight and not even the turn of an ankle revealed to any man until they were married.

But Miss Tessa Harrison's legs, the soft curve of her booted calf, the long, firm muscles of her thigh, the twin globes of her buttocks, all rippled beneath the fine stuff of her breeches and her eyes looked challengingly into his, not caring, or so it appeared, for her own reputation, nor indeed considering whether she had one.

When she reached where he still stood rooted to the bottom step of the stairway which led up to the counting house, she stopped. There was a deep silence for several tense moments as she waited for him to move aside. Her gleaming grey eyes, or were they silver he wondered in awe and confusion, cat's eyes, the pupils outlined with a thin black line, stared directly into his. In that first fleeting moment he felt a strong urge to step hurriedly out of her path, to fumble with his forelock as the inferior orders were expected to do to those above them, to go bright red and mouth some humble greetings—but something in him would not allow it and his eyes refused to drop away from hers.

53

'What are you staring at?' she asked rudely, her eyes pale and dangerous. The small riding crop she carried slashed against her leg and he had the distinct impression she would like nothing better, indeed would have not the slightest hesitation in using it on him or on anyone who stood in her way, but he did not move. His mouth curved in an amused smile.

'At you, my lass,' he answered softly, watching the hot colour flood beneath her white skin. 'As is every man in this yard and can you blame them?' Deliberately he let his gaze travel down the length of her body.

'You insolent ...' Her mouth gaped in amazement and the scathing words with which she obviously longed to flay him lodged in her throat. Tessa Harrison was not often lost for words of any kind, and she knew many more than a lady should, but it seemed they had become misplaced somewhere between her brain which leaped wildly to consume this presumptuous millhand, and her mouth which hung foolishly open. Her eyes blazed into his whilst her furious mind considered some way in which she might reduce him to his proper and inferior place in life. But even whilst it did so, some tiny core of her woman's sensibility, independent and extraordinarily wilful, pondered on the pleasing shape of his hard mouth, the smoky brown depths of his eyes which had the most curious amber flecks in them, the brown smoothness of his freshly shaved face and his smile, an odd slanting smile which gave him a decidedly whimsical expression. He was a head taller than she was, with wide muscular shoulders and yet his waist and hips were slim. He leaned indolently against

54

the door frame, his manner saying quite plainly that it was of no particular interest to him whether he had offended her or not and it was perhaps this which intrigued her the most.

'You are unforgivably rude,' she managed to say, foolishly, she realised.

'Mebbe I am.' His smile deepened into an amiable grin. 'But you can't expect men, if they are men that is, to be unaffected by the sight of such . . .' Again he let his gaze wander speculatively up and down her lovely, quite audaciously displayed body, 'such splendour,' he finished softly.

'I could have you flogged for this, you know that, don't you?' she said, just as softly, and somehow, though the words they were saying were quite clear in their meaning, their expressions seemed to imply something else, something which neither could quite grasp.

'Nay, hardly. If you don't want to be looked at, my lass, then you shouldn't make a spectacle of what no sane man could resist taking a peep at, or even two.' Will's grin became even wider, showing the strong white teeth which were a legacy of the pitchers of milk and lumps of cheese he had consumed as a boy and she found herself watching his mouth with a surprising intensity. 'You mun be used to taking offence, I dare say,' he went on engagingly, meaning no impertinence now since what he said must be the truth. 'Dressed like that every man between here and Oldham would be hard pressed to keep his eyes off you.'

'Who the devil are you to air your views on my appearance?' she managed to gasp. 'What I wear is nobody's business and certainly none of yours, whoever you are.' She had recovered herself now,

55

the hot flash of her temper exploding quite visibly. 'And I should be obliged if you would stand aside and let me pass.' Her face had gone strangely white, a pale translucent white as her fury increased, and her eyes had become almost transparent. She lashed her riding crop about her leg, in danger of hurting herself so menacing was her rage. Her nostrils flared and her soft pink mouth had thinned into a hard line, straining to find the words to punish him, to spit them out and turn them on him, whoever he might be. No one, except perhaps her Uncle Joss and he was hardly ever at home, had ever defied her dangerous spirit, had even had the courage to try to curb it. From the first nanny in whose arms she had been put at birth when her mother had hurried back to the mill which was her greatest concern, to the last young governess who had been employed to educate her, not one had had the resolution which was needed to discipline Tessa Harrison and so she had come to young womanhood believing herself to be infallible. She pleased herself, barging her way through whatever obstacle was put in her path. Her cousin Drew was the same, knocking aside or breaking any opposition which threatened him. Pearce, though just as bent on his own way, was a shade more subtle, perhaps a shade cleverer than they. He had a knack of climbing *over* a hurdle, of getting exactly what he wanted but with less wear and tear on the nerves, the temper, the peace of mind and sanity of everyone involved in their upbringing. She and Drew often admired the way he did it, watching as he teased and cajoled until he had what he wanted, marvelling at his patience but not caring to try it themselves. She had moved, as

56

they did, through sixteen years of her life expecting and getting everything she had ever wanted from it. It might be a nuisance in the evening when her mother insisted she wore a dress instead of her customary boots and breeches to the dinner table, but it was worth the bother for the freedom she was allowed at other times. She did not know, and did not care to ask lest it be curtailed, why her mother was so liberal, so different from the mothers of other girls of her acquaintance. It was enough for Tessa that she was: she took advantage of it and of every moment of liberty she could, blessing the mills which kept her mother so preoccupied.

'Get out of my way, you ill-mannered lout,' she hissed now, 'before I take my crop to you and wipe that foolish grin from your face. I don't know what you are doing here loitering in the doorway when you should be about some labour, but I intend to let my uncle know and you will be fired immediately.'

'Now then, lass,' Will said mildly, 'there's no need for that. I were only telling you the truth and well you know it, else why should you get in such a tantrum? Any lass who dresses . . .'

'By God, I won't stand here to be insulted by some . . . some yard labourer in my mother's mill. Are you to leave now or am I to have you thrown out?'

Will's face hardened and the amused and perfectly amicable expression in his eyes disappeared. He moved down from the bottom step and out into the yard. The sunlight fell on the short, rough cap of his hair, shading its pale brown to a pleasing, glinting fairness. He wore plain kersey breeches of good grey with stout black knee-boots and his jacket was of dark green corduroy. His shirt was a paler grey than his breeches and in the open neck was knotted a jaunty, freshly ironed red neckerchief. He looked just what he was: a labouring man who had come up in the world and certainly not the yard-hand she had thought him to be. He was a man who had, by hard work and self-education, risen from the thousands of faceless, nameless operatives who minded the mules and looms in the cotton factories of Lancashire; a man who could claim a position of responsibility, perhaps not yet of the manager class but not too far below it. He was about twenty-seven or eight with a look of good-natured tolerance, an easy-going man and yet there was a keen intelligence, a tough-fibred shrewdness about him which said he would be a hard man to take advantage of.

'Well?' Miss Harrison of Greenacres demanded loftily. 'Shall I call these men to throw you into the street or will you go unaided?' But her eyes studied his height and width somewhat uncertainly for now he was out of the shadows she could see he was taller, heavier, stronger, than any man in the yard.

'I think I'll stay just where I am,' he said softly.

'Very well.' She turned away from lifting her chin with the disdain of the young thoroughbred she was. She raised her hand and beckoned to four brawny men who had stopped work to watch, giving their undivided attention, as did every man in the yard, to the scene at the foot of the counting-house stairs.

'I would be obliged if you would throw this man into the street at once,' she told them imperiously. 'See, you four over here, if you please.'

'I'd save your breath if I were you, lass,' Will said

58

pleasantly enough. 'You don't want to make more of this than you already have. I am here to see Mr Greenwood and I doubt he'd take kindly to a brawl on his counting-house steps.'

'*You*! To see my uncle? Rubbish.' She did not even bother to turn her contemptuous glance on him but continued to gesture towards the four men who were reluctantly moving towards her, their eyes on the uncompromising man who stood at her back.

'They will not take me on, lass, believe me.'

'They will if I tell them to and when my family hears of the insulting way you have addressed me my cousins will give you the biggest hiding . . .'

'Lass, lass, give over. You're only making a show o' thissen. I meant no harm when I said every man in the yard was looking at you, nor offence. I was merely stating the obvious and surely to God you must know it, if that's the way you always dress. What man could resist it? They've never seen such fine . . .' Despite himself he could not help but grin and she turned, her expression menacing and her crop darted towards his chest, snapping against the knot in his neckerchief.

'Yes? Fine what?'

Will pushed his hands through his hair in exasperation and wondered how in hell he had got into this ridiculous situation. Why had he even bothered to speak to this girl when all he had to do in the first place was step aside and let her pass? She evidently believed she was above every consideration, every rule, every discipline with which life was ordered. It was nowt to him what she wore, how she spent her days or into what trouble, as a rebel, they led her. He had meant no

59

disrespect, none at all. He had been amused and strangely stirred by her appearance, as any man would be, but she had turned on him like a wildcat, creating this explosive situation in which not only he and herself were involved, but every damned man in the yard. There was not one moving, from nine-year-old boys, delighted by this diversion in their humdrum day, to older men who should have known better.

'Miss Harrison, will you not lower that riding crop?' He grinned for it was all so foolish, so childishly foolish. 'I'd not want to have to take it from you.' Instantly he could have bitten his tongue for it seemed she could resist no challenge; that everything said to her which she did not care for, must be opposed.

She grinned.

'Try! Go on! Take the crop and I shall say nothing to my uncle or my cousins of your insolence.' The end of the small whip just tickled his cheek and he felt the irritation in him stir to something else. He was a man slow to anger, equable, since his size and strength made other men reluctant to tackle him. But this bloody girl was like a persistent wasp: nothing to be afraid of but ready to sting if she could, to hurt him in any way she could, and no matter how many times he waved her away, she buzzed in again and again to attack wherever she found an opening.

'Oh, for God's sake, lass, be off about your business and let me take care of mine ...' The whip lashed out to sting his cheek sharply. She smiled brilliantly, her eyes vivid and mocking, her lips curved maliciously over her white teeth as a trickle of blood ran down his face.

60

'You were saying ...?' She danced away from him, her pert breasts lifting delightfully against her shirt.

The smoky brown softness of his eyes darkened dramatically. He put up a hand to his cheek, then looked at the blood on his fingers. His voice was ice cold and round the yard there was a concerted hiss from a dozen or more throats as the men pressed in closer.

'You need a good thrashing, Miss Harrison, and have done for a long while, that's what I'm saying, and if you were mine I'd see you had one before this day was out. And every day until you had learned some manners.' Before she could close her astounded mouth or blink her incredulous eyes he had taken her crop away from her and with a gesture of contempt snapped it in two over his bent knee. He threw it to the ground and her gaze followed it, the expression on her face quite unbelieving.

The yard was as silent and still as the cemetery on the outskirts of the town. There was no movement beyond that of the horse's tail as it swished at the flies which tormented it. The men waited, stunned by the big man's impudence. They waited for Miss Tessa to erupt into the savagery of which they knew her to be capable but the sound of another horse entering the yard turned all heads except those of Will Broadbent and Tessa Harrison, who continued to stare challengingly at one another. Not until Charlie Greenwood spoke did Tessa Harrison tear her gaze away.

'Tessa, what are you doing here?' He threw the reins of his horse to the waiting boy and walked tiredly towards the doorway, his eyes somewhat vague as though he had things on his mind other than his mill and was merely being polite.

'Charlie, this man has ...' She turned angrily to him.

'Not now, sweetheart, I have been ...'

'But, Charlie, you cannot mean to let this pass. He has ...'

'What pass, Tessa?' He had reached them by now and as though he had only just become aware of the tension in the yard he turned to look about him and at once every man and boy sprang into action and the yard became alive again.

'What's been going on here, Tessa?' he asked, but his slumped shoulders and strained expression said he really did not want to know and at once, to Will's surprise, she went to him and took his hand.

'It's nothing, Charlie, really. Some small disagreement, resolved now but what ...? Is there news of ...?' Her voice was soft, amazingly so, Will thought, the flashing eyes and furious clenching of her jaw completely gone as her concern for her uncle showed in her face.

'Aye, two hours since ... but ...' He sighed deeply.

'Not ...?'

'Yes, dead, poor little mite ... a girl ...'

'Oh, Charlie, I'm so sorry. And Laurel ...?'

'Sleeping now. I stayed with her. That's why I'm late.'

He turned away from her abruptly and found himself face to face with Will Broadbent. Conscious suddenly that he was saying more than was decent before a stranger, his voice was sharp.

'Do you have business here, Mr ... er ...?'

'Will Broadbent, and I believe we have an

62

appointment, Mr Greenwood, eight thirty sharp, but I can come back, sir, if you're ...' Will was polite and yet he showed no humility for he was a man who knew his own worth. He was courteous as a man should be, not just with this man who he hoped would give him the vacant post of under-tackler, but with anyone who, in his opinion, deserved it. Unruffled, honest of expression and sure of himself, but in his eyes was a look which conveyed his sympathy, the sympathy one man shows another who is grieving. Mr Greenwood was not himself and though Will had taken precious time to come to see him, it would not be right to press the man at this moment.

Tessa Harrison might no longer have existed for all the notice he now took of her. He was here by appointment, one made by Mr Greenwood only yesterday when Will had approached him in the yard. Naturally, he was well aware that employment at the Chapman factory was hard to come by for every job which fell vacant had two dozen applicants waiting to fill it. It was like working in heaven, it was said, compared to the dozens of other mills in the valley. Besides the decent working conditions in their mills the Greenwood family had built a school and all those who worked here, into the second generation now, could read and write, were well set up, healthy and cheerful, with none of the deformities which were to be found in the mill where Will presently worked. That was one of the reasons he wanted to leave it and be decently employed without the dreadful necessity of trying to get a day's work from operatives who were underpaid, underfed and exploited by the unscrupulous owner.

63

The repeal in 1846 of the hated Corn Laws, which had made rents high and living low, had alleviated matters somewhat for the lower classes as the price of bread came down, but there was still hunger, disease, squalor, long hours and hard labour in most textile mills. There were still strikes in which strikers' families starved and men, maddened by despair, ran amok, smashing, killing. But the 'hungry forties', as they were calling them, were surely done with now as trade boomed, mills prospered and unemployment was on the decline. The cotton towns, though they were for the most part a hideous, unplanned sprawl of delapidated cottages, broken pavements, rutted tracks and open drains, would surely improve with the Greenwood family's living example of how things might be done. A decent day's work would be rewarded with a decent wage.

'You're after the job in the spinning room?'

'Aye, sir. I want to work decent and ... well, where I am now ... it's not to my liking, but if you're ... I can come back ...'

'No ... no, come up, Broadbent, and we'll talk about it.' Charlie Greenwood turned to his niece who still held his arm. 'You'd best be off home, sweetheart. Nay, don't pull your lip at me, lass. You shouldn't be here in the first place, you know that.' He smiled affectionately, then without allowing her to speak again turned away and, indicating to Will to follow him up, began to climb the stairs.

*   *   *

He was on the top road which led from Crossfold to Edgeclough where he had lodgings, when she

64

rose from the spiky bushes of gorse which lined the track and amongst which she had been sitting, coming, it seemed to him in that moment, from the very ground beneath his feet.

It was almost noon and the sun fell directly on the glossy cape of her dark hair which had escaped the chenille net. The beauty of it caught his breath, then his irritation, at himself for being so affected by it and at her for her fool-hardiness in being here, alone, sharpened his voice.

'Good God, Tessa Harrison, what the devil are you doing up here by yourself? Don't you know there are all manner of ruffians on these moors? Have you no sense? And what is your family thinking of to allow it?'

She shook her head and shrugged as though to ask what that could possibly have to do with him.

'Did you get the job?'

'Why should you care?' His voice was set and closed.

She smiled and he felt his heart lurch against his breast-bone; then he turned away so that she might not see his face. It appeared that she bore him no ill-will for what had happened in the yard, indeed, now that it was over and done with, she found it amusing. She had a quick, hot temper, her smile said, but she was not one to harbour a grudge nor to sulk over it, as many women would, and her refreshing candour moved him in some strange way.

'It's nothing to me, really,' she answered lightly. 'Just put it down to curiosity. There were fifteen applicants, you know. I wondered what you had that they hadn't.'

'And have you decided?'

'I was hoping you would tell *me*.'

He sighed and turned back to her. 'Don't you think you had better get on your horse and go home as your uncle suggested?'

'I rarely do as people suggest, as you must have noticed.' She lifted her autocratic head then grinned impishly and he could not help but smile back.

'That's true, and yes, I got it. I start next Monday. Nice chap, Mr Greenwood.'

'I know. We all are in the Greenwood family.'

'Really?' His smile was rueful now and he raised his eyebrows.

'Mm. Though I'm not related by blood, of course.'

'Oh, aye. How's that then!' He found himself responding to her completely natural manner. It seemed not to occur to her that they had met for the first time only that morning, or even that he was to be employed in the family mill. She found him intriguing. He interested her and so she satisfied that interest in the only way she knew how. She asked questions regardless of his station in life, or hers.

'My mother was adopted. She has no idea where she came from.' She sat down on a sun-warmed rock indicating that he should sit beside her and again it seemed an entirely natural thing to do.

'Oh, aye.' His eyes were very soft as he studied this amazing girl who could in one moment be a bold-faced minx, and the next almost demure. He hesitated for a moment as though debating with himself on whether to speak, then:

'I was t'same,' he said quietly.

'The same?'

'Aye. Came with a cartload of others to Abbotts when I was no more than a nipper and I've bin there ever since. Mind you, I was a strong lad. God knows where I'd come from but wherever it was they'd fed me well, so I survived. I think that's why I love these hills so well, this moorland . . .'

'Why, Mr Broadbent?' She was quite enthralled and again he was bewildered by the mercurial changes in her moods. He felt a thrill go through him to have captured her complete attention, then a surge of irritation at feeling it, but he went on nevertheless for it was delightful to have those incredible eyes gazing so earnestly into his.

'Because we were shut up so much. It wasn't until I was a man grown that I could please myself, you see, then I discovered all this.' He waved a hand in the general direction of the great sweeping moorland which lay all about them and her own eyes followed the gesture. 'When I was a child I spent my Sundays, first at church where the mill-master's wife seemed to think it her duty to send me and my companions, then cleaning the machines on which the following day we were to labour. We had no time for tramping the moors, I can tell thee, even if it had been allowed, which it wasn't, or we'd the strength, which we hadn't. Apprentices, as we were called, were not well fed, Miss Harrison, and we had to be in the loomgate or jennygate from five in't morning until eight at night. It was a long time for a child.'

'You seem to have done well on it, Mr Broadbent.' It was not meant as a criticism, merely a statement of fact. Her eyes ran over his broad shoulders and the long strength of his limbs and as they did so they narrowed approvingly and she felt a not unpleasant flutter in the vicinity of her throat as the pulse there quickened. He really was a most unusual man with his strong, good-humoured face, his lazy, slanting smile. He had a way of talking, articulate and open, and though now and again he fell back into the way of speech of the working man he appeared to be, he was what she supposed would be called well educated. He was looking at her now in that gleaming, speculative way which she recognised, despite her youth, as the admiration of a man for a woman. He liked her, she could tell that, despite the battle they had fought in the mill yard. And that was another thing. Not many men would have had the daring—which she admired—to stand up to her in that way.

'Aye, well . . .' He grinned disarmingly and she leaned closer to him, her eyes filled with her curiosity. 'If you promise not to send for the nearest constable I'll tell you how I came to thrive where others didn't.'

'Oh, please.' She hitched herself even closer and he wondered at the trust and confidence of this girl. Though he was to be an employee in her family's mill, like hundreds of other men, he could very easily mistake her friendliness as an invitation for something else, which would not be hard to do, he admitted. A man might take advantage of what she seemed to offer and though it was doubtful any man would achieve much with this firebrand, he thought wryly, she would be seriously offended. And yet why should it concern *him*, he asked himself as she smiled winningly up at him, her eyes like grey crystal in the vibrant beauty of her face, and he did not know the answer.

'Should you not be getting home?' he asked,

suddenly aware that he himself was not immune to her attraction, to the interest she showed and the pleasure she seemed to find in his company. What man can resist a pretty woman who hangs on his every word? Though he knew it was probably only the reaction of a girl bored with her own class and curious about his. *He* could not resist *her*.

'Oh, no, please go on.'

He allowed himself to smile again, his eyes on her curving mouth. 'Well . . . I used to steal from the larders of those who had more to eat than I did.' His face became serious and her soft . . . dear God . . . soft pink mouth dropped open in awe.

'Where . . . ?'

'Every place I could find with a window I could open. Not the poor, of course, since they had nowt worth stealing anyway, but on most nights I would slip out when the others fell into their exhausted sleep and find a house which looked as though the occupants fed on more than cold-water oats and pigswill.'

'*Pigswill?*' She shuddered and pressed her shoulder against his.

'Aye, for that's what the others ate, lass. At first I'd hardly the strength to walk the necessary miles, for these houses were not close to the mill, as you can imagine . . .'

'No, indeed.'

' . . . but gradually, with the food I ate, and I only stole what was nourishing, and the milk I drank, I became stronger and could go further afield. I was a very resourceful lad, Miss Harrison,'—and you are a resourceful and strong man, Will Broadbent, and will go far, she had time to consider—'and I meant to survive. I used to enjoy those walks,

69

striding out in the summer night when it was warm and all scented with the aroma of wildflowers, or the heather drifting down from the hills. I had known only the stink of the mill, you see, and the spinning room and all the unwashed people who worked there.'

'Of course.' Her eyes were enormous in her pointed face, a face bemused and wondering, and he had the most overpowering inclination to place his mouth on the one which parted in fascinated interest as he told his tale. He tore his gaze away to stare into the sunlit valley below, then he grinned.

'Promise me you won't breathe a word to your uncle or I'll lose me grand new job afore I start?'

'My uncle? Why?'

'One of the larders I robbed was at Greenacres.'

'Oh Lord, you didn't?' He could see he had impressed her enormously, as would anything which was out of the ordinary, different, or smacked of defiance of authority.

'I did, Miss Harrison. I helped myself to a turkey leg which I knew would not be missed, a lump of the most delicious cheese which I have since discovered was from our own Lancashire, drank a pitcher of milk, thick with cream, and some plum pudding. It was Christmas, you see.'

He had not said it to gain her sympathy, just to demonstrate why he had remembered the exact meal on which he had dined that night in the house in which she herself was probably upstairs sleeping. But somehow his words moved a soft and dangerous thing inside her and she took fright at it since this man was a stranger after all.

She cleared her throat and blinked her eyes as though to clear the fog of curious emotion which

70

blurred them, then stood up quickly and turned away for she did not want him to see and wonder over her sudden agitation. In her mind's eye she could still visualise the tiny scar he had on his chin, no more than a small indent, and she wondered wildly how he had come by it in his deprived and loveless childhood; then, even more wildly, why it should concern her.

'I'd best get you home, Miss Harrison,' he said abruptly.

They were the exact words needed to release her from the strange enchanted spell his voice had cast about her. She was no weak girl who needed a man's help to get her from one place to another. She was Tessa Harrison who could ride gloriously to hounds and keep up with the best horseman in the county. She could leap the highest hedges and the widest streams. She could shoot fifty birds with fifty shots and had been known, though her family were not aware of it, to dress herself in her cousins' clothing and frequent a bare-knuckle prize fight and even a bear baiting with Drew and Pearce and Nicky Longworth. She had not enjoyed either, but she had *seen* them, had proved herself as strong and resolute as any man and she did not need this chap to escort her home.

'I need no help to get me home, Mr Broadbent,' she said sharply, her eyes flaring in a burst of annoyance which came from nowhere to attack him.

'As you like, Miss Harrison.' His voice was just as curt for he had found himself to be quite devastated when the softness, the sweet womanliness of the past few minutes was dashed away coldly as the affronted Miss Harrison leapt

71

lightly on to the back of the small mare she whistled up.

'Safe journey, then,' he could not help adding for it seemed to him it was a long, hard road she was to take.

'Heavens, Mr Broadbent, I am to go but to Greenacres, after all.'

'I doubt it, Miss Harrison.' Turning swiftly away from her, his face curiously stern, he strode off in the direction of Edgeclough.

CHAPTER FOUR

They stood in the office of the spinning-mill manager, their faces set in identical expressions of boredom, young gentlemen impeccably suited in the sober uniform of a businessman: black frock coat, light grey trousers, plain grey waistcoat and a shirt front which was immaculate. Each wore a pearl tie-pin in his neck cloth, a present from their mother on their seventeenth birthday, just gone. Their loathing of commerce could not have been more evident and Mr Wilson sighed, for what was the use of it? They wasted *his* time, which was valuable, and their own, which was not, but Mr Greenwood had insisted upon it and there was nothing the manager could do. He had worked at Chapman Manufacturing for nearly twenty years, starting as a spinner, then overlooker, a promotion to foreman, then manager of this mill two years ago, answerable to Mr Charlie Greenwood himself.

For the past few months, ever since they had left school, the twin sons of Mr and Mrs Joss

72

Greenwood, who owned Chapmans, had been coming to the mill each morning at five thirty. Slowly, week by week, they were moving through the whole process of preparing and spinning yarn, starting in the blow room where the bales of raw cotton were opened, cleaned and blended ready for combing. Here the impurities and short fibres were removed until the cotton was ready for spinning. There were five more procedures to be gone through—winding, knitting, warping, sizing and drawing in—before the spun yarn was ready for weaving and the cloth finished. All must be thoroughly learned by Masters Drew and Pearce, and though they presented themselves each day and were seen to be there in the flesh, so to speak, it could not be said that either of them had the slightest notion of how the simplest process came about, nor the slightest desire to be told.

They had been lounging against the stable-yard wall, just beyond the laundry, when nemesis had fallen. A pretty laundry maid stood between them, all three giggling over some nonsense the boys were pouring into her willing ear, when Joss Greenwood had come across them. He had arrived at Greenacres unexpectedly, perhaps for a purpose, who was to say? Certainly not the two boys whose eyes had widened in alarm as his hands fell on their shoulders, the expression on his face freezing the blood in their veins.

'You will settle down to some decent occupation,' he said when they stood before the desk in his study, 'and that means, naturally, in the trade which employed your maternal and paternal grandfathers. Your place is in the mill. You are to be commercial gentlemen as not only your father, your grandfather but your great-grandfather were before you, not young squireens like Nicky Longworth or Johnny Taylor who were born to it. Do you understand?'

They said they did.

'*You* were born to be manufacturers and manufacturers you will be. That is why you were educated at the local grammar school and not at public school as your friends were, so that you might get something in your heads other than a bit of Latin and Greek. Do I make myself clear?'

They said he did.

'Now I appreciate that you have no particular aptitude for it; that you have no inclination towards machinery, nor the adding up of profit and the subtraction of loss. But you will learn, for that is what you are to do with your lives now that your schooling is ended. Is that clear?'

They said it was.

'You will accompany your Aunt Jenny and Charlie to the mill each day, starting at five thirty, as they do, and you will learn to get on with those about you. To start with you will go with Wilson on his daily round of the mill at Chapmanstown, since it is the largest, and make yourselves conversant with all the processes of spinning, and work with Aunt Jenny in the counting house getting to know the overall business strategy. You will travel to Manchester with Charlie to acquaint yourselves with the trading side of the business, see to the purchase of raw cotton, learning from him, and others, how to judge *when* to buy and how much to *pay*. There will be the organising of credit to our customers, the collection of trade debts in world markets and the proper knowledge of how to husband your resources. You will agree, will you not, that there is a lot to be learned and the quicker you get started the sooner you will be able to take over when the time comes. Is that understood?'

They said that it was.

'You will go to the Cloth Hall each week, or perhaps more often, depending on trade. Your lives will be controlled, not by your own whims and fancies but by the factory bell. There will be no galloping off to join the Squire's hunt at the first hint of autumn. You will work in the spinning rooms and weaving sheds and get yourselves dirty, as I did, as your Aunt Jenny did, as Charlie did, as your own mother did, and you will become millmasters, the manufacturing gentlemen you were destined to be. Do you understand? And if I hear you have disobeyed me I shall have you whipped into the mill yard and keep you permanently without money until you stay there.'

*   *   *

Mr Wilson was droning on and Drew yawned.

' . . . designed to spin and wind automatically. It will also make the necessary adjustments between successive draws to take account of the growing size of the cop and the decreasing length of the bare spindle blade, as you will see when we go into the spinning room . . .'

What is the old fool blethering on about? Drew's eyes signalled to Pearce. God knows, he was answered, and could you care less? The two handsome boys, just seventeen years old and destined never to go to Cambridge, never to go on a Grand Tour as Johnny Taylor's father had promised *him*, never to go *anywhere*, their despairing expressions said, but across the yard and into the spinning room, or to Broadbank and the weaving sheds, stared desperately into one another's eyes.

'Now have you any questions before we go into the spinning room, young sirs?' Mr Wilson asked genially, short-sightedly, hopelessly, since he knew there would be none.

They said they hadn't.

'Right, then if you will follow me we will step across the yard and Broadbent will show you the self-actor in motion.'

Pearce told himself that this time it would be better. No one had warned him on that first day two months ago when they had entered the spinning room, and so the shock had been all the greater, and he had felt that he could not really be blamed for the way he had reacted then. He and his brother had been reared like the young colts up in the paddocks of Greenacres and the contrast had been appalling. Suddenly they had been transferred from the lush meadows where they had bucked and kicked their high-spirited heels since the day they were born. Taken from the sun-dappled freedom, from the joy of being skittish with their own kind, it had seemed to Pearce, they had been put, like the pit-ponies they had heard about, in the black confines of the underground mines. That was how the spinning room had appeared to Pearce, used as he was to wild moors, high-vaulted skies and the pungent smell of heather and gorse in his nostrils.

There had been a general darkness at first, a lack of the fresh air and sunshine to which they were both accustomed, though the windows of the mill stood wide open. The noise was indescribable; clatter, rattle, bang, the swish of thrusting leavers, the crash of carriages 'letting in', the shouts of the minders as they summoned a piecer or a scavenger. What seemed to be hundreds of people crowded down the long rows of spinning mules with literally thousands of spindles and the heat was such he could distinctly see the oil bubble from the pinewood planking of the floor. Little piecers ran barefoot repairing broken threads, skidding and slipping, some of them, with the speed they went, rolling instinctively to avoid the gliding carriages, well aware of the consequences should one of the advancing monsters catch them.

A film of flock, or 'fly', as it was called, immediately settled on the fine coats of the two young gentlemen and dusted their smoothly brushed hair. Pearce felt it invade his mouth as he took a deep breath, settling in his throat and drifting into his nostrils. His stomach lurched uneasily and the breath became trapped somewhere in his lungs. He knew himself to be suffocating. If he did not get out of here he would either vomit the substantial breakfast he had eaten all over his new, pale grey waistcoat, or faint right away like any languid maiden. The mass of interested faces, the noisy spinning mules, the straps and belts and wheels, the constant movement of women and children and machines all ran together, blending into a misted haze which floated before him and about him, and he had time only to fling himself backwards, down the steps and into the yard before nausea overtook him. He clung to the wall, watched by men who nudged one another slyly, their prediction that these two fine young gentlemen would never last the course becoming true on their very first day, it seemed. His face sweated and so did his body inside the immaculate crispness of his clean shirt. He felt dirty and wretched, a sensation he had never known before and he had not liked it. But he had been forced to go back, time and time again, and it had never got better. Never. The walls closed in on him; the machines appeared to glide towards him the moment he entered the room, hemming him in between their lethally moving parts. He swore he would overcome the sensation and was ashamed when he could not. He was afraid of nothing, just like Drew. They had ridden frighteningly wild horses ever since they had been big enough to climb on their backs. They had jumped hurdles higher than their own heads. They had gone out with the hunt and taken many a tumble, broken a bone or two, clambered back on and continued as though nothing had happened, smiling through the pain. They had fought boys bigger and stronger than themselves, had their eyes blacked and blacked a few in their turn, bloodied noses, and known no fear. The bleak, open barrenness of the moorland, vast and empty and cruel at times, an enemy of those who did not respect it, was their territory, a place he loved and roamed with Drew and Tessa, but it held no terror for him, unlike the hot, clammy, airless hell of the spinning room. And his terror grew with every visit, a terror he was forced to hide from everyone but Drew, and it shamed him.

On this day, as he followed Drew inside, the din and confusion which met him at the door instantly stunned him, taking his mind and his determination. His step faltered. His eyes went black and sightless and but for the broad back of his brother ahead of him he would have lost his way. He was like a sleep-walker, but some tiny, still-intelligent part of his mind told him he must just follow that back wherever it went: hang on to that thought, to that solid, dependable shape ahead of him, the brother who had never in all their young lives together let him down or deserted him, who had been his other half for sixteen years and who would lead him from this place which, with every second, was closing in on him.

But it was no use, his last desperate thought told him, as the greyness about him became black. He felt himself slip on the oil-soaked floor, his stomach heaved and the blood began to drain away from his head.

'Just bend ower, lad,' a light voice said and he felt a pressure on his arm and across his back and though it was not forceful he found himself obeying. He was hanging, head down—how in hell had he got here?—over a motionless machine. He could see nothing but oil and cotton-waste and the face, young and cheeky, of a little piecer who had crept beneath the machine to get a better look at him. There were bare feet everywhere, dirty and splayed, ugly some of them with swollen veins and joints, but the pair nearest to him, though just as dirty, were small and fine, narrow and really rather shapely. He sensed dozens of pairs of curious, probably amused eyes on him; then he was gripped again in a violent spasm of nausea.

'Come on, old chap,' a gentle voice said and familiar, strong brown hands, duplicates of his own, grasped his. He clung gratefully to them as they began to lead him, blind and ill, towards the doorway at the end of the interminably long room and out into the yard.

'Fresh air'll see 'im right,' a voice said briskly, as though the owner of it really had no time to be wasting on him, then he was out ... thank God, thank God ... out of the smell and the din and the enveloping walls, the hellish confusion, and at once he was recovered.

He lifted his head and looked into Drew's concerned face, which grinned at once, letting him know that though he did not really understand what ailed his twin he was quite willing to try, and to stand shoulder to shoulder with him should anyone turn awkward over it. There was a girl there, small, light-boned and thin and yet giving the impression, strangely, that she was as sturdy as the weeds which grew in the hedgerow. Her face was pale, and plain as a bleached yard of cotton. Her eyes were a sharp and almost colourless blue and her fine, mousy hair was dragged back from her face into what must surely have been a painful knot at the back of her head. Her bare feet stepped without concern on the bare cobbles and he knew that this must be the person who had, with her quick thinking, saved him from losing consciousness.

'Tha'll be reet now. Tek a few deep breaths,' she ordered, wiping her hands down her sacking apron. She did not look away when his eyes met hers, nor shuffle about awkwardly as the lower orders often did in the presence of their superiors, but met his glance steadily. He had never seen a girl less comely and yet she had a quiet dignity which was unusual in someone of her age and class. 'Tha'll get used to it, like we all 'ave to,' she added ready, now that he was recovered, to get back to her work.

'Like hell I will,' he answered harshly, wiping his arm across his sweated face. 'I'll run away to sea before I'll go in there again.'

'Hold on, brother.' Drew's lazy drawl and narrowed eyes indicated to him that the undertackler, Broadbent, was not far away but Pearce was beyond caution.

'No! You hold on, brother. It's not you who turns faint like some puling woman . . .'

'I never 'eard such nonsense in me life. Turnin' sick ower a bit o' stink. We none of us like it, Mr Greenwood, but we've no choice. It's work or starve wheer I come from an' let me tell thi, we're glad o't work. 'Ave thi ever bin in Abbotts mill or any on 'em in this valley? 'Ave thi? Conditions 'ere are like a palace compared to t'other 'uns. Thee'd 'ave summat ter be sick ower if thi 'ad ter work theer.'

Both young gentlemen turned to stare at the girl who spoke. She might have been some creature from another world, or a gatepost which one does not, naturally, expect to speak, so deep was the amazed consideration they gave her now. Indeed, despite their close proximity to them, the two boys had never actually *noticed* an operative in the weeks they had been working in the mill. The girl stared back at them grimly, such a plain, drab little thing, resembling nothing so much as the sparrows which nested in thc ivy on the walls of Greenacres, a sparrow which, nevertheless, was prepared to take on two magnificent soaring eagles. Her expression asked quite plainly what else could you expect of

81

these pampered young fools who were playing, reluctantly she had heard, at being commercial gentlemen. Their aunt and uncle knew exactly what she and the hundreds of others in the mill endured day after day, though this was a good mill. Both of them knew the meaning of *work*. These two young bucks, quite evidently, would soon tire of the discipline, the sheer physical discomfort of the factory floor and take themselves back to their old pastimes of shooting everything that took wing and riding like madmen with others of similar inclination, chasing the fox through the farmer's cornfield.

'I'll get back ter me machine, then,' she added coldly. 'Time's money ter me, an' I've already lost 'alf an 'our wi' thee.' With that she turned on her heel and walked away, her thin back straight, her narrow shoulders squared.

'Sorry about that, Mr Broadbent,' she said to the overlooker who still leaned in the doorway. He was watching the two young men. They were laughing now, quite amused, it seemed, by the strange girl who had given them the sharp end of her tongue but not the least offended since, really, did she matter? They had got themselves, through her, out of the damned spinning room and why not take advantage of it? They strolled towards the gate with the appearance of gentlemen who, having done their day's work, were off about more important matters, though it was barely seven o'clock.

'Nay, Annie, don't fret, lass. It's not the first time it's happened and it'll not be the last.'

'Does't tha think they'll come back, then?' she asked, surprised.

'Oh, aye. Their father's set on it, it seems. It's to be their mill, after all.'

'God 'elp us, then.'

'Happen he'll get over it, the sickness.'

''Appen, but that'll not mek 'im into a millmaister, Mr Broadbent.'

There was a sudden commotion at the closed gate and the man who had charge of the key ran frantically across the yard to unlock it. Every morning the gate was locked on those late-comers who had no legitimate excuse, such as the illness of a child, and not opened again until eight o'clock, but the girl who was shouting to be let in was not one of those and the gatekeeper knew better than to keep her waiting. The mare was restlessly sidestepping, catching her rider's impatience, and the gatekeeper fumbled with his keys whilst the voice on the other side urged him to get a move on. At last he had it open and in she came, hair flying out in a banner behind her, scattering the same men and boys Will had watched her disperse a few weeks ago. He had not seen her since that day but she was just the same. Heedless of those who got in her way, she went straight as an arrow towards her target, her two cousins who had turned to look at her.

She did not dismount. Drew put up a hand to her mare's nose as she leaned down to him. All the men in the yard, grumbling beneath their breath, had turned to look at her, as Will was sure she intended. Her mare moved sideways again, nervously shying away from the enormous waggon which was just entering the yard, but she held it in expertly, her gloved hands firm on the rein, her slim, muscled legs strong and lovely in their dove-grey breeches.

Her eyes narrowed as she caught sight of him across the heads of the men and there was a burst of laughter as she said something to her cousins. All three turned to look at him and he could feel the hard knot of anger tie itself beneath his breastbone. The two young men lounged indolently against the mill wall, their hands shoved deep in their trouser pockets, their dark eyebrows arched, their eyes gleaming in identical amusement. He saw their good white teeth flash in their sun-darkened faces and then, with the insolence of the lordly young gentlemen they considered themselves to be, they turned away. He was nothing to them, merely that breed known as overlooker in their mill, a man *under* the man who was in charge of the spinners, but not of *them*. Pearce left the other two for a moment, making some sign to the boy who hung about the yard and whose job it was to attend to the horse of any caller. In a moment the boy returned, leading the two restive bays which the brothers rode. They all three turned to look at Will again, the girl grinning now to let him see that this was really *her* doing. The boys mounted gracefully and one turned to him, grinning, his voice flippant since they all knew he was lying.

'Some urgent business. Tell Wilson, if you please.' With their coat-tails flying and the girl's hair and ribbon streaming out behind her, they galloped madly from the yard, down the street towards the edge of town and the wild moorland which was the only place they really wished to be.

Mr Wilson came slowly down the steps from the first-floor spinning room, his face resigned but not unduly concerned since they were not *his* problem, thank God.

'Where the devil have those two gone now?' the men in the yard heard him say out loud, shrugging, for what else could you expect? It was no good trying to tame a bird which has flown free since it came from the egg and in their opinion, their good-humoured north-country faces seemed to say, best save your breath to cool your porridge. It was too late. A flogging once a week starting in the nursery was what those two had needed, her an 'all, really, then happen they might have shaped themselves. Too late now, they repeated as they resumed the work which had been so violently disrupted, bloody glad it was nowt to do with them.

'Urgent business, they said, Mr Wilson,' Will answered him, eyebrows sardonically raised, and was not surprised when Mr Wilson swore quite rudely beneath his breath before turning back to the stairs.

CHAPTER FIVE

She had given her mare her head, letting her go flat out over the rough stretch of moorland known as Besom Hill, seeing the coarse grass blur beneath the animal's hooves. Her face was pressed close to the mare's neck as she bent down with her into the wind. Her dratted hair had come loose as usual, whipping about her head and eyes, blinding her for a moment, and she did not see the half a dozen rabbit holes until her mare swerved to avoid them. She felt herself move forward over the animal's neck, her co-ordination gone completely with her balance; when she hit the ground, though she landed in a clump of heather which broke her fall somewhat, the breath was knocked from her body. She lay for a minute or two, gasping for air, watching the sky swing in sickening loops above her, then as it steadied and became still and serene again, she sat up, looking around for her mare.

She was high up here, almost at the top of the moorland sweep with a splendid view of the rock-strewn stretch of moor which went on endlessly as far as the eye could see. It was bleak and treeless, rough ground pierced with mosscovered boulders, submerged in gorse and bracken, with a dozen shades of green from the paleness of the ferns which sheltered by a dry-stone wall, to the dark, cloud-shadowed foliage on the far side of the deep clough which split the land. A soaring, grey-green landscape, hard and enduring, cut with water and rocks, where a bird or two wheeled above her head, and nothing else.

There was no sign of her mare.

'Damnation,' she said softly, swinging back her mane of hair. Then, feeling for the ribbon which confined it and finding it gone, she pulled her scarf from around her neck and carelessly bound up the troublesome locks. She stood up and dusted off her cream, doeskin breeches. Shading her eyes from the sun, she looked about her, her eyes penetrating the vast landscape for a sight of her mare. There was nothing to be seen, no movement of any kind beyond that of the birds above her head.

It was not cold and the clouds were broken and low, some enfolding the top of the highest peaks. They moved quickly allowing the sun to show through, and for half an hour she sat on a rock and stared out across the tops, to the next and the next, whistling now and again to attract her mare, should she still be in the vicinity. But the mare was not inclined to show herself and would, no doubt, be well on her way to the stables at Greenacres by now. There was no alternative but to walk: almost five miles, she reckoned, skirting Edgeclough and Harrops Edge and following the rough moorland track to the back of the Greenacres parkland.

It was warm walking but very pleasant. She removed her jacket and was tempted to hide it under a rock, picking it up the next time she came this way for it was cumbersome to carry. She draped it over one shoulder, climbing steadily up the next rocky incline until she reached the brow, then, carried by her own momentum, almost running down the far side.

Her boots began to chafe her heel. She was used only to riding in them; in fact, come to think of it, she really had no footwear suitable for striding out across the hills since she rarely did it. She walked over the Squire's moor when she accompanied Drew and Pearce on one of his shoots but that was in a much more leisurely fashion, more of a stroll than a walk.

She skirted Edgeclough an hour later, clambering over a dry-stone wall to walk on the rutted path, once a 'salt-way', she had been told, which led past the town, or hamlet as it had been in the old days. The clamouring of factory bells and whistles announced the changing of shifts and far below she could make out the patient crowds of ant-like men, women and children streaming through half a dozen factory gates.

The moors were deserted, achingly empty, and

the sun had gone completely as the summer's day began its slide towards twilight. Her boots were really rubbing now as she began the descent from Edgeclough towards Chapmanstown. Damn it, she would have to stop a minute and take them off. She must have blisters the size of a guinea on her heels. But if she took them off would she be able to get them on again, she wondered? Well, she'd rest for a moment and then go on. Her mare would have reached home without her by now and Walter would be running round the stable yard raising the alarm. There'd be a search party out in half an hour and she wanted to be well on her way before she met up with it. How very demeaning to have taken a tumble on this relatively easy stretch of moorland! Drew and Pearce would crow over it, saying she was not fit to be let out alone, which would bring the whole matter to her mother's attention. There would be hell to pay, probably an ultimatum to take Walter with her on future rides or some such nonsense.

They came over the brow of the hill just as she stood up, half a dozen or so of them. The man was of medium height but painfully thin and a washed-out, ferret-faced woman shuffled behind him pushing a broken-down hand-cart on which rattled and shook a festering pile of what Tessa could only describe as rubbish which threatened to fall off with every turn of the wheels. Slung out behind was a miscellaneous rabble of children of various ages and sizes, all scratching and picking at themselves, with sore eyes and no teeth to speak of in their wizened, little old men's faces, small and stunted with rickety legs and no shoes to their dirty feet.

They all stopped when they saw her, as though

she was some mirage shimmering ahead of them, which, in a way, she was. Who would expect to see a girl such as herself alone up here, a girl in a pure silk shirt, in breeches of the finest quality doeskin and boots of the finest quality leather, all of which would fetch a decent price in any market?

The man's eyes, which had been vague and empty, sharpened to flint. He did not turn to the tribe behind him, merely put out a hand which said 'leave this to me, we'll have us a grand supper tonight', and they all stood obediently, well used to taking his orders, it seemed.

'Good day to yer,' he said cheerfully, his Irish brogue so thick it was difficult to understand. ' 'Tis a great one, ter be sure.'

'Indeed,' she answered guardedly, beginning to walk towards him for he stood on the track down which she must go to reach Crossfold.

'Could yer spare a copper or two fer a starvin' family?' His eyes ran over her like the fleas which so evidently swarmed on himself and his family, to judge by the way they were scratching, and she dug her fingers into her own suddenly prickling scalp.

'I don't carry any money with me,' she said shortly, wishing to God she'd brought the dogs with her, cursing her own stupidity in leaving them at home. She'd imagined, as she had always done in the past when she had come across a vagrant or a tramp or one of the itinerant families she met, such as this one, that she had only to touch her heels to her mare's flank and she could outrun any man with dubious intentions towards her.

She began to edge past them. The man made no move to stop her, merely watching her with the child-like curiosity of someone set down amongst beings he had never before clapped eyes on, and she began to breathe a little more easily. The woman even sketched a curtsey, though there was no respect in it, and it was not until she reached the last figure, a weasel-faced, cross-eyed, runny-nosed lad somewhat bigger than the others, that the whole family moved. The man must have made some signal behind her back and as she passed the boy, trying hard not to look into the nastiness of his face, his foot shot out and neatly inserted itself between her boots, bringing her down with her face in the dry-baked hardness of the track. They were all over her then, like a pack of squealing rats, hands and small, filthy feet pressing her down until the man's voice, harsh and expecting to be obeyed at once, shifted them all.

'Turn 'er over an' let's see what we got,' he commanded and several pairs of hands obliged until she was glaring up into the dirt-ingrained face, the cunning, jubilant eyes, the mouth in which there was nothing but blackened stumps, of the head of the family. For several minutes they all laughed and chattered evidently unable to believe their good luck and though Tessa struggled wildly, threatening them with everything from a flogging to transportation, even the gallows, they took no notice. In her heart where up to now there had been no more than outrage, alarm began to grow. She had believed that though they might take her boots, her beautifully cut and tailored tweed jacket, she had nothing more to fear than that: they were a family and therefore, though they might be thieves, would not use violence. But the man and the boy who had tripped her were looking at her in a nasty way, licking their cracked lips, their eyes on her freely moving, almost exposed breasts which strained through the silk of her shirt. The woman had become uneasy, shifty, watching her menfolk with the resignation of one who has long given up defiance or argument, and when told would obey without question.

The man did not speak, just lifted his eyes to those of his son and smiled. The boy smiled back at him and when the man, with a curt movement of his head to the woman and the rest of the group indicated that they were to move on, the gesture saying that he and the lad would be along presently, they obeyed at once.

Tessa began to scream. It was no more than the shrill cry of a rabbit when faced with a stoat, a despairing cry, but the woman turned back, her woman's sensibility giving her, for a moment, the pity one female feels for another who is to suffer as perhaps she once had done, as perhaps her own female children had done, despite their age.

'Get on, woman, 'tis nought ter do wi' you,' her husband, if that was what he was to her, said and struck her across the face. For a second, only the boy held Tessa; he was looking away towards his parents, waiting eagerly for what he was to share with his father, impatient for his mother to be dealt with as he had probably seen her dealt with a hundred times before.

Tessa was up then, and free of his grasp, pushing him out of her way since she was stronger than he was, bounding in terrifying leaps down and down the steep stretch of moorland, tearing herself on the spiky gorse, banging her ankles on angry rocks, her breath hot and cutting in her throat and chest, her back cringing away from what was behind her,

91

her flesh flinching, expecting at every step to feel their hands. There was another wall ahead of her, higher than she was, dangerous with loose stones, crumbling and waiting only for an unwary hand or foot to bring it down. She had her fingers on the top cam stones, pulling at them to lift herself up and over, but her pursuers were at her back now, their hands reaching for her. She could smell their foul, unwashed bodies, the stench of the rotting teeth in their opened mouths, then she was carried backwards, flung into the waist-deep fern and bracken and her cry, her feeble cry of anguish, was strangled by a cruel hand.

The roar of rage could be heard as far away as Edgeclough, or so she believed later. Now she was conscious of nothing but a great, heavy shadow looming over her, of hands which she tried weakly to resist: then air and space and light, emptiness, no sound but that of men's voices and men's bodies blundering away into the distance, becoming fainter and fainter, a blessed 'nothingness' which wrapped itself about her peacefully. She dared not look, of course, for fear she had imagined them to be gone and they would be standing over her, grinning, taunting. She curled herself up, her arms wrapped about her knees, pulling them high to her breasts, her head tucked into her shoulders, prepared to stay there until Drew or Pearce, or even Walter came for her, but a voice spoke up sharply.

'Nay, they've gone now. You've nowt ter be feared of. Mr Broadbent'll mek mincemeat of 'em, tha'll see.'

She peeped out from beneath her folded arms. A young girl was peering over the wall at her with

92

an expression of disapproval which seemed to ask what else you could expect of a lass who wandered the hills all by herself, dressed up like she was, and if she had her way, a good thrashing would not go amiss. She was about her own age, a girl whom you'd not recognise tomorrow if you spoke to her today, so colourless was she. A girl with a pale face, pale eyes and pale scraped-back hair, wearing a clean, drab shawl and a bodice to match. The rest of her Tessa could not see.

'Are yer ter stay theer all day, then?' the girl asked tartly.

Tessa stood up slowly, turning anxiously towards the steep incline where, she supposed, the men had gone, then back to the girl.

'Who was it?' she quavered, a violent fit of shocked trembling beginning to shake her from head to foot. Even her teeth chattered.

'Come over't wall,' the girl ordered and Tessa obeyed without question. She was wrapped snugly in the girl's shawl. Her flowing hair was tied back again with the scarf, the hands which performed the task strangely gentle. She leaned gratefully against a shoulder which was thin but apparently strong and when the girl began to walk in the direction of Edgeclough, still with her strong young arms about her, Tessa went with her.

'Tha've nobbut thissen ter blame, tha' knows,' the girl said crossly, just as though Tessa had become involved in a minor tumble brought on by her own foolishness, as in a way she had. 'Theer's nowt in't world'd make me cross them moors on me own. Mr Broadbent lives up near me so me an' 'im always walk together, but if 'e's on different shift I wait while Aggie or Rose is ready. I used ter

93

walk wi' me Mam but she . . . well . . .' She shook her small head fiercely, not prepared to reveal anything more of herself to a stranger, it seemed. She continued to scold Tessa in the sharp voice of one who is used to being in command of others, taking no 'lip' but at the same time patting her shoulder awkwardly, giving her time to pull herself together, soothing her, not with obvious sympathy but with her own sensible belief that there was no use in crying over spilt milk so best get on with mopping it up.

They came to a small house in a row of similar houses: all neat and tidy, decent, with a bit of garden in front, the windows polished and the steps donkey-stoned. There was an air of spartan cleanliness about the one her rescuer entered. It smelled of carbolic and beeswax. The hearth was freshly brushed, the brick floor freshly swept, the table all set out with decent crockery, and floating out to greet them the smell of something cooking on the sparse fire. At the table sat four children. They all turned expectantly as Tessa's friend opened, then shut the door firmly behind her, the gesture saying quite clearly that what was done inside these four walls was no one's business but *theirs*.

'This 'ere young lady 'ad an accident so put kettle on't fire, our Nelly,' she said brusquely. Tessa found herself placed with little ceremony in the rocking chair by the fire, a cushion at her back, a buffet at her feet and all done with the minimum of fuss and no regard at all for her higher station in life. She might have been a casual acquaintance, perhaps another mill-hand, but made *comfy* just the same.

94

She still shivered and shook and when the tea was put in her hand she could scarcely hold it. She was settling into a badly shocked state now and the girl looked anxiously at her and kept going to the window to stare out into the darkening street.

'Get on wi' thy tea, our Polly,' she said to one little girl who was inclined to stare in awe at Tessa.

'Are tha not 'avin' any, our Annie?' the third girl asked. 'I put a bit o' scrag end in wi't carrots. Do thi good,' she added with the same business-like air of their Annie.

'Aye, but I'll wait while Mr Broadbent gets 'ere, Gracie.'

'Where is 'e then, Annie?'

'Never you mind. Get yer tea down yer. There's many a lass'd be glad o' that, so shut thi trap and gerron wi' it.'

When the knock on the door sounded she was there to answer it at once, apparently having seen the caller come up the garden path. She flung it open with evident relief and the enormous man who entered smiled at her for a moment, telling her, since she was really no more than a child herself, that everything was as it should be. He turned instantly to Tessa, squatting down on his haunches before her.

'Lass,' he said softly. They all gathered round, the scrag end forgotten in the wonder of the moment: Annie, the one who had brought her home, their Nelly who had made the tea, Polly, whose endeavours with the scrag end were being so ungraciously ignored, Gracie and a boy who looked to be a year or two younger than Annie. Their expressions were solemn, their faces as plain as their older sister's, but sharply intelligent.

95

'Are you . . . did they . . . hurt you, lass?' the man asked, putting up a hand to smooth back her tangled hair and was relieved when she did not shrink away from him, though she did not answer.

'Are you all right, Tessa?' he went on and at the sound of her name she turned and a faint semblance of sense began to show in her empty grey eyes, the first Annie had seen since she had ordered her to climb over the wall.

'Yes, thank you,' she said politely.

'They . . . they didn't touch you?'

'No . . . only . . .'

'Only what, Tessa?'

'They knocked me down.'

'They'll not do it again, my lass.'

'Oh . . . ?'

'They'll be half-way to Leeds by now, I shouldn't wonder. I gave them a helping hand, like. But if they've hurt you in any way I'll fetch them right back and hand them over to the constable,'—but not before I've given them summat they'll not forget in a hurry, his bleak expression said.

'Oh, no, don't bring them back.'

'No, that's what I thought.'

He stood up then and looked about him, so tall and broad he seemed to fill the scrupulously polished kitchen from wall to wall. He said a word or two to the boy who nodded his head in understanding and after flinging a cap on his pale hair, left the cottage at once.

It was then Tessa recognised him. She had last seen him in the mill yard when her cousins had run off with her to the moor. They had all three laughed at him since he had Drew and Pearce in his charge that day and their defiance of him had

96

excited them. He was watching her steadily now, his soft, smoky-brown eyes concerned, with no hint of the coolness with which he had looked at her then, and not only then but the first time they had met when he had threatened to put her over his knee and spank her, like a naughty child.

'I've sent Jack to let your family know where you are. When you're ready I'll take you home . . .'

'That you'll not. Not while you've summat inside thi, both o' thi.' Annie began to crash plates about, sending their Nelly to stir the stew, their Polly for some peat for the fire and their Gracie to bed.

'Aah, Annie . . .' It was not often anything as exciting as this happened to the little girl, ' . . . can I not stop up . . .' Gracie began but Annie, whose word, it seemed, was law, would brook no argument and the child, taking a candle from the dresser, went obediently up the stairs.

Tessa was put on a bench by the table, shoulder to shoulder with Nelly. A plateful of stew with the precious scrag end plainly on view—most on *her* plate though she didn't notice—was set before her and she was told sharply, as the child had been, to 'eat up, lass'. To her surprise she found the food quite delicious.

She was feeling better now. No one took any notice of her. Polly was telling the big man, Mr Broadbent, they all called him, apparently well used to his company, about some wondrous thing she had become acquainted with at Sunday school the day before. Annie moved briskly between the table and the hearth in which an iron basket, fixed to the back of it, held the open fire where the cooking was done. When the meal was eaten Polly and Nelly took up a bit of plain sewing, mending

97

what looked like a cotton sheet, whilst Annie moved about, performing tasks the function of which were a mystery to Tessa, with the energy and vigour of a whirlwind. Mr Broadbent lit his pipe. The room was peaceful, warm with nothing of tension in it and Tessa looked about her with growing interest.

She had never seen a room so small and cluttered and yet so achingly clean. Where did they get their water, she thought, and how did one cook on that . . . that contraption in the hearth? And what on earth had been in the tasty meal she had just eaten? Who were these people, the girl and her family who, now that they had become used to her presence, acted as though she was one of them? Where was the mother, the father, and what was Mr Broadbent who was an overlooker at the mill doing here? Surely *he* could not be the father? The girl, Annie, had said he lived up her way which did not seem to mean with her. She studied the tall oak settle to one side of the fireplace, used as a seat but with a cupboard underneath. There were barrels against the wall and stoneware storage jars and on a shelf what looked like wine in glass bottles. She watched Annie take a spoonful of salt from a pinewood box mounted on the fireplace wall, then select a few dried mushrooms from a net which hung from the beam above the fire.

'Isn't bread done, lass?' she asked Polly and when the girl nodded, as sparing with words as her sister, Annie opened the door of the baking oven beside the fire. She nodded her head approvingly in Polly's direction, apparently well pleased with the girl's efforts and Polly, perhaps six or seven years of age, though she did no more than nod her own head, looked gratified; Annie's unspoken praise was something to be treasured.

The clock on the wall struck seven; they all turned to look at it and as they did so the boy returned, nodding in Mr Broadbent's direction.

'That lass'd better be gettin' off 'ome, Mr Broadbent,' Annie said firmly as she pushed her brother into a chair and put a plate of the stew in front of him. When she was satisfied that he was filling himself in what she considered to be an adequate manner, she turned in a bustling, efficient way to Tessa, her attitude so completely like Nanny in the nursery of her own younger days that Tessa began to smile. 'See, put that there shawl about thi ... no, give over arguin' wi' me. I've another. It were me ... me Mam's.' Her voice was almost ungracious but Tessa was getting the measure of this Annie by now and did as she was told. Nor did she say much in the way of thanks for somehow she knew Annie would not care for it.

'I'll si thi in't mornin', Mr Broadbent,' Annie said, wiping her hands on her coarse apron.

'Aye, lass. Five sharp at the top o't street.'

'Right. Well, good night then,' she said and before Tessa and Will Broadbent were hardly over the doorstep the door was shut resolutely behind them.

They walked in silence for five minutes or so. Tessa was inclined to look stealthily over her shoulder, keeping close to Will Broadbent's strong left arm and when she stumbled he took her hand and tucked it into the crook of his arm. She clung to it gratefully, still fragile in a way that surprised her. She was a young woman, tall, and strengthened by the hours she had spent in the

99

saddle, by the outdoor life she had led. She had been afraid of nothing in all her life since, she supposed, nothing had ever threatened her until today; but the ordeal she had suffered, though no harm had come to her, had for the moment sapped her confidence in herself and she was glad of this man's quiet, unflaunting strength beside her.

'You're not to come out alone again,' he said definitely, another who believed he was not to be disobeyed, apparently.

'Indeed I won't,' she answered readily enough, not adding that from now on, when she was not with her cousins, she would bring the dogs, knowing that was not what he meant.

'Good lass.'

There was silence again for another few minutes, then she broke it.

'Who is that girl, Mr Broadbent?' In the darkness she did not see Mr Broadbent's smile at the sound of this imperious young girl, who thought herself to be only a stratum or two below the Queen up in London, addressing him so respectfully.

'She's called Annie Beale. She works in the spinning room at Chapmans.'

'Really? She doesn't seem very old.'

'They start young, lass. She's been a piecer, then a spinner since she was nine. Their Nelly pieces for her now. I think Annie's about sixteen.'

'But why are she and her family alone?'

'Her mother died a while since. I don't know what happened to her father. Annie never speaks of him. She and Nelly are the only earners.'

'How on earth do they manage?'

'They rent that cottage from Chapmans. Your
100

mother lets her have it cheap, and they live off the land. Jack goes full time to the school at the factory. He's a clever lad and Annie wants him to have his chance. You saw the peat they use on the fire? Well, he collects that from up on the moor. Coal's too expensive, you see. He has an allotment and grows potatoes and onions, carrots and such.'

'But how can they afford wine?'

'Wine? Dear God, they only just scratch by as it is. What makes you think they drink wine?' He was laughing out loud and she felt the strength of her recently wounded spirit return to her.

'I saw it in the bottles on the shelf.'

'Nay, Miss Harrison.' At his words she realised that though she clung to his arm in the most intimate way he was telling her that they must now resume the relationship they had known before the attack. 'That wasn't wine, t'was cordial. Nelly and the others gather field and hedgerow fruits, cowslip and sloe and elder, and Annie makes them into . . . well, what you thought was wine. She's a grand lass. She made up her mind when her Mam died she'd keep her family together and she's doing it. It's a bit of a tight-rope at times, one slip and they'd all be off, but she works hard and gets on with life especially when you consider what happened to Nelly . . .'

He stopped speaking suddenly, his face expressing his irritation at himself, it seemed, and even in the enveloping darkness she sensed it.

'What is it, Mr Broadbent?'

'You'll not want to hear it, Miss Harrison, not after . . .'

'Oh, please, I'm all right now, really, I am.' Something told her that whatever it was that had happened to Nelly had a connection with today's events.

Will hesitated, evidently made uneasy, not only by speaking of such a thing on this occasion, but of perhaps revealing a confidence which was not really his to disclose.

'It was your uncle told me . . .'

'Charlie?'

'Aye. He was involved . . . well, not involved but it was brought to his notice. He didn't like it, you see, not in *his* mill and I think he felt responsible. That's why he asked me to keep a . . . well, you might say a *brotherly* eye on Annie and the children.'

'Yes?'

'Nelly's only a little lass. You saw her. An overlooker took her into the cabin . . . a few months back . . . you know, the one in the spinning room.'

She didn't since she had never been in the spinning room but she nodded just the same. The skin on her arms and the back of her neck began to prickle.

'I'll not go into detail, lass.' Will's voice was quiet and he put his other hand over hers where it lay in the crook of his arm. 'But . . . well, Mr Greenwood didn't get to her in time. Nelly wasn't as lucky as you.'

'Dear God . . .'

'I reckon *He* was looking the other way that day.'

'Yes.'

'But Annie cleaned her up, made no fuss, nor did Nelly and that's what infuriated Mr Greenwood, I reckon: that they should just accept it as though they'd no rights to be defended and

102

must take whatever life chucks at them without protest. They would have been back on their machines a few minutes later if Mr Greenwood hadn't sent them home. He paid them while they were off an' all. A grand chap, Mr Greenwood.'

'Yes, yes, he is. Thank you for telling me, Mr Broadbent. It seems you are meant to reveal a side of life I know nothing about. First yourself and how *you* survived . . . no, indeed, I had not forgotten . . . and now about Annie and Nelly.'

'You'll not let on I told you, Miss Harrison? Annie doesn't even know your uncle told me. She'd not like her private family business discussed, even by those who mean her no harm. You saw how she was?'

'Indeed. She is a . . . proud person, I'd say.'

'You're right there so we'll say no more.'

They had reached the outskirts of Crossfold by now, just where Reddygate Way led out on to the bit of moorland between there and Edgeclough. There were lights and a carriage or two, the beginning of paved streets and Tessa halted, turning Will towards her. Her face was earnest in the street light.

'Do you think she would be offended if I . . . took her something. As a thank you, I mean?' Her eyes were deep and shadowed but he could see a pinprick of light in each one, like a tiny star and he felt that sweetness, that lurching tenderness she had awakened in him the last time brush against his heart.

'I think she might, Miss Harrison.' His voice was soft.

'I would like to show my gratitude, nevertheless. She was very kind.'

103

'I imagine the only thing she would take from you would be your friendship, Miss Harrison, if you could spare it. Why not start by returning her shawl next Sunday?'

She looked up at him, astonishment plain on her face, even in the shadowed darkness.

'My friendship?'

'Aye, for she's got little enough of that and it'd cost you nowt. And, by the way, I sent a message to your Mam to say there was nothing to worry about; you'd had a tumble from your horse and you'd be late home—that Will Broadbent'd be bringing you. I knew that'd satisfy Mr Greenwood and it's the truth.'

*   *   *

He was sitting by the fireside reading from a book, the three girls at his knee, when Annie's astonished face peered at Tessa through the open door. Somehow she was not surprised to see him and was glad that she had tied up her hair with a bright knot of scarlet ribbon before she left Greenacres. The ride over, with the dogs, had put colour in her cheeks to match the ribbon and her silvery grey eyes were brilliant as they searched out his. With an effort she dragged her gaze away from him and back to Annie.

'I brought your shawl,' she said awkwardly, standing on the doorstep. Her usual high-handed assumption that she was immediately welcome wherever she went was sadly lacking this day.

'You've not come on yer own, not after what 'appened t'other day?' Annie gasped, her disbelief in this girl's daft and foolhardy ways taking her

104

breath away. 'I've never known 'owt like you, really I 'avent.' She peered over Tessa's shoulder as though fully expecting to see a complete battalion of soldiers guarding this feckless girl; when none appeared she 'tcched-tcched' angrily, reaching out to draw Tessa in before she was attacked by some dreadful mob which must have followed her across the moors. 'And I 'ope that animal out theer won't eat me daisies,' she added crossly, referring to Tessa's mare, 'an' them dogs 'ad better not mess me clean step, neither, or I'll tek me broom to 'em. Look who's 'ere, Mr Broadbent, an' after all as we said to 'er.'

She shook her head, shoving Tessa quite rudely into the chair opposite Will, taking the neatly wrapped, freshly laundered shawl from her and throwing it impatiently on to the table where she was evidently making blackberry pies.

'Tha'd best pour thissen a cup o' tea for I've no time ter bother, what with them childer ter see to an' pies ter get in th'oven . . .' Without further ado, just as though Tessa was the last person alive she could do with right now she continued, with a curiously delicate hand considering the noise she made with pots and rolling-pin and dishes which all got in her way, to roll out the pastry. But in her cheek was a touch of colour and her eyes were soft with pleasure.

Tessa chanced a swift glance at Will and her insides turned right over in the most unusual way as he winked at her.

CHAPTER SIX

She sat on the round-topped stool in front of her dressing-table and stared at her own reflection in the mirror while Emma brushed her long, difficult hair. At each stroke her head snapped back on her neck and the maid watched her anxiously. Miss Tessa's temper was always uncertain: she could be sweet-natured and generous, carelessly bestowing ribbons and lace-trimmed handkerchiefs on her maid when she was in the mood. Lately she had been somewhat softer, dreaming and seemingly unaware of Emma's presence, allowing her hair to be brushed and brushed for the required five minutes without uttering a word of protest, her face absorbed, deep in some reverie. Emma was grateful for a moment's respite in the drama that was often enacted in the dressing hour before dinner.

It was almost dark now as autumn took hold. Emma had lit the lamps and stoked up the fire for as the nights drew in it was becoming colder up here in the harsh northern climate of the Lancashire Pennines.

A great flock of blackbirds prepared to roost for the night in the depths of the rhododendron bushes which grew wild amongst the trees, making an enormous clatter as they imagined all kinds of danger menacing them. Sparrows squabbled over possession of a cosy niche in the ivy growing against the walls of the house and the noise of the birds seemed to bring back her mistress from the daydream in which she was enveloped. She jerked her head irritably and the maid sighed knowing the moment's peace was over.

'That will do, Emma. You'll have it out by the roots if you go on much longer. Fix it up anyway and quickly, if you please. I'm in a hurry.'

'There's plenty of time, Miss Tessa. Dinner's not for another hour yet.'

'Oh, I've something to do before dinner so do hurry. Tie it up in a ribbon and then pass me my breeches.'

'Your breeches! For dinner! Dear Lord, your mother will . . .'

'I'll be back in time to dress for dinner, Emma, but I've somewhere to go first. I hadn't realised the time and you let me sit here daydreaming . . .'

'Not me, Miss Tessa. I was only brushing your hair as I've been told to do each night and morning.'

'Oh, for God's sake, girl, give me the brush and a bit of ribbon and I'll do it myself.'

'Oh, please, Miss Tessa dear, be a good girl. You know your mother likes to see you dressed nicely with your hair done properly,' and not in the outfit of a bold lad with your hair hanging down your back like some gypsy. The unspoken words hung on the warm, scented air but Tessa did not appear to notice, or if she did was so accustomed to the maid's silent accusations they no longer troubled her, if they ever had.

But Emma meant it this time and meant to have her own way. Usually she merely stepped aside and shut her mouth and allowed her young mistress to do exactly as she pleased. It was easier that way with less damage to her own nerves and to the many pretty ornaments in the bedroom. What did it matter anyway, for when her mother was at the mill no one questioned what Miss Tessa did or said or where she went, so why should Emma wear herself to a shadow trying to make her into an elegant young lady? That, of course, is what she had been employed to do. Emma saw that her mistress was clean and tidy; that her clothes— mostly shirts and breeches, for heaven's sake— were neatly pressed and mended, and then sat back and enjoyed the peace and comfort of the pretty room without Miss Tessa Harrison in it.

But Mr and Mrs Joss Greenwood were home again now that the House was no longer sitting, and would be at dinner and all three of them, Master Drew, Master Pearce and Miss Tessa, would need to be on their best behaviour. She had laid out her young mistress's new dinner gown, a white muslin this time, pretty and trimmed about the sash with white satin rosebuds, slightly off the shoulder but with a modest sleeve. All of Miss Tessa's gowns were quite lovely, in Emma's opinion, and very expensive but she had a way of throwing them on hurriedly, irritably, since, her manner said, it would be so much easier simply to go down to dinner in her breeches, as her cousins were sometimes allowed to do when their parents were absent, with her hair tied back in a careless knot of ribbons.

'No, Miss Tessa, no!' the maid continued. 'I am to do your hair and put you in your new dress, your mother said, otherwise your uncle will naturally be upset and questions will be asked, and you know what will happen then.'

Tessa scowled and thrust back the flowing cape of her hair with both hands, knowing that her maid spoke only the truth. No one, not even her cousins, knew of her 'brush' as she casually called it *now*, with the tinker family. Should they find out—and might not her uncle do so if probing questions were asked?—her freedom would be severely curtailed. All her family were considered quite appallingly unconventional by the rest of the Penfold Valley and though her mother and Uncle Joss, as head of the family, were aware that she rode astride like a man, if they should discover that she had been in *danger* because of it, a vastly different attitude would be taken. They had all been rebels in one way and another, Jenny Greenwood, Joss Greenwood and his wife Kit, earning themselves reputations as trouble-makers in their defence and support of the exploited operatives, the brutalised children, scandalising the Penfold Valley with their carryings-on. Perhaps because of that they had understood, and allowed her own fight for a measure of freedom but she was certain they had no idea of the jaunts on which she accompanied her cousins, or even that her cousins *themselves* participated in such activities, and she had no wish for them to become acquainted with the true picture of her life.

'So we'll brush your hair and dress it at the back of your head with your new tortoiseshell comb, Miss Tessa,' her maid continued slyly, 'and your mother will be so pleased with you. Now, sit you down again while I get the pins.' Tessa had no choice but to grit her teeth and place herself before the mirror again.

Emma brushed back the hair which was as rebellious in its disorder as her mistress. When it was as smooth and tangle-free as she could get it, she began to pin it up on each side of a centre

109

parting, then brushed it into a huge and intricate coil at the back of Miss Tessa's head. But it seemed the style was determined to be awkward tonight and the maid clucked her tongue irritably, pulling quite forcibly at her mistress's head. The trouble was that the hair was so thick, so straight and slipping; no matter how she struggled, strands of it would keep escaping out of the coil and hanging down Miss Tessa's back in the most wilful fashion. The maid's face was red, her mouth full of pins as she patiently adjusted the tortoiseshell comb for the third time but the girl had had enough and she sprang up, scattering pins and combs and the hairbrush about the bedroom floor.

'Oh, for heaven's sake, Emma, does it really matter *what* style you achieve as long as it's tidy? Won't a simple knot on the back of my neck do? You could put some rosebuds in it like you did the last time,' she wheedled, genuinely trying to be helpful. She really did want to slip down to the stables, for a minute, no more, to join her cousins in what was happening there. She had never seen a foal born before, nor indeed any animal, not even one of the dozens of kittens which skittered about the stable yard. She knew she might be prevented, not by her family who, due no doubt to their working-class, down-to-earth, no-nonsense *practical* heritage would see no harm in it, but by the stable lads and grooms, the coachmen themselves who would be shocked to have a female amongst them on such an intimate, *physical* occasion. And if she told Emma where she was going there would be such a caterwauling the whole estate would hear of it.

'You must be fashionable, Miss Tessa,' the maid

said sternly, quite enjoying this momentary power she had over her young mistress. 'This style is right up to the minute and your aunt is bound to notice coming straight from London as she has.'

'Dear God,' Tessa moaned, sitting down again obediently, but before Emma could lift the brush to begin all over again, she turned and smiled. The maid's heart sank for she knew that smile so well: it meant mischief, there was no doubt of it, and the often wicked temper which followed if she was not allowed her way.

'Why do we not cut it, Emma?' she asked vividly, her eyes joyous in her expressive face, an expression which said she wondered why she had not thought of that before. It was such a simple solution to a tangled problem since Emma would have no further need of pins and combs and she would really have no further need of Emma.

'Cut it?' the maid gasped.

'Yes. Why not? Mother has short hair and she is not thought to be unattractive. Aunt Kit and Uncle Joss are used to seeing her as she is, as we all are ever since I can remember, and they find nothing strange in it. Uncle Joss wouldn't mind at all, nor Mother since I have heard her remark a number of times on how easy it is to manage.'

'Oh no, Miss Tessa, oh, no, I cannot allow it.'

'*You* cannot allow it? And what has it to do with you, pray?'

Tessa's face had turned truculent and she stood up, a head taller than her maid and not at all sure she might not strike her for her insolence.

'Please, Miss Tessa, don't, don't, I beg you. Your beautiful hair . . .'

'Mother's hair is quite beautiful, in my opinion.'

'Maybe it is, Miss Tessa, but your mother is an elderly lady and a widow. She is allowed to be . . . to be eccentric and no one notices any more but if you were to do it, a young, marriageable lady, how will you ever attract the attention of a husband . . .'

Tessa turned away in disgust, her still-maturing body somewhat brittle and vulnerable and yet eager, for though she had no intention of marrying, not for years yet, she wanted to live life to the full, its joys and triumphs, even its disasters should they come, and how could she if she was perpetually harassed by those who would stop her getting at them?

'Where are the scissors, Emma?'

'Oh, please, Miss Tessa dear, don't, I beg you . . .' Emma was almost in tears now and wishing in her heart, as she had done a hundred times in the last couple of years, that she had been given any job other than this in the great house of Greenacres. It was simply impossible to mould Miss Tessa into a young lady of fashion. She had been allowed to run wild for too long, you see, making it extremely trying not to say downright *punishing* for those who had her in their charge. As Emma was fond of telling her own mother who had once been in the service of the Chapman family but was now pensioned off in one of the Chapman alm-houses, she felt she had aged ten years in the two she had served Miss Tessa.

This house had once belonged to the great Barker Chapman who, with his father, had begun the Chapman Spinning and Weaving Concerns. When he had died, murdered it was said by a group of rioting men calling themselves the 'Onwardsmen' who had fought for better conditions and wages for themselves and others in the textile trade, the great wealth he had left, his mills and weaving sheds and many other business concerns, this house, had all come to his daughter, this girl's aunt. Emma's mother, who had been parlourmaid then, had often spoken of the scandal which had set the Penfold Valley aflame when Miss Chapman had married the man some said had been involved in her own father's murder: Joss Greenwood, no more than a working man himself, a hand-loom weaver, a radical and a revolutionary and now a Member of Parliament. He and his wife spent most of their time up at Westminster, coming home only when the House was not sitting.

Firebrands, both of them, and so was this girl who was no blood kin, which was strange. She was stamping about the bedroom now with every appearance of darting off to the kitchen to fetch a bread knife to her hair if the scissors did not immediately come to hand. Dear God in heaven, what was she to do? Doubtless she would be the one to get the blame should Miss Tessa arrive at the dinner table with her hair cut like that of a child from the poor house.

Emma looked desperately about the room as though searching for something which might distract her young mistress from the course she was set on, but there was nothing forthcoming.

It was a lovely room situated on the first floor of the house, on the corner with windows on two sides facing south. The furnishing of it was completely feminine, expressing not Miss Tessa's taste but that of her aunt's mother who had, years ago, decorated and furnished it for her own sixteen-year-old daughter. The furniture was of glowing rosewood;

113

slim-legged tables, a rococo desk, though Emma had never once seen Miss Tessa so much as write a note at it in the two years she had been with her; low, rosewood-framed chairs, armless and with the backs and seats embroidered in delicate pinks and creams. There was a dressing-table softly swathed in white muslin, a rosewood chest and the walls of the room were lined with blush-pink silk. Ornaments were grouped tastefully on tables and shelves; ivory combs and silver-handled brushes, a manicure set of mother-of-pearl, a jewel box of engraved gilt with a Sèvres china plaque set into the lid, cut-glass toilet bottles and jars with silver-gilt tops.

The stuffily draped four-poster of the beginning of the century had been replaced by the half-canopied bed with a high, prettily draped canopy and curtains at its head only. There was a feather quilt and a silken counterpane and enormous white pillows edged with lace. At the windows behind pelmets trimmed with ball-fringes hung lavishly draped damask curtains matching the colour of the walls, and the light from the windows was further softened by swathes of white muslin. The predominant colours, even of the huge carpet which covered the whole floor were cream, white and blush-pink, delicately lovely as Mrs Hannah Chapman, now dead, had once been, restful and dainty and not at all suited to the temperament of Miss Tessa Harrison who was neither.

Emma tried again.

'Come now, Miss Tessa dear, sit down and I'll dress your hair in a simple knot.' Her voice was coaxing for anything was better than a shorn head. 'And when you see your mother tonight you can ask

114

her permission to cut your hair like hers. See, it won't take but a minute . . .'

'But it will all be over if I don't go soon.'

'Only a minute and I promise you you'll be off to wherever it is you're going.' And the sooner she went the better in Emma's exasperated and nerve-torn opinion. 'Your dress is laid out and Polly will be up in a minute to lend a hand with your stays and it will take no more than a second or two to get you into it. Now, will you have the white rosebuds in your hair, or the satin ribbons?'

'Dear Lord, will you stop babbling and pass me my breeches and boots. Surely even you will agree that white muslin is hardly fit attire for the stables and . . .'

'*The stables!* Merciful heaven, what d'you want in the stables, Miss Tessa?' Emma was immediately suspicious since it was not unknown for her young mistress to say she would be only a second or two, promising to be back in time for dinner and then simply to disappear, and then lads with her. It was rumoured she had been seen at a cock-fight, wearing her cousin's jacket and top hat with her hair pushed up inside it, but Emma, even knowing Miss Tessa as she did, found that hard to believe since their father would have skinned them lads alive if it was true.

'Oh, damnation, I had not meant to . . .'

Enlightenment dawned on Emma's face. 'It's that new animal, isn't it? The one that's in foal. Percy told me it was ready . . . You're not going there, my girl, you can take my word for it.' In her agitation Emma went so far as to forget her place and the respect she had been taught to show her betters. She had an 'understanding' with Percy, the

115

head stable lad at Greenacres, who had told her in a discreet way, of course, for even servants, particularly of the superior kind like Emma, were treated with a bit of common decency, of the foal's imminent arrival.

She began to flutter about the room, wringing her hands. Tessa hesitated for though she knew she was a trial and a tribulation to her maid and had seen her near to tears a time or two, she had never seen her quite so badly distressed.

'Look, Emma,' she said irritably for really the girl was a damned nuisance and time was pressing if she was to get to the stables and back before the dinner gong sounded. 'Why don't I just tie my hair up for now as the girls in the mill do, and then when I get back you can dress . . .'

'Because you're *not* a mill girl, Miss Tessa, that's why.' Emma rounded on her, goaded beyond endurance, her face a bright pink in her effort to restrain herself from smacking this silly child's face.

'Mother was once and she's allowed to wear her hair anyway she likes and I don't see why I shouldn't. All this dressing up . . .'

The perilous sound of her voice was interrupted by the resonant noise of the dinner gong from the hallway downstairs and the relief etched on Emma's face was quite comical. Thank God, oh, thank God, she repeated over and over again to herself as Miss Tessa sighed in heartbroken resignation, or so she would have her maid believe, and began to move dejectedly towards the bed and the inevitability of the pretty gown which lay there. She'd put her in the damn dress *without* her stays, for where was Polly? And do her hair in a simple coil on her neck. Make her presentable for a family

116

dinner. But if she brought up this ridiculous notion of cutting her hair again Emma would go right to Mrs Harrison and ask to be relieved of her duties, really she would. The privilege of being a ladies' maid was not worth it, not to this one, it wasn't, and if it came to it she'd rather scrub the bloody scullery floors than go through what she suffered day after day with Miss Tessa, really she would.

*   *   *

The foal was on its feet, its shy, liquid eyes, fringed with deep brown lashes, looking anxiously at the entranced group of humans who hung over the stable door. The mare was inclined to be despotic in her protection, tossing her head challengingly and Tessa laughed with delight.

'Is she not brave? I do believe if one of us was to go in there she'd kick and bite until we took ourselves out again. And what a little beauty her baby is! Look at those legs and the colour of her. She's like the mahogany table in the hall. Honestly, I could cry when I think we might have been here to see her born had we not been made to eat dinner at the prescribed time that every one else in the valley dines. Would you not think that just for once we might have been allowed to absent ourselves so that we could have seen her born? Percy could have come for us . . . Oh, look at her, will you? She is going to—what is the word, Walter?—suckle. There is no need to blush . . . and see how she goes at it. Even with those fragile legs she can stand to do it. What was the exact time of her birth, Walter?'

She turned to the stable lad who leaned with

117

them over the loose-box door, the expression on his face as foolishly doting as a mother with her firstborn, his head to one side, shoulder to shoulder with the Greenwoods, social position forgotten in the wonder of the shared moment.

'T'were just gone eight, I reckon, Miss Tessa.'

'There, you see, we were half-way through the soup.' Her expression was dramatic.

'Well, *we* were here for almost an hour before dinner, but you didn't show up.' Drew's voice was scornful. 'I suppose you were preening yourself in that delectable creation you have on and had not the time for something of *real* interest. Your own reflection in the mirror must have been altogether fascinating . . .'

'That's not true, damn you.' Tessa's face had turned a furious red and her raised voice caused the new mother to stamp her feet in anger and alarm.

'Keep your bloody voice down, cousin. If you make her nervous she'll lose her milk. And it doesn't really matter to anyone whether you came or not since we all missed the big event.'

'I tried to come, I really did. It was all the fault of Emma and her absolute refusal to allow me to cut my hair.'

'Your hair, Miss Tessa?' The stable lad was clearly mystified.

'Oh, take no notice, Walter.' Pearce's eyes were narrowed in admiring contemplation of the mare and her foal, and not a little envious of Drew to whom they both belonged. He had won the animal in a bet, a wager with Nicky Longworth. Drew had declared his bay to be capable of jumping higher than Nick's magnificent roan and since the bet had

118

been Drew's bay against Nick's mare which had been in foal, they had set up the practice fence in the Longworth paddock immediately. The great deal of money his father had paid for his bay did not even cross Drew's mind and if it had there was little doubt he would not have allowed himself to be concerned over it. Nor did he consider that if he lost he would be without a decent mount. He *would* win, whatever the cost, to himself or his animal. A wager was a wager and a gentleman would honour it, as he would any challenge.

'How high shall it be, Drew?' Nicky had enquired lazily.

'As high as you please, old fellow.' The pole had been at its highest, just over seven feet when the hooves of Nicky Longworth's roan had clipped it, sending the Squire's son over its head to hit the ground with a force which stunned him.

Without a moment's hesitation, ignoring the Squire's grooms who had been about to dash across to the lad who was, after all, the son of their master and should be checked for damage, Drew thundered towards the pole, lifting his bay over it with half an inch to spare, narrowly missing Nicky Longworth who had the presence of mind to roll out of the way.

The handsome little mare was in the Greenwood stables by nightfall but the talk was that Joss Greenwood had better watch that touch of instability in his sons or they would not survive to see twenty. They were all wild, the young gentlemen who rode hard and took no heed of danger to themselves, but the Greenwoods had something about them, particularly since they had begun work in the family mills, which was more

119

than foolhardiness. They seemed ready to fling down a challenge on the slightest provocation, strung high on nerves which surely would snap one day.

But the mare was lovely, and so was her foal. Pearce watched them together and though he was not awfully sure *he* would have attempted such a height, unless dared by his own brother, he would dearly love to own her.

'It's true, Pearce. It was all that damned arguing about my hair and how it should be dressed. Would I have rosebuds or ribbons and on and on until I could have struck her. Left to myself I would have tied it up and been down here at least half an hour before the dinner gong.'

'You still wouldn't have seen her born, just as we didn't.'

'I know, but I would have been here with you and witnessed some of it. She must have been nearly ready to give birth . . .'

'Oh, for God's sake, shut up, Tessa. It's done with now so what does it matter?'

'I'm only explaining why I didn't come.' Tessa gritted her teeth: it was most unfair of them to take this attitude just as though she hadn't tried and tried to get down to be with them. They had no idea how difficult it was to be a *girl*. 'It takes Emma *hours* to decide what I should do with my hair and then hours actually to *do* it. Plaited or coiled . . .'

'Christ, Tessa, all we ever hear from morning till night is you moaning about that bloody hair of yours. If you are so persecuted by it why don't you do what you are always threatening to do and cut it off?'

'No one will do it, damn you.'

'I'll do it.'

They all turned to look at Drew, even Walter who had no idea what they were talking about and, really, was it any wonder? Their minds were like the sleek and beautiful blood animals they rode: fast, complex, skittish when checked, moving too quickly for him. Though he spent some time with them each day in the stables and paddock and was as adept as they in the saddle, he could never follow where they went.

'*You*? What with? The gardening shears?'

'If you like.'

'Don't be a bloody fool, Drew.' Pearce's voice was rough.

'All right, then. If Tessa runs back to the house for her scissors I'll cut it for her with those.'

Tessa looked into the indolently smiling face of her cousin. There was nothing she wanted more—was there?—than to be rid of the fuss and bother attached to getting herself ready for the day and how much time and argument she would save if she were not subjected to Emma's ministrations, yet she hesitated. Drew was such a devil you were never quite sure where you were with him. He had a way of looking at you that dared you to gamble—which was how he had won the mare—if you had the nerve. His violet-blue eyes were clear and innocent but his mouth slanted in a sardonic smile which she did not quite trust.

But she was a Greenwood, brought up as one anyway, and when had any of them ever turned away from a challenge?

'Wait here,' she said turning towards the door which led out into the dark stable yard and she knew by the way his eyes gleamed and the broadening of his smile that she had won his admiration.

'Don't be stupid, Tess.' Pearce tried to put a hand on her arm but she shook him off. He shrugged and turned away so that neither of them could see the doubt in his eyes. Though she might be as undisciplined as himself and Drew when the opportunity offered, including herself in all the light-hearted escapades they thought up, she was still a *girl*. Despite the breeches she wore and her desperate attempts to follow wherever they went, one day she would be stopped and that day must surely be soon. She was almost seventeen years old and ripe for the pickers in the marriage market. What the hell would her mother do with her, and *them*, if she turned up at the breakfast table in the morning with her hair cropped like a man's?

The scissors were in Drew's hand when Pearce turned back to them. Walter, knowing at last what they were about to do, had reared off, his hand to his mouth, his face white, his horror so great Drew might have been about to plunge the blades into Tessa's breast.

'Eeh no, Master Drew, you don't mean ter . . . ?'

'Be quiet, Walter, this has nothing to do with you.' Tessa's voice was feverish as she placed herself within the reach of Drew's hands and the snip-snip of the lethal scissors.

Walter moaned deep in his throat as the first gloriously shining strand, so thick and lovely he felt the urge to beg if he might have it, fell to the cobbled floor of the stable. Another went and another until all about the recklessly laughing young girl was a carpet of hair, the rich chestnut glints in it quite extinguished as though they had

122

derived their life from the girl herself.

'Dear God, you'll catch it from Aunt Jenny,' Pearce said softly and, like Walter, his young heart ached with something he could not describe as his cousin was stripped of her most obvious claim to femininity. What was left of her hair stood out in differing lengths, tufty, like the shorn skin of a rabbit, and beneath it her face had become as pointed and fey as a pixie's. Her cheekbones appeared to have widened and become higher and more pronounced. Her eyes were enormous, glittering, so clear and pale a grey as to be almost colourless, piercing the semi-gloom of the stables like two of the new 'electric rays' which were, Pearce had heard, being used to illuminate Vauxhall Gardens up in London. Not that he had seen them, you understand, but surely they could not be more brilliantly lovely than Tessa Harrison's eyes? Her small chin thrust forward challengingly and she laughed.

'Well?' she said, tossing her head which felt so light she thought she might float away.

'*Jesus* . . . !'

'Aah . . . Miss Tessa . . .' and Walter looked as though he might weep.

'Just a shade more here, I think,' Drew said cheerfully, 'and then under the tap with you.'

'The tap? What on earth for?'

'Trust me, little cousin.'

He towelled her wet hair with a bit of old horse blanket rubbing the short stubble which suddenly, miraculously, was no longer stubble but a moving cap of smooth darkness, clinging about her head, not in curls as her mother's did, but in short and springing waves. They fell over her forehead and

123

about her ears, hugging the nape of her long and shapely neck, outlining her neat head and producing in her a strange and bizarre beauty the likes of which had never before been seen in the Penfold Valley. It accentuated the width of her forehead and the delicate strength of her pointed chin, the pretty shells of her ears and the pale velvet-grey of her eyes.

'Bloody hell, it actually suits you,' Pearce blurted out in amazement and the curious and speculative expression on his face was mirrored in that of his brother. It was the look of a man confronted, for the first time, by a new and exciting woman, a look which says quite plainly that he is intrigued and more than a little willing to get to know her, to have her look at him with as much interest, and if she did not, the added thrill of persuading her to do so.

She did not see it, only the approval written on his face and that was all she wanted.

'And what about you, Walter?' She grinned at the stable lad who was staring, open-mouthed and slack-jawed at this dashing young lad who was very definitely *not* a young lad. Though her hair was shorter than his own, its boyishness merely served to emphasise the thrusting peaks of her high young breasts, the smooth white skin of her shoulders above the disarranged neckline of the dinner-gown she still wore, the slender shapeliness of her bare arms which he had never really noticed before, and the sight of it all took his breath away.

'By gum, Miss Tessa,' he breathed admiringly, letting his masculine appreciation show in the way his eyes ran over her, then blushing furiously he turned and blundered from the stable.

'Well, cousin,' Drew's voice was somewhat husky and his fingers gripped the scissors fiercely, 'it seems you have at least one admirer should the rest turn tail at the sight of you.' They wouldn't, of course, his eyes told her.

'Fiddlesticks! I want no admirers.' Her heart beat fast and joyously as she ran her hand through the delightful softness and lightness of her hair. 'Come on, let me slip inside and up to my bedroom before Mother sees me or I'll be for it. I'm sure you will want to ride over to the Hall tomorrow to tell Nicky Longworth of your new foal and I want to come with you. We'd best lie low until then or we're bound to be stopped.'

For a second only she lost her nerve at the thought of her mother's dark anger, then she tossed her head again as another thought followed, much more exciting.

What would Will Broadbent think? Would he look at her as approvingly as her cousins and Walter had done? Would his eyes warm with admiration, then narrow in that quite thrilling and masculine way which happened sometimes? Or would he laugh, treat her as an enormously amusing child, naughty and wilful and deserving of a spanking?

Well, what did it matter what Will Broadbent thought? His opinion meant nothing to her, she told herself, and if he so much as smiled when next she saw him she would . . . what would she do? As she lay in her bed, having avoided the servants and her family and gained the privacy of her room quite safely, she grinned wickedly in the dark at the thought of the fun there would be tomorrow.

CHAPTER SEVEN

The fox, being a night feeder, provides no sport early in the day and it would give her the greatest satisfaction, she decided, to arrive at the Hall amongst the Squire's Friday-to-Monday guests before they set off in its pursuit. There would be aristocratic ladies and gentlemen, manorial families from Lancashire, Yorkshire and Cheshire and perhaps even further afield come for the start of the hunting season, booted and spurred, languid and bored and ready to be amused by anything for a lark, particularly the gentlemen who would approve of her own boldness in defying every convention enforced by society. It would give her even more satisfaction to see their faces when she whipped off her top hat to reveal the splendour of her new hair style which nobody but Drew and Pearce and Walter had yet seen.

No, she wouldn't wear a hat. She would gallop up to the Hall with her short hair all about her head as she had seen her cousins do and would enjoy the vast consternation and be as outrageous as she pleased. She would ride with the wind intoxicatingly in her face and hair, through farmyards and over fences, showing them her daring and endurance, showing them that she was as able and strong and durable as any man there. Why she should want to do so never crossed her mind.

It was a clear and glorious day. The trees were almost naked now and the fallen leaves made a dry, rustling sound beneath the hooves of the horses, a splendid carpet of red, gold, green and brown. The fields had been harvested, then ploughed and the long, neat furrows reached into the distance, orderly and somewhat business-like. Bright-eyed jackdaws disappeared in and out of them, hopping up and down with sprightly steps, and on the edge of the fields stood trees holding the former spring nests of rookeries.

The mellow October day was perfect, acting as a barrier between the last of the autumn and the bitter weeks of winter to come. There were still wild flowers bobbing their last blooms in the cool sunshine: the yellow buttons of tansy and orange of toadflax, the deep pink and white of fumitory, its fern-like leaf so fragile it looked like smoke from a distance.

Though she rode like the wind, leaping and diving, the thundering explosion of horses' hooves in her ears, flat on her mare's back across pasture and meadow, her companions close about her, hounds ahead, the clarion call of the horn, the spray of mud and river water, the scatter of earth thrown up by their passage, she was scarcely conscious of it, or them, as she moved through the day in some dream world, their noisy presence jostling about her like discordant ghosts. Her cousins were nowhere to be found when later the stable yard at the Hall was filled with the wild-riding end of the hunting party, hoof-beats erupting against the cobbles, the smell of steaming horse-flesh, the well-bred shouts of the fox-hunting set applauding the success of the day. Her own cheek carried the brown stain of dried fox-blood for she had been the first lady to reach the kill. There was to be champagne and they pressed her to stay but, for some reason, she found that the great and glorious sparkle with which the day had begun had evaporated. She could not have said why since she had been a huge success, showered with compliments on her appearance, her bravery and the glory of the kill, but really, she said politely to the Squire, who could not take his eyes from her flaunting and extraordinary beauty, she must be getting home since her 'people', speaking as *they* spoke, would be expecting her.

She was on the top road which led from Longworth Hall to Crossfold and Greenacres when he rose from the flat stone on which he had been sitting. It seemed right, somehow, as though everything had been moving towards this moment: the frustration of yesterday, the cutting of her hair as an act of bravado which had been a statement of some pressure within her; the dream-like quality of today, leading up to her meeting with this man who had trembled on the edge of her conscious thought ever since she had opposed him in the mill yard.

She reined in her mare, ready to smile, the afternoon, though drawing in towards nightfall, brighter suddenly. She had her back to the lowering sun which shone directly into his eyes and she could see the expression in them, warm, glad, she knew, to see her, as she was to see him.

'Miss Harrison.' His uncompromising jaw which told the rest of the world of Will Broadbent's intention to succeed, to get on with his life in whichever way it took his fancy, softened for her. She felt herself become disentangled from the complexities which seemed to beset her, and life slowed down and simplified to this moment, to this quiet stretch of moorland and she knew he made it

128

so. She sat for several long, tension-free seconds, looking at him, at the understanding he had of her which showed in his quiet smile, glancing away smilingly, then back at him, recognising that there was no need for haste nor impatience.

'Will you not get down?'

'I think I might.'

'I hesitate to help you.' He grinned, absurdly pleased with himself for some reason which seemed not to matter in the lingering end of this lovely day, though she guessed it had something to do with her.

'Perhaps I might not mind today.'

'Miss Harrison! I can hardly believe my ears. Have you lost your senses?' He was still smiling and warm. 'Where is the independent young lady who needs assistance from no man, or so she told me?'

'I . . . I found that to be untrue, Mr Broadbent, if you remember . . . ?' Both their faces darkened suddenly as they were reminded of her encounter with the tinkers from which he had saved her. She still woke in the night, her body drenched in sweat, crawling with the memory of those filthy hands, the rank stench of unwashed bodies and decaying teeth in her dreaming nostrils. Only the deliberate bringing back of this man's controlled strength which he had shown her twice now, could dissolve the nightmare.

The quiet, almost tender moment shattered and his face closed up.

'Aye, I remember it and it occurs to me you made me a promise on that day. Have you no concern for your own safety, girl? At least when you came over to Annie's you had the sense to bring your dogs but now I find you riding hell for leather along a lonely track which no sane woman would attempt. Have you no sense at all?'

'Apparently not, Mr Broadbent,' she began, ready to smile, to soothe his sudden irritation with an unusual apology, a warm glance, a reference to Drew and Pearce who could not be far behind her. But the image of her as he had seen her then, fragile, defenceless, made him harsh in his fear for her, careless of the lovely moment they had just created.

'You did not mean to keep your promise then?'

'Yes, I did, but . . .'

'Then why are you here completely alone, with no one, not even those dogs to protect you?'

'If you will allow me to speak . . .'

'To make further promises which you have no intention of keeping?'

'No, I would just like to . . .'

'You are like a child who must be forever watched . . .'

'Dear God!' She was as maddened as he now without really knowing why. The strange sense of unhurried tranquillity, the smiling calm he had instilled in her had gone and she felt her resentment rise sharply to swamp her previous pleasure. What right had *he* to tell *her* where she might or might not go, and with whom. She was at liberty to please herself how she went about, her haughty expression said. To tell the truth, in the excitement of the last twenty-four hours she had given no thought to the danger which could stalk these moors and which recently she had been careful of. She had expected to ride home with Drew and Pearce, later on, much later on, and it was only her own curious unease which had brought her home early.

But that had nothing to do with Will Broadbent. Just because he had rescued her from those Irish tinkers—whom she had now convinced herself she could have dealt with on her own anyway—he imagined he owned her. Well, he didn't and she would tell him so. Sensing her anger, her mare began to move restlessly, stepping sideways in a circle round the standing man until the sun which had been at Tessa's back now fell on her face.

'I would be obliged if you would get out of my way,' she said, high-toned as any of those with whom she had hunted that day. 'You are making my mare nervous,' which was not true. 'I cannot imagine what you can be doing hanging about on this path like some wandering vagrant ...' Her voice, which had been loud and defiant died away slowly as the expression of ill-humour on his face drained away and the corners of his mouth twitched. His whole manner altered miraculously. His eyes became warm again and alive with amusement and his mouth stretched in a wide smile over his white teeth.

'What the devil have you been doing to yourself, lass?' he laughed, shaking his head in disbelief. 'My God, if there was another girl like you in the whole wide world I'd eat me damned cap. Peak an' all.'

For a moment she felt her anger dissipate and pleasure moved in her again for she took his words as a compliment. But he had not done yet. 'If you were mine I'd take a strap to you for you're surely the most contrary female in Christendom. There must be a thousand women in Lancashire primping and preening with the curling irons, or whatever it is you women do in an effort to catch the eye of us

131

men, and they would all, like as not, give their souls for hair such as you had. But you! You have to throw it away like some unwanted . . .'

'It *was* unwanted and is none of your business besides,' she said tartly.

'Dear God,' his eyes had lost their glow, 'd'you think I'm not aware of that?'

'Then why is it that every time we meet you find it necessary to threaten me with a thrashing and spend all your time lecturing me on how foolish I am?'

His voice snapped in exasperation and he made a sudden movement towards her mare, catching the bridle and bringing the animal to a halt. He was breathing hard and his face had darkened.

'Because that is the feeling you arouse in me with that capricious and flighty manner you have. *And* the careless way you put yourself in danger. And for God's sake get down off that damned animal: I've a crick in me neck from looking up at you.'

'Again I say what I do does not concern you and *no*, I will not get down. I am on my way home so let go of that bridle before I am forced to lay my crop about you.'

He sighed and stepped away. His face was without expression now, the warmth and laughter she always seemed to have the power of inspiring in him, emptying from him.

'You're right, it's nowt to do wi' me so I'll move on and you can do the same, Miss Harrison.'

He watched her turn, ready to guide her mare away, her head, so strangely defenceless in its short, close-fitting cap of tumbled waves, held in high disdain. He was struck by the way the loss of

132

her hair, which was said to be a woman's crowning glory, had made her somehow more and not less feminine and the words were out before he stopped to think about them, or the effect they were to have on his life.

'It suits you like that. I don't know why it should, but it does.'

'Your approval is of no concern to me, Will Broadbent. I'm sure you know that?' Her lip curled disdainfully but she did not move on.

'Indeed I do, Miss Harrison. You don't give a damn what anyone thinks, or so you keep telling me and who am I to argue?' His mouth began to twitch again and she looked at him suspiciously, not at all sure whether to be offended again. He smiled as his eyes went to her hair, but they admired it now, and *her*, and she was somewhat mollified.

'Well, then,' she said, not quite sure what she meant by it.

'Come on, get down and let me look at you properly. I'm certain there must be some quite fascinating explanation on how it came about and, really, I can't wait to hear it.'

'If you're going to make fun . . .'

'No, really. I would like to know how you persuaded your mother, who must be a remarkable lady, to let you have it cut, and besides, we cannot be at each other's throats every time we meet. I thought we were to be friends when we were at Annie's . . . No, no . . .' He stood back, his hands upliftcd in a placatory manner, his grin broadening, ' . . . I'm not going to lecture you, really. If you are intent on risking yourself . . .'

'Mr Broadbent . . .' Her voice had a warning in

it, but she swung her leg over her mare's rump; then, fastening the bridle to a clump of gorse, she moved to stand beside him, looking out over the darkening valley.

There was a mist coming off the river, tinged a soft rose-pink by the last of the sun's rays, and further along the valley bottom was the dark smudge which was Crossfold. Lights pricked the smudge but up here they were still in full daylight. They had moved together, sauntering towards the flat rock on which he had previously been squatting, lowering themselves into the same sitting position with their arms about their drawn-up knees. Neither spoke as they allowed the soft-hued ease of mind which Will Broadbent seemed to generate, to slip comfortably over them again. It was satisfying, tranquil, with no need of words to fill the silence and yet they were both aware, Will more than Tessa, that there was more to it than that. He acknowledged her as she was, awkward, stubborn, wilful, and did not judge her nor condemn her, for he understood her striving nature which in many ways was like his own. And sensing his understanding and acceptance she was untroubled, with no need of the defiance she showed to others. She could be herself, perhaps the self no one had ever seen before, allowing the friction with which she challenged life to be gladly set to one side.

'I really *do* take the dogs with me when I ride out alone, Mr Broadbent, and having seen them that day at Annie's you must realise that I am quite safe with them. But today, though I set out with my cousins I decided to come home early. We had been with the hunt . . .'

134

'So I see by the blood on your face.'

'You don't approve?'

' 'Tis a cruel sport, lass, and the custom of rubbing the brush of the poor little beggar on your face . . . well, it's what I would call barbaric.'

She bristled and he put a hand on her arm. 'Nay, don't let's start again. See, wipe that mark off your cheek . . .' He pulled a clean white square from his pocket but instead of handing it to her he turned her face towards him with a big, gentle hand and rubbed at the dried blood which had turned a rusty brown on the smooth skin of her cheek. It was stubborn and he clicked his tongue, his eyes engrossed with his task. She watched his face with an odd breathlessness and a feeling of expectancy, her eyes bemused, and as he felt her gaze on him his breath shortened. He cleared his throat.

'It doesn't seem to want to come off.' He tried to sound casual. The hand which held her chin trembled.

'Try a bit of spit.' Her voice was soft and there was a quiver in it and he knew he must be very careful with her. She was a woman, but yet a child: innocent and trusting with him, but not, he was sure, ignorant. She was of an age when most girls were thinking of marriage, but still a child and he must be careful.

He made his voice merry though the effort was great.

'A bit of spit! Miss Harrison, whatever next?' She smiled then put out her tongue and when he had rubbed his handkerchief across its pink moistness, he carefully cleaned off the offending stain, not meeting those incredible eyes which were looking so earnestly into his.

135

'What do you do on your day off?' she asked him presently and though he had resumed his contemplation of the shadowy valley he was aware that she was still studying him.

'Nowt, really. I walk across the hills if I feel like it or go to political meetings, but there's not a lot to do in these parts when the mill's closed. There's talk of forming a football team in the mill but they'll not want me in it since I've never played the game in me life and I'm too old to start now.'

'How old are you, Mr Broadbent?'

He turned to smile at her and watched the comers of her mouth lift in answer to his. 'I must be twenty-eight or nine, I suppose.'

'Really!' and her sixteen-year-old face conveyed pity. 'What else do you do?'

'Sometimes I take the train to Manchester and then in the summer there's the fairs. I read a lot but more often than not after I've been in the mill all week I feel the need to get out and let the wind blow in me face and even the rain . . .'

'I know.'

'Oh, aye.' He turned to her in surprise for though she was a forthright, independent and, some said, entirely too free a young lady for her own good, he had not realised that she shared his own deep attachment to this bleak environment which was their heritage.

'Indeed. I can think of nowhere I would rather be.' As she spoke she felt a sense of surprise for she could clearly hear her own voice, accompanied by those of Drew and Pearce, bemoaning the fact that they were forced to remain here, tied to the family inheritance. It really was amazing. What was it about this man which brought out something in her

136

which she had not even known was there? That made her say things which were sometimes insolent, disdainful, mocking as only she could be and the next moment seduce her into a state of well-being in which she brought forth statements she had certainly not meant to make, nor even knew she had believed? And yet she *did* love this high patch of Lancashire despite her constant reiteration to Drew and Pearce that she wanted only to get away with them to some magical world which she had convinced herself existed beyond it.

She turned to look at him, a large and personable man, smiling, his expression steady, interested, humorous, concerned with what she had to say and finding it worthwhile. 'But that doesn't mean I wouldn't like to travel, to see some of the world beyond the Penfold Valley, as long as I could come home to it.' As she spoke she knew that what she said was the truth though she had not been aware of it. Her voice had become somewhat defiant again, irritated with herself for allowing him to glimpse a part of her which was not really meant to be seen.

'No indeed.' His voice was grave.

'Don't smile, Mr Broadbent.'

'I'm not smiling, lass, but do you think you could bring yourself to call me Will?'

*　　*　　*

The fire had been built up, the logs crackling and fragrant, the flames glowing into the high ceiling and casting shadows on the rich rosewood panelling as she entered the hallway. It was quiet and deserted, warm, secure and so ... so *homely*

137

she felt her heart wrench and she stopped, one foot on the bottom tread of the stairs.

She turned and looked about her, studying this home of hers which she had never before really noticed. A hundred hundred times she had raced up and down these stairs; skated along the tiled floor in pursuit of, or pursued by her cousins. She had laughed and cried, screamed in temper and skipped for joy. She had toasted marshmallows in the flames of the fire, sat on a stool and dreamed into it, played all manner of games and tricks and all the time the house had been here, as steadfast and reliable as ... as Will—now why had she thought that, she wondered, confused—or her mother, always here when she really needed her. As safe as houses, that was what they said, and that was exactly what she felt here. She always protested that she didn't *want* to be *safe*, but she realised in that moment, perhaps just for that moment, that everyone needed a place, or a person, in whom they felt secure. There had always been this house *and her mother!*

And tonight she knew she was going to distress her mother, take from her the pleasure her brother's visit brought her just as surely as if she were to strike her full in the face. And all for a childish whim. No more. That was what it had been, an impulsive, infantile caprice which was not worthy of her mother's daughter. Her mother would be upset, she knew full well she would when she saw the state of her hair; she had known full well when she had allowed Drew to cut it, but it had not stopped her.

And that was what had taken the lovely glow, the excitement of the day from her when the hunt was finished, that and the unspoken regret in Will Broadbent. Though he might tell her she looked well with her hair shorn like a ragamuffin—and perhaps she did, perhaps it suited her in its strangeness—but she had sensed that he deplored the loss of the long, shining splendour of the hair which she had discarded so lightly last night. As her mother would. No doubt Drew and Pearce would be back soon for not even they would dare risk their father's displeasure should they not be home for dinner. Drew would defend her, try to take the blame; he would say he had encouraged her, own up to his share in the horror for it had been his hand which had held the scissors.

She could hear Uncle Joss's laughter in the drawing-room. It was almost dark. They would be having sherry perhaps, Charlie and Laurel, her mother, Aunt Kit and Uncle Joss, her family, before going upstairs to bathe and change for dinner. The mills would have closed at six the night before, the boilers not to be fired up until five tomorrow morning, Monday. She and her cousins had been invited to ride to hounds any day they pleased now that the season had begun and she had heard Drew promise carelessly, thoughtlessly—since when would Uncle Joss allow his sons to hunt on a working day?—that they would all be at the Hall tomorrow. Between then and now she must try . . . try to explain—was there an explanation?—to her mother; make an effort to clarify . . . well, demonstrate to her mother *why*—was there a logical reason?—she had acted as she had. To say she was sorry. That she hadn't given it any *real* thought. That she hadn't really *cared*, at the time. To plead with her mother to understand.

In that moment Tessa Harrison began the difficult process of growing up. For the first time in her young life she felt compassion for *someone*, an adult, not a sickly kitten or an orphaned puppy or a rabbit caught in a trap, as children do, but a person who, by *her* action would be wounded. Somehow she must let that person know that she was sorry; not sorry that her hair was cut short, but that the cutting of it should cause her mother distress. And now was as good a time as any to begin. She knew quite positively that this remorse on another person's behalf would not last, that it was not in her to bend her will to another's, to put the wishes of someone else before her own, to curb the wilful need to get away from the restrictions her sex, her age and her class put upon her, but right now she was experiencing these emotions and she must do what her often-stormy heart told her before she changed her mind.

She did not fling open the drawing-room door as she normally would, noisily, a child still in her exuberant need for life and excitement, but moved into the room in a manner so sedate it would have gladdened Miss Copeland's heart.

They all turned to smile, her family, welcoming her and had she not, for the moment anyway, been this new and strange Tessa she would have laughed out loud as their smiles slipped away like ice melting in the sunshine. They sat like figures carved in stone for several moments then very slowly her mother put down the glass she was holding, not once taking her eyes from her, and raised a trembling hand to cover her mouth. She seemed unable to move beyond that, her eyes enormous in her bone-white face, her body still, her brain atrophied and unable to function, or so it appeared.

'Tessa . . . child . . . have you had an accident?' her Aunt Kit faltered and her Uncle Joss rose slowly to his feet, ready, should he be needed, to move rapidly across the carpet to catch his niece when she fell, as fall she undoubtedly would.

'Dear God . . . sweetheart . . .' Charlie sprang to life, pushing aside Laurel's trembling hand, striding with his great long legs after his brother until they both stood before her their hands lifted, eager to comfort, to support, to hold, but not sure where to lay them since they did not want to cause further damage.

'What happened? Jesus, lass, what happened?'

'Nothing . . .'

'But look at you. Your riding habit is covered with blood or . . . or is it mud? And your face . . . you're as white as a sheet. What the devil . . . who . . . ?'

Slowly her Uncle Joss's eyes rose to her hair and she became aware that her unkempt appearance . . . yes, she remembered now, she had come off her mare in the ditch beside Jenkinson's oat field . . . well, it would be the Squire's oat field since Jenkinson only rented it from him—her appearance, stained, muddy, bloody from the fox had somehow distracted them from the real injury of the day. The injury to her beautiful hair.

'Who did it?' Charlie whispered, his mind racing to all kinds of horror, to vagrants and gypsies, tinkers and ruffians, rapists and those who . . . who . . . and surely this child had been in some pervert's hands for who else would take from her her lovely hair, and if they had taken that, what else

141

had she lost?

Her mother's face floated, she could think of no other words, towards her, stationing itself besides Charlie's shoulder, grey and amazingly agonised and for a moment Tessa was confounded by its strangeness, its utter, utter horror.

'Now, Jenny, it's all right, lass,' her Uncle Joss said, moving rapidly to take her mother's arm and Tessa was made aware that there was something in her mother's absolute terror that had nothing to do with her. 'Tell us who did this to you, Tessa, tell us . . .'

'I did it,' she protested harshly and again they were all struck dumb. And all the softness, the love and remorse with which she had been going to approach them evaporated in her own terrified distress for matters had all gone so horribly wrong. 'I was tired of having Emma forever nagging me to have it brushed and washed . . . and pinned up . . . put into nets . . . and things. Well, I asked her to cut it . . .' Her voice had become high, childish in her defiance.

'Are you saying Emma cut your hair?'

'No, oh, no, Uncle Joss, no, she wouldn't so . . .' boldly, ' . . . I did it myself.' She lifted her shorn head, 'And I like it even if no one else does.'

'Well, no one else does, that's a certainty,' and Charlie, her beloved Charlie on whom she had always counted to defend her when no one else would, turned away in disgust.

There was a clatter in the hallway and a cheerful voice shouted that it was going to see if there was a chance of a drink in the drawing-room. The door burst open and with all the enthusiasm of two boys let out of school, Drew and Pearce Greenwood

142

catapulted into the room, just as mud-spattered, just as tumbled, just as wild-riding and wild-natured as she herself had been, and in their path stood Joss Greenwood and his sister, Jenny Harrison.

'Whoops,' said Pearce frivolously, still laughing from the overflow of champagne which had run like water from a tap in the Squire's great hall and of which he and Drew and several other of their young companions had drunk deeply.

'You have been at play with the young lordlings, then,' their father asked ominously, 'and have just this moment decided to grace your mother's drawing-room with your presence?'

Drew laughed and swaggered, somewhat unsteadily, in the direction of the nearest chair but his father's voice cut about him like a whip.

'Stay where you are, lad, unless you want to feel my hand in your face.'

'Joss ... darling ...' Kit murmured but her husband for once did not listen to her voice.

'I would like to know, and by God, one of you had better be quick in telling me, what has been going on here today. First we have missy here,' he waved a heavy hand in Tessa's direction, 'coming in looking like some waif from the bloody workhouse, frightening everyone into thinking she had been robbed or ...' he shook his head like some beast tormented by three troublesome flies, 'or worse, and then you two swagger in as though you were lords of the bloody manor, and as drunk ...'

'Joss ...'

'Don't Joss me, Kit Chapman,' he roared and the wild temper which none of them, including his wife, had seen for years, made them all wince.

143

'What's going on here and what's this damned girl had done to her? Because if you think for a moment I believe she cut her own hair just for the hell of it . . .'

'I did, Uncle Joss.'

'No one asked you to speak, girl,' he thundered, turning on her, and Jenny put out a hand to him, the first stirring of alarm, not for her daughter but for him, moving in her. Now that she had determined that Tessa was not physically hurt, she could feel her own outrage growing: an inclination to drag the girl upstairs, put her across her knee as she would a child and give her a long-overdue thrashing. What she had done was childishly defiant and though she herself had cut her own hair short against all the then rules of decency, it had been done for a completely different reason.

Or had it?

Jenny Harrison looked back for a moment to that wilful, resolute girl she herself had been more than twenty-five years ago. Resolute in her determination, she had told herself to protect and support her mother, her younger brother and sister whilst Joss had been fighting the injustice inflicted by the oppressive millowner. She had been forced to go into the mill when her father was killed at Peterloo and her brother had gone out on the rampage, wild with grief and his need to take Joshua Greenwood's place. She had been the only wage earner in the family and the responsibility had made her strong, self-willed, defiant of convention. She had told herself that to cut her hair was a measure of safety in the spinning room where machinery was waiting to drag in any careless hand or unbound length of hair, but, if she

144

were honest, had she really cared about that when she had taken her father's shears to her own waist-length mass of curls? Had she not been impatient of control—as her daughter was—the control that said that whilst Joss might spend his time marching with the rioting men, smashing machines and windows in his challenge of the masters, she must stay at home and guard his family? It had been no more than a display of her own revolution and when it was done and she had enjoyed the shocked stares and whispered disapproval she had had no choice but to leave it as it was.

The memory brought a measure of understanding.

'Go upstairs, girl,' she said quietly to her daughter. 'I will be up directly.'

When Tessa had gone she turned to the tableau which still stood, tense and ready at any moment to explode into a scene of great violence. The two young men had somehow arranged themselves shoulder to shoulder, not exactly with their fists up and clenched, but giving the impression that they were prepared to fight should they be pushed to it. Her brother, she realised with something of a shock, was no longer taller than his two lean young sons, and she recognised, if he did not, that though they were no more than seventeen they were at that inevitable stage in a man's life when he is no longer prepared to be dominated by his father. They were young men now, the two of them, each a part of the other, a double commitment of conflict; young cubs yet, showing their teeth to the old lion but not prepared for much longer to back away from his superior strength.

'Leave it, Joss,' she said.

145

'No, by God! These two have been inciting that lass of yours for years now, dragging her along on their wild skylarking . . .'

'She'd not need much dragging, Joss.' He took no notice.

' . . . treating her as though she herself was a young lad and this is the last bloody straw . . .'

'Joss, Tessa is my responsibility . . .'

'As these two are mine and it seems to me that I've been sadly lacking in that direction, but I mean to change that right now. They've been up at the Hall drinking, aye, seventeen years old and carrying on as though they were the Squire's sons and with a perfect right to live the lives of landed gentlemen. I'll have a word or two to say to Longworth the next time we meet. *His* son might be allowed to act the rake-hell if he wishes but mine certainly will not. Don't think because I'm in London I know nothing of how you joy-ride about the countryside on those damned thoroughbreds of yours, which were bought, by the way, from your Aunt Jenny's and Charlie's efforts on *your* behalf in the mill. And now Tessa is becoming the same. It's time all three of you settled down to the realisation of who you are: the sons and daughter of a *millowner*. You drift in here as though you're doing us a bloody favour by bestowing your company on us. Your mother has been most upset,'—which was not true for Kit Greenwood, though she loved her sons, barely gave them a thought as long as her husband was with her—'and I'll not have it. Now I don't know whose idea it was to crop that child's head like some sheep at shearing time but I've absolutely no doubt that one of you or both, had something to do with it.'

146

He passed a hand over his eyes and there was a visible tremor in it. Jenny frowned, for suddenly something seemed not quite right about the shape of her brother's face, and the smooth amber of it, the look of glowing health which had always been his, appeared to be draining away, leaving it grey and clammy. He put out a hand, blindly seeking some support and in that moment before they began to move towards him in alarm, he seemed to shrink so that not only were his young sons as tall as he but exceedingly taller.

'Joss!' The scream which came from his wife's throat had all the despair and terror of a child who has been confronted with a dark, unimaginable nightmare. It was heard quite clearly in the kitchen, freezing every servant to immobility, and up in her room where Tessa sat disconsolately on her dressing-table stool, sighing over the punishment which was surely coming, the sound brought her to her feet.

Drew and Pearce Greenwood, with the rapid reflexes of the young, had their father by the arms, one on either side of him, their own faces as pale as death itself, their strength the only support which kept him from crashing to the floor like some poleaxed animal. They were quite appalled, panic-stricken, for it seemed their reckless insolence so evident in the unabashed rebellion they had shown, was killing their father before their very eyes.

'Father . . . ?' Pearce's voice, no longer that of a man but of a frightened young boy, followed close on their mother's scream. They loved him, their distraught young faces said; they were sorry, dear God, how they were sorry, and if he would just stand up straight and give them both a good hiding

147

they would never defy him again. But as their mother flung herself across the room, her arms outstretched to hold him, not only upright but in this world since she could not live without him, her expression said, he slipped quietly from their grasp into a crumpled and surprisingly small heap on the carpet.

*   *   *

The doctor had gone, swearing that if Mr Greenwood put a foot out of bed within the next month, Mrs Greenwood would surely be a widow. He would call the next day, he said; a light diet, perhaps a bit of fish or chicken, and certainly, now that he had been bled he would improve. Mrs Greenwood was to take this potion to make her sleep, or *she* would be his next patient. Yes, undoubtedly Mr Greenwood had been overworking but it was only a slight inflammation of the head and, given time and rest, he would recover.

Kit Greenwood was drifting protectively over the still-sleeping figure of her husband, her violet-blue eyes enormous in the suddenly old and waxy pallor of her face, ignoring the doctor's advice regarding herself with the contempt it deserved. *Sleep*, when the only person who had ever meant *anything* to her in the whole of her life, might slip away whilst she closed her eyes! Was anything more ridiculous? She attached herself to his bedside, not quite touching him, but certainly willing into him the very breath of her own lungs should his not prove adequate.

They sat in the drawing-room, none of them speaking for what was there to say? It was their fault, of course, his sons and his niece knew, for had he not been so goaded by their waywardness, he would undoubtedly not be lying inches from death at this very minute. Laurel held Charlie's hand, badly frightened and in need of comfort, blaming them as much as they did themselves. She was seen to lean her bright head against the sombre darkness of his shoulder, sighing tearfully, for though Joss Greenwood was not her father by blood, she loved him dearly.

They were side by side on the sofa, the three culprits, Drew and Pearce with Tessa between them, still in the mud and muck of the hunting field and they all jumped guiltily when Jenny spoke.

'This is not your fault, you know.'

'Oh, Mother, it was, it was.' Tessa began to weep noisily, no longer, now that the crisis was over somewhat, able to contain herself.

'We've always made him wild, Aunt Jenny, and now look what we've done.' Pearce's voice was distraught and Drew put his head in his hands, filled, it seemed, with the deepest shame.

But Jenny Harrison, though she recognised this as an ideal opportunity to hit them with the stick her brother's 'turn' had presented to her, was too honest a woman to use it.

'No, lad. Joss has always had a quick temper. We all have, let's be honest, and if it were that which had cudgelled him as it did, he would have been struck down years ago. Your father has driven himself for the last thirty years doing what he set out to do when your grandfather died on St Peter's Field. He swore then he'd take the fight wherever it was needed to try to get a decent living for the "afflicted poor", as we were called. Aye, I say "we" because he and Charlie and me were among them when the hand loom became obsolete. He fought himself to a standstill, did your father. He went to gaol twice, as you know, and for the past twenty years he's never given up hope of a fair deal for the working man. Twenty hours a day he's worked and I reckon he's just paid the price for it. He wanted to see the rest of the men he fought beside get a vote of their own, you see, not just those with property and influence, but it's not come and I think it's taken the strength from him. So you're not to blame yourselves, any of you. But that's not to say you've no need to mend your ways. I want to see you two at the mill gate at five thirty sharp tomorrow morning and as for you, miss, you'll go nowhere without a bonnet to cover that head of yours until your hair's a decent length. D'you hear?'

Tessa said fervently that she did but even as Jenny Harrison looked into the tearful face she was aware that though her daughter meant what she said, and honestly meant to obey her, it would not be long before she forgot her bonnet, or lost it, or simply threw it away, since she was *her* daughter after all.

That night as Tessa lay restless in the tangled covers of her bed, the house hushed and uneasy about her, she brooded on the shape and colour of her own nature. Why had she done it? Why did she do so many wild and challenging things? There was no need. She was allowed so much more freedom than the girls of her acquaintance and yet she abused it, gambled with it, risked losing it just for the sake of some excitement, which, after all, caused nothing but sorrow to her family whom she loved dearly. That moment of reflection in the hallway before she had entered the drawing-room had been, probably, the first feeling of uncertainty she had known in her life. She had found it uncomfortable and so had ignored it. But perhaps they were right, those who bade her shape her restless activities into a more lady-like pattern. Perhaps she should stay at home and ... and ... *what?* What should she do? Sew and paint, play the piano and write interminable letters ...? Oh, dear Lord, the thought appalled her. She couldn't do it but she really would try to be a little more as her family wanted her to be. She would ... she ... would ...

CHAPTER EIGHT

They were seventeen years old when they really *saw* her for the first time and strangely, or perhaps not in view of their closeness, they did so at exactly the same moment.

'I think we'll give a big Christmas party this year,' Laurel said, 'not just the family but friends as well. We could empty the salon and line the walls with chairs, put a dais at one end and engage a small orchestra so that we might dance. Not a grand ball since we haven't the space and not a dinner party either but something in between the two.' She turned anxiously to Charlie who was studying a newspaper whilst coffee was being served after dinner. 'Do you think it might be possible to invite the Squire, darling?' She sat down beside her husband and looked up entreatingly into his face, begging his support, her tense look implying how dearly she would love someone to show some interest in this splendid idea of hers. There was nothing she feared more than being overlooked in this family of arrogant males—except Charlie, of course—and self-possessed women and yet, unless she stamped her foot and pouted, made a great to-do, that was exactly what happened.

'There's no reason why he shouldn't be sent an invitation,' Charlie answered her absently, 'though whether he accepts is an entirely different matter.'

'Drew, Pearce and Tessa are frequent guests at the Hall so do you not think he might be persuaded to allow us to repay his hospitality? It would be only good manners on our part after all.'

'Nothing ventured, nothing gained, sweetheart.'

'We might even make it into a fancy-dress affair, everyone masked until midnight. That might tempt him,' she continued, for she was desperate to get into what she called 'good' society. If she did she was convinced she would be more ... well, more ... assured and less prone to this foolish— she knew it—belief that she was going to be, that they were *all* going to be, flung back to the old days when the Greenwoods had been nothing but lowly weavers. If she could just claim the patronage of the Squire and his lady, if she could drop it casually into the conversation of her afternoon callers that she had more than a second-hand acquaintance with the leading family of the Penfold Valley, how grand it would be and how special she, Laurel Greenwood, would feel.

'It sounds delightful, Laurel,' Drew yawned, then turned to look at his brother for he was well aware
152

of his sister's longing for social recognition in the gentrified class of Crossfold. He raised an enquiring eyebrow at Pearce asking if it might be possible for the two of them to slip away to some more congenial surroundings but Laurel intercepted the look which passed between them and her face became thoughtful.

'Why don't you put it to Nicky Longworth?' she said after a moment. 'The three of you have been thick as thieves for years.'

'You mean ask Nick to ask his father and mother if they would kindly agree to attend my sister's party?'

'Oh, Drew, you know what I mean.' She sighed tremulously. 'Naturally you and Pearce will be there . . .'

'Are you certain, my pet?' Pearce grinned amiably.

'I am *positive*, Pearce Greenwood, am I not, Charlie?' The dreadfulness of their father's collapse, though he had recovered now, still remained vivid to both young men and they became instantly restrained.

Her husband laid down his newspaper and turned politely to her. He was always polite to his wife.

'I beg your pardon, dear?'

'I am begging your support, Charlie, in the matter of my Christmas party and I must insist that you compel Drew and Pearce to be there. Aunt Jenny . . .' She twisted anxiously in the direction of her aunt who glanced up reluctantly from some papers she was studying. Tessa watched her mother's eyes turn from warm interest to cool appraisal of her brother's wife. Her mother always

153

looked like that when she was brought face to face with Laurel's hunger for social advancement: cool, expressionless, disinterested as though the trivia with which Laurel concerned herself was mindlessly tedious.

' . . . you do agree with me, don't you?' Laurel was saying, apparently unaware of her aunt's slightly jaded opinion of her, and Tessa wondered at Laurel's absorption with her children, her husband, her position in the society of Crossfold and the Penfold Valley to the complete exclusion of anything else.

'Agree with what?'

'That Drew and Pearce must be made to attend my party and to use their influence and advantage as friends of Nicky Longworth in persuading the Squire to accept my invitation to it.'

'What party is that?' Tessa felt a surge of interest for was there to be an argument to alleviate the boredom of the hours between dinner and bedtime?

'Oh, Aunt Jenny, please listen. And you, Charlie. It will be Christmas in four weeks' time and I would love to give you a Christmas party—something entirely different from the usual family affair, particularly as Father and Mother will be unable to attend. Mother tells me Father is settling down nicely in Italy but the journey back for Christmas so soon after arriving there is completely out of the question.'

'I appreciate that, Laurel, but what is wrong with just having family for Christmas dinner?' Jenny said suspiciously. 'It is what we have done for the past twenty years and I see no reason to change. The children enjoy it and it would be a shame to

154

have a party which excluded them.'

'They could still have their party on Christmas Day but we could have *ours* on Christmas Eve. A Christmas Eve fancy-dress ball with masks ... a champagne supper ... decorate the salon. Heavens, it must be years since it was used. It would be when Father was re-elected in ... when was it? Ten years ago. Oh, please, Charlie, you must say yes.' She turned to him, her white skin flushed with a lovely rosy glow, her green eyes sparkling up into his, her whole body surging enchantingly towards him. Tessa saw him soften and lean somehow towards her, the movement at once conveying something which made her look away awkwardly and her cousins exchange knowing glances. A promise between them, from her to him, something she pledged to give him if he would back her up on this against Jenny who was bound to be awkward on general principle. Not that Charlie ever denied his wife anything. She had a way with her sometimes that was hard to resist, so soft and pretty and gentle, and Charlie viewed it fondly. Or did he just do it for the sake of peace? A peaceful man was Charlie, who hated discord and loved his wife.

Tessa grimaced in embarrassment and turned away from them and at that moment both Drew and Pearce looked at her. To her amazed bewilderment, instead of grinning and pulling a face as they would normally do when confronted with one of Laurel's little play-acting performances, they continued to stare at her as though they were hypnotised. Two pairs of vivid eyes held some strange expression in them, unreadable in the soft glow of the lamplight and

155

she felt the discomfort rise up in her until it reached her heart which began to thump against her breastbone. What was the matter with the pair of them? Had she grown another head, or was it her hair which Emma had arranged with a complicated array of pins and a knot of bright ribbon in an attempt to disguise its short and springing growth? It had increased by an inch or so in the last month and could now be pushed behind her ears but it was still difficult to contrive a style which could in any way be called normal. She knew her mother sighed when she looked at her but then she had never been a young lady concerned with fashion, had she? She was too tall for one thing, where small and dainty was the vogue, with a long-limbed grace which was quite delightful had she but known it. She had broad shoulders, a bosom which had continued to bloom until it was quite splendid. She was dark with what she knew was a big mouth, when fair hair and rosebud lips were considered the thing. Tall, dark and well-rounded, then, with a comical hair style, but that did not give her cousins the right to stare at her as she had seen them stare at many a pretty girl. She was *not* a pretty girl: she was their cousin and companion of many years. To show her disapproval, first making sure no one was watching but them, she pulled a face and poked her tongue out at them.

At once they folded into silent laughter, both of them spluttering into their after-dinner port and a great wave of relief washed over her as Pearce winked and inclined his head in Laurel's direction, sighing dramatically.

Drew, however, turned courteously to Laurel.

'I think it is a splendid idea, big sister, and I for

one am all in favour of it.'

'Why, thank you, Drew. There you are, you see.' She turned in triumph to Jenny. 'Someone else is on my side.'

Pearce, knowing instinctively that Drew had some reason, which no doubt would be revealed in a moment, for this turnabout, spoke up in his support.

'I am with you, too, Laurel. It would make a splendid change to have a party to which one could invite one's friends.'

'Really! You mean it?' Laurel was enchanted. 'And you would sound out Nicky Longworth?'

'Oh, indeed. I dare say all our acquaintances'— meaning, of course, in the fox-hunting society of the Penfold Valley, which he knew quite well was what Laurel referred to—'would be delighted.'

'It sounds daft to me,' Jenny muttered irritably, turning back to the report she was reading, 'and if you think I'm going to dress up as Good Queen Bess or Mary Stuart, you can think again.'

It was plain from Laurel's face she cared not a jot or tittle what Jenny Harrison did, nor even if she attended *her* Christmas party at all. Important people would be there, people with whom she longed to mix, people of fashion and good breeding, considered to be gentry in the Penfold Valley. For most of her life she had been on the same footing as the local towers of trade and commerce, rich and powerful men, many of them, but it was the 'ancient' families of south Lancashire on whom she had her sights, those who were not merchants, shopkeepers, industrialists; whose money had come to them not by way of anything which could be bought and sold, but was inherited

157

wealth. And the head of the local society, of course, was the high Tory Squire Longworth, the greatest landowner in the district. The only way the new railway route to Crossfold could effectively proceed was across the Squire's vast estate and by allowing it he had become almost as wealthy as the Greenwoods themselves. The Squire had never accepted an invitation to any of the homes of the local millocracy but if Laurel Greenwood, through her younger brother's connections with them, could coax him and his lady wife to hers, what a feather in her cap that would be. A triumph indeed for would she herself not have a foot in the door of Longworth Hall, and where, her excited thoughts wanted to know, might that lead her?'

'So it's settled then?' she asked breathlessly, her hand gripping Charlie's arm in a passion of joy.

'Indeed it is, if Aunt Jenny agrees.' Drew sipped his port peaceably.

'It's nothing to do with me, lad.'

'Well, then, all we have to do now is to decide what we are to go as. I must admit I can quite see myself as a Regency buck: I would look well with a powdered wig. As for Tessa, what would suit her more than one of those delectable, high-waisted draperies of shimmering fabric I am told the Empress Josephine used to wear? I can quite see her . . .'

'Yes, yes, how splendid.' Laurel was not really listening though both Jenny Harrison and Pearce Greenwood turned to look at Drew with narrowed, uncertain eyes. 'What will you wear, Charlie?'

Laurel's delight was very appealing and Tessa saw Charlie's hand go out to touch the back of her neck, resting there in a warm caress, and again,

158

when she looked away, her eyes met those of both
her cousins who had also seen it. Their expressions,
so similar it was quite uncanny, were speaking of
something which caused a strange but not
unpleasant fluttering in her throat.

'And what will you go as, Pearce?' she heard
herself say, surprised at the ordinary sound of her
own voice.

'I had not thought . . .'

'Oh, come on, Pearce,' Laurel was laughing now,
animated and lovely, looking no more than
nineteen again in her excitement. 'How about
Henry the Eighth?'

'Please, Laurel . . .' He tore his eyes away,
reluctantly Tessa thought, from her own, his face a
warm brown, his mouth beginning to curl in a
familiar, whimsical smile, 'I have hardly the figure
to play Henry the Eighth. But we shall see, shall we
not, brother, what the evening will bring?' There
was something in his voice which seemed to say he
was not referring to costumes.

*   *   *

She wore a dress of incredibly light chiffon, high-
waisted with satin ribbons tied beneath her breasts,
as Drew had described so accurately. The narrow
skirt fell in straight folds to her sandalled feet and
she floated all in white like a wisp of swansdown,
the hem of the dress drifting and fluting about her
naked ankles. Her arms and shoulders were bare
though her mother insisted that the deep plunge of
the neckline be draped to hide the swell of her
smooth white breasts. Her hair was brushed up on
her head, arranged with false pads and curls into a

reasonable copy of a Grecian hairstyle, an intricate arrangement of glossy swathes and ringlets threaded through with white satin ribbon.

'Who are you supposed to be then?' her mother asked, quite amused now that she had ensured her daughter was as decorous as propriety demanded, though what Crossfold would make of it she could not imagine.

'I am a Grecian lady of great renown.'

'Dear Lord, who's that then?'

'Diana the huntress.'

'Didn't she have some kind of an animal?'

Tessa's face fell. 'Yes, she did. Do you think I could take one of the dogs?'

'Now Laurel *would* have something to say about that.'

Tessa laughed, then turning abruptly, leaned down to kiss her mother's cheek hurriedly. They were not given to demonstrations of affection, but she felt a great flow of it well up in her for this woman who, she was fully aware, had always gone against the code of her society in allowing her daughter so much freedom.

'Thank you, Mother.'

'For what, child?'

'I don't know, really, I just want you to know . . .'

'I *do* know, Tessa. Now come on, lass, we don't want Laurel to steal all the limelight. Not that she's likely to, the minute those downstairs clap eyes on you.'

Even now it was uncertain whether the Squire would attend. He had answered Laurel's invitation with a brief note to say he had a prior commitment on that date but if he could manage it he and his family and Christmas guests might look in for half

160

an hour to wish the Greenwood family seasonal greetings. It was almost in the style of a manorial lord bestowing a visit on a deserving tenant.

Laurel was delirious with joy, almost insufferable in her pride. She was unaware that had it not been for Nicky Longworth who had reminded his father of the charm, the wit, the good looks and good manners of the three Greenwood youngsters who were often included in the Squire's hunt, he would have thrown the invitation to the back of the fire where it belonged.

They went downstairs together, mother and daughter. Jenny, who vowed she was far too old for dressing up, appeared serene and elegant in stark black velvet, relieved only by a magnificent diamond choker about her smooth neck and long earrings to match. She made the perfect contrast for her exquisitely, simply dressed daughter and the two young men who watched for her at the foot of the stairs were bound in her spell, caught in the shimmering magic of her.

'Drew, Pearce, good evening,' their aunt said to them, offering a cheek to each in turn, which they kissed without once taking their eyes from Tessa. 'You both look very dashing. And what a cold evening it is. I do believe it might snow before morning. A white Christmas would be lovely for the children.'

'Indeed.'

'Where are Laurel and Charlie?'

'In the drawing-room. The first guests are due to arrive any moment.'

'Well . . .' She glanced from one entranced face to the other and a small pang of misgiving struck her. She had seen that look on a man's face many,

161

many times, directed not only at her daughter as now, but at other women, including herself. It came in different guises from pure lust to the deep and endless love, strong, steadfast and beautiful to see, that her older brother felt for his wife, the mother of these two young men. And if it transpired that one or the other of her brother's boys should make up with *her* girl she would have no objection. They were wild and reckless, hot tempered and arrogant, but good-natured withal. And her girl was strong, stronger than both of them, though that was not yet immediately apparent; she would tame and control, shape into a steady man, the one who would be her husband. It would be a good match, but with which one, for God's sake? They were both looking at Tessa as though she was the Christmas fairy come to life.

Jenny shook her head, smiling at her own absurdity, for they blew hot and cold, the pair of them, changing their minds as often as they changed their splendid jackets. Tessa looked superb tonight, older than her years and eternally feminine, and would not any man with a drop of red blood in his veins stare as these two were doing?

'I'll join them for a sherry, then,' she said, wondering why she bothered, and left the three of them knowing that none had even noticed she had gone.

The young men were dressed identically in tight black riding breeches and a white frilled shirt open at the neck. Their tall boots reached their knees and they wore gold earrings looped on thread about their ears and a red bandana most rakishly tilted over one eye. Their brown skin and white

162

teeth added to their startlingly effective appearance, as did the mock cutlass they each wore at their belts. Laurel had decided against masks as she wanted none of the company to be in any doubt of the identity of the peerless guests she hoped to entertain this night.

'Pirates or gypsies?' Tessa asked impishly.

'He's a pirate and I'm a gypsy.'

'How clever.'

'We thought so, but not half as clever as you, little cousin,' Drew stepped away from Pearce to stand in front of her as she moved down from the bottom tread of the stairs. Pearce frowned and fingered his cutlass, ready to plunge it into his brother's back, but she stepped lightly between them, moving towards the towering Christmas tree which stood at the foot of the stairs, adjusting a strand of tinsel on its bough, allowing them to study her whilst she stood gracefully on tip-toe to reach the branch.

'You *have* grown up since we saw you an hour ago,' Pearce murmured, his eyes narrowed, 'and in a most delightful way. Mind you, we have noticed for the past week or two that you have become quite the young lady, have we not, Drew?'

'Indeed we have.'

'And in what way is that, Pearce?' she asked innocently, immensely pleased with her own womanhood which had come on her so suddenly and so splendidly. She smiled over her shoulder, scarcely troubled, as she had been on the night the party had been discussed, by their speculative glances, for did she not know what scamps they were? Charming scamps who would flatter any pretty woman, and she knew now, and was pleased

163

with it, that she was pretty. And she was almost in her eighteenth year so why should she not try out this amusing pastime of mild flirtation, even if it was only with her cousins? They were exceedingly handsome, both of them, and quite willing, it appeared, to go along with the game.

'Come over here and we will show you.' He grinned wickedly and a small shiver of delight ran through her. His teasing eyes were so lovely and blue, so blissfully familiar, and this nonsense made her feel so grown up.

'My turn first, I think, brother, since I am the oldest,' Drew said softly and there was something in his tone which was not teasing at all. He had followed her as she drifted away from the Christmas tree, leading her resolutely in the direction of the mistletoe which hung by the drawing-room door. When his cool hand fell on her arm she turned, smiling and ready for her very first kiss, glad that it was Drew—or was it Pearce?— then realised that it made no difference. His lips were warm as they rested on hers and she could taste his wine-scented, cigar-scented breath and the sharp smell of his freshly shaved skin.

'Merry Christmas, sweetheart,' he whispered amazingly, his cheek against hers. Then before she could open her eyes which she had closed in pleasure at the loveliness of it, he kissed her again, a delightful repetition of the first time. His hands were firm on her upper arms and she felt herself sway for an instant against him, then he was gone. She opened her eyes and knew they were shining as she waited for Pearce to take his turn, as he surely would, wondering if his kiss would be as pleasant as Drew's. But he was standing next to his brother, shoulder to shoulder as they always did, grinning audaciously.

'Well, then, little cousin, which one did you like the best?' they teased, but in both pairs of enquiring eyes and about each smiling mouth was that strange expression she had seen a month ago and she knew they were in deadly earnest, in deadly contention as they so often inexplicably were.

'Which . . . but I thought . . . I did not know that you had . . .'

'What are you trying to say, my pet?' Pearce's eyes wandered to her mouth and with a sense of amazement she understood that she had been kissed by *both* her cousins and, amazingly, their kisses had been identical, so identical she could not have said which was which. Or perhaps it was that way with all men. A kiss was a kiss, no matter who gave it to you. But Pearce was waiting for an answer and she must cover her confusion for she did not want them to think her a silly female flustered by her first encounter with a male.

'That you are both exceedingly impertinent and I cannot for the life of me understand what all the fuss is about.' Her voice was teasing. 'Both were quite . . . pleasant,' she tossed her head to show her supposed indifference for it, 'but that is all.'

'So you are saying you do not care for it, then?' Drew's mouth opened on a shout of laughter, then he stepped forward and, as the cousin he was, kissed her soundly on both cheeks. 'Well, then, we shall have to wait until you are a bit older,' he declared from the elevated position his six months' seniority gave him, 'shall we not, brother?'

'Merry Christmas, Tessa, and a happy New Year,'

Pearce offered her his arm and they were as they had always been, impertinent and infinitely dear to her, both of them.

The evening was a huge success, Laurel positively purring as she moved amongst her guests for they were all aware that the Squire had favoured her with a promise to 'look in' on her small party. The house was luminous with candlelight and fragrant with blooms from the greenhouses at the back of Greenacres, hundreds of flowers lining the stairs which led up to the gallery and salon, and in the lovely room itself great swathes of ivy, garlands of mistletoe, holly and red satin ribbon.

There was chilled punch and chilled champagne, claret, Madeira and sherry; salmon and game, lobster and pigeon pie, oyster patties, mayonnaise of trout, paté and prawns; tipsy-cake and fruited jellies and mountains of ice-cream mixed with almonds and cherries, the laden tables decorated with a dozen epergnes burdened with fruit and edged with trailing ivy and pale pink rosebuds from the Greenacres hothouse. Quite, quite exquisite, everyone agreed. Had not Laurel Greenwood done well? the whispers echoing about the salon hissed as she came in on the arm of the Squire, his lady behind them with Charlie.

'Dear God, there'll be no holding her now,' Pearce drawled as he lounged indolently on one side of Tessa against the tall windows looking out on to the icy winter garden. Drew, from her other side, sipped his champagne and agreed lazily, his eyes not on his sister as she was led out on to the floor by the man she obviously considered her own personal endorsement of having 'arrived', but on

166

his cousin. They had taken it in turns to dance with her though they had been forced, when it could not possibly be avoided without a scene, to allow Nicky Longworth and one or two others to take a turn round the floor with her. They had vied with one another to make her laugh out loud, causing heads to turn to see what Jenny Harrison's undisciplined daughter was up to now. And that 'get-up' she had on was scarcely decent. Her ankles were on display for all to gawk at and it was obvious to anyone with eyes in their heads that she wore no petticoats beneath that shockingly diaphanous gown. It was well known that Jenny Harrison was an unorthodox woman, capricious in her own youth, it was said. Well, weren't they all? Kit Greenwood had been a law unto herself from the day they killed her father and it seemed her sons and their headstrong cousin were to be the same.

And yet when the Squire favoured her with a dance, taking her in a graceful dip and sway about the room, evidently as intrigued with her as her madcap cousins appeared to be, she was as demure and modest as any sixteen-year-old should be, smiling innocently, speaking, one supposed, when spoken to, her eyes, on a level with his, cast down quite shyly. He was so delighted with her, remembering her skill and bravery on his own hunting field, that he took her round again, returning her to her mother most reluctantly. He had a word and a smile for Drew and Pearce who sprang to attention respectfully as he approached, his own son with them, and though Laurel was none too pleased at the amount of time, almost twenty minutes, he then spent chatting with them, it really was a triumph for the family.

167

The Squire and his lady had been driven away in their carriage when Pearce took Tessa's arm and drew her to one side.

'Meet us at the bottom of the stairs in ten minutes,' he whispered.

'What for?' she whispered back.

'Never you mind. It's a surprise. Just be there.'

They were there waiting for her. They led her along the back passage to the side entrance of the house, one carrying her warm, fur-lined cape, the other a stout pair of boots, and when she was snugly bundled up they opened the door with a flourish.

'Just for you, little cousin, and a very happy Christmas from us both,' Pearce said softly, revealing the magical garden beyond. It had been snowing for more than an hour. At first small, frozen pellets had stuck fast to the lawns and paths, turning within half an hour to huge, soft flakes which had laid themselves, like the swansdown which lined the edge of her hood, three inches deep in a smooth and silent layer across the estate and the moorland beyond, transforming it into a world of such perfect, unspoiled beauty she drew in her breath with delight. It was eerily quiet. The lamplight stretched out in a pale yellow path across the glistening snow, gold and silver shimmering where the light reflected from it. The sky was a deep, mysterious purple and from it tumbled and whirled enormous fat snowflakes. Trees and bushes were captured in their dazzle, stretching out graceful arms to take on the shape of smooth, white, diamond-studded statues. It was all glitter and dazzle and when she stepped out in it, a hand in each of her cousins', it closed in around her,

168

caressing her with the infinite tenderness of a lover.

They were quiet at first, almost reverent, stepping softly across the wide lawn beneath the salon window, looking back at the three sets of footprints they had made, those in the middle blurred by the dragging of her cloak.

But the peace did not last. How could it? They were young and in love with life and enjoyment and their own immortality, and when Pearce picked up a handful of snow and moulded it into a hard, round ball, warning his brother to beware, it did not take long for the other two to respond. Their shrieks of joyous laughter were heard even above the sound of the orchestra, drawing an amused crowd to the window. Within five minutes Laurel Greenwood's salon was emptied of every gentleman under the age of sixty, her own husband included, and even a dozen of the most daring young ladies, those who could escape or ignore their mamas' eagle eye.

It was said by many of the young guests to be the best party the valley had ever known, with the snowfight allowing those young ladies who had the inclination for it, more freedom than their mamas—or husbands—would have thought decent. More than a few lovely gowns were ruined and satin dancing slippers in tatters. Cheeks were rosy and warm despite the snow which danced against them and the laughter and shouts of triumph rose as snowballs found their mark. When it was done and a smilingly frozen-faced Laurel, who had declined to go outdoors and make a fool of herself, served hot coffee and mulled wine to those gentlemen who remained, Tessa curled herself up under her quilt, the firelight picking out the

169

snowflakes which still floated against the window, and tried blissfully to decide which of her cousin's warm, Christmas kisses had pleased her the most.

CHAPTER NINE

Will Broadbent's tiny house, rented from the Greenwoods when he had begun work at the Chapman Mill as an overlooker, was set in a bit of garden at the end of a row of similar houses. Each had a parlour, a back kitchen which led out into its own yard, two bedrooms above, a good dry cellar beneath and a privy to each family.

Will's cosy parlour in which he had placed a couple of comfortable wing chairs, one on either side of the fireplace, and a round table covered with a red chenille cloth, was as warm as he could get it on this cold, snowy Christmas Day. The shelves in the alcoves beside the chimney breast were filled with books and the fireplace had a cast-iron surround with a brass fender and gleaming fire-tools. The polished floorboards were partly covered by a square carpet and before the fire was a hearth rug. There were curtains at the windows, red chenille again with a fringed pelmet, and on the walls were several commemorative plates, one produced to mark the 1832 Reform Bill and another the Chartist Movement of 1838. Will had been no more than a lad at the time of the first event but he had grown up with tales of the daring and recklessness of men of the Radical movement which had aimed to help other men, like himself, women and children too, to work with dignity and

170

fulfilment in the cotton mills of Lancashire and, indeed, in many other parts of the country. Deeply interested in reform, though not perhaps with the fervour of Joss Greenwood or the late William Cobbett, he attended political meetings, union meetings, liking to hear an argument from every side before making up his own mind and went each week to the library in Chapmanstown, erected by Mrs Joss Greenwood for the betterment of the minds of her workers, to read the national newspapers from cover to cover.

Sir Robert Peel, the greatest of all English statesmen in Will's opinion, had died three years ago when he was thrown from his horse, and his death had affected Will deeply. Indeed, the whole nation had mourned the great man. It was due to him that the hated Corn Laws had been abolished, thus alleviating to some extent the conditions of the poor, though the deed had lost him his own office in government. An enormous loss to his country, Will had read, and he agreed with the statement wholeheartedly.

He sat before his own cosy fire, aware at the back of his mind that he was lonely, acknowledging to himself that man was not meant to live alone and that he should be thinking of taking a wife. For twenty or more years he had lived in the Penfold Valley and for the past six months, ever since he had gone to work for Chapmans, he had lived in this little house, his first home and one that could so readily be shared with the right lass, perhaps children. And hc had made it what it was. Unlike most men who would have been content with a bed, a chair and a table under which to put their feet, he had found a great deal of satisfaction in

171

turning it into his own place.

Feeling somewhat foolish at first, he had scoured the second-hand furniture shops of Crossfold and Edgeclough, sorting through the sad treasures of women who, perhaps, had fallen on hard times, finding pieces which pleased his eye. Knowing nothing of craftsmen such as Hepplewhite or Sheraton, nevertheless Will recognised a decent bit of polished wood when he saw it. The lustre of mahogany and rosewood and walnut, the glowing colours in the tapestry of his wing chairs, gave him immense pleasure. The hard-wearing Brussels carpet, made in Halifax, though worn in places was swirled in patterns of faded rose and sage, and the hearthrug, come from somewhere in the Orient he had been told by the owner of the pawn-shop where he had bought it, was soft and warm to his stockinged feet.

In the small scullery behind the parlour was a pine dresser on which he had set out dishes, plates, cups and saucers bought at the Crossfold country fair during the summer. There was some durable pewter and a copper pan or two and he had smiled as he placed them on the shelves, chiding himself for an old woman, but pleased, just the same, with his first *real* home, his kitchen, simple in pine and deal. The bedroom upstairs he had furnished in what was, to him, luxurious comfort: a big brass bed with snowy linen and warm blankets covered with a splendid Welsh quilt stitched in hearts. Again he had laughed at himself, glad that the men with whom he worked could not see his pride and pleasure in what, surely, was a woman's domain. The fact was, he liked beautiful things. He didn't know why and certainly did not disclose the fact to

172

anyone, even though his handiness with his fists and his great strength, well known and appreciated in the mill, would have discouraged any man from making a disparaging remark about it.

They were well built, these houses, he mused, as he strode for the third time to the window to peer out at the snowy world beyond, aware that he was becoming increasingly restless. The road outside his gate, though knee-deep in snow at the moment, was paved and well lit on a dark winter's night. There was an air about the houses not exactly of prosperity, for none of the Chapman employees could be said to have wealth, but of care, pride even, in each well-maintained, well-polished cottage. The windows shone, the gates were intact and oiled, there were curtains, mostly clean, and steps which were donkey-stoned each Saturday. Gardens in the summer produced a flower or two and at the back was a row of allotments where men like himself grew cabbages and potatoes. The privies stood by the back gates of the yards, the cleanliness of each depending upon the family it served. For the most part, they were scrupulous, since every house had its own piped water and the sewage was adequately taken care of by the splendid drains.

He sat down heavily in the chair and picked up a book. He put his stockinged feet on the fender, lit his pipe and prepared to have an hour or two with Mr Charles Dickens' *David Copperfield*. It had come from Mrs Greenwood's library in Chapmanstown, where the many young men and women who could read and write were allowed to borrow books.

But it was no good. Somehow David and

Steerforth and pretty Dora could not hold his attention and he knew it was because, today of all days, Christmas Day, he was alone. Why should it concern him now, he wondered, when for the past seven or eight years, ever since he had left the apprentice house, he had been on his own, living in lodgings, without family or friend?

His eyes drifted to the holly he had hung above the fire-place and the mistletoe pinned to the door-frame between the parlour and the scullery. He smiled ruefully, asking himself which young lady he had hoped to catch in a Christmas kiss when not one soul had crossed his threshold since he had taken up residence here. That was not to say he did not enjoy the company of a pretty woman. He was friendly with the landlord's wife at the Dog and Gun, a bonny woman a year or two older than himself with a husband of almost fifty who had lost his appetite for his wife's curving flesh. Strange, since she was extremely obliging—to Will and, he suspected, to several others whom he was certain shared her favours.

He nearly dropped his pipe when someone hammered on his door and was severely handicapped for a moment or two as he attempted to brush away the hot ash from its bowl which had fallen on his cord trousers. His expression was quite foolish as he stood indecisively on his own hearth rug, wondering who it could be when all it took to find out was a stride or two across the parlour and the opening of the front door. Of course, he could peep from behind his chenille curtains to see who was mad enough to wade through the drifts which were certain to have piled up where the wind had blown them. It had snowed heavily many times in the past for the winters up here on the edge of the Pennines were fierce and stormy and those of the spinners and weavers who lived in Chapmanstown and must trudge up to Crossbank, Highbank and Broadbank had tales to tell of finding themselves up to their armpits in snow banks. Mrs Harrison, a woman of ingenuity he had heard, and to be admired, had organised them into groups so that they travelled together, and if one got into difficulties the others could form a rescue party. It had been quite hilarious, it seemed, and certainly a novelty, especially as Mrs Harrison had arranged for them to have a bowl of hot soup to restore them to a working condition before they switched on their mules or looms.

And last night there had been just such a blizzard.

She was on his doorstep when he opened the door; not Mrs Harrison of whom he had been thinking but her daughter. She was dazzling, brilliant with delight, like a child who has achieved the impossible. Her eyes glowed into his, her mouth wide and sweet, parting over her white teeth in a huge grin. Tessa Harrison: the young girl who had, in the last few months, become his friend.

Friend! Dear God, if anyone of her family became aware of it, particularly those reckless cousins of hers, he would be hounded not only from the mill, his job there and this snug cottage, but from Lancashire itself; and yet their relationship was completely innocent. It had begun on the moor, on the top road from Chapmanstown to Edgeclough. It had begun an hour or two after she had snarled her wild Greenwood temper at him in the mill yard. It had begun when he found her

175

waiting for him to enquire whether he had got the job he had asked for. It had begun when she had shared her family history with him, who had none, and had been enthralled by the tale of his sad beginnings. It had begun and flourished on the few occasions they had met when her cousins had ridden off without her, she said mutinously, refusing to include her in some wild and reckless folly. He had walked the moors every Sunday, not looking for her since she was no more than a child, he told himself, and a child of the class to which he, as a millworker, had no access. When they met it was by accident, an encounter neither looked for nor planned, but which both enjoyed; perhaps for only a few moments in which she enquired of his job and his progress in it, he to admire her growing hair, to joke about her cousin's cutting of it, to ask politely after her uncle's health. After the incident with the Irish tinkers he had been somewhat short with her, subconsciously recognising that his exasperation was more than one human being's concern for another, but she seemed not to notice. Sometimes they sat on the rough grass together, saying nothing, at ease in their silences with no need to make the small talk they both found so irksome. He was often amazed that he found such pleasure in the company of a young girl, one in whom, he told himself, he had no physical interest, nor shared interest at all, really, for she was no reader and had neither heard of, nor was concerned with what he read. He did not care about the hunting of the fox, nor the shooting of game birds, which it seemed she did and was good at, she boasted, but somehow they met on a bit of common ground, neither realising what it was, relishing one another's company. They had come across one another at Annie Beale's cottage, sharing a cup of tea and a joke, easy with one another, and with her, as a mutual friend.

But there was something different about her today.

She was beautiful: not in the way a child, or even a young girl, was beautiful, but as a woman. Alive, vibrant with her own joy of getting here against almost overwhelming odds, the tenacious hold she had on life which gave her the strength and courage carelessly to thrust aside whatever obstacle might be thrown in her path. There was not another female in Crossfold, in Lancashire, he believed, like her. Not one of them would have tackled the walk from Greenacres to Chapmanstown, a distance of more than three miles, on foot over ground which, though it was not exactly high moorland, was rough and hazardous with deep hollows and sharply rising inclines, and in three feet of freshly drifted snow.

'Look,' she beseeched him before he could speak, lifting her feet, first one then the other, on which she had strapped what looked like a pair of round, flat, mesh sieves, something the gardener would use to riddle his soil free of large objects. They had a handle protruding from somewhere at the back, made of wood, clumsy and comical, but she was clearly beside herself with her own ingenuity.

'What the devil are they?' The delight, the wondering emotion, intact and perfectly shaped and which had become quite clear to him at that moment was mercifully hidden from her by the obligation to admire what she obviously considered her due.

'They're bats of some sort. I found them in the cupboard where Drew and Pearce keep their cricket things, fishing tackle, walking sticks, stuff like that. I think they play tennis with them. You know tennis, don't you? The Squire has a covered court . . . Anyway, when I was deliberating on how I might get here I saw these and remembered a picture in a geographical magazine, in Canada or North America I believe it was, and the man in it had these on his feet so I thought what a splendid idea to strap them to my boots. Briggs found me some leather straps . . . the mesh is ever so strong and when I stepped on to the snow—well, you could see the servants all expected me to vanish from sight or at least sink up to my waist but I walked on top of it. Can you imagine? Lord, it was wonderful. I've never been out before, not on the moors, I mean, when it was like this, and if you could have seen it! Oh, Will, I wish you could have seen it . . .' Dear God, so did he, so did he . . . Her voice became hushed and her eyes were like crystal, a clear-cut grey with a darker grey rim and around the iris the most incredible white, as white as the snow over which she had just tramped to come to *him*.

He felt the pain spear him in his fierce masculine need to sweep her off those ridiculous things she had on her feet and into his arms. Into his heart, for that was surely where she would be from this moment. He could feel his arms begin to lift and his body sway towards hers. Though she was tall her head would fit neatly beneath his chin and her long body curve itself snugly against his. He could feel it there already and his rose to meet it, his

178

maleness instantly knowing the rightness of it and demanding to be recognised. Dear, sweet Lord, but she was beautiful and no matter what they said of her in the valley, her heart was good, her nature warm for who else had taken the trouble to remember Will Broadbent on Christmas Day?

'It was like magic, Will,' she was saying, 'or like poetry, not that I really know any, but what I imagine it must be to those who do. You know the feeling you get when a song is sweet? Your skin prickles ... it was so ... so pure and clean, untouched white everywhere, and if I had not known the landmarks I should have been lost.'

He felt the familiar anger ... no, it was fear ... for her rise in his chest. She was so dear and the risks she took, the risks she was allowed to take, were almost more than he could bear. Was there no one to watch over her, to care as he did, for her safety? But as he gazed, quite bemused, absurdly so, he knew he could not approach her, not now, not today.

'And yet there were great patches of blue where the shadows lay. A landscape of pure, sparkling white and blue and the trees were like ... like filigree, like lace almost, against the snow and the sky, and there was nothing else. There were patterns in the snow where the wind had moved it as though someone, a child perhaps, had tried to draw a picture ...'

'Should you not come inside, lass?' he interrupted gently.

'Oh, Will, do you not think you could fashion another pair like these,' she asked, lifting her feet clumsily, 'then I could show you? It's like walking on clouds ... yes, that's it ...'

179

'I've never walked on clouds, my lass, and I reckon I never will, nor anyone, so perhaps ... But come in first and have a cup of tea, then we'll see. You must be cold.'

'No, I'm not, that's the wonder of it. I'm as warm as toast, feel.'

She put the bare palm of her hand against his cheek and without thought, since he was beyond it, he turned his warm mouth into it, moving his lips softly along the base of her thumb.

Her words froze on her lips. She simply stood there, her hand thrilling to his touch. Something as vivid and as simple as a flicker of lightning seemed to shiver between them. Her eyes were big and wondering, her lips still parted in startled delight, and when he drew her inside she took her marvellous footwear with her, scattering snow across his carpet. She made no objection when he sat her in a chair, nor when he knelt at her feet and removed not only the 'bats' but her stout black boots as well. She held out her feet to him, obedient as a well-brought-up child, her eyes on his bent head, waiting, just waiting for the next step in this delightful condition which had sprung up between them.

But when he had removed her boots he stood up abruptly since he found his hands were inclined to linger caressingly about her shapely stockinged foot and ankle. He made himself busy with the coal-scuttle and fire-tongs, heaping up the already dangerously high fire, arranging her boots to dry. She wanted him to turn and look at her again, to lap her about in that amazing but delicious sense of expectancy she had felt when he kissed her hand, but he moved away and she felt an illogical wave of

180

disappointment wash over her.

'I'll put the kettle on,' he said, in what he hoped was a normal tone of voice, conscious that she was looking at him, conscious of her stillness, her breath held in, for she was a young girl with no experience of such things and the kiss he had placed in her hand had been a mistake, an impulse a man of his age should have resisted. She was not sure of it, or of him, or of what was expected of her, so she was waiting for him to take the lead in whatever was to happen, if anything *was* to happen. It was up to him to return them to the casual friendship which was all that could ever be allowed between Tessa Harrison and Will Broadbent.

He tried to keep up what in other circumstances he would scornfully have deemed 'small talk' and when he came back from the scullery, bringing teacups and milk, she was stretched out with her feet on the fender, her toes wriggling in the warmth. He placed the kettle on the fire, careful not to touch her, keeping a wary distance, his chest filled with the distressing weight he carried within him.

She took the cup of tea he handed her looking about her curiously at the cosy room, this parlour which was that of a *working* man, just as though it was the most natural thing in the world to be doing, the most natural place to be on Christmas Day. She was the daughter of a wealthy millowner, he was an overlooker in that same mill, twelve years her senior, a man from only God knew where, and yet she seemed to be conscious of no disparity in their hugely different circumstances, nor of the impropriety of being here in a bachelor's home, alone and unchaperoned. He had, he admitted to

181

himself, not worried unduly over it in the past months when they met on the moors or at Annie's where the artificiality of social conduct seemed so trivial. He had been attracted to her. She was a lovely young woman and there would have to be something wrong with him had he not been, but now in the short time it had taken him to open the door and look into her enchanted, enchanting eyes, all was changed.

'It was good of you to come,' he said formally and she turned to look at him, surprised by his tone.

'Don't be silly, it's Christmas Day. I knew you would be alone so when Mother and the rest started a game of whist and Laurel's children were removed to the nursery I slipped out of the side door. I knew no one would miss me.'

'What about your cousins?' His voice was curt for though their father's collapse earlier in the year had made Drew and Pearce Greenwood, for a short time at least, more conscientious in their duties, it had not taken them long to fall back into their old ways. They turned up at the mill long after the factory bell had rung. They were missing, one or the other of them but more likely both at the same time, just when they were supposed to be busy at some task in the spinning room, the carding shed or the counting house. Long before the appointed hour at which Mr Greenwood or Mrs Harrison left the mill, they were reported to have been seen riding off on their fine bays, doubtless in search of mischief. On some days they simply didn't turn up at all. It did not unduly interfere with Will's work as an overlooker but Mr Wilson was often put in a most embarrassing position when some business gentleman with whom one or other had an appointment was left high and dry with only Mr Wilson—which was really quite adequate—when he had expected to be greeted by the son of the owner. It was said in the mill that they might as well let them do as they pleased since they did it anyway, and if they were no longer to come to the factory at least everyone would know what to expect. Now the foreman and managers with whom the young sons of the business were relied on to co-operate, were all at sixes and sevens, calling them a damned nuisance and wishing their father would give them leave to spend their days with the hunt, or whatever it was young squireens did with themselves.

'Oh, they took themselves off as soon as Christmas dinner was eaten. God knows where they've got to since they don't always tell me these days.' She sighed, exasperated by her cousins' defection but then she turned to smile at him, making his heart turn over, letting him know that right now she didn't really care. 'They'll be back by tea-time and the opening of presents, which brings me to . . .' She grinned and getting up to move to where he had hung her coat on the back of a chair, reached into her pocket and drew out a small package. It was roughly wrapped in some bright paper and tied with a length of scarlet ribbon.

'Happy Christmas, Will,' she said cheerfully and handed it to him, putting into his suddenly trembling hands the first gift he had ever received. He stared at it, quite numb, unable to speak or even to think clearly, unable to look up into her face lest she see what was written in his.

'You're supposed to say thank you and then

183

open it, Will,' she said impishly, sitting down opposite him again, clearly delighted by his reaction

'Aah, lass,' he managed to mumble, the package resting in his big hands which were reluctant to disturb its loveliness.

'Will, for heaven's sake open it. I'm sorry it's so poorly wrapped but I'm not much good with things like that. All fingers and thumbs. I'm just the same with sewing and painting. That's why I never do any.'

It was a scarf. Bright red, wide and long and hand-knitted, the pattern of it was complicated and skilfully done. He allowed himself a quick glance at her face, his own bemused, and she laughed.

'No, I didn't do it, Will. Miss Copeland, who used to be my governess, or one of them, I had so many, knitted it for me last Christmas and I've never worn it. I hope you don't mind but it seemed just right for you. And perfect for this weather.'

He shook his head, beyond words, appalled by his own inclination to weep like a baby, studying the scarf as it glowed richly across his hands, unable to move or even glance at her lest the tears pricking his eyes should escape.

'Let's see how it looks, then.' When he made no move to put it round his neck she took it from him, standing before his seated figure while she wrapped it about his neck, tying the fringed ends beneath his chin, unaware of the rock-like stillness of him.

'There, that looks splendid,' she said briskly, 'and now I really do think I should be going. It will be dark by four.'

'I'll walk with you . . . an' wear me new scarf.' He

184

grinned. 'I'm only sorry I've nothing for you. I didn't know, you see . . . I'd no idea . . .'

'Rubbish. I've got heaps of presents at home.' She reached for her boots and coat and though he would dearly have loved to help her with them he knew quite simply that it was impossible now. That everything was impossible now. All that had been sweet, and, he realised, precious to him, was clearly out of the question, for the person of Miss Tessa Harrison was beyond his reach. She appeared to have regained her composure which had fled away with his unexpected kiss, but she was not aware that the last half-hour had separated them as sharply as the sudden closing of a heavy curtain separates an audience from the players on the stage. He must avoid her; keep out of her way, treat her as the young mistress, daughter of his employer when encounters at the mill, for instance, were unavoidable. She would be bewildered by it since he knew she had taken their strange companionship for granted, but if it hurt her so much the better for she would keep out of his way then. But today, this last day as her friend, must be allowed to continue in its magic for a little while longer.

'Oh, I forgot to tell you about the ball, Will.' She whirled to face him, her eyes eager and excited, and he stepped back from her for surely she would sense the need in him?

'So you did, lass. Was it a huge success and did all the young gentlemen fall swooning at your feet when they saw you in your splendid frock?'

'Frock!' She laughed, still holding her coat before her, waiting as young ladies did, for the gentleman to assist her on with it. 'What a word to

185

use! It was not just a frock, Will, but the most enchanting outfit, all gauze and satin ribbons, and everyone simply stared when I entered the ballroom. Well, you will have seen the pictures of Diana the huntress in one of those books you forever have your nose in . . .'

Yes, he had, and the thought of her in a flimsy garment like that the goddess of Roman mythology wore, made his skin tingle and his breath shorten and he felt the need to smash in the face of every man who had seen her in it.

' . . . and I had nearly every dance with Drew and Pearce who simply wanted to fight every gentleman who approached me, even the Squire, I suspect, though they were forced to let him take me on the floor. Heavens, it was like being in a magical world and when those wicked cousins of mine whispered to me to meet them at the side door . . .'

He felt his jaw clench and knew he really must get her coat and her boots on her and open the door to the world outside. Dear Christ, she was a child, prattling on about a party with no thought in her head but what fun she had had. No more than a young girl and should be left that way.

And yet she seemed to have gained something since he had last seen her up on Badger's Edge; an indefinable impression which was probably an illusion, a trick of the firelight and the snow reflecting through the window, but which seemed to say to him that she was not *quite* the girl he had chatted with amongst the winter bracken of the tops. What was it? What was in her eyes, the flush of her cheek, the soft turn of her lips as though she smiled at some secret memory?

She was looking at him strangely too, assessing

him in some way, her gaze reflective, a glow of something in her eyes which were a pale grey velvet now, the crystal gleam gone all of a sudden.

'We went out into the garden, Drew and Pearce and I,' she continued, her voice almost a whisper so that he had to lean towards her to hear it. Dear God, what was she saying?

'We walked, the three of us, across the snow when, all of a sudden, everyone was there. They had seen us from the window and came out, dozens of them, throwing snowballs, the gentlemen pushing one another about in the drifts which grew. It was glorious, quite glorious. There were gentlemen kissing ladies ...' She stopped and waited, smiling, then, 'It was Christmas Eve after all, Will. It's allowed, you see, particularly if there is mistletoe.'

Her eyes drifted from his to the small green bough which was just above his head in the doorway.

'A merry Christmas, Will,' she said softly, still smiling. She put her coat on the chair and, quite deliberately, moved across the small room towards him. When she was directly in front of him she lifted her hands, resting them on his shoulders.

'Well, are you not going to wish me the same, Will Broadbent?'

'Lass,' and his eyes narrowed, 'you don't know what you're doing here. I'm no lad to giggle with under the mistletoe.'

'I'm not giggling, Will.'

'What the hell's that got to do wi' it?' he said roughly, since he knew exactly what she meant.

'Drew and Pearce kissed me, Will. I liked it.' Her smile deepened.

It was perhaps this, the knowledge that some other man had sampled what he was so busy denying himself, that shattered his control and his voice was beset with peril.

'I'm not Master Pearce, Tessa Harrison, nor his brother. Are you sure you want to continue with this game?' But his hands were about her waist now, big and gentle but ready to be rough since she felt so lovely beneath them. He wanted to grip her tightly, perhaps hurt her a little though he didn't know why, to savour the warm smell of her skin and hair against his face, to blend her limbs into his. But she was only a girl testing her female strength and power over the male and he did not care to frighten her. She knew nothing of passion, true passion, nor what she did with her light-hearted flirtation and he must put a stop to it . . . he must . . .

'It's only a Christmas kiss beneath the mistletoe, Will,' she breathed, her soft young face lifting to his, her eyes beginning to close in what she thought to be the accepted fashion.

' 'Appen it is,' his voice was husky, 'and 'appen it isn't . . .' Then her mouth reached his and he took it as gently as he knew how. Her lips were trusting, innocent, and he held back, desperate not to offend her in this game she was playing, appalled at the back of his mind by his own behaviour, but her lips parted and clung and her arms crept about his neck. She shifted her body, drawing it closer to his and his mouth became more urgent, more demanding since, *his* body said, he was a man holding a woman who was willing in his arms. He crossed them at her back, lifting her up against him, feeling the roundness of her breasts press

188

against his chest and when she seemed not to mind he lifted his hands to the back of her head, his will beginning to master hers, his male body to dominate. His hands moved to her neck, caressing the soft flesh of her throat beneath her chin and his mouth travelled about her face, warm and moist on her cheeks, on each closed eye, her jawline.

'Oh, God,' he moaned in the back of his throat, pleading with her to stop him, for someone must.

'Will . . .' Her breath was warm on his brow and her own mouth found, somehow, the tender place beneath his ear, and the hot desire which might have been stopped, flowed madly through him. She was so lovely; her skin was smooth, like satin and smelling of wild flowers, and her shoulders which were revealed . . . somehow . . . Oh, Christ . . . were a pale golden silk in the fire's glow. Her breasts . . . her breasts . . . her nipples round, sweet, pink and hard with her longing, swelled into his hands which closed eagerly about them. She arched her throat and small sounds of delight came from it. He pressed his mouth against it before moving down to take her peaked nipple between his lips.

'Tessa . . .' Her name was sweet and soft on the air, 'I love you, girl . . .'

'Love me . . .'

Her clothes lay in a feverishly abandoned heap about her feet. Her body was a pale amber column and for a moment he stayed his demanding, compelling hands, and hers, to look in wonder, his eyes worshipping the beauty of it. Her splendid shoulders, smooth, womanly and yet strong; the high peaks of her young breasts, rosy and eager and full. Her small waist and slender hips, her long tapering legs between which was the dark,

189

flowering centre of her and which she was, though she was not quite sure how, longing to give him, longing for him to take from her. She was one of those rare creatures of her own sex, he realised, marvelling, who are ready for love, for loving, with no need of the complexity of wooing, of coaxing; a freely giving, enthusiastically taking woman who would match his own ardour once he had taught her how.

'Will . . .' Her naked body swayed towards him, enclosed his like a flower clinging to the trunk of a tree. His own emerged quite miraculously from its wrappings, beautiful, hard, the muscles of it standing rigid beneath his brown skin.

'Sweetheart, sweetheart,' he heard himself murmur, terrified somehow that this loveliness, this forbidden sweetness would be snatched from him. He was beyond reason, beyond any thought, any concern other than that he must have this girl, this woman, wherever he could lay her.

'I love you, Will,' he thought he heard her say as they clung together and then the worn fabric of the fireside rug was beneath them and when he took her they both cried out with the pain and joy of it.

They lay for a while in silence, the firelight dappling their entwined limbs to gold and amber and rose and he heard her sigh in pleasure.

'I do love you, Will,' she said, in that natural, free-spoken way she had. She had not learned to be subtle or artful, and all her life had said exactly what she felt or meant, and it seemed she could see no reason to be different now.

He lifted himself on one elbow and looked down into her rosy face. His heart was straining to free itself of his love for her, to pour it over her in

190

endless waves, to wrap it about her, to hold her within it, with him, for the rest of their days and his eyes were deep, filled with his pride in having her love. He cupped her cheek with a gentle hand and smiled.

'Aye, I reckoned you might, after what we've just done. There was no holding you, nor me neither, for which I make no apologies. But what's done is done, lass, and there's no turning back now.' He turned to look about him at the room which was no longer just a room but a shrine—dear God, what had she done to him, to make him so fanciful?—a shrine to their love. He let his eyes study each piece of furniture, each picture and ornament, before he brought his gaze back to her. She lay against his arm, her eyes unfocused and dreaming, the short crop of her hair in a cloud about her head and he put up a hand to brush it back from her forehead.

'There'll have to be a few changes but I've got a bit put by so you must get whatever you need to make this place just as you want it, sweetheart. I know it's not what you're used to but you an' me'll be happy here.' His face was very serious. 'I'll make you happy, Tessa Harrison, I swear it, for if ever a lass was loved it's you.' He grinned and ruffled her hair again. 'But do one thing for me, will you? Grow your hair for the wedding. I'd like to see it a bit longer, maybe with a flower in it, you know, like a proper bride . . .'

She had been smiling, still woven in the fabric of love, not really listening to what he was saying, just the pleasant sound of his deep voice, but gradually through the languorous mist she distinguished a word or two. 'Wedding' was one; 'bride' was another.

191

She sat up slowly and his eyes dropped to the soft weight of her breasts as they fell forward. He raised a hand to cup first one, then the other, but she pushed it away.

'What did you say?' she asked him warily.

He looked momentarily perplexed, the hand she had refused hovering somewhat uncertainly as though her rejection of it had sown a sudden seed of doubt.

'Say?' He tried a smile but even then her expression alarmed him. 'What about?'

'You ... you mentioned ... a wedding.' She drew away from him a little, shrugging off his arm and his alarm grew stronger, surging quite sickeningly through him, seizing him by the throat. Really, this was mad, for had she not just ... well, any girl of her upbringing ... she would hardly have allowed him ... encouraged him, surely, if she did not mean to ... she had said she loved him ...

'That I did, sweetheart.' He forced his voice to be steady and put out a hand to draw her back into his arms. 'We must be married now. I want it more than anything, Tessa, and so do you, else why should you ...?'

'Married!'

'Aye. As soon as she'll see me I'll speak to your mother, or should it be your Uncle Charlie, seeing as how he's the man of the family? They'll not like it ...' His face became anxious then. 'You don't think they'll refuse, do you? Make you wait until you're of age ...'

'Married,' she said again. Her enormous eyes left his and wandered about the room. In them was such a look of terror he reached out to her, not certain what was frightening her so but ready to

192

protect her from it with his life.

'Aye, what else? We're handfast now, my love. More than that, I reckon. It'll be hard but your mother was a working lass once, and Charlie Greenwood came from . . .'

'*Married! To you!*' Before he could stop her she had scrambled to her feet, reaching urgently for her clothes which she began to drag about her. Her eyes were haunted, her face so drawn she might just have been recovering from some dreadful illness.

He stood up slowly, magnificent in his manly beauty but her eyes would not look at what had, only minutes before, delighted her. His voice was harsh.

'You'll not marry me then, Tessa Harrison?'

'I don't want to marry anyone.' She began to laugh, the sound tearing hatefully through the small room. In his agony he did not recognise the panic in her, the desperate beating of her wings against the bars which he had imperiously put up about her, the bars which were closing on her freedom. He only heard what he thought to be her amusement, her scorn, her rejection of the gift, the precious bounty of the love he had for her.

She had gone, blundering blindly into the snow when he himself began to laugh, the sound gaining volume, on and on until it died away into the empty lonely silence her going had left.

*   *   *

The snow had nearly gone when she came back, the sudden, almost spring-like sunshine clearing it from rooftops and garden walls and revealing the track between Greenacres and Chapmanstown.

'Will ...?' Her eyes were enormous in her hesitant face and she tried a tremulous smile.

'Yes?' he replied coldly, but already he was opening the door wider the more quickly to have her over the doorstep. The book he had been reading fell to the floor as his arms lifted to take her inside and he groaned as her body nailed itself to his.

CHAPTER TEN

The lead up to the big strike was long. Wages had been cut in the recession of seven years ago but promises had been made by the millowners to return to the old levels when trade improved. Trade was improving, the operatives said, but against a background of rising food prices and the non-appearance of the increased wage they had been promised, in March 1853 a general wages campaign began. There were mass meetings and parades to rouse and mobilise those who were unorganised and the resolution was formed to demand nothing short of an unconditional advance of ten per cent in their weekly wage packet.

In October of the same year employers in Preston locked out their entire workforce and in many other places 'short time' was introduced. The lock-out in Preston began to create hardship and anxiety, not only in the town itself but amongst many of the people not actively engaged in dispute. Most had become involved without really understanding what their union leaders told them, willing to obey since the hardships of the 'hungry forties' must not be repeated. If they were told this course was best for them, that this was the only way to show the masters that they were a solid, unbending army, no longer prepared to be trampled beneath the millowners' feet, then they would obey; but they had not known, they whispered to one another, that the struggle would take so long.

Six months had passed now and each week the benefit they lived on, collected from men and women still in work, not just in the textile trade but in many others, including the shopkeepers who if they did not keep the millworkers' custom would go down with them, was reduced and men who had earned two pounds a week were trying to keep a family on no more than ten shillings.

Every man who still worked in a strike-bound mill, and there were a few, was branded with dishonour; not a man, but a 'knob-stick' who was subjected to the most harrowing forms of intimidation. Many of them sincerely did not believe in the strike, and said so, and the tales of beatings and other brutalities were reported each week in the news-papers. Often the 'Bashi-Bazouks', as the gangs of youths who perpetrated these outrages were called, had been arrested and charged not only with criminal assault, but conspiracy. They roamed about in groups of thirty or forty, under the guise of 'body-guards' but in reality terrorising any man or woman who tried to work.

In February 1854, the masters said they would re-open their mills if the workforce would be prepared to accept the wages they had earned before the start of the lock-out in the previous October, but when the mills were opened none of their operatives reported for work.

Agents were sent to Ireland and to various agricultural areas of England to fetch men and women who were starving and would therefore be glad to do anything to put food in the mouths of their children. Thousands arrived by train and were then carried in covered carts to the factories of Lancashire, escorted by police constables.

Again arrests were made as many of the strike leaders tried to stop these new hands from entering the mills and taking the jobs they themselves were trying, or so they said, to protect. Lord Palmerston had been appealed to by the striking men but he could do nothing to help them, stating that their employment was still available to them if they cared to take it up again.

The situation was becoming more ugly as each week passed and now it was said that the union tax, 'voluntarily' paid by those in work to support the strikers, was to be put as high as eightpence a week on each loom or mule. The rumblings were beginning to be heard as far away as Colne or Burnley and indeed in all the towns where cotton was manufactured. Families, hard up themselves, were forced to support what they had begun to realise was not a just cause.

A young widow with two children and not a penny to spare had refused to pay last week at Abbotts when the collector came to her loom-gate. When she returned to it after her breakfast she found her shuttles had mysteriously vanished and when she complained those about her merely looked away, saying it were nowt' to do wi' them.

She was now out of work and on 'relief' and the unions were not collecting for *her*.

Written threats had been nailed to walls where any operatives not complying with the union men could not miss seeing them.

'IF THAT OILER AT CROSSBANK MILL DOES NOT PAY UP A CALLER WILL BE OBLIGED TO COME AND PUT HIM IN THE COUNTY COURT.'

'IF THOSE HANDS AT ALLSOP AND GREENS DO NOT PAY UP THEY WILL GET SOMETHING THEY DO NOT LIKE.'

'IF THE BLOW ROOM HAND AT BRIDGEFOLD MILL DOES NOT PAY UP "PUNCH" WILL SEND A FINE TROOP TO HIM.'

There were men, women and girls in many mills with a will on them like iron, short of cash and not a little impatient with those who were on strike for no good reasons that they could see, and who would be bound to say so, and refuse their eightpence a week to those who demanded it of them.

It was a week later when the first of the bad troubles began. Chapmans had not experienced any problems since the unions had scarcely a toe-hold there. For twenty years the operatives had held themselves apart from other mills, their better working conditions, shorter hours, decent wages and the neat and sturdy company cottages most of them occupied instilling in them no desire, or need, to associate with those who wanted what they had. They were content with their labour and what it brought them and like those who believe that another man's fight is best left alone, especially if that fight made no sense, they walked by when the street-corner meetings, and the men who formed

197

them, demanded they fight the injustice which was being done to their fellows. The unions had become strong with spinners' unions, weavers' unions, combers' unions and in the past twenty years many wrongs had been put right but the Preston operatives' strike was a hardship of their own making, so most of those not involved believed.

It was said that young men and boys were turning to petty crime, stealing and getting into fights which were more than youthful squabbles, with nothing better to do than roam the streets and look for mischief. Young girls might be had at any street corner for the price of a loaf of bread. These girls had no other way to keep themselves alive and some, finding they had a taste for such a life, were unlikely to give it up when times were better. They were innocent, most of them, when they began their new trade, inexperienced, and when the strike was finally over and the cost of it counted the number of illegitimate babies was found to have increased and who was to pay for their upkeep? Certainly not their mothers who were little more than children themselves, and so they fell on the parish like hundreds of others whose lives were drastically changed by the lock-out.

Annie Beale was at her mule when the man approached her. It was three years since her mother had died, taking the child she had just borne with her, leaving Annie to support the four she left behind. And she had done so uncomplainingly for they were her responsibility. A great one for responsibility and duty was Annie and if, with hard work and an obsessive sense of loyalty, she could give them a bit of decency and a start in life, then she would. There was Jack, three years younger than herself, and bright and he'd make more of himself than her own father had, wherever he was, for he'd run off and left them when his wife had told him he was to be burdened with yet another child. Nelly, who was eleven, had never been 'right' since she had been interfered with by the overlooker but she worked besides Annie without complaint. The two youngest, Polly and Grace, not yet old enough to work, were champion in their tireless and sadly mature preoccupation as guardians of their home in her absence and somehow or other the family managed. She was proud of her honest, independent, hardworking brother and sisters. They were obliged to no one, paying their way as decent folks should, but only just.

On that day she was blind and deaf to all but the movement and sound of her two machines, keeping an eye on Nelly, who was piecing for her, and when the man touched her arm she was disposed to be irritable for she had neither the time nor the inclination to turn and gossip.

'Will yer support t'Preston strikers, lass?' The man mouthed genially. He was a working man, dressed as one, since he did not want to be thought of as a cut above those from whom he collected though it was plain from his confident, swaggering manner that he considered he was. His teeth glittered in his full, red face—no hunger there—as he showed them in a false smile. 'Eightpence a mule, that's all, an' the men an' women o' Preston will bless yer for it.' He shook his collection box persuasively but when she turned to look at him his eyes were cold, ready to be hostile if she refused.

'I can't. I've four childer ter support,' she said curtly and turned back to her machine, the matter done with as far as she was concerned.

But not to him. He touched her bare arm again, only lightly, but she flinched away for though the room was hot his hand was like hard ice against her flesh.

'Now then, lass, yer wouldn't turn yer back on those in need, would yer? You're a spinner thissen an' will know the history o't cotton trade. Maisters 'ave trodden down t'workers long enough in our opinion an' must be taught that us'll not 'ave it.'

'I've no time ter stand an' argue. I've nowt ter give yer. I just told thi, I can't afford it.'

Her face was expressionless. Indeed, she felt nothing, not pity for the workers, many of whom in her opinion were too bone-idle to get out of their beds in a morning; nor even resentment, for all her emotions were concentrated on her need to get on with her work, her resolution to support her family, not those of another. If everyone was the same there'd be no need for all this hullabaloo, and if she had had time to turn off her machine and tell him she would have done so.

But his face had become set in a perilous smile and it was clear he was not prepared to be brushed off as if he were of no more importance than a troublesome fly.

'Come now, my girl. Yer mun 'ave a bit put by fer a rainy day an' them in Preston are sufferin' it now. Share it wi' 'em an' when time comes, an' it might, when yer in't same plight, they'll do it fer thee.'

Annie could feel her irritation growing, thrusting through the layers of attention she must pay her
200

labour since she was on 'piece' work and every minute she lost would mean a smaller wage at the end of the week. She could feel her hard-won equanimity slipping away and her pale eyes narrowed.

'I've none ter give,' she threw over her shoulder, 'an' if I 'ad I'd think twice about it. They've only themselves ter blame, them as is locked out. Most on 'em was offered a rise last year but unions forced 'em ter stay out, goin' on about a standard rate o' pay, whatever that might turn out ter be. They've 'ad chance ter go back last month an' they turned it down. I've no time fer 'em, nor yer collection, so clear off an' let me gerron wi' me work.'

Her face was cold and tight, and around her women were peeping furtively over their shoulders at her, wishing they had her nerve. Most had paid the 'tax', though the eight-pence they had been 'asked' to hand over could be ill-afforded. They were frightened by the tales of what had happened to those who didn't, of beatings and harassment, of women being jeered at by alarmingly large gangs of youths, and even physically assaulted, and they did not want their own families to suffer. Surely to God it would soon be over, they whispered to one another, and in the meanwhile best tighten belts and pay up.

From the end of the room where he stood in the cabin doorway Will watched carefully, ready, should he be needed, to intervene on Annie's behalf. He'd not have his operatives intimidated by this new breed of union men who were really no more than troublemakers, denouncing tyranny and yet, in their own way, upholding it with their

201

menace.

'You've no call ter talk like that, my lass. Yon are thy people an' they depend on't benefits they get given by their own kind. If yer can't find it in yer 'eart ter support 'em, there's them hereabouts what'll reckon yer as bad as them "knob-sticks" in Preston. Will yer not, me lasses?'

He whirled about and smiled at the mass of women who had turned to watch Annie, and in his corner Will took a step forward, then another, waiting for some sign from Annie that she was being harassed, reluctant to interfere since the man had a right to go about the cotton workers as he chose; but he would have no violence.

The man smiled smoothly at the nervous women. He spoke in a voice just loud enough for them and Annie to hear above the noise of the machines.

'Thee thissen'd not like ter work beside a "knob-stick", would thi?' His meaning was clear and they all looked away from him quickly, though one or two shook their heads in sympathy with Annie. He turned back to her. 'So will thi change thi mind, lass, an' give ter them what's in need?'

'No, I won't,' and she turned a contemptuous back on him.

'Right, lass, I 'eard yer,' and he smiled at the back of her head before moving on to the next machine where the spinner already had her eightpence in her hand.

'IF THE SPINNING HAND AT CHAPMANS DOES NOT PAY UP CALICO JACK WILL SEE TO HER.'

It was pasted on the wall by the side of the gate the following week, along with a dozen others, for Annie was not the only one to refuse to pay her

202

'voluntary' contribution in aid of the Preston strikers. In the worry of how long it would take her to save up for a new pair of boots for their Jack who was shooting up like a weed, it had little impact on her. She lived from day to day in her practical way, ekeing out her wage to feed hungry mouths, making do and putting a bit by when she could. Nothing much mattered beyond getting from one pay day to the next; beyond the necessity of completing at the end of her ten hours the household tasks which were too much for her young sisters; of seeing to the children; of listening to their Jack telling her of the clever things he learned at school where he went *full time*, worth every minute of her precious time for he'd make something of himself, would Jack, or she'd know the reason why; and of cobbling together all the bits and pieces of her life which were so fragile.

They were hanging about on the edge of Chapmanstown when she finished her shift. The last houses were at her back and the empty track which curved over the moor towards Edgeclough lay before her when she saw them. Half a dozen or so young men, brawny and brash, larking about, laughing, jostling one another as young men do, nothing to do with her, and her heart did not even miss a beat as she strode past them.

It was March, cold and blustery, the clouds torn into long shreds by the wind, and through which a thread of blue tried to creep. The newly budding heather and bracken was caught by the gusts, bending earthwards, and her fine hair was torn from her shawl, whipping about her head like pale fibres of cotton. She pulled her shawl more closely about her, tucking her arms inside it, and stepped

203

into the teeth of the wind which met her as she climbed higher.

She was glad their Nelly was not with her. She'd caught her finger on a 'picking stick' last week and it had festered and swelled, making it impossible for her to piece, so Annie had made her stay at home today. Best place for her on a day like this and Annie wished with all her heart she could stay there for a couple of years more. She was so little, thin and quiet, without the stamina she herself had, especially since she had been abused by that bastard of an overlooker.

Badger's Edge came up on her left and soon she would be in the lee of Besom Hill and just half-way home. It had begun to rain, spilling in a cold sheet directly into her face. She wrapped her shawl more closely about her head, bending down into the face of it, hugging herself as she quickened her step. She could still hear the shouted laughter of the men whom she thought must be drunk, the way they were carrying on, and she wondered where they were going. She had never seen them before but she supposed they could live in Edgeclough. For once she had not waited on Will since there were others on the track with her, turning off to Dingle, Moorside and Linthwaite, small villages in which some of them lived, but suddenly she was alone and she heard the men coming up fast behind her.

They were still laughing as one fell against her, not hard enough to knock her down but with a force which sent her staggering almost to her knees. She regained her balance and her pale, pointed face became a vivid, indignant flame and her eyes narrowed angrily.

' 'Ere, what d'yer think your up to?' she cried, rounding on him fiercely. 'Why don't yer look where yer goin', yer great oaf? Just come from 't Ship, 'ave yer . . . ?' But before she could finish she was shoved from another direction, propelled quite violently towards the man who had first pushed her, his grinning face thrust into hers as he caught her arms.

'Well, if it ain't little lass as what refused ter support 'er brothers an' sisters in Preston,' he smirked. 'Look 'ere, lads. Look what we 'ave 'ere.' He turned her about so that she faced the rest of them, holding her for a moment before shoving her towards them. Her shawl remained in his hands but he threw it to the ground and trampled it into the muddy track. When the next one caught her he tried, leering and malevolent, to kiss her before she was pulled from his embrace.

For five minutes they pushed and shoved her from one to the other, laughing at her anger at first, becoming more dangerous as her anger turned to fear and they sensed it in her. She broke away once and began to run, in which direction she didn't know, anywhere to get away from the mauling hands, the loose, open-mouthed laughter, the mud with which they had daubed her, the rain running down her face and through her hair wetting her to her undergarments.

They watched her go, still shouting with laughter for she was headed back in the direction from which she had originally come, and when she had gone fifty yards they started after her. Her skirt, heavy with water and mud held her back and her scattered, frantic thoughts dwelled for a moment on simply stepping out of it and running like the

205

wind in just her drawers, for she was sure she could outrun them then. She was fit and strong, used to exercise, but what if she should fall and they should catch her without her skirt, in nothing but her sodden drawers and bodice? Would not their thoughts turn to something of a more menacing nature than a 'bit o' fun'?

'Calico Jack's right be'ind yer,' a grunting voice said. 'Yer should've paid up, lass, when yer 'ad chance. 'Appen tha will when't collector comes round next week, ay?' and a foot tripped her. She landed flat on her stomach with her hands stretched out in front of her as she tried to save herself and for several moments she lay on the spiky wet grass, completely winded. They were all about her again, their heavy clogs moving and slipping on the grass, their laughter loud and ugly. She could see those clogs fidgeting as the men moved from foot to foot, waiting for her to get up so that they could knock her down again, so that they might devise some way to humiliate her further, to intimidate and frighten her, a lesson to others who would not comply with the rules which they had written. Her head reeled and the horizon lifted in a sickening motion and on her right the stones of Badger's Edge seemed to move towards her.

They had her by the arms then, picking her up to dangle both feet off the ground, between two of them. She was coated from the top of her head to her bare feet in mud. It stuck to her wet body, outlining her small, peaked breasts, her nipples, the thin but shapely length of her legs and she felt the fear paralyse her as the laughter died away and they fell silent as every pair of eyes ran down her body.

One licked his lips. Dear God, is he Calico Jack? was her last despairing thought, then the world exploded about her and she fell like an empty sack to the wet earth. There were shouts and the movement of enormous shadowy figures, the vague and quite senseless sound of a woman's laughter, dark shapes so big and filled with vigour, with colour and movement, she could make no sense of it. Something crashed within an inch of her face which was pressed to the pulped grass and a voice told someone to, 'watch that bloody horse of yours, brother'. Then there was quiet, an absolute stillness and calm, and all she could hear was the soft patter of rain against the rocks which littered the ground where she lay.

The peace went on and on, how long she did not know. Five seconds, five minutes, five hours perhaps, she did not care in the wondrous release from the terror which had been forced on her. Then the thunder came back, moving the ground on which she lay and she cowered away from it, unable to lift her head to see which one it was who had come back to torment her.

'Dear, sweet Jesus,' a voice said, soft and filled with compassion.

'The bastards! I've a good mind to go after them again.'

Men's voices but not like those who had brought her to this. Voices she had heard at the mill. Cultured and yet harsh with the anger of young men who would not damage a woman, any woman, for they had been brought up to protect those weaker than themselves. To be gallant and courteous, to honour a woman's virtue, to take it, certainly, if given permission, to take it willingly, merrily, but with sweetness, not violence.

'Put my cape about her, Drew.' A long, flowing garment was placed over her as four strong young hands lifted her to her feet.

'Let me have her,' a girl's voice said and she went willingly into the curve of strong, female arms. She was held fast against a tall, slender, woman's body, safe, familiar and infinitely comforting for she could still feel those hard masculine hands and hear the sound of hard masculine laughter.

'Are you all right, Annie?' the girl's voice said quietly in her ear, meaning have they interfered with you as men do? She spoke so softly the young men could not hear her and Annie was grateful for she did not wish to be burdened just yet with such thoughts.

'Yes, they did not ... hurt me.' Her voice was muffled against the girl's shoulder and she clung to her for a moment longer, then stepped back and looked up into her face: Tessa Harrison and at her back would be Drew and Pearce Greenwood.

'Thanks.' She had recovered somewhat and her voice was brusque.

'Are you sure?' Tessa smiled and in her vivid face still lingered the excitement of the last few minutes, the enjoyment she had known as she chased the attackers across the moorland, and yet there was understanding, sympathy, for had she not suffered what Annie had, in the grasp of the tinkers? 'We were up on Badger's Edge and saw them chase you. We weren't certain whether it was ... well, what it was they were after. From up there, covered in mud as you ... sorry, Annie ... we thought you were . . .' She shook her head and became brisk. 'But really, should we not be getting you home? One of my cousins will take you up, will you not . . . ?'

She turned to the young men who stood awkwardly at Annie's back. They were not quite certain how to treat this child they had just rescued, this poor, bedraggled, mud-spattered little rabbit, and were only waiting for orders from Tessa who seemed to have taken command.

'Pearce.'

'Of course.' Pearce leaped forward and in a moment Annie was in his arms, the mud which rubbed on to his fine woollen jacket of no consequence as she was lifted to sit before him on the back of his tall bay. She did not know which was worse, the ordeal through which she had just gone or the dizzying heights in which she now found herself and the restless movements of the horse beneath her. Then he sprang lightly up behind her, placing his arms on either side of her to take the reins. She shrank from his touch and he was most careful with her as they walked gently in the direction of Edgeclough as Tessa directed them.

The small cottage seemed about to burst apart from the press of people who crowded within it. Nelly, Polly and Grace fluttered about like three pale moths, appalled by the sight of their sister, whom they had never seen other than calm, unruffled and immaculate, in such a sorry and mindless state, whilst Jack, not yet a man but no longer a boy, seemed undecided whether to weep or go and fight the devils who had done this to their Annie.

Pearce and Drew shifted from foot to foot, ready

to do anything which might be asked of them, for Annie was not herself at all, as anyone could see, since she clung to Tessa in a most unusual way.

The men were got rid of, the tin bath lifted down from the scullery wall and filled with hot water by the three frozen-faced, tearful little girls. It was warm and quiet. Female hands washed her hair and soaped her back whilst Tessa's soft voice chatted of this and that and nothing at all, as though she knew that, at this moment, this was what Annie needed most. Female things, female voices, soft, gentle, the faint perfume of her own skin, the fine silk of her shirt, the commiseration of her sisters, the friendly, almost casual attention which asked nothing of her and brought the familiar order which was the stuff of life, back to her. Tessa watched the strain leave Annie's face and when she began to give instructions to her three young sisters, it left theirs also since they recognised that she was herself again and the tension in the room eased.

'Are you feeling better?' Drew enquired politely, as young English gentlemen are trained to do with a lady. They were all drinking tea, cramped together in the tiny room for Annie would not hear of them leaving without 'sumat inside 'em'.

'Aye. I weren't hurt. They was just lads ... bullies ...'

'Tell me who they were and we will deal with them.' Pearce moved to lounge against the table, standing close to her, towering protectively over her slight figure.

'Nay, I don't know their names.' Annie was alarmed by his nearness and masculine aggression, of which she had had more than enough today, and edged away to a safer place behind her teapot.

'They belong t't union, sent ter frighten me an' t'other lasses inter payin' towards Preston strike fund. I were tellin' Tessa about 'em only last week . . .'

Pearce turned to stare, bewildered, at Tessa, for how did this factory girl come to know his cousin and, more to the point, have the privilege of calling her by her Christian name? But Tessa frowned and shook her head, indicating that she would explain later, wondering as she did so why she had not spoken of their acquaintance to her cousins, or even her mother who would surely have understood. The reason probably had something to do with Will: they were sometimes together in Annie's cottage and the secret part of her life, with Will, seemed inexplicably linked to Annie and the friendship the three of them shared.

Annie was clattering about the kitchen now, awkward and ungracious, tidying away the pans which had heated the water for her bath, waiting for them to take themselves off and leave her to recover with her family with whom she was at ease. The bath stood before the fire, the cooling, muddied water still in it, embarrassing her. Her sisters were inclined as yet to cling about her impatient figure and when Tessa nodded towards the bath Pearce and Drew instantly sprang forward to lift it, laughing now that the drama was done with.

'Where . . . ?' they queried, for really, what did one do in these circumstances, since they had known only the comfort of an upstairs bathroom, with hot and cold piped water.

'The back door, you idiots,' she mouthed at them and as they tussled with the bath between them

211

even the children began to smile despite the god-like proportions of these two gentlemen, circling about them as they edged towards the door.

'Sit down, Annie,' Tessa beseeched her, 'just for a moment.'

'Give ower, lass. I've them childer ter see to . . .'

'Oh, sit down and tell me all about this union thing. I'm sorry to say I didn't take much notice last week when you and . . .' she turned round to make sure they were not overheard, ' . . . when you and Will were talking about it.'

'No, I didn't think you was listening,' Annie replied dourly but there was a glint of amusement in her eyes.

Her cousins, returned from their mastery of the bath water, listened, fascinated for the first time by this aspect of mill life of which they had previously known nothing. They had heard it mentioned a dozen times around the dinner table but what had it to do with them, they had asked one another, yawning? Now they had an almost proprietary interest in this quaint thread of a girl who was as sharp of voice as she was sparing of words.

When they had gone to fetch the horses Tessa took Annie's reluctant hand and from her own superb height and splendid good looks, smiled down into her face.

'You have nothing to be ashamed of, you know,' she whispered, 'and nothing to fear now. My cousins will see to that. Something like this appeals to the gallant in them.'

'Aye, so I noticed,' Annie answered shortly.

'Will you be all right now?'

'O' course. I've got ower worse n' this.'

'Would you like me to . . . ?'

212

'Nay, you gerron 'ome.'

'I'll call to see how you are.'

'Give over, there's no need.'

'Nevertheless, I will. We *are* friends you know, Annie, though you make it very difficult at times.' She smiled to take the sting out of her words.

' 'Appen yer right,' Annie agreed grudgingly, the light in her eyes soft.

Tessa lifted her head in that haughty gesture Annie knew so well as though to say that all was now settled to her satisfaction.

'I shall come on Sunday on my way to . . . well, on Sunday.'

*   *   *

She had explained to her cousins, to her own satisfaction at least, how she had become friendly with Annie, leaving out all mention of the tinkers who had frightened her last summer, and naturally, of Will Broadbent.

'I visit her now and again,' she said airily, 'and take a few things for the children. Well, you can see how they are placed,' she added, making it sound as though she was the lady of the manor distributing munificence to the poor and they seemed to find no reason to question her further.

They rode home companionably side by side, the three of them taking up the width of the rough track which led over Besom Hill and beyond Badger's Edge to Crossfold. Those they met on the way were forced to step off into the grass to let them go by, but it is doubtful the three riders noticed or, if they did, thought anything much about it.

There would be no more collecting in the mill, Pearce said ominously, for the out-of-work operatives at Preston. Besides, had he not been told that they were slowly drifting back to work, those who had been on strike for the best part of thirty-six weeks? They had won nothing beyond a long, hungry winter. The strike leaders, it appeared, had no option but to capitulate and the masters would soon be celebrating a victory. It was being said that labour, as a commodity, could obtain no higher price than the purchaser was willing to give for it and the strongest party would, in the end, win.

The March wind ruffled through Tessa's growing hair, flicking a damp strand across her mouth. Her eyes were a soft grey velvet musing on the plight and appearance of Annie Beale, and her thoughts were full of admiration. A nasty experience, but Annie had made herself recover, for the sake of her family. Not many young girls in factory life today would have had the strength, of mind and body, to evade those bully boys, for so long, as she had, and then pick herself up and reassure her sisters that she was not in the least hurt, just madder than a wet hen, or words to that effect.

Tessa smiled, then glanced down at her own slim legs which were becoming wetter every minute in the persistent drizzle which fell. She had flung her cape about her, fastening it carelessly as she left Annie's cottage but it had become loosened, riding back over her shoulders, allowing the damp to penetrate her clothing beneath.

'Just a minute, you two,' she said, falling back a pace. 'I want to fasten my cape. This drizzle is getting heavier and I'm going to be wet through by the time we reach home.' She made her horse stand whilst she undid the cloak, lifting and whirling it about her head and shoulders, allowing it to settle but not before the two men who had halted obediently had seen the joyous lift of her breasts, very obviously unconfined, the dark and peaked circle of her nipples through the damp silk of her shirt. Two pairs of vivid blue eyes narrowed. Two brown throats dried up, the breath within them becoming trapped, and when they each turned away and their eyes met it was with the murderous rage which springs up between two dogs who covet the same bitch.

'What the devil are you staring at?' Drew snarled, just as though Pearce had been found ogling Drew's woman. His hand closed viciously about the crop he held and it was quite certain, if he had been within range, that he would have sliced it across his brother's cheek.

'I might ask you the same question.' They drew their horses up hard against one another, nose to tail, and as Drew lashed out with the crop, Pearce caught his arm. The bays, unused to such rough and menacing handling, reared and pranced, their thoroughbred eyes rolling in fright, their long and fragile thoroughbred legs clattering across tumbling stones and treacherous rabbit holes. But still they came at one another, their well-muscled arms and strong brown hands looking for a hold, for something to hit, to damage, to destroy, in their mindless, unreasoning jealousy.

A sharp lunge brought Drew from his mount and he slid beneath the belly of Pearce's kicking, enraged animal, but in a second he was up, his arms reaching for his brother, his feet digging into

215

the soft ground, finding enough purchase to heave Pearce down with him.

'You filthy bastard . . . you filthy bastard,' he was snarling, his eyes slitted with rage, his mouth hard and cold and cruel. His arms were about his brother, lifting him bodily from the ground; then they both went down, rolling against the legs of the screaming horse, sending it, and the other, racing away in terror in the direction of Crossfold and the safety of the stable.

'I'll kill you,' Pearce sobbed in the back of his throat, his hands reaching for his brother, his teeth searching for his jugular, his booted feet for anything, preferably in his breeches, which might do him the most harm.

'Drew . . . oh, dear God . . . Pearce . . . Stop it, stop it. What is it? . . . Dear Lord, what is the matter? Stop it, stop it . . .' She tried to get between them, her cape hampering her so she flung it off. She had done no more than secure the top button when her cousins had, unaccountably, gone for each other's throats, and it came undone easily. The rain was coming down harder now and she slipped in the wet grass, falling heavily on her back, drenched to her skin, her bold breasts almost naked, but the two men who fought over her were too concerned with killing one another to see. Splattered with mud and blood from a wound one had inflicted, they grappled fiercely, flinging unco-ordinated blows, some of which found their mark but most ending ineffectually in the ground. If they could have kept their feet, face to face, doubtless they would have half-killed one another since, both being skilled at bare-knuckle fighting, they would have fought to a standstill, but scuffling on the wet

216

and slippery grass as they were they did little damage.

During the five minutes the fight lasted Tessa did her best to stop them but it was they themselves who ended it.

They rolled away from one another as though sense and reason and sanity infiltrated their fevered minds at the same moment. Slowly they sat up, several feet apart, their heads bowed on their arms which were draped across their bent knees. They did not look at one another, nor at her.

'Well,' she said indignantly, 'what the devil was that all about? You realise you have terrified your horses into stampeding, I am wet through and covered in mud and one of you, or both, is certain to have a black eye or a bloodied nose. What happened? What were you fighting about? Did one of you say something the other did not care for, was that it? You're like a couple of schoolboys, always ready to scrap over nothing. One of these days those tempers of yours will get you into serious trouble. Oh, I know I've a temper too, but nothing like the exhibition I've seen here today. Now you'll have to walk home and I hope to God those bays of yours have come to no harm or Charlie will . . .'

'Go home, Tessa, there's a good lass.' Pearce's voice was drained of all expression.

'*Go home!* Don't you start ordering me about, Pearce Greenwood. Just because you and Drew have had a spat it doesn't mean you can . . .'

'*Go home, Tessa!*'

'Dammit, I will then. Why should I stay, or even concern myself with either one of you?'

'Quite, cousin, so go home.'

217

She had gone, her cape enveloping her from head to toe when Drew spoke.

'What are we to do, brother?' he said softly, still staring at the ground between his legs.

'God knows, for I don't.'

CHAPTER ELEVEN

'We can't go on like this, dammit, and well you know it. It's nearly six months since we became . . .'

'Lovers. Is that the word you hesitate over, my lad?'

Tessa rolled on to her stomach, draping her arms across Will's broad, naked chest, smiling languorously into his face. Her eyes were soft, filled with the sighing warmth of the aftermath of their love-making and he felt a great desire to shake her, to fling her off and climb out of the vigorously crumpled depth of the feather-bed, to stand up and bellow his frustration, to stamp about the small room and bang himself against the walls, to hurt himself physically, as his sore heart was hurting now.

'Don't turn away from me, Will,' she said plaintively, moving herself up his body until her lips were an inch from his. She put up a hand to his face, forcing him to look at her then took his bottom lip between hers, sucking it gently into her mouth, tracing her tongue along the inside of his lips in the way he had taught her. She smiled into his eyes, inviting him to begin again, then lifted herself on to her hands until her breasts touched his face, each nipple brushing sensuously across his

218

parted lips.

'Open your mouth wide,' she ordered breathlessly and when, unable to refuse, he did so, she pressed each one in turn between his lips, the rosy peaks finding his tongue. He licked them slowly, rolling his tongue about the soft flesh which hardened and filled. He felt his body begin to respond to her, as it always did, rejoicing in the way hers pleased it, again as he had taught her, and inside him something tore loose and broke away in pain. Whore's tricks, his anguished mind told him before he could stop it, then it thought of nothing as the wicked skill she brought to his bed overcame him. She was expert in the art of love-making now, bringing him and through him, herself, to peaks of glorious, shouting delight, not once, not even twice, but several times at each encounter. Sometimes it was a quiet, shivering, almost lyrical experience. A soft rejoicing in the way their bodies met and joined, so perfectly balanced in their need and fulfilment, he felt a great desire to weep at the beauty of it. Then she was tender, as gentle as a dove on his hand, submissive and willing, he thought, to be anything he wanted her to be.

'Marry me,' he would say then, even as he spoke the words knowing the foolishness of them, and he would watch her, hopelessly, as she became restless beneath his gaze. 'Marry me and we'll go away. Emigrate to the colonies. They want strong, healthy men and women to begin a new nation in Australia . . .'

'Among the felons?' she would laugh.

'There are men of importance there now. Land to be had for those prepared to work. You'd love it there, sweetheart. There'd be no restrictions on you as there are here. An outdoor life in a world so big and empty and free you could ride that mare of yours for evermore and never meet another living soul. A farm of our own . . .'

Her gaze avoided his, or worse still, to him, became filled with a mischievous gleaming, that look of smiling ardour, of passion which would, without question, render him to the depths and heights where her need took him. Always it was the same. She answered his questions, his pleas, his demands with the certain persuasion of her body, diverting his masculinity to the attention, not of their future, but to the rapture of now.

From the day it had begun she had set the pace, the rhythm, made the rules, giving him everything he wanted of her body, taking everything she needed of his, fulfilled to such glowing beauty he had been amazed, on the next occasion he had come face to face with her mother, that she had not approached him on what he had done to her daughter. She was seventeen now and certainly ready for marriage and her body, nourished by his, for as the saying goes, 'man feedeth woman', became a woman's, magnificent and proudly flaunting. And each time he tried to speak of the future, even though he knew inside himself where practical common sense lay that his hopes were forlorn, she would fling herself upon him, her mouth reaching greedily for his so that the words were kept locked inside him. She made *his* body desire *hers*, filling his mind not with what he recognised as a pathetic dream of the future, but with forthright and lusty desire.

But not this time. This time he would not be seduced into that mindless abandonment of

220

thought and sense which her magic wrought in him. This time her body and her use of it would not come between him and what he had to say to her. He meant to make her understand that he wanted to be not her lover but her husband. He could not go on like this, week in and week out, hiding away in this cottage the love he had for her, delightful though their hours together in this bed were. It was a marvel to him that their relationship, which surely to God must be known to those who lived nearby, had not yet reached the ears of her family. She was discreet, too discreet for his liking since if it became generally known that she was seeing one of her uncle's employees in secret, would it not force the confrontation he hoped would end this deceit and make her his wife? They would not like it, especially those two lordly cousins of hers, but the Greenwoods had come from working stock and might that not incline them to look more kindly on him as a husband for the daughter of the house! He was strong. He had a good brain and that most driving whip of them all, ambition. He would be more than overlooker or foreman in someone else's mill, by God, he would. His clever brain, and he knew it was clever, would find a way to make him his own master one day. He wanted none of their money and, if he were honest, none of it for Tessa though he supposed he could not deny her her inheritance. It was only recently that he had been made up to foreman with a decent wage to suit his new position. He could afford to rent perhaps a small villa on the outskirts of Chapmanstown, or at least something a bit better than this cottage. He was realistic enough to know that Tessa was used to luxury beyond his imagining

221

but if she loved him, and she told him over and over again that she did, she would be prepared to make some sacrifice, surely? He would even try to get in a girl to help with the heavier housework. Allow her to have more freedom than the wives of other foremen. Freedom to ride her little mare up on the moorland road and . . .

Here his thoughts became confused for how was he to afford to feed and stable a horse, and besides, would he care to have his wife galloping about the countryside as Miss Tessa Harrison did? He knew he wouldn't and if that was the case, could he hold her to him, reined in and locked in a cage, which is how she would see it, if he dared not allow her the freedom she needed? Was he being selfish in asking this child-woman, since that was what she was despite her sexual maturity, to set herself down into the life a woman of his class must live?

He turned away from her then. Easing her body to one side, he slipped out of the bed and strode to the window, staring blindly out into the pale spring sky. The candle on the small bedside table which she had insisted upon lighting so that they might study one another more intimately, turned his hard, muscled body to the colour of amber, the light emphasising the broadness of his shoulders, the lean beauty of his narrow waist, buttocks and shapely legs. He did not look back at her but he was conscious of the tight-clenched impatience and distinctly heard, as her breathing slowed, her long drawn-out sigh of resignation.

'What are you doing over there?' she asked softly, knowing quite well what was coming for had it not happened a dozen times before, but attempting to avoid it with lightness. 'Come back to

222

bed, sweetheart. I shall have to go soon if I'm to be home for dinner and you know we won't see one another until next weekend. Come here, Will, and put your arms . . .'

'Stop it, Tessa. Stop wheedling like some sixpenny strumpet. Don't demean yourself, or me, or what we feel for one another with these . . . these silly games. Get up and put your clothes on.'

He turned without looking at her and began to fumble his own way into the trousers she had removed from him two hours since, the shirt which, playing the temptress, she had insisted she would unbutton, slowly, one by one, her mouth on his chest and shoulders, his flat stomach and strong thighs. A witch and a wanton, if he were honest, she had lifted him to a groaning, quivering summit of joy.

'Oh, Will, don't . . .'

'Put your clothes on, Tessa. We must talk.'

'I don't want to talk, Will. I want to . . .'

'I'll be downstairs so be quick about it.'

Her face was sullen as she entered the parlour, still buttoning up her shirt. Her hair lay in a gloriously dishevelled cloud about her head, dark as the midnight sky. Her breeches were crumpled from the careless disorder in which they had lain for the past two hours and in her hand she carried her riding boots.

'I don't want tea,' she said coolly, 'so don't bother with the kettle. Besides, I thought on an occasion such as this a lady and gentleman were supposed to sip champagne from a crystal slipper, not drink a mug of tea round a . . .'

Before she could finish the sentence he had stepped dangerously across the room. The palm of

223

his hand, when it hit her, made the sound of a pistol shot and her head rocketed to one side with the force of it. Her hair lifted and flung itself in a shimmering curtain across her face and when she turned back to him her eyes burned through it, as fierce and baleful as those of a tiger in the night.

'Don't ever speak to me like that again, my lass,' he said, his voice warning her to be careful. But this was Tessa Harrison and should he not have known she was a woman, no matter who struck her, who was not to be intimidated by it? She sprang for him, her nails reaching for his eyes, her bare feet flailing at anything they could find for a target.

'You bastard,' she hissed. 'I thought you were a man but it seems you are no better than those louts who pick on anything smaller and weaker than themselves. But I should have known. I should have known from the first that you could never be anything but a product of your own upbringing, a bully and a tyrant who would hit a woman . . .'

'Stop it, Tessa, don't be any more foolish than you already have been.' He had her easily in his grasp, his arms pinning hers to her side, his body forced against hers so that she could not move. Her face was just beneath his, white with rage except for the flame print of his hand across her cheek, her eyes brilliant, like sparkling, lamp-lit crystals between her narrowed lids.

'Let go of me, let go of me,' she spat at him and when he did she almost fell. He pushed her unceremoniously backwards until she was forced into the wing chair by the fire, keeping her there easily merely by holding her shoulders with both hands and placing his knee on her lap to prevent those lethal feet from finding their target between

224

his legs.

'Let me up. I wish to go home.' Her face was set against him, cold and expressionless now, the hot fury turned to ice and she no longer struggled.

'Not until you have heard what I have to say.'

'Nothing you have to say is of the slightest interest to me and I would be obliged if you would take your hands off me at once.'

'My dirty, working man's hands, you mean?' He smiled grimly.

'Something like that.'

'You were happy enough to have them on you half an hour since.'

'That was different.'

'Of course. Then I was what you wanted me to be.'

'And what is wrong with that? You made no complaint then, as I recall. You were more than happy to let me . . .'

'Stop it. Let's have no more of this. You know what I want to talk about but you're afraid of it so you divert me with . . . with whore's tricks . . .'

'So I'm a whore, am I? No wonder you have been so willing to let me into your bed. Not only a whore but one who costs you nothing. You don't even have to walk down to the nearest inn where I believe such women are to be had. You have one come to you. How convenient . . .'

'You're doing it again, Tessa. Listen to yourself. You know you're talking rubbish, I can see it in your eyes. You know what you say is untrue but you're so afraid of the truth you're prepared to tarnish what is precious, good, between us so that you don't have to hear it. Go then, if you must . . .' He stood away from her abruptly, lifting his hands

225

to show that he would not try to prevent her. 'Aye go, but if you do, don't come back.'

She had stood up as he moved away from her, her bare feet whispering on the carpet as she strode across to where she had dropped her boots, her face stormy, every line of her offended body telling him in what she hoped was no uncertain manner that it would take a lot of coaxing on his part to make her forget this. But his words stopped her and for several moments he watched her haughty back as she struggled with the hope that he was bluffing. She wanted desperately to pull on her boots, to shrug into her jacket, toss on her tall beaver hat and without looking at him again, sweep disdainfully from the house. She wanted to, oh, yes, she wanted to, but he could see the indecision, not in her eyes, since her face was turned from him, but in the slight tremor of her shoulders, the clenching and unclenching of her fists.

She turned then and he felt his heart move painfully with his love and thankfulness. She *did* care. Despite her restless changes of mood, the fidgeting with which she treated his attempts to find some bedrock on which to stabilise their relationship, she was not, thank God, reckless enough to walk out on it. She was ready, albeit reluctantly, to hear what he had to say.

'Sit down, lovely girl,' he murmured softly.

'Tell me what you have to say,' she said but her eyes had melted, despite herself, at the endearment, and her love shone through them.

'Sit down, please.'

The delicately woven, fragile stuff which bound them together was stronger now and he grinned ruefully, boyishly, the breath he had been holding

226

sighing out of him as she sat down in the chair she had just left. Her face was still truculent, her mouth mutinous, but she turned her smoky grey eyes on him, watching him warily, waiting for him to speak.

He picked up her jacket which lay on the table and held it to him, looking down at it without seeing it, stroking the rough tweed with patient hands, strong hands, a working man's hands, and she found herself watching them, remembering their smooth and erotic passage over her own body. She shivered and looked away.

'What is it, Will?' she asked, though, of course, she knew.

'We must be married, lass.'

'*Must*?' He saw that she was offended again and his own hard-won patience stretched itself uncomfortably. She was like some prickly hedgehog which, at the first hint of threat, thrusts its spines to hurt the hand which meant none. He sighed and bent his head, his strong face soft with his love.

'I love you, Tessa, and you say you love me.'

'Don't you believe me?' She threw back her head defiantly.

'Sometimes.'

'Only sometimes? Why do you think I come here and get into your bed?'

'Aaah . . . !'

'And what is that supposed to mean?'

'Only that a woman does not have to love a man, or indeed the other way round, for them to . . . to please one another in a sexual way. There would be few partnerships if it depended only on love, Tessa.'

'I *do* love you, Will, and I don't know what you mean.'

'I mean we must move on. We cannot stand still

227

like this. Dear God, for nearly six months now every time I've spoken about it you've shied away like some nervous colt. You're young, I know . . .'

'I'm seventeen . . .'

'And I reckon I'm twenty-nine or thirty and I want a wife . . .'

'So I'll do, is that it?'

'No, it's not. Why the hell must you turn everything about the way you do? I believe it's meant to put me off but this time I'll not be denied my say. I love you. I want you. I want to wed you, lass. Bloody hell, is that not clear enough? You've been my . . . my mistress, there, does that satisfy you since you seem to like to use the right words? . . . for long enough and I'll wait no longer. And the risk . . .'

'What risk?' Anything, *anything* to sidetrack him.

'Don't be childish, Tessa. You know you take a risk every time you leave that blasted animal of yours tied up in my back yard. D'you think no one notices? It will come out soon enough and then you'll have no reputation left at all. Not that I care about that. You'd be my wife and there's not a man in the valley would dare say a word about you, to me or to each other. But there's other risks, lass. What if you should conceive? I try to be as careful as I can but sometimes you're a bloody challenge to any man with your wildness and I'm put to . . . well, you'll take my meaning.'

'No, I don't.'

'Never mind, then, but it's bound to happen and I want us to be wed when it does.'

There was a deep, endless and, to Will, quite dreadful silence. That was what he felt. *Dread*. She continued to look at him, her expression

228

unreadable, saying nothing, and the misery began in him then, the sheer, bloody, hopeless misery which lapped through the layers of his skin. It not only racked him from within but surrounded him like a black shadow through which he could hardly see her. She did not answer and he knew it was because she didn't know how.

He answered for her.

'You can't bring yourself to do it, can you?' His voice was harsh and she felt a great longing to go to him then, to put her arms about him and draw his head to her shoulder, to comfort him in the only way she knew how. They were lovers. She had spent the last months in the most delightful occupation of being loved, of being made love to by Will Broadbent and she had gloried in it. She loved him, or at least she thought she did, and she did not want to lose him. She could not bear to consider the prospect of a life without him in it but she was not at all sure she wanted to be married. Not yet. Not to Will. Not to anyone. She was quite old enough for marriage and motherhood but it was not for her, not yet. She had thought about it in the quietness of her own bedroom, away from the hard beauty of Will Broadbent's body which delighted her so and which she must have, but the prospect of living in this tiny house, in the primitive conditions which, when one was not compelled to it was *fun*, simply appalled her.

And yet, could she live without what he gave her, not just with his body but his loving spirit? So was *that* love? She knew she was treating him as some men treat certain women, as a diversion, a sweet and thrilling pastime which had nothing at all to do with her real life. She was not sure whether it was

Will she wanted . . . loved . . . or what he could give her, and she was desperately afraid to set herself the task of finding out. Now he was determined on marriage and she knew she could not go through with it. Perhaps when . . . well, in a year or two . . . or when . . . when . . . *When?*

It was no good and she knew Will could see it in her face. He picked up her jacket and held it out for her. She slid her arms into the sleeves, then, as he reached for her boots, stood like a child as he eased each foot in turn into them. He brought her cloak and tucked it about her shoulders, then stepped back from her, unsmiling, his eyes unreadable.

'Goodbye, lass.'

'Will, don't send me away. I do love you and one day . . . when . . . Dear Lord, I cannot bear to let you go . . .'

'Then don't.'

'Let me have some time to . . . Oh, surely there must be something, some way . . .'

'You know what I want.'

'But, Will . . .'

'Nay, say nothing more. It's in your face. Don't come back unless it's to tell me we'll be wed. I love you, Tessa, and I'll wait for a while. You're young . . .'

It began to rain, a soft spring rain as she rode along the track which led from Chapmanstown to Edgeclough, the freshness of it sliding down her cheeks and mixing with her warm and anguished tears.

The knock on the door startled Annie. She had not been expecting anyone this late in the afternoon since Tessa usually came earlier, and she

230

had been hoping to get the last of her spring cleaning finished before the children came back from Sunday school.

'Oh, it's you,' she said tartly when she opened the door, then stood back to allow Tessa to enter. 'Wipe yer feet. I've just done that there floor,' she added and was mildly surprised when Tessa meekly did as she was told. Tessa's face which was always a clear, creamy white had an overtone of grey in it and her eyes were shadowed. Annie studied her carefully.

'I'll put kettle on,' she said moving towards the fire and when she had done so she returned to her scrubbing of the deal table, treating it with the demented fervour which she gave to every job of cleaning she tackled. From the corner of her eye she watched as Tessa picked up first a teacup, then a spoon, putting each back where she found them without seeing them, then flung herself into Annie's rocking chair, her unfocused gaze on the dancing flames in the grate. She put one foot on the fender. Her head was slumped between her shoulders and she did not speak, even when Annie put a mug of weak tea in her hand.

'What's up?' Annie said, sparing of words as always.

'Nothing.'

'Then get out o' me road an' let me gerron wi' me spring cleaning.'

Tessa looked up in surprise, then sighed deeply.

'I'm sorry, Annie, I know you have things to do but I just didn't know where else to go.'

'Thanks.'

'No, I didn't mean it like that, it's just . . .'

Annie watched Tessa brood silently on whatever

231

it was that troubled her, though she knew she'd not have far to look to find the reason for it. The whispers were already rustling like the wind through the bracken on the tops, going from machine to machine. Whispers about their newly made-up foreman and—they hardly dared breathe her name—this young woman who was crouched in Annie's kitchen chair. Annie had given the spinner who had hissed of it into her ear a withering look and told her sharply not to be so daft and to mind her own business, but it'd not stop there. Just let Mr Greenwood or Mrs Harrison hear of it and Will would be out on his ear quicker than you could say 'picking stick.'

'Best tell me, lass.'

Tessa sighed again and Annie shifted impatiently, banging her mug of tea down on the newly scrubbed table. Some of the tea slopped over the rim of the mug, staining the fresh surface and Annie stamped into the scullery, tweaking the wrung-out cloth from its nail by the scullery door where she had just hung it up to dry. Muttering darkly she wiped up the tea, returning the table to its immaculate condition, then stood back to admire it.

Tessa watched her, then began to laugh for, really, was there another like her?

'Oh Annie, you'd make some man'—probably the one I've just left, she thought sadly—'a wonderful wife. You're sensible and ... and domesticated with no longing to ride over the brow of the next hill just to see what's on the other side.' She stretched out her hand to touch Annie's arm but Annie drew back, uncomfortable with demonstrations of affection, though she would give you her last farthing even if it meant she herself would starve.

' 'Ow d'you know what I want?'

'I'm sorry, you're right. How do any of us know what ... what others want and if we do, it's not always possible to give it to them. How can we ...?' Her voice drifted away uncertainly.

'Nay, don't ask me. Yer talk in riddles sometimes an' if yer've nowt better ter do wi' yer time but sit about and gossip, I 'ave.' But Annie's plain face was soft with compassion.

'Life's a bloody riddle sometimes, Annie.'

'An' I'll 'ave no bad language in my kitchen neither.'

'I don't know why you put up with me, Annie, I really don't.'

'Nor me neither. Reckon no one but me'll 'ave yer.'

'You're right.' They smiled in perfect understanding at one another.

'It's Will, isn't it?'

'Yes.'

' 'E's ready fer marriage an' you're not, is that it?'

'Yes.'

'Not good enough for thi, is that what yer sayin'?'

'No, Annie, oh, no. You know I'm not like that.' But Annie was not so sure. Tessa was 'gentry' and spent a large part of her life with gentry. Could she give up the social position she had, which was bound to happen if she married Will? Mrs Will Broadbent would be a considerably less important person than Miss Tessa Harrison.

'Then what's ter stop yer?'

'Annie, I don't want to get married. I'm not even

233

eighteen and the thought of living for the rest of my life . . .'

'In a foreman's cottage, is that it?'

'No . . . well, yes, up to a point though I'm sure if we were married Charlie would promote him to something more suitable to . . .'

'To th'usband o't millowner's daughter. D'yer know, Tessa Harrison, I can't fathom you. Social position, or so you say, don't seem ter bother thi'. I'm a spinner, wi' clogs an' a shawl an' yet yer seem ter like me company, so why, when yer love the man, a man what's the same class as me, will yer not wed 'im . . . ?'

'I do love him, Annie, at least, I think I do . . .'

'Then wed 'im, fer God's sake.' Annie sat down and hitched her chair closer to Tessa's, her sharp little face a bright pink in her earnestness. 'Can yer not see what a good match it'd be . . . ?'

'*A good match!*'

'Don't tek that tone wi' me, lady. 'E's as good as any man in't valley. An' when yer Mam's gone, an' yer Uncle Charlie, who better ter run them mills than a man what's bin fetched up in cotton?'

'And what about Drew and Pearce? Are they to be disinherited?' Tessa drew back abruptly, deeply offended by Annie's contempt for her cousins' capabilities as millowners. 'They'll take over when . . . well, when they're ready.'

'Give over.'

Tessa stood up. 'If you're going to insult my family then I think it's time I left. Thank you for the tea. And I don't think I shall be able to call next week.'

'Suit thissen.'

But as Annie watched Tessa ride away her face

234

was sad and filled with pity, not only for the girl—
for what else could you call her?—who seemed
unable to reach out and hang on to the happiness
which was offered to her, but for the man who
offered it.

CHAPTER TWELVE

The first awareness Tessa Harrison had had of the
'trouble' which existed between Russia and Great
Britain was last November when the newspapers
reported that the Russian fleet had fired on seven
Turkish frigates and three corvettes at Sinope—
wherever that might be—and nearly four thousand
men had perished. She couldn't understand it,
really she couldn't, she had said to her mother who
had read the account out loud to them. Why should
the sinking of Turkish ships and the killing of
Turkish sailors have anything to do with them, for
heaven's sake? But everyone seemed to think it did
and it was apparent the British public was highly
indignant. Now it appeared the French and British
had declared war on Russia and troops had
embarked for Varna.

The news about the war excited Drew and
Pearce. They had known from the start that there
was to be one, Drew said, and naturally, Britain
should be drawn in if she was to protect her
interests out there.

'Out where?'

'In the Balkans.'

'Well, it's a mystery to me and I can make
neither head nor tail of why Britain and France

should declare war on Russia over it.'

They were all three sprawled before the drawing-room fire. Laurel and Charlie were dining with commercial acquaintances and as always when Laurel was absent they all took advantage of it, even Jenny, turning up at table in whatever they had worn during the day. They were relaxed, quiet, a family with no need of the bright social conversation which Laurel insisted upon.

'They've made their camp on the northern slopes. The French have 15,000 men and 520 guns. It says the Russians have already retreated from Silistra and the British and French have pitched camp at Varna. It's rumoured to be quite a glorious sight: white tents and green fields, broad sweeps broken by a great many fine trees overlooking a shining lake, or so the papers say, and all surrounded by meadow land and backed by the rugged outlines of the Balkans.'

Pearce's soft voice trailed away and his eyes seemed to gaze, not at the valley he described but at some image only he saw. His brother looked away, his own eyes shuttered.

Jenny lifted her head from the newspaper and her voice was startled.

'You sound as though you'd like nothing better than to be there, lad?'

'The thought had occurred to me, Aunt, that it might be rather splendid to see something other than mill chimneys and loom-gates before I die.'

'You've been to Italy to visit your mother and father. Why should you wish to see . . . where was it? . . . Varna? I don't even know where it is.'

'Varna is on the Black Sea, Aunt Jenny, half-way across the world and a long way from Chapmans

236

mills.'

'But your life is in those mills, Pearce, you know that.'

'Indeed. I am only too well aware of it.'

'And what is that supposed to mean?'

'Why, nothing. Only that Pearce and I are not the stuff you and Charlie are made of, Aunt Jenny.' Drew's voice was smooth as he stepped in quite instinctively to support his brother. 'We are neither of us, or so it appears, naturally cut out to be industrialists, as you are, as our own mother was. Father became a politician, despite his humble beginnings . . .'

'Humble beginnings, is it, Drew Greenwood? And don't we all come from those, you included?'

'Oh, indeed we do, Aunt Jenny, but I hardly think Tessa, Pearce and I fit into the . . .'

'Oh, don't talk daft, lad. Your grandfather and your father planted taters to see them through the winter and even in 1826 during the power-loom riots they brewed nettles to make a bit of nourishment for Charlie and Daisy who was our sister. They were only children then . . .'

The three faces about her had taken on that faint and uneasy look of the young when confronted with the awkward and tedious reminiscences of the old. It was all history, their expressions said, and nothing to do with them and their generation. But she had lived through those times, riots and machine-breaking and the fight for a decent standard of living for the working man. And the father and mother of those two young men who were staring so irritatingly at her, had been in the forefront of that fight. Yet here their sons sat, careless, restless, ready, it seemed, to take a ship, if

237

they had the choice, to some far-flung spot on the globe just for the hell of it. Just as though they were Nicky Longworth or Johnny Taylor, with no other obligation but to amuse themselves.

'Don't you care?' she asked coldly.

'About what, Aunt Jenny?' Drew's voice was polite, genuinely puzzled she could see.

'About what happened to your family. To all the families around here thirty years ago.'

'Really, Aunt Jenny, it is all so long ago. The future . . .'

'Depends on the past, my father always said.'

'How very quaint.'

Drew's face had assumed the haughty expression of a young prince and her own became a bright pink in her anger.

'You supercilious young devil! Your grandfather was a great man with a wisdom and a feeling for others which I suspect you wouldn't recognise. He was a working man, as I am a working woman, as *you*, both of you, are from a working-class family, and you will not expend your so-called humour at his expense. You really do amaze me, yet I don't know why you should for you've always shown a marked reluctance to take up your responsibilities in the mill. And I suppose you feel the same, do you?' She turned savagely on Pearce. 'About . . . what were the words your brother used? . . . the need to see something other than mill chimneys and loom-gates before you die?'

'Well, it would be splendid to travel but I don't know whether I'm prepared to go all the way to the Balkans to . . .'

'To escape your heritage, is that what you're saying? To live like young lords without having to

238

do a day's work in your lives? Shooting grouse over the Squire's moor . . .'

'The Squire works hard, Aunt Jenny,' Drew protested angrily. 'He is busy from morning till night seeing to the needs of his tenants, just as you do your operatives. His people, he calls them. He is Chairman of the Bench at Quarter Sessions, a magistrate and is always occupied about the estate . . .'

'Oh, that,' Jenny Harrison's voice was contemptuous, reducing Squire Longworth's busy day to the proportions of a tea-party which, if he did not care for it, he had no need to attend.

'Yes, that!' Drew was beyond caution now and though Pearce made a movement towards him, one that said he should take care, he chose to ignore it. 'And, I can tell you, the life would suit me admirably. Out in the sunshine instead of inside that . . . that . . .' It seemed he could find no word strong enough to describe his detestation of the mill. 'In the rain, if you've a mind to, not bound by clocks or bells but merely the seasons, the needs and desires of one's own inclination which certainly would not include the amassing of more and more money which one can scarcely need, surely?'

'That's because you have plenty already which others have worked for.'

'But there is no need of it any more. There is enough and to spare for us all. We can live in luxury for the rest of our lives . . .'

'And what happens to your workers? Are they to be thrown out like old bobbins, or will you keep them in this luxury as well?'

'They would not lose their jobs. If we were to sell the business whoever bought it would continue to

239

run it just as it is.'

'Really! So you would cast off your responsibilities just as though you were talking of a herd of cows or a flock of sheep to be sold to the highest bidder? These are people you are concerned with: men and women who have worked loyally and faithfully for your family, some of them for over twenty years; young men who are beginning to make something of themselves because of the chance they have been given. Your family have shown all these people the opportunity to move forward, to find a change of place, each generation taking another step up. Yet you want to throw them all away so that you might walk in the rain whenever you have a fancy for it.'

'You will not understand, will you, Aunt Jenny? You will not even try to see what I am, what Drew Greenwood is. That we are not all the same. You are one of them . . .'

'And proud of it, lad.' She stood up and with quiet dignity walked from the room.

'Well, you have put the cat amongst the pigeons,' Pearce said softly, wondering how the war in the Balkans had led to the passionate argument between his brother and his aunt on the eternally recurring theme of the trials of the working 'poor'.

The scene between Jenny Harrison and her nephew was not spoken of the next day or the next, and by the end of the week Drew and Pearce had convinced themselves it had been forgotten. The weather had turned quite glorious. It was almost the end of May, Whit Monday and a holiday, and they with Tessa were to stroll down in the bright sunshine to watch the Whit walks.

Tessa had seen nothing of Will and made no

240

attempt to. She missed him quite dreadfully. Her body, now that of a woman with the needs of her awakened sexuality, was even more restless than usual and she rode the moorland with all the wildness which had always been in her, but doubly so now without Will to soothe her to peace. She startled many a tramping family as she flew past on her fleet-heeled mare, her dogs about her feet, her unconfined hair growing longer now and streaming about her head like a dark and whipping pennant. At night she lay in bed, tossing her stimulated body from side to side, or fidgeting at the window for the rose-flushed dawn to break over the hills.

He had steadied her, she was aware of that now, making her think of things which had nothing to do with the wild excitement which had once been important to her. Now, without him, she needed it, or him, again. Several times during the week, as the spring evenings drew out towards summer she had been tempted to ride over to his cottage. She longed to fling her arms about him in a passion of love, to declare that she would marry him, despite her doubts, since she really could not manage without him and his quiet strength. Perhaps, in a week or so, if she still felt as miserable, she would drop by and talk to him, ask him to be patient with her, give her time to think. The thought heartened her, glowing like a tiny candle flame in the surprising darkness his absence left her in. Drew and Pearce had grown somewhat cool with her in the months she had known Will, going, she thought sadly, knowing nothing of their secret, on their own masculine and hell-bent pursuits from which she was firmly excluded. She had ridden to hounds in season, the last hunt in April, and joined the

Squire's shoot over his moorland during weekdays when her cousins had been forced to the mill, accompanying them when they managed to elude her mother's and Charlie's disapproving eye, but they were different with her now. They had their share of milliners, dressmakers, actresses and parlourmaids, those who were fair game to young gentlemen such as they, and appeared to be completely preoccupied in their man's world in which, she was aware, she no longer had a place.

On the day of the Whit walks the houses in Jagger Lane and Reddygate Way were decorated with flags and banners, with mottoes which read 'God save Good Queen Victoria'. There were processions of Sunday school children in their Sunday best, the girls in white starched pinafores, the boys in white starched shirts and all provided, to those who could not afford them, by the ladies of the many church committees formed to help the deserving poor. Those who could pay for the new outfits of their children, a custom at Whitsuntide, did so, naturally, and even put a ribbon on the end of a glossy plait, or a rosette in a buttonhole.

The Mayor and Corporation marched manfully into the market place. When silence was obtained and the children, who were inclined to be boisterous on this day of freedom from loom or mule or schoolroom, were hushed, the Mayor said a prayer for Whitsuntide, since Pentecost was a religious festival after all.

The bands, of which there were at least half a dozen, struck up 'God Save the Queen' and when they were done the children who had been practising for weeks sang it in piping voices, most out of tune and not one finishing at the same time as his neighbour.

Led by a marshal on horseback supported by two stalwarts with spears, both on foot, the procession moved on then for it was felt that some of its members were becoming restive. It must have been two miles long, Tessa grumbled to Drew, and did they really need to stand and watch this endless assembly of Wesleyan, Methodist, Primitive Methodist, of Latter Day Saints, Catholic and established religion as church after church went proudly by carrying its own treasured banner? There was to be a fair on Crossfold green with stalls, dancing and puppet shows, prize-fights and side-shows, a fortune teller and later, when it was dark, a display of fireworks.

There were three or four annual fairs held at Crossfold, where trading took place, where household goods were bought and sold, where menageries and travelling shows drew folk from miles around, and the excitement was intense. There would be clowns, they had been told, acrobats, peep-shows and freak exhibitions. Percy had whispered to Emma who had breathed of it to her young mistress as she brushed her hair—almost back to its original length, thank God—that there was to be a goldfish pulling a boat in a glass tank, could you believe it? Oysters smoking a pipe apiece just like a man, and, giggling, dancing girls exposing themselves to the public gaze for money.

Tessa had lately taken, much to the surprise of the Penfold Valley, to wearing an elegant gown when she was seen about Crossfold and had even been noticed coming out of Miss Maymon's dressmaking establishment, her mother's coachman behind her staggering beneath an armful

243

of packages. They could not, of course, explain it and neither could Tessa herself, seeing no connection in her new preoccupation with how she looked and her love for Will Broadbent. It was as though that part of her which had been subdued for years as she rode madly at the heels of her cousins had begun to drift lightly, awakened by his hands and lips, to the surface of her woman's sensibilities. Now that she was a woman in the truest sense of the word, she needed to look like one, even to act like one at times.

She had gone a time or two to Annie's cottage in her new, stylish gowns, and to the Hall with Laurel, who had been invited to tea by the Squire's lady. Stepping down from the carriage in crimson taffeta, amethyst silk, honey-coloured velvet, turquoise satin; in cashmere of the softest hyacinth blue, tarlatan of palest peach, as bewitched by exotic and glowing colours as her mother, it seemed, she appeared as an elegant, suddenly fashionable young lady when it pleased her to be, delighted by the sensation she caused.

Now, on this annual day of celebration she wore a gown of rich cream, simple and beautifully cut, fitting closely to her breast and waist, the skirt so full it had filled the carriage. Her hat was like a flower garden of cream and apricot rose-buds, made from silk and lace. Her gloves were cream and so were her high-heeled kid half-boots and the dainty, lace-trimmed parasol it amused her to carry. She was playing a game, as both Drew and Pearce were aware, delighted with its novelty, basking in the admiration which turned every head in her direction and brought an appreciative gleam to each male eye which fell on her. When she was

244

tired of this part she played she would discard it.

The green at Crossfold was an enormous pasture on the edge of town, reached by walking up the steep slope of Reddygate Way. It was packed from fence to fence with hundreds of tents and side-shows, with stalls selling everything from sweetmeats to the very latest Bowie knife, made in Sheffield but fashioned, it was advertised, for American and Indian fighters. Painted and gaily dressed clowns tumbled about the spaces between the tents. Acrobats performed the most amazing and seemingly impossible contortions with their elastic bodies. Jugglers juggled and showmen screeched of the wonders of fat ladies and thin men, of sheep with two heads and a fish with a woman's body. Bands played and the sky was blue and cloudless and when she saw him she felt her spirits lighten and her curiosity sharpen but she would not, of course, show him that for one didn't with a *real* gentleman.

'There's Nicky Longworth and Johnny Taylor,' Drew said.

'Who's that with them?' Pearce asked

'I don't know,' she murmured and it was not to Nicky and Johnny that her eyes were drawn but to the indolent figure of the man who strolled beside them. He was looking at her with the exaggeratedly cool expression gentlemen of his class always seemed to assume when presented with a pretty woman but there was a leap of pleasure in his eyes which she knew was answered in hers. He was tall, loosely put together, half a head taller than she, with crisp fair hair cut short and brushed smoothly about his well-shaped head. His eyes were a deep chocolate brown, narrowed and speculative in his

245

bronzed face, and when he smiled as he did now his lips parted on teeth which were white and perfect. His manner said quite plainly that his ancestors, like those of Nicky Longworth and Johnny Taylor, had been of the privileged class, generations of them stretching back into time, of landed gentlemen, great soldiers, men of superiority and honour, but his whimsical smile told her that it did not matter since what was it to her, whoever she was, and to himself at this special moment?

'Drew, Pearce, good to see you,' Nicky Longworth said enthusiastically, just as though he had not drunk himself into a stupor with them the night before, pumping their hands, terribly glad to have them for his friends, it appeared.

'And Miss Harrison . . . Tessa. How splendid you look, doesn't she, Johnny?' But Tessa, her hand bowed over by both her cousins' friends, had not yet torn her eyes away from those of their companion.

'Oh, do forgive me. May I introduce an old school chum of mine . . . well, we were at the same school though Robby was at the end of his learning as Johnny and I were just beginning. He was somewhat of a god to us, I can tell you. He has come up for the . . . Oh, I do beg your pardon, Tessa, here am I rattling on . . .' To tell the truth Nicky was quite bowled over by young Tessa Harrison's striking beauty. He was accustomed to seeing her in her riding outfit, mud splattered and a bit of a tomboy, really, and now here she was looking as elegant and . . . well, there was hardly a word to describe her radiance as she waited for him to complete his introductions.

'May I present Robby Atherton? Robby, this is

246

Miss Tessa Harrison . . .'

'Miss Harrison.'

'Mr Atherton.'

He bowed over her hand, his manners exquisitely good humoured, his education obviously expensive, as the Squire's son's had been, his air superior but his impudent smile irresistible.

' . . . and her cousins, Drew and Pearce Greenwood.'

For several moments there was well-bred confusion as introductions were completed and it was perhaps this which kept concealed from Drew and Pearce the attraction which had flared up between their cousin and the gentleman to whom they had just been introduced. The polite conversation, the charming smiles and meaningless small-talk, hid the tension. Then Mr Atherton turned courteously to Miss Harrison, drawing her a pace or two away from the rest.

'You have been acquainted with Nick and Johnny long?' he asked her, placing a confident hand beneath her elbow, leading her even further ahead of the others with the manner of a gentleman who has the perfect right to do so if he wishes, but without being in the least discourteous.

'For quite some time, Mr Atherton. Squire Longworth has been kind enough to allow my cousins and myself to join his hunt.'

'Really? They are a charming family. Mine have been on friendly terms with them since before I was born, I believe, though this is the first time I have visited this part of the world.' But it certainly will not be the last, his admiring eyes said. I have never seen such beauty, such style, such splendour and having found it I do not mean to give it up

247

lightly.

'Oh, and why is that, Mr Atherton?' She could feel the excitement effervesce inside her, foolishly perhaps, even dangerously, for such headlong and immediate attraction could not possibly survive, but when had Tessa Harrison ever considered danger?

'I have been in the army, Miss Harrison, and away from home since I was eighteen. A death in the family, my father's brother, brought me home and I was compelled to give up my commission. The estate, you understand.' He shrugged his shoulders on which, his manner said, the whole burden of his family inheritance now rested. He was sure she would know what he meant. 'And then there is the hunt in Leicestershire, and my own in Cheshire. The grouse, of course, and we have a lodge in Scotland. Deer stalking, you know?'

Oh, yes, she knew, for was it not the life she herself admired and should she not have known that this man was the kind to lead it? He was so amazingly handsome with his long and elegant mouth and that whimsical half-smile lifting the corners, the smiling brown gaze from eyes that said everything his words, so polite, so correct, could not say, not to a lady such as she was.

'My word, you must lead an active life.' Her own trite answers were just as hidebound.

'And you, Miss Harrison? What do you do with yourself? I know you ride to hounds for you have just told me, but surely that does not occupy all your time?' So could not you and I be somewhat more enjoyably employed away from these people, somewhere quiet and sun-filled, song-filled, and suitable for the delights we could show each other?

248

But naturally, a gentleman conversing with a lady to whom he had just been introduced could not speak the words out loud.

Her smile was dazzling. 'No, indeed. I fill my days most pleasurably.' But not, of course, as they were meant to be filled, the slanting, cat-like grey of her eyes told him.

'I'm sure you do. Painting and fine embroidery.'

'Not particularly.' Her eyes dropped of their own volition to his curving mouth.

'My word, Miss Harrison.'

'Yes, Mr Atherton?' she said breathlessly.

'If we carry on like this for much longer I swear I shall be forced to believe you are as foolish as the rest of the young ladies whose aims and conversation are all the same and to whom I have been introduced by the score, and I know you are not. So why are we conversing in this absurd manner, do you think?' He grinned down at her engagingly, wickedly, then winked and her heart soared with delight for it seemed his wit matched his looks and breeding.

'You are teasing me, Mr Atherton.'

'Am I, Miss Harrison? I believe I am, but please, my name is Samuel Robert Atherton, Robby to my friends and if I may I shall call you . . . ?'

'Tessa.'

'Tessa . . . Tessa, may we pretend we were introduced, let's say three months ago, and are well acquainted. So well acquainted your cousins are looking at me with the obvious intention of calling me out or beating me to death with their bare fists . . .'

She turned, startled. 'Drew and Pearce?' Why should they be concerned since she was so evidently accompanied by a gentleman of the highest pedigree, a friend of the Longworth family and surely in safe hands? Then her enchantment with this new feeling was too strong to let her attention wander for another moment and she turned her brilliant smile back to him.

' . . . but I'm sure they will not mind if I snatch you away and escort you round the fair. Now tell me what you would like to see first, Tessa . . .' His voice deepened on her name and his eyes assessed her in that completely male but gentlemanly fashion he had been brought up to assume with a lady. His admiration was very evident. He was quite old, she thought, twenty-eight or nine, with wide shoulders which fitted his elegant coat with that perfection such English gentleman seemed so easily to achieve. His face was finely chiselled and his body delicately balanced, every portion of him matching exactly every other. Moulded by the same culture as Nicky Longworth to repress embarrassing emotion, nevertheless his interest, his approval, the warm excitement with which he regarded her, the open-hearted, light-hearted charm, a touch perhaps of complexity, a boyish air overlaid with the maturity of an experienced man, was overwhelming.

'Tessa,' he said again, quite urgently, 'call me Robby. Say my name.' She knew precisely what he meant.

'Robby . . .' Her eyes smiled into his. Then, for the first time in her life, Tessa Harrison looked shyly away from a man.

* * *

250

'We are to dine with the Squire tonight, Tessa,' Drew said casually the next morning but his eyes were careful and Pearce's, who had followed him into the breakfast room, were the same as though, curiously, they were both waiting to judge her reaction.

She kept her face somewhat averted, pretending a great deal of interest in the fruit on her plate, making a determined effort to calm the tumult of her nerves, the exultation which surged through her at the thought of seeing him again so soon. Of course, this was *his* doing, she knew it. It was he who had instigated, somehow, this invitation to the Hall, and though the three of them dined there quite often, the suddenness of this command had surprised Drew and Pearce.

'Well, and I may not be able to attend,' she said airily, foolishly, for nothing in the whole world would keep her away, she knew, so why had she said it? She could find a dozen reasons to stop her from going, couldn't she, she asked herself, for even now something inside her called to her to halt this startling thing which had happened to her. It told her to be patient and wait. Yet it was not like her to hesitate, to be cautious, particularly when it was something she wanted so desperately. It had caught her off guard, probably because it was so soon after Will, she told herself, and really, should she not restore her heart to a sound and carefree condition before risking it again?

No such thought was in her head as she sat next to him that evening. Though they were the conventional distance apart at the dining table she could feel the warmth of his body strike hers, smell the fresh, lemon-scented aroma of his shaving

251

lotion and was acutely aware of the texture of his brown skin, the movement of his muscled shoulders beneath the well-fitting evening coat, the shape of his smiling mouth from which came the courteous and correct words a dinner guest is expected to address to another and the fierceness of his desire which lay deep in his brown eyes.

They met again the following weekend when the Squire ended the season with a hunt ball to which Miss Harrison and her cousins were invited.

She had marked time all that week, chafed by her need to see him again, to see if he was as she remembered him, consumed by the span of the days which dragged from second to everlasting second, from hour to endless hour. She had been unable to sit still for longer than thirty seconds, to sleep for longer than an hour, her mind dwelling on the colour and shape of his eyes, the tilt of his eyebrows, the soft brushed gold of his hair and the absolute certainty that when his mouth found hers, as she knew it would, she would know the absolute and supreme truth of life itself. She rode for hours on the tops, demanding of her mare impossible speeds, then standing, shivering, as the animal did, in a fit of remorse. She could not understand the way that she felt, nor, if she was honest, did she care to wonder about it since it could not be altered by wondering and marvelling. She fretted through every long hour which kept him from her.

She wore an evening gown of stark simplicity, a sheath of poppy-red taffeta, cut so low there had been a murmur as she entered the ballroom between her cousins. She wore no jewellery though it was known there were many fine pieces in the family, owned by her aunt, and her aunt's mother,

Hannah Chapman. Since Drew had cut her hair so dramatically, it had grown again and she wore it now low on the nape of her neck in an intricate coil in the centre of which was one enormous red silk poppy. Drew and Pearce were elegant at her side in their black evening attire, handsome and superior as thoroughbreds and glaring about them, those in their vicinity declared, as though they might strike any man who so much as spoke to her, though why they should since they were known to be light-hearted themselves, was quite an enigma. But it was agreed that they made a most arresting trio as they stood at the top of the Squire's splendid staircase waiting in line to be received by him and his lady, their commercial background scarcely showing.

He was at her elbow almost before her hand had been released by the Squire's and for the next three hours, to the chagrin of every lady present, to the swelling, dangerous, and surprising resentment of her over-protective cousins, and to the mortification of the Squire's lady who could not understand how a gentleman of such impeccable breeding could be so ill-mannered as Robby Atherton, they danced every dance together, ate supper together; bemused, bewitched, the Squire's lady said acidly to her husband, raising pained eyebrows as they floated past her once more, and, really, if her husband did not intervene and remind their weekend guest of his obligation in return for their hospitality, she would.

CHAPTER THIRTEEN

She thought about Will in those weeks of enchantment more than she had ever done since their last bitter quarrel and she wondered on the reason for it. Was it because in this new and rapturous love, this giddy joy she knew each time she and Robby Atherton met, she could at last understand what Will had felt for her and, in a strange way, sympathise with him? How would she feel if she were to be deprived of the man, the handsome, complex, lovable man who was Robby Atherton? Would she not have felt and acted in exactly the same way? Would she not have been empty of hope and joy, as Will had been? Would she not have been angry and bitter because the love which had filled her days, and her life, had been savagely ripped away from her? As Will had been. But surely Will must have known that eventually what they had must end, for how could he, an employee in her family's mill, hope to become the husband of one of its daughters? He would have known in his head, where reason and logic was, that one day she would marry one of her own class, or even above it, for she was a woman not only with physical attraction but a splendid dowry which would be enough to earn her a grand catch in the marriage market. She was, if not by name then by birth, a Greenwood, a member of a family which had clawed its way from weavers' cottage to what it was today, and certainly she could not be expected to go back a step, which was what she would do if she married Will. That is, if she had wanted to!

She looked back curiously to that period in her life, no longer than three or four months really, in which she had been bewitched, she could think of no other word, by the splendour, the hard masculine beauty of Will's body. Though she tried to tell herself that it had been no more than the awakening sensuality of young womanhood—since she knew about that now—an inherited recklessness which all the Greenwoods seemed to possess and which she had been unable to deny, she was honest enough to admit that it had been more than that. True, she had been delighted with the amber glow of his smooth skin, the steady gaze of his smoky brown eyes, the warm strength of his firm mouth. She had desired only to be across the threshold of his cottage with the door shut firmly behind her; shut herself and Will Broadbent on one side of it, leaving on the other reason and sanity; shut out the world which, she admitted to herself, she wished to remain ignorant of what she did with a man who was no more than her uncle's overlooker. All she had wanted, desperately needed, was to have her arms about his neck, to be clinging to his strong shoulders whenever they met. It had been a folly in which she had indulged herself, a folly she had thought never to undertake. She had wanted him. She had wanted his brown and muscled body, the hard yet tender love he had offered her. She had wanted it and she had been prepared to do, or say, anything to have it.

But there had been another side to their relationship and she must not scorn it. Will Broadbent was a man who had been given the ability to sharpen his own intelligence. He was keen, shrewd and with a warm spirit to add

255

balance. He had possessed the knack of giving her, as she knew he gave others, not self-esteem exactly, since she had that, but a worth which had nothing to do with how she looked or who she was. He had argued with her, naturally, since they were both stubborn with a belief in the rightness of their own opinions, but he had given her the realisation that her mind and her emotions were as important to him as her fine body. He had made her laugh, his wit often audacious and irreverent. He was well read and had told her tales she had never heard from Miss Copeland, adventures of men like Columbus and Marco Polo and more recently of the great David Livingstone and his discoveries on the continent of Africa, holding her in his arms in the deep feather-bed until other, more pressing matters had overtaken them.

So, a man worthy of loving was Will Broadbent, but not to be compared with the dazzling splendour of Robby Atherton.

He called the following Friday, giving the appearance of a man who has been hard pressed to contain himself for the required period polite society demanded of a gentleman, arriving in the Squire's carriage which he had borrowed, he told her, since he could hardly carry 'these' on his roan. 'These' were roses, masses of velvet-textured, heavily perfumed buds of every shade from the palest cream through delicate pink to deepest scarlet, a carriage-full begged, he said ruefully, from the Squire's garden. Not to be compared with *her* velvet-eyed beauty, of course, his eyes told her, smiling down at her with that easy, lounging charm she found so irresistible. She was so indescribably happy she could barely speak.

256

'I know I should not have called unannounced but I thought if your mother was receiving . . . well, I would dearly love to . . .' he shrugged his shoulders, telling her without words that her family was of the utmost importance to him now. As the astonishing image of her mother 'receiving' slipped in and out of her mind, the roses were placed carefully in her arms, thorns catching in the fabric of his superbly cut, superbly tailored coat and in the soft ivory muslin of her afternoon gown, fastening them together for a breathless moment, his mouth close to hers, his hands hovering as he delicately disentangled them.

'My mother is not at home but I believe Laurel . . . my cousin . . . is receiving callers. That is if you would not mind . . . well, there are other ladies . . .'

'I should be delighted to meet Laurel,' he said gravely.

The ladies, wives of manufacturing gentlemen, naturally, for Laurel had not yet been successful in enticing those from the gentry on whom she had set her heart—the Squire's lady, Mrs Celia Longworth, related to a minor earl, it was said; Sir Anthony Taylor's wife, Lady Prudence, a lady in her *own* right—were flung into an absolute turmoil of genteel confusion at the arrival of such an obvious member of the ruling class. So well mannered, they observed, so well bred, so patently interested in Jenny Harrison's girl it was almost indecent. And would you look at her with her arms full of roses and her eyes with stars, and which way was the wind blowing *there*, they wondered to one another.

'Laurel, may I introduce Mr Atherton? He is a

guest at the Hall.'

At the Hall! Did you hear that? The ladies were positively agog, casting sidelong, knowing glances as he bent his head courteously over each hand. As for Laurel Greenwood—well, if she had been a dog she would have wagged her tail, so great was her satisfaction. He sat amongst them, perfectly at ease as he balanced a fine bone-china teacup and saucer in one hand, a fine bone-china plate on which Laurel had placed a dainty macaroon, in the other. He listened to every word they each addressed to him. They were delighted with him and his pedigreed presence in their midst and when he begged Tessa if he might be shown the gardens, they watched, with sighing regret, as he went down the steps from the drawing-room and on to the wide green lawn.

Tessa felt her face soften with blissful satisfaction. She had known from the first, of course, but it was miraculous to realise that her instinct about him had been right. He was not only handsome and charming, he was amiable. He was kind. No sunshine had ever been so warm and bright, dancing on her skin as she walked beside him on that afternoon—a bright blue afternoon shading into a golden evening and the dazzling prospect of what was waiting for them, though not to be spoken of yet, naturally. How did she know? What was it about him that was so in tune with *her*, with the intricate bone and muscle, tissue and nerves of Tessa Harrison? Why did she feel so at *one* with him? She neither knew nor cared. It was there, it had happened and why should she question it? What did they talk of that afternoon, she wondered later? They laughed at the same absurdities, she did remember that, until, with a suddenness and a fierceness that surprised her, Drew and Pearce were there, like two boisterous, roistering, foolish schoolboys, or so they seemed in contrast with the complete man who was Robby Atherton. They invaded the magic circle which had wrapped itself around them; became surly when she was disinclined to notice them, her haughty manner telling them quite plainly to take themselves off, for could they not see that just for this one time, this enchanted moment, she could well do without their presence?

They only scowled, placing themselves on either side of her.

'You're in these parts again I see, Mr Atherton,' Drew said, rudely, Tessa thought. 'Or have you been a guest at the Hall since last weekend?'

'Please, call me Robby. And no, I have been home but the Squire invited me to meet some friends he has coming for the weekend.' And what has it to do with you? his coolly arrogant expression asked before he remembered that these were Tessa Harrison's cousins of whom she was, presumably, fond, and therefore must be treated politely, difficult though that might be. He knew, naturally, being a man, what caused their antipathy.

'Indeed.' Drew sounded as though he couldn't quite bring himself to believe him.

'Indeed. A champagne picnic is planned for tomorrow afternoon, and a party in the evening. But are you not invited?' he asked somewhat urgently, turning to Tessa, his whole demeanour implying that if she was not he could scarcely be expected to attend himself. 'I was given to believe that you . . .'

'Oh, yes, we shall be there, shall we not, cousin?' Pearce took Tessa's arm quite savagely, much to her surprise and annoyance. 'We shall *both* be there, Mr Atherton.'

*   *   *

'I believe you had a gentleman caller this afternoon, Tessa?' Her mother's look was keen and Tessa turned eagerly to her, her radiance shining about the candle-lit drawing-room, her expression that of all those who love and long to talk of the beloved.

'Yes, did Laurel . . . speak of him?' She and her mother had dined alone that night, Drew and Pearce galloping off into the darkening night, only they knowing where they were going and why they rode at such a breakneck speed to get there.

'No. She and Charlie had already left for the Abbotts when I got home. It was Briggs who told me. You know what an old gossip he is. Quite beside himself with it, he was. A gentleman caller, he said, making sure I knew exactly what he meant.' Her mother smiled for there was no worse snobbery than that which existed amongst servants. 'Who was he, lass?'

For some reason Tessa turned awkward, assuming the casual air of a hostess who has been called upon by an acquaintance of no importance and who is really not worth the mentioning.

'Oh, no one really. A friend of . . . a mutual friend of Nicky Longworth's and, I suppose, of Drew and Pearce. They were here to greet him.' It was almost true.

'Someone I am likely to know?'

'No, not really, Mother.'

'Is he likely to call again, d'you think?' Jenny Harrison was intrigued by her daughter's capriciousness. As far as she knew, Tessa had shown an interest in no man beyond a willingness to engage in flirtation of the very lightest kind with her cousins' friends, and here she was fidgeting about the room, restless as a colt and with a flush on her cheeks to shame the almost overbearing show of roses which stood in the hallway.

'Heavens, how am I to know? Why do you ask?'

'Charlie and I are to go to London for a week or so. There is to be an exhibition and Charlie is eager to see this new combing machine designed by James Noble. We are off first thing in the morning. It is said to be . . . but there, you are not interested in that, I'm sure. I did tell you we were to go several days ago,' she added gently, for she could see her daughter was not really listening.

Tessa was not. Already she was dreaming against the window, gazing down the dusk-filled garden with the air of someone who has been transported to another world, one in which less fortunate mortals such as her mother were certainly not included.

Jenny smiled.

*　　　*　　　*

They had met a bare two weeks ago and when he moved urgently towards her as she entered the Squire's ballroom she was touched with an almost unimaginable terror. It was too soon; it had happened too quickly. Then he smiled and her terror fled away as though it had never been. She was dizzy and bemused with love for him. She adored him. There was nothing she would not give him, or do for him. Nothing.

'Come into the garden with me. The moon is shining and if you promise not to scream I shall kiss you,' he teased, but their desire tightened the air about them with such force they were both overwhelmed by it.

Her eyes were twin stars, brilliant, the expression in them letting him know how very willing she was. She had waited for him for so long, since when one was deep in love an hour is forever. Each time they were apart she was in turmoil until she saw him again. Had she imagined him, she agonised, endowed him with graces which existed only in her mind? But as she took her hand from the Squire's and put it in his, he was exactly as she remembered him, knew him, wanted him to be, his eyes were almost black with his love for her, his mouth smiling, not just at her, but at himself and his own eagerness to take her in his arms before the whole company, for what else could it be but a declaration of his intent?

And they had not spoken a word as they glided away from the suddenly silent group of watchers for they had been dazzled, mesmerised by the enchantment of being in one another's arms.

'Why, Mr Atherton, you are no gentleman to say such a thing to a lady. If he were here I would inform my uncle who would certainly take his whip to you, but since he is not I may be forced to . . . to allow it.'

'It would be worth it if he took the skin from my back.'

'And if he did I would . . . soothe it with . . .

salve.'

'Tessa.' His breath was sweet on her upturned face. 'You really are ... you must be a witch. Before you left home this evening admit you brewed some potion which you have slipped into the champagne I drank, for I believe ... yes, I believe ...'

'What do you believe?' Her lips were no more than an inch from his and the Squire's lady declared to her husband that she really meant it when she said she would *never* allow that hussy in her home again. Her husband pointed out drily that she would have to ban the whole Atherton family who had been landed gentlemen for as long as his own, for if he was any judge young Atherton would be making an announcement before the week was out, if he had not already done so with his behaviour tonight.

'That I am falling in love with you.' Robby Atherton told Tessa Harrison.

'Mr Atherton, how you do go on ...'

'Stop it, Tessa.' His voice was sharp suddenly and his face had lost its smiling impudence and for a strange moment she was struck by a feeling of familiarity, a feeling that she had seen that expression somewhere before, a likeness to someone she knew. But the sensation passed in the bewildering, overwhelming emotion which fevered her skin and prickled her spine. His hand was hard on her back and the one in which hers rested gripped it cruelly.

'Robby ...'

'Go to the ladies' room ... for God's sake, make some excuse. Dammit woman, can you not see I am serious? I will meet you ...'

263

He bowed her off the ballroom floor, evading politely the hand of the Squire's lady, the beckoning finger of Nicky Longworth, the restraining clasp of old friends and over-enthusiastic mamas with daughters in tow.

She thought she would have a fight on her hands, not certain whether it was to be between herself and them, or just between the two enraged young men themselves as her cousins accosted her, surrounded her it felt like, in the quiet passage which led from the main hallway to the ladies' retiring room.

'What the hell d'you think you're up to?' Drew hissed menacingly, his hand hot and vicious on her arm.

'Making a bloody show of yourself.' Pearce was just as violent and for a moment she felt the ominous shadow of something cold and icy pass through her, then her heart reminded her that her love waited and she had no time to bother with her cousins' tantrums. God only knew what had got into them now, and she really didn't care. She only knew she must get rid of them as carefully as she could before their ugly mood erupted into the ballroom and stopped her escaping.

She made her voice aggrieved. 'Drew, Pearce. Where have you been all evening?' And before they could answer, taken aback by her tone, she hurried on to the room set aside for the ladies and where they could not follow, calling over her shoulder, 'Wait for me at the entrance to the ballroom. I'll be about five minutes. The hem of my dress is torn.'

She left them and when they had gone, slipped back to the side door, fleeing beyond the lights of the Hall, beyond the formal garden and across the smooth lawn to the summer house, led there by the absolute certainty that that was where he would be, and she was not surprised when she found him waiting there for her.

'Tessa . . .' He seemed uncertain now, no longer the hard and masterful man who had ordered her to meet him here.

'Robby, perhaps we should go back?' In her new-found maturity and bountiful love, since she *did* love him, she gave him the opportunity to draw back while there was still time from this confrontation which he had demanded.

'Tessa, you look so beautiful. The moon has taken your colour and made you into a silver maiden.'

'I don't quite know what that means.'

He took her hands in his and with a simplicity which was astonishing to her in a man of his years, his experience and knowledge of life, he told her, 'I'm so much in love with you.'

'Robby . . .' She could not speak for the tears in her throat.

'Could you love me, d'you think?' It was so different from what she had expected she could not answer. His words were quiet with a gentle sincerity in them she could not have believed existed in this mature, complex, quite dazzling man. She had thought he would sweep her off her feet, run with her exhilaratingly across the dewed grass, perhaps barefoot, plying her with champagne. Kiss her until her head spun, demand, take, his masculinity assertive, but he was trembling with need, his hands lifting to her shoulders. She was a lady, his manner said, and he was a gentleman. He had been made as he was by traditions which told him a gentleman treated a lady with respect, courtesy, chivalry, gallantry. Beneath his well-bred, well-polished shell was a virility which was without question; which seethed to escape and crush her to him, to take her since she was so lovely, so willing, so exactly what he had always wanted, yet he would not. Ladies such as she, despite her wicked humour which delighted him, had a purity not just of the flesh but of the mind, an innocence which must be protected from the coarseness of the male until her husband, the man who loved her, himself in fact, taught her with gentleness the meaning of desire.

We'll go back now, my darling,' he said quite sternly, holding out his arm to her. 'I will call on your mother next weekend, if she will allow it, but until then I think it best that you be returned to where the Squire's lady, and your cousins, can see you.'

Blindly, her will for the first time submissive to another, she took his arm but at her touch he trembled violently. She heard his breath rasp in his throat and he groaned.

'Bloody hell . . .' Then, 'Forgive me, my love, but I just can't do it. I meant to take you back to them. You're so sweet, so lovely. I only wanted to hold you for a moment. Just one kiss, but then I was afraid . . . of you . . . and what I might do to you. You're young, inexperienced,' he laughed shakily, 'and have no idea what I'm talking about or what you're doing to me but I'm damned if I'm going to let you go in without one kiss to . . . to mark the . . . we will be married soon . . .'

He put his arms about her, crossing them at her

266

back and drew her softly against him, his love so strong and glorious she would have gladly died for him then and there, if he had asked it of her.

He placed his lips against hers, their first kiss, and liquid honey ran hot and fierce and sweet along her veins and into every part of her awakened woman's body. They breathed their longing into one another's mouth, tongues touching, lips clinging, then parting reluctantly.

'I love you.'

'Oh God, and I love you.'

And several miles away, in a candle-lit cottage, a man lifted his head from the book he was reading and shivered.

They saw each other every day. He took rooms at the brand new Station Hotel, built to accommodate those who now rushed about the country by the comparatively new method of travel, the railway, whilst he awaited her mother's return.

'I cannot impose on the Squire, my darling, not without telling him of my intention towards you and I must speak to your mother first. You cannot, of course, come into the hotel but I can hire a carriage and take you driving. Your reputation may be somewhat damaged, I'm afraid, but as we shall be engaged by the end of the month and married by the end of the year it can hardly matter.'

She wore her most elegant gowns and extravagant French bonnets, brought at great cost from London, lovely colours of pale amber, peach, apple green, cream and cornflower blue, white lace and white silk rosebuds on her parasol, as dainty, perfumed and feminine as she had ever been in her life. A female, submissive and obedient to male dominance, catching her breath at the almost

267

primitive, animal-like docility she knew.

They left the carriage and walked, moving slowly, dreamlike, smiling at her strange awkwardness in her cumbersome petticoats and wide skirts, her high-heeled white kid boots, Tessa Harrison who had strode these moors in breeches and a man's shirt, hands clasped, hearts clasped.

He kissed her many times, each one becoming sweeter and more difficult to end, hurting her sometimes in his passion for her. His body trembled against hers, and hers responded and when he stood away from her his breath would be short and harsh, his eyes a deep, deep glazing of brown.

'Dear God, I cannot ... I shall do something damnable if I do not take you home,' he whispered against her throat, and she could barely stop herself from pulling him down into the waist-high, sweet-smelling fern. Only the awareness that he would be appalled, much as he wanted it, stopped her since she knew that to him she was as white and virginal, as untouched and innocent as a newly budded snowdrop.

On the day before her mother was to return he had business to attend to in Manchester. Restless and impatient without him she called for her mare and rode over the moor to see Annie.

CHAPTER FOURTEEN

' 'As tha told Will?'
'I have not seen him.'
'Tha owes it to 'im, Tessa.'
'Dear God, Annie, are you my keeper? It does
268

not matter what I do or don't do, there you are, an expression of disapproval on your face, telling me where my duties lie.' Her guilt made her sharp. 'What have I to tell Will? What is there I can tell him?'

'Eeh lass, I knew thi ter be 'eartless at times but never cruel. This is cruel and well yer know it especially after what's bin between yer. D'yer love this chap? If tha does, yer mun tell Will. Are thi ter wed this chap? If tha is, tell Will an' let 'im gerron wi' 'is life . . .'

'Don't keep calling him *this chap*. He is named Robby Atherton. You speak of him as though he was some fortune hunter who is merely after my wealth. He has money and land and . . . and he wants to marry me. He is to speak to Mother tomorrow.'

'Tha's in a rush, the pair o'yer. I thought you said you met 'im at Whit walks. Tis only a month since . . .'

'I know, oh Annie, I know, but we love each other so.'

Tessa stretched her tall, slender body in an ecstacy of joy, her arms above her head, ready to soar up to the ceiling and beyond, away from the earth which bound her, dipping and swaying the full skirt this new Tessa Harrison felt the need to wear, about Annie's stone-floored kitchen, rapturous as Annie had never seen her, her face lit in a way Will Broadbent had not, it seemed, been able to achieve. Poor Will, and yet what a pitiful word to apply to the quite devastated strength, the clench-jawed, savage-eyed pain of the man who had snarled his way about her kitchen only last night, very much as Tessa was doing now, but for a

269

very different reason.

'What the hell's she playing at, Annie? Christ, it's been weeks and she's not been near me. Oh, I know I told her not to come back until she was ready for marriage but I thought she would realise . . . I was convinced she loved me, you see. That given time . . . she is so young . . . I stayed away from her . . . Dear God, Annie, I love her. That is all there is to me . . .'

'Give over, Will Broadbent . . .'

'It's true. She's had me in a thrall since the very first time. I wouldn't have her unless she married me, I told her,' he laughed harshly, 'so she came to my house and made short work of that statement. You understand what I'm saying?'

She did. She had known from the first of the physical nature of the relationship between Will and Tessa but he was not a man who would go in for 'dallying'; a steady man who would give his heart wholly to one woman and love her until the end of his days. He was strong, self-reliant, enduring, but Tessa Harrison had brought him to his knees, taken what she wanted from him for as long as it pleased her, then drifted on to the next sensation, the next adventure, the next pleasure to take her fancy and this time his name was Robby Atherton. The son of a gentleman and therefore much more acceptable to the Greenwoods and their status, to Tessa who could now, if she chose to it seemed, live the life of a gentleman's wife, shooting and hunting in season, parties, the hunt balls, all the exciting pastimes the gentry got up to and which Will Broadbent's wife could never have.

'I asked her every time she came to me to let me speak to her mother, her uncle, or her cousins, or whichever male relative their class insist on, but she put me off. Mr Greenwood has promised me manager of the spinning mill at Highbank when old Fishwick retires at the end of the year, aye . . . me . . . a pauper child, a little piecer and scavenger to be manager at Highbank. There'll be good money, Annie, and a fine house. There's a plot of land out New Delph way that I've got my eye on. We could build . . . anything she wants. She loved me, Annie, else why would she . . . ?'

His voice was harsh, no longer caring about any finer feelings Annie might have, nor of the children upstairs who could hear what he said, ' . . . else why would she come to my bed? You've not loved a man yet, lass, but I reckon you'll know what I'm talking about when I say that woman is my life and without her I'm nothing. Now there's talk of her . . . of her making free with some chap up at the Hall . . . in a red dress and walking the moors dressed like a bloody lady, hand in hand with . . . but that I'll not believe. Not even of her, wild as she is. Dear Christ, she was in my bed only a couple of months ago. It's said she was . . . that he . . . that they are lovers . . . but she'd not do that, would she, Annie . . . ?' Annie had shaken her head numbly, horrified to be the witness of such suffering, unwilling to be made a part of this turmoil and yet how could she avoid it, for they were both her friends.

Now, the very next day, here was Tessa floating about on air, it seemed, over some haughty, self-opinionated gentleman of enormous superiority, an aristocrat of the highest order. Handsome, oh aye, and oozing charm and wit and, by God, Tessa was dazzled by it.

271

But this Robby Atherton wanted to marry her she said and was to knock at the door of Greenacres tomorrow and tell her family so.

'Is 'e thy lover an' all?'

'That is none of your business.' Tessa was appalled.

'I reckon it is when it were only a month or two back you were in Will Broadbent's bed.'

'Who the devil told you that?'

'Will.'

'He's no damn right . . .'

'It's true, in't it?'

'It makes no difference.'

'It does if tha's sharin' thissen between this chap an' Will.'

'How dare you, how dare you?' Tessa's face was white with rage as she turned and strode from Annie's cottage without another word. How dare Annie besmirch her love with comparisons to what she had done with Will? How dare she speak so coarsely about the miracle which was softly curled inside her, the feeling she held to her, within her, silent, sweet, secret? She was in love this time. Not in the way she had once loved Will for that had been strong and lusty, a pure, white-hot passion that in no way could be compared to the delicacy and fragrance of what she and Robby felt. She and Will had suited one another, she told herself, taken one another as one does a meal when one is hungry but he was not a man she could marry, for God's sake. She wanted, as Robby did, to place her body against his in some private world away from this one, to discard the wrappings, one by one, of their clothing, to gaze with awe and rapture, to touch and hold and finally possess. Robby had not said so, naturally, not yet, but she had seen and recognised it in his eyes. But they were to be married first. She was to be his wife and one paid respect to the lady one was to marry by taking her virgin to the altar.

She had agonised over this, her memory scalded by the touch of Will Broadbent, wishing with all her heart that she could have given Robby this gift which men seemed to set such store by but it was too late to worry about. She had not loved Will as she loved Robby, so surely it did not count?

She was still seething with indignation, swearing she would not go near Annie Beale's cottage again as she urged her mare up the slope towards a great outcropping of rock. She crossed a shallow, slow-moving stream which, when it reached the bottom, would wind along the valley floor. She paused for a moment on the old wooden footbridge, then cantered along the narrow track before she moved on to the rough, uneven surface which led to Badger's Edge. The bracken stood tall, nearly as high as her mare. There was a mist moving in the hollows below her, but the sky was a delicate pink on the hills shading to a pale blue vault above her head.

The sun was low since it was late and would soon be setting on this early summer's day. The air was sweet, smelling and tasting as sharp as wine, and she dragged great mouthfuls into her lungs, leaning back in the saddle, allowing her mare to go as she pleased as she fell into a daydream.

Her eyes were vague as she looked towards the trees carpeting the valley below her. As the shadows lengthened their shaded green turned slowly to a smudged and darkening grey. Her dogs padded silently beside her, accustomed to her changes of pace, ready to slow, to stop and doze or, almost beneath the mare's belly, to race with the wind as she did. Soon, too soon, it would be high summer, then autumn with winter not far behind, the cruel Pennine winter which prevented only the most foolhardy from venturing out in it, but what did she care now? Long before that, long before the month of June was out, as she and Robby eased themselves further into the deep, soft-textured rapture of their new love they would move on to the next step in their delicate courtship. They would inform her mother and his family that they loved one another. Long before the snows came she would be married to Robby and living far away from here in Cheshire.

But before then she would become his 'fiancée' and once she was that, she would be changed into the young lady Samuel Robert Atherton of Atherton Hall, a gentleman, was to marry. She would be a valued possession which must be guarded every minute of the day and night, a treasure which would be prepared, wrapped up in its wedding finery and given to him in the sanctity of the great wedding ceremony for all to see. A virgin bride in her white, *his* bride, and though it was himself who would take that virginity from her, until then, innocent. She was his lady and though she knew he was mad to possess her, his reverent love made him draw back. She was not to be treated like some obliging wench from his mother's dairy and he would wait, as a gentleman should, until she was his wife.

How she loved him. He was her 'parfit gentil knight', the man most girls dream of, so dashing, so gallant, handsome and strong but with a wit which delighted her, a mind which somehow had the keenness of her own north-countrymen, despite his upbringing. He had a contempt for the often shallow and superficial qualities of his own class which surprised her. He worked hard, he said, on his grandfather's estate which would one day be his since his father's older brother had died childless and his own father had died when he himself was a boy. He took it seriously, hunting and pursuing the activities with which gentlemen of his class amused themselves but only when his duties allowed, he told her earnestly.

They loved the same things, shared the same interests. He was, in a way, her cousins all over again, rolled into one man, but without their wildness, quite amazingly appearing to know who the person inside Tessa Harrison was, and what she needed. He was the other half of her, fitting her and she him as though they had been made each to complete the other.

He rose almost from the ground at her feet, making her mare shy so that for several moments it was all she could do to stop the animal from bolting. The dogs snarled menacingly and her voice was high as she called them to her. The alarm she felt gave her reason to be sharp and she was glad of it for the unexpected sight of him on this weekday evening badly frightened her.

'Will, for God's sake, you really should not leap out from behind a rock like that. You know my mare is nervous and the sudden ... Why did you not ... well ... stand out where you could be seen?'

'Would you have ridden over to greet me or

275

would you have turned round and pretended not to see me, avoided me as you have done these last few weeks?'

'Don't be silly, Will.'

'Silly? what does that mean, Tessa? But perhaps you're right. Happen it is silly for a man to hang about hoping to catch a glimpse of a woman he thought had some feeling for him.' His voice was toneless, his face quite without expression but in his eyes was the flare of madness which comes to a wounded beast when the hurt is almost too much to bear. His face was drawn, looking older than his years. He had not shaved and his shirt was creased as though he had put it on several days ago and not removed it since.

'I've not come to harm you, Tessa,' he said at last, when the silence in which she fidgeted nervously seemed long enough, 'so you can get down off that animal's back.'

'I . . . well, I really cannot stay, Will. It will be dark soon and . . . well, Laurel is . . . another child, you know, and there is so much to attend to . . .'

'And you are to attend to it, is that it?'

'Well . . .'

He sighed deeply and passed a hand across his pale, shadowed face. 'Don't lie to me, Tessa. Not now. Let us be honest for this one last time together.'

'What . . .?' Still she did not dismount and he smiled wearily.

'Don't fret, my girl. I've not come to hurt you though the devil knows you deserve it. I said last year that a good thrashing now and again in your childhood would not have gone amiss but I'll not give it you, nor take, as you seem to think I might,

276

what now belongs to another man . . .'

'Will . . .'

'Don't Will me. The whole spinning room is whispering about you and that popinjay up at the Hall . . .'

She sprang hotly to her love's defence. 'He's not a popinjay . . .'

' . . . and we all know what goes on up there amongst the gentry.'

He straightened his back as though for the past few weeks it had been bowed with the weight of a heavy burden which he was about to throw off. His eyes were like granite now, cold, the smoky brown humour gone with his love. They were filled with his contempt for her. His lips curled and the expression on his face told her he despised her whole class which treated so lightly men such as himself. 'It seems you have found some other man to warm your bed . . .'

'*No* . . .'

'Aah, so you have not yet played the whore for him as you did for me . . .'

'It's not like that . . .'

'Dear me, Miss Harrison, has he been able to withstand your charms as I seemed unable to do? Of course, he is a gentleman, they say, so perhaps he is made differently from the rest of us.'

'Will, please . . .'

'I don't want to hear what you have to say, Tessa. I would have listened to you if you had come to me and told me honestly that you no longer . . . that you and I . . . that your feelings for this . . . him . . . were stronger. I might not have liked it, nor understood it, for I truly believed there was something fine between us but I would have

277

respected you for being truthful. I might not have given you up easily . . .'

He bowed his head and she could see the tremble of his powerful shoulders and the working of the muscles in his throat. 'You were so young but time would have remedied that and when it did I thought . . . hoped you would recognise what we could do together, where we could go together. I'm not a man to be content with the place in life the parson tells me God meant me to have.' He lifted his shaggy head, uncut and unbrushed, and stared at her as he might at some creature which he had found beneath a stone. 'I meant to move on and *up* and I would have done it with you since it would have been *for* you. But it seems I didn't recognise you for what you are. How foolish I was! I could have enjoyed the simple and uncomplicated use of your body without the agonies of remorse I suffered after we had made love. I idolised you, could not believe my good fortune in having you love me. I did not realise that you were simply amusing yourself with me, passing time which must hang heavily on ladies of your class in the tedium of the day. Most paint water-colours, I believe, or do fine embroidery but it seems you like to . . .' Here he used a word she had not heard before but whose meaning she instantly understood, an obscene word so coarse it was spoken only between men. 'You *are* a whore, Tessa, and even that insults those who go by that name for they are at least honest in their profession. You are a liar and a cheat and I am saddened to think that I spent useless hours longing for you, loving you, weeping . . . oh, yes, I wept for you. So go back to your latest lover'—his face jerked in pain but his eyes still dwelled on her

278

face in contempt—'and tell him from me that I can recommend you as a splendid . . .' Again he used a word she did not know but whose meaning was clear. 'But your morals leave much to be desired. It's a long and vexed road you tread, Tessa Harrison. I shall get on with my life now and you get on with yours, whatever it might be. And God help you when you fail to find what you look for, since no one else will.'

He turned then and began to stride away across the springing turf, his own step light, as though he had freed himself from the load he had carried and laboured under for so long. He did not look back. His head was held high and proud, almost jaunty, and Tessa felt her heart move painfully beneath her ribs, aching with some strange and sad emotion in which shame and sorrow were mixed. Why had she been afraid of the steadfast man who now walked away from her and their brief life together? That was what had kept her from him, she realised now. She should have gone at once to him and told him of Robby since it was his right to know but the fear of hearing the words he had just spoken had held her back: the fear of seeing on his face the scorn and disdain he felt for her, the knowledge that he found her worthless. She had dreaded it, avoided it by avoiding him, and as she turned her mare towards Greenacres her face was wet with tears.

*   *   *

The expedition to invade Sebastopol led by Lord Raglan reached the Crimea at last. He had been informed that a safe and honourable peace could be obtained in no other way. The nation thought so

279

and the government thought so and he was not to delay his decision to attack. Despite the sickness of the troops and their complete lack of preparation for war, he set forth bravely to do as he was bid.

The first mistake was caused by the misunderstanding between the systems of the French and British armies. The British, as Wellington had always done in France, were prepared to purchase at a fair price the carts and bullocks they needed, having brought no transport of their own, from the simple country folk who came into their camp. The French, on the other hand, believing that stores belonging to the government of one's enemy are a fair prize, entered and plundered villages within the British lines, abusing men and even women, and like snow before the sun the supplies on which they had counted simply melted away.

That was the first mistake but certainly not the last as Lord Raglan looked about him for the transport needed to carry the expedition consisting of 61,000 soldiers and 132 guns. Somehow it was accomplished and on a soft and sunny day a week later, they prepared to set off but, staggeringly, it was found that the British were not ready. They should have been in lines of seven and where was the delay, they were asked. No answer seemed to be forthcoming but at last they were prepared for the daring exploit of invading the Peninsula. They marched gloriously towards the banks of the Alma where a great battle was fought and despite the initial blunders, was won in triumph and the Russians were forced to retreat.

Pearce Greenwood read the account of it in the newspaper and his eyes gleamed in his sun-browned face. He savoured phrases such as 'irresistible vigour in all parts of the field', 'immediate advance' and the words spoken by Brigadier Sir Colin Campbell: 'It is better that every man of Her Majesty's Guards should be dead upon the field than that they should turn their backs upon the enemy.'

What splendour! What magnificence, the newspaper reports declared. Did it not describe exactly what every right-minded Englishman, if he had hot blood in his veins, which Pearce did, was thinking as he ate his bacon and eggs that morning? The names of the divisions of which the British army was composed were enough to make any man reach for his rifle and his horse and travel immediately to the Crimea to see for himself what was going on: 'the Light Division', 'the 2nd Battalion Rifle Brigade', 'the Grenadiers', 'the Fusiliers', 'the Coldstream Guards', 'the Light Dragoons', 'the 11th Hussars'. They painted pictures of flags snapping in the breeze, the sun reflected on polished sabres and boots; the flare of the kilt above brawny knees; scarlet coats and sleek, well-bred horses and the roar of battle-hardened men, the cream of Britain's finest, for surely that was what they were, as they whipped the enemy from the field.

He sighed forlornly as he lowered his newspaper and looked about the room. Briggs and Dorcas, one of Mrs Shepherd's clean, respectable and efficiently trained parlour maids, stood to attention by the sideboard, their eyes somewhere over his head, their faces expressionless. He wondered what the hell they thought about as they waited for him to tell them what he would eat for breakfast, if he would eat anything at all from the dozen silver platters which stood under their silver covers on the sideboard.

He was alone at the table. Laurel ate breakfast in the peace of her own small sitting-room and his Aunt Jenny and Charlie had gone to the mill an hour ago, as he was only too well aware. His brother . . . well, God knows where his brother was at this moment. Some actress in Manchester, he had said vaguely, as he had ridden off into the night, and to expect him when he saw him.

The door opened and the subject of his thoughts lurched across the threshold, dressed as he had been last night before he took the train to the charms, one supposed, of the actress. It was obvious to Pearce and to the servants that he had been drinking heavily, and alone, by the look of sullen oppression which hung about him like a mist. Pearce, in his own misery, recognised his brother's, and the unhappiness was made worse by the knowledge that for the first time they could not share it. How could one console a man who suffered the same malady as oneself? In one way he did not care about Drew since his heart ached only for himself and yet, in this ludicrous situation, they were the same person.

The thought gave him the strength to speak sympathetically to his brother. Really, he thought, with a sardonic twist of his young mouth, one could almost laugh about it had it not been so painful.

'Do you want something to eat?'

'No.'

Drew sat down heavily and stared moodily at the empty coffee cups in front of him and the two servants exchanged glances which asked quite

282

clearly what the devil the young master had been up to now? If he had nothing better to do than fiddle with a teaspoon all day, they had, and if he was not to break his fast why didn't he beggar off and get changed for his day's work at the mill and leave them to theirs?

He lifted his head suddenly as though seeing them there for the first time. 'You two can go,' he muttered. 'If I need anything I'll help myself.'

The servants, all bustle and activity now, left the room smiling, relieved to escape for the time being the uncertain tendencies of the Greenwoods' volatile nature which could, at a moment's notice, turn from the blankness of utter boredom to the sheer exuberance of some anticipated escapade. God knows which would take shape today with the pair of them looking as though they'd lost a guinea and found a farthing.

They sat for five minutes without speaking, then Pearce cleared his throat painfully.

'What are we to do, brother?'

Drew laughed harshly. 'Only God knows and He's not speaking to me.'

'Perhaps not, but we must speak to one another.'

'Oh, absolutely.' He twisted round in his chair to stare blindly out of the window. 'Do you know, when I was having a quiet drink with myself last night—I couldn't face the actress, you see—out on the moor actually, I had the strangest thought.'

'Oh, yes, and what was that?'

'What would have happened if she had chosen one of us?'

'The irony of it has not escaped me, either.'

They were silent for a distressing moment while Drew blinked rapidly.

'I would have killed you for her.'

'I know, so at least that has been averted.'

'Yes.'

'One must try to see the bright side, I suppose, or so they say, but I'll tell you this. I'm not hanging about to see her go up the aisle with that bloody . . .'

'You think it will come to that?'

'He's calling tomorrow, isn't he, with the express purpose of seeing Aunt Jenny. What else could it be but . . . ?' Pearce could not continue and felt his heart constrict with angry pain. My God, was this what it did to you? This raging, savage jealousy which ate into him. It had him in such a damaged state he could not think beyond the desperate certainty that he could not stay here to see her married to another man. And the laughable thing, the almost hysterical thing that had him nearly in tears was that he was suffering it *twice*, for himself and his brother, and he knew Drew felt exactly the same. They had shared most things: their hatred of the mill and their hopeless attempts to escape it; their love of this land, this harsh north-country land which had bred them; their light-hearted disposition, their arrogance, their hot heads and warm hearts which had fallen in love a dozen times, often sharing the favours of the same pretty girl. And now, irony upon irony, they were in love, both of them, with Tessa Harrison.

'Seen the newspaper?' he went on curtly.

Drew turned to stare at him. His face was drawn, unshaven, his eyes quite blank, dead somehow, and yet in them was a prick of bewilderment as though his brother's question was beyond him just at the moment. His shoulders sagged.

'I can't say that I have. Is there something interesting in it?'

'Read that.'

'I don't think I can drum up a great deal of concern.' Drew turned away again, then stood up and walked slowly to the window. Putting a hand on either side of it he leaned against the frame and stared down the long sweep of lawn towards the lake and the trees on the far side.

'I love this place, you know,' he said almost dreamily and Pearce knew, with a kind of surprise, that his brother was near breaking point and that it was up to himself to provide the answer for both of them; that for the first time in their eighteen years, one of them must take the lead.

'Listen, Drew,' he said quietly. 'Listen to this.' And he read the report of the Russian defeat at Giurgevo.

There was a long, almost death-like silence. Then Drew turned to him and this time Pearce knew he had his attention.

'Stirring stuff.'

'You know what I'm saying, don't you?'

'Oh, yes.'

'An adventure at last. We have always, since we were boys, dreamed of one but we were forced into the mill. Made to see where our duties lie. And for the past year we have done it. Now, for a little while at least, I think it is *our* time. It might put Charlie and Aunt Jenny in a bind but I'm certain our combined contribution to the running of the mill could be easily taken care of by one little piecer! There will be someone to take our place for a . . . well, however long it takes. A month or two, perhaps . . . until the . . . wedding is . . .'

285

'Don't.'

'It has to be faced, dammit.' Pearce's voice was hard and angry. He was suffering pain for the first time in his life and he was angry. He did not know how to deal with it beyond getting away as far as possible from its source.

'How are we to manage it?' Drew's voice still dragged but he had straightened up. There was a look almost of hope about him, as though the torpor had shifted somewhat like a mist when the breeze touches it, revealing a path which might be explored, a path which might lead to a way out of it.

'Get on our horses and simply ride away.'

*　　　*　　　*

It was, strangely, Will Broadbent who drew to the attention of their uncle when he returned from London that Drew and Pearce Greenwood had not been seen for a couple of days.

'Maister says 'as 'ow he wants to see them lads of 'is,' the young lad who had been sent to deliver the message, told Will.

'Well, they're not here, tell him,' Will answered flatly, not at all sure he wanted to be involved with *any* of her family just now. 'I was told by Mr Wilson they'd gone away.'

'Gone away?' Mr Greenwood repeated to him ten minutes later. 'Gone away where?'

'Nay, don't ask me.' Will's voice was short, curt even, but Charlie did not notice as the first trickle of annoyance ran through him. 'Who told you they had gone away?'

'Well, I suppose it was Mr Wilson, but he'd been

286

told by ... Nay, I don't know. It seemed to be just sort of ... accepted ...' To tell the truth he could not for the life of him remember how he had come by the knowledge, or the rumour, if that was what it was. It seemed that all those in the manager's office, each one assuming it had come from the other, were convinced those 'damned lads' had been given permission to absent themselves and yet here was Mr Greenwood looking madder than a wet hen. Perhaps this time he'd give 'em what for.

'Have they not been home, sir?' he said calmly. Dear God, they'd bred a pack of wild cats, untamed and unreliable, this family of decent, hard-working, *working-class* folk, for that was what they were. Yet from them had come these uncontrollable lads and that ... that lass whose claws had raked his own heart almost to shreds.

'I've not seen them, Will, but then they often don't dine with us, or breakfast either, come to that, so I wouldn't expect to. They come home late ...' He shook his head in exasperation. 'Has no one seen them at the mill?'

'Not that I know of, Mr Greenwood, but I expect they've gone off on some junket ... some adventure which has taken their fancy ...' He stopped, realising who he was talking to, realising that he was talking about two young men, eighteen years old and no longer schoolboys who were expected to indulge in such nonsense. They had never grown up, never come to the maturity expected of most men. For the past year they had been made, half-heartedly, to present themselves at the mill and it was a wonder to him that they had lasted as long as they had. No doubt they were in London or Paris, living high and dangerously, recklessly risking their young lives on anything which seemed foolhardy. And so he was not surprised a week later to hear that those 'damned lads' had fetched up with Lord Raglan's army in the Crimea.

CHAPTER FIFTEEN

She was at the door to meet him when Briggs opened it. Her mother waited in the drawing-room, promising nothing, she said, for it was far too soon, declaring she would reserve her opinion on this 'Robby' her daughter spoke of, until she had met him. Tessa was seventeen, ready for marriage and, from the look of her, rapturously in love with this man she had met on Whit Monday and, she admitted, a time or two at the Hall. She would see him first, a proper introduction, question him about his intentions, his family, his suitability as a husband for her daughter, and Tessa had her permission to ask him to call.

Briggs took his top hat, bowing reverently for this was a gentleman and not many of those stood in this hall, not real gentlemen. Then obeying Miss Tessa's instructions, he left them alone together. There had been talk about her—when had there not been?—and the Squire's Friday-to-Monday guest, which had reached the servants' hall, and now, it seemed, there was more to it than talk for as he closed the door behind him Miss Tessa flung herself into the gentleman's eager arms.

'There's something in the air, Mrs Shepherd,' he told his only confidante in the kitchen, the housekeeper, 'and I wouldn't be surprised to see a wedding very soon and on a very grand style. A gentleman, this one.'

Tessa wore a day dress of muslin in a tawny shade of amber. The skirt had a dozen flounces, each edged with black velvet ribbon; the pagoda sleeves were frothed beneath the wrists with a mass of lace; the bodice was tight and plain. Her hair was smoothed back into a glossy chignon, unadorned but for a tawny ribbon of velvet. Emma was delighted with her for it seemed her young mistress was a lady at last, a lady who cared about fashion and elegance and the need to allow her maid to take as long as was necessary each day to groom her, to change her as many times as was necessary from one outfit into another.

'Darling, you look beautiful,' Robby whispered.

'And so do you.' Her breath was sweet on his lips. He was correctly and immaculately dressed, his olive green frock-coat exactly the right length, the lapels wide, the collar high. His dove-grey trousers were tight to his long, lean legs, clinging to the calf muscle, his boots polished and his frilled and pleated shirt-front ironed to perfection. He smelled of lemon soap, his face freshly shaved, glowing and brown with health, and his gold-blond hair was smoothly brushed, not a curl of it out of place. His brown eyes worshipped her and she thought she had never been so exquisitely happy in her whole life.

He grinned engagingly. 'Do I look good enough for the daughter of the house?'

'She will simply fall in love with you, just as I did.'

Her answer was still on her smiling lips as he

opened the drawing-room door for her, stepping back a little to allow her to enter before him. Her mother stood up, her face serious for this was a serious business. She had never met this young man and she would not be charmed by any facile and good-natured fool who thought he might get his hands on her daughter's inheritance, since one day she would have one. It looked somewhat suspicious to her that this gentleman who had only just come into her daughter's life was already making his intentions known having swept her off her feet, it seemed, in a matter of weeks. She would size him up, as she sized up any man who came to do business with her at the mill and draw her own conclusions. That was why she had not wished to hear any of Tessa's gloriously coloured notions on what a paragon of virtue he was, what a marvel, indeed a miracle of perfection, and from such a splendid family, or so Tessa would have it. She would decide what he was when she met him: from long experience she could read a man, his motives, his beliefs and values, his pedigree and breeding as easily as she could read a balance sheet.

He walked towards her, coming from the past as savagely as the fist of a pugilist swinging up from nowhere, the blow hitting her between the eyes with a force which took her senses, her breath from her lungs, the strength from her legs. She could feel the movement inside her head as her mind began to go round and round, darkening the space about her, blinding her eyes, reeling and dipping, flinging her about sickeningly, nauseously, as though she was a child on a swing which goes far too high. She put out a hand to ward him off, both hands as she felt herself fall, and her last thought as the blackness slipped mercifully over her was that she had burst her heart and would be dead before she hit the ground.

'Mother . . . Dear God, catch her, Robby, she's fainting. Mother, what is it? Ring the bell, Robby . . . Dear God, Mother . . . Robby . . . ask Briggs . . . fetch Emma . . . smelling salts in Laurel's drawer, she always has them. Mother, oh, darling . . . speak to me . . . tell me what . . . ?'

She could hear her daughter's voice spiralling down the length of the tunnel which led into her head, the words hollow and echoing, and even see her terrified eyes peering through the darkness. She was sorry she had frightened her. She had never, in the whole of Tessa's existence been anything but calm, unruffled; not the perfect mother, perhaps, since she spent all her days at the mill, not always there when Tessa had needed her in her childhood, but never anything other than perfectly controlled. She had left this girl to others to bring up, hoping it would be all right, not knowing how to do anything else, not being awfully sure she could be anything else. But she had always, always been strong, steady, and had never swooned before in her life. But the sight of the man her daughter loved had taken away the props, the crutch on which she herself was balanced, and somehow she must find it again, or make another.

He was looking at her, concerned, his eyes bewildered, his face just as she remembered it, his expression telling her that he was willing to be anything she wanted him to be for as long as it suited her, the young and endearing manner she knew so well. His mouth slanting into a smile of encouragement, his hand on her arm, ready to lift her wherever it pleased her to go, a gentleman at the disposal of a lady, and she did not know whether to love him or hate him.

Her face was the colour of putty, somewhere between beige and gunmetal, it's youthful elasticity gone, the flesh drooping, sweating, and she trembled violently. She was on the sofa, her head propped on a cushion, her skirts bunched uncomfortably beneath her as though she had been picked up quite urgently and bundled on to the nearest resting place. Tessa knelt beside her, chafing her hands anxiously. The room seemed to be full of people: Briggs hovering distantly as he always did by the door; Emma, her daughter's maid, wringing her hands, and Dorcas, a sensible lass and the only one to show calm, holding the smelling salts which a moment before had brought her back to her senses, and *him*, the man her daughter wished to marry—which, of course, was impossible now.

'I'm all right,' she managed to whisper but her eyes could not tear themselves away from him. He stood to one side, a visitor, a stranger, really, who had been involved in a small family emergency, had helped out but who, knowing his place, had moved away to give the family, her daughter, some space and air to breathe.

'What happened, Mother?' Tessa continued to worry her with her hands.

'I . . . I would like to go to my room, lass.'

'Of course, Mother. Emma and Dorcas will help you but . . .' Her gaze turned, radiantly, even now, towards the man she loved . . . Oh, dear God . . . dear, sweet God . . . 'may I not introduce . . .'

'I'll go now, daughter.'

292

'Please, Mother . . .'

'If you will give me your arm . . . see, Dorcas, lift me up . . .'

'May I help, madam?' A true gentleman, he was beside her as she tried to rise, offering her his arm, his support, anything she might need as a lady and which he, as a gentleman, was willing to give her.

'No, no . . .' She broke the spell she herself had made, the link her eyes had forged with his, by turning abruptly away, rudely the rest of the assembly were inclined to think, particularly her daughter who loved him. He fell back, startled, genuinely puzzled by her apparent distaste for him, then bowed, his impeccable code of conduct keeping his face politely expressionless.

He had gone, she had been told an hour later as she lay in her darkened room, not undressed for she simply could not face the task. He had sent his good wishes for her speedy recovery, Tessa said coolly as she sat beside her, and the hope that they might meet again to discuss his and her daughter's future, when she was feeling better able to manage it. Perhaps the next day, if she could spare him an hour, since he wished to get the matter settled before he discussed it with *his* family.

'He loves me, Mother.' Her daughter's voice came to her out of the darkness and she thought her heart would break, just as she was about to break this child's. All these years and the past dead and buried, she had thought, hopelessly at times, but more easily as the years moved on and now, on an explosion of anguish and joy, of despair and winging ecstasy, it had come back to destroy them all.

'I can see that, lass.'

293

'Will you meet him tomorrow, then? If you feel better that is. He has to get back . . . the estate . . . his grandfather is not well so he cannot remain here indefinitely. I want to . . . we both want to make plans and there is his family. If I bring him up to the mill, to your office . . . or perhaps here if you feel up to it?'

'No, my lass. I'm afraid not.'

She saw the shadow who was her daughter lift herself from the chair in which she had waited, keeping quiet with a great deal of self-control until her mother was herself again. She moved across the room, graceful and lovely in her tawny gown, her face bewildered, her eyes mutinous, her expression saying she would have this man no matter what her mother said, or did, to try and stop her. She stood beside the half-drawn curtains, then flung them open with a great clatter and moved back across the room to stare with narrowed eyes into her mother's. She found them steady and unflinching, clear and honest as they had always been with no inclination to look away.

'Why? What's wrong with him? He comes of a good family and . . .'

'I know that, Tessa.' She saw the startled movement of her daughter's arms, both lifting fractionally, almost a shrug as if to say she wished she could understand what was in her mother's mind for, really, this was so foolish when anyone in their right minds could see how perfect she and Robby Atherton were for one another.

'How do you know?'

'Would you obey me if I told you that I didn't want you to see him again?'

'Of course not.'

294

'Could you not trust me to know that he is not the man for you, Tessa?'

'You know I could not. Do you expect me to give him up without any explanation? To give him up *at all*, with or without any explanation, a reason? There *is* no reason. Mother, please, Mother, will you not tell me what happened in the drawing-room? I have never seen you faint, or even be ill. Heavens, I don't think you have had a day off from that mill since the day I was born. You were yourself when I left the room to greet Robby, even as I returned, but suddenly you keel over like a . . . Why, what was it? It can have nothing to do with Robby since you have never met before so . . .'

'Tessa . . .'

'Mother, I must insist that you see him tomorrow, or if not then, as soon as you feel well enough. We are to be married and there is a lot to do.'

'You must never see him again.'

Tessa whirled away in exasperation, sensing her mother's urgency but refusing to accept it, throwing it back at her forcefully since it made no difference. She would marry Robby Atherton, with or without her mother's consent or approval. She would not listen a moment longer to this foolishness, this stupidity, this *insanity*, this unbelievable refusal of her mother, not only to accept her love, but to give an explanation for her opposition. She would leave now. She would go . . . somewhere . . . Robby would find a place for her . . . and as soon as they could they would be married; not with all the pomp she knew would have been the choice of his family but in a little church somewhere. Her mother could disown her, disinherit her, what did it matter? She

295

had only one life, one chance, and this with Robby was it. They were so alike, so perfectly in accord, some lovely bond between them making them the one spirit and flesh the Bible talked about though they had not as yet made love in the full sense of the word. But they would. Tonight. She would go now. Let herself out of the small side door and ride over to the Station Hotel where Robby was . . .

'No Tessa, you can't do it.' Her mother, it seemed, had read her mind, but it didn't matter. If they locked her up, which was unlikely, her mother knew she would escape. A hundred times in the past she had climbed down a conveniently placed tree, swinging from bough to bough to join her cousins in some wildness and she would do it again if she must. Put on her breeches and boots and . . .

'I can see I must tell you the truth, girl.' Her mother's voice was harsh and grating, just as though with the prospect of telling what was to come her mouth and throat had dried up and become like the sands of the desert.

'I wish you would, Mother, then perhaps I can give Robby a decent explanation of why we must marry without you.'

'No, lass.' And now she was gentle, her disciplined, composed mother, so gentle Tessa was suddenly very afraid but still she fought on, for what else was she to do? She would have Robby Atherton.

'Mother, please understand. I don't care *what* you say about him. Tell me he is a . . . a murderer, a . . . a . . .' What was worse than murder? She couldn't think, but if Robby had done it, she didn't care, she would still have him.

'He is, I'm sure, a perfectly acceptable young
296

man, with no criminal record. He will make some woman a good husband one day but it cannot be you, my darling, not you, ever.'

'My darling'. Her mother had called her 'darling'.

'Please, Mother . . .' Her voice was the voice of a frightened child, frightened by some unknown monster which hid in a cupboard and was about to leap out on her.

'Robby Atherton, as you call him, has another name, Tessa. Once, long ago, until he was three years old he was known as Lucas Greenwood.'

'Lucas Greenwood . . . what . . . who . . . ?'

'He is my son, Tessa, and your brother.'

*   *   *

She lay in the dark, in the complete and utter dark which was her hatred, her despair, her hopelessness and fear. Her mind seemed to be infested with the words her mother had spoken, senseless, of course, but making perfect sense when you saw the picture her mother painted. She had refused to believe it, naturally, screaming out that same hatred—of her mother—the despair and hopelessness, the fear in which she now lay. But then there had also been the enveloping belief that her mother was lying to her, that she was mistaken—for how could she tell after all this time?—that she was out of her mind. Indeed, she grasped at any explanation which occurred to her to prove her mother was quite mad.

She could hear her mother's voice now, patient, kind, filled with sorrow and yet there had been a kind of joyousness she had not understood, had been crucified by, and she had said so in her dementia.

'He is my son, lass. Would not any mother's heart be glad to have her son, who she had thought to be dead, returned to her? I am torn between grief for you and gladness for myself. Dear God, there is a great need in me to run after him and turn him about to face me, to look into his eyes and tell him who I am.'

'How can you be sure?' Her voice was flat and toneless for she knew her mother told the truth.

'He is exactly as his father was at that age.'

Her mother had been a spinner, long ago when times were hard and the poor oppressed. That was what they called them, her mother said: the oppressed poor. And it was for his efforts to help them, to win them a decent life, that her Uncle Joss had gone to prison. His family had survived. Tessa's mother. Charlie, no more than a child. Daisy, the younger sister now dead. Their mother had starved, and to keep her family warm and fed Jenny Greenwood had contrived, that was the word she used, to get what they needed from Harry Atherton, a manager at the mill and to whom, for a while, her Aunt Kit had been betrothed.

'It's a long story, Tessa and I'll not bother you with it now. He was a scoundrel, charming and ruthless in the pursuit of what he wanted. He wanted me. I was pretty then, and strong, so I gave him what he wanted in return for the things my family needed. You understand what I'm saying? He went away. Kit sent him. I was never quite sure how she did it . . .' her mother's voice was vague as she lived again in that haunted past, ' . . . and I bore his son.'

298

'Why did you . . . give him to his . . . father?' Her voice was flat and lifeless.

'He stole him from me. He came to the house when I was alone and took him.'

'And you let him?'

'Things . . . were done to . . . to me. There were . . . other men. Afterwards Joss and Charlie and I went to Atherton Hall. We were deceived. We saw a child, a little girl Harry said was his. She wore a bonnet . . . I couldn't see her face. She was the same age as Lucas . . . I thought . . .'

Hope shone for a moment in Tessa's eyes, then was extinguished.

'I was . . . I did not know for certain Harry had him. I thought he might have taken him somewhere else . . . revenge, you see, for what he thought had been done to him by the Greenwood family. Put him to a chimney sweep or . . . but now I know. My son was here today. If you cannot accept it we will . . . I will question him. He must have some memory. We will go to Atherton Hall. But don't you see, he believes he is the son of a gentleman, the heir to a great tradition. This will not . . . not please him. It will inflict great pain on him and you will still not be able to . . . to marry him. But we will do it if . . .'

'No.'

'How will you explain your decision not to marry him?'

'I shall not.'

'Something must be said to him.' Just as something should have been said to Will Broadbent, a voice inside her head whispered, and wasn't, and here was her punishment. She could not stop loving him, her 'parfit gentil knight'. Her

299

mind might know he was her brother, but her heart and body did not and they would mourn his loss, grieve for him and . . . dear God . . . long for his touch just the same. The flesh was no different, the mouth she had kissed, her flesh, her mouth which did not recognise that it was a sin now even to *think* of, what they had almost done and what, God help her, she still wanted more than anything. What was she to do? Where was she to go? The rest of her life lay before her without him in it and how was she to manage travelling through it alone?

She tried to weep for perhaps it would relieve the heavy weight of suffering which rested in her chest, crushing her and her shallowly breathing lungs, the pain which twisted viciously about her heart and head and indeed in every part of her tortured body, burning her eyes which would not see him again, her ears which would never hear him whisper her name, her fingers which would never clasp his.

And there was so much hatred in her. A hatred of the fates which, smiling slyly and nodding at one another years ago, had brought her and Robby to this. On the day her mother had met his father how the gods must have chortled knowing the devastation that encounter was to bring, not only to her mother but to the children she was eventually to bear. And her mother. She hated her mother with a frantic loathing which filled every cavity in her body, oozed from every pore of her flesh. It had been her, her carelessness, her disregard for the consequences, despite her protestations that she had done it for her starving family, which had brought this on them, this agony of spirit, this poison which was festering into her soul, this grief which would never be assuaged since Robby *was* her spirit and her soul.

The tears would not come. She sprang from her bed where she had lain fully clothed, motionless for the best part of the night. The dawn was near for she could hear a sleepy bird-twittering close by her window where the sparrows nested and there was a thin line of light along the top of the hills in the east to the back of the house. She could see the two dark and towering pine trees outlined against the pale sky. She did not think now for the part of her which could reason had closed down, deep in shock and no longer able to cope with logical thought. The world had gone mad, her world which had collapsed about her in a lunatic fashion and left her marooned in some place she did not know, in which she was alone. She must escape from it and she must do so in the only way she knew how. Her mare . . . up there it would be clean and empty . . . her mare would take her and if she should not come back the animal would, eventually, find its way home, or someone would take it in . . . steal it, sell it, what did it matter? Her breeches . . . but that would take too long . . . a saddle . . . but that would take too long . . . How had she got out here? As she crossed the stable yard the stray thought penetrated her mind, fragmented with no meaning nor answer so she cast it away. She threw her leg across her mare's back, the skirt of her tawny gown bunched up about her thighs, her bare feet and legs not feeling the chill of the early morning, her hands gripping the mare's mane to guide her.

She rode through the trees, moving across the thick green carpet of dewed undergrowth. The full weight of summer foliage brushed her head and a

301

squirrel darted amongst the leaves, abusing her angrily before dashing back to shelter. As she came out of the spinney and started up the track towards the high moorland, a breeze blew into her face the smells of yesterday's summer sunshine, a hint of the warmth that was to follow but which had not yet risen from the misted ground.

Her mind was quite empty now, pain and pleasure gone, hate and love gone, perhaps a beginning of acceptance though no such thought entered her head. Her mare was nervous, not caring overmuch for the feel of her rider's gown about her flanks, the bootless feet and bare legs, the absence of rein and saddle and stirrup, of not being guided in the way she was accustomed. She shied at everything in her path from the moving, breeze-blown bracken to a harmless clump of heather which had rooted in the hollow of a rock.

Where was she going? Not to Friar's Mere, nor Dog Hill nor Badger's Edge for these were places where she had known happiness, laughter, companionship, love and what had they to do with her now? Great hills stood around her, their flanks clothed in a tapestry of purple and gold and green. The faint track on which she moved, trance-like, was no more than deep ruts and pot-holes but she did not see them as her mare picked her way around them. She came to a place where on one side the track had collapsed in a torrent of rain and it fell in a scree over the precipitous slope. The animal, with an instinct of its own, clung to the bracken on the opposite side.

She had no idea where she was when she finally slid from the mare's back. Not that she coherently thought about it. There were stones, a jumble of them on the top of a barren fell, wild and with a thin, whining wind which found its way beneath her dainty afternoon dress and touched her skin unkindly. She sat down, mindless, senseless, looking out over but not seeing the thickly wooded vale far below through which the glint of water shone. She leaned her back against the rock and the veil, dragging and thick and cold, fell over her and she could neither see nor hear.

CHAPTER SIXTEEN

'I must see her, Mrs Harrison, really I must. There is something strange here and I will not go away, as you say I must, until you have told me what it is. I must apologise for my obstinacy but . . . well, she will have told you, Tessa and I are very much in love. I am not a boy, madam, in the first flush of calf love but a man of nearly thirty . . .'

'I know that . . . Mr Atherton . . .' Jenny's voice trembled and almost broke.

'You know?' He looked surprised.

'I . . . I had guessed you were . . . older than . . .'

'Then you will know that I do not take my feelings for your daughter lightly.'

Dear God, he was just as she had known in her heart her son would be, had he lived. Though his father was Harry Atherton, a man who had given thought to no one's needs but his own, who had been greedy and cruel, heartless and dealing only in easy charm, this man, her son, had a strength, surely, at least a stubbornness that would not easily be turned away from the woman he was certain he

303

would marry. He had waited a long time for the right, and fit, bride to come into his life, his haughty manner said, and no one would deny him. But she, Jenny Harrison, must, and do it in a manner that would give no hint of his true birthright. He was to lose his love and though it broke her mother's heart and put an almost intolerable ache in her mother's arms that longed to lift and enfold this son of hers, she could not take his life away from him as well. Somehow he must be made to return to the world he knew, to pick up the living he knew, to resume without Tessa, what he had before he met her.

Her daughter was not in the house. Her mare was not in the stable. They did not worry unduly for it had always been her habit when she was unhappy to take to the moor and stay there all day sometimes, returning calmed, perhaps not accepting whatever troubled her but better able to bear it. That was where she would be now, up on the tops weeping for her lost love and when she was ready she would come home and somehow she would survive. As her mother had survived.

There was some fuss in the house over the non-appearance of her nephews, her tired mind had registered, not caring overmuch for when had those scamps not caused trouble? Really, she had enough to grieve her without worrying where *they* might have got to.

'She is not here, Mr Atherton.'

'But where is she? Surely she would not have gone away on this day . . .' on this special day when she and I were to be betrothed, his bewildered face asked. 'She must have known I would return to see you, to ask you to consider me as . . .'

304

He pushed his hand through the bright tangle of his unbrushed hair and she watched him hungrily, glorying in his masculine beauty, the way he lifted his head, the turn of his smooth jaw, the slender strength of his horseman's hands. She would not see him again after today and though the thought was a pain barely endurable there was a tiny floating joy in her which told her that she had been returned from the dark place into which his kidnapping years ago had flung her. He was a man now and she knew it. He was alive and healthy and she knew it. Another woman's son, but Jenny Greenwood knew, at last, at last, he was here on this earth still, not dead as she had thought, not murdered or maimed as young boys were in the mills and mines and chimneys where she had feared he might be. He was *her* son, though he did not know it and never would, for the knowledge would torment him, cause chaos in his life which would be hard enough to bear, for a while, without her girl.

'I think she may have gone to visit a cousin in Liverpool. Yes, I believe that was what she had in mind. She was under the impression you were to go back to Cheshire and decided to go and stay for a while. She won't be home for . . . well, I cannot really say. They are very sociable there, parties and such . . .'

His eyes turned a cold, putty brown and he straightened slowly.

'You are lying, Mrs Harrison. I don't know why but, by God, I mean to find out. A cousin in Liverpool! After what happened yesterday you expect me to believe a tale such as that? You took against me from the start and somehow you have

305

persuaded Tessa . . .' A look of confusion shifted across his face and Jenny Harrison felt the tears seep to the back of her eyes and knew she would weep soon for her son, and her daughter, and their broken hearts.

'But how . . . why . . . ?' he continued helplessly.

'Really, Mr Atherton, I must ask you to leave my house.' If he didn't go soon she would break, break up into a thousand pieces as she was hurled hither and thither by their separate and yet bonded pain. 'It really does no good . . .'

'Mrs Harrison.' He sat down in the chair close to the fire, his face, had he but known it, looking as hers did when she was absolutely determined on a course of action which nobody but herself considered right. His voice was quiet and very polite. 'Mrs Harrison, I shall not leave, you know, until you tell me the truth. I shall sit here in this chair until Tessa returns from her trip to Liverpool, if necessary.' He raised sardonic eyebrows. 'And I shall have the truth from *her*. She will not lie to me.'

Jenny Harrison sat down in the chair opposite her son knowing that something fine and . . . yes, the word was 'sweet' was to be taken from him in the next few minutes. And she herself was to lose the last, the very last slender belief that there was goodness somewhere in the harsh world around her. She had tried to spare him, her son, her beloved son, but even that was to be taken from her in the bewilderment, the disbelief, the amusement, she supposed, that he would feel at first before she convinced him. Then would come the horror, the total horror and loathing as she stripped him of all he loved in his life; of his life

306

itself, really, for how would he bear the destruction of the man he thought himself to be?

She tried one last time.

'Believe me, Mr Atherton, when I say I am sure Tessa will contact you when she returns from . . .'

'Mrs Harrison.'

There was silence for a moment as the mother looked for the last time into the still dauntless eyes of her son.

'I will tell you the truth now, Mr Atherton,' she said hopelessly.

*   *   *

Her mother was in the stable doorway as she clattered into the yard, a darker shadow in the darkness of the night which was illuminated by the myriad of stars in the navy-blue sky. They did not greet one another. Her mother moved to one side as Tessa led her mare through the doorway, watching silently as she rubbed the animal down. When all was done Tessa turned and began to move towards the stable door, brushing past her mother as though she was not there.

Jenny put her hand on her daughter's arm, feeling it flinch away and her own heart recoiled from the rebuff.

'Tessa, you must speak to me, lass.'

Tessa shook off the restraining hand and continued to stride towards the side door of the house. Jenny thought she would crumple up and die with the pain of it, and indeed wished she could as it hit her again and again. Then anger stirred.

'He's my son, damn you,' she called after the retreating back of her daughter, following her

307

across the yard. 'Do you think you are the only one to hurt? You have not borne a child, Tessa Harrison, and so you cannot know the strength and the agony of a mother's love when she loses that child.'

But Tessa walked on as though she had not spoken. When she reached the door her hand did not seem able to turn the door-knob, but fumbled with it blindly. Jenny opened it for her and they moved into the dimly lit quiet of the passage which led to the main hallway and staircase.

'Tessa ...' She took her daughter's arm, firmly this time, driving down the anguish which came to her. 'We must speak to one another. We cannot go on as though this had not happened. I ... have never said this to you before ... but I love you, girl, and ...'

Tessa whirled about violently, flinging her mother against the panelled wall and Jenny was frightened by the expression on her face as the lamplight fell on it.

'Do you think I care about that? Do you? Do you imagine that your ... your love ... can make me feel better again? Pick me up, brush me down ... kiss where it hurts ...'

'No, no, lass. I didn't mean that ...'

'At this moment I feel I will never be well again, Mother. I will never recover. That is what I feel and how *you* feel means nothing to me. My head tells me that you're not to blame, but my heart'— she struck her chest violently with her clenched fist and her mother winced—'says it will never forgive you for what you have done to me and Robby.'

'Darling ...' Her mother's voice was an anguished whisper. 'I'm sorry, dear God, I'm

308

sorry ...'

'Leave Him out of it, and leave me alone. Let me go ... now.' She made a huge effort to control herself. 'Perhaps later ... but for now. Leave me alone.'

They sat in different rooms, the two women, but in exactly the same attitude as they mourned the same man: a rocking chair by a window moving slowly backwards and forwards, heads back against a cushion, hands folded, eyes staring out towards the east as a pink dawn crept along the tops and the sun rose on another day.

*   *   *

The sun rose earlier in the Crimea than it did in England that day. The dawn of the twentieth of September was soft, balmy and sunny, glowing from behind the snows of the Caucasus at about five o'clock, outlining the fleet of war steamers, eight French and one British which sailed towards the mouth of the River Alma. Their guns opened fire with the ferocity of ravenous beasts about to fall upon their prey and the two young men who stood beside their horses recoiled sharply, trying to hold the bridles of the animals which reared in fright. It took them several minutes to calm the terrified beasts, then with the fluid grace of born riders they mounted them, turning this way and that indecisively.

'It's started, Pearce. By God it's started. We missed the scrap at Giurgevo but we're to be in on this. Where the hell should we go, d'you think?'

'Where the hell will they *let* us go? Surely to God you don't intend to climb to some vantage point and watch as so many seem to be doing? That chap we spoke to yesterday had brought his mistress to see the spectacle, I was told. Anyway, in this smoke we should see nothing.'

'They are to go up to the plateau which stands above the valley, so I believe, but I should like to be closer, wouldn't you?'

They were yelling at the tops of their voices as they galloped away, manoeuvring skilfully to avoid soldiers who darted everywhere, tents, carts, guns and the chaos which had sprung up as bugles sounded from every quarter.

'D'you think we'll get any breakfast?' Pearce shouted jubilantly, not caring whether he did or not.

'Well, the troops certainly won't so really we shouldn't either, old man. It's only fair.'

'You're right. Now where should we go first? No one seems to mind our presence and perhaps we may be able to help in some way. We are both good shots.'

'Indeed, and excellent horsemen so I suggest we follow the cavalry.'

'Dear God, this is better than the mill, wouldn't you say, Drew?'

'You never spoke a truer word, brother, and won't we have something to tell them when we get home?'

The smoke had cleared somewhat when the great Lord Raglan arrived and as he rode off with his staff along a pathway leading round the western side of the heights, Drew and Pearce Greenwood removed their hats respectfully, as they had done for no man before. He was calm and steadfast, it was said of him, his resolution higher when danger pressed. He and his soldiers were children of a proud and obstinate race and would advance through the jaws of death if needs be.

'He's bloody marvellous, isn't he?' Pearce whispered reverently.

'They say he's waiting for three more battalions to arrive but due to the rain in the night it will take some time to get them here. They may be glad of us yet, brother.' Drew's face was tense and boyish in his excitement.

His words were drowned by the sudden thunder of the guns from the artillery of both sides. Two eighteen-pounders had been brought up and as they beat on the senses, the eardrums, the blood and flesh of every man within a radius of ten miles, order and sense was blown away. If either of the sons of Kit and Joss Greenwood had been asked to describe that day they could not have done so with any coherence. They had begun it as two excited schoolboys out for a spree, a lark, something to describe to those back home, an adventure which they had both craved. They ended it as men, frightened, sickened, devastated, but men at last.

The allied armies spent two days on the battlefield of the Alma. When it was done the dead and wounded lay within a space only a mile and a half square while about Telegraph Hill the bodies were piled so high it was impossible to see over them. No one alive on that bloody field had ever seen such a spectacle, except perhaps Lord Raglan himself who had fought and lost an arm at Waterloo. Men, seasoned soldiers, fell ill when they looked about them and the effect on Drew and Pearce Greenwood was to shape them for the rest of their lives. They had become separated from

311

each other as the first sweep of men and horses pushed them apart. Pearce's horse was shot from under him as he turned it about, his face ludicrously bewildered, wondering where he should go in this mad world which had suddenly erupted about him.

When he got to his feet, already quite deep in shock for despite his declaration to the opposite he had not really meant to *fight*, he found himself defending his own life with no more than the shot gun he had brought with him, the one he used against the grouse on Longworth Moor. An instinct for self-preservation luckily took over what was left of his senses. Finding, first a musket, then a sabre, each clutched in the hand of a bloody and quite-dead soldier, for an hour he parried and shot wildly, carried along blindly until the man beside him began to shout that 'they were on the run now'.

It was then, as he staggered along behind the retreating Russian army, so stunned he merely did what others did about him, he realised what he had done, where he had been, how he had spent the past few hours of his life. He had seen men, *real* men scream and crumple in front of him. He had felt the steel he held slide sickeningly into other men's flesh. He had seen blood, torn flesh, shattered bone, and worse, erupt from bodies broken and mutilated. The images penetrated his clouded mind—he sank slowly to the ground and began to vomit.

They stepped over him, still chasing the Russians, cheering now for they had won a victory, but Pearce Greenwood wept for he had lost his brother and how was he to live without him?

'Pearce . . .'

The voice brought him back, a hand lifted his face from his own vomit and the blood-soaked earth on which he lay. He turned slowly but there was no one there he knew, only a soldier in a blood-stained tunic, his eyes staring and haunted in a blackened face.

'Dear God, Pearce . . .' The soldier held out his arms and they both began to weep.

CHAPTER SEVENTEEN

She sat by the tightly closed window of the pretty bedroom, a soft white shawl about her thin shoulders, another thrown over her legs. A fire burned brightly in the grate, its flames heaped with an abundance of coal, and on the white ceiling and rose-silk walls shadows danced and wavered. Outside a flurry of hard-pelleted snow flung itself against the window but when Tessa turned to look there was nothing to see but a wall of whiteness, shifting and leaping, slowing as the wind died down, then hurtling as fast as one of the railway trains which ran through the valley bottom, across her vision as the wind sprang up again.

She was impassive now, dry-eyed and silent in her self-induced calm; rigid of mind and body, free for the moment of the punishing memories which came so often to devastate her as she gathered her small reserve of strength together. If she concentrated hard on the top of Emma's small, frilled cap as it bent over some mending in her lap she could empty her mind of everything but the will, the resolution, the absolute effort that was needed to drive Robby Atherton's face from every corner of her mind.

But she must have Emma's cap on which to set her mind. It was a trick, of course, because anything would do really: the Meissen figurine on the mantelshelf, the silver candle-holder by the bed, the gilt-framed miniature of her cousins as children. But somehow Emma's cap, simple, pretty, fluted, quite foolish, really, but always the same, seemed to have the knack of emptying her mind of the pain.

She had flung herself about at first in the dangerous rage which had come to consume her, just as she had once done as a child. She had frightened poor Emma as she had fought, time and time again, to live without his memory inflicting its vicious pain upon her.

'I cannot bear it another moment. I must go . . . I must and no one will stop me,' she had screeched in her anger at what had been done to her and her mother had sat beside her, for the first time in living memory leaving her mills to manage as best they could without her. She would not lose this child, not this child as well, her terrified mind had implored some god, her own face pale as the death which threatened her daughter. Tessa had taken a fever several weeks after Robby Atherton had gone. The heat of it had burned her flesh away like the tallow of a candle and Jenny had despaired for the child no longer cared to live, it seemed. But she was strong and she had recovered to make the lives of those around her more miserable than they cared to contemplate.

'Let me get up, Mother. I cannot stay here with nothing to do but think.'

314

'Be patient, Tessa.'

'Let me at least walk out to the stables and see my mare.' This, when she could barely sit up.

'Be patient, child.' Her mother's reply was laughable really, if it had not been so sad.

But she wouldn't be told. She fought them all violently, hurting herself, breaking everything she could lay her hands on as she threw exquisitely fine figurines at those who tried to stop her. Emma had the feeling in the back of her mind that it was not all to do with the fever which for weeks had brought her so low; this was a weakness not just of the body, but of the heart, or Emma missed her guess. They'd all seen, or been told of, the handsome young gentleman who had come a'calling and Miss Tessa's happiness had shone through the house, affecting them all for, really, it was true what they said about 'laugh and the world laughs with you, cry and you cry alone'. They'd heard her laughing and singing for days on end before he'd called on Mrs Harrison. Then all of a sudden he'd gone tearing down the drive on Mr Greenwood's horse, sent off with a flea in his ear, though God only knew why, a fine, well set-up gentleman like him, and *she'd* gone off her head because of it, if you wanted Emma's opinion. It was a mystery, it really was, and Emma almost broke her heart over the state of her since.

But her temper, unpredictable and dangerous, was back with a vengeance now as they all knew to their cost for they suffered it at close quarters.

'She threw the teapot at me, Mrs Shepherd,' Emma sobbed. She had thought Miss Tessa to be a hellion before her illness but it was as though those days had been all sweetness and light compared to

315

now. 'If the tea had run on me I would have been scalded. As it was a bit of broken china hit me on the hand, see, just there.' She pointed to where a trickle of blood ran. 'If it goes on much longer I'm giving in my notice . . .' This was a drastic thing to contemplate in the climate of unemployment which prevailed in the valley.

'Now, Emma, don't be daft, lass,' Mrs Shepherd said sharply.

That was how their young mistress was now. Tormented, that was the word which came to Emma's mind, one minute and then the next staring vacantly at nowt, not even answering when she was spoken to. Aye, had they not all suffered in one way or another at the hands of the three wild youngsters who had dominated this household in the past? Though they were sorry for the plight of the poor lass since she'd been so badly, the girl could be a danger, now that her mother had returned to the mill, a danger not only to herself, but to the servants who had been left to look after her.

'I don't care what you say, Mrs Shepherd, if she don't get out soon God knows what she'll do. She's as wild as an animal in a cage at times.'

Emma had been to the Zoological Gardens at Liverpool once when her family had stopped there for a while on their way from Ireland and the famine which continually seemed to rage there, before moving on to Crossfold. The restless padding and infuriated snarls of some beasts, the listless apathy of others had made a great impression on her and had lingered in her young mind. Miss Tessa reminded her of them. Not the padding, of course, since she could do no more

316

than stand weakly by her chair as yet, but the snarling, the wildness, the sudden, depthless silence were enough to make your blood run cold.

And Miss Laurel did her best, poor thing, and her with another little one to see to.

'I do wish you would stay in bed, Tessa. Don't you think it would be wiser to rest instead of . . .'

'Taking up everyone's time and energy with my constant demands? It would be so much simpler if I were to remain here, mim as a mouse, hidden away and a nuisance to no one, wouldn't it? It must be so peaceful at table now without Drew and Pearce and myself to . . .'

'That is not what I meant. In my opinion, this determination of yours to leap out of bed so soon after what has been a very serious illness . . .'

'*Leap?* If only I could! Why am I so weak?'

'It cannot be good for you, all this anxiety to be on your feet. Why don't you stay in bed and I will fetch you a book from the library?'

'A book! Dammit, Laurel, I don't want a book. I want some excitement, some noise, something going on. Why don't you send the children down to see me?'

'They would jump all over you, darling.'

'I don't care. I want them to.'

'Now, Tessa, you know what the doctor said. Besides, Robert and Jane are at their lessons and Nanny would not like it if I woke Henry and Anne from their nap. And baby is too young . . .'

'Laurel . . . please . . .'

'Just rest, Tessa.'

'*I don't want to rest!*'

It was March before she was completely recovered, nine long months before she was able at last to walk with her usual proud carriage and not just the lurching stagger from one piece of furniture to the next, with Emma and Dorcas hovering at each elbow. At last she could pass out of the bedroom which had been her prison for so long; away from the cosy, fire-warmed comfort, the feather quilts and lace-edged pillows, the soft carpets and soft voices, away from safety and into the wide hallway towards the stairs.

'Let me do it alone,' she begged Charlie who would have held her arm.

Down the shallow steps of the stairs, one by one, she went, her hand refusing the banister, her legs like jelly but her face hard and determined in her triumph. She wore a pretty gown of scarlet delaine, the colour giving her a bold and gypsy look which belied her fragility. It had been made to fit her new slenderness and the bodice clung to her small breasts. The skirt was full and plain with fifteen feet of fabric round the hem. And beneath it were half a dozen fine cambric petticoats, each flounce edged in white French lace. Fastening back her flowing hair was a scarlet ribbon.

The front door stood open to let in the sunshine and she stepped through it into the fresh light of spring. Gardeners raised their heads from their planting and touched a finger to their caps and she nodded to them, but it was not them who held her attention.

On the gravel driveway, stamping and blowing through her nostrils as though she knew what a great day this was, stood her mare, saddled, her coat glowing, her mane tossing, her eyes rolling in her mistress's direction. Walter held her bridle, beaming from ear to ear, his face as red as Tessa's

318

dress.

'She's ready for thee, Miss Tessa,' he said, then wiped his nose on the back of his hand.

She walked down the steps, her legs no longer like jelly but strong and sure and when she put her face against that of the animal's she was smiling since she knew she would survive now.

'Give me a week or two, Walter.'

'Happen less, miss?'

'Aye, happen . . .' and they both grinned.

*　　　*　　　*

The valley of Balaclava lay desolate and melancholy. The road to the camp was a track of liquid filth. The town itself was as muddy as the plains which surrounded it. The tideless harbour was no more than a common sewer in which floated not only the waste of the bodies of thousands of men but the carcasses of soldiers, horses, dogs, cats and every other discarded and decomposing matter which could be found no other resting place.

For weeks now those who still survived had been without proper clothing, fuel or food and to worsen matters further in this vast and mystifying war, the reason for which the soldiers themselves were not fully aware of, there was a virulent outbreak of cholera. In the camp hospitals the men lay down to die upon the bare ground and in the hospitals themselves, ignorance, dirt and confusion prevailed for want of doctors, blankets, medicines, bandages, fresh water, beds and space to put beds. Even had these been available, there was still the need for someone with the sense and energy to arrange

319

them all together.

The weather was appalling. There were heavy squalls with winds so strong they brought down every tent on the plateau. No fires could be lit and no food cooked and the sick and wounded lay exposed to the elements which were no respecters of rank. Generals, officers, soldiers, sick, wounded, hale and hearty lay together in the deluge and when the rain turned to snow 300 men died in one day.

But worst of all, far worse than anything which had previously befallen them, four steam transports, ten sailing transports and four freight ships, caught by the violence of the weather were dashed to the bottom of the harbour.

And those who were left, without blankets or rugs, socks, boots, biscuit, salt beef, or even corn for the horses which survived, must face the winter in the liquid mud on which the camp floated. Every victim on the muddy and half-frozen plains of the Crimea sent home doleful and angry accounts of his own and his brother soldiers' suffering. It was always the same. They lived from hand to mouth with the minimum of ammunition to keep them safe from the enemy. Their lives were unendurable and when they lost them it was from overwork and exposure, not as soldiers in the heat of battle but like deserted children abandoned by cruel parents. In two weeks the number of sick increased from 13,000 to 16,000. What had become of the fine army, they asked one another, sent off so dashingly, for no other reason, it seemed, than that there had been no war for forty years and it was time for another?

It was about this time that Miss Florence

Nightingale arrived at Scutari and the hospital there.

The two young soldiers had, with what remained of their strength, dug a hole in the hard ground, just deep enough and wide enough for them to sit, or lie side by side, drawing over it a sheet of canvas from another such hole in which four soldiers of the 2nd Hussars had frozen to death several weeks before. Thousands of men had died but the loss of life had become a condition of life itself and they concentrated the whole of their physical energy, which was scant, and the whole of their mental energy which was not much better when there is nothing to do all day but turn their minds to their memories.

'Do you remember the day she'—they never mentioned her name by unspoken mutual agreement—'challenged us to a race from ... where was it? ... Badger's Edge or Friar's Mere? ... I forget, to Greenacres? She jumped that bloody gate as though it was no more than a foot or so from the ground then turned to grin at us. It was May. The sky was so blue that day and it was warm ...'

'Warm? Warm? What the devil does that mean, d'you think, brother? How does it feel? It is so long since we enjoyed it I have forgot. To be warm and dry and clean ...'

'And can you remember the time we went with Nicky Longworth and Johnny Taylor to that dog fight at the Craven Heifer?'

'She didn't like it, as I recall ...'

'No,' the voice was soft and smiling, 'and, really, would you have expected her to? She only went because we did.'

'The poor brute was nearly disembowelled . . .'

'And she brought her dinner back and then tried to pretend she had eaten something which had disagreed with her.'

'Eaten something! What do those words bring to mind, Pearce? To eat something. Actually to put in your mouth some delectable, tasty, delicious, *palatable* food. What, though? What would you order if you could have anything you wanted?'

'Roast beef.'

'Yes, yes, or smoked salmon with . . .'

'No, a saddle of lamb with mint sauce . . .'

'Pheasant done in . . .'

'Followed by . . .'

'Washed down with a good claret . . .'

'And then a warm, clean bed . . .'

They fell silent. Their shoulders touched and they huddled in the faint and grave-like light cast through the heavy canvas, their backs to the wall of the dugout. They had a candle which they did not light, ever, except in the emergencies created by Pearce's nightmares where he dreamed he was buried alive beneath a growing mound of dead and injured soldiers, as he had been at the tail end of the battle of Alma. Drew had been beside him for they had made sure as the frenzied day had eased towards nightfall that they did not become separated again. When the bursting shell had lifted a dozen or more soldiers, shredding them to an assortment of bloody torsos, arms, legs and heads, and threw them by some strange chance over Pearce, burying him for ten appalling minutes with the softness and wetness and obscene weight, it had been Drew who had dug him out. Pearce dreamed of it often, screaming as he had done then, clinging

322

to his brother until the candle was lit and sanity returned.

They had a blanket between them, their most treasured possession since not many were so lucky. They had an upturned wooden crate on which stood the pathetic bits and pieces so dear to a soldier far from home and which once they would have laughed over: a miniature of their mother as a girl, a few letters from their aunt and Charlie, a length of satin ribbon with a faint smell of some woman's perfume and which neither would acknowledge to be hers, a box with brushes and a comb, razors and a tiny, prized sliver of soap.

They each wore mud-stained breeches, knee-length boots, an army greatcoat and a peaked soldier's cap. They were dirty with a sour odour about them for neither had washed, let alone bathed, in weeks. Their beards were dark and stiff and their blue eyes, once so vivid, clear and devilish with merry arrogance, were dulled and staring from faces old and tired beyond their years. They had seen and heard sights and sounds they would never forget. They had lost their horses and every fine thing they had brought with such high expectations from England and in each one was the common longing to survive and get home. Nothing more. To survive the cholera and the dysentery, the shot and shell the enemy rained upon them, the siege and the enemy which besieged them. Somehow to get up that invisible track to Balaclava and on to the first transport they could arrange to England. They had been taken for soldiers and had not argued since that was the only way to be fed. They existed, when they were on the duty they were forced to do, in the mud and rain and bitter cold of the trenches, returning to sleep in wet clothes on the wet ground of their dugout.

'D'you remember the fatty-cakes Cook used to make for the servants? We used to turn up our noses at them as some quaint dish of the working class.'

'They'd be bloody welcome now . . .' But the rest of what Drew Greenwood said was cut off by the clear call of a bugle and with a muffled exclamation both young men leaped to their feet, threw aside the canvas of their 'home' and with a hundred others began to move towards the source of the sound.

*   *   *

Tessa read Drew's letter again then stood up and strode towards the door, gathering up her crop and jacket as she went. She would ride over to Edgeclough and visit Annie. It was a week since she had seen her and in that time she had done nothing but tear about from one place to another in search of some occupation which would keep her from going mad with boredom . . . and grief. There were, after all, only so many hours in which one could ride to hounds, and besides the season had ended with the coming of early summer. She had ridden for hours across the burgeoning moorland grasses, called time and time again at the Hall with the excuse that she brought news of Drew and Pearce and though the Squire and his friends welcomed her warmly, the Squire's lady could not quite forget Tessa Harrison's behaviour at the ball last year. She and Robby Atherton had been the talk of the community then and after all it had come to nothing.

March had seen the allies making preparation for the bombardment against Sebastopol. In April there was what Pearce called a 'skirmish' at a place called the Mamelon. In May an expedition was despatched to Kertch with the express purpose of seizing the strait which led into the Sea of Azoff through which the Russian supplies were sent, and in June the Mamelon described by Pearce was captured. In July and August the Allies crept nearer to victory, and on the 'glorious twelfth' Tessa accompanied the Squire and his guests, shooting grouse, partridge and pheasant, drifting very pleasantly through the late summer and autumn days, the depth of her sadness hidden away beneath her wild, high-strung laughter. It was a pity about her cousins, they said, still, for some reason known only to themselves, out there fighting in the Crimea when they might have been having such fun with them, but they had Tessa to amuse them. She was so exhilarating, reckless and willing to do *anything* they did in her search for pleasure, careless and indifferent to the opinions of others. She wore her new outfit, designed by herself and made up for her by a disapproving Miss Maymon who had never created such garments in her life, of black riding jacket, sleek, skin-tight breeches and a white, watered-silk waistcoat. She wore a black top hat, a white frilled stock and black riding boots and was vastly amused, she told an admiring Nicky Longworth, by the consternation of the commercial and manufacturing society of the Penfold Valley who had, no doubt, thought her roistering days had come to an end with the departure of her cousins for the Balkans. She caused a sensation on the

325

hunting field at the start of the new season, in the company of the wild and, in her mother's opinion, unstable fox-hunting set of Crossfold who were, they thought, beyond being amazed at anything Tessa or her missing cousins did.

She was herself again, in other words, arrogant, conceited and charming and the harsh desolation of her nightly weeping was known to no one. They were not aware, those who condemned her wildness, that only in such desperate frivolity, the light-minded and heedless search for 'fun' which was the sole aim of the set of which she was a part, could she momentarily displace her deep unhappiness. The despairing misery which washed over her when she was alone was held at bay only by the total abandonment with which she flung herself into their giddy lives. What else was she to do, she asked herself hopelessly, when she was alone with her ghosts? The brief fling she had enjoyed with Robby Atherton, who had not been seen at the Hall since, was over with neither the worse for it, they were saying, though of course *her* reputation would never be the same again. Only *she* knew that *she* would never be the same again.

In short, she fitted again into the world of the squirearchy, the gentry and the lesser aristocracy as she and her cousins had always done, preferring ploughed fields and recklessly taken ditches, damp drizzled mornings of moorland, wind and foul weather to the polite and civilised world of dinner parties, soirées and evenings of culture which her aunt by marriage, the socially ambitious Mrs Charles Greenwood, thought she should favour. She was known quite definitely to join the gentlemen in their after-dinner billiards and claret

and to have won quite a large sum of money at
some card game at the Hall. A restive colt again,
she appeared to be, impatient of all restraint,
though those who spoke of it agreed that at almost
twenty she was long past the age to be coltish.

'She's trying to kill herself,' they said, not at all
surprised for it was known they, meaning herself
and her cousins, had always been mad.

'She *will* kill herself,' Laurel declared when the
wild, hell-raking stories of Tessa Harrison's disdain
for her own life and limb became common
knowledge and her mother grew old before their
eyes, agonising not only on the peril to her
daughter's physical safety, but on that to her mind.

'Why don't you come to the mill with me, lass?'
she asked carefully one day in September. 'Come
and see what you make of it.'

'Drew and Pearce made nothing of it, Mother,'
she answered in that coolly impersonal voice in
which she addressed Jenny Harrison, 'so why
should I?'

'You have more sense than the two of them put
together, if you'd care to put it to some use.'

'At the mill, you mean?'

'Aye, why not? It helped me when I was . . .'

'What, Mother?'

'When I needed my mind taking off things.'

'And is that what I need?'

'You are still . . . still not yourself, lass,' she said
awkwardly. Neither am I, she thought and can you
wonder after what has happened to us both? The
very foundation of their lives had been disturbed,
roots which they had thought to be securely settled
almost torn out, roots which were still shaky and
prey to any stray breeze which might blow against
327

them. It was as though the rock to which they had both thought themselves firmly fastened had become dislodged and they must take care, in their fragile relationship, not to tumble down the scree which loomed beneath them.

'I didn't hear you come in last night, Tessa, and I was awake until past midnight. I know it's the acceptable thing for young men to go skylarking into the early hours, but it won't do for you.'

'It's a bit late to be concerned about my reputation, Mother, if that's what's bothering you, and I was not out all night. And besides, Nicky and Johnny are as good as brothers to me, just as Drew and Pearce were, and until they return home I'm quite safe with their friends.'

'That's as maybe . . .'

'We only rode up to Friar's Mere to see if the ghosts of the monks really do walk as they say they do when the moon is full.'

'Why, in heaven's name?'

'Why not, Mother? It is no more senseless than your going each day to the mill to watch cotton being spun and woven.'

'That cotton buys the fine blood horses you ride and that outrageous outfit you wear.'

'Mother . . . if you don't mind I am due at the . . .'

'Lass, I'm only trying to help you. To give you something . . . a purpose, a road to set your feet on again.'

'Really, Mother, I have a road . . .'

'No, you have not. A wild track, that's all, and where will it lead?'

'Can you honestly see me doing what you do all day? Sitting at my desk planning business strategy,

328

dealing with commercial gentlemen from Manchester or wherever it is they come from? I would not know a bale of raw cotton from a . . . from a carding machine, nor a mule from a loom, and as for the financial side, well, it's as incomprehensible to me as how to sew a fine seam.'

'You could learn, child, and it would give you some diversion other than riding about the countryside with that wild pack of your cousins' friends. You need something else besides . . .'

'I have something else, Mother. I have been invited to go down to Leicestershire with the Longworths. The Squire's lady seems to have relented and pardoned me my lapse of good manners of last year. She seems to be of the opinion that having been . . . been jilted by a gentleman whom I, a member of the manufacturing classes, should not have had the ill-breeding to monopolise in the first place, I can now be forgiven. I can consider myself under *her* patronage, she says, providing I don't try to marry her son.'

*   *   *

The young soldier lay on the narrow cot. Every time he twisted his racked body the blanket which covered him was thrown violently aside and each time it fell, the second soldier who sat by his bed patiently recovered it and patted it tenderly back into place.

The enormous room was filled with the subdued murmur of men's voices, some, like this soldier, babbling in delirium, others whispering, mumbling, staring upwards into the high, vaulted ceiling, some perhaps praying, others on the road to recovery or not so badly hurt or ill, talking quietly to one another.

There was a mixture of odours, the overall stench of putrefaction and vomit, of blood and excrement, almost but not quite masked by the smell of good carbolic soap and antiseptic.

A nurse stopped and put a hand on the brow of the soldier in the bed, smiling at the man who sat beside him. She was decently dressed in a neat grey gown over which she wore a huge white apron. Her hair was confined in a white cap and she reminded the soldier of a capable nanny he had had as a child. There were a dozen or more just like her, moving from bed to bed; others were scrubbing floors, up to their elbows in buckets of lye-soap as they patiently attempted to keep at bay the cholera, the typhus, the dysentery and the half a dozen other diseases which were killing more men than had been cut down in battle.

The war with Russia was almost over. Sebastopol had finally fallen but out of the 405,000 men committed to the Crimean War by the British and the French, almost 26,000 were killed on the field and a staggering 39,000 from disease.

'Does your wound need dressing again, Mr Greenwood?' the nurse said gently to the man by the bed.

'No thank you, nurse. It's almost healed now. You have been most kind.'

'You really should go back to your lodgings, you know. Your brother is in good hands and should there be any change I will send an orderly for you.'

'I would be most grateful if I might be allowed to stay for a while longer. We were ... are ... very

330

close and if he should ... Well, we are twins, you see.'

'Yes, that is very evident, Mr Greenwood.' The nurse smiled and hesitated, her kind eyes studying the thin, paper-white face of the young man by the bed, then the flushed and hectic one on the pillow. 'Very well, a few more minutes, but the surgeon will be here soon and ...' She hesitated again as though weighing her words before speaking. 'I ... well, I'm sure you are aware of the seriousness of your brother's condition.'

'Yes.'

'The stump has not healed and is ... I'm so sorry, Mr Greenwood, but I'm afraid the gangrene has taken a firm hold and the surgeon is certain we will have to ... cut again.'

The young man bowed his head, no immediate expression of any sort crossing his young/old face and the nurse felt an urge to put out a hand to him for he was no more than a boy. He raised his head and smiled as though he was trying to spare her pain and she felt a hint of the charm he must once have possessed in another world than this, shine through to please her woman's heart.

'Yes, I understand, nurse. I will remain, if I may, until the surgeon has been.'

The soldier on the bed began to fling his arms about and his hands clawed desperately at his face. His head moved frantically from side to side on his sweat-stained pillow.

'Get them off me ... Sweet Christ, I can't breathe ... please, oh, please ... I can't breathe ... heavy ... get them off me ... Jesus, oh, Jesus ... It's the mill all over again, the bloody mill ... suffocating ... I won't go in again, Charlie, I swear it . . .'

His voice ended on a despairing scream and the nurse looked about her hurriedly, for the morphine with which he was drugged was evidently wearing off and some more must be administered by the doctor.

'And you shan't, old fellow, you shan't. Do you think I would let them take you in there again, knowing how you hate it?' The young man's voice was soft and filled with love. The soldier calmed somewhat as his brother's hand smoothed his hair back from his fevered brow and his eyes, almost submerged in the swollen flesh about them, opened a little.

'Brother . . .' He managed the semblance of a smile.

'I'm here, lad, I'm here.'

'I was having one of those damnable nightmares.' His expression was apologetic.

'I know.'

'I'm . . . glad you're here . . .'

'You can't get rid of me, lad. The proverbial bad penny . . .'

'I'd . . . I'd have liked to see her again.'

'You will, old chap, just as soon as we get you on your feet.'

'You'll make sure she knows I love her.'

'You'll tell her yourself . . .' But the soldier's vivid blue eyes had become unfocused again and the brightness of delirium had returned as his voice rambled on about the loveliness of the golden bracken and the swiftness of his bay which would take him to her. He did not want to spend his life in that accursed weaving shed, he declared irritably, when there were so many other more pleasurable

332

things to do. The fox . . . it was away . . .

He was drowsy now as the drug administered by the doctor took effect and it was only then that the man beside him broke down. What fools life made of us, was his agonised thought, when his brother's life could now be measured only in hours.

*　　*　　*

It was to Annie that Tessa first spoke of Will Broadbent.

'What of Will?' she asked carelessly. 'Does he still call on you?'

'Aye, whenever 'e can.'

'And is he well?'

'Champion.' And nowt to do with you, her manner said but Tessa was never one to be put out by Annie's close-mouthed asperity.

'Is he . . . did he become manager? There was talk of it the last time we met.'

'No.'

'*No?* Then who got the job? And why didn't he?'

'It weren't for 'im, 'e said. 'E were after summat else an' so 'e 'opped it.'

'''Opped it? Whatever does that mean, for God's sake?'

'Look, my girl, I don't press you ter tell me what came o' that chap you was to wed and then never, so don't you go pokin' yer nose in Will Broadbent's business. It's nowt ter do wi' you.'

'Annie . . . Dear God, don't . . .'

Instantly Annie was sorry. She had not meant to be so unkind. Had she not been aware that though Tessa had spoken not one word about the surprising disappearance of the man she was to marry, his going had devastated her? She had been ill and Annie had made enquiries about her and had even sent a note but she had received no reply. Not that that concerned her but she had never quite forgiven Tessa for her indifference to Will Broadbent last year. Now here she was asking casual questions just as though he had been no more than an acquaintance.

' 'E's gone.' Her manner was short, since, like affection, humility was hard to demonstrate.

'Really, Annie, if you don't stop this ... this foolishness I swear I'll throttle you. Can you not just answer a simple question with a simple answer instead of all this evasiveness?'

'I don't reckon I know what that means but 'e's gone an' I were told yer Mam an' Mr Greenwood were right upset when 'e went. 'E's an 'ead on 'is shoulders 'as Will and Mr Greenwood told 'im so 'an all.'

For some unaccountable reason Tessa felt her heart begin to thud in her chest and she was reluctant to let Annie see the awkward and stiff set of her shoulders. She stood up and moved to the window, staring out into Annie's scrap of garden.

'What is he doing then?'

' 'E's gone up Rochdale way. 'E's brought the Chadwick spinners and weavers together to form a co-operative and run their own industrial enterprise. Will set up a committee, apparently with 'imself as chairman. They've found t'capital, Will said, by selling shares at five pounds each an' all't shares were sold within't week.' Annie spoke with the care of a child who repeats some passage she has learned by heart but does not really understand.

'They bought some land at a penny a yard, close to't railway where there's a siding an't mill were built an' in business in six months. There's 400 looms fer weavin' and 20,000 spindles fer spinnin'. Will ses that at the first 'alf-yearly meetin' of't company an' the 450 shareholders, they'd already med a decent profit an' look set fer a prosperous future. Will's managin' director an' the last time chap what I were talkin' to saw 'im he were ridin' in a carriage wi' a pretty woman at side of 'im. Whether it were 'is carriage or 'ers I couldn't tell thi. Now then, did y'ever think ter see't day when a pauper's brat, fer that were what he was, could rise ter such heights? Mind, he were a good tackler, were Will. 'E knew engines an' e' knew cotton from't minute it come from't bale right through t't piece goods. An' 'e were fair wi' people. Now it seems as 'ow 'e's got a feel fer business an' all.'

Annie turned triumphantly to Tessa as though to say, 'There, see what can be done with what you considered a mere working-class man not fit for the likes of you,' but Tessa was staring out of the window, her mind far away, scarcely listening and Annie sighed heavily.

Later Tessa rode down the long slope from Badger's Edge to Crossfold. The sun was red as it sank over the Pennine hills. There was a great stillness in the air, as there was in her heart and she wondered about it: was it a sadness about what might have been, or was it indifference to what had been?

She could hear a dog bark at the back of the house as she rode towards it and some bird singing in praise of the beauty of the autumn day. For a moment in the poignancy which drifted like

335

cobwebs about her, through which, if she was not vigilant, she might have to fight her way, she let Will's face etch itself sharply on her mind. A strong face and arrogant. Not with the arrogance of Drew and Pearce Greenwood nor of Nicky Longworth who all considered themselves to be somewhat above the rest of mankind, but with the sureness of a man who knows his own strength and what he will do with it. Not a handsome face. Vulnerable at times in his love for her since she admitted now that he had loved her. Smoky brown eyes flecked sometimes with green and at others with amber. Curling hair, ordinary, cut short to his head so as not to cause him any trouble. A slanting, humorous smile to his curving mouth, a sardonic twist to it, a lifting of his heavy eyebrows, a smooth and freshly shaved brown cheek.

Will Broadbent, then. A man she had admired and in a physical sense of the word, loved. A dependable man, truthful, sensuous, gentle, all these words described him and once, years ago it seemed, all this had belonged to her. She had turned away from him, chasing a dream of her own, careless of his hurt and the days which would be so empty for him without her. There were other women in the world for him to love, she had told herself as she had wound herself into Robby Atherton's arms, and now he had found one. What was so bewildering was the hard knot of something in the middle of her chest which she could not identify and which would not go away.

336

CHAPTER EIGHTEEN

The tall, extremely thin young gentleman had changed trains at Manchester and Oldham on his long journey from London. His bearing was very evidently that of an army man though surprisingly, since he *was* a gentleman, he was not an officer. He was dressed in a motley collection of clothing: the peaked cap of a soldier of the line with the greatcoat of a foot guardsman. His boots were of the Household Cavalry but they were unpolished. There was an air about him of indifferent disregard for his appearance as though that morning he had taken the first garments to hand, whatever they may have been, and flung them on his uncaring body.

He got off the train at Crossfold and walked slowly along the platform. The station clock was five minutes fast, for every village and town in Britain kept its own time, several minutes before or after that in London, and idly he wondered why.

The journey had been comfortable. Despite his extreme shabbiness he had travelled first class in a coach which was based on the style of the old stage coach. Through his inertia he had felt a slight pang of pity for those who had travelled third class for the weather was wet and extremely cold. The poor devils had sat in waggons which, unlike some which had sides and seats, were open to the elements and any stray spark from the engine was a definite threat. Passing through tunnels which poured down floods of dirty water, they must have arrived so wet, bedraggled, and begrimed it was a marvel to him they travelled at all.

The station was almost deserted. A trolley heaped with trunks and boxes indicated that someone of importance had arrived while another was piled with milk churns which a porter was trundling briskly towards the goods van. The gas lights had been lit for it was almost dusk. Soon spring would be here but this March day reminded him of the winter he had spent—was it only a year ago—on the harsh Crimean plains with . . .

His face moved jerkily and his hand was seen to reach out as though to some unseen companion but he continued his slow and steady pace towards the ticket collector. He handed the man his ticket and briefly their eyes met. The man had seen a hundred such as he in the past six months, dragging themselves back from the Crimea, many worse than he with no coats to their backs, no boots to their feet, no feet, unemployable and bitter. This one, however, he knew personally. Well, not personally, but who in the Penfold Valley was not familiar with the Greenwood brothers? Those blue eyes which were said to have dazzled and charmed the ladies from here to Burnley, were not so bright now, not so insolent as once they had been.

'Mr Greenwood, sir,' he said respectfully, for they were all aware that these two lads had fought for Queen and country and were to be recognised for their bravery.

Two lads? Then where was the other? He stared after Mr Greenwood's retreating back, arrow-straight and with not so much meat as it had once carried, and wondered which one it was who had been left behind. Not that it mattered really, for there had not been much to choose between them

338

for devilment.

It was dark when the hansom cab he had hired reached Greenacres, the early dark of a dismal March day. As he stepped from the cab he could smell the rich, damp earth and the faint aroma of daffodils. Daffodils have no perfume, he thought wonderingly, and perhaps it was his imagination but he knew he could smell them just as clearly as he could see them in his mind's eye, bobbing and dancing merrily in the wind which whipped straight down from the bleak moorland.

Light streamed from every window of the house, lying in bands across the garden: lamps lit in rooms in which no one would sit, fires glowing where no one would linger. So it had always been since he was a child and before, he supposed, in this household where once there had been no mistress to supervise what the servants did and so they had done what their previous mistress had told them. There was comfort and warmth, always, and an abundance of good, splendidly prepared and cooked food which the servants ate too, naturally, and he pondered on it for the first time in his life.

The great oak door opened when he rang the bell and Briggs was there, his face smooth and expressionless, though it was certain that in his mind was the disapproving thought that it could be no gentleman calling, unannounced, at this time of the evening.

His jaw dropped and he put a hand to his own heart and for a moment there was a warmth in his eyes, almost, one might say, a hint of moisture.

'Sir . . . oh, sir . . .' he gabbled, ready to move forward, to grasp the young gentleman's hand. Then he remembered himself. He straightened and

339

stepped back, his duties recalled but the gladness still gleamed in his eye.

'Welcome home, sir. It is indeed a pleasure to have you home.'

'Thank you, Briggs. It is good to be home.'

The butler waited for a moment, holding the door wide open as the young gentleman stepped inside, smiling, looking beyond him to the porch, the beginning of bewilderment on his face as the hansom disappeared into the darkness of the drive.

'Master ...? Er ... you are alone, sir?' he ventured, slowly closing the door on the cold and windy darkness, reaching out to his young master, eager to take the shabby army greatcoat from him, to relieve him of the quite battered cap and his one piece of pitiful hand luggage. Beneath the greatcoat he wore the torn and mouldering battle-dress, once a brilliant scarlet, with one epaulette missing, of a common soldier of the line.

In Briggs' eye flashed the picture of the last time he had seen Joss Greenwood's sons, immaculately dressed then in expensively tailored coats and breeches, fine cambric shirts and peacock, watered-silk waistcoats, with boots as superbly polished as the tall bays they rode. Their faces had been dark and dashing, excited by something known only to them, laughing, heedless and reckless as they galloped off madly down the drive intent on some mischief, he had thought sourly.

And in the two years they had been away something dreadful had happened to them. Here was Master Drew—or was it Pearce?—looking as though he had had the stuffing well and truly knocked out of him, and where was Master Pearce, or was it Drew?

340

'Is my aunt at home, Briggs?'

'Indeed, sir. She and the family are at dinner.' He was about to ask should he announce him, for really he was a stranger but this was his home and he was at liberty to go where he pleased.

His master swayed slightly and Briggs put out his hand solicitously.

'Miss . . . Miss Tessa . . .?' he whispered so softly Briggs could barely hear him.

'Indeed, sir.'

Master Drew—or was it Pearce for heaven's sake? He must ask him, Briggs thought irritably—continued to stand in the middle of the hall, quite incapable, Briggs thought, or so it appeared, of deciding whether to go or stay.

'Are you unwell, sir?' he asked, wondering whether to offer his master a seat.

'Miss Tessa, you said . . .?'

'Yes, sir.'

'And her . . . is she alone?'

'Alone, sir? I'm afraid I don't understand.' Dear God, surely he had not been . . . well, damaged in his head? He seemed quite dazed, and yet so quiet no one could be afraid of him.

'Has her . . . is her . . .?'

'Yes, sir?'

'Is her husband with her?'

'Husband?' Briggs' mouth fell open. 'Why, sir, Miss Tessa has no husband . . . Dear me, what made you . . .?' Then he stopped for it was not his place to question the son of the house on his obviously confused state of mind.

The young master began to walk unsteadily across the hall. 'I'll go in then, Briggs.'

'Very well, Master . . . er . . . I'll fetch Dorcas

out, sir, for you and ... you'll want to greet your ...'

They all stood up, pushing back their chairs quite violently. Dorcas sketched a frantic curtsey as she passed him in the open doorway, her own face wet with sudden tears. Then Briggs closed the door quietly behind him as he always did.

There was complete silence for the space of ten seconds, though it seemed longer, then Tessa's voice murmured something in a hushed whisper. It was not clear what she said, even to herself, for it had been no more than a devastated recognition, a wailing cry of torment deep inside her at the realisation that whereas two of her beloved cousins had gone to war, only one had come back.

'Charlie ... Aunt Jenny ...' He stood, like a small whipped boy, not awfully sure what he should do to get himself across the vast expanse of carpet to the comfort he so desperately needed, the haven from the pain, the hoped-for refuge in which to hide whilst he attempted the healing of the part of him which had been torn away at the hospital in Scutari.

'Oh, dear, sweet Lord ...' Charlie began to walk towards him and Laurel sat down again abruptly, her eyes enormous and glittering in her ashen face. His Aunt Jenny put her hand to her mouth and for the first time in his life—another first, he thought dully—he saw her weep. She seemed to be incapable of movement, standing beside the table in her elegant silk gown, crucified, it seemed to him, by some dreadful emotion which surely could not have been aroused merely by his homecoming.

'Oh, my sweet boy ...' he heard her say, amazingly, then he saw nothing else, felt nothing else but the strong, steady, infinitely loving, endlessly compassionate arms of Tessa Harrison as she put them around him, enfolding him in the first scrap of peace he had known since his brother had died in his arms. His own arms were about her, clutching desperately, for surely the strength which had held him upright from Scutari to this moment was about to slip away, finally, and only she could keep him on his feet.

'Tessa ... Tessa ... Tessa ...' he said over and over again, his face buried in her shoulder, the soft, sweet-smelling curve of her neck, her gown already wet with his agonised tears.

'Sit down. For Christ's sake, sit him down,' Charlie was saying harshly, his own arms ready to support him should Tessa's prove inadequate.

'Darling, come ... let me hold you ...' He felt her turn for a moment, frantically, to Charlie who hovered beside them, bidding him open the door ... the morning room ... more comfortable ... more coal on the fire ... hot coffee ... Then he was in the depth of the soft sofa, the fire warm on his bare feet—he had no socks, of course, but where had his boots gone?—and her arms were still about him, her shoulder there for him to lean on. His aunt's hand, steadier now, was holding a cup of something hot and delicious to his lips, while Laurel ... and Charlie ... were weeping and all the time he shook like the trembling aspens which lined the lake. He must pull himself together, regain his composure for at least as long as it would take to tell them of what had happened, and suffer again that frozen state of senseless, unfeeling shock he had known for the past eight weeks and in which he could endure the telling.

343

Then, and only then, would he let it all wash over him, re-live it, fall into the nightmare which, when it was told, would surely once and for all be done with.

'Darling, can you speak of it now?' Tessa said, her lovely grey eyes as soft and shadowed as the drifting veil of the mist which so often covered Friar's Mere. There was a lingering desolation in the expression on her face, as if she knew what he was to tell her and was not certain she would ever recover from it, but it must be said. 'We are not sure . . .' Her voice was but a whisper. She looked up swiftly at her mother, not smiling for that would be impossible now, but with a memory of the past when Drew and Pearce Greenwood had played boyish pranks, changing places as easily as two coins from the same mint. They had relished the confusion, or sometimes the lack of it for quite often no one was aware that a trick had been played.

So, who was this in her arms? Which loved man? No matter which one, she would mourn the other until her dying day.

'Which . . . who . . . ?' Her voice cracked with the depth of her sorrow.

'Pearce died in the hospital at Scutari.'

It was said and she could not bear it, and neither could he.

They sat for almost an hour with their arms about one another, saying nothing. On the other side of the fireplace Jenny Harrison sat in a low, velvet, button-back chair, a ladies' chair in a ladies' room, and watched them compassionately. Charlie had his arms about Laurel who was weeping as though her heart was broken. The morning-room

344

had long been a family room, less formal than the drawing-room where guests were received, and it seemed appropriate now that the family should begin their grief here. The room had a lived-in air, homely and slightly untidy with books lying about, today's newspapers crumpled on a low table, sheet music standing open on the piano, playing cards in a box, not opened since Pearce and Drew went away. It was here that Drew Greenwood began to feel the emptiness, the dead and sterile shell which had been left when Pearce died, begin to fill with what he knew would be his own agony. He must speak of it before the pain became too much for him.

'We were in the last bombardment of Sebastopol,' he said simply, staring into the fire, his eyes far, far away on the barren plain which they had come to know so well. 'What a lark, we thought, on that first day. What fun to be there, amidst the excitement and adventure, away from the mills and the deadly boredom of the hours we spent in them,' and away from you whom we both loved, Tessa Harrison, though he could not say it, of course. 'We couldn't wait to leap on our mounts and follow the soldiers, the cavalry, to fight in the glorious battle we were convinced it would be.'

He paused, capturing that unbelievable, almost forgotten, carefree youthfulness. 'We lost our horses on that very first day. Do you remember them, Tessa? Such lovely animals who had not been trained for ... They were terrified ... We killed them, Pearce and I, just as surely as if we had put a revolver to their heads. It would have been more humane if we had done so. Mine got a sabre thrust in his belly ... he was screaming. I don't know what

345

happened to Pearce's: I didn't ask. You got like that, you know. You never asked anyone what had happened to them. At the end of the day you simply slipped into your tent and if the next time you were mustered there was a face missing, a dozen faces you had known the day before, you didn't ask.'

'No . . .' Tessa's hand soothed his forehead.

'I saw Lord Raglan once, you know.' His voice was soft, his thoughts not marshalled into any particular order, just uttered as they came into his head.

'Did you, darling?'

'We were always wet. For months we were wet. In the trenches . . .'

'Why were you in the trenches, Drew? You were not soldiers.'

'No . . . I don't remember now.' He passed his hand over his face as though in a dream. How could he tell them the reason he and Pearce could not come home? How could he tell them the reason they went in the first place? 'It was . . . there was nothing else to do. They thought we were soldiers so they fed us what there was.' He looked down at the odds and ends of his uniform. 'We lost all our clothing . . . a shell, and the dead have no use of . . . what they wore. Those boots belonged to an officer. I did him a kindness so . . . as he lay dying he said I must have them. A decent fellow. From Norfolk I believe.'

'And then . . . Pearce . . . ?'

'Yes. Well, we survived two years almost though thousands and thousands didn't and then . . . there was to be an attack on the Redan. There were 12,000 men there to defend it, we were told and we were to send only 4,000 stormers and supporters. If it had been . . . different, we might have laughed. A handful of men expected to take and hold an open work defended by thirty-two battalions of Russian infantry! But we did it . . . we did it. The Light Division and the 2nd Division. We got in but instead of storming on after the retreating Russians we were ordered to extend on the parapets and begin to fire . . .'

His voice tailed away as in his memory he re-lived that fatal day, that fatal hour, that fatal order which had, finally, cost his brother his life.

'They came back at us. They pressed us closer and closer. We ran out of ammunition and were forced to throw stones . . . stones against bullets and shell and sabre and bayonet . . .'

There was a long and dreadful silence as the five people in the pleasant room observed quite clearly the pictures one of them had conjured up.

'We were forced over the parapet and into a ditch, every one of us who was left. Those who could, scrambled up, running the gauntlet of fire, of grape and musketry. The Russians were cheering, manning the parapets which we had just left, firing into the chaos of bleeding, falling soldiers, into the heaps of our men who lay in the ditches unable to crawl out. They even brought up two field-pieces and . . .'

Again he fell silent, his mind beginning to close instinctively against the pain of what came next, knowing he must tell it, but not sure that he could finish.

'Leave it, Drew. Let it rest now. Let us get you to bed . . .'

'I felt a blow to my arm. I thought . . . I didn't

347

know I'd been hit until I fell. There were dozens of us there . . . one on top of the other, dead and wounded. Pearce was shouting that we should make a run for it but something pinned me down. I didn't seem able to extricate myself though I felt no pain. I didn't know I'd been hit, you see. "Come on, brother," he shouted again. "Don't just lie there or must I carry you, you lazy devil." He was grinning, you know how . . . he was. He had bent down, ready to heave me to my feet when the shell hit the . . . a dozen yards away. He caught the full blast . . . his legs . . . were . . .'

'Oh, God, oh, dear God . . .' Was it Tessa or her mother who cried out?

'When I came to I couldn't find him. I went crazy, I think. My arm . . . my arm was . . . I don't know . . . bloody and . . . somebody held me down while they dressed it. Then I ran from man to man . . . hundreds of them lying on the bare ground. It was a lovely day . . . autumn. The sun shone on them . . . Dear God . . . I found him two days later. They were about to put him on a ship for Scutari. His . . . feet . . . please, Tessa, hold on to me . . . his feet were gone, both of them, and . . .'

'Drew . . . oh, Drew . . . please, I cannot bear it . . .'

' . . . so I went with him. I stayed with him on the hospital ship but . . . the surgeons tried . . . he would not heal . . . the gangrene had . . .'

Tessa wept blindly, clinging to him now, tortured by the picture of handsome, dashing Pearce Greenwood brought down to the pitiful agonised creature, dying by inches in a foreign land with no one but his brother to care what happened to him. And yet, who else would he have chosen, had he had the choice, but this man who was part of him, who had shared the same womb, the same cradle, the same rip-roaring childhood and reckless youth? This brother he had loved and who had loved and comforted his pain until the end.

'He died in November. It took him two months. They kept . . . taking off a bit more. But I was with him, he was in my arms when he went.'

His voice was spent, his head drooping, his face quite blank, empty of pain, of regret, of everything but the need to fall, for the moment, into oblivion.

'What have you been doing since then, lad?' Charlie's voice was neutral as though he was holding himself, and Drew with him, by a tight and tenuous thread to the world of reality, to this world in which they now were and in which they must spend the rest of their days without Pearce Greenwood.

'Nothing much, really. We buried him . . . the nurses were kind. They came to his funeral. Then I stayed on. I could not bear to leave him, you see, by himself in that land which had killed him. I helped in the hospital . . .'

'Why did you not write?'

'I wanted to tell you myself . . . about him.'

'We were so anxious. Your mother was . . . and your father tried to find out what had happened to you . . .'

'Did he? How strange.'

'Why do you say that? You are his . . . were . . . his sons . . .'

'He took no great interest when we were here.' It was said with no rancour, just a great and engulfing weariness. He sighed, his face grey like the ash in the fireplace, his eyes deep in liver-

349

coloured hollows.

*   *   *

She heard him screaming from his room along the corridor. She had fallen into a light, haunted doze, the night almost gone, exhaustion and grief overtaking her at last, and when the sound began she sat up in bed with her heart pounding, disorientated, with the tail end of the dream she had been in still lingering in her frightened mind.

They had been up on Badger's Edge, the three of them, sharing the easy laughter which was part of their companionship. The horses had cropped the grass close by, their reins dangling and the dogs sprawled about them, dozing with their muzzles resting on their paws. How lovely it all was, she had been thinking, as Pearce's eyes, as blue and brilliant as the turquoise in the necklace her aunt wore, smiled into hers, when the sky, the great familiar vault which had hung over them all their lives in every colour from the palest oyster to the deepest purple, simply erupted, emptying hundreds of bodies from its glorious arch, pouring them down upon their heads, flinging them willy-nilly about the plateau until they were heaped in great obscene piles. Heads and limbs were twisted in unnatural angles from their torsos, flaccid and writhing, and from beneath them, sticking up into the soft summer air, was one living hand. It clenched and twisted, begging to be let free and she could hear his voice ... Pearce's or was it Drew's, from somewhere beneath ... Pearce ... ?

Oh, God! Oh, dear God. It *was* Drew and his voice was becoming more shrill with every passing
350

second.

She bumped into her mother on the landing. The night was as black as pitch, no light filtering through the heavy curtains which shrouded each window. Briggs, as was his duty last thing at night, had extinguished every lamp and the corridor was like a long, dark tunnel. There had been no thought in her mind of lighting the candle at her bedside nor any of the lamps which stood about her bedroom, since her instinct had been to get to him as quickly as she could, to extricate him from the mass of corpses which were slowly burying him alive and under which his mind was slipping into madness.

How did she know? *How did she know?*

There were tables along the passage, each with its own lamp, and after crashing into her mother, no more than a pale, shapeless shadow against the open doorway of her own bedroom, her hip caught one, sending it in a spray of splintered glass to the floor.

'Sweet Jesus,' she heard her mother gasp and from some dark place above them came the sound of quavering female voices asking what was to do and a deeper one, male, ordering them to be quiet and get back to their beds where they belonged.

He was still asleep when they stood over him, she and her mother, his mouth a blacker hole in the blackness in which he lay. He was clawing at his bedclothes, his hands tearing and twisting, his arms pushing at something, his head moving frantically from side to side as he gasped for air. The screaming had subsided to a low, frantic moaning and when her mother lit the lamp at his bedside his eyes flew open and stared up into the flickering

351

shadows the light cast on the ceiling. He became perfectly still, not even breathing for a moment, then his head turned slowly on the pillow, so slowly and carefully it was as though he was desperately afraid of what he might see.

Tessa knelt down beside him and put a hand on his cheek, stroking it, brushing back his sweat-drenched hair, making small noises in her throat, the noises all mothers make to frightened children, saying nothing which made much sense, but soothing him with the sounds, calming him.

'Tessa, oh Tessa ...' His breath shuddered violently in his throat.

'Yes, darling, I'm here.'

'I was ...'

'I know ...' With delicate tenderness she put her arms under his head and drew him towards her, cradling him against her with a little sigh. She put her lips gently to his brow and he lifted his own arms and clung to her, his face in the soft, sweet-smelling division between her breasts, her hair falling about him like a protective shield. She felt his stiff body fall slowly into peace and his breath drift from his mouth against the curve of her breast. He was thin, frail, and his bones felt brittle beneath her hands. Her heart was squeezed with love and pity and on her face was a look her mother had never seen before.

She watched them for a moment, Jenny Harrison, then, making a decision which even then she was not sure was right, turned and walked from the room, closing the door behind her.

CHAPTER NINETEEN

Laurel watched them anxiously as they walked hand in hand from the terrace and down the smooth sweep of lawn which led through a series of terraces, flower beds and smoothly clipped box-hedges; beyond the massed rhododendrons and ornamental rose beds to the rougher grass which surrounded the lake. Her face was creased with doubt and in her eyes was an expression of unease.

'Really, Aunt Jenny, do you not think it is time Tessa put away those extraordinary garments she insists on wearing and dressed in a manner more suitable to her station in life? I had hoped she might be going to do so recently but since Drew returned she is as improperly dressed as ever. She is nineteen now and surely too old for such things.'

She stood at the window of the morning room. It was Sunday and breakfast, a leisurely affair on this one day of the week when the mills were closed, was almost over. She would go up to the nursery floor soon to direct the activities of her nursemaids, of Nanny who was in charge of baby Joel, of Henry and Jane, of the governess Miss Gaunt who gave lessons to six-year-old Robert and five-year-old Anne, of Miss Copeland who had been her own governess, and Tessa's, and still helped out in the schoolroom. Miss Copeland was over sixty now but still very useful in her own supervision of the young woman who had come to take her place and Laurel would not have dreamed of pensioning her off to some cottage on the estate. Anyone who was able to perform some task which would leave Laurel

353

with more freedom for her many social obligations would always be found a place in her household.

'What were you saying, dear?' Charlie was deep in yesterday's newspapers and did not even look up. He was well accustomed to his wife's anxiety over almost everything her cousin did, or said, and was once again reminded of the deepseated and strange feeling of insecurity she had unconsciously acquired as a child. It made him gentle with his wife, perhaps more indulgent than he might otherwise have been. He held her in considerable affection, a protective and obligatory affection which had never faltered. He made love to her when she would allow it, not often for she had conceived six times in nine years, bearing five live children, and she wanted no more. He knew she did her best, running this house and her children with efficiency and a certain good humour; this was what she wanted and was a way of life she understood. But, and he knew he must be honest about it, she was somewhat jealous of Tessa Harrison, and it soured her life.

'I was remarking to Aunt Jenny that it was time Tessa grew out of the notion that she is a boy and not a young woman and gave up wearing those ridiculous breeches. Will you look at her . . .'

They made a stunning couple, there was no doubt about it but Charlie could see what it was that made his wife so uneasy. Tessa simply drew every male eye to her wherever she went. She had become a gloriously sensuous woman, there was no other description for her, and yet she was still no more than an innocent girl. Where did she get that flaunting, outrageous, and fascinating—and Charlie was aware that there was not a man who

354

came within a hundred yards of her who was not fascinated—magnetism? He drew in his breath sharply, then looked away, not wishing his wife to see him admiring such splendour. He caught his sister's eye and grimaced, aware, awkwardly, that she knew exactly what was in his mind. She did not blame him for it since, though he was Tessa's uncle, he was still a man.

'She does no harm, Laurel,' Jenny said mildly, folding her own newspaper and standing up to move towards them. 'You must admit she has done wonders with Drew in the last three months.'

'But everyone is talking about them.'

'I can't see why. They have done nothing they have not been doing all their lives.'

'But alone. Just the two of them.'

'What are you suggesting?' Jenny's voice had become cool.

'I am suggesting nothing, Aunt Jenny, I am only repeating what has been implied to me in every drawing-room in Crossfold. They are never apart. He clings to her hand wherever they go for everyone to see and she makes no objection.'

'He is her cousin. His brother died in harrowing circumstances. He is only just beginning to recover. And who else would he turn to but Tessa? She is the closest to him after Pearce.'

'Oh, I know all that, but I must say I find it extremely embarrassing having to listen to my friends, not in so many words, naturally, for they are ladies, but intimating nevertheless that there is more to it than cousinly affection.'

'Fiddlesticks.' Turning on her heel Jenny swept from the room but not before Charlie had seen the uncertain expression on his sister's face.

'And shouldn't he be back at the mill by now?' Laurel continued, allowing her voice to rise plaintively now that there was only her husband to hear it.

'He'll go back when he's ready.'

'Heavens, he's been home three months already. How much longer is he going to lark about like the young squire?'

'He needs time, Laurel. You know how close he was to Pearce.' Charlie tried to be patient, realising that Tessa, and now Drew, threatened Laurel's security in some curious way which was not even clear to herself.

'I think he is making it an excuse not to go back to the mill.' Charlie thought so too, but with far more understanding than Laurel since he had seen his nephew's distaste for the work they had been expected to do there. Neither of them had been true 'commercial men' as he and Jenny were, and he tried to imagine how he would feel if he was forced to work at something he loathed. But then hundreds and thousands did so for it was that or starve and not many were as privileged as Drew Greenwood.

Drew had changed quite dramatically from the pale, devastatingly thin and hollow-eyed shadow he had been on his return. As handsome and strong as ever, his old audacity showed in the brilliance of his vivid blue eyes when he and Tessa rode to the top of Badger's Edge, the ghost of Pearce Greenwood always at their shoulders, to look out on the lovely stretch of summer moorland which swept down to the busy valley, the chimneys of the growing town. It showed in his eagerness to do what he, his brother and Tessa had always done: in their search

356

for anything which might erase the memory of the past two years. But only with her. She was his 'partner', a 'steadier' to the other self Pearce had taken away from him. For three months no one had spoken of the past, nor of the future, knowing his loss and suffering, allowing him to do as he pleased, what best suited him, what best mended him.

Tessa protected him fiercely. He was not to be pressed to resume his duties in the mill, she commanded. Indeed, no one was to mention the mill. They rode out when and where they pleased as the weather improved. He had quickly recovered his boundless health and the humorous, engaging charm he had shared with his brother. Country life, country pursuits that had nothing to do with warp and weft, with yardage and quality, with frames and looms, boilers and steam engines, these were what he sought. He had not survived the hell of the Crimea to spend his days in the hell of his family's mill, his manner said, though he did not voice such an opinion out loud, and no force, no coercion was put on him to do so.

The peace treaty with Russia had been signed at the end of March and guns were fired in all major towns of Lancashire to signal the end of the hostilities. The armies of the Allies were to return to their own countries as soon as possible, they were told, and there was to be great rejoicing and fireworks on an enormous scale in London.

A naval review by Her Majesty the Queen at Spithead, one of the finest sights the country had ever witnessed, those who saw it reported, showed exactly what England could do in times of war. The fleet was so large it extended for several miles

357

across the Channel and people travelled on the new and exciting railway trains from all parts of the country to see it.

It was not until the end of May that a day was appointed as a national holiday to celebrate this new thing called peace. Hardly before the day had started the guns were booming from Oldham barracks and in every church tower bells rang, fit to wake the dead, Briggs remarked gloomily, and what was the point of it when the war had been over since September? There was to be a celebratory procession with bands and flags, banners and mayoral speeches and Tessa spoke to Charlie on the advisability of risking Drew in the intense fever of patriotic joy which would undoubtedly abound there.

'I don't know if he'll be up to it, Charlie. All the hurly-burly, the noise and confusion, all those people celebrating what was to him ... well, you will know what I mean. The memories ...'

'You can't go on cosseting him forever, lass. You know, you're like a mother cat protecting her kitten whenever anyone threatens his peace of mind. He's bound to think of Pearce, as we all will, but sooner or later, preferably sooner, he must rejoin the world. You and he spend all your time up on the tops, playing with those thoroughbreds of yours in the paddock and racing that curricle you've acquired. Just the two of you, lass, and it really won't do. He's a man and must mix with other men, do what they do. These months have been good for him and have returned him to full health but he needs other things now. All men do, Tessa.' His voice became very quiet. 'And no matter how you both refuse to face it, one day he must return to the

358

mill. It will all belong to him, and when the time comes he must be able to run it alone. With Pearce gone he has no choice but to learn how to go about it.'

'Charlie . . .' Tessa's face was soft with pity.

'No, lass, he must face up to life again. Take him to the celebration. Put on your prettiest gown'— and let him see you as you are and not as a replacement for Pearce Greenwood, Charlie thought—'and go and have some fun. I'm sure the Squire's lad will be there.'

*   *   *

'Drew, my God, old chap, it's good to see you. We had heard you were back and have been looking forward to . . .' Nicky Longworth, with more sensitivity than Tessa would have given him credit for, said no more than that, pumping Drew's hand enthusiastically, terribly glad to claim him for a friend, for was he not something of a hero amongst those with whom he, and Pearce, had once roistered?

'And Tessa. How absolutely splendid you look, doesn't she, Johnny? Why have we not seen you both at the Hall? Why don't you come over . . .'

She held Drew's arm protectively, waiting for the sudden trembling to subside, and when it did and his face broke into a tentative but pleased smile, she relaxed her grip somewhat. His right hand, when it had been shaken by several more of the 'fellows' who had come over to see the fun, closed over her own where it rested in the crook of his left arm and he squeezed it gently to let her know he was all right.

359

And they did indeed look splendid, both of them. She wore blue, a lovely cornflower blue that was almost violet. Her jacket fitted neatly to the sweet curve of the bosom she had regained when her flesh returned after her illness, and her enormous skirt was looped about its wide hem with tiny bunches of silk cornflowers. Her bonnet was the same colour, decorated under its brim with masses of white tulle and her blue lace parasol shaded the grey velvet of her eyes.

Drew's face, in the sun-warmed breezes of the days spent in the saddle, had regained its brown smoothness. His dark curly hair was cut short, glossy and thick, tumbling across his wide forehead. His eyes narrowed in a deep and brilliant blue as he smiled at his friends and his mobile mouth curved across strong white teeth. He wore dove grey with a well-cut watered-silk waistcoat. His shirt front was snowy and his boots polished. He had removed his top hat and his tall frame was straight and yet easy, graceful. He looked quite beautiful, she thought proudly as she looked up at him, just as though it was all her doing, and in a way it was. She was the one who walked with him through the tortuous memories which harrowed him, who shored up and filled the gaping hole left by his brother's death, who held him in her arms in the black of the night when his cries brought her from her bed. She it was who had coaxed him to eat, to rest, to doze in the sunshine with his head in her lap, to get up on the new bay he bought and ride again as he had not done for two years. She had brought him back to this hesitant willingness to be a part of life again and she felt a most proud and proprietary self-esteem settle about her.

360

In the weeks they had been alone together, he talking, weeping, but speaking at last of what he and Pearce had seen in the battles they fought, she listening, weeping with him, he had finally asked her about Robby.

'When Pearce and I left ... you were to be married,' he said diffidently. Just that, nothing more. A few words which invited her to speak of it if she wished.

'Yes.'

'He ... you changed your mind?'

'I ... I was ill.' It was no lie and yet not the full truth. Her face was averted from him and she knew he could not see the expression of pain which flickered across it. Robby Atherton still lay uneasily in her heart. A hard and often despairing desolation struck at her when she least expected it. She loved him still: that was a fact of her life which would not change. How could it? Her mother had told her, from experience she said, that time would heal her, would lessen the ache in her heart, and during the last three months with Drew she had found a certain measure of content. His need had overridden hers. His pain had pushed hers to the back of her conscious mind, tamped it down to bearable proportions in her breast, not lessening it, as her mother said, but easing it somehow as she poured what Robby had left into her compassionate love for Drew. What a tortured pair they were, she and Drew Greenwood, she thought as she turned back to him, the sharing of their misery perhaps making it more bearable.

'I had a fever. I was ill ... off my head for weeks. You know about it, don't you?'

'Yes. Aunt Jenny told me.' His expression was

361

gentle, steady, with something in it which invited her to confide in him, if she wanted to, as he had done with her. They were friends as well as cousins, it said. He was not the young man he had been when he rode away, not yet, but he was more than willing to give her a hand to cling to, if she had nothing else. But somehow, despite his dearness, she could not tell him the whole truth.

'I was not myself. At times it seemed I was not to recover and he did not ... return.' Dear Robby, forgive me for the lie, she whispered in her heart, but it lay easily on her conscience for what else was she to say?

'When you were recovered, you did not let him know?'

'No.'

'Why not, if you wish to tell me?'

'I ... it seemed we were ... no longer suited.'

She looked up and smiled and was startled by the intent expression in his eyes as they stared into hers. A deep and concentrated watchfulness showed there and waited for her answer as though its meaning, the content of it was of the utmost importance.

'You love him still?'

Again there was that breathless attention to her words, a diligent alertness which placed a faint prickle of surprise in her. His eyes studied her minutely, blue, she had never seen them so blue, and he seemed to hold his breath. And she knew, suddenly, though she could not have said how she knew, that her answer was vital to him and for his peace of mind it must be the right answer.

'One must have a love returned for it to flourish, Drew,' she said softly, knowing as she said it that he

362

was satisfied.

They began to widen their activities. He took her to see a play at the assembly rooms in Crossfold, *Richard III* which was staged quite splendidly considering that it was not put on at an established theatre such as those in Oldham or Manchester. He was quite shaken by the press of his family's acquaintances who rushed to shake him by the hand, expressing their joy in seeing him 'himself' again, not mentioning Pearce, perhaps warned against it by the savage look on Tessa Harrison's face. She held fast to him like a tendril of clinging ivy, they noticed, those mamas whose daughters might, now that he was home and apparently settled down from the hellion he had once been, be pushed in his direction. Was there any truth in the rumours that circulated about them, the wondered to one another? True, they had always galloped wildly about the countryside ever since they had been children, but there had been three of them then, which made a difference, one must admit, from just one man and one woman! And they did seem completely wrapped up in one another since it was noticed that his eyes followed her every movement. Was Jenny Harrison keeping something from them, they asked one another. But the question was still unanswered.

Nicky Longworth remarked to Johnny Taylor as they discussed it over a bottle of his father's best claret that there really could have been nothing in the rumour that had circulated some time ago that Tessa Harrison and Robby Atherton were to be married. And if there had been shc'd damned soon recovered from it. Most women went into a decline when they were jilted but there was no sign of it

363

about Tessa. What a splendid creature she was and if she weren't so firmly attached to that lucky cousin of hers he wouldn't mind giving her a whirl himself.

*   *   *

At the start of the hunting season, when he had been home for six months, they rode over to Longworth Hall. She was dressed in the superb outfit which had been made for her by Miss Maymon and which had caused such a commotion last season, a magnificent study in black and white. But for the high swell of her breasts, she and her cousin might have been the two brothers, one of whom lay in his grave at Scutari.

She was instantly surrounded by admiring gentlemen the moment she put her booted and spurred foot to the ground and none of them noticed the ominous clenching of Drew Greenwood's jaw. She was breathless with laughter, swaggering amongst the men, one of them, it seemed, as she accepted a glass of punch. She was completely at home in their company, unaware, as indeed were they, of any gulf between them. She had been welcomed here, despite her commercial background, from an early age. She had dined, with her cousins, in the medieval great hall, had watched them play wild games, and even joined in on occasion, down the long gallery lined with ancestral Longworth portraits. She had danced with them at their last Christmas party before Drew and Pearce rode away and dreamed here in the arms of her love, before the great darkness had fallen in on her. Now, it was as though she had

364

come home.

'Tessa.'

His voice was like a whip, snapping about her and the group of laughing men. They all turned, their faces still wreathed in merriment, their eyes glowing with that particular look gentlemen bestow on a pretty woman, especially if she is as spirited as Tessa Harrison. He could see it in their eyes, that slight hint of coarseness only another man will recognise, a look of speculation as these boisterous and brash young gentlemen eyed the long and lovely body of his cousin.

'It's time we were mounted,' he said harshly. His voice sounded strange even to himself for he could not bear, simply could not bear her even to speak to these men who were clustered about her. He was eaten up with jealousy and had not the least idea how to cope with it. She must come to him, she must come at once, his arrogant manner said, or he honestly thought he might break down in some way. His legs which had so easily swung him on, and then off his new bay were rigid with the necessity of keeping himself upright. But at the same time he could feel that familiar snapping rage, that savage temper, the Greenwood temper, the Chapman temper, he had been told, that had been his mother's, begin to race through him. *She was his*. Tessa Harrison had belonged exclusively to Drew Greenwood for the past six months. She had folded herself in all but the physical sense about his wounded soul and body and had begun the process of healing within him.

She knew, of course. Though he said nothing more and they were all looking at him in amazement—for had not Drew Greenwood always been the most amiable of fellows, except in a fight?—she knew, and miraculously she put her glass in the nearest hand and came to him.

'I'm ready, cousin, if you are.'

That night, just as though the terror he had lived in for several minutes that day had awakened the sleeping beast of his nightmare, he screamed for her, calling her by name, urgently, though he still slept.

Jenny Harrison stood by the door of his bedroom watching the now familiar scene as Tessa rocked him against her breast. Laurel was at her back, and Charlie, and over Laurel's head their eyes met in understanding. Jenny closed the door quietly.

'You're not going to leave them there alone?' Laurel was aghast, genuinely shocked by her aunt's attitude towards something which was not at all proper. Both Drew and Tessa were in their nightclothes, almost lying together on the bed, and how could Jenny Harrison countenance such a thing, turn a blind eye to what was becoming a scandal in the Penfold Valley? It must be stopped, this gossip which was on everyone's lips and which might affect her own standing in the community. It must be put an end to, preferably, in Laurel's opinion, by sending Tessa to her own mother and father in Italy for a few months until it had died down, and returning Drew to the mill where he belonged. This attachment between her brother and her cousin had begun to frighten her as she recognised its potential for dislodging her from her present position as mistress of this house. One day, of course, Drew would marry, some shy, submissive sixteen-year-old who would be safely and easily

366

managed by someone as proficient as herself. But if she and Tessa, who was headstrong and wilful, were bound together in the running of Greenacres, how could Laurel possibly retain the control which had been hers for so many pleasant years?

'Well, you might be able to overlook such behaviour, Aunt Jenny, but I certainly cannot, not under my own roof with innocent children sleeping in their beds not a dozen yards away.'

With a crash she flung open the door, her hand which held the doorknob losing its grip so that the door hit the wall violently. A draught of air eddied in with her, lifting the lace curtains at the open window, whispering about the quiet room and making the flame of the candle dance and flicker, casting dreadful shadows on the ceiling and walls. Before Jenny could stop her, or even catch her breath to speak, Laurel strode into the room, her small figure casting a huge shadow.

Drew had begun to move slowly away from the horror of the bodies which clutched at his own, from the weight which he knew was his brother Pearce, his brother who had no feet, indeed no legs; away from the tortured screams of men and horses and into the warm, scented presence of the woman whom he knew would be there, ready to welcome him back. His breathing had slowed to a peaceful calm, his turbulent body becoming quiet, and he sighed thankfully. He did not awaken, merely moved from one level of sleep to another, from the nightmare into the state of dreamless peace she brought him.

He awoke to confusion: to wildly dancing shadows, huge and distorted, to harsh cries and angry voices. There were people struggling. He did

367

not know who they were in that first awareness and for a few moments he floundered, ready to call out to Pearce to come and give him a hand, or to Tessa to gather him into her arms; one of them, either would do, to be there for him, as there had always been someone. He struggled to sit up, to make some sense of it and he felt a calming hand on his shoulder, hers, and in that moment he knew what he must do to make himself complete again, secure again.

'What the devil's going on?' He was ready to leap from his bed though he had on only a nightshirt, and casting modesty to the wind he threw back the bedclothes and stood up. Charlie, incredibly, was struggling with Laurel who was beseeching his Aunt Jenny—dear God, it was like a bloody circus—to do something before the good name of the family was completely ruined. It would be best, really it would, she cried, if Tessa went to Italy—couldn't she see it?—and later, when Drew was settled in the mill, perhaps with some suitable young lady, Tessa could come back and . . .

'For God's sake, Mother, will you tell her to be quiet before I smack her silly face?' Tessa was furious. 'How dare she come in here with her vile insinuations, upsetting Drew . . .'

'I'm not upset,' he said and he meant it. For the first time since he and Pearce had left this house two years ago he felt filled with well-being, eager to fight with anyone who cared to take him on. He had no idea what was happening. He knew he had been dreaming, well, having one of his nightmares, and that for an awful moment his dream world had followed him from sleep, creating a fog of swirling shadows about his bed. Now he saw it was only

Aunt Jenny, patient and enduring, Laurel and Charlie having some kind of argument, familiar and everyday . . . and Tessa.

'You won't be satisfied until you have driven us all to the point of madness with your stupid and quite unbelievable implications, will you?' Tessa was shouting. 'Have you no humanity in that self-centred mind of yours, or does the whole universe begin and end with what you consider proper? You listen to those feather-brained friends of yours who have nothing better to do than gossip over their teacups, ruining reputations with as much compunction as swatting a fly. Dream it up, if it does not exist, as you have decided to dream up this fantasy that Drew and I are . . . well, whatever that nasty mind of yours . . .'

'Charlie, are you going to let this niece of yours insult . . . ?'

'Insult? That is where *your* talents lie, Laurel, that and your gift for seeing villainy where there is none . . .'

'I really believe you are quite mad, Tessa,' Laurel said coolly, raising a fastidious eyebrow. She had decided, it appeared, to treat Tessa's outburst with the disdain one shows to a child in a tantrum. Her husband's reluctance to support her in this was really unforgivable and she would not forgive him, nor Tessa, her manner said. It was not in her nature to brawl like a fish-wife, particularly with the servants within earshot, as they were certain to be. But Tessa, driven at last to lose the patience and temper she had sworn to keep under control at least in Drew's presence, had no such compunction.

'I must be to have lived in the same house as you

369

for nearly twenty years, and if I am you have driven me to it with your double-faced, double-tongued hypocrisy . . .'

'How dare you.' Laurel was white-faced, her eyes pure green slits of outrage but still her training as a lady, which Tessa surely was not, held her in check.

'Tessa, I will not have this,' Jenny said, trying to signal to Charlie to get his wife out of the room. 'It cannot be good for Drew and it certainly makes me feel . . .'

' . . . and if you think I shall allow you to . . .'

'*Tessa*, that is enough.' Her mother's voice was like a pistol shot for though Tessa was perhaps only voicing Jenny's own thoughts it did no good, none at all, to bring them to light now. Not now.

'Thank you, Aunt Jenny. She really does deserve a good thrashing and if she were mine she would have one.'

'That is for me to say, Laurel, not you.'

'A baggage such as she is deserves . . .'

'And what does that mean, Laurel Greenwood? What are you implying now, pray? That I stand on street corners like any common . . .'

'*Tessa!*'

'I do not imply anything, my girl.' Laurel was incensed beyond care now, ready to say anything, anything, regardless of the truth: to wound her cousin in any way she could, and the more painful it was the better. 'Dear God, it is no more than two years since you were disporting yourself all over the valley with that gentleman, if one can call him that, from the fox-hunting set of the Squire's. God alone knows what you got up to with him but whatever it was, it surely must have escaped no one's notice that he did not offer marriage. Really, Tessa, one can only hope that there is someone somewhere who has not heard of your reputation since the likelihood of your marrying seems very remote.'

The silence which followed was like the endlessly grey, endlessly deep waters of the lake in winter. Small, cruel ripples washed against the stricken girl who drowned in the centre of it. Her face was as white as her demure lawn nightgown, rigid, clenched with anguish, and she seemed unable to move, to speak, to defend herself. Her fiery temper, the strong and heedless defiance she had shown had been defeated, blown out like a candle, her vividness quenched, her spirit torn from her.

'I would be most obliged, Charlie old chap, if you would remove your wife, my sister, from my room.' Drew's drawling voice was insolent in its intention to insult. 'She really does need taking in hand, you know, and if you have not the backbone to do it, I would be delighted to give her the beating she deserves. One would think a woman of her age—what is it now, Laurel, thirty-two, thirty-three?—would have learned tact and indeed some common sense. And she is quite mistaken, you know.'

He moved lightly across the space which divided Tessa and himself, turning her to face him. He cupped her face gently with his hands, looking down into the deep, glacial grey of her stricken eyes. In his was the warm certainty of his intentions.

'She is quite wrong, my darling,' he said, heedless of the the three people who watched. 'I have known you and everything there is to know about you from the day you were born and it would be my joy and my honour to marry you. That is, if
371

you will have me.' Then he grinned impudently, just as once he had done, his humour and charm concealing from her the urgency with which he waited for her answer.

They saw the wretchedness leave her. They watched the stiffness, the awful steel-edged tension drain away and with a sigh of thankfulness she simply leaned into the arms which were held out to her.

CHAPTER TWENTY

'You don't have to marry him if you don't want to, lass,' her mother said to her, her expression one of gentle understanding for only she knew of her daughter's anguished love for Robby Atherton. To the rest of the household and community it had been no more than a girlish romance, the short-lived excitement of a gentleman whose curiosity and attention had been aroused by a pretty girl somewhat beneath his station in life; a restless, spirited girl who should not have been put forward, nor attracted his notice in the first place if she had been properly brought up. And the whole thing had come to naught, as these things have a way of doing, but leaving Tessa Harrison with a reputation irretrievably tarnished, which was why this marriage to her cousin was so timely.

'I want to marry him, Mother. I love Drew, you know that, and he needs me. And I have no one else in my life, no one else I could share my future with. What better way to spend my life than with a man I have loved ever since I was a child? There is nothing else for me, Mother, *you* know that.'

'But that is no reason to marry Drew, child. He is recovered now.'

'That is because he knows I'm here to ... protect him.'

Jenny looked surprised, then disbelieving.

'No, Tessa, you mustn't think that. If you believe that he can only live his life with you by his side then you are being ... well, I was going to say coerced into marrying him. Oh, I know not deliberately since Drew wouldn't do that to you, but unwittingly. You have been his ... his crutch— no, don't argue with me for that is the right word— ever since he got home. You have taken Pearce's place by his side and have helped to heal him. Now I'm not saying I'm against the marriage, but I don't want you to do it for the wrong reason. Drew is ... a wild young man and you're no meek and mild miss yourself, my girl, and I reckon when he gets over this gratitude he feels towards you and you overcome the sense of responsibility you seem to have for him, there'll be fireworks. You're a strong girl ... woman ... Tessa, and you'll not take kindly to bonds ...'

'*Bonds?* Drew would not bind me.' The uneasy calm which existed between Tessa and her mother flared up instantly into the tense friction left over from the grief they had share two years ago. She was polite with Jenny, enough to hide the rift between them from the rest of the family, but the ease had gone from their relationship and would never be as it once was. She was aware that the devastation, the desolation had not been caused by her mother, just as the shell, aimed by a soldier's hand, which had killed Pearce, could not be blamed

373

for his death, but the bitterness remained in her heart just the same.

'Drew is a man, child, and has all the male characteristics of possession, pride and pigheadedness. And you are a beautiful woman, yes, you might well stare and smile, but there is something about you, not just to do with the way you look, that men like.'

'Oh, come now, Mother. When I'm Drew's wife I'm hardly likely to attract men to my side.'

'Why not? You have always been . . . different from other girls, mixing with that free and easy lot up at the Hall. Oh, yes, I hear about the goings on . . . Now don't pull your face at me, my girl, since I know you, and I know you wouldn't do anything to shame your family or yourself . . .'

Tessa turned abruptly away so that her mother could not see, and wonder at, the expression on her face.

' . . . but your name is linked with it just the same. Drew is a friend of Nicky Longworth. The Squire seems to have taken a fancy to you both and at the moment, with Drew not entirely himself yet, there has been no discord. No . . . problems, shall we say. But let me tell you this: when you are his wife things will be very different. He is his father's son with a capacity for enormous emotions, whether love, hate, jealousy or rage, of the most red-blooded kind.'

Tessa listened to her mother with every appearance of disbelief but her mind returned to that moment when she had been laughing with Nicky Longworth and the others at the Hall as she had done a dozen times before in the past. They accepted her cheerfully, as they had always done,

374

seeing her not as a girl when she had tagged along with them, but as an appendage of Drew and Pearce. But she was a woman now and she had sensed the change in them, the speculation in their eyes. Admiring certainly, and still respectful for dare they be anything else in the company of Drew Greenwood? But assessing just the same, since she was an unattached girl whose reputation was somewhat questionable.

And Drew had not liked their recognition of her attractions, nor the way she had responded to it. It had amused her and, if she was honest, pleased the female in her, that was all, but he had not known that and his displeasure had been very evident. She had thought at the time it was his own fragile condition and state of mind but now, as she listened to her mother she recognised there had been something else there, something she had seen once before.

On the face of Will Broadbent!

'I cannot let him down. He does need me, Mother.'

'I think it might be you who needs him, Tessa. I think that is what you are saying. You have made up your mind there is no one else for you and so, because he has asked you and you feel beholden, you will marry him. To comfort yourself as well as him.' Her mother's voice became urgent. 'But there will be someone for you one day, lass. Don't rush into this thing because it is expected of you.'

'Don't be ridiculous, Mother.' Then her manner softened somewhat. 'Don't you see it would be suitable for both of us . . . ?'

'Suitable! That is no reason for marriage, not in my opinion, though I daresay there are those who

375

would argue with me over it.'

'I only mean Drew and I really are alike. We are suited by our temperament and upbringing. We admire the same things, activities and . . .'

'Yes?'

'He knows I cannot abide housekeeping and doing all the things Laurel does . . .'

'And what about Laurel? You and she do not get on. Are you prepared to live under the same roof with her for the rest of your days? This house is Drew's inheritance and will one day be his. Laurel has run Greenacres for a long time now, and very competently, if we are to be fair to her. She looks on it as her home and unless you and Drew are prepared to ask her and Charlie and the children to find other accommodation you will have her at *your* dinner table, which she will consider to be *hers*, forever.'

'I will not interfere with her. She is mistress here.'

'No! You will be mistress. Your husband will be its master, *is* master now with Joss and Kit permanently abroad. You would do better with a housekeeper who could run the place, and Laurel in her own home elsewhere. Charlie could afford to buy a grand house where she could be in complete charge but it would mean you would have to settle to domestic duties . . .'

'Good God, I couldn't bear it. I'd rather have Laurel queening herself about the place.'

'You could perhaps share the responsibility . . .'

'Merciful heaven, how appalling. No, she does it so well, as you say, and I should be bored to death within a week. Besides, I want to help Drew.'

'To do what?'

'Well,' she shrugged her shoulders since she was not sure, 'in whatever it is he is to . . . to do.'

Jenny looked at her sadly, not awfully sure her daughter knew what marriage to Drew Greenwood entailed, and not awfully sure she wanted to tell her. He was a complex man, particularly since the death of his brother, always youthfully self-willed and ready to challenge any opinion which opposed his own. Now that he was a man would he not be doubly so? Pearce's death had shattered him in a particularly subtle way, for they were not only brothers but twins. And the manner of Pearce's death had been harrowing for in the back of Drew's mind was surely the thought that his brother had died from wounds sustained as he rescued Drew from the Redan at Sebastopol. What nightmares dwelled in the mind of Drew Greenwood? What frailties remained to bring him down? What weaknesses which he might be unable to withstand? He had, almost overnight, become himself again, confident, positive, audacious even, his wit and charm a delight at the dinner table. He had even apologised to Laurel and Charlie, begging their forbearance, claiming the strain of his recent illness, for what else could it be called? His good humour, at least to Charlie, proved irresistible, though his sister was less inclined to be forgiving.

The three months betrothal was something which must be got through with the best possible grace, he said to Tessa. It was expected of them. They were members of a family with obligations not only to each other, but to his father and mother, to her mother and to their position in the community. There would be parties and dinners in

377

their honour and it would be churlish not to comply. Joss and Kit Greenwood were to come home at once, to see their only son married and also to attend to several legal matters which now arose because of it. There were many preparations which must be attended to, not the least Tessa's wedding outfit and trousseau for her mother declared, despite the peculiarity of the betrothal, her daughter would not go to her marriage without a new shift to her name. And Laurel, her mouth grim, her face set in a mould of cold disapproval, was nevertheless determined to snatch every advantage she could from her brother's connection with the gentry and would entertain as many as could be crammed into Greenacres in the three months prior to the wedding.

They had ridden that day up to Friar's Mere, guiding their mounts amongst the browning, mist-soaked bracken which dripped about them. It was cold that autumn, almost winter though September was barely done with, and they both wore warmly lined capes and gloves. Their own breath wreathed with the horses' about them and when they dismounted to look over the shaded valley, she shivered suddenly, not with cold but with some sudden disquiet which came from nowhere to trouble her.

He draped a companionable arm across her shoulders, wise in the ways of women. Best not to startle her too soon with his own needs, and so he remained, despite the magnificent diamond on her finger, just as he had always been, cousin, companion, friend.

'Are you cold, sweetheart,' he asked lightly, 'or just contemplating the future as Mrs Drew

378

Greenwood and finding it somewhat daunting?'

She looked up at him sharply. She was not always sure lately when he was teasing. In his new role as her 'fiancé' she supposed he had the right now to be somewhat more . . .' familiar with her, not intimate, for that was reserved for their wedding night, but not exactly the same as he had been as 'cousin'. But he was just the same. Both of them had suffered a great loss. They had been bruised and lonely, needing, probably, to be loved and they had given something to one another on the day when he had asked her to marry him and she had accepted gratefully. She needed warmth and some emotion he seemed to be offering. She rested easily when she was with him, trusting him as implicity as she had always done and she was aware that in her he found something he had lost with Pearce.

'Oh, really, Tessa, don't tell me you don't find this somewhat strange?'

'Well . . .' She knew what he meant and was grateful that he was treating it with humour and lightness.

'It is new to us both, this "betrothal".' He grinned down at her, making her smile as he exaggerated the word.

'I'm not afraid, Drew Greenwood.' Immediately she began to bristle, shying away from him indignantly but he pulled her back, laughing, his eyes narrowed and shining.

'Yes, you are, just a little bit. Afraid that things might be changed between us because of . . . well, because you will be wife, but I promise you they won't.' He grinned wickedly. 'Would you like to try something?'

'What?' she said suspiciously.

'Well, we are betrothed, as they say, so surely it would be allowed?'

'What?' she said again.

'A kiss to seal our . . . pact.' He smiled even more engagingly, turning her so that she faced him. He reached up to tuck a damp strand of hair behind her ear, his gaze moving across her face, resting on her smooth brow, the puzzled depths of her eyes, the touch of rose in her cheeks put there by the cold, and finally, her soft, parted lips.

'What pact?'

'To marry, of course, and besides, it won't be the first time. Remember that Christmas when Pearce and I caught you under the mistletoe? We each stole a kiss from you. In fact, I do believe we had no need of theft.'

Her mouth curled up in a wide smile and as it did so he placed his own carefully against it. It was a smiling kiss, light as thistledown with no more in it than a friend might give to another. He tasted the sweetness of her breath and felt the warmth of it drift into his open mouth. She leaned against him, willing to go on, her eyes so lovely and trusting told him, and he caught his breath.

'Did you know that in this light your eyes have the palest, softest blue in them?' he said wonderingly. 'Like the smoke you see against a summer sky. Transparent almost.'

'Oh, Drew, stop teasing.' Her arms crept up behind him, her hands gripping one another in the centre of his back. His were across her shoulders and he pulled her into them, tucking her head into the hollow of his neck.

'I need you, Tessa,' he said quietly, his breath

moving her dark hair.

'I'm here, Drew,' she answered and when she looked up at him, smiling, his face was serious. He held her gaze for a moment, then bent his head and took her lips again and this time it was different. For a moment she wanted to draw back for this was how Robby had kissed her. This was warm and filled with desire and she was not really ready . . . no . . . not with this man who was her cousin. She closed her eyes so that Drew could not read the expression in them, the expression which surely would reveal to him that . . . that other kisses had been left there, and in her heart, and that no one, no others could replace the ones she had lost.

But when she opened her eyes again there he was, Drew Greenwood, her beloved cousin, grinning delightedly, dashingly handsome, familiar, loved, winsome and dear.

'There you are,' he said, 'how was that?' Taking her lead from him, she pretended to bob a curtsey, dimpling in laughter.

'Very nice, thank you, sir.'

'Have you another to spare, d'you think, since I must admit to finding it very pleasant myself?'

He was breathing rather more heavily than usual when he drew away, but he merely looked into her face as though to check that she had not taken fright and when he could see that she hadn't, he pulled her gently back into the circle of his arms.

'That's enough for today, cousin,' he said, his voice soft and inclined to tremble over the top of her head.

The next time was a week later. They had dined with the Longworths, just the two of them invited, much to Laurel's chagrin since she had expected, as

381

Drew's sister and closest relative until Joss and Kit returned from Italy, to be included in any celebration given for the newly engaged couple.

They had drunk an excellent wine with dinner, and champagne to toast the happy pair who really made a splendid picture, everyone agreed. That girl of Jenny Harrison's was quite superb in her white lace gown, and the effect of the broad scarlet sash wound tight about her slender waist and the matching ribbons in her dark hair, dressed in tumbled curls, was simply stunning. She was almost as tall as her bridegroom-to-be in her white satin high-heeled slippers, and he was immaculate in his black and white evening clothes, a perfect contrast in his male beauty for her loveliness. How magnificent they were, how handsome, and could anyone fail to believe that they were not made for each other and that their future together could be anything less than perfect?

They had held hands in the carriage on the drive home, still laughing and inclined to fall against one another in the hilarity produced by several glasses of champagne. Like children they were, giggling over the rather pompous but kindly speech the Squire had made in their honour, and the number of times they had been told how well suited they were, perhaps, as Drew remarked gleefully, because they were both from the class known as 'trade' and therefore, one supposed, to consummate the perfect union.

It was dim in the hallway. Briggs had left one lamp at the foot of the stairs before retiring, as he had been ordered to do since they were to be late. The logs in the enormous fireplace had smouldered down to whispering ash, a golden flame here and

382

there, and a curl of smoke. It was warm, intimate, a place where they were both relaxed, at home and secure.

'I think I'll have a brandy before I go up,' Drew drawled. 'Would you care to join me?' An eyebrow arched questioningly.

'Why not?' She was light-headed and pleasantly tired, ready for bed but unwilling somehow to let go of the content that lay about her.

The brandy made her gasp and the heat of it rose from her stomach where it had found the champagne, and put flags of scarlet in her cheeks to match the ribbons in her delightfully tumbled hair.

'Slowly, cousin,' Drew laughed, putting an arm about her shoulders as they sat side by side on the sofa before the dying drawing-room fire. 'Sip it slowly and then, when you are almost asleep, I shall take you up to bed.'

The words meant nothing to Tessa beyond what they said: it had not yet occurred to her to think of her cousin in 'that way', and the implication which sprang instantly to Drew's more sexually alert mind completely escaped her. She felt a quiver run through him and the clear image of Will Broadbent came surprisingly to her mind. Why, she thought, at this particular moment, should she think of him? Then she was conscious of the suddenly taut presence of Drew beside her, his arm rigid across her shoulders.

'What is it, Drew?' she asked though really she knew. How could she not when she had been loved by Will Broadbent, who had caressed every part of her, sweet and secret parts which had set her on fire for more?

But Drew, though a man too, was her cousin, and had been all her life. That was who he was.

The simple and, to her, quite logical thought slipped into her mind, to be followed by the equally logical and obvious reply that they were to be, not just cousins, but man and wife. In that moment she knew they must take that next step *now*, before she had time to dwell on it, before she had time to consider the *mechanics* of it, before she had time to jib at it, to get cold feet and turn away from it, since he *was* her cousin, dammit. It must be done without thought, without design. It must be done *now*.

Blindly she turned to him, not knowing where to begin, and as swiftly as he had come Will Broadbent winged away, and her heart, on which he was still engraved, was filled with Robby Atherton. Kisses ... oh, Robby, Robby, my love, that was how ... how it had begun ... sweet, warm ... Dear God, how she loved him still, but she loved Drew ... she did ... she did, but not, sadly, in the way she had loved Robby ... Robby, Samuel Robert Atherton ... and with none of the passion she had given to Will Broadbent.

His mouth was there waiting for hers and wisely—how did he know her so well? understand her as he did?—wisely he let her take the lead, sitting almost passively, there, his arm relaxed now about her shoulders, waiting. She was aware in that moment that if he had responded eagerly, attempted to move at a faster pace than she could manage, she would have let Robby Atherton into her soul, and refused him.

She could taste the brandy on his lips. They were warm and very soft, moist on their inside. They

384

moved with hers in little butterfly motions, soft and fluttering, waiting, smiling, she could see that, in pleasure.

'You are very dear to me, Tessa,' he murmured, again the right words, with no mention of love. He put up a hand, a brown, familiar hand which she had known all her life and placed the palm against her cheek. He began to guide her then, holding her cheek gently as he kissed her, his fingers warm against her skin. Sighing, his lips moved to her eyes, resting against each one before going on to her eyebrow, the line of her hair, a soft whisper of breath in her ear, his mouth trembling, lingering on her jawline and into the soft hollow at the base of her throat. She arched her body without thought, feeling his lips move across her skin and the arm which had been resting lightly across her shoulders tightened as he turned her towards him. His hand was under her hair, pulling at ribbons and pins, caressing the back of her neck, still gentle, without urgency. She could see the outline of his dark face above hers and the blue glow of his eyes.

For a moment he hesitated, lifting a questioning eyebrow, giving her, she knew, time to draw back, to wait for another time. It has to be done at sometime, his quizzical expression said, and why not now, in the spontaneity of now?

He turned her then, taking her stillness for acquiescence, resting her across his knee. His arms were strong and positive, lifting her up, and his kisses were demanding, opening her lips beneath his own. His tongue teased hers, his hand was smoothing her shoulder, her upper arm, the other holding her since the moment had come and gone when she might refuse.

'Tessa . . .' His fingers moved slowly, saying there was no hurry, no need to rush this sweet moment, caressing her throat, smoothing her skin until it reached the soft upper curve of her breast.

'Not here, Drew.'

'In your room, then. I have to have you now before you change your mind . . .'

They stood up awkwardly, then he swung her up into his arms, his lips finding hers, allowing no shrinking away and her arms clung about his neck, her mouth clung to his mouth, afraid to detach herself from the physical junction which was the only one she knew about her cousin Drew.

Her room was warm and sweet-scented, familiar, scattered with the things she had left there before setting off for Longworth Hall. Emma had made up the fire and drawn the curtains, even turned back the bedclothes, and when he placed her on the bed it seemed it had been waiting there for them, for this which was to happen.

Though he was breathing hard now she could see he was making a great effort to hold back for her sake, since was she not virgin, inexperienced in these matters? She wanted to cry out to him to hurry, to get it done, to get it over with. She wanted it behind her, that first time, so that they could be Drew and Tessa again, cousins, friends and, one supposed, lovers.

He gently drew down her dress, exposing her breasts and when she closed her eyes in confusion he put up a hand and cupped her cheek.

'Don't look away, sweetheart,' he whispered, kissing her softly on her mouth and cheek and chin. 'We have nothing of which to be ashamed. Look at me, look at my eyes. See in them what I feel for

386

you.' It was there, his love, his admiration for her as a woman. Not as Tessa Harrison, cousin, but Tessa Harrison, woman, *his* woman. 'I should be patient with you since you have the look in your eyes which says you will grit your teeth and endure it, as women are expected to, but there is no need . . .'

When he had undressed her completely he stood for several moments exploring with his eyes every part of her body, lingering at her breast and thighs, not touching yet but completely absorbed in the loveliness of her. He began to undress himself and she watched him, diverted by the beauty and fineness of his body, so different from Will's. Will had been broad, heavy, hard, so strong he made Drew seem a lightweight in comparison, but Drew Greenwood was slender, arrow-straight and yet with a fluid grace. Easy and lean as an athlete, smooth-skinned with a fine matt of crisp chest hair which travelled down his belly to between his thighs. Will had been . . . Dear God, why should she think . . .? And in that last moment her mind, amazed, was filled with the memory of him, then Drew bent over her, his candle-lit body eager, his eyes searching hers. She lifted her arms urgently and wound them round his neck, wanting to blot out everything but him and pulled him down to her. His body entered hers and it was done. He groaned and shuddered and called her name as he took possession of her, and it was done.

They lay for a while and she stroked his back, feeling the satiny strength of it and the muscles bunched beneath the skin. A moment ago they had been rigid with need, now they were relaxed and spent. It was as though he had poured into her all

387

his strength, the boyish strength which was Drew Greenwood, leaving him defenceless, weakened, vulnerable, as he had been when he returned from the Crimea. She was the one with undiminished power now, her strength gained from him, her body unbreakable, not weakened as his appeared to be. She wondered if this was all that was to be between herself and her cousin, this . . . tenderness she felt, this warm and gentle love, just the same as it had always been, even after what had just happened, for Drew Greenwood. Was she never to know again that lusty delight she and Will had shared, that joy, that abandonment, their bodies clasped together in the sensuality a man and woman can know?

He sighed and sat up, studying her face in the pale glow of the candlelight. He bent to kiss her, cupping her breast with his strong hand.

'You are quite beautiful, my darling.'

'If you say so.' In her body, deep down, was that familiar sensation connected with his fingers which rolled her nipple gently. It began to stir and she felt a great desire to lift her hips, to move them up towards him, but he lay back on the pillow, putting an arm about her and the feeling fled away. She put her head on his chest and when he pulled the quilt up around them she knew they would fall asleep with the greatest of ease, fitting together even in this new environment, as they had always done.

They made love again and again in those months before their marriage, wherever and whenever they could find the opportunity, each time more easily, each time more surely, each time more enjoyably, and she was grateful that he seemed to find such joy in it and in her. Though he did not say the

388

words, she knew he loved her, not just as he had always done, but in the way a man loves a woman. And she was thankful, thankful for that love and for his need of her. It warmed her, gave her comfort and pleasure, made her soft with him, and for him. She would devote her life now to being what he needed, to giving whatever it was he wanted. Not submissive for it was not in her nature, she told herself, but ready, always, to take him in her arms, to love him, to support him, to allow him to support *her*, which was much more important. Robby Atherton was dead now, dead and buried in the grave of her heart, and Drew Greenwood had sprung up to take his place, and the whisper that was Will Broadbent, which came sometimes to ask what of *her* joy, and *her* fulfilment, was scarcely noticed.

CHAPTER TWENTY-ONE

She had seen nothing of Will for two years, not since she had ridden over to Annie's on the day before Robby Atherton was to speak to her mother, so when he rose casually from the chair before Annie's fire as she entered the cottage she felt her breath leave her body in an explosion so violent she thought she was about to swoon.

She was to be married the following Saturday and the invitation, written in Miss Copeland's beautiful copperplate and sent to Annie over a month ago, had still not been answered. She would be awkward, Tessa knew, stubborn and ungracious, declaring herself not the sort to attend a grand

389

society wedding, and absolutely unconvinced that Tessa should marry Drew Greenwood anyway. She had said so a dozen times ever since Tessa had told her she was to wed her cousin.

'He's got thi on't rebound, lass, an' tha should 'ave sense enough ter know it. Tha was ter wed that other chap, tha said, then all of a sudden it were off . . . No, I want ter know nothing about it, lass, so don't look at me like that. What 'appened is thy own affair an' nowt ter do wi' me,' she declared, for Annie had a horror of seeming to interfere in another's life at the same time fiercely defending her own privacy. But she could not resist giving her opinion, nevertheless, particularly when she firmly believed, as she did now, that Tessa was about to make a mistake. And she was not eager to put on her best bonnet, which was her *only* bonnet, and traipse over to the parish church of Crossfold and watch her make it.

Tessa could sympathise with her reluctance to come to Greenacres to join in the celebrations: when one is no more than a lowly mill girl it took courage to place oneself amongst those who consider themselves to be one's betters. She had not dared to offer Annie the 'loan' of a decent bonnet and gown since she knew where that would lead, but if she would just come to the church, see her married to Drew, Tessa would be content and she meant to try to persuade her to do so today.

She had known, though nothing was ever said, that Will still called at Annie's cottage when he was in the district and she had relied on her friend to let her know when that was so that there would be no awkward confrontations. Yet now, in that first moment when she realised that this visit must have been unforeseen, just as Annie had not known that she, Tessa, was going to call, she felt an unexpected surge of incredible gladness.

'Tessa,' he said coolly. 'Are you well?' No more than that, leaving her in no doubt that whatever there had been between them was not only dead but decently buried. He was a man who had, unwillingly, his imperturbable manner seemed to say, lost his head over a pretty girl. That was folly from which he had recovered as one recovers from a heavy cold or a fever, debilitating at the time but not dangerous. So he could greet her quite calmly now, just as though they were no more than acquaintances of Annie's who found themselves together in her kitchen.

'Thank you, yes, and you?' With a great effort she kept her voice just as neutral, her manner just as off-hand.

'I'm well, thank you.'

'I'm glad to hear it.'

'And what brings you over to Annie's so unexpectedly?'

At the back of the room Annie drew in her breath sharply and when one of the children, Tessa could not have said which one, erupted into the scullery from the back of the cottage, Annie moved quickly to the back door and ushered whoever it was out again, whispering something which neither the man nor the woman in the kitchen could hear.

Tessa was stung by Will's familiarity since it was nothing to do with him when or why she visited Annie. So she was not expected, was it any of his concern? Her head lifted imperiously and she turned away from him, tossing her riding crop and cloak to a chair beside the table. She was aware of the silence. She could no longer see him as she stared out of the window to where her mare cropped Annie's few winter plants, but she could feel him there and the dread grew in her, for a small part of her wanted to turn round and touch him. To put out her hand and . . . and have him grasp it.

Dear God, was she mad? She believed she was for it seemed there was still something in her which called out to something in him despite what had happened since she had seen him last. She did not love him, of course she didn't. She loved Robby and she loved Drew, though in a completely different way, naturally, so why, her suddenly anguished mind asked, was she dithering about in Annie's kitchen allowing herself to become upset at the sight of Will Broadbent?

'My dear Tessa,' he said, amusement in his voice, 'you seem quite agitated. I do apologise if I have . . . startled you.'

'There is no need to apologise.'

'Good, nevertheless you are startled?'

'Of course not. I . . . did not expect to find you here.'

'Nor I you.'

She allowed herself to turn to him then, conscious of the softening in his voice and was just in time to see the strange expression which deepened his amber eyes to a smoky brown, then it was gone and he smiled. He took a cigar case from the pocket of his well-cut jacket, selected a cigar, lit it and when it was drawing to his satisfaction, blew smoke into Annie's kitchen ceiling. His smile deepened as he saw her look at it.

'Aah, yes. As you see I have acquired the . . .

er . . . trappings of the business gentleman. The good suit, the cigar, the . . . well, other things.' He gave a sardonic twist of the wide, strong mouth, a lifting of the heavy eyebrows as though to say it was all a performance put on for those who were impressed with such things.

'Congratulations.'

'And to yourself.'

'I beg your pardon?'

'Are you not to be married shortly?' The sudden swerve unnerved her.

'Yes.'

'How splendid. I do like to hear of good fortune. So, it seems we are both . . . doing well.'

'It seems so.'

'Oh, indeed. A good marriage is not a thing to be scorned.'

'No.'

'You mean it is not to be a good marriage?' He leaned forward or did she just imagine it? His expression did not change. His face was just as suavely smiling but there was still the remainder of something curiously tense in his narrowed eyes.

'Of course it is.'

'Not like the . . . er . . . other one?'

'What . . . ?' Please don't, her heart cried out to him. Please don't hurt me, or try to, and in her anguish it did not occur to her to wonder why he should try to do so.

'I do beg your pardon.' He was immensely civil now, all traces of feeling of any sort wiped from his face. 'It has, of course, nothing to do with me. Now,' he turned to Annie who still hovered at the back of the scullery, 'I must be off. I have an engagement this evening which I would not like to miss.' And his manner, and smile, told them both quite clearly that it was with a lady.

He had been gone for several minutes when she felt Annie's gentle touch on her arm. She had been brooding out of the window into the street along which his broad-shouldered back had disappeared and she jumped when she felt Annie's hand, then turned, attempting to smile.

'It seems Will Broadbent has gone up in the world, Annie.'

'Tessa, lass . . .'

'Don't say it, Annie.'

'Say what, Tessa Harrison?'

'I don't know. You have a look on your face which says you are going to argue with me about . . . well, whatever it is you feel must be argued about.'

'Yer can't do it. Yer can't wed Drew Greenwood. Not just because of Will an' what you an' 'im 'ad. But because that cousin o' thine is . . .'

'Will's nothing to me and I am nothing to Will. Heavens, it's two years. *Two years*, Annie. I can't just keep drifting from man to man like some aimless butterfly . . .'

'Nobody ses yer should, but wait . . . give it a month or so, lass . . .' and see what comes of this reunion with Will, her anxious eyes said, but Tessa flung her off roughly.

'I can't.' Her face which, an hour since, had been filled if not with joy then with peace, was now devoid of all expression.

*   *   *

She was married to Drew Greenwood on a white

394

and frosted morning just before Christmas. There was a crunch of new snow underfoot as she walked up the path on the arm of Joss Greenwood and above them the sky was streaked in delicate layers of palest pink and blue. The sun shone hazily through the slight curling mist and when they moved inside the dusty parish church it was scarcely warmer than the crisp air outside.

She wore ivory velvet and carried rosebuds of the same shade from the Greenacres hothouses. Her veil was a marvel of white lace and seed pearls and in her ears and about her neck were the lustrous pearls her bridegroom had given her as a wedding gift. Her wide skirts flowed from her supple waist, whispering across the worn flagstones as her uncle put her carefully beside his own son, and the massed congregation agreed they had never seen a lovelier bride. She looked fragile and mysterious, although of course she was not, for she was tall and had junketed about the high tops and deep valleys of the countryside with her recklessly wild cousins since she was old enough to sit on a horse.

Her family were arranged on both sides of the church since she and her groom were cousins, with their guests in descending order of importance behind them. The Squire with his lady and their family sat in the second pew, naturally – a feather in the Greenwood cap there, by God, with the young Squireen, who was known to be one of those with whom the Greenwoods had made merry, acting as groomsman. Among the mainly commercial congregation were one or two members of the fox-hunting set, those who had taken a fancy to the Greenwood girl, as she was known, over the past few years. She had proved to be not only their equal on the hunting field, but damned amusing as well, with the lofty arrogance they both admired and shared since it was the characteristic which set them apart from the lower orders. And Drew Greenwood had shown the courageous foolhardiness on the battlefield which was the stamp of the pedigreed and ruling class to which they themselves belonged. A rare couple and one they were more than ready to take up.

It was all most gratifying and despite Laurel Greenwood's fierce disapproval of the marriage it was apparent that she considered herself to be getting only her due as she greeted ladies and gentlemen known to be related to the lesser aristocracy. She had been attempting to get her toe in the door at Longworth Hall for three years now, ever since her Christmas fancy-dress ball which had been honoured by the Squire's presence. Surely this meant a further and renewed warmth between her family and that of the leading gentry of the Penfold Valley? The young Greenwoods and the Longworths were so obviously the best of friends and Laurel had sons and daughters of her own whose future hopes might well be furthered by her acquaintance with the local Squire.

Kit Greenwood, doing her best to signal to her husband that no one would think the worse of him if he sat down, looked quite splendid in one of the new hooped 'cages' or 'artificial crinolines' to support her vast skirt. The bodice of the outfit was separate and worn over it was a 'gilet' or waistcoat, considered a little fast by the ladies of Crossfold where the Paris and London fashions had not yet arrived. It was in a lovely violet-blue, the exact shade of her eyes which had sadly lost their brilliance since the death of her son. Her bonnet, worn at the back of her head, had a dip in the centre of the brim, on the underside of which was a froth of blond lace. She watched her boy, for surely he was still that despite his twenty years, lean against his cousin, his wife now, and as he made his vows his mother was seen to reach for her sister-in-law's hand as though she herself was sorely in need of support. They sat quietly together, the mothers of the bride and groom, perhaps dwelling on their losses as a family, on the past which had led to this marriage, which, if they were honest, neither had wanted for their children.

The wedding breakfast was of such splendour it was talked of for weeks by those, and there were well over one hundred, who sat down to share it: the Squire and Mrs Longworth, Sir Anthony Taylor and Lady Prudence, Nicky Longworth, Johnny Taylor and numerous ladies and gentlemen of their society rubbing shoulders with Abbotts and Jenkinsons and others of the manufacturing classes. Annie Beale had not been persuaded to come. There were flowers everywhere amidst the warm, scented comfort of Greenacres and Drew Greenwood proposing a charming, witty and quite emotional toast to his lovely bride.

It was a moment of great beauty, of great poignancy, when one remembered the son who had been left behind on the battlefield of the Crimean Peninsula, but perhaps with the responsibility of a wife and no doubt a child within the twelvemonth, Drew Greenwood would now buckle to, and become a part of what he would one day inherit.

Jenny Harrison watched them, her daughter and

397

her new son-in-law, her mind not on wedding cake and champagne, on laughter and toasts and kisses, but on what Joss was to say to his son and his new daughter-in-law the next day before they set off on their wedding journey.

*   *   *

They gathered in what had once been the study of Barker Chapman, Kit's father, then in turn hers, her husband's, Jenny's and, occasionally, Charlie's, but never Drew's. Kit, still beautiful despite her fifty-one years; Joss, his face brown with the Mediterranean sun, but lined; Jenny, looking older somehow than her own brother; and Charlie, his pleasant, good-humoured face wondering on what this meeting could be about. Laurel, his wife, making sure of everyone's comfort in the way a good hostess should; making sure everyone understood, particularly Tessa, that she was mistress of this house, at least for the time being.

And Tessa and Drew themselves, sitting close together in the deep leather chesterfield, Drew ready to whisper and giggle, treating the whole event with the light-hearted frivolity he directed towards anything which smacked of the serious. He was eager to be off to the railway station and the start of their grand wedding tour: Italy, France, Austria and wherever their careless search for pleasure took them. They might tarry in Paris since he had a fancy to deck Tessa out in the most fashionable and expensive gowns money—and they had a lot of it—could buy.

Joss smiled at them all, reaching for his wife's hand which was there, as it had always been for

398

thirty years, waiting for his.

'You'll be wondering what all this is about,' he said, 'especially you, Drew.' His son blinked in surprise since he was not wondering at all. He supposed it to be some gathering, a family occasion in which a toast was to be drunk to the health of the bride and groom, wishing his father would get a move on since he and Tessa were to be off within the hour.

'We've been through some rare do's, your mother and me, and we've always managed to overcome them, haven't we, lass? But we're none of us getting any younger and there's still some ends want tidying up, eeh, my love?'

'Rubbish, Joss Greenwood. You might be in your dotage but I'm in my prime yet.' Kit held his hand fiercely, her eyes clinging to his with a passion which was quite extraordinary, even somewhat embarrassing in Laurel's view.

'Aye, well, that's as maybe, but best get things sorted out.' Tessa suddenly realised that what she had always considered to be her aunt's mills, her aunt's house and fortune, in fact belonged entirely to Joss Greenwood since on the day of their marriage, by law, everything she had owned became his, even herself. She had no existence, she did not exist in the eyes of the law except as Mrs Joss Greenwood, and what had once been hers could now be disposed of by her husband as he thought fit.

She felt a warning prickle at the base of her spine and her grip on Drew's hand tightened. The room was so quiet she could distinctly hear the voices of the servants in the breakfast room as they cleared away the table.

'We're not short of a guinea or two.' Her uncle grinned boyishly and his wife shook her head. 'I reckon Kit and I can live very pleasantly, luxuriously even by my standards remembering I was brought up in a weavers' cottage'—he winked at his sister and Tessa could swear she saw a glint of moisture in her mother's eye—'with what the mills have brought us and the investments we've made. The railways have . . . well, I'll not go into details except to say the shares we bought have made a pretty penny. So . . .' He paused and though it was of no concern to her, Tessa found she was holding her breath. 'My wife and I have decided to let go, to make over the business to those who deserve it. A partnership. Drew, as our . . . our only son will have a three-quarter share but the rest is to go to my sister and brother who, for the past twenty-five years, have kept the whole bloody lot together. They will hold their share, half each of the remaining twenty-five per cent, until their death and then they may leave it to whoever they please in the family, or sell it back to Drew. As the largest shareholder Drew will be general manager but Jenny and Charlie will now be partners in the business. These arrangements were made some time back, before you and Tessa decided on marriage, Drew. There was a proviso which, at the time, was not fully completed and until it is Drew does not become the head of the firm as is his right. Jenny and Charlie are in control as it stands. All the decisions made are theirs alone, but Mr Dalton, the lawyer, is to come here this morning and everything will be put in order, so I would like you all to be present. Naturally, for the time being Jenny and Charlie will continue to advise since

Drew has not the experience to do what they have done for so many years. But when the papers are drawn up he and he alone will be in charge of Chapman Manufacturing.'

'*No!*'

They turned as one, all heads moving as one to look at the drained and pallid face of Joss Greenwood's son. He sat beside his wife, his hands wringing hers most piteously. Gone was the look of indolent amusement, of unruffled carelessness, and in its place was an expression so haunted Jenny was reminded of the day he had come back from the Crimea.

'I cannot work in the mill, Father.' He lifted his proud head but in his eyes was the terrified look of a child about to be shut up in a dark cupboard. His bravery on the field was beyond question, both on the hunting field and on the field of war. His courage had been spoken of by several returned officers, acquaintances of the Longworths and the Taylors, but the horror and dread which the one word 'mill' conjured up had, it seemed, unmanned him.

'Then what will you do?' his father asked him, his voice steely.

'Must I do anything, Father? Could we not sell the mills? We could use the money to buy an estate ... land ... farm land ...' His face brightened and the expression of horror began to fade from his eyes. 'I could live as the Squire does, not farming, of course, but looking after the tenants, acting as a magistrate ... a gentleman's life, Father, to which I am particularly drawn ...'

The echo of a conversation—a hundred years ago now, surely?—slipped into Tessa's mind and the day on which it had taken place became clearer with every minute. There had been just the four of them dining that night. Her mother had been there, yes, and this man who was now her husband, Drew Greenwood, and another—his brother, his *twin* brother who was dead but who surely lived on in the man who had just spoken. Her mother was looking towards her as though the thoughts in her head were the same as her own. Drew, as always, had met the confrontation with his aunt that night head on, arguing that what had been in the past should remain there and did not concern those who lived in the present and the future. But it had been Pearce who had sworn he would sell his heritage, sell it without a thought for the men of his family who had made it. Sell it and live as the Squire did, close to the land which bred him.

And now, in almost the same words, Drew had pronounced that that was his hope, that he wanted nothing more than to live the rest of his days in idle luxury, *as Pearce had said*. Where was the Drew Greenwood who had taken up any challenge flung at him? Flaunting and arrogant and sure of himself, was he now, sadly, merging slowly into the weaker, or perhaps gentler character his brother had possessed?

He was still babbling on: ' ... we could sell Greenacres. There are a dozen new manufacturers who would be only too glad to take it off our hands,' he added contemptuously 'and buy an estate where there is a bit of rough shooting, farming land ...'

'Don't be foolish, Drew.' His mother's voice was more amused than angry, for had anyone ever heard such nonsense and could anyone be expected to take it seriously? Sell the mills? Sell Greenacres! One might as well decide to sell one's own flesh and blood to those who dealt in the slave trade as sell this heritage of theirs, her smile said, and when her husband chose to ignore his son's outburst, she was not surprised.

'You would let others support you then? For that is what you are saying. Your Aunt Jenny and Charlie would do the work whilst you spent the money they earned?'

'Could I not employ a man to do my share? To ... to do whatever it is you are asking me to do?' Drew was sullen now, his grand scheme which, Tessa was completely aware, would suit his nature better than any other, flung back in his face.

'Jenny and Charlie can do that,' his father's cool voice told him, 'most efficiently too, and there are a score of managers under their directorship, but do you not think it unfair that they alone should take the responsibility of what belongs to you?'

His son twisted about like an animal trapped in a cage which is far too small to accommodate it and for a dreadful moment Tessa thought he was about to spring it and flee, away from his father and mother, away from the prison they were preparing for him, away from his new wife who was all that was holding him together. But her hands steadied his and she drove her unfrightened will directly into his wild eyes, telling him with her own that she was here, that they were together, and the boy who had, for the first eighteen years of his life, been one half of a whole part and had thought he would never survive the loss of the other, sat back and the fear fell away.

'I'm sorry, sir. Forgive me. I was somewhat
403

stunned and spoke without giving the matter any thought. You must not worry about me, about us.' He turned to smile at his Aunt Jenny, then at Charlie and they all relaxed quite visibly.

'Aunt Jenny, Charlie and I will, I'm sure, work out some arrangement convenient to the three of us. After all, the mill belongs to us all and we would not see it go to the wall for the lack of a decent commander, would we?'

His manner was vital and confident, a complete reversal of his terror of a moment ago, letting his parents see that, though he might not have the slightest idea how he was to do it, he would run *his* concern as he damn well pleased. It was a gamble he took for the documents which were to make the mill his were not yet signed. Yet his father appeared prepared to take that gamble, for surely it would make a responsible man of this valiant son of his?

'Then it only needs all our signatures then me and your mother will be off back to that sunshine which, they tell me, is keeping me alive. And you and your bride can be away on your wedding journey which I'm sure you're eager to begin.'

He made love to her that night and indeed every night of their stay abroad with an intensity that told her he was in some desperate straits which only the act of love could assuage—the act of mindless, greedy lust which, though he loved her, was really nothing to do with her, nor him, but the dread of what hung over him and which must somehow be hidden. He groaned and shuddered, giving no thought to her desire, should she have had any, nor her pleasure, should she have had any of that, lying against her, still trembling. His face in the lamplight was drawn, his eyes staring sightlessly to the corners of the shadowed room. When she touched his shoulder he turned again to her, violently, nuzzling his face to her breasts, curling his body about hers, a hurt child seeking comfort and reassurance, protection from the demons which had come to plague him.

'I can't do it, you know,' he said unnecessarily.

'It would be difficult at first.' Her voice was careful.

'You aren't listening to me, Tessa. *I cannot do it.*'

'Then what are you to do, my darling? You heard what Uncle Joss said.'

'Yes.'

'The papers are signed.'

'They are nothing to do with me, Tessa.' His voice had become sullen. 'I didn't ask for this.'

'Then . . . will you refuse?'

He flung back the bedcovers and with a rapid stride moved to the table beside the fireplace. His tall, naked body was brown and beautiful in the lamp's glow. He poured himself a whisky, throwing it down his throat in one neat swallow. He had another, then turned to her, his face irritable, his eyes perilous but very sure.

'Oh, no. If I refuse my income will without a doubt be taken from me and I will be forced to manage on some schoolboy's allowance, or whatever they think I am worth. They must give me something since I am the son, but the bulk will go to Aunt Jenny and Charlie, and wouldn't Laurel be pleased about that?' His laugh was harsh.

'Does that matter?'

'It does to me. She is not a true Greenwood.'

'Neither am I.'

'You are my wife and will have what is your right.'

He stood by the fireplace, his body brooding and taut, staring into the fire which still blazed. 'Besides, there must be more than enough for us all. Let us say *my* contribution will be to help them spend it.'

She lay beside him as he tossed and fretted the rest of the night away, her mind struggling to retain the pleasant pictures of her wedding day. She wondered desperately if Joss Greenwood was aware of the box of imps he had opened and set free in his damaged son. She knew he had thought to provide Drew with an incentive to take up his duties by making him head of the firm, whereas he had merely turned his son from an irresponsible, but engaging pleasure-seeker, into a cheat and a liar.

CHAPTER TWENTY-TWO

The machinery in the mill had been running for twenty hours, two shifts of ten hours each, when it was turned off at eleven o'clock on Saturday night. Tomorrow was Sunday, the one day of the week when the mill was quiet, and as the operatives poured out of the gates their wooden-soled, steel-tipped clogs made a merry clatter on the uneven cobbles.

The evening, though dark by now, of course, was still warm with the residue of the heat left over from the day and the navy blue sky was clear and punctured by the light of a million stars.

They were weary, all of them, especially the women who, after a morning of washing and mangling, of cleaning and donkey-stoning the steps of the neat houses they rented from Mrs Harrison, had stood for ten hours on their shifts, spinning, carding, weaving, or toiling in the bleaching and dyeing processes which created Chapman cloth.

But tomorrow was their day off and with the prosperity which had come in the past few years as the textile trade of Lancashire flourished, many of them would be taking a train on an excursion to Preston or Blackburn, Bolton or Oldham where there might be a fair or a circus, a band playing or an open-air troupe of travelling players. Parish Jack, a singer, fluter and fiddler, was a great favourite, appearing regularly in Lancashire cotton towns at 'stirs' and merry-making, in beer-houses and inns. There might be games, a country wake or two, quoit playing, bowling, wrestling, 'bumble-puppy', bull-baiting, all contrived to entertain those who, in the last decade, had the means now to jingle a few spare coins in their pocket.

There were railway day trips to Southport and Blackpool, costing rather more than the working class could afford at two and sixpence a head, but on special days the fare was to be reduced to a shilling for children, one and sixpence for women, and two shillings for a man. With the increased wages the unions were promising them, another ten per cent it was said, it would not be long before they would all be paddling in the sea which few, as yet, had ever seen.

Life had changed since their parents' day when times had been hard. Not that they were easy now but at least families did not starve as once they had.

And conditions would continue to improve as their 'Association' fought to achieve an even better standard of living. A pair of self-acting spinning mules which one man or woman could mind had brought about a higher wage trend that was gaining for the minders an aristocratic position within the industry. They had to work harder, naturally, for the higher spindle speeds made for a greater intensity of labour, but in one ten-hour day they earned more than their fathers had in sixteen.

The overlooker in the blow room, a man with the necessary half-crown to spare for such things, was off to Blackpool himself the next day. He had been dwelling on the delight of taking off his boots and dipping his feet in the sea, or even, greatly daring, changing in one of the bathing huts he had heard tell of and immersing his *whole* body in the sparkling wavelets. There might even be some lass with whom he could strike up an acquaintance, leading to who knew what pleasures. He was adjusting the small wheel on the carding machine which laid the raw fibres of cotton parallel, and further cleaned them, when the factory bell began its clangour signalling the end of the shift. Wrapped up in his dreams of tomorrow, the tool he had used for the adjustment was left carelessly teetering on the extreme edge of the machine.

What caused it finally to lose its precarious balance would never be known but when it fell it struck the metal wheel with which the overlooker had been tinkering.

The enormous building was empty by now. The nightwatchman had said good night to Mrs Harrison an hour since, and one by one the managers and Mr Greenwood, the last to leave, had nodded to him as he touched his cap to them. He'd go and have a 'brew' as soon as the gate was locked, he told himself, for though the night was warm and a pint of ale would have been more welcome, Mrs Harrison and Mr Greenwood allowed no strong drink in the premises.

Although it was dark in the blow room the outline of the machinery showed up clearly in the light of the stars and the splinter of moon which hung in the sky just above the window. It was quiet and when the spark jumped as metal struck metal, the flare no greater than that of an instantly extinguished match, the sound seemed quite loud. After that there was a hush, almost as though the ghosts which peopled the room—of those workers who had just gone thankfully, wearily, even blithely if they were off on a jaunt the next day—were holding their breath, waiting for what would happen next.

The machinery, once so lethal to small, unwary children, was now properly and securely fenced with wooden casing, miles of it, not just in this room but throughout the factory. The machines were cleaned regularly, of course, for cotton fibres collected inside, mixing, if they were not taken away, with the oil used to grease the parts. There was dust and fly and a collection of flake almost an inch thick in some places and it was to this that the spark jumped.

Like a small but voracious animal it fed on the dust hungrily, disposing of it in seconds before looking round, considerably grown by now from a spark to a flame, for something else with which to feed its appetite. As it grew so did its hunger, and gathering strength it gathered speed.

When the flame reached the soft fibre within the casing it ignited like gunpowder, only a small explosion as yet but loud enough to turn the head of the nightwatchman whose kettle had just come to the boil. He listened intently, prepared to guard against intruders as was his duty, but the sound was not repeated and the hot water was ready to pour on to the tea leaves. He poured it, sniffing the aroma of freshly brewed tea, then sat down and reached for the newspaper which he had found left behind by some manager. It was *The Times*, costing only threepence now the newspaper tax had been abolished. It was not a newspaper he himself would have chosen, *Frazers Magazine*, or *Punch* which both had pictures in them being more to his taste since his reading was not all that good. Still, this was better than nothing and he'd just pick out the headlines whilst his tea mashed.

The fire in the blow room, on the far side of the building from where the watchman drowsed over his *Times*, spelling out words with a calloused forefinger, had devoured the whole room now. If the inhabitants of the cottages in Chapmans Row had turned to look in the direction of the mill they would have seen at least a dozen windows lit up like the hobs of hell, but most of them were tucked up in their beds, getting a good night's sleep in preparation for tomorrow's enjoyment. There was to be a cheap trip to Manchester and Belle Vue Gardens, starting at seven, and they'd need to be up early if they were to get there in time to see the great Fife and Drum Contest, as well as look round the splendid gardens. They dreamed about the visit, those who were to go, as the fire, having devoured the blow room, passed through shaft after shaft, all horizontal and encased in wood. Backwards it surged to the room in which the raw bales of cotton were stored, pouncing on them and causing such an explosion the roof of the building directly above it was lifted twenty feet into the sky; then forwards to the carding room where every drum was stretched tight with cotton and every can filled with the soft rope of yarn which came off the machines.

As the explosion lit up the sky every person within three miles sat up in their beds exclaiming in unison though not perhaps in exactly the same words, but with the same apprehension, 'Good God, what the hell was that?'

Drew and Tessa had been making love, their sweat-slicked bodies entwined on the rumpled bed, the pale moonlight streaming through the drawn-back curtains and open window to touch them with a strange and unearthly beauty. He was at peace for the moment as though the spilling of his seed into his wife's empty womb had released the devils which came more and more often to plague him. Though neither was consciously aware of it, each month both breathed more easily when it became apparent that Tessa was not pregnant. Sometimes Tessa reflected upon it, wondering why she had never conceived and why, now that she was safely married, she did not desire a child. If she cared to dwell on it she supposed the one she held in her arms at this moment was as much as she could manage. Drew, if such a thought were to enter his often confused mind, was aware that he could share her with no one. She was *his* mother, giving him security in a shaking and insecure world, as mothers should he believed, though he had not

411

experienced it with his own. She was the only friend he had for despite his 'pals', the fellows with whom he roistered, he had no others. She loved him unquestioningly and he loved her. Since their marriage he had never been unfaithful to her, despite the many opportunities that had arisen, and he found great satisfaction in that and in the pleasure she now gained in his arms. She had become, in a completely feminine way, the twin he had lost and when their bodies were joined it was as though he and Pearce were returned to the safety of the womb.

'Good God, what the hell was that?'

It took them no more than seconds to fling off the bed-clothes and pull on shirts and breeches. Afterwards Tessa brooded on her own absolute certainty that disaster had struck though at the time she could not identify what it was that had them in such a panic.

'Good God, what was that?'

The words were but a whisper in Jenny Harrison's lamplit bedroom for did she have any real need to ask? Her experience told her. Her years in the cotton trade, her knowledge of mills and their workings had brought with them the fear which lies at the back of the minds of all manufacturers whose buildings are crammed with dangerous machinery, dangerous materials and substances which, if treated carelessly, bring the lot together in disaster, a chain of disasters which was the millowner's nightmare. Of course, it might not be *her* mill, or even a mill at all, but the explosion, for that was what it was, had come from the east and in that direction lay Chapmanstown and Crossfold.

Charlie was out of the bed he shared with Laurel and across the room to the window almost before the echoes of the explosion had begun to resound from hill to hill, those which stood guardian about the Penfold Valley. Even as he anguished on the certainty that disaster had struck *his* mill, for really, when he considered it, he had not actually heard the explosion since he had been deeply asleep, he was struggling into his breeches, hopping from foot to foot in his quite comical efforts to thrust the first one down the leg of his trousers.

'What is it, dear?' his wife asked, not particularly concerned since she had heard nothing.

'I don't know. Go back to sleep. I'll just go and . . .'

The flames leaped merrily from machine to machine in the spinning rooms on each floor of the mill, racing each other to be first to the weaving shed. Bobbins ricocheted like bullets from wall to wall and just as lethally, exploding into a hundred tiny shards of wood on impact. Beams above the machines, wooden and impregnated with nearly thirty years of oil and cotton flake, caught fire, burned through and crashed down in the space of two minutes.

The nightwatchman, with his mug of tea still in one hand and his newspaper in the other just could not believe it, and stood with his mouth hanging open thinking he must be dreaming. It was no more than ten minutes since he had brewed up and whilst his back was turned, so to speak, someone had fired the whole bloody mill. He watched as the tape-sizing plant where the beams were full of yarn being sized to stiffen and strengthen the threads, became an inferno, the size bringing fresh life to

413

flames which were already twice as tall as the building itself. The heat took his eyelashes and brows and he could smell his own hair beginning to smoulder and he moved then, screaming a warning, far too late, dropping his 'brew' and his newspaper as he raced for the mill gates.

The weaving shed was reduced to an unsteady, smouldering skeleton with a dozen huge tottering beams which once had supported whole floors now sticking up like the fingers on a hand against the brightening sky. The warehouse and despatch room were completely gutted when they arrived in the carriage, driven at a dangerously run-away speed by Drew himself. He was charged up to fever pitch with excitement, his face quite devilish in the lurid flames of the fire. Just for a second, before the horror of the disaster rooted her to the soot-blackened square of ground on which she stood, Tessa was quite appalled by her husband's terrifying intensity. He seemed bewitched, clasping her hand like a small boy who had come across some strange and alarming sight and is unsure whether to be afraid or exhilarated. The fear excited him, and the excitement frightened him, combining to produce a dangerous state of mind in which, it appeared to her, he might dash recklessly into the flames to save some small, quite unimportant item, risking his life to do so. And at the same time she sensed a gladness in him, a delirious relief as though he was overjoyed to see, at last, the destruction of the one thing he hated more than any other on earth.

Then the fury and savagery of the fire took everything from her mind. Her mother stood like a statue in the higgledy-piggledy collection of clothing she had flung on, her eyes following the line of useless water-filled buckets which passed from hand to hand, directed by a frantic Charlie; and then, amid the confused shouts and the realisation of those who operated it that it was a waste of time, her gaze turned to the large hand-pump which had required fifty men to haul it here and pump the water from the nearby river.

Dawn came early for it was not yet autumn and still her mother stood at the top of the brow which led down to the mill, now no more than a blackened, smoking pile, spread over an enormous area of what could only be described now as rubbish. There was nothing identifiable in the stinking debris: the outline of what might have been a spinning mule, melted down in the fierce heat to no more than a lump of metal; a half-burned-through beam, the unexplained mystery of why half of it was barely touched whilst the solid steel had melted.

Scores of silent onlookers stood about with no thought in their minds of going to Preston or Manchester, conscious only of their jobs which had gone up in the flames along with the mill. Men moved about aimlessly through the pools of filthy water, scratching their heads for want of a better occupation, their clogs sinking into the water and the mud as they wondered what to do next. Children watched awed but thrilled, as Drew Greenwood had been, unaware of the consequences which would surely follow this night. And over it all the sun shone benignly from a cloudless sky.

Tessa could not seem to get her stunned and senseless mind beyond the wonder of how much

415

space the mill had taken up. Across the acres and acres of wasteland she could now see the tidy row of cottages, the village church and its graceful spire, the smithy set beside the small row of shops and, to the left, the fields on which the men played cricket and the children ran in the meadow grass. Why, it's open countryside here, her astonished gaze told her, only the mill making it seem like any other small cotton town. There were trees and a park which she had never noticed before, a whole community which had lived under the wing of Chapman industry, nurtured by the thrift and common sense, the foresight and business acumen of women like her mother and men like Charlie.

She stood with her arm about Jenny's shoulders, drawn to her with compassion, their past animosity forgotten, watching as Charlie began to walk in the direction of the ruined mill, his long stride taking him down the slope and through the wide open gateway into the filthy yard. Jenny began to follow and Tessa went with her, both still stunned by the enormity of the destruction. Drew was helping the men push the hand-pump from the area. Pearce, his brother, had loathed—and been afraid of—the factory in his youth. Now Drew, who had been part of him, certainly did not feel the need to poke about in its remains as Charlie seemed intent on doing.

'Charlie,' Jenny's voice was nervous, warning her brother not to go too near.

'Don't fret thissen, our Jenny,' Charlie answered in a strained, ragged voice, the broad vowels of his Lancashire heritage strong now in his distress. 'I'm nobbut tryin' to see if there's owt in't . . .'

'What, for God's sake? Everything's burned to a

416

crisp. What can there possibly be left worth risking getting yourself burned for?'

'Th'office were here, lass. Happen there's a file or two . . .'

'Don't be daft, Charlie. Please come back. The wood's still smouldering and your clothes might catch alight.'

'Give ower. The men've cleared a path through theer to mek easier access for't hosepipes. I'll just . . .'

'Charlie . . . please . . .' Jenny begged, then turned to the men who stood in dispirited groups in every corner of the yard. Some had come for miles and some seemed not quite so downcast as others, since it was not their mill which had burned down nor their jobs which were lost.

'Is it safe for him to go in there?' she asked them irritably for, really, her brother was so pigheaded sometimes and would listen to no one. Perhaps if another man told him, one of those involved in the fire-fighting, he might be persuaded to stop poking aimlessly around and come home for a hot bath and a rest. Heaven only knew what he would do with himself, nor she either, until the mill was re-built: the four other mills, the old ones built by Barker Chapman nearly eighty years ago, were small and with only enough managerial work to keep those already employed there fully occupied. But that was for tomorrow. Today must be got through and they were all in a badly shocked state. They needed food and sleep and the sooner they left this desolation the better.

The smoking beam, though as solid as one of the rocks up on Badger's Edge, made from the strongest wood, twelve feet long and at least two feet wide on each of its four sides moved ever so slightly. It stood bolt upright from the dense mass of melted machinery which supported it and though Charlie was at least six feet away and standing quite still as his eyes darted about in search of something he might salvage, a ledger perhaps, a wages book or some record of the work done here only yesterday, it seemed to line itself up with the menace of a wild animal ambushing its prey. It fell so slowly all those who watched were quite convinced Mr Greenwood could easily have side-stepped, and they stood waiting for him to do so, shouting a warning nevertheless, just to be on the safe side. It struck him squarely on the back of the head, falling with a sound like thunder, taking him with it into the muck and filth and water-soaked ashes, the charred wood and melted steel, the stinking ruin of what had once been the best and safest mill in the whole of south Lancashire.

For a moment that seemed to stretch on forever more there was an appalled silence. Then Jenny Harrison began to scream and it was not until her daughter gripped her savagely, pulling her into her own desolate arms—for how could any of them survive if Charlie, dear, dependable Charlie was lost to them?—that she fell into chilling unconsciousness.

*   *   *

The funeral of Charlie Greenwood, little piecer once, in the mill that he had for less than two years owned in partnership with his sister and nephew, was attended by high and low from every part of Lancashire and even beyond into Yorkshire where

418

he had been well known for his clear business head and his reputation for fair dealings. Piecer he might have been, years ago, but when he died, besides being a wealthy man, his wealth now inherited by his distraught widow, he had also been the brother of the illustrious Joss Greenwood, once and for many years Member of Parliament for Crossfold.

The ladies were in black silk with corsage and sleeves ornamented with jet, and skirts with no more than seven flounces, for one did not want to seem ostentatious on such a sad occasion. The gentlemen wore black coat and trousers, mourning bands and tall black top-hats. Black, black everywhere except for the wisps of white cambric and lace, black-edged, which many of the ladies lifted to their eyes though they could not say they had exactly known the dead man.

His sister stood beside Joss Greenwood, erect, composed and quite, quite still, no sign of tears for her dead brother, though her face was paper-white behind her black veil. Her sister-in-law, once Kit Chapman who had built the destroyed mill, wept quietly, more, one felt, for the passing of so young a man than in grief, clinging to her husband's arm, not looking round at the mourners nor the hundreds of operatives who jostled for a place to watch the burying of the man most of them had known only as their millmaster. The remaining four Chapman mills were closed for the day in respect for Charlie Greenwood and the press of spinners and weavers was so great that the hillside on which the church stood was black with them.

His niece was impassive. Her eyes stared stonily at the coffin being lowered into the grave as she supported, or so it seemed to those nearest to them, the sad weakness of her husband and cousin, Drew Greenwood. His behaviour was strange, or perhaps not, when one remembered him as a wild youth. Despite the efforts of his family to persuade him to his proper place in the business, or so it was said in the valley, ever since his father had made it over to him this young and vigorous man had managed to live as though it had nothing at all to do with him. He had never been near the factory, now gone, which was his inheritance, since before he and his equally reckless brother had ridden off to the Crimea. Even marriage to his cousin had not steadied him and at the age of twenty-two he had not, to anyone's knowledge, done a hand's turn in his life and by the look of him drooping at the graveside, his hand in that of his beautiful wife, was not likely to do so in the immediate future.

The mourners had gone and the six adults who remained of Charlie Greenwood's family sat stiffly about the drawing-room wondering how soon they might, without giving offence, be allowed to leave: Kit Greenwood eager to return to the comfortable solitude she and her husband shared in the sunshine of Italy, her son to get his wife upstairs and into the private world he and she wove in their wide double bed and where he felt secure. The graveside had reminded him too sharply of that other one in Scutari, dark and silent and menacing. He needed sweet-scented flesh, pliant and warm, soft-hued with life, the feel of silk and the smell of sensuality to reassure him that he was not dead, and only with Tessa could he find that.

Jenny and Laurel sat side by side on the pale velvet of the sofa, the stark black of their mourning quite shocking against its soft prettiness. For once

420

they were united in their stunned grief, not exactly leaning on one another but both conscious of the sympathy they shared. If she were honest Laurel would admit, only to herself, mind, that her sorrow was strongly laced with the fear of what was to happen to Laurel Greenwood without Charlie to ease the awkward path she trod. What would be her position now in this house where she had been mistress for so long? She could hardly picture her flighty cousin, Mrs Drew Greenwood, wanting to take over but at the same time could she, Charlie's widow, continue as what would now be, with Charlie gone, no more than housekeeper in Mrs Drew Greenwood's home?

Kit clicked her tongue disapprovingly as her husband asked the question she had been dreading. Though she might be his mother, she was not blind to the ... well, shortcomings was a mild way of putting it, of her only son and there was certain to be discord which would only serve to distress Joss Greenwood further. Jenny was fifty-six now—or was it fifty-seven?—and how much longer could she go on, particularly without Charlie? Kit felt she no longer cared. The mills which had once been her whole life could go to the devil, just as long as Joss took no harm from it. Let them get on with it, Drew and Tessa, and run the damn place into the ground. All she wanted was for the few years she and her beloved husband had left to be peaceful.

'Son, you will take Charlie's place now?' his father asked, but it was more of a command than a question, his manner saying quite plainly that, this time, there was really nothing clse for it and Drew Greenwood might as well make up his mind to it.

Tessa closed her eyes and waited. She could feel

421

her husband's hands clench over hers and his whole body seemed poised ready for flight. Already the day had placed a great strain on his slender reserve of stability, surely his father could see that? She herself was only too well aware that someone must run the business but surely he knew after all these years that it would never be Drew Greenwood? Never! They had been married for two years almost and in that time she had faced and learnt to accept what he was. Could not they? Providing no one obliged him to do anything other than what he did so well and easily, which was to be a country gentleman with thought for nothing but the care of his guns and horses, the cut of his jacket and the paying of his gambling debts, which he did quite without effort now, he would remain the pleasant, engaging husband she loved. But force him, if it were possible which she doubted, into the mill, and he would simply be unable to face it.

'Tessa . . .'

'Yes, darling?'

'I am ... do you not think ... there is something ... the stables ...?'

'Of course, sweetheart.' She turned and kissed him on the cheek, just as one might a large child who has asked politely to be excused from adult company. 'I know Percy wants to check with you on the condition of your new hunter. But don't be too long for your mother and father are to catch the train to London shortly.'

'No indeed. Excuse me, Mother, Father, Laurel, Aunt Jenny.' He smiled endearingly, his manners exquisite as he stood up. 'I shan't be but half an hour. This damned hunter of mine has developed a cough and I said I would look in to see how he is.

At the price one is forced to pay for a decent mount, one cannot afford to neglect it.'

There was a great and sorrowful silence when he had gone as the three who were most concerned contemplated, finally, the awful consequences of the Crimean War on the surviving son of the family. This was the heir; the one who, as was proper, would take up the reins of the business; who should, five years ago, have been compelled with his brother to take up the reins of the business. Tessa wondered at the naïvety of her aunt and uncle who, for some curious reason, had believed up until this very moment that he would. Could they not have seen, years ago, the weakness in *both* their sons? The lack of tough-fibred tenacity which every mill-master, whatever the size of his concern, needs to make a success of it? Joss Greenwood had had it, though he had channelled it into another undertaking. His wife, Kit Chapman had had it, refusing, thirty and more years ago to let a man take over and run her business when her father was killed. And in the veins of their sons had run their blood, the blood of the blunt, outspoken, stout-hearted north-countryman who would fight for his own bit of ground until they buried him in it. Her own mother, no kin of theirs except by the kinship of love, was the same, and so, sadly, had been Charlie. Now there was only Jenny Harrison left to carry on the great tradition and how was she to do it without her much-loved brother beside her? She was approaching sixty, a great age for a woman, and the task of rebuilding the mill at Chapmanstown, of organising into some semblance of order the huge financial commitments, of handling the hundreds of their customers who would now have to look elsewhere for the piece goods and dress goods with which Chapmans had supplied them, the enormous task of painstakingly putting together what the holocaust of the fire had smashed to pieces must now fall on her shoulders alone.

Jenny Harrison lifted her eyes from the pretty Meissen ornament she had been gravely studying and sighed. Her hollow-eyed face was a pale and dusty grey. Her flaunting mass of short curls was covered by her black mourning bonnet and she looked extinguished, the guttering flame of the candle of her life gone out at last. She had lost her brother whom she had loved. They had shared so much, she and Charlie, from the day when as a young boy nearly thirty years ago he had strode out manfully beside her to his place at the mill. He had suffered so much with her, even more than Joss: the bitter hardships, the hunger, the cold, the brutality of the work he was forced to, the desolation of the 'afflicted poor', doing his best despite his tender age to be a man. Now he was gone. She had lost her son, not only the memory of the merry-faced three-year-old who had been taken from her, but the haunted, hate-filled man he had become, who said he would never forgive her for what she had done to Tessa, her daughter, and to him, her son. She would live with that memory until she died with no other to soften it. The two men she had loved more than any other, both gone and, her expression said, she could stand no more.

'I've had enough, Joss,' she said simply, looking only at him.

'Jenny?' Her sister-in-law's voice was unsteady.

'You cannot ask it of me, Kit. If he . . .' she

jerked her head in the direction of the door through which Drew had just gone, 'cannot manage, then you must sell it.'

'We cannot sell what has been in the family for almost a century, Jenny.' Kit Greenwood's voice was anguished, her indifference of a moment ago regarding the mills' future apparently fled away.

'Your family, not mine.'

'Dear God, Jenny . . .'

'It's no good, Kit. I'm finished. I can take no more. I want to sit in the sun, as you and Joss do, all day long with no decision to make but which hat to put on or how to fill the hours from breakfast to bedtime. It's gone now, lass, the force, or the need, or whatever it was that drove me on. Merciful heavens, I'm fifty-seven. That mill's had me since I was a girl and now it's taken Charlie . . .'

Laurel began to sob broken-heartedly, the thought of her future and that of her children looking more and more bleak with every word Jenny spoke. Dear God, if Jenny went, presumably giving her share to Tessa, what would happen to them all? To herself whose world was tottering like a house of cards and to her children who were not only to be fatherless, but homeless and forced to manage on the tiny share she would be entitled to if the other mills were sold?

'Oh, be quiet, Laurel,' Jenny said sharply. 'There's more than enough for you to set up house somewhere and give your boys a decent education, providing you're careful.'

Careful! Laurel sobbed even harder and Kit moved over to her, patting her shoulder carelessly, at the same time keeping an eye on her husband for signs of his distress.

Tessa sat quite still and waited for the blow to fall and when they all turned to look at her, as she knew they would, inside her something shrivelled and died away. She had a life that she enjoyed with a man she loved and who needed her. There was nothing now that she wished desperately to do except to go on in the same pleasant way with no great joys and, more to the point, no great heartaches, with her husband and companion, Drew Greenwood. Her heart began to race madly out of control and the palms of her hands became sweat-slicked and yet were icy cold. Nausea rose to her throat. She knew exactly what they wanted, it was written in three pairs of eyes, since it meant they could all continue to drift through the lives they had chosen for themselves, as she had done since she was a small child. They were to take her freedom away from her. That was what terrified her. They were about to beg her to do her duty, as women of her class and heritage were bred to do. They were telling her they were entitled to her consideration. A sacrifice, then, and was she prepared to make it, three faces begged her to tell them. Her mother seemed to care neither one way nor the other, staring vaguely out of the window as though, now that she had made her stand, she really could not be expected to take any further interest in the outcome.

But could not the mills be sold as Drew had suggested, she beseeched them silently. There must be insurance, a great deal, to be collected for the burned mill. As for the other four, as far as she knew they were prosperous for had she not heard her mother say time and time again that the demands for higher wages by the spinners and

426

weavers must, if it was at all possible, be met since trade was great and expanding? Well, then, four thriving mills. Easy to sell, she would have thought, and surely her uncle, or his wife, who was a clever woman with many contacts in the textile industry, could see to it? There was other property, land in Northumberland she had heard, shares in the railway, in mining and banking which would keep Drew Greenwood in horses and cravats for the rest of his life, surely.

She said so.

Sorrowfully, they replied, that though this was so Joss Greenwood's years in politics had not been without a price. The entertaining alone which was needed to keep a Member of Parliament where he was most likely to be noticed, had whittled away his wife's inheritance. And then there was the villa in Italy and years ago the enormous cost of knocking down Barker Chapman's old property, and building decent cottages in which their operatives might live. The mill at Chapmanstown had cost a pretty penny, expensive machinery, all paid for from the wealth her father had left Kit Chapman. This house was naturally, unmortgaged, but if the profit from the mills were to dry up . . . well . . .

'Tessa?'

'No, please, you cannot ask it of me. Besides, I know nothing of cotton or the commercial world. I wouldn't know where to start.'

'We would advise you, dearest . . .'

'From Italy?'

'We must try, Tessa. Those mills were built by my grandfather . . .'

'Your grandfather, Aunt Kit, not mine. You and I are not related, not by blood. The responsibility is

427

not mine, in any case. And then there is Drew. I must be here when he comes home, always.'

She glared angrily at his desolate mother and father, growing old before her eyes, since they knew only too well now what their son had become. 'You do understand, don't you? I would . . . would willingly help but . . . I am all he has . . .' Her voice petered out, the sharpness suddenly gone, and about her was the air of a cornered animal. When Briggs entered the drawing-room, after first knocking discreetly, she jumped quite violently, her nerves frayed and painful, her head aching so dreadfully she could barely see him.

'There is a gentleman to see you, sir.' He said the word 'gentleman' in such a way it was clear that in Briggs' opinion he was no such thing. 'Are you at home?'

'Who is it, Briggs?'

'A Mr Will Broadbent, sir, come to pay his respects.'

CHAPTER TWENTY-THREE

He looked prosperous, his black coat and trousers immaculate, his mourning bands correct in every detail. He did not even glance in her direction.

'Mr Greenwood, sir.' Briggs announced him to the master of the house but the visitor moved gently to take Jenny Harrison's hand.

'Mrs Harrison. I had no wish to intrude on your grief but I felt the need to come and tell you, and your family, in what high regard I held your brother. He was a fine man and will be sorely

428

missed. I was at the funeral along with a great many men who admired him but I did not speak to you then, not with such a throng.'

Joss was on his feet, his hand outstretched, his face showing his sadness at the death of his younger brother but pleased that this man, a man he did not know, had taken the trouble to go out of his way to show his respect for him.

'We have not met, Mr Broadbent. You are . . . ?'

'I was overlooker, then manager for a short while in Mr Greenwood's spinning room at Chapmanstown. He was a fair master and a good man. I can say no more than that.'

'No, indeed. That is a praise enough and a decent epitaph for there are not many of those, I fear. You are acquainted with my wife?'

Will Broadbent bowed his head in Kit Greenwood's direction, courteous and respectful but in no way humble.

'Mrs Greenwood.'

'Mr Broadbent.'

'And this is my brother's wife and my daughter, Mrs Laurel Greenwood.' Laurel bowed coolly for surely as the widow it should have been to her the first condolences were paid?

'Mrs Greenwood.'

'And my niece, my son's wife, Mrs Drew Greenwood.'

'Mrs Greenwood,' he said for the third time and nobody seemed to find it strange that he did not bow to her. His eyes looked directly into hers and she flinched away from the cool hostility in them; from the height and breadth of him which filled the dainty room; from the terrible blankness of his face which had once been warm with his love and the

429

almost cruel firmness of his mouth which had once covered hers with soft kisses.

She did not speak, indeed she could not, merely inclined her head towards him. He was a stranger after all, known only to her mother in whose employ he had once been, and nothing more was expected of her.

'We were about to take tea, Mr Broadbent,' her aunt said, not unduly concerned with the proprieties at a time like this, or indeed at any other. 'Will you join us?'

'Oh, no, thank you all the same, ma'am. I will not impose on you . . . on your . . . I was passing the house, that is all, on my way to Hepworth and felt I could not go by without paying my respects. My carriage is at the door and I will be on my way but before I do . . . I hope you will not be offended, Mrs Harrison . . .' His manner had become awkward, his face flushed but his eyes were clear and warm as he turned again to Jenny. 'If there is anything I can do to help you, perhaps some . . . well, anything at all.' He straightened his already straight back, beginning to move out of the room. 'You have only to ask, ma'am.'

'That is good of you, Mr Broadbent.' Jenny's eyes grew soft and she lost that faint air of vagueness she had worn since her brother's death.

'Aye . . . well, you and Mr Greenwood were good to me, ma'am.'

Tessa's jaws were clenched so tightly together she felt her teeth begin to ache with the pressure. A small shiver of pain shot through her right temple. Her thoughts spun wildly round and round in her head, one following hot on the heels of another, so closely they over-ran and became confused, but

430

one was clear, dominating over all the others, and she clung to it desperately.

She must say something. She must keep him here, at least until she had arranged her chaotic mind into some sort of order. She must not sit here like a painted image over which the ice has set, frozen to her chair, her hands clamped to her lap, her lips sealed and grim. Her uncle was shaking Will's hand again and her aunt was nodding politely as they walked towards the door. Their voices came at her from a great distance, faint and disintegrated, and she knew that if she did not do something now, though God knows what it should be, her life would turn on to a path which would be ill-fitting, like some garment made for another. She stood in the middle of a great and barren expanse with nothing to indicate which was the best direction, the right direction for her to escape from it. She had reached a crossroad but with only one route, a route along which she was being inexorably forced. And Will held the answer to her critical situation. She did not even know why. It was all shadow and illusion, as life itself was, a cruel farce cheating its players contemptuously, the injustice of it scarring them badly, as she had been scarred, as everyone in this room had been scarred, even Laurel whose awkward nature was surely the result of what life had done to her as a small child in the mills. Always it came back to them: the mills. They were the cause of all the turmoil and heartbreak that was in this family. They were the sword which hung over them all, the prison from which none, it seemed, could escape. And she was to be their next prisoner.

Her uncle had his hand on the door handle,

ready to usher their guest away to his carriage, to his life, wherever that was, when the door opened inwards and the handsome, apologetic, endearingly smiling face of Drew Greenwood appeared. He had the air of a small boy who knows he has been 'out to play' for far too long and is bound to get a scolding, but could they not see how much he had enjoyed himself and, really, would they begrudge it to him on this sad day? He had been extremely fond of Charlie, as they well knew, and if his heart was distressed was he not entitled to ease it in the comfort of the stable with his beloved hunter? Later, when it could be arranged, it would be in the comfort of his own bed with his beloved wife.

'I beg your pardon.' He sprang to attention with all the grace and good manners bred in him by a succession of nannies, tutors, schoolmasters and, more extensively, his close contact with Nicky Longworth and his friends up at the Hall. 'I was not aware we had guests.' He looked Will up and down, his arrogant superiority showing quite plainly for this man was not their kind, but he smiled and waited courteously to be introduced.

'This is Mr Broadbent, Drew. He was acquainted with Charlie and . . .'

'I worked in his mill, lad.'

'Indeed? My word.' Drew was not at all sure how to deal with Mr Broadbent's bluntness and, never having shaken the hand of a working man before, was not quite certain how to go about it.

'This is my son, Drew.'

'I believe we have met before, Mr Greenwood. It was in the spinning room when I worked for Chapmans.'

'Indeed.'

There was an awkward pause. Will stood quietly, composed, merely waiting politely, as a guest should, to be shown the door but before anyone could move towards it Tessa sprang up, turning all heads in her direction, and rang the bell.

'Really, Uncle Joss, we cannot allow Mr Broadbent to make that long journey to Hepworth—that is near Rochdale, is it not, Mr Broadbent?—without some refreshment, can we?'

Her uncle hesitated and his wife waited, as she always waited, for his answer. Then taking Will by the elbow he began to urge him, reluctantly on Will's part, towards the chair by the small fire.

'No, of course not, Mr Broadbent.'

She had no idea, not the slightest, what she was to say, or do, or on what topic she wished to address him, if there was one. She only knew that this man held the remedy to her desperation; that he was the one to get her out of the corner into which she was backed. Dear God, *how*? she beseeched silently, but no sign of her agitation showed on her impassive face and her eyes did not once lift to his as the conversation flowed slowly, politely, somewhat awkwardly among the company.

They drank tea and ate small cakes and Drew spoke enthusiastically on the virtues of his hunter, on the anxieties of the cough which afflicted the animal and on his chances of taking him to Leicester when the hunting season began.

'You are not to take over the immediate running of your mills then, Mr Greenwood?' Will asked courteously, the first spark of interest pricking his eyes.

'Good God, no. I am no millmaster, Mr Broadbent. I know nothing of spinning or weaving.'

433

Tessa held her breath. The room was as hushed as a church and she saw from the corner of her eye Will's interest quicken even further.

'If I am not being presumptuous, then who is to take Mr Greenwood's place?' he asked. 'Surely, ma'am,' addressing Jenny Harrison, 'you are not to manage alone?'

Jenny shook herself lightly, as though coming back from some distant place where she had gone to escape the bird-twittering of the drawing-room.

'I? Oh, no, Mr Broadbent.'

'Then ...?' He was very polite but clearly confused.

'My sister is to come to Italy with us, Mr Broadbent. She is ... not herself yet, after the death of our brother, and feels in need of a holiday.'

'I see,' he said, though clearly he didn't.

'The managers will attend to such things as are necessary, I believe. It shall all be left to them.' Drew's voice was careless.

'Indeed, that sounds well enough, Mr Greenwood, but in my experience that is a quick way to ruin. There is only one man to control a business and that is its owner.'

'Really? And you are qualified to give such an opinion?' Drew enquired insolently and Tessa saw Will's face register anger as his hosts' son reached for a cigar, lit it without permission to do so in his mother's drawing-room, then blew smoke slowly from between pursed and smiling lips.

Will's voice was quiet. 'I am a businessman myself. Some years ago I formed a co-operative spinning and weaving concern which I run for its owners who are, of course, the shareholders. As I have a considerable number of shares myself it is in my own interest to ensure the business prospers. I would not care to see it in the hands of men who work solely for a pay packet at the end of each week.'

Of course, he had heard—as who in the Penfold Valley, indeed in south Lancashire had not?—of the reluctance to take up his responsibilities as the Greenwood heir. Had it not been for his uncle, just buried that day, and his aunt who, it seemed, had lost not only her will but her desire for a commercial life, the business would long ago have gone the way of all such mismanaged ventures. Despite the expansion in the textile trade and the ensuing profitable business, it was to no purpose if there was no one to snatch an opportunity when it presented itself, some enterprising player to gamble, to take a chance, to recognise an opening, and that only the man at the top was capable of doing. Seemingly, amazingly, it was not to be Drew Greenwood.

'Then . . . ?' Will began.

Drew's voice was high, haughty, the privileged class answering one of its inferiors who had no right to have spoken up in the first place.

'I can only repeat that the managers at the mills are highly regarded by the family and will continue the running of them as they have been employed to do. I can see no reason to do the work when one employs, and pays, others to do it Mr Broadbent. My wife and I are agreed on it, are we not, Tessa?' He took Tessa's hand possessively in his where it lay passively. Not even Tessa saw the sudden clenching of Will Broadbent's strong jaw.

'I see,' he said coldly, 'then I wish you well, Mr
435

Greenwood, and I must also bid you good day. I have presumed for too long on your hospitality.'

In the polite confusion of leave taking no one noticed that not only did Mr Broadbent avoid Mrs Drew Greenwood's hand, he managed to avoid addressing her at all.

*   *   *

She waited two weeks before she called on him.

'Mrs Greenwood?' Though he was clearly surprised it in no way shattered his icy disdain. His office was small, not at all the splendid affair her own mother had worked in at Chapman Manufacturing and which now, if she could not arrange it to her own satisfaction, awaited her.

It was a cool, blustery day, a shower or two and the wind disturbing the tops of the trees which crowded the floor of the valley in which the mill stood. A small fire burned in the grate at his back and before him was an enormous desk taking up a great deal of space, the rest of the room crammed with shelves in which were hundreds of books of a highly technical nature. On the desk were papers, ledgers, account books, one assumed, pens and pencils, a tray filled with dozens of small wooden cups in which the operative's wage was presented to him. There was a 'piece' or pick glass used to examine cloth construction. The base formed a one-inch square frame, she remembered her mother telling her during one of her attempts to interest her daughter in life at the mill, to count the threads per inch in the cotton. A clock ticked loudly on the wall and as though to remind her that he was a busy man, to state her business and be off,

436

he took out his pocket watch and looked at it. He remained standing behind his desk and did not ask her to sit.

'What may I do for you, Mrs Greenwood?' he asked her coldly.

It was not going to be easy. He was not going to make it easy for her. His steady eyes told her he didn't like her much but he was a man who was not rude to a lady, particularly when she might have come to do business with him, for above all, where she was concerned at least, he was a businessman.

'May I sit down, Will?' She tried a smile but she was nervous and the muscles in her cheeks did no more than twitch. She was in mourning, of course, of the deepest black but her gown was elegant with a wide skirt and flowing sleeves and her large brimmed hat was piled high with black tulle roses. She looked, she knew, slightly frail, pale-skinned, her dark hair smoothed back into an intricate chignon by Emma, her face veil turned up to allow him to see the velvet grey of her long-lashed eyes. She meant to make use of every advantage she possessed.

'What is it, Mrs Greenwood?'

He was telling her he had no time to waste on pleasantries, indeed he had no time to spare for her at all. He was busy with his own concerns, his manner said, and he could see no reason for her to be here in any case. She would be best served to state her case and be on her way.

'I have come to ... well, you know how I am placed, Will, with the mill, now that Charlie is dead and my mother gone to Italy?'

'I had heard, yes.' And he was not particularly concerned.

'I am sure you realise how difficult it is, for the family, I mean.'

'Really! In what way?'

She leaned towards him, smiling her brilliant smile. If he would just invite her to sit down, perhaps drink a cup of tea with him, it would make matters much easier. She had held him once in the palm of her hand, had him eating out of it, as the saying went, willing to do everything she asked providing she did not leave him. He had loved her, wanted to marry her, and there must be some of that feeling left, surely? He would not, could not turn her away without hearing what she had to say, and how much more relaxed it would be if they were to chat, civilly, if not warmly, over a cup of tea. They had parted cruelly. He had spoken bitter words then and she felt herself curl up inside at what she must say but, really, she could think of no other solution and so she must swallow her pride and hope that he had forgotten, or at least allowed the memory of that day to fade. They had met since at Annie's and he had called her Tessa then. They had been ... polite. There had been ... something. Could they not be ... perhaps friends?

But she still felt the need to tread warily, knowing that this man could be dangerous if he chose. She had thought him easily managed, gentle, a peaceful man, a man who would be happy to go through life in a moderate and tranquil way. He was strong, certainly, strong-willed and tough-fibred and would let no man own him, but surely she, as a woman, should be able to reach that core of decency which was the essence of Will Broadbent?

'Though it is some time ago now I have not yet

congratulated you on your marriage, Mrs Greenwood. Allow me to do so now,' he continued smoothly, swinging her cruelly off balance with the sudden turn of conversation, 'though as I said when we met previously, I must admit to a slight bewilderment at your choice of husband. When first I heard your name mentioned in connection with matrimony it was linked with that of some landed gentleman from Cheshire. You were to be married to *him*, I was led to believe, or was he too found to be unsuitable?'

It was as though he had cut the ground from beneath her feet opening up a hole, deep and black, which she did not care to contemplate and into which, if she did not take care, she might tumble. Robby Atherton had not been seen nor heard of since the day he had been told of his true parentage. It seemed that her 'parfit gentil knight' had not the heart nor stomach to face her again, either as her brother or her love, and though she had not blamed him, her heart had never quite recovered. He had been forgotten now by the Penfold Valley, as though he had not existed, but not by this man, it appeared.

He smiled and his face took on a musing expression. 'Do you know, Mrs Greenwood, if I live to see ninety I will never understand the ways of the gentry, since I suppose that is what you call yourself, particularly the gentlemen. Now, if I were your husband there is one thing you could be absolutely sure of: under no circumstances would I allow my wife to come begging favours of another man. Because that's what you're here for, isn't it? You want something from me, don't you? You would hardly drive all the way from Crossfold to
439

Hepworth otherwise, looking fragile and wan in your mourning gown, doing your best to seem helpless when you have never been helpless in your life. Really, Mrs Greenwood, it doesn't suit you, this pretence that you are no more than a weak and helpless female. You should try being honest sometime, as I told you once before, I believe. You might find it to your advantage in the long run.'

'Will, please, you have not heard . . .'

'Nay, and I don't think I want to. It seems the young gentleman whose heart you captured and who was so uniquely suited to your life-style and station in life and whose charms far outshone my own, and for whom you were willing to run to the ends of the earth, barefoot if needs be, no longer found favour in your eyes and that your cousin, the estimable Drew Greenwood, took his place. Really, Mrs Greenwood, one cannot hope to keep up with you. Three men in your bed already and you barely in your twenties . . .'

'Will, please . . .'

'No, really, you are to be admired for your tenacity, Mrs Greenwood. I suppose when you consider it, your cousin would be the better prospect: sole heir to the might and wealth of the Chapman concerns whereas a gentleman whose estate would simply devour any money you brought to him might not be such a catch. As for the simple over-looker in your family's mill . . . well, need I go on? I only hope your husband has the stamina and backbone to take on not only you, but his inheritance, that is if he is to do so. Or are you, perhaps, to take up your mother's position?'

He grinned wickedly, lifting a sardonic and knowing eyebrow.

440

She did not wait any longer to be invited to sit down but sank into the nearest chair, the thudding in her chest painful and taking her breath away, echoing in her temples, at the hollow of her throat and the pulses in her wrists. She felt dizzy, weary, as wave after wave of futility and defeat washed over her. She had thought it would not be easy, that she might have to beg and plead a little, make him realise that she had changed—had she really?— that she would make it worth his while perhaps. Would that have worked? But now she could see it was impossible. He hated her, despised her, or not even that. He was indifferent, and that was worst of all. He no longer cared if she survived or not. He was unconcerned with her future or even if she had any, and certainly had no softer emotion lingering in his heart which had once loved her.

'Who's to look after it all, Mrs Greenwood, whilst your husband chases about the countryside on that thoroughbred hunter of his, or tramps the Squire's moor shooting pheasant and grouse, or indeed everything that takes wing? It's been three weeks now and those mills won't be looking quite so profitable, I dare say, not without Mrs Harrison or Charlie Greenwood at the factory gate before the bell goes.'

'The managers . . .'

He made a contemptuous movement with his hand and sat down at last, lifting the tails of his splendidly fitting coat. Though his face had none of the masculine beauty of Robby Atherton or Drew Greenwood, nor the etched and lean superiority of Nicky Longworth, it was infinitely more virile with a compelling strength which said that no matter what life cared to fling at *him*, he would never yield

441

to it. His hair was still short and inclined to roam about his head as though he had cut it himself, carelessly, with the first pair of scissors which came to hand, but his smoky amber eyes were steady, firm, his skin brown and smooth. His whole appearance spoke of his rise in life. He was a businessman now, a man of consequence with a new, detached villa on the outskirts of Hepworth, she had heard, set in half a dozen acres of landscaped garden. He had a well-bred bay to ride when he cared to, and a carriage and pair for when he did not. He was an exceedingly attractive and successful gentleman and she wondered idly why he had never married.

'You cannot leave it to your managers, you know. If you do you will go under.' It was said irritably.

'What else am I to do?' She was more composed now, though her heart was still inclined to miss a beat. Now that they had left behind the delicate issue of Robby Atherton and were addressing themselves, she hoped, to the problem of Chapman Manufacturing, Will appeared to be, if not agreeable, at least prepared to discuss what might be done. If she could just get him to listen she was certain she could persuade him to what she had in mind.

'You are recovered now?' He spoke sharply and again his change of direction disconcerted her. Just as she was about to breathe more easily, thinking that she might at last get round to what she had come for, he led her somewhere else, giving her no time to get her thoughts into any kind of order. Recovered? What did he mean? Surely he was not talking about the fever she had contracted over two years ago? He had gone away just before, Annie had said, come up here and started his own venture, far too busy making his own life to bother about hers which had been smashed apart, but then had she herself not been far too busy with the loss of Robby Atherton to bother about *him*? Well, they had both lost something all those years ago but now he had found something to replace it and so had she and she would not spend the rest of her days in the mills which had taken Charlie's life, and her mother's too, in a way, though she still lived. She would find something, someone, she was determined on it, to look after what she and Drew had been left.

'Yes.' She smiled for she must keep on his right side. 'I was ill for a while but I am a tough north-countrywoman and so I recovered.'

'Your . . . friend did not care to stay then, to see you back to health?' His voice was harsh, scornful.

'My . . . friend?'

'Your lover, if you prefer?'

'Please, Will. Must we continually go back to something which happened a long time ago? It's over now and I . . . we must all move on, must we not?'

'I dare say, but now I must ask you to state your business for I've not got all day to sit and gossip.'

'No, indeed. You are a man of some importance, I am told and . . .'

'Give over, lass. Let's get to the point. I'm not one of your pedigreed nincompoops who needs to be buttered up before he can be asked to do anything. Speak plain and be done with it.'

She sighed for at last it had come and, as he said, best be done with it.

'I've come to offer you a position, Will.' There, it was out, thank God. She did not like it but the devil drives where the need must, or some such twaddle, and the devil was certainly driving her when she must grovel to this man who had once grovelled to her, well almost. But it was done now and when they had talked of wages and all the other difficult but necessary things—she would leave that to him, having no idea what they might be—she could get on home and tell Drew that he and she could continue to play as they had done, she realised, all of their lives.

'A position? And what might that be, my lass?' He had begun to smile now, his eyes narrowing in amusement, his slanting mouth turning up at the corners. His eyebrows lifted and she could feel the sudden tension in the air, coming not from him but from herself. He was vastly pleased about something, his bold expression said, his whole lounging body said, and again she felt awful uncertainty nibble at her. But what the hell? She was not afraid of him, or his damned insolence. She lifted her head imperiously.

'I would like you to be my general manager, Will. In charge of the mills, I mean. Of course there are only the four smaller ones at the moment but once you get the rebuilding of Chapmanstown under way you would be fully occupied, I'm sure. There will be a lot to see to, arranging with builders and whoever else is concerned with such things, and I'm sure you are right about the men in charge at Crossbank and the others. They will be lying in their beds until nine each day, leaving it all to the overlookers and . . . well, you will know what I mean. The sooner they are all under the direction

444

of one man the better.'

'Indeed you are right, Mrs Greenwood. I couldn't agree more.'

'Oh, Will, I'm so glad.' She smiled in gratification then became business-like again. 'Now I will leave the question of wages to you since I know you will not cheat me. I have no idea what a manager earns but . . .'

He began to laugh then. Lifting his head in genuine enjoyment, highly diverted, it seemed, and not at all concerned that he might be offending her. His laughter echoed round and round the room and there was a warm, dancing merriment in his eyes as he turned at last to look at her.

'Tessa, there really is no other woman in the world who would have the damned impudence to come here, after all that's happened between us, and offer me a job as manager in her mill. Does your mind dwell on nothing but what is best for Tessa Harrison, or did it not occur to you that I have my own mill to run, my own business to attend to? I've built this concern up until it's become one of the most productive in south Lancashire, for its size. Oh, not to be compared with Chapmanstown, I'll grant you that, but I'm damned proud of it just the same, and of myself. I've dragged myself up by my bootstraps, aye, and done a few things I'd tell no one about to get here, and not just get here, but to stay *alive* when I was a lad, and if you think I'm going to jeopardise it all for the sake of a lass who isn't worth a hundred of them in my mill then you must be dafter than I thought.'

'But, Will . . .' She ignored the insult which she found she did not care about just now. 'You told us it was a co-operative and that means it's not really

445

yours . . .'

'I own the majority of the shares.'

'I don't quite know what that means.'

'It means that if I left it on its own while I concern myself with your business, mine would suffer and my shares be made worthless.'

'But you said yourself that Chapmans needed to be under the direction of one man.'

'Aye, and so it does, but I'm not that man.'

'Please, Will, please. I would pay you anything you asked.'

'*Anything*, Tessa?'

Again his eyes danced with evident enjoyment. 'I really cannot think there would be anything at all which might tempt me. Not now. My life has gone on, you see, leaving you where we last met and what you have done and what I have done no longer matters to the other. I am no longer at your beck and call . . .'

'Will, please, think it over . . .'

'I have no wish to think it over, and no need.' His eyes had turned cold again, cold and disdainful. 'You really must become used to the fact that you can't have what you want, whenever you want it, Mrs Greenwood. You mean nowt to me, and neither does that damned business of yours. You and your fine husband can go to the devil for all I care . . .'

'Will, for God's sake, Will.' Her voice cracked painfully and she stood up, hauling herself to her feet as though she was clawing her way to the surface of a boiling torrent which was dragging her under. Her eyes had turned a brilliant, quite incredible silvery grey, like crystal, in her despair and her breasts rose, drawing his eyes to them. Her

446

face had flushed to rosy pink and the soft flesh of her mouth was moist and swollen. She put out her hands to him in desperation and he felt himself begin to move towards her, his body answering the appeal of hers. 'I'm ready to pay you any wage you ask.' Her voice was husky, just as it once had been in the fierceness of their lovemaking. 'I'll give you shares in the mill, which, I believe . . . I have been told, though I really know little about it, will give you a small part of the ownership. Apart from the ones left to Laurel by Charlie it all belongs to Drew and me and he would give anything you name not to have to go in the mill.'

'Would he indeed?' His own voice sounded strange in his ears. His eyes gleamed, an intense speculative gleam which she was not sure she cared for. The lazy unconcern had gone completely, as had his indifference, and she felt the first feather of alarm touch the nape of her neck.

'He . . . you will have heard of his brother's death, no doubt?' Her mouth had dried up and she seemed to have trouble forming the words but he merely continued to watch her, allowing her to stumble along at her own pace. 'Well . . . they were . . . being twins, you understand, they were very close and Pearce's death hit him hard.' Dear Lord, why was she telling him all this unless it was to dissipate the curious tension which had sprung up from somewhere? 'He was himself wounded and it has left him . . .'

'You really have no need to explain, my dear. Your husband's . . . afflictions are well known to me. Remember we worked . . . I use the term loosely, you understand . . . together in the Chapman spinning room.'

447

'So you will help him then?'

'Not him, Tessa, oh, no, not him.'

'Then . . . ?'

'You and I . . . once . . . had a very delightful arrangement, did we not? Do you remember?' His voice was like silk and his eyes had become a warm and appreciative brown and she knew immediately, of course, with what coin he was asking her, no demanding her to pay and she felt the fury explode in her, not just with him and the effrontery of what he implied but at the sudden excitement which stirred in her at the idea.

She had never been so humiliated in her life, she told herself, whipping up her own temper until her cheeks were scarlet with her outrage. His eyes were merry now, maliciously so, and he had the greatest difficulty, she could distinctly see it, in preventing himself from grinning broadly at her discomfiture. Her rage struck even more deeply, a scorching blow which had her savagely struggling not to hit him. If she had held a pistol in her hand she would have shot him in his smiling face and been glad to see the flesh shatter, the blood flow. Her heart was banging and crashing inside her—*why, for God's sake, why?*—far too big for her chest, and deep, deep within her, where no one could see or even know of its existence, the core of her female self, that which had lain dormant for many, many years, began to unfurl and throb, and she hated him, hated him for it.

She lifted her head and though her eyes were hot and baleful with her need to hide from him what was in her, she managed to keep her words cool and contemptuous.

'May I ask what you are suggesting, Mr

448

Broadbent?'

'Come on, my lass. Don't play the innocent with me. I know you better than any man, I would say, and certainly better than that husband of yours. You know exactly what I am saying or do you want me to spell it out to you? Not only do you know, you're excited at the thought, aren't you? You're a woman, Tessa, and though I've had my share before and since, there's been none to match you when it comes to . . . pleasing a man, and to taking pleasure from it yourself. I'm sure you know what I mean. I can see it in your eyes right now. So what d'you say? Shall we strike a bargain? You come to my bed and I'll see to those mills of yours for you. You and Drew Greenwood can skylark about to your hearts' content, if you've a mind, and I'll keep your mills running to pay for it, but I'll want a share of the profit, and a share of Drew Greenwood's woman to go with it.'

He grinned, then, with all the time in the world and the unconcern to go with it, reached into the silver cigar case on his desk, selected a cigar, lit it and when it was drawing to his satisfaction, leaned back in his chair and waited.

'*You can go to hell, Will Broadbent,* and the sooner the better as far as I'm concerned. I'd see the mills in ruins before I'd let you touch me again.' She gathered her pelisse about her as she leaped up, snarling and dangerous, ready, should he put out a hand to her, to bite it off at the wrist but he merely grinned more broadly. He took another puff of his fine cigar, his long legs stretched out indolently beneath his splendid desk.

'Just as you please, Tessa,' he said as though it was nothing to him, one way or the other. But when

449

she had gone, sweeping regally from the room, elbowing aside the clerk who would have guided her down the steps to her carriage, he leaned forward in his chair and pressed a trembling hand across his suddenly sweating face.

CHAPTER TWENTY-FOUR

'I shall go alone then. If you cannot or will not come with me, which seems to me to be nearer the truth, I shall go alone. You know that Nick has set his heart on this holiday, and on having you there. You are a great favourite, darling, not only with the gentlemen of whom, by the way, I am inordinately jealous, but of the ladies. They seem to find us immensely amusing because of our industrial background and the way, one supposes, we have risen above it. You make them laugh, my love, with your outspoken ways and your quite careless disregard of their belief that they are superior to us. Oh, come with me, Tessa, please. I know we are still in mourning for Charlie, but he wouldn't mind. You know how he was. We have never been stag-hunting before. They say that runs of eighty miles are not uncommon and not a third of the horses which start out are in at the death. What a challenge, eeh? You and I against the others. What d'you say?'

Drew Greenwood paced his wife's sitting-room with all the fire and intensity of a beast which, having been caged, is searching, snarling and dangerous, for the way out. He had just ridden back from the Hall where he had spent the day

450

riding to hounds with the Squire and his guests. He was over-excited as he seemed to be so often these days, Tessa thought. Either that or bored to distraction, casting around for something to amuse him, petulant and churlish at times and at others boyish in his eagerness to tempt her to come and share his play. But slowly, she knew, he was becoming increasingly hostile to what he saw as her stubbornness in the matter of the mills. She felt there was something barely harnessed within him and if she let go he would not be able to hold on to it without her, but she must put the factories into some kind of order before she could resume the pleasurably careless life-style they had enjoyed together before the disaster of the fire and Charlie's death. No matter what she said, how she tried to explain to him the need for someone to be concerned, he still insisted that managers were employed for that particular purpose and that he could see no reason for this ridiculous obstinacy on her part. And he was becoming isolated from her in a quite frightening way. She who had been his 'steadier' was accused of being tedious and not half the fun she once had been. He would not listen to her when she explained patiently that though they had the managers in whom he set such store to see to the running of the sheds at Broadbank and Crofts Bank and the spinning rooms at Crossbank and Highbank, the four older mills, *someone* was needed to oversee *them* until order was restored. There was the re-building of Chapmanstown to be considered, insurances, she had been told vaguely by her mother before she left for Italy, and who was to do it if she did not? Her own sense of responsibility towards the accursed business which, after all, belonged to the Greenwoods, irritated her beyond measure and she wished heartily that she could do as Drew wished and just leave the whole damned lot to go to the devil. But something stopped her. Something only half-understood which had perhaps to do with old Joshua Greenwood who had died at Peterloo and all those who had come after him—her own mother, her Uncle Joss, Charlie. Or perhaps it was her own stubborn will which would not allow itself to be beaten, plus the certain knowledge, finally, that Drew would always be just as he was now, never able to be the Greenwood *they* had been, and which, surprisingly, she *was*.

She had said as much to Annie when she had ridden over to her cottage, shortly after she had been to see Will. Drew had gone to the races with Nick and Johnny, sick to death with her long face, he said, and set on escaping it.

'I don't know where to begin, Annie,' she moaned. 'It's like turning a three-year-old loose in a kitchen with instructions to prepare and cook a fifteen-course dinner for thirty people. I have never been in the counting house except to call on my mother and only in the yard to pick up Drew and Pearce and I have never once set foot in a spinning room or a weaving shed. I have heard my mother speak of carding and drawing frames but if you should ask me what they meant and my life depended on the answer I could not describe them. Will you not at least come with me for a day or so to start with? You are a spinner and have some idea as to what I might be looking for. We could walk round the mills together and you could tell me what is happening . . .'

452

'Yer overlookers could do that, Tessa, much better than me, or one o't managers.' Annie's voice was blunt.

'But I don't want them to know I'm so ignorant. Dear God, Aunt Kit had her father to guide her through it all and Mother had Aunt Kit. Dammit, I've no one.'

Annie hesitated. ' 'Appen if you was to speak polite-like to Will . . .'

Tessa's face set in an icy mask of contempt. 'I have already offered him the position of manager but he declined. He does not care what I do, he said. I can go to hell in a handcart before he would lift a finger to help me.'

'Yer can't blame 'im, lass. Yer tried him sorely a few years back an' 'e'd not forget in a hurry. Still, I thought 'e might 'ave given thi some hint, some idea where tha might begin. Mind you, 'e said nowt ter me when 'e were 'ere last . . .'

'You've seen him?' Tessa felt her heart lurch painfully.

'Aye. 'E comes over now an' again, like 'e always did, an' we 'ave a chin-wag. Just because you an' 'im 'ad a fallin' out years ago, doesn't mean 'im an' me 'ave to do't same.'

Tessa's face was stiff, she could not have said why since what was it to her if Annie and Will had remained friends? She had known, of course, so why did the mention of it cause this agitation in her?

'You never mentioned him.'

'Would it 'ave made any difference if I 'ad?' Annie, quick to take offence at the implied criticism and letting it be known that what she did was her own business, lifted the kettle from the fire

453

and banged it down on the dresser just as though the innocent utensil was the cause of her pique.

'No, indeed. None at all.'

'Well, then?'

'Indeed.'

'So what are we arguin' about?'

'We are not arguing, Annie, and certainly not over Will Broadbent who is not worth giving the time of the day. I don't want to hear another word about him. I'm going to get out the carriage tomorrow and go to Crossbank and show *him* and everyone else who thinks I shall fall flat on my face that I'm as much a Greenwood as my mother.' She lifted her head challengingly but in her eyes was the dreaded anticipation that that was exactly what she would do, and if she was to fall who would pick her up?

Annie sighed sadly. 'I'm right sorry. I wish I could 'elp thi, but I can't.' It was said simply, the truth of her words, the certainty of them very obvious. 'I 'ave me own life ter sort out now.' Tessa, absorbed with her own problems, did not hear her. Annie put out her hand. 'Is there no other way? Could not that 'usband o' thine not 'elp out, or 'appen yer could sell the mills?'

'I suppose I could try but I don't even know enough to guess at an asking price. Dear God, if only Aunt Kit or Uncle Joss or even Mother had remained for long enough to tell me what to do.'

'From what thi tells me, Mrs Greenwood can't do wi' 'avin' yer uncle worried. She only cares about 'im an' spendin' what days they 'ave left together in peace.' In a way, Annie could understand that: a bit of peace must be a wonderful thing to have. Not that she'd ever known any, what with her mam dying and four children to be fetched up somehow, but a thing to be treasured was peace of mind. ' 'Ow old d'yer reckon they are?' she asked, more to take Tessa's mind from her problems than her own curiosity.

'Who cares?' Tessa's voice was irritable. For God's sake, Annie was really the limit sometimes. She could think of the most foolish things just when sensible advice was needed. What did it matter how old her aunt and uncle were? It was *now* that concerned her and what *she* was to do, if she could only think what that was. Perhaps it might be an idea if she were to go and see ... the bank manager ... or that lawyer chap in Crossfold her mother had dealt with. Would it not be practical to find out about the mill's financial position? That sounded sensible. Its financial position. How much ready cash there was available. Would it be in the bank, hers and Drew's inheritance, and if so could she get hold of some of it? Briggs had already intimated that one or two tradesmen had presented their accounts. No hurry, naturally, since the Greenwoods and Harrisons were valued customers who normally settled their debts immediately they were incurred, not like the gentry who seemed to think next month, next year or even never would be quite agreeable and who could take serious offence, and their custom elsewhere, if pressed.

She felt quite pleased with herself. She stood up and smoothed down the tight-fitting black breeches she wore, smiling a little for she had made a decision and had a sensible plan of action. That was what she would do tomorrow. She would call on the bank manager and the lawyer and then, step

455

by step, one action surely leading to another, she would gradually take a hold on the unwieldly package her mother had left her and which was loosely tied together and called 'the mills'. She'd show them, all of them, meaning, of course, Will Broadbent who had so insulted her with his nasty proposition. She'd show him that she needed no one's help, especially his, to keep the profits flowing from the business which had been the most efficient and productive in the Penfold Valley for almost a hundred years. It only needed that first step to get her going. Everyone had to take it. Her Aunt Kit and her own mother had done it and if they could do it so could she. She'd let no one guess at her complete lack of knowledge or her fear and though they might suspect they would never know for certain. Bluff, it was called, and she would learn to be good at it. Damn him to hell. She'd show him.

'You off then?' Annie asked.

'Yes, I've had an idea. I'll go to see the bank manager. He'll tell me where to begin. Uncle Joss did say something about consulting him and I'd clean forgotten in all the ... well, I'm sure he'll give me some clue where to begin. Thanks for the tea, Annie. I'll be over again soon and if there's anything you need just let me know,' she added for Annie, Nelly, Polly and Gracie had all been thrown out of work by the destruction of the mill. 'By the way, where are the girls? They're usually helping you with something. Don't tell me you've let them escape your tyranny for once?'

'They're workin'. All three o' them.' Annie stood up, moving the pans on the fire, setting the tongs to a more precise angle in the hearth, her face

456

expressionless, her manner defensive, the very air about her rigid with her determination that everything should be in the perfect order she liked. 'And I'm ter be off in a day or two so I'll not be 'ere when yer call.'

'Oh? You never told me you had a job.'

'I'm tellin' yer now an' yer'd best be off or it'll be dark soon.'

'Never mind that. What are the girls doing and where are you going? I thought we'd agreed I'd fit you in at one of the other mills, you and the girls.'

'Oh, aye, an' what about them as was laid off because o't fire? 'Undreds of 'em. Are yer to fit them in an' all?'

'You know I can't do that. There isn't enough work.'

'They know that, an' so do I, that's why I'm off ter . . .'

'To where?'

'I've found work in Manchester.'

'Manchester! But you can't go all that way. I need you here.'

'What for?'

'Oh, Annie, you know you're the only one with any sense I can talk to. You are . . . aware . . . of how things are with Drew at the moment.'

'Aye, I reckon the 'ole valley knows.'

'Well, then, I must have someone to . . . to discuss my problems with. Is it not possible to find work closer than Manchester? And how are you to get there and back each day? It's nearly ten miles . . .'

'We're moving. I've sold up an' we're movin'.' Annie's face was gaunt and hollow-cheeked and Tessa wondered why she had not noticed it before,

457

but her voice was tart and quite resolute. 'We've got lodgings in Salford. I've got rid o' most o't stuff . . . we 'ad to eat, tha' knows . . .'

'But you know you had only to ask me . . .'

'Mebbe so, but we've always managed on our own, like, an' I'll not take charity.' She lifted her chin menacingly as though daring Tessa to try pressing it on her. She was looking for no sympathy. She stated a fact and that was that and there was absolutely no use in Tessa attempting to change her mind. 'The girls are . . . pin-heading in Brown Street an' I'm ter do pin-sheeting . . .'

'Pin-sheeting?' Dear God, what was that?

'Aye, just 'til summat better turns up. Our Jack's in a warehouse in Portland Street. It tekks brass to keep a lad articled. The lawyer in Crossfold kept 'im on as long as 'e could but . . . well, 'e's a strong lad an' when things is better 'e can go back. 'Till then us'll manage.'

Tessa fumbled her way into a chair, her face like paper and somehow, though her mind told her it was foolish, this appeared to be even worse than the death of poor Charlie and the chaos she herself was in. She had no one, *no one* in whom she could confide her absolute terror, her sense of being caught in some ghastly nightmare from which somehow she must escape. Only Annie. Only Annie and now Annie was to leave her as well. Drew was . . . well, Drew had a contempt for the commercial world so great and so condemning he would beg on the streets rather than submit to it. He was, in the opinion of Crossfold and the Penfold Valley and to himself, if she were to be truthful, too fine a gentleman for the life of a millmaster. He had simply been waiting, they told

458

one another, to get his hands on his considerable share of the Chapman fortune when he would be off, with or without that dashing wife of his, to more exciting climes than Crossfold.

'We are rather rich now, are we not?' He had grinned amiably, daring her to deny it, his vivid blue eyes quite beautiful in the deep, smooth brown of his handsome face. He really is quite flawless, she had thought, from the outside, for she had no illusions about her husband's unstable mind. She herself was wild and just as carelessly imprudent, but where Drew exposed himself to danger with no thought to the consequences, not even aware that there were any, she had, in the past, done it quite deliberately, challenging the gods to stop her. And now the gods had stopped her and she must find a solution without even Annie to give her a hand.

'I didn't know,' was all she could find to say in response to Annie's news. 'I really had no idea.'

'Thi 'as enough on thi mind, lass, wi'out me ter think on. But we couldn't just sit 'ere an' wait fer summat to 'appen. It's same fer us all, them as worked at Chapmans. Mouths ter feed an' no wages ter do it. Anybody with a bob or two put by 'as spent it. Now it's pawnshops' turn, then, fer them as can do nowt else, poor relief. You'd not noticed, what with all you 'ad on yer plate, but I've 'ad ter let me mam's things go.'

Tessa looked about her dazedly noticing for the first time that the dresser on which Annie's willow pattern had once proudly stood, probably bought at one of the pot fairs which toured the north of England and not worth a great deal but dear to Annie, was empty of all but a couple of chipped

459

mugs, the old kettle and a frying pan with a broken handle—a few things not even the pawnbroker would consider. The room was bare somehow, though she could not have said what else was gone, and when she turned back to Annie her friend began to polish the dresser vigorously, wanting nothing said, nor willing to receive pity and indeed showing quite plainly she would be deeply offended if any was offered.

'There's no need ter look like that, my girl. We'll be all right, me an' the childer.' She always called them that though Jack would be eighteen now. 'It's only temporary, o' course,' she asserted, warning any fates which might be listening that she'd know the reason why should it prove otherwise.

Tessa stood up again, the colour seeping slowly back into her pale cheeks. For a moment she had allowed Annie's news to bring her close to fainting, the awful prospect of not having this sharp-spoken, sharp-faced woman right here where Tessa could find her whenever she pleased, taking her wits. They had been friends, or as close to friends as Annie would allow, for years now, a faintly uneasy relationship since Annie was extremely sensitive to what she thought of as 'decent' and 'proper' and in her opinion persons of a different class did not mix. She was a good listener, becoming involved in all Tessa's troubles, conveying her opinion with grunts of scorn, irritable shrugging of her shoulders, unbelieving shaking of her head, sharp tuttings, an ability to let you know exactly how she felt without saying a great deal. And yet when she did speak she demonstrated her north-country shrewdness, cunning almost, with bite and humour. What was she to do without her?

460

But she was right, of course. Tessa could not find employment for the hundreds of operatives who had been thrown out of work by the fire until the mill re-opened and only the Lord knew when that would be, but though she might be unable to do anything about the rest she would put this family back to work by the end of the week.

'You get down to the pawnshop and get your things at once,' she said briskly, 'because if you think I'm going to drink out of those dreadful mugs you are mistaken. See, here's a guinea, it's all I have on me. Then get the train to Manchester and fetch those girls back. And Jack. I'll see to the lawyer. Jack's had too good an education to waste it in a warehouse and I'm sure when . . .'

'You can stop right there, Mrs Greenwood, if you please.' Annie's face was taut with displeasure. Her pale brown hair was dragged back severely into a small bun with not a wisp allowed to escape and the style gave her an added sharpness. She laid her calloused, hard-working hands on the table top—where had her handsome chenille cloth gone? Tessa had time to consider—and her eyes were quite astonishingly vivid in her colourless face. Her voice almost splintered it was so icy. 'We can manage right nicely on us own, if yer don't mind. We've takken no charity, me an' me family, ever, an' we'll not start now. Any road, all't arrangements've bin made an' I'll thank you not ter come 'ere interferin'. You sort out yer own life, my lass, before yer start on mine.'

She sniffed loudly, then turned away as though to imply that there was nothing more to be said on the subject. She'd brook no argument, not from anyone: not from her brothers and sisters who'd set

461

up such a caterwauling you'd have thought she'd asked them to jump off Badger's Edge instead of take up the decent employment she'd found for them, and she'd brook none from this woman who would insist that they were friends. Just as if the likes of her and Annie Beale could ever be truly that. She'd not say she wouldn't be sorry to . . . well, to lose sight of her since she'd given Annie many a good laugh on the quiet, but as for allowing her to order their lives, just like they belonged to her or summat, that would never do.

'Annie, please. I really am not offering charity. You will all be working . . .'

'Aye, an' who'll get t'sack ter give us that work, tell me that?'

'Oh, Annie, please let me . . .'

But Annie would not be moved. She'd keep in touch, she promised grudgingly, and no, Tessa wasn't to visit them—Annie tried to picture the elegant Mrs Drew Greenwood in the small cellar room she rented in Salford—but first chance she got she'd come up to Crossfold and . . . well, it were no good frettin' over what couldn't be helped and Tessa must stop making a fuss over nothing. But when her friend, and she admitted to herself *now* Tessa was her friend, put her arms about her in farewell, Annie allowed the gesture.

Tessa and Laurel sat one on either side of the cheerful drawing-room fire that evening waiting for Drew who had not yet come home from the races. Was that where he had said he was going, or was it off on a day's hunting? She couldn't remember. The episode with Annie had upset her more than she cared to admit and her face was bleak as she sipped the sherry Laurel insisted upon before dinner. Her thoughts were scattered dwelling on the awful disruption in everyone's life caused by Charlie's death. She felt guilty that her own overlying emotion was not one of sadness for Charlie, for his widow and five fatherless children, but for herself who had lost with his death, not only her freedom, her friend who had kept her afloat on more than one occasion when life had seemed quite intolerable, but her husband too, for where on earth was he at this time of night?

'My brother is not to dine with us, then?' Laurel enquired tartly. Her mourning black was deep and sombre, allowing not even a jet bead. She was playing for all it was worth the role her husband's death had cast her in, knowing full well that the deep black gave her an air of fragile vulnerability, a defencelessness which said she would simply break and shatter into a hundred pieces should anyone speak a harsh word to her. She was a widow, a woman for whom the deepest respect and sympathy was expected, and she expected it. She was also a shareholder in Chapman Manufacturing now, or would be when the estate was settled, small certainly, but with a voice in the running of things and she was waiting, unable to comprehend the true state of Drew Greenwood's heedless indifference to the fate of the firm, for him to step into the shoes her Aunt Jenny and her own husband had left vacant. And where was he? And at this time when his disregard for the convention of mourning was really quite indecent. Gadding about still with Nicky Longworth and the other wild-riding young men of his acquaintance, she supposed. It really was too bad and her manner said so.

'He will be here soon,' Tessa replied shortly, not at all prepared for one of Laurel's eternal lectures on the behaviour which was expected at a time like this of a gentleman, which, one presumed, Drew was.

'May one ask where he has gone?'

'One may but I cannot promise to give the right answer.'

'Are you saying you don't know where your own husband is?'

Tessa sighed a long, wavering sigh. 'That is what I am saying.' And, really, I could do without your disapproving face and air of displeased resignation, she thought. Indeed, she had begun to worry for though he had been late home on several occasions he had always sent a message to let her know. She did not want to share her anxiety with Laurel, constrained by pride and a reluctance to let her sister-in-law crow, but when Briggs announced that dinner was ready and they moved into the dining-room, the third place set for Drew proclaimed even more loudly his absence.

'I do think he should make more of an effort to be here on time for meals,' Laurel grumbled, picking delicately at the tiny portion of turbot her widowhood allowed her to manage, her manner saying that really, in her state, should she be asked to put up with such thoughtlessness? 'I suppose he is drinking with Nicky Longworth and has not noticed the time, or has probably become so absorbed with whatever those wild friends of his get up to all day, he cannot bring himself to remember that he has a family at home grieving the loss of one of its members,' meaning herself for who but Laurel Greenwood, she seemed to say, mourned her husband?

'I'm sure you're right but there is nothing to be done about it.'

'Really! Well, if he were my husband I know what I would have to say to him.'

'Since he is not your husband perhaps you would keep your observations to yourself,' Tessa hissed. Then, realising that with poor Charlie in the ground no more than six weeks it was hardly the most tactful thing to say to his widow, she began to rise, to go to Laurel who had her black-edged handkerchief to her face. But she had gone too far, it seemed, and Laurel was out of her chair and gliding towards the door, deeply affronted and in no way to be mollified should Tessa even try.

Dear heaven, what had happened to the pleasant, hedonistic, she admitted it now, life she had led in the past with Drew? Her despair was deep as she waved away the poker-faced Briggs and Dorcas with a request for coffee and brandy in the drawing-room, seeing the disapproving twitch of the butler's eyebrows, since no lady drank brandy, but not caring. Her world was disintegrating about her so why should she care that, knowing the servants' grapevine as she did, it would be all over the Penfold Valley by this time tomorrow that, among her other shortcomings, the high-stepping Mrs Drew Greenwood took hard liquor, and on her own?

She stared into the fire having further displeased Briggs by telling him curtly to leave the decanter, she would serve herself and would ring if she needed him. The brandy smoothed its warm descent into her stomach, soothing a little the fluttering butterflies of what she recognised quite

465

plainly as fear. The fumes of the drink reached her head, blurring her sharp thoughts, of Drew and where he might be, of Annie and where she was to go, and of Will.

Will. Dear Lord, why should she give a thought to that perfidious scoundrel? It was he who had brought her down to this. If it was not for him she could even now be with Drew, wherever he was, or at least have him here with her, where he should be, observing the proprieties of mourning for a month or two. It was only because she had been forced since Charlie's death and her mother's flight to Italy to address herself to the wearying problem of the mills, that Drew had ridden off—where did he say he was going? her confused mind asked again—and left her to the tedium of Laurel's false and easy tears. If Will Broadbent had had an iota of compassion in him he would have accepted her offer of manager, *no*, directorship of the Chapman mills thus leaving her to devote herself to the care and constant attention which her husband needed. Will had loved her once, she told herself as she poured herself another brandy, and surely, for the sake of what they had once known and for the simply splendid salary she would have been prepared to pay him, he should have taken her up on her offer. Instead, he had laughed at her, made the most insulting suggestion, humiliated her. God, she could feel the red flames of outrage scorch her body even now for that was what it was that made her so ... so inflammable. Her skin prickled and shivered to her own touch. She was restless and on edge and it was all his fault, the bastard, and if she could get back at him, in any way, by God she would. And all this time he had been going to

Annie's, gossiping no doubt the pair of them about Tessa Greenwood and the hard-drinking, rashly gambling, arrogantly riding society she moved in. Well, to hell with them. Both of them. And good riddance. She was going to bed and she didn't care where Drew was either, or what Will Broadbent and Annie Beale had been up to behind her back. She didn't give a damn if he'd taken Annie Beale to his bed as once he had taken her; if he had laid those hard hands and that hard body against the frail but fighting spirit which dwelled in Annie. What was it to her? Damn them, damn them . . . she'd show them . . .

She knew she was drunk as she stumbled up the stairs to the warm, candle-lit intimacy of the bedroom she shared with Drew, but she didn't care. If it blurred the pictures of Will and Annie . . .

She felt her way to the dressing-table, shaking her head, trying to clear it of the ugly thoughts which muddled it. It was nothing to do with her. Annie must be lonely . . . and Will . . . and how convenient . . . She swung back blindly, knocking over an ornament which fell to the carpet with a gentle thud. She felt quite sick and trembling, which of course was due to the amount of brandy she had drunk . . . She must get into bed . . . where, for God's sake, was Emma . . . ?

She awoke in the night, alone for the first time since her marriage, and frightened. Deeply, disturbingly, terrified. Where was he? Merciful heaven, where was he? He was a grown man, strong and vigorous, but wilful and defenceless as a child without her and what accident might have befallen him in his scorn for anything he considered smacked of caution or common sense?

467

She was no saint herself, as anyone in the Penfold Valley would confirm, but deep inside her was that spark of self-preservation, that instinct which told her when she had reached the limit of what might be called foolhardy and could be considered insane, and that Drew lacked. She had restrained him to that limit but on his own, or in the company of only his breakneck friends, where might he have ended up?

She sat up wincing as her head rattled painfully about on her shoulders, then began to thud to the rhythm of her heartbeat. Getting out of bed she moved to the window and stared blindly out into the wavering darkness of the garden, trying to penetrate it for some sign that Drew had come home and was, perhaps, sprawled drunkenly in the drawing-room or at the foot of the stairs. She had not heard his bay or the sound of the dangerously light curricle he drove. It was solidly dark and quiet, the only movement a faint blurring where the bare bough of the tree outside the window shuddered in the wind. It was cold and sinister out there, beyond the walls of the park and the woods which surrounded Greenacres. The wild moorland, the rapid rushing of icy water, the stony hillside was no place for a man, particularly if he was drunk as Drew was bound to be.

He came in with the dawn, trembling slightly from some excess he did not care to speak of, not quite sober but grinning impishly, pleading for forgiveness, slipping naked into their bed, nuzzling into her shoulder. She held his long, lean body in her arms, her cheek resting on the damp thickness of his matted hair, soothing him to warmth and sleep. She felt the tension—caused by what? she wondered despairingly—drain from him, and as it did so her own body relaxed, and her mind, suddenly clear, suddenly impatient with her previous turmoil, knew what she must do, for no one else would.

CHAPTER TWENTY-FIVE

She was standing in the middle of the cleared site at Chapmanstown, staring in hopeless bewilderment at the plans the clever young architect was explaining to her when the carriage drew in through the gateway. She glanced at it without much interest. It was probably another of those infernal men from the bank or the insurance company come to fill her mind with incomprehensible figures; to talk of assets and liabilities, of titles and securities and after weeks of being bombarded by such imponderables she felt she really could not take one more.

The man who descended from the carriage was overwhelmingly familiar as he stood for a moment beside it seeming to give some instruction to the coachman. When she looked again she was not at all surprised to see Will Broadbent.

He was quite splendid in a well-cut business suit of dark cloth, his shirt front snowy and his greatcoat thrown back from his heavy shoulders in a most dashing way. His tall hat was held against his chest and he bowed before walking towards her with a light tread which came, she assumed, from his experience of being a thief. Now why should she remember that? she wondered dazedly. Then he was beside her, his white teeth startling against his brown skin.

He smiled and his smoky eyes, filled with some secret amusement, ran over her.

'Mrs Greenwood,' he said politely, 'may I say how well you are looking?'

She stiffened and gave him a frigid stare. 'What are you doing here?' she asked rudely and the young architect turned to look at her in surprise. 'I'll just go and . . .' he began, but she put a hand on his arm to restrain him.

'No, don't go, Mr Talbot. This gentleman will not be stopping.' The memory of her humiliation at his hands made her go hot then cold with anger and she did not wish to be reminded of it nor left alone with its instigator. What was he doing here, anyway, looking so prosperous, with his own carriage and coachman and nothing at all to do with his day, it seemed, but ride over and inspect what she was doing in her own mill yard?

'Are you here on business, Mr Broadbent?' she asked haughtily, her manner implying that, if not, he could take himself off and look sharp about it.

'Indeed I am, Mrs Greenwood, and if we can find somewhere more congenial to discuss it I would be obliged.'

Not by a flicker of his cool eyes nor a muscle of his smooth face did he convey that he even remembered their last meeting. It had been nothing to him; an event of so little importance it had slipped completely from his mind. She was of so little importance to him in his new and distinguished career, in his busy and successful world, that had it not been for the certainty of profit to himself he would not have been here at

470

all.

'I cannot think that you and I could have common business interests, Mr Broadbent, but if you would like to call on my managers at Crossbank or at one of my other mills I'm sure one or other of them could spare you a moment or two.'

She heard Mr Talbot draw in his breath sharply. In the past four or so years Will Broadbent had carved out for himself quite a place in the business community of south Lancashire, creating and enlarging the now-prosperous co-operative over Hepworth way. He was known to have a share in several very profitable schemes and had been successful in more than one gamble to do with the railway, so Mr Talbot had heard. It was Mr Talbot's firm which had drawn up the plans for the mill in which Mr Broadbent was one of the major shareholders and he was a highly respected businessman where businessmen were known to be hardheaded, shrewd and extremely ruthless. Men called on Mr Broadbent these days, not the other way round, which was a fair indication of how well he had done for himself. Now, it was well known that Mrs Drew Greenwood had a high opinion of herself, indeed her fine husband was what could only be called arrogant, but to speak to Mr Broadbent as though he was no more than a weaving-shed overlooker surely smacked of foolhardiness?

Mr Broadbent evidently thought so too, and Mr Talbot watched uneasily, wishing he could slip away and let them get on with whatever it was that was between them, but Mrs Greenwood still had his arm in a grip of steel and short of rudely tearing it

471

from her grasp he was forced to remain where he was.

'I don't deal with managers, lass,' Mr Broadbent said warningly.

'And I don't deal with overlookers, Mr Broadbent.'

Mr Talbot watched in growing horror as Mr Broadbent, for a moment, looked as though he would like nothing better than to strike Mrs Greenwood full in her contemptuous face. Then, miraculously, he smiled, a smile of such good humour Mr Talbot thought that he could not have heard exactly what Mrs Greenwood had said.

'Is that meant to insult me, Tessa?' His smile broadened into a delighted grin. He shook his head and, without so much as an 'if I may' or 'do you mind?' he reached out and plucked the plan for the new mill from the architect's hands.

'You go too far, Will Broadbent,' Mrs Greenwood hissed and as she whipped forward to retrieve the plan Mr Talbot stepped back, thankfully, moving to stand several yards away with the site foreman and the master builder in charge who were also present, mouths agape, slack-jawed and wide-eyed, avid spectators of the incredible scene. They were treated to the sight of the imperious and beautiful Mrs Greenwood, wife of the owner of Chapman Manufacturing, dancing at her full height as she stretched up to reach the set of plans which Mr Broadbent held above his head.

'You are being exceedingly foolish, Tessa,' he laughed, 'and undignified too. These men are wondering what on earth can be going on between Mr Broadbent and the exquisite Mrs Greenwood that she has to create such a scene over a piece of paper. Calm down, for God's sake. I only want to study the damn thing.'

'Who gave you the right to walk into my yard and help yourself to the plans for my new mill, Will Broadbent?' she snarled, her eyes narrowed in her angry face. She wanted to stamp her foot and strike out at him, to fly at him with hard, furious fists for he was doing it again, he was humiliating her, but this time in a yard full of curious men.

'Stop it, Tessa, and stop acting like a child in a tantrum.'

'Tantrum, is it? I'll show you who . . .'

'All you are doing is showing these men a side of your nature, which, if you are to go into business, would be best kept hidden and which, if you don't control yourself, will be all over the valley by nightfall. Direct me to your office . . .'

'I haven't got an office,' she snapped perilously.

'Then the foreman's hut will do.'

'You must be out of your mind if you imagine I am about to discuss my affairs with you, and in a workman's hut.'

'Don't do this to yourself, Tessa. Smile and allow me to hold your arm.' He looked about him, one dark eyebrow raised, his eyes beaming with good humour. 'Now, where is the . . . aah, there it is.' He nodded politely to the startled builder. 'May we borrow your office for a moment, Mr . . . er . . .

'Of course, sir.' The man touched the brim of his tall hat, wondering as he did so why he had called Will Broadbent 'sir', for he himself, as a *master* builder held a position of some importance in the business community of Crossfold.

He closed the door of the small wooden hut behind him and leaned against it. His eyes, almost

473

the colour of treacle in the dim light, were bold now, impudent and full of stifled laughter. She flounced out of his grasp, putting up a hand to her bonnet and adjusting a stray wisp of shining hair.

She had discarded the black of mourning in the month after Charlie's death. She could not have said why she had worn it in the first place except perhaps in deference to her mother, her Uncle Joss and Aunt Kit, who she knew somehow, despite their own unconventional ways, would have been distressed by what the community would have seen as a lack of respect and grief. She felt both for she had loved and respected Charlie as a good and steadfast man who had tried to do his best in the awkward and often trying circumstances created by his wife. But she did wear a dress instead of her breeches and jacket, her instinct telling her she might gain some advantage in this man's world into which she had been flung so unceremoniously, if she appeared womanly. They would be insulted if she careered into the mill yard on her mare, dressed like a lad who seemed more likely to gallop over the moor following the wind, than to do business with them. Today she was in a respectable blue, a deep French blue, demure and ladylike with a touch of sparkling white in the crisp lace at her wrist and throat and beneath the brim of her unadorned bonnet.

But nothing could quell the brilliance of her eyes nor the gloss and burnish of her hair, the satin smoothness of her white skin and her poppy-red mouth which Drew had kissed to bee-stung fullness only that morning.

'Don't go,' he had murmured, his mouth tasting her cherry-hard nipples, his tongue teasing and

474

moist as it travelled down the length of her arching body. She could feel him drawing that glowing thread of excitement from the base of her belly, pulling it taut, making it quiver in anticipation, eager, greedy in its desire to be stretched to its full extent before it snapped in that complete and rapturous climax which she had never yet quite achieved. Each time as it struggled to reach what he reached in his own shuddering orgasm, it slipped away, aching sometimes, and angry, and Drew would fold himself about her, warm and for the moment calm, and she would tell herself that next time it would happen.

'Don't go, stay with me,' he had said this morning and his hands had reached for her as they did every morning when she rose early in order to meet the bank manager, the lawyer, the architect, one or other of the managers at the four working mills. He would turn from her when she tried to kiss his resentment away, pulling the fine lace-edged sheets about his amber shoulders, burrowing his head in the fine, lace-edged pillow.

'Go if you must but don't, for God's sake, expect me to be concerned. If you insist that the managers cannot *manage* without your expertise to guide them, by all means give it to them. I'm sure you are right, Tessa, for you always are, but I am off to Northumberland in the morning with Nicky so don't be surprised if I am not here when you return.'

And increasingly he wasn't!

Now she drew herself up to her full height and the look she gave Will Broadbent was one of icy disdain. He had dragged her, there was no other word for it, into this ... this shack and she had

475

allowed it since with his considerable strength and indifference to what others might think, he was quite likely to have flung her over his shoulder and carried her here.

'I would be glad if you would state your business, Mr Broadbent, for I have a lot to do today . . .'

'Aye, so I heard.'

'I beg your pardon?'

'Your . . . doings are the talk of the valley, lass.'

'And exactly what is that supposed to mean?' She had tossed away the 'Mr Broadbent' by now, too incensed to keep up the ice-cool demeanour of a lady confronted by a man who was certainly no gentleman.

'It means that your absurd pretence that you know just what you are about is discussed in every quarter where businessmen gather. They are taking bets at the Cloth Hall on how long you will last and at what price the Chapman concerns will finally be sold. It is very low, Tessa. In one way, they are ready to admire you for doing your best, which is more than can be said for that husband of yours.'

'You keep your foul tongue from my husband's name, you bastard,' she whispered, relieved that the crushing pain of his insult to Drew prevented her from facing the fury of the feared ridicule about herself. How dare they criticise Drew, her dear Drew, who could no more help his nature than they could help being the fools they were. Drew was fine, fine and good, and it was not his fault that he was as he was.

Her face was like a mask, hiding the painful, scalding truth. Oh, yes, she could imagine what they whispered but from no one, *no one* would she allow one word of criticism. He was her cousin, her husband and she loved him as she loved no other person. Let them dare to attack him and she would defend him until she fell wounded, bleeding, dying.

He watched her, allowing no intimation of what was in his heart to show in his impassive face. Her intensely protective love for the emotionally damaged Drew Greenwood glowed through the shadowed bareness of the wooden hut and he marvelled at it, at the same time despising its under-serving recipient with the masculine aggression of a strong man for a weak.

'Nay, lass, what that lad gets up to is nowt to me, nor you for that matter, but I can't abide to see a decent mill such as Chapman's has been, go under. I admired Charlie Greenwood and your mother. They worked damned hard to make something fine of this business. They were well respected, fair and honest as any man in cotton will tell you. They could drive a hard bargain, mind, especially Jenny Harrison, but always to be trusted. And they treated their operatives fairly. And that's another thing. I can't stand by and see a lot of good folk who could be in decent work, forced to apply for poor relief, and that's what they're being driven to by your ham-fisted methods. These walls should be shoulder high by now, with the prospect of your spinners and weavers being back at their machines by summer. A good mill it was, and could be again. I know because I worked here and it fair sets my blood to boiling to see the way it's going . . .'

'Which has nothing to do with you and if you don't remove yourself from my property I shall have you thrown out.' The words could scarcely get beyond her gritted teeth so tightly was her jaw clenched. There were white patches about her mouth and he knew she was holding herself back—just—from springing at him.

'Happen you're right, my lass, but don't let it go. Don't let it slip away from you for the sake of your pride. Get yourself some men together, a board of directors with you as chairman. Men who know what the word 'business' means. Men who know one end of a loom from the other. Men who understand money, and the cotton trade and who can show *you* what to do, or even that husband of yours if you can get him off that bloody horse of his for half an hour . . .'

'I've warned you once and I won't do it again.' She was trembling, so great was her rage. 'Get out of my yard or I'll have you thrown out.'

'Nay, Tessa, you've said that to me a time or two and I'm still here. Remember the first time? You were a slip of a lass, sixteen or so, and you took offence like you always seem to do when someone doesn't move out of your way fast enough. You hit me with your little whip . . .'

'By God, I wish I had it now. Stand away from that door and let me out. When my husband hears about this, as he surely will for I will tell him, he will give you the thrashing of your life . . .'

'Tessa, give over, lass.' He looked highly amused. The very idea of the lightweight Drew Greenwood who did nought from morning until night but gallop about on a bloody horse or shoot at bloody birds taking on Will Broadbent who had learned from the age of five how to take care of himself, was evidently something of a joke.

'Get out of here, Will, or I swear I'll get a gun and kill you myself.'

He became quiet then, his strong face settling

478

into a look of bewilderment. 'Why should you do that, Tessa? What is it in me, and in you, that arouses this ... this loathing you have of me? I have offered you no injury, ever, and if you are thinking of the last time we met when I made you a certain proposition, which you refused, then I can only say I meant you no insult. Rather the opposite. I admire a man who knows what he wants and goes directly for it, whatever the consequences, so why should I not feel the same for a woman? And you really are a splendid woman. I said so and admitted then that I would be more than willing to resume the ... the friendship, for want of a better word, we once knew. We were splendid partners then, well matched, if you take my meaning, and could be again. We could give a lot to one another, my dear. So, you see, I am at a loss as to why you seem to find me so objectionable. I mean you no harm. Far from it. You are married now and I hope to be in the same happy state myself one day, so why cannot we be at least polite with one another?' He was grinning, moving forward into the shaft of pale, dusty sunlight which fell through the grimed window of the hut. 'There may be an occasion in the future when we will do business together and you can hardly glare at me as if there was nothing you would like better than to see me dead at your feet. Forget what has happened in the past and look to the future. It could be good for both of us.' There was no mistaking the meaning of his words. 'Don't ignore the advice I'm giving you, Tessa. Don't fight me. Accept it and ...'

She put up her hands, palms facing him, as though to ward him off, as though he was about to make some physical attack on her. She was white-faced and trembling and for a moment he was alarmed but in her eyes was the blinding brilliance of her rage, making them almost transparent.

'I need neither your help nor your advice and as for doing business with you, *in any way*, I would sooner starve and see my family homeless.'

'Tessa, come now . . .'

'Get out, Will, get out . . .'

Her face which had been so pale became suffused with the deep red blood of her killing rage. She sprang towards him with an incoherent cry which brought the hum of voices in the yard to a sudden silence. Swift as a leopard Will moved to meet her, his arms tight about her waist. She struggled fiercely, her wide-open mouth ready to shrill out the madness of her hatred, but he silenced her, his mouth coming down on hers, capturing those stretched lips, holding them, moving warmly, strongly until he felt them soften beneath his own. She still struggled against him wildly, trying to kick his legs, twisting every way she could against the steel of his arms, her heart pounding in her breast. He held her roughly, hurting her, only his mouth gentle as it moved about her face, then returned to recapture her pliant lips.

'Darling, darling,' he was murmuring and his long, hard body pressed against hers urgently. One hand moved to the back of her head, flinging her bonnet to the corner of the hut, and as her hair came loose his hand was in it, holding her where he might more easily have access to her warm, urgent, demanding mouth.

'Will, dear God . . .' Her arms were about his neck, clinging to him, terrified that he might slip away, that he might leave her, that the hot sweetness which flowed through her body, so familiar and for which she had waited so long, might be taken from her.

He backed her up against the wall of the hut, their bodies still welded together, the hot need of them burning even through the layers of their clothing. Their mouths clung desperately, honey-sweet and swollen. She was moaning deep in her throat and when his mouth moved beneath her chin, smoothing down the soft flesh of her throat, she arched her back, holding his head to her, offering her breasts to him as she had done in the depths of the bed they had shared five years ago.

They might have gone on, mindless of everything but their bodies' longing, for though both had known love during the years between, they were starving for this. His hands were at her breast, cupping the soft weight and she pressed eagerly against them when from beyond the closed door Mr Talbot cleared his throat noisily.

'Will . . .' She would have fallen but for his arms about her.

'Darling . . . ?'

'No, no, I'm not . . .'

'Yes . . . ?'

'Please, let me go.'

'Never, not now.' His lips came down on hers again with all the masculine possession of a man who knows a woman is his.

She was weak, soft and lovely in his arms. 'Mr Talbot . . .'

'Damn Mr Talbot!'

'My bonnet . . . please . . .'

'Here, smooth your hair.'

'Dear God, I can hardly stand. Don't let me go or I shall fall.'

'Not you, Tessa Greenwood. You will never fall for I shall not let you.'

*   *   *

'And how was your day among the industrialists, my love?' Drew smiled sardonically, sipping the pale golden wine with which Briggs had just re-filled his glass. 'Did we make another fortune to add to the one we already have or are we to sell the family silver to buy that hunter I have my eye on?'

'Oh, Drew, you are not to buy another horse, surely? The stables seem full of them already and why you should need another is beyond me.'

Drew turned lazily to Laurel, his lounging manner, his smile, the lift of his dark eyebrow, the curl of his lip, insolent and begging to know exactly what it had to do with her how he spent his own money. He had been in the saddle all day for the hunting season was almost over and he intended to make the most of what remained. After the hunt ball at the end of the month the Squire and his family would be off to some other sporting pursuit in which, naturally, Drew Greenwood would be included. And his charming wife too, if she could be parted from this somewhat astonishing occupation she had taken up with matters of a commercial nature. Like Drew, the Squire was of the opinion that if one was unfortunate enough to be of the industrial world, the world of trade, was it not only sensible and more seemly to leave the distasteful running of the business in the hands of one's employees? There was no need, surely, for

482

the delectable Mrs Drew Greenwood to occupy herself personally with the rebuilding of the mill in which her unfortunate uncle had perished and Drew was to impress on her that they missed her enormously. They would be most distressed if she did not show herself on her superb mare the very next day and in that stunning riding outfit she wore, since the last three months without her had been quite tedious, and he was to tell her so.

'Laurel dear, I do not question the purchases you make and so I would beg you not to question mine.'

'I do not question it, Drew. I am merely pointing out that as you can only ride one horse at a time it seems imprudent to own half a dozen all eating their heads off in the stables.'

'They are all ridden, Laurel, except, of course, those ponies which were brought for Robert and Henry and Joel and which you will not allow them to mount.'

'Robert and Henry are far too busy with their studies and Joel is too young . . .'

'Rubbish! They must be allowed to play sometimes, Laurel, and as for being too young, Drew and I . . . no . . . Pearce and I for I am Drew . . . Pearce and I . . . when we were the same age as Joel were . . .'

His voice faltered suddenly and his face took on an expression of uncertainty. The wine in his glass slopped over the rim and dripped on to the lapel of his immaculate evening jacket as his hand trembled and he turned at once to Tessa.

'You remember, don't you, darling? We were all up in the saddle long before we were five years old . . .'

483

'That may be so, Drew, but my sons are to be millowners'—since you don't appear to be producing any of your own, her tone said—'and not urchins who are allowed to romp . . .'

He continued as though his sister had not spoken and when his hand reached for hers, Tessa took it soothingly appalled by the confusion he was in over his own name, the words she had been preparing all day regarding the running of the mill dying away in the back of her throat.

' . . . and when Tessa was six she was following us out on the moor, weren't you, sweetheart? What times we had, the three of us, didn't we?'

His face had become sweated, just a fine sheen on the glowing brown of his skin as though from some fire within him, and his eyes were the brilliant blue of a sapphire. He gripped her hand fiercely, then, tipping back his head poured the wine, almost in one swallow, down his throat. He held out the empty glass to Briggs without turning and the butler filled it once more to the brim, his own face impassive. This was the second bottle of wine he had opened and they had not yet finished the fish course.

Will Broadbent's face, his hands and lips and . . . yes, the emotion he had allowed her to see were pushed savagely to the back of Tessa's mind as she looked into the faltering face of her husband. Her body which had been wild with longing only that morning, grew still and empty.

'Indeed we did, my darling, though I had to fight you every step of the way to let me be part of it. You thought me nothing but a nuisance until I could prove to you both that I could do everything as well as you.'

484

'You mean the gate?' He pushed his plate away, grinning, the splendid trout on it barely touched, leaning forward to gaze admiringly into his wife's lovely face as he hitched his chair nearer to hers. He had soon given up sitting at the head of the table as Laurel had wished him to do and as was proper for the master of the house, placing his chair next to his wife's at its foot, declaring he could not shout from one end to the other when he wished to address her.

'What a devil you were when you took it into your head to beat us, which was most of the time. But I really did think, for a moment only, believe me, that that bloody gate would be your undoing.'

'Drew, please, must you bring such language to my dinner table?' Laurel raised a fastidious eyebrow.

'I'm afraid I must, dear sister. If my wife does not object, which I'm sure she doesn't, do you, my pet? ... there, you see ... then I cannot think it concerns you.'

He indicated to Briggs to refill his glass and Laurel sat up straighter, her face even more rigid with disapproval.

'And if I might just point out, Laurel, whilst we are on the subject, that as mistress of this house, this is my wife's dinner table.'

'Drew, be quiet.'

'No, I will not be quiet, Tessa. I am acquainting Laurel with the fact that she no longer . . .'

'Drew, how could you?' Laurel's eyes filled with tears and in the background where they discreetly hovered Briggs and Dorcas exchanged glances. 'With Charlie hardly cold in his grave, is it kind to remind me that I must relinquish what has been

485

mine for so long?'

Drew's eyes narrowed and the slightly cruel humour which he acquired when he was drunk, curled his mouth.

'Really?' he drawled, lounging back in his chair, but though he gave the impression of the dashing young man-about-town, cynical, arrogant, carelessly indifferent to anyone's feelings including his own—for had they not already suffered irreparable damage?—he still clung quite desperately to Tessa's hand. 'I cannot recall under what circumstances you undertook to be mistress of Greenacres. My mother, who is the wife of its master, is still alive and now, in her absence and in view of the fact that my father has deeded the property to me, as my wife, Tessa must take my mother's place.'

'I will not stay here to be treated so cruelly.' Laurel rose to her feet, ready to glide from the room as she had done so often since Charlie died and with him the championship which was her due as his wife, and the daughter of this house.

'Laurel, sit down. Drew did not mean to be cruel and, whatever he might say, you *are* mistress here. You know you are splendid at it and that I would be hopeless.' That was true. 'Besides, I am to be fully occupied with the . . .'

She had not meant to speak of it, really she hadn't. She had seen the lost expression cloud Drew's eyes, the uneasy confusion and even worse which came to plague him. It was mixed with bravado which was meant to let her know he could manage very well on his own if she persisted with her lunatic scheme to run the mills, and yet it told her of his awful fear that, if she did, he might lose

486

his way again without her by his side.

'With what, my sweet?' His voice was deceptively mild and yet again his glass was held out to Briggs who hurried to refill it. 'Let us guess. Come on, Laurel, sit down and we will discuss the . . . what is it, darling, that you are to be occupied with? Can it be the charitable works with which married ladies concern themselves, as Laurel herself does, do you not, sister? Or are you to begin making social calls, leaving cards and receiving them, spending your afternoons gossiping about fashion and the perfidy of gentlemen? Are you to accompany your husband as once you did, so pleasantly and with such devotion, or, as I suspect, is it something else entirely?'

Laurel's tears had vanished, dried up mysteriously at the prospect of not only watching the entertaining diversion of Tessa and Drew quarrelling but of discovering what was to happen to her share of the Chapman fortune. As Charlie's widow she owned twelve and a half per cent and surely she was entitled to know how soon she could reasonably expect to get her hands on it when the mills were sold, as sold they must certainly be? Drew was incapable of running them as Charlie and her Aunt Jenny had done, not only by reason of the serious instability of his nature which, though always wild and rebellious, had grown to gigantic proportions since Pearce's death, but by his absolute contempt and antipathy towards anything remotely commercial.

Tessa sighed, wondering why Drew was not able to propel her into the fury which Will Broadbent could awaken in her, nor the hot desire of bodily need, her secret mind slyly added before she could block it. Was the delight of it, the harmony of her marriage, cooled to mere pity and irritation, or were the last few months of frustration to blame for the slight wearing in the fabric of her marriage? The truth of it was she longed, yearned, for someone to whom she could pour out the great wave of her fear and frustration: of her distaste for the days ahead in which somehow she must turn chaos into order, turbulence into the smooth and pleasant life she had once led with Drew. She needed with all her heart to hear someone say, 'Leave it, Tessa, I will see to it for you. There is no need for you to bother your head about it. It is safe with me. Go and play with your husband who needs you more than the mills need you. He will not be able to function without you to hold his hand and lead him through life, so go, go and leave it all to me.' She would have liked nothing better than to wink audaciously at Drew, to joke and tease and take him to bed safe in the perfect knowledge that tomorrow they could do as they pleased, as they had always done. Lie on the rug before the bedroom fire and make love until he was satiated with it. Saddle their horses and gallop the moors until they were exhausted with it. Ride over to the Hall and amuse themselves with their friends, watch Drew drink and gamble feverishly until he was ready to come home, to sleep in her arms, safe in her arms, loved and needed, both of them in their shared brittleness. For that was fast what they had become; easily broken, running away from responsibility, spoiled and worthless, impatient with those who had their feet firmly on solid ground—like Will—restless and forever seeking some diversion to relieve them of that mortal affliction, the affliction of boredom.

Or was she firmly to grasp this nettle which scorched her hands, hurt her quite dreadfully, and if she was, if she was to burden herself with it, the question was *why*?

Will Broadbent's face danced in the shimmering flame of the candelabra which stood in the centre of the table. He was smiling quizzically, the question in his eyes unreadable. *Unreadable*! What had been in his eyes and in his mind was as clear as the light from the candles at which she gazed, and she had almost succumbed to it. Dear God, she had almost given in to the lust he had shown so impudently. He had asked her weeks ago to be his mistress and, clear-headed, she had refused. This morning he had tricked her, confused her, got her into his arms before she knew what was happening, his body telling her exactly what it wanted of hers. But he'd not get it. She was Mrs Drew Greenwood who loved her husband, wasn't she, and Will Broadbent could go to the devil. She despised him and his wild idea of forming ... what had he said? ... a company, a board of directors, perhaps taking on a partner who had business and managerial expertise ... shares, small but shares as an incentive ... what had he said? ... with herself as ... as chairman. She could learn from them and if she learned she would make damn sure they did not cheat her ...

The chair on which her husband was sitting crashed backwards to the floor and across the table Laurel squeaked in alarm as Drew leaped to his feet.

'Goddammit, Tessa, what's come over you, lolling there with your chin in your hand and your

489

mind obviously a million miles away from here? You've barely said a word this evening beyond a remark or two about nothing in particular. Do you know what, Tessa? You have become a bore. Ask yourself when you last made me laugh, or indeed when you yourself smiled at something? You used to be so splendid, always ready for anything, riding with Pearce and me, with Nick and Johnny and the others. They all thought you were the best sport, one of them, and now look at you.'

His voice had become ugly and his eyes were an unnaturally livid blue as he waved his wine-glass towards her, spilling most of the contents on the carpet. At the back of the room Briggs sighed inaudibly for it would not be Master Drew who had the cleaning of it.

'You look ... you look ...' Her husband searched about in his mind for an insult cutting enough to wound her, as he was wounded by her defection. 'You look and sound just like a bloody millowner.'

'Well, that's what I am, darling. That's what we both are and if you won't accept it, then someone must.' She stood up and smiled, not at all put out, it seemed, by his slashing attack, the invitation in her eyes plain enough for everyone in the room to see and understand. 'So why don't we just forget it for tonight? Bring some champagne—see to it, will you, Briggs?—and we'll have a toast, just you and I in our sitting-room. Come. Have you ever made love to an industrialist, my darling? No, well neither have I,' they heard her say as she led her suddenly laughing, suddenly dazzled husband across the wide hallway and up the stairs. 'It shall be a new experience for us both, I'm certain of
490

that.' And surely, her puzzled heart asked, it would drive the image of Will Broadbent's smiling face, his warm lips and hands from her mind forever?

CHAPTER TWENTY-SIX

The young architect, Mr Talbot, accompanied by the builder, Mr Hale, called on her several days later to ask her opinion on one or two alterations to the plans for the new mill. Just small changes, they assured her, but if she was to study them she would see immediately the enormous benefits they would make to the access of raw materials from one department to another, the easy movement of one process to another, the added safety of her operatives and, she would be happy to hear, they would be advantageous to her financially, shaving several hundreds of pounds from the cost.

'Why were these not thought of months ago when the plans were drawn up?' she asked sharply.

'We have had time to . . . to go over them more thoroughly, Mrs Greenwood, in relation to the site which was not cleared when they were first drawn up. And with this latest development we also find we shall be able to begin building at once.' Mr Hale twisted his tall hat in his hands, his eyes somewhat inclined to look, not at her, but through her.

'But you said it would be another month at least before you could start the foundations.'

'Indeed I did, but with some reorganisation it is now possible to dig out the footings at once.'

She was inordinately pleased with herself, taking this latest development as an omen that at last

491

things were about to improve. In fact, almost overnight progress surged forward: the mill was invaded by a positive army of brawny Irish labourers, the footings were dug out, the foundations laid and the walls began to grow with a speed which was nothing short of miraculous; and at home Drew was convinced that it was only a matter of time before she would be his constant companion once more. Indeed, he had been so delighted with her plan to form a 'company' of dependable, knowledgeable men to run the mills, he had even promised airily that he might be persuaded to sit on the board with her.

'Providing I don't have to go in the spinning or weaving sheds amongst all that infernal machinery, and providing it doesn't interfere with the hunting season, naturally, I can see no harm in it. Mind you, my darling,' his old mischievous smile, the merry humour he had been blessed with before Pearce's death, warmed his handsome face, 'I cannot promise to understand what they are talking about. Profit and loss was never my strong suit and when it comes to adding one figure to another I am hopeless. I have no head for it, you see, but I'm sure I would recognise it if I was told we had made a profit of a guinea or two. There, that's a bargain then. I shall accompany you to a . . . what do you call it? . . . a board meeting now and again and you will come with me when there is some excitement at the Hall. My goodness, won't Mother and Father be delighted with me? Their son in business at last? Now that's decided, come here and entertain your husband as he deserves. Take off that gown . . . no, no, let me undo the buttons. What a divine creature you are . . .'

492

And so, in the weeks which slipped from spring and into summer, as the mill walls grew as high as her shoulders, then ever upwards, forming one storey ... two ... four ... six, her life continued pleasantly enough, balanced quite easily, it seemed, now that Drew was prepared to be patient and share a little of her time with the demands of 'the business' as he laughingly began to call the forming of Chapman Manufacturing Company Ltd.

It was really quite amazingly simple when you knew the right way to go about it, she found. Her bank manager, Mr Bradley, when approached, declared himself more than willing to suggest several gentlemen of unquestionable reputation who might be prepared to sit on her board, men who knew the cotton trade and the commercial world in general. Naturally, with the inducement of directors' fees and a chance to purchase some Chapman stock, it could only be in their own best interest to see the five mills prosper. Her lawyer, Mr Dalton, would be delighted to draw up the necessary papers, he said, to ensure that she, her husband and her sister-in-law, and their inheritance, were protected in the most water-tight, *legal* fashion, the major shareholder in the new company being, naturally, Mr Drew Greenwood himself. In fact, he would be pleased if she would consider himself as the company lawyer to ensure that all the legal aspects of running Chapman Manufacturing Company Ltd were completely safeguarded. She was not to concern herself with the complexity of the insurance which had proved awkward but to leave it all to him.

The new mill was quite splendid, six storeys high, oblong in shape and solid, with thirty windows on each of its two long sides and fifteen at each end. There was a chimney, tall and imposing, with the name CHAPMAN MILL in bricks of a contrasting colour, and the whole building had a most pleasing *permanent* look. It would be some weeks before the new machinery could be put in but in the meanwhile those operatives who had not found other employment, and even those who had, were alerted to the forthcoming opening of the mill and the reinstatement of their old jobs.

The next day the company's first board meeting was to be held, but at the bank premises since the brand new board room at the mill would not be ready. Drew had ridden over to the Hall saying ruefully that if he was to be concerned with business tomorrow then he'd better prepare by clearing his head on Longworth Moor with Nicky. She'd smiled to herself reflecting that one would think he was to be involved in the practicalities of running the mill, taking the burden of all that entailed on his own elegant shoulders, instead of spending, as she knew he would, an hour or two yawning at the first and probably the last board meeting he would ever attend.

The meeting was to begin at ten o'clock and as Mr and Mrs Drew Greenwood entered the bank the clock on the tower of the church opposite struck the hour.

'What on earth does one wear for such an occasion?' Drew had questioned languidly as she coaxed him from their bed at seven thirty. He had not come home until the early hours of the morning, for the wild riding gentlemen had celebrated the splendour of the day with

494

innumerable bottles of the Squire's champagne. He had been good humoured then as he sometimes was when he drank, amiable and boyish, but determined, despite his drunkenness, to make love to her. She had submitted to it, unwillingly for the first time since they had become lovers, sensing that it would cause less dissension simply to lie still and allow him his fumbling way. He had fallen into effortless sleep on her shoulder, the deed half done, his naked body heavy on hers, not stirring when she had slid out from beneath him, but the good humour was gone by the morning light.

'Is it really necessary for me to go with you, Tessa?' he asked peevishly, his aching head in his hands, his still-naked body appearing curiously defenceless in its shrunken, flaccid state as he crouched on the edge of the bed.

'I'm afraid it is, darling. You are the largest shareholder.'

'Christ, what on earth does that mean?'

'You know what it means, Drew. There will be . . . well, decisions to be made . . .' she ventured hesitantly, not at all sure herself on the proceedings of a board meeting, so how was she to explain them to Drew?

'Hell's teeth, Tessa, I'm in no state to make decisions.'

'Not decisions exactly. They will . . . plan what is to be done at the mill, the board, I mean, but it is all to be voted on. You and I between us have the major holding . . .'

'Oh, Jesus, Tessa, don't go on. Just send Briggs to get me into my things and when I'm dressed I'll try to drag myself into the carriage. I promised I would come and so I shall but, believe me, this will be the last time. I had no idea such affairs began at dawn. Dear God, why cannot these people conduct their business affairs like gentlemen, at a decent hour of the day? Better yet, could they not have come to the house?'

'Darling . . .' Her jaw ached with the necessity to stop the hot words from pouring out of her mouth and all over him. Dear God, she had seen often enough in the past months that if she lost her temper he would lose his, there would be a stormy exchange and he would refuse to come at all. Dammit, if she could arrange it in some way—she must ask Mr Dalton if it was possible—she would find some means so that he need never attend a meeting again. Once a month, Mr Dalton had said, but the chairman of the board, in this case Drew or his agent, must be present. Could she be his agent—what was it called? Her mother had mentioned it in one of her letters . . . proxy, that was it—then she would have no need to trouble Drew with anything beyond putting his signature on whatever papers Mr Bradley and Mr Dalton, the lawyer, presented to her.

Her mother, her Uncle Joss and even Aunt Kit who was not awfully sure that she wished her frail and precious husband to be troubled by the problems of the reorganisation, wrote her long letters of encouragement. Perhaps in her niece Kit Greenwood recognised herself as she had been over thirty years ago when she had taken up the role of 'manufacturer' on her own father's death. Her words of support, of pleading, really, since she did not want to see all that her family had built up crumble away, did their best to let Tessa know she understood her frailty at this time.

'You can do it, Tessa,' she wrote, 'and I promise you that when the challenge, for that is what it is, is taken up and overcome, there is no greater satisfaction to be had. Gentlemen have told us for so long that we are not made as they are, that our minds are not as theirs, that we are inferior to them in all but one thing, that our brains are incapable of dealing with anything more complicated than a menu, but *you* know that is not true, my dear. Your mother agrees . . .'

Jenny did, but her letters were softer, more tender, less pressing. She was the only one to know the desperate unhappiness Tessa had suffered through her love for Robby Atherton. No one's fault, of course, but what mother can resist blaming herself for her children's misery, dwelling interminably on what she might have done to prevent it? 'Don't allow yourself to lose hope, Tessa. *Never* lose hope for it is all we have to get us through the day. Always, *always* the strength to overcome life's adversity is found and I know you to be a strong woman. Take hold, daughter, and you will win through. If there is anything I can do . . .' But Tessa was aware that her mother was saying any help she gave would only be sent *by letter* from the soft, sun-filled world into which she herself had escaped.

She wrote back, letter after frantic letter, begging to be shown the way to 'take hold', to 'meet the challenge', to 'overcome', but though they always replied kindly, optimistically even, she knew that, at their age, they really could not provide the impossible support she begged of them. They had done it once, Kit Chapman, as she was then, and Jenny Harrison, and could not Tessa

497

Greenwood do the same?

In every letter which passed between them not once was it suggested she should turn to her husband.

He grumbled languidly, petulantly the whole time Briggs was dressing him, protesting that his boots hurt his feet, his cravat was too tight, his shirt front far too stiff and how could he be expected to show himself in a business suit, for that was what it was, when he was not a businessman and had no intention of ever becoming one? His head ached abominably and what he needed was fresh air, not the stuffy confines of some damned office. She could see that he was genuinely nauseous, the requirement of being what he hated above anything else, turning his smooth brown face hollow-eyed and pallid. Should she have told him to change into riding breeches, to take up his crop and saddle his horse, to be off on the moorland and up to the tops and that she would go with him, he would immediately be as charming and lovable, as smiling and generous-hearted as he frequently was, sweet-tempered and terribly sorry he had been such a bad-tempered swine. He would be willing to do anything she asked, to go wherever she pleased if only it was not to the mill, which was what this meeting represented.

Mr Bradley and Mr Dalton were in the doorway of the bank waiting to welcome them, holding out their hands to be shaken by Mr Greenwood who complied reluctantly, quite startled, it seemed, by the novel idea.

'The members of the board are waiting for you, Mrs Greenwood, if you would like to follow me,' Mr Bradley told them officiously whilst Mr Dalton went ahead to ensure that doors were opened and a smooth passage was cleared for these important personages. Though neither he nor Mr Bradley would dream of cheating the owners of the Chapman mills since both they and the other members of the board which they were about to form to run the company were all honest, hard-working businessmen, there would be a great deal of advantage to be gained in being associated with such an undertaking. Particularly as Mr Drew Greenwood and his wife and, one supposed, the third member of the family who had a small share in it, Mrs Laurel Greenwood, were all totally inexperienced in the running of the mill and would therefore, one supposed, leave the whole concern to himself and the rest of the board.

'What a delightful day it is, Mrs Greenwood,' Mr Bradley murmured politely, 'quite warm for the time of the year, though one should expect it in July, I suppose.'

'Indeed,' she answered, keeping one hand on the arm of her husband who was inclined to wince away from everything on which his eye fell, from the half a dozen clerks at their high desks who stared at him and his wife with a great deal of impolite interest, he was inclined to think, to the steep stairs he was forced to climb to reach the corridor which led into the board room.

'Is this going to take long, Tessa?' he was heard to say with no attempt to lower his voice, as he followed her up them, and as they moved along the corridor Mr Bradley exchanged glances with Mr Dalton since it was evident that this meeting was going to be even more trying than they had anticipated.

The board room appeared to be filled with gentlemen. They stood in pairs engaged in serious conversation, or sat engrossed in papers about a large, well-polished table, those who were seated springing to their feet as she entered. They were soberly dressed in dark business suits, all of them, important of expression and shrewd of eye, about a dozen of them she could see now, men of obvious worth and standing in the community, whose resolute expressions told her they would be well able to protect the interests of any business in which they had a hand.

Only one smiled and her heart lurched in her breast as she looked into the narrowed eyes of Will Broadbent. She could distinctly feel, and hear, her own breath quicken and the hand which still rested on Drew's arm trembled slightly as the emotive picture of the last time they were together crept stealthily into her mind.

Mr Bradley was leading the way across the smooth Turkey carpet, doing his best to usher the reluctant owner of the Chapman mills towards the gentlemen who were to sit on his board. Mr Dalton, as Drew moved forward, had Tessa by the elbow, a gentleman paying her the respect a lady deserved despite the strangeness of having one where none had been before. His hand guided her and his voice soothed her since she seemed somewhat alarmed by the seriousness of this meeting and the overwhelming mass of commercial gentlemen to whom she would be unaccustomed. Indeed, he could feel the trembling of her arm as he placed her in her chair and he smiled to let her know she was in safe hands with Mr Bradley and himself.

The glance she and Will exchanged went unnoticed. She had not seen him since the morning in the mill yard, three months ago now, and though she had been expecting him to follow up and take advantage of the incident—for that was all it had been, she told herself, an incident—in the foreman's hut, he had not done so. His embrace had been ardent and her own response to it surprising, but it had meant nothing to her, she had repeated time and time again to herself, and evidently nothing to him either. He had realised, she supposed, that she was happily married and was not the sort of woman to be treated as a convenient release for his own nasty lust. She had been relieved that he had finally accepted her refusal and the last few moments of their encounter, which she must have imagined, she told herself, when he had seemed to imply that there was more to this than the desires of the flesh, were pushed firmly to the back of her mind.

In the ensuing moments of introduction his eyes holding hers let her see quite openly, that it was not so. I told you you were not to fall, did I not? they seemed to say, warm and expressive with some deep-felt emotion. You are here with that diminished man you call a husband because of me; because I showed you the way to do it. A few words, no more, were all that were needed to put you on the right path since you are an intelligent woman. These men have been assembled at your command. Let no one tell you differently. They are here to do *your* bidding so show them from the start that you are as strong and forthright as other women in your family have been. Do it, Tessa. It is all yours, so grasp it with both hands and let no man, *no man* pull you down.

' . . . and this is Mr Will Broadbent, Mrs Greenwood. He is a millowner from Hepworth who has been invited to take a seat on the board.' She smiled since she was well aware now that Will Broadbent would not have waited to be invited and the sardonic gleam of humour in his eyes confirmed it. 'He is a man who knows cotton,' Mr Bradley was saying, 'is that not so, Mr Broadbent? . . . and will, I'm sure, be an asset to the newly formed Chapman Manufacturing Company Ltd.'

'Mr Broadbent and I have already met, Mr Bradley.'

'Is that so, Mrs Greenwood?'

Will took her hand and bowed over it but his eyes continued to smile audaciously into hers. They were a lovely pale brown, flecked with amber and gold, the colour they had been, she remembered, when they had made love in his small overlooker's cottage, the colour of love. And she knew, suddenly, as he held her hand just a shade too long, that everything that had happened in the last three months had been his doing: the miraculous suddenness with which the building plans had been re-designed and completed; the increasingly smooth growth of the building itself, the absence of hitches, the wondrous removal of the obstacles and snags which had plagued her in the beginning. Every man on the site from the master builder himself right down to the lowest hod-carrying labourer had worked hard and fast, and in unison, to get her mill up in record time—why did she now think of it as *her* mill, she wondered curiously—and now it was complete and within weeks would be

502

manufacturing the cotton which her family had manufactured for almost a century. Engineers had been employed, sent ostensibly by Mr Bradley or Mr Dalton who had vouched for them. Managers and overlookers found who had been connected with the old mill, all eager and willing to work with, and for, Mrs Drew Greenwood.

And it was all thanks to Will Broadbent who was turning away now to take the reluctant hand her husband held out to him.

The tiny flame of quite giddy joy burned deep within her as the meeting began and she was afraid to look at him. Drew sat beside her, refusing the chair at the head of the table as though the seat might prove to be red hot. On his face was an expression of ill-mannered boredom which she knew hid his painful fear that somehow, while he was not looking, so to speak, he might find himself embroiled in the machinations of the mill again. He barely listened as Mr Bradley began to speak of the advantage in terms of the future development of Chapmans' to be found in the forming of a limited company. He showed some interest when the words 'chairman' and 'managing director' were mentioned for did they not imply that someone, not himself, naturally, nor his wife, was to take over the running of the business? He voted with the rest, as Tessa had told him to, staring quite openly at Will Broadbent who came, of course, from the lower classes, despite his expensive, well-tailored suit, when he was put forward as managing director. It was incomprehensible to him that such a man, a man who had once worked, so he had been told, in one of his own family's spinning rooms, should hold such a position of authority.

Still, if the rest of them thought he could do the job who was he to argue? As long as he had enough money in his pocket to continue his own pleasant life with his wife he didn't give a damn who earned that money for him. A Mr Entwhistle, whose wealth came from breweries, Mr Bradley whispered in his ear, as if it made any difference to Drew Greenwood, seconded the motion, and Drew's brief interest flagged. Mr Dalton was proposed as company secretary, seconded by Mr Bradley and Drew put up a languid hand to indicate that he agreed. It was not until his wife's name was mentioned that his unfocused gaze which had wandered to the patch of streaked blue sky beyond the window, swung sharply back to the proceedings.

'What was that?' His arrogant, well-bred voice brought the vote taking place to a halt.

Mr Bradley smiled smoothly though it was evident from the expression in his eyes that he had been hoping young Mr Greenwood would remain in the imperceptive doze into which he appeared to have fallen in the last half-hour. He was far less trouble that way. It was necessary for him to be here at this first meeting of the board for appearances' sake if nothing else, and when Mrs Greenwood was made chairman, with the signed agreement of the biggest shareholder, Mr Drew Greenwood himself, giving her the right to chair the proceedings and vote in his place, there was no need for him to attend a board meeting again. And with Mrs Greenwood under the ... ah ... wing, if one could call it that, of that astute businessman, Mr Will Broadbent, Chapmans could once again be the thriving concern it had been under the direction and guidance of Mrs Jenny Harrison and Mr Charles Greenwood. Dear God, the lengths he had had to resort to, the secrecy to which he had been sworn by Mr Broadbent, of course, in order to get this far in the business dealings. He and Mr Dalton, both as close-mouthed and discreet as men of their respective professions had to be, had worked closely with Mr Broadbent on Mr and Mrs Greenwood's behalf and it was not up to him or Mr Dalton to ask why. This was a business transaction; a helping hand to get a thriving business over a sticky patch and to find the means to keep it the profit-making concern it had always been, and for which, naturally, he and Mr Dalton would be suitably rewarded.

'What is what, Mr Greenwood?' he asked patiently, somewhat alarmed by the wild cast in Drew Greenwood's eye.

'You mentioned my wife's name in connection with . . . what was it?'

The whole room held its breath as the lovely Mrs Greenwood turned to her husband, her expression one of concern. She smiled at him, a brilliant smile and yet softly reassuring, and there was not one man there who did not envy Drew Greenwood that look. They watched him with expressionless faces but their indignation and impatience could be quite plainly felt. Had it not been for the esteem in which they had held his aunt and uncle and the presence of Will Broadbent who had assured them that there was a profit to be made, it was doubtful if any of them would have agreed to sit on this board. They had expected nothing less, of course, from this young gentleman whose concern it was, since his inflammable nature was well known in the Penfold

505

Valley, but Tessa could see in their cold eyes that in their opinion the quicker the proceedings were got through the better they would like it.

'Mr Bradley is asking for the agreement of the board to . . . well, myself as chairman of the board.' Her voice was patient and the room held its breath.

'*You?*' His face was comical in its amazement.

'Someone has to . . . to chair the board, is that not the correct expression, Mr Bradley?' She turned her charming smile on the bank manager who assured her that it was.

'I don't give a damn about the correct expression, Tessa, nor who the hell does the job as long as it is not you nor myself. Let one of these . . . these gentlemen see to it, for God's sake. That's the whole idea of this arrangement, surely, so let's get the . . . the positions allocated and get out of here.' He turned to Mr Bradley, making a decent attempt to be civil she could see, yet letting it be known nevertheless that he was not accustomed to dealing with tradesmen, which these gentlemen were. 'Can we not just appoint someone, sign a paper or something, Mr . . . er . . . You will know how these things are done, I'm sure, since that is what I pay you for.' His rudeness was inexcusable but only his wife knew that it was caused by fear. 'My wife and I have an important engagement and really cannot remain any longer.'

'Drew . . .'

'No, Tessa, this has nothing to do with us, really it hasn't. A chairman must be employed . . .'

'That is what we are trying to do, darling.'

'Then let it be done.'

'It must be the major shareholder, Drew. That is how Mr Dalton has arranged it, legally, I mean . . .'

506

The gentlemen about the table, except for Will Broadbent who looked as though he might, for some reason known only to himself, spring from his chair at any moment, were grim-faced, clinging, Tessa could see, to their equanimity with the greatest difficulty. And all the while Drew was becoming more restless, his face showing his absolute disdain for these trumpery business dealings. After all, he had only come because Tessa had promised him that it would be just this once, to appoint members to the board and would soon be done with. Now they were taking the liberty of begging his own wife to be employed on it. How dare they even suggest it when it was well known that she was Mrs Drew Greenwood, a lady, and though she had been forced to move amongst them for the past few months, the purpose of this bloody meeting was to ensure that she need do it no longer?

'Don't talk nonsense, Tessa. Any of these fellows could do it. They are all qualified, I'm sure . . .'

'No, we are not, Mr Greenwood, or we would have no need of you at all.' The quiet voice from the end of the table was Will Broadbent's. Tessa could see the dangerous gleam in his now-darkened eyes and she put out an instinctively protective hand to her husband. Will's jaw clenched perilously when he saw it and she knew she must get Drew away from here at once.

'I think it's time we left, darling, or we shall be late for our engagement.' Her voice was light and airy. 'I think our business here is concluded but I believe Mr Bradley has some papers you are to sign, and myself too, is that not so, Mr Bradley? In fact, I think it might be appropriate if we dealt with

507

that now, if it is convenient, then we can take our leave. There is no other immediate business, is there, gentlemen? We have a managing director . . .' She dare not look at Will lest they see the tiny glow which shone not only in her eyes, but in his, ' . . . and a chairman . . .' Without revealing to Drew the chairman's name but letting them know that she would be taking the position herself, she turned to Mr Bradley and smiled.

Drew signed his name carelessly to every paper put before him, ignorant of the fact that, witnessed by a dozen of the valley's leading businessmen, he had just signed away his inheritance to his equally ignorant wife.

'Good morning, gentlemen,' she said breathlessly to each one whilst her husband chafed at the door, a curt nod in their direction all that he considered necessary.

'Good morning, Mrs Greenwood.'

'Good day to you, ma'am.'

As he held her arm courteously, leading her across the room to the protection of her husband, no one but Mrs Greenwood heard Will Broadbent murmur in her ear of his habit of walking the moorland high above Friar's Mere each Sunday.

'Well, thank God that's over. Now perhaps you will come with me to Johnny's Friday to Monday next weekend. You will not believe me when I tell you that poor old Johnny has fallen hook, line and sinker for one of the Henderson girls and has invited her family down from God only knows wherever it is they live, to view his prospects. He means to marry her and she not more than fifteen, so they tell me. Can you believe it? Though why I should be surprised I cannot imagine as I have

508

extolled the virtues of the married state to them all for the past three years. But then they cannot all have the good fortune to be married to the most beautiful and charming woman in the whole of Lancashire, can they?'

The offensive scene in the board room might never have taken place. Indeed, like all the tiresome irritations which came to trouble Drew Greenwood's feverish spirit, it was cast already into a deep hole and covered over with all that was frivolous and amusing and with which he filled his life.

He pulled her to him in the carriage, his boyish face filled with good-humoured satisfaction that at last all that dreadful business was behind him. He could not wait to return to the carefree life they had enjoyed together before Charlie's death and to which now, now that affairs were in other hands more suited to them than his own or hers, they could return.

'I'm pleased for Johnny, and the Henderson girl, whoever she may be,' she answered carefully, not wanting yet to disturb his triumphant belief that she was to be his completely from now on. She knew she would be forced to compromise, to share some of her time with him in his hedonistic pursuit of pleasure; to keep an eye on him, she supposed, but she could not forget that small budding of pleasure she had enjoyed when those men round the board room table had treated her with the respect and care one man will show to another who has power. They would wait to see if she would fail dismally, not displeased if she did since she was a woman, but she'd done damn well so far in her handling of the Chapman venture, they believed.

The forming of the company to look after her husband's concerns was good sense since anyone with half an eye could see he was incapable of doing more than pursuing the life of the gentleman he thought himself to be. The mill was to start up again, which none of them had predicted almost a year ago, and she had been clever enough to get some decent advisors, themselves in fact, to guide her along what would be a hard road to tackle.

They had believed *she* had done it. Will Broadbent had given her that. He had let them all believe that *she* had done it and they admired her for it. She had liked their admiration since, until now, both as a woman and a girl she had earned nothing but scorn for her wild ways, her complete lack of judgement, her inability to do more than skylark about the county with her two reckless cousins.

It did not occur to her that at the time she had delighted in that scorn she earned from all those in the Penfold Valley, whom she in her turn had held in contempt for their conventionality. And she certainly did not connect the change in her attitude with Will Broadbent who had told her that he would be on the path above Friar's Mere next Sunday at noon.

'Well,' her husband said, pulling away from her impatiently, 'are you to go or not?'

'Go where, darling?'

'Hell's teeth, Tessa, will you pay some attention to what I am saying or I shall begin to believe you actually enjoy being an industrialist?' He was laughing now, amused at the lunatic idea that Tessa Greenwood could possibly be entertained by anything other than what she had done so successfully for most of her life. 'Come on, sweetheart, it's all behind us now. You have absolutely no need to go into that mill yard again, and neither have I. Oh, I understand that we may have to attend a board meeting or two, as directors of the company.' He could accept it now that it was over, even believe that he would do it. He grinned endearingly as though to ask if he was not clever at remembering it, 'But that is all and we will celebrate our freedom with our friends next weekend. You must have a new gown, something to turn their heads and make them stare. Cause a sensation as you have always done.'

He made love to her that night, jubilantly, calling her name over and over again, but when she lay sleepless beside his restlessly turning body she knew, despite the triumph which he thought had been his that day, he was still haunted in his dreams by the past.

CHAPTER TWENTY-SEVEN

She would not go up to Friar's Mere, she told herself, on that first Sunday after the board meeting nor on any other. Despite what Will had done for her and her deep gratitude towards him, she loved her husband dearly and had no wish to chance the fragile equilibrium which held him, but only just, to the rationality of his day-to-day living. He had been uneasy of temper for several days following the meeting as though considerably unnerved by the narrow escape he and his wife had had from a life of utter degradation in the mill.

511

Filled with high spirits one minute and with wild ideas on how to make Johnny Taylor's weekend memorable, then cast down in the next and wanting nothing more than his head on her breast, her arms about him in the complete privacy of their room. His instability of temperament was growing beyond even her controlling, she was ready to admit, and if she were to chance a meeting with Will, even if it was only to thank him for his help, to tell him how deeply grateful she was to him for shouldering so much of her burden, how might it affect her husband should he come to hear of it?

Sunday came and for the first time in her life she begged off riding over to the Hall, claiming a headache as an excuse.

'But you go, darling, for I shall only lie here quietly with the curtains drawn until I feel better.'

His immediate and loving concern almost undid her. He would stay with her, he whispered softly. He could not bear to leave her when she was unwell. How many times in the past had she been beside him when he had been 'afflicted', the word he used when the nightmares came to terrify him. He would soothe her temples with cologne, her forehead with a cool cloth, hold her head, lie beside and comfort her, kiss her better—smiling— and would not dream of leaving her, no, not if Nicky Longworth and Johnny Taylor came themselves to drag him away.

For an hour he hovered about her, moving restlessly from the bed to the open window, twitching aside the drawn curtains to stare out into the garden, hurrying back to her side each time she moved, begging her hoarsely to tell him she felt better, wondering if he could fetch her anything,

512

until she pleaded with him to go since she really did think she would be better on her own. He was quite visibly relieved.

'Are you sure, dearest? I wouldn't dream of going, you know that, but if you're certain you'd be better alone . . . ?'

'I'm certain, sweetheart. You get along and when you come home I shall be completely recovered.'

'I won't be late, I promise.'

'Stay as long as you like. I'm poor company today.'

'I've never known you have a headache, my love.' He was still hesitant to leave her but dying to be off, disturbed perhaps by the remembrance of another illness in another place.

She heard the wild gallop of his bay's hooves on the cobbles of the stable yard at the back of the house and the pounding on the turf as horse and rider headed off across the parkland towards Longworth Hall. She lay for a while, convincing herself that her 'headache' really did exist and that she would stay and cosset herself, much to Emma's amazement, for the rest of the day. Yet in her heart, which thumped quite madly, and in her mind from which all reason had long since gone, she knew she would be high above Friar's Mere by noon.

'I think I feel a little better, Emma. I might even go out for a breath of fresh air.'

'A walk in the garden would do you good, madam.' The incredible thought that Miss Tessa, or Mrs Greenwood as she should really call her, was breeding, had leapt into Emma's mind and she was pleased that at last her mistress had acquired some sense. It was well known that ladies in the family way should not climb up on a horse's back and Miss Tessa did look somewhat peaky; a bit pale and strained about her mouth, though her eyes were quite feverishly bright.

For half an hour her mistress allowed herself to be treated like an invalid, just as though she really would rather stay in the seclusion of her home and garden on this day when the sky was streaked with torn clouds and a mist like a silver veil shifted uneasily about the tops. It was not fit to be out in, Emma said cheerfully, even if it was July, placing more coal on the small fire which had been lit. But when she came back from the kitchen with the dainty tray of coffee and toasted muffins Miss Tessa had ordered, her mistress was already in her breeches and riding jacket, her warm cloak over her arm, her hair bundled up into a loose knot and tied carelessly with an emerald green ribbon.

'Send a message to Walter to saddle my mare, Emma. I have decided to go riding after all.'

'Oh, Miss Tessa, please don't.' Setting the tray down Emma moved to take the cloak from her mistress, her face distressed. She'd never forgive herself if Miss Tessa had an accident, out there all by herself, and damaged that precious burden Emma had persuaded herself she was carrying. It was many years since Miss Tessa had gone out alone, in fact not since Master Drew had come home from the Crimea. 'It's not fit to be out in, Miss Tessa. You'd never think it was July. Percy,' who had been Emma's 'intended' for many years now, 'has just told me how nasty it is and the master'd not like it if you was to go out without him. You know how he is . . .' Her voice trailed off lamely. They all knew how he was, those who

514

worked in his house. Doted on his wife, he did, hardly able to bear her out of his sight, and he'd not be best pleased if she was to go galloping over the moor on her own, especially if she was in an 'interesting' condition.

'Do as I say, Emma. I might even ride over to the Hall to join him.'

But when Mrs Greenwood cantered decorously out of the yard and across the stretch of pasture which led to the small wood and on to the beginning of the wild moorland she had three of those fierce dogs with her that she and her husband had bred from the original pack and she was not going in the direction of the Hall.

The mist swallowed the dogs as they raced ahead so that she was constantly obliged to call them back to her. They were fresh and enchanted to be out of the stables, reluctant to come to her whistle, their sleek black shapes slipping in and out of the trailing edges of the mist and cloud which came down to meet her.

He would not be there, of course, since he would not expect her to venture out on such a day. She had not meant to come herself but something had whispered that this was as good a way as any to prove the ethereal nature of his purpose towards her. A dalliance was what he was after, she told herself, with a married woman who would have no claim on him; who would prove no threat to his good name for she would be guarding her own.

He was leaning against a pile of rocks, his face quiet and serious as he turned towards her. He made no move to help her down from her mare and when the dogs circled him, baring their teeth menacingly since they did not know him, he

515

remained still.

'Call them off, Tessa,' he said at last and when she did and they were lying peaceably against the base of the rocks he turned back to his contemplation of the valley which revealed itself as the mist drifted in eddying patches.

'I was hoping you wouldn't come,' he said absently, and she took no offence since she knew exactly what he meant. 'I wanted you to, of course,' he continued, 'more than anything I've ever wanted before. I came up here hours ago, long before there was any possibility of seeing you, and I dare say I would have waited all day.' He began to smile, turning back to where she stood, still holding her mare's bridle, 'So you may be well aware of my feelings for you, Tessa Harrison. Do you feel the same?'

'I have not come . . . lightly.'

'I hoped you would say that.'

'I love my husband.'

'No. You love your cousin, not your husband,' he replied and she knew at last that he spoke the truth. She had always loved her cousins, both of them, and the damaged man who was her husband held a special place in her heart, as did Robby Atherton. But she had loved neither of them with the true, enduring love that exists between a mature man and woman. Girlish love, young love, a bright, shining wonder had been her feelings for Robby Atherton. Compassion and gratitude and need had led her into marriage with Drew. And this man. This true man. What had she to give to him? What was it that he wanted and could she give it to him?

She moved towards him almost unwillingly

though her heart was bounding joyfully ahead. She leaned her back against the rocks beside him, her shoulder an inch from his and when he took her rain-wet hand and raised it to his lips she felt the sweetness move in her veins. The gesture was so courtly, so gentle, so sad even, as though he was fully aware of the great and awful gulf which stood between them and she felt the sorrow of what they might have had prick to tears at the back of her eyes.

'Tessa, my Tessa, what are we to do? We cannot pretend, either of us, though I fancied otherwise several months ago, that I want you merely as my mistress. It is more than that. We are back all those years to when you were seventeen and I fell in love with you, and yet look what stands between us now. We have come together again inevitably as I suppose I knew we would for what we had was not something given to many. Its only fault then was that you were too young for it; for the commitment it needed. I was ready but you were no more than a girl and now it is too late, now that we are both . . . of a mind . . . oh, yes, we are, my girl, so give me no argument. I can see it in your eyes, and in the reality that you are here where anyone will tell you it is madness to be. Why have you come if you don't love me? Not to say thank you as you would have me believe. Why have you risked your marriage, the life you lead and which you seem to find so pleasant, and now, your husband's inheritance for without you it will certainly fail?'

'Will . . . for God's sake . . .'

'What is it, my lovely lass? Are you afraid?'

'Desperately.'

'Not you, Tessa. You are the bravest woman I

517

know, or do I mean the most stubborn?' He turned at last and with a groan pulled her into his arms. His voice was shaking as he tucked her head beneath his chin, holding her so close she could feel a pulse in his throat throb against her cheek.

'I did want to thank you, Will.' Her voice was muffled against his chest. 'I couldn't have done it without you, you know that. I don't even know why you changed your mind. When I first came to ask you for help it took you all your time not to knock me to the floor of your office . . .'

'I know. I hated you even while I loved you for your bloody nerve in coming. That bright look you gave me, half-afraid, defiant and haughty, for were you not Tessa Harrison who was accustomed to her own way? Yet there was a wariness about you, a readiness, if you like, to run like hell if I turned nasty. But you came just the same and that took courage. God, you were so maddening, with your chin up and your eyes flashing, just as you had always been. It almost broke my heart. It took all my strength not to sweep you into my arms and kiss that supercilious smile from your face.'

She tilted her head and looked up at him smiling. 'I didn't know I looked supercilious.'

'You don't know you're doing it, my darling. It comes so naturally to you. That's why the men in the yard scurry around to do your bidding. You are Mrs Greenwood and your manner tells them that they would be wise to jump when you tell them to. It will stand you in good stead in the months to come.'

'You think I can do it then?'

'I know you can.'

'Even without you there to . . . to clear the way?'

He smiled down at her ruefully. 'How did you know I had . . . put in a word here and there?' He held her away from him, making no attempt to kiss her, the embrace they had just shared quite without passion. She had never seen him like this before, so introspective, as though he was looking inwards to a man he had not known existed. He seemed surprised at his own actions on her behalf, wrapped in thoughts of the past and of the future in which, his manner seemed to say, there could be no room for Will Broadbent and Tessa Greenwood, at least not together. She was frightened by it for suddenly it was inconceivable that he should go out of her life again for she knew she could not manage, not now, not ever, without his arms about her.

'Will . . . ?'

'What is it?'

'Why are we here?' her voice was urgent and he turned to her, surprised.

'I don't understand.'

'Why are we here, Will? Why did you tell me to come? It is this which frightens me, not the mill, though that is bad enough. It would be simpler, far simpler, if we walked away from one another. I don't want . . .'

'To love me?'

'Yes . . . no . . .'

'Then you do love me?'

'I . . . we cannot . . .'

'Say it. Goddammit, Tessa, say it, but mean it this time.'

'I . . . I love you. I love you, Will Broadbent. Can you doubt it now? This is no adventure, as it was the last time.'

'I wish it were, my love, it would be far easier for

us both.'

'I dare say.' She moved to stand closer to him, looking up into his stern face. She placed her hands carefully, one on either side of his smooth, freshly shaved cheeks, then her mouth lifted to his as sweetly and softly as a sigh, lingering, tasting the texture of his lips, carrying in her mind the passion of their past but holding back from it.

'Will you stay with me, my darling?' he whispered against her mouth, still not touching her.

'For as long as I can.'

'Aah, Tessa . . .'

'I know, I know. I have never felt so sad and yet so blindly, rapturously happy.'

'Where . . . ?'

She shook her head and the misted drops of moisture in her hair scattered, some running down her forehead and across her wet cheeks. She blinked as they dewed her eyelashes and he watched with all the fascination and bewitchment of a man under a spell. She was like some water sprite, dewed and shimmering palely in the mist, and yet her mouth was poppy-red and full.

'When?' he said more urgently and she felt the instant unfolding of their desire. His arms drew her to him, a home-coming now, a return to the place where she was always meant to be, and his mouth, wet with raindrops, came down hard on hers, merciless in its aggression. She was his, *his* and he would take her now, put his own special mark on her, his woman, before she could change her mind. 'When, Tessa, when?' His lips parted to take hers and the rain which was falling steadily on them now tasted sweet in their joined mouths.

'I don't know . . . there is nowhere . . .'

'Dear God, how I've loved you, wanted you, all these years, and now the bloody weather . . .'

They began to smile as they kissed, then to laugh, holding on to one another, the skin of their faces wet and sliding, their hair dripping, their hands which were longing to explore, to touch, to caress what was dear and familiar, cold and wet. The whole loving encounter was becoming impossible, amusing even, so that their laughter released itself high and merry into the grey sky.

After a while they grew quiet, content for the moment to stand within the circle of each other's arms and talk softly of the past, the question of where, or how, or even when they would meet in the future, still unresolved. It would happen, they both knew it. There would be turmoil ahead, they both knew that too, since he was not a man to share another man's woman. He might have believed, in the past, that they could become lovers, live a clandestine life of deceit and lies, of messages passed from one paid hand to another, of hurried meetings and hurried farewells, but Will Broadbent, deny it now as he might, was not a man to live such a life. The day would come when Drew Greenwood's wife, Will Broadbent's *woman*, would be forced to make a choice.

'We could go away, you know,' he said abruptly. 'I have money. We could move away from here. I am not a man without experience. There are other mills . . .'

'Don't . . . don't, Will.'

'You could not bear to leave your husband, you are saying?'

'He could not bear it.'

'He is a grown man though one would not think

521

it to hear him speak. He would survive.'

'No, he would not. He is . . . not strong . . .'

'He looked well enough to me at the board meeting. Somewhat highly strung but then he and his brother were always that. The mills could be run by those men . . .'

'You told me a little while since that they would fail without me.'

'I only meant that *he* could not do it.'

She held on to him tightly, her face buried against his chest, her eyes tightly closed against the pain and fury in his. So soon, so soon. It had been but an hour and already he was demanding, begging more of her than she could give. They had done no more than kiss and declare their true feelings, hold one another, thanking the gods which had given them this small, shared part of their lives. Somehow she must make him see that they could never, *never* have more. Only she knew what Drew had become, how far down the slippery road his darkened mind had sent him, the death of Charlie accelerating that journey a hundredfold. He was desperately vulnerable, likely to be further weakened by anything which threatened that vulnerability, and knowing this she had come here joyfully to throw herself into Will Broadbent's arms.

'Will, you must listen to me.'

'To hear you tell me how much he means to you?' he said roughly, holding her to him desperately, crushing her, hurting her in his sudden illogical anger. The sweet reason with which he had viewed their relationship was swept away on a flow of savage jealousy.

'You must listen to me. Don't you see we might

as well part now, and forever, if you will not see reason?'

'I want you, that is reason enough . . .'

'No, Will.'

There was a great weight on them now, a bewilderment that this had come upon them so suddenly. It was as though a pendulum had swung them, first high on a delirium of delight at finding one another again, falling slowly to the sober realisation of what it would mean to them as they lived that secret life, then high again in possessive, jealous rage. Will was not naïve enough to believe that Drew Greenwood's wife would not make her body available to her husband whenever he required it and in his mind's eye he could picture them, perhaps no more than an hour from now, sharing the sweetness of what he himself was denied. He and Tessa could find a place somewhere, discreet and hidden, he was certain, but for how long! They could meet up here now and again where no one came but the birds and the moorland animals, but for how long? How long would it be before the situation provoked disillusionment, impatience, and a refusal to suffer it any longer?

'Perhaps we should remain . . . no more than business acquaintances then?' His voice was cold and he let his arms drop heavily to his side.

'If you think it best.'

'I can see no alternative.' The numb misery in him washed over her.

'Nor I.'

'We had best be on our way then.'

'Indeed.'

'You are . . . we are both getting very wet . . .'

Their eyes met for that last fatal moment, glazed

523

with pain and the need to hide it, to bury it deep where it could be neither seen nor felt, for it was too much to bear. A moment, an instant, then without coherent thought they flung themselves into one another's arms, crying both of them, that whatever the cost they could not part. His hands were at her face and hers at his, stroking feverishly, then clinging again until their bodies met and strained together.

'I can't wait . . .'

'Nor I . . .'

'Here . . . ?'

'There is nowhere else, my love.'

He tried to spread his cloak and hers upon the wet, spongy turf, using the overhang of the rocks to protect them from the drizzle which still fell, but the garments were already damp before he laid her on the makeshift bed. It was not cold and though the skin of her naked body rose in tingling gooseflesh it was at the delight of the new and erotic sensation as wet flesh met wet flesh. Her breasts lifted ecstatically, the nipples peaked and rosy to his hands and lips. They had waited a long time and they could not hold back, either of them. He entered her at once and that taut thread which had tightened so many times in the past for Drew Greenwood snapped in two releasing in her a languorous breathless pleasure which left her laughing and weeping with her joy.

'Again,' she told him, lifting her body greedily, and he plunged into her, his own laughter joyous and triumphant. This time the rapture caught them both by surprise as it exploded within them simultaneously.

'Truly, you are perfect,' she breathed when she

could at last speak.

'Together we are, my love, my sweet love.'

'Hold me in your arms.'

'Always.'

'Always. You will always love me?'

'How can you ask?'

He wrapped his warm, wet body about hers and drew the damp cloaks about them. His head rested in the curve of her shoulder and as they lay quietly the sun drifted out from behind the wisps of cloud which moved across the sky and the light rain stopped. There was no sound except for her mare as she cropped the grass. One of the dogs yawned noisily and moved into a patch of sunshine and Tessa knew that it was time to leave. She must be home before Drew. She would, of course, tell him she had been for a canter up behind the house but he must not know how long she had been gone.

Will drowsed against her and she studied his relaxed face intently, the hard, flat planes of his cheeks, the strong mouth, half-smiling in sleep, the firm chin unblurred by excess flesh though she knew him to be thirty-five or so. The face of a man who has known hardship and adversity but has overcome it; who has shouldered aside the barrier of class and education and become a man other men respect, a man other women—other than Tessa Greenwood—could love. Only his eyelashes seemed out of place in his man's face for they were long, silky and fine, like those of a sleeping child, giving him an air of defencelessness which was not apparent when he was awake, and which moved her heart to anguished love. His short, straight hair lay spikily on his forehead and she brushed it back with loving fingers. His smile deepened as she dropped light kisses on the corner of his mouth, on his eyes until they opened, and he made love to her again, slowly, softly, gently, without urgency and time simply stopped for her as she fell into the rapture again.

They dressed hastily. She was aware that she must get home before Drew, that it was probably already too late; he was conscious of her anxiety and resented it. She caught his rancour but did not dare to stop and allay it. How could she? It would always be like this and they must both accept it. Don't let him be hurt, her heart begged over and over again, don't let him be hurt *too* much. Don't let me wound him again as I did the last time. But already she knew the pain was there, the pain of letting her go to another man.

He pulled her roughly to him.

'Will you . . . ?'

'What, my darling?'

'Is it too much to ask that you won't . . . ?'

She knew what he was trying to ask, trying *not* to ask for it diminished him in his own eyes, but she could make him no promises and he knew it in his heart. She drew his head down to her shoulder, amazed that this strong man should be so frail.

'I love you, Will,' she whispered. 'No matter what . . . happens between Drew and me, you are the one I love.' She could promise him no more than that.

She thanked God that Drew's horse was not in the stable. Though it probably meant that he would come home the worse for drink, that his earlier solicitude for her had been forgotten, indeed that she had been forgotten, at least she would be saved the complication of explaining where she had been for so long. It was almost six and the intervening hours with Will had drifted by without her noting their passage. Even Walter, she felt, as he took her mare from her must sense the tension in her, the guilt, she supposed, since she had just committed the sin of adultery. Drew in his more reasonable state was aware of her every mood, but if he was drunk, whether merry or surly, it would be easier for her to get through that initial encounter. For the first time, she realised, she was praying that her husband would come home in his cups!

He did, just as the watery sun slid beyond the charcoal grey tops.

'It was a splendid day, sweetheart, quite splendid. We played cards and sampled the Squire's claret and then old Johnny rode over and bored us all to distraction waxing lyrical on the charms of his Alicia. Yes, that's her name, the future Mrs Johnny Taylor, of Hadden Hall. So we plied him with claret and took several guineas off him . . . well, I did until Nicky had a run of good luck and ended up the winner by . . . now don't look at me like that, Tessa darling. A gentleman must pay his gambling debts . . . only 200, sweetheart, and now that the mill is to be back in business and old Bradley is looking after all our investments, we can well afford it. Then, after we had finished the claret Nicky brought up a bottle of . . .'

His good humour made him mercifully unaware of her own tenseness and gradually it drained away as she realised that her husband had spent such a pleasant day he had completely forgotten her own reason for not accompanying him.

' . . . so all in all it should be a splendid weekend. Freddy Piggot is to be there. You remember

527

Freddy, don't you, darling, and that horse-faced sister of his, who, I suspect, is a strong candidate for Nicky? His mama is set on seeing him married and if she can arrange it to her own satisfaction poor old Nicky will be saddled ...' he shouted with laughter. ' ... did you hear that? Saddled, how very appropriate ... with Freddy's wealthy sister ...'

She listened smilingly, able now to look into his flushed face, to meet his bright and merry eyes. When, after half an hour of lounging by her sitting-room fire, a glass of brandy in his hand and the decanter close by, since the night had turned decidedly chilly, he said, he dredged up from his bemused mind the memory of the morning and her indisposition, he was almost reduced to tears in repentance.

'How could I? Oh, my darling, all these hours you have been alone. What a swine I am, and you with a headache ... Will you ever forgive me?'

'I had a ride out ... to clear it.'

'Oh, darling, I'm so glad. You're completely better, really?' With his contrite head in her lap, her hand smoothing his tumbled curls, she sighed, remembering the wiry hair she had caressed that afternoon, studying the face of Will Broadbent as he smiled at her from the dancing flames of the fire.

CHAPTER TWENTY-EIGHT

It was just over six months since Annie had gone to Manchester and with the new mill to be opened the following week Tessa searched for the scrap of paper on which her address had been scribbled, intending to write to tell her that her job was waiting for her and that she was to come home immediately.

But the memory of their last meeting and Annie's pig-headed refusal of employment at Crossbank or one of the other mills; her absolute determination to do what she thought right and not what Tessa considered best for her, made Tessa leave the note she had begun to write and move thoughtfully to the window. Annie was quite likely to turn awkward if she thought she was being 'ordered' home. She might even be settled happily in her new place and job and be disinclined to return to the cottage—which Tessa had kept vacant for her—and her job at the rebuilt mill. Tessa was not awfully sure what 'pin-heading' or 'pin-sheeting' was. Perhaps it was a splendid job which Annie had found more to her liking and in that case it would need all Tessa's powers of persuasion to get her to come home.

She had missed her. Annie's forthright common sense and practical, realistic outlook on what life could fling at you had often been a lifeline for Tessa in the years they had been friends and she needed her now as she had never needed her before. She was not awfully sure why since Annie was bound to disapprove of her renewed relationship with Will, but there would be comfort in having Annie there in the cottage at Edgeclough, even if it was only to scold.

She had wondered vaguely, now that the mill was to be working again, whether Annie could be employed with something other than her spinning machine. There were hundreds of girls who could do the work Annie had done before the fire. Annie

529

was so bright and sensible, surely she could do something besides mind a couple of self-actors? And her sisters. They were growing up now and were ready, she supposed, for marriage and how much better they would do, back here with their own people. Strangely, she never thought of marriage in connection with Annie. And, of course, there was Jack whose place at Mr Dalton's, the lawyer, had already been arranged and was waiting for him.

No, best get over to Manchester and talk face to face with Annie, make her see what wonderful opportunities were available not only to her, but to her family. Tell her she would be doing them an injustice if she allowed such chances to slip from her grasp. In the most diplomatic way, of course, knowing Annie!

She told no one, not even Will, that she was going. Drew had ridden into Crossfold to see his tailor and would be bound to tarry at the Dog and Gun, and so on a fine day at the end of July she took the train from Crossfold, changing at Oldham for Manchester, arriving at Victoria station as the clock struck noon.

The day was warm and though she wore a light-weight sprigged organdie gown of the palest grey she was immediately aware that not only was the close, smoke-covered pall which hung over the city about to make her perspire in the most uncomfortable and unladylike way, but that her light-coloured gown would be stained and grimy long before she arrived at Annie's. The huge crinoline cage, though cooler than the old fashion of the six or seven petticoats she had worn to hold out the width of her skirt, was awkward to manoeuvre. As she and Emma, whom she had been compelled to bring with her to avoid the attention a lady alone might attract, crammed themselves into a public carriage, Emma was quite appalled by its condition.

'We can't ride in that, Miss Tessa.' Her voice was indignant, but at the same time somewhat apprehensive since, never having travelled in anything other than her mistress's splendid carriage, she was not at all sure of the rough fellow who was to drive them. 'Mr Drew wouldn't like it at all, not at all,' she added tearfully.

'Mr Drew doesn't know so he cannot form an opinion and if we are not to ride in this carriage are you prepared to walk?'

Emma eyed the curious men who seemed to have nothing better to do than lounge about the station yard and stare and the barefoot, filthy-faced urchins, inclined to beg or throw stones, she was sure. Reluctantly she climbed into the carriage.

'Where to, madam?' the driver enquired politely enough, though evidently not accustomed to driving a lady and her maid in his conveyance. When she told him, giving him the name of the street which Annie had written down, she was bewildered when he turned to stare at her.

'*Pike* Street? What, Pike Street what runs by't river?' he asked, his expression quite astounded.

'I do not know where it runs. I merely wish to be taken there.'

'Are yer sure yer mean Pike Street?' he repeated, eyeing her elegant gown, her white, lace-trimmed parasol, her pretty pearl-grey bonnet on which an enormous white silk tea rose bobbed and the dainty white kid boots to which already some quite unrecognisable substance adhered.

'I do and I would be obliged if you take me there at once.'

'Well, you know best,' he remarked cheerfully, turning out of the station yard and into Victoria Terrace which led into Victoria Street.

They proceeded at a steady pace along the pleasant thoroughfare until the carriage turned a corner and there, in the centre of a vast square, stood the imposing building of the Royal Exchange, the very heart of the cotton industry and without which, it was said, the sprawling body of its trade which spread over most of Lancashire, would cease to function. Radiating out from the Exchange like the spokes of a wheel were dozens of streets in which lay the thousands of warehouses, factories and sweat-shops connected with the cotton industry, and all within five minutes' walk of its hub. The Royal Exchange was the focus of buying and selling cotton and on market days, Tessa had heard, its huge halls were crowded from one end to the other with buyers and sellers, not even the least self-respecting of them without his tall silk hat for this was the most important cotton market in the world. She would come here one day, Will had told her, for she must learn everything there was to know about cotton if she was to become the manufacturer her mother and her Aunt Kit had been. All around it, enormous warehouses were crammed with cloth, some of it her own, brought from surrounding towns: Bolton, Bury, Oldham, Stockport, and Crossfold! The excitement began to grow in her at that moment.

The streets became increasingly narrow and twisting the further they went and the buildings were so tall it was almost impossible to see the sky. There were waggons heavily laden with cotton cloth, with piece goods and dress goods, with huge bales of raw cotton and all the commodities on which Manchester had built its reputation as the centre of the cotton industry. Waggons lumbered in and out of wide gate-ways, the patient, plodding dray horses which pulled them bending their heads with the weight of their huge loads.

'Oh, Lord,' Emma gasped as their own carriage swayed quite dangerously in the frantic rush which seemed to pervade the area. A hurrying multitude crowded about the conveyance and the impassive animal which pulled it, and surely the massed sea of people were in danger of being run down by the dozens of vehicles which crammed the streets, all of which were involved in the many and complex layers of employment the industry produced. Brokers, yarn merchants, dyers, waste dealers, merchants, manufacturers, buyers and sellers, all were hurrying in the direction of the particular street or region which dealt with their own section of the trade. Stockport and Salford were 'making up'; Piccadilly and Portland Street where the great warehouses were situated; Brown Street was 'shirts' and Stride Hill 'underwear'. It looked just as though some careless foot had kicked over an ant-hill, scattering the human ants in every direction, but there was a strange kind of order about it for each ant knew exactly its own destination and business.

'Oh, Lord,' Emma said again, inclined to be even more tearful as rude, inquisitive faces peered in at them, some leering at the sight of two pretty women in a place where the only females were those drabs who worked in one of the hundreds of small factories, sweat-shops most of them, which crowded the cellars of every street, and were allied to the cotton trade.

The bustle of the town centre began to die away as they crossed the river Irwell, turning left to follow what was really no more than a cobbled track running beside the river. It was here that the stench invaded the carriage, faint at first and causing no more than a tendency to sniff and turn one's head in an effort to identify it and its source.

'What is it, Miss Tessa?' Emma whispered.

'God knows, Emma, but whatever it is it seems to be getting worse by the minute.'

They each held a dainty scrap of perfumed lace to their nostrils and Tessa felt her stomach begin to move distastefully as the stink became so strong she could not only smell it, but taste it.

On one side of them ran the river, slow moving, evil looking, with unidentifiable objects floating sluggishly just below its surface. Along its banks great piles of rotting garbage swung in the gentle eddies of river water which had carried it there. The smell was appalling and Tessa had the strongest desire to scratch at herself just as though the deeper they penetrated into the squalid district the more loathsome the miasma of filth grew on her skin.

' 'Ere we are,' the driver of the carriage told them. He had a look about him which said he would be glad to get away from this place himself. Already attracted by the sight of the carriage, the area was beginning to swarm with what must have been inquisitive children but which looked for all the world like small, scurrying monkeys, grey-

534

coloured, pallid, furtive. He could not imagine what two such elegant ladies wanted here, but a fare was a fare though if they asked him to wait he'd have to refuse. These urchins would pick his cab clean, wheels an' all, if he stood still for more than two minutes.

They were in a courtyard, large and square with immensely tall houses on three sides of it, each floor-level of the buildings contained by an iron-railinged balcony and each connected by narrow stairs up to the sixth and top floor. The courtyard was unpaved and in its centre a huge pool of water had collected in a hollow, unable to run away to the river in which sewage was dumped. Directly in the middle of the water was a broken building with an opening, evidently once a doorway from which not only the door but the frame was missing as well. It was from here that the stench came, an invisible eruption to which those who inhabited the court seemed impervious but which brought stinging tears to Tessa's eyes. Everywhere was filth, mud, rotting carcasses of what must once have been a living cat or dog, and in it the children played, barefoot, almost naked, and men and women lolled, the smoky sunshine and warmth lulling them into a somnolence which gave them the appearance of living corpses.

Emma began to choke and gasp as the foetid air entered her lungs. 'Merciful heaven! Miss Tessa, please ... we can't stay here ... call the carriage ... don't let him go, Miss Tessa ... We'll be murdered where we stand ... or worse. Please, oh, please, Miss Tessa ...'

Tessa felt the smarting tears clog her eyes but she clung to Emma's arm, convinced that if she did

535

not keep a hold on her the maid might make a run for it. They moved jerkily towards the left-hand side of the courtyard. Her pretty, pale grey gown now had six inches of brown filth about its hem and the ooze of something quite dreadful seeped into her boots. Emma continued to weep loudly.

'Be quiet, Emma,' Tessa said through gritted teeth, 'or I swear I shall strike you. We shall just enquire here for Annie.' She indicated a doorway above which was a sign stating that 'Good Beds' were available, but Emma was beyond caring and continued to cry loudly. The children screamed in play and Tessa wondered how such under-nourished bodies could make such a noise as they threw whatever came to hand at one another. Slime ran down every wall, seeping into the unpaved ground, but a woman leaned casually by the doorway, inured, one supposed, to the horror by its familarity.

'I'm looking for Annie Beale,' Tessa said firmly, her manner letting the woman know that she would tolerate no impertinence.

'Who?' The woman smiled pleasantly, or so she thought, but the sight of the blackened stumps in her mouth made Emma recoil against her mistress's shoulder and reminded Tessa of that day on the moor, long ago now, when the tinkers had chased her.

'Annie Beale. This is Pike Street, isn't it?'

'Aye, it is.'

'Well, then, do you know her? She's about twenty-four and has three sisters and a brother. She came here six months ago . . .'

'Oh, that one.'

'You know her then?'

536

' 'Oo doesn't, stuck-up cow.'

'Where is she then? Where does she live?'

The woman indicated with her head towards a doorway which stood below ground in the third house along the road. Down the flight of area steps which led to it trickled some thick brown liquid, gathering at the bottom and leaking under the fragile door and, Tessa assumed, into the cellar beyond.

She had turned away, her manner brisk and undaunted, wanting somehow to show this woman who eyed her with such amusement that despite her own upbringing she was quite able to cope with the difficulties the woman lived amongst every day.

'She'll not be in,' the woman said.

'Oh . . . ?'

'Well, she'll be at work, won't she, now she's better.'

'Better?'

'Aye, from't fever.'

'Fever?' Emma moaned and Tessa felt the dread move in her.

'What . . . fever?' There were so many. Cholera, dysentery, and dozens with no name but all rife in places such as this and carried indiscriminately to strike down where they were least expected, for they were no respecter of class or privilege.

'We gerrit regular round 'ere.' She smiled more broadly, revealing most of the obscene interior of her mouth. 'Sorts out weak 'uns, they say. Mind you, I've seen a strong, well-set up lad go whistlin' off to't mill in't morning' an be lyin' wi' 'is toes turned up by nightfall.'

'Who . . . did Annie . . . her family . . .?' Her mouth was so dry she could barely speak but the woman continued to grin slyly.

'She'll be at Spicers in Earnshaw Street.'

'And . . . the rest . . . ?'

'Nay, they've gone.'

'Gone?'

'All on 'em in one day. Seen it 'appen a lot. 'Ole families kick t'bucket an' one left ter tell t'tale.'

Oh, dear God, sweet merciful God . . . She felt the ground tilt and for one dreadful moment thought she was about to go down into that foul, slime-coated horror which lay about her, but somehow balancing against the half-fainting Emma she kept herself upright.

'Where . . . where is . . . Earnshaw Street, if you please?'

'Just up yonder.' The woman turned away, her interest in the visitors at an end.

They walked to Earnshaw Street for there were no cabs to be found in this pestilential jumble of rat-ridden cottages in which ten, fourteen, sixteen persons slept habitually in one room, this area of tottering tenements where the residents lived in rows side by side and on top of one another, where a hundred rooms housed more than a thousand destitute outcasts.

'Just up yonder' proved to be back over the bridge which spanned the Irwell, another rickety building with the name SPICERS PINS over the door, and needing no more than a stiff breeze to have it down, Tessa was convinced. The large room which led directly off the street was filled with small tables at each of which sat four children. None of them appeared to be more than six or seven years old, small, pallid, their eyes quite blank and incurious,

538

and the sound of their wheezy breathing in the foetid air reminded Tessa of the sound of the engines at Victoria station, but that had been cheerful and energetic and this was not. There was a kind of frame fixed before each child on which was suspended what appeared to be a heavy weight. Under each table was a treadle and as the child pressed it with a bare and bony foot, the weight came thumping down with a deafening clatter. They were 'pin-heading', applying heads to the shanks of pins, the heads tightened by a blow from the weight hanging before them.

Annie was not among them.

Emma clung like a child herself to Tessa's hand. She had been brought up in the vicinity of mills and the men and women who worked in them. She was from such a family herself but what she had seen today had sent her senses reeling and she could do no more than follow where Miss Tessa led, praying to her Methodist God to deliver her soon from the horrors she was witnessing today. She winced, sidling even closer to her mistress as a man appeared from behind a machine.

'Ere, what d'yer think you're up to?' he demanded to know, not recognising in that first moment and the dim haze of the work room that Tessa and her maid were 'quality'. 'You've no right in 'ere an' I'll thank yer to be off,' he added roughly, his manner marking him as the owner of the factory and the children who worked there.

'I'm looking for a friend of mine.' Tessa's tone was peremptory. Her eyes were riveted to the sight of one small child, her back bowed in the form of a letter 'C', her head no more than six inches from

539

the table, falling into what appeared to be a deep and comatose sleep. The man gave the child a casual but stinging blow about the ear and her head hit the table top but in an instant her tiny hands were reaching automatically for the pin shanks and her filthy feet for the treadle.

The man scratched his head and Tessa watched Emma do the same. She herself had never felt quite so filthy in all her life. Her skin itched and prickled and she longed to be at home in front of her own bedroom fire, a bath of hot water standing ready to receive her, to soak for an hour in its perfume, but would she feel clean even then?

'Surely there is no need to strike the child like that?' She spoke coldly, using the telling weapon of her class, the only one she had.

'There is if I'm ter keep 'em awake, lady. They're no use ter me asleep. Anyroad, what's it ter do wi' you?'

She sighed for there was nothing she could do, not for this child, but she could help Annie, if no one else in this sweat-shop.

'I believe you have a friend of mine working here,' she said haughtily.

'A friend of *yours* madam?' the man said incredulously. 'What, in 'ere?' He eyed her expensive gown and boots, her imperious bearing and the expression on her face which told him she would find her friend or know the reason why.

'Annie Beale. Is she here or not?'

'Annie Beale? A friend of yours?'

'Do you employ her or not?'

'Aye, she's in pin-sheetin' room.'

'Lead me to her.'

'Nay, missus, she's busy an' so am I.'

'Emma.' Emma cowered against her mistress, too appalled and terrified to do more than keep herself upright, just. 'Emma, go and fetch a Peace Officer. I'm perfectly sure these children are all under age, certainly underpaid and definitely undernourished. You will have heard of the Factory Act of 1833, I presume?' The man stood open-mouthed but managed to nod and indicate that he had. 'Then if I am not led to my friend at once I shall report you to the Factory Inspectorate. In fact, I shall probably do so anyway.'

She could hear her mother's voice in her head, saying the words she herself had just spoken about the Factory Act and the Inspectorate, and she marvelled that though her ears had not heard them years ago when they had been discussed, her brain had both noted and retained them.

Annie was the last in a row of girls and young women, all sitting at a long bench with their faces to a grimy, soot-stained window. There was a vice before each one and in the vice was a paper folded previously by the overlooker. The pins made in the outer room were placed carefully, a dozen at a time, in the holes which had been especially punched in the paper, and when the paper was full it was removed and the procedure repeated. The room was damp and packed from wall to wall with similar benches and females, and something else was there too which, though she had never been in such a place before, Tessa recognised as despair.

Annie seemed unable to grasp who Tessa was. When the man tapped her on the shoulder, his truculent face indicating that she was to stand up and shift herself, she did so slowly, her reflexes slack and unco-ordinated. The face she turned to

Tessa was grey and narrow, her eyes deep in bony sockets above her cheekbones. Her threadbare skirt and bodice was sweat-stained and sour and her dirty feet were bare.

'Hello, Annie,' Tessa said softly and before the amazed stare of the factory owner and the dozens of women who were his slaves, she drew the drab and unknowing figure of Annie Beale into her own elegant and compassionate arms. She held her for a moment then began to guide her between the benches but strangely, it seemed, Annie did not want to go.

'We're going home, Annie. Home to your cottage in Edgeclough,' Tessa murmured, taking Annie's hand.

'What about them?' Annie's voice was harsh and filled with something Tessa could not identify.

'Who, Annie?'

'Them.' Annie's hand lifted, swinging in a tired arc to indicate all the hopeless faces who were staring dazedly at her and the fine lady who had come so incredibly amongst them.

'What . . . ? I don't understand.'

'Yer never did, lass.' Annie sat down again and drew a sheet of pins towards her.

'You mean you want to take . . . to take them as well?'

The man at her back began to laugh. He had never enjoyed anything so much for years. The idea of this fine madam trailing up Earnshaw Street with this bloody lot at her heels was the funniest thing he'd ever heard. Just wait until he told his missus in that fine villa in Cheetham Hill which 'this lot' had earned for him and his family.

'They're in as bad a state as me, Tessa Harrison.'

'Dear God, Annie, I might have known you'd be just the same. Even with all that's happened to . . .'

'I'll not come wi'out 'em.'

'Very well.' The factory owner smirked for he'd have summat to say to Annie Beale when her 'friend' had gone, but his smirk changed to amazement when Tessa turned to the young women at her back and addressed them just as though they were human beings and not the dregs of the streets which he knew them to be.

'I am Mrs Tessa Greenwood,' she said vigorously, 'the owner of the Chapman Manufacturing Company Ltd in Crossfold. Have any of you heard of Crossfold? It is near Oldham.' One or two nodded their heads hesitantly. 'I will give work, decent work, to any of you who can make your way there. Do you understand?' Again a couple nodded their heads and it was to these that she addressed herself. 'I have several mills, spinning mills and weaving and the work is easily learned. Annie here will help you . . .' It was then that Annie's new position in life became clear to her and she reached out and clasped her friend's hand.

*   *   *

Really, Mr Briggs remarked fretfully that evening to Mrs Shepherd in the privacy of the housekeeper's small but cosy sitting-room, one wondered what the world was coming to when the gentry—if you could call them that, which he doubted sometimes—brought what one could only term a 'common' person into the house and the mistress of it treated her as though she was her dearest friend: ordering the bath to be placed in front of her own bedroom fire, totally ignoring Miss Laurel's cries of alarm, and the maids running up and down the stairs with jugs of hot water and warm towels, with milk and eggs and soup. And to cap it all sending off a carriage-load of servants, who were, after all, in *his* charge, to some dreadful little cottage in Edgeclough to prepare it for her friend's immediate return, she said. Light the fire, she told them, Mrs Shepherd, and scrub the place from top to bottom. There's some unused furniture up in the attic, Briggs, she said, beds and chairs and things. You will know what is needed, just as though I had the arranging of such like. I want the place to be warm and as clean as a new pin. Mind, when she said 'new pin', Mrs Shepherd, she shuddered quite visibly, though I can't think why. And then off they go, the pair of them, three hours later, in madam's carriage and the whole house in an uproar, and the stables with horses got out, and carriages in and out of the stable yard, and on top of it all Emma having a fit of hysteria, screaming about lice, if you please, tearing at her hair as though she was demented. And as for Miss Laurel, *she* was in a faint after shrieking for the whole valley to hear that if any disease had been brought into the house to harm her children she would never speak to Miss Tessa again. And *he* agreed with her, the master, I mean, though knowing the kind of acquaintance he favours in those low gin shops I hear tell he frequents, I can't imagine why.

'I'll stay with you, Annie,' Tessa said when Annie was settled at her own hearth. 'I'll sleep in the chair by the fire.'

'You'll not.' Annie's face was calm now and her

544

eyes were lucid. She sat in a wing chair, old and somewhat faded, brought over hastily by carriage with several other pieces by the maids, her head resting against its padded back. She was clean, her skin stretched tightly over her delicate bones, pale and thin, but clean, and her own pleasure at the comfort of it showed in the way her eyes lingered on every shadowed corner of the room, on the warm flames licking against her old kettle; in the way she smoothed her hands down the faded but spotless skirt and bodice rummaged from somewhere in Tessa's wardrobe, far too big, but *clean*.

'I'm not taking orders tonight, Annie, you are, and besides, the carriage has gone.'

'I'm all right now, so you can get off home.'

'You don't change, do you, Annie?'

'Not where it shows, lass, and I'm not ready to talk . . . about . . . about them, not yet. 'Appen in a day or two . . .'

'Annie, oh, dearest Annie . . .'

'Give over, Tessa.'

'Why didn't you let me know? You know I would have come at once. You make me feel ashamed . . .'

'Nay, you've nowt ter be ashamed of. Yer've bin a good friend ter me.' It was the nearest Annie could get to a declaration of affection. 'Yer've 'ad enough on thy plate, so I 'eard, ter be botherin' about me an' mine.'

'But it's all done now, Annie. Everything's running beautifully. I've . . . we . . . we had help . . .' She looked down at her hands which gripped one another tightly. Her face was soft and smiling and her skin flushed to a lovely rosy hue. 'The mills are a limited company now and there is a board of

545

directors. Will Broadbent . . . you remember Will?' She looked up at Annie and her eyes told their own story and Annie knew, of course. But this was not the time to ask questions, even if she had cared to.

'That's why I came to fetch you, Annie,' Tessa went on, not aware that her love for Will Broadbent shone in her flushed face. 'The mill is to be opened next week and your job is waiting for you if you want it. But that's not what I wanted to talk to you about.'

'Yer know I'll do what I've always done an' that's work at mill an' earn me own livin'.'

'But what about those girls from Spicers, and all the other young women who need someone to help them?'

'You'll help them.'

'No, you will.'

'Me? What can I do?'

'You'll think of something, Annie. We could . . . open a small factory . . . do pin-heading, but in decent conditions . . .'

'But I'm a spinner . . .'

'Does that mean you can do nothing else? Would you not like to give a hand to girls who have no one else to help them?'

'Aye.' Annie's face had become quite pink and her eyes glowed.

'But you're to have a rest first, Annie.' Despite Annie's sudden interest it was apparent she was very tired. Beneath the false glow there was a waxy look of strain about her mouth and sad eyes.

'Aye, a day or two, 'appen, then . . .'

'Annie, will you stop being so stubborn? You're in no fit state to . . .'

'I'll decide what sorta state I'm in, if yer don't

mind and . . .'

The soft knock on the cottage door made them both jump but even as she moved to open it the image of Will Broadbent slipped into Tessa's mind and her heart began to beat joyfully.

His enormous frame filled the doorway. He was dressed in a rough jacket and cord trousers, the legs pushed into the tops of his knee-length boots. His shirt was opened at the neck and his hair was dishevelled as though he had ridden at speed. He looked exactly as he had done on the day she first met him: a working man with a brown face and hands, a bit rough and ready with none of the smoothness he acquired when he put on his business suit, but clean, dependable, steady, with a curl to his mouth which said he was ready to laugh easily and a soft glow in his eyes when he saw her at the door.

She loved him. Dear God, how she loved him.

'I thought you would be here,' he said, ready, she knew, to take her in his arms, indeed they lifted involuntarily and she almost stepped into them.

'Come in, Will.' The voice from the kitchen was weary and instantly they moved away from the embrace they both longed for. 'Come in, Will, an' tell me 'ow the dickens yer knew I were back. News don't 'alf travel fast 'ereabouts. I'll be 'avin' the Mayor of Oldham knockin' on't door next.'

He knelt at Annie's feet and though she turned red with embarrassment and was stiff and awkward, he drew her slight figure into his arms and hugged her. The gesture was spontaneous, warm with affection, and Annie allowed it. She even smiled and when Will stood up and turned to Tessa her eyes were deep and knowing as he took Tessa's

547

hands in his.

'I might have known this was your doing, Tessa Harrison,' and I love you even more for it, his eyes told her, 'but I'm only sorry I didn't do it myself. I thought she was . . . comfortable . . . with a decent place . . .'

'Don't talk about me as if I wasn't 'ere, Will.'

'I'm sorry, lass,' he tore his reluctant gaze away from Tessa, 'but I feel that ashamed . . .'

'That's what Tessa said but it were no one's fault. If we'd . . . if the fever, well, wi' first one then t'other goin' down . . . cholera, it was said . . . I couldn't work. Nay, I'm not goin' ter weep again. See, Tessa, give Will a cuppa tea, I'm off ter me bed. 'Appen Will'll see yer back 'ome, lass.' She stood up slowly, her gaunt frame showing the effort required to control her straining emotions.

'I said I'd stay . . .'

'An' I said I want to be on me own, Tessa.' Her voice was sharp and painful, then it softened. 'Just fer a day or two . . .' She could not put into words her need for peace and privacy in which to do her grieving and she begged Tessa to understand. 'I'll be right as rain, lass. I just want ter . . . 'ave a bit o' rest. Come over in a day or two, if yer've a minute ter spare. Now don't come out 'o yer road, only if yer over this way . . .'

'Oh, stop it, Annie. One more word and I'll not come again, ever.'

'I reckon I'd manage on me own if yer didn't.' But Annie was smiling as she made her slow and weary way up the stairs which Tessa's maids had scrubbed, to the warm, herb-scented bed they had made up for her.

'Shall I come up with you, Annie?'

548

'Nay, my lass. I've bin puttin' meself ter bed since I were a bairn.'

'How did you know she was home?' she asked when Annie had closed the door quietly on her spartan bedroom.

'Oh, it's not easy to move about this valley undetected, my darling. In no time at all the news that Annie Beale was being treated as a valued guest at the home of Mrs Drew Greenwood reached the ears of my head clerk who informs me of anything he thinks might be of interest to me. And knowing Annie as I do, I was pretty certain she wouldn't be happy until she was in her own place, by her own fireside. I came over at once.'

They both smiled at Annie's stubborn pride. Tessa was still dressed in the soiled organdie gown she had put on that morning—was it only such a few short hours ago?—but she had left her bonnet, her parasol and gloves on the bedroom chair where she had tossed them as she had helped Annie inside. Her hair hung about her face and shoulders in damp drifts and there was a streak of dirt across her forehead where she had pushed a frantic hand through it.

'You've had a hard day, Tessa.' The very words she had longed to hear, and who but Will would know her needs, how utterly exhausted she was? How lovely it would be to sink into the chair Annie had just vacated, to kick off her filthy boots and put her feet on the fender, to have a cup of tea put in her hand and pour into some sympathetic ear the dreadfulness of what she had seen that day.

'Sit down, my darling.' When she did his hands were at her bootlaces removing her filthy boots. Then they caressed the arch of her foot, her ankles,

549

smoothing the skin and taking from her weary bones the memory of the recent horrors. The tea was forgotten as he lifted her up and drew her into his arms. Their mouths met for a brief moment and she sighed for Will knew just what was in her heart and troubled mind, as he had always done.

The woman who lay sleepless in her bed above them listened sadly to the silence.

CHAPTER TWENTY-NINE

The formal betrothal between Johnny Taylor and Alicia Henderson was announced at the ball his father gave at the beginning of August, and his weekend guests, amongst them Mr and Mrs Drew Greenwood, were fulsome in their congratulations.

Hadden Hall was a fine old country seat in the parish of Middleton, Sir Anthony Taylor, Johnny's father, being a great landowner in those parts. Like Squire Longworth he had sold a tiny corner of his land to the railways so that the Manchester to Rochdale line might proceed unhindered through Lancashire and had made himself enormously wealthy in doing so.

By chance, as the navvies prepared the track, which was several miles from the Hall, coal was discovered on his land. Fortunately the colliery winding-gear built to get his coal out of his land would not be seen from the windows of his home, so he allowed the necessary work to go ahead, and his income tripled.

Drew and Tessa rode over in their splendid carriage, another following behind packed with their boxes, and with Emma and Hibberson, the footman who was to 'do' for Drew. Behind the second carriage rode Walter on Drew's bay and leading Tessa's mare, for there was bound to be some sort of sport on horseback and though Sir Anthony had a fine stable Drew had declared he would prefer to ride his own animal.

It was a glorious day, the sky across the moors a vast and endless bowl of blue. The summer had been fine with warm, sunny days and a good deal of rain at night and the moorland was a wonderful sight, swathed in the deepest purple heather, the verdant green of the springy turf and the yellow of gorse. The banks of the lanes as they drove through villages and hamlets were covered with harebells, toadflax and hackweed, the occasional field hedge laced with long streamers of honeysuckle and sweet-scented bedstraw.

Drew dragged the clear air deep into his lungs, looking around him contentedly. He put his arm about Tessa's shoulders, indifferent to the eyes of the servants, and drew her more closely to him, smiling down into her face.

'This is better than that damned factory, don't you think, my pet? Just smell the air.' He took another deep breath and obediently she did the same.

'It's lovely, Drew,' she agreed.

'And you look quite glorious, my darling. I shall have to keep a watchful eye on those fellows at Hadden: not one of them would hesitate to steal you from me if they could.'

'Fiddlesticks, Drew, and you shouldn't joke about such a thing. Besides, I might not want to be "stolen", have you thought of that?'

551

He grinned and bent his head to drop a light kiss on her upturned mouth. He was at peace with himself this morning, and with her. He had made love to her last night, finding nothing lacking in her submissive acceptance, pouring his terrible nightmares from his body into hers, releasing the tension which came to grip him, and sleeping like a child in her arms for the rest of the night. He did not know what his nightmares were any more for it was five years since Pearce had died and six since the horror of the battles he and his brother had fought side by side. In a way his terror had something to do with Tessa which was strange for she was the hand which led him from the shaking quagmire that threatened him. But during the last twelve months she had shown a strange and quite unbelievable attention to the mill, and in that time he had felt his fears begin to grow again. Fears of what? he asked himself in his more lucid moments, and he could not answer. But she was here with him now. The new mill was running smoothly, he had been informed, the directors had it all in hand and he and his wife were to take up their pleasant life again from now on.

'This will be a splendid weekend, sweetheart,' his voice was soft in her ear, 'and there are such good things ahead. D'you know, I think this is my favourite time of the year. The grouse next week and then at the beginning of September the partridge, with hunting to follow. Did I tell you we are invited to Scotland again?'

They were all there to meet them on the imposing steps which led up to the wide front door of Hadden Hall: Johnny Taylor, Nicky Longworth, all Drew's insolently aristocratic friends who

552

welcomed them enthusiastically, young lords at play, not one of them under the age of twenty-five, Tessa thought, and all acting as though they had just been released from the school-room.

'They are high-spirited, Mrs Greenwood.' Sir Anthony took her arm benevolently but his eyes ran appreciatively over the soft swell of her breast inside its cream silk, finely-tucked bodice, her splendid shoulders and slender neck, the bright flame of her lips and the extraordinary colour of her long-lashed eyes. She felt his speculative gaze and knew clearly and suddenly, however he might deny it, that she and Drew would never be completely part of this wild-riding, hell-raking, self-assured and overbearing class of society. Though he might welcome her warmly, Sir Anthony Taylor considered it not at all discourteous to let his glance roam quite openly over her body, to let her see that he thought her charms were there for anyone to admire just as though she was no more than a maidservant in his fine old home. All these years she and Drew had imagined that they were the same as these people, part of their society and accepted by them, whilst in reality they were no more than an amusing diversion. They were welcome wherever they went: both were well-mannered, attractive and charming, with money which Drew lost regularly at cards, and were prepared to join in any mad escapade, showing that wild courage which the privileged class admired, but they were not *of* them.

What had opened her eyes to it, she wondered, as she moved about the elegant bedroom she was to share with Drew, directing Emma in the preparation of the gown she would wear for dinner, the choice of her jewellery, the consideration of how her hair should be dressed. Perhaps she had always known but had chosen to ignore it for what else could she and Drew do with the rest of their lives? They had been brought up as neither fish nor fowl belonging in neither the industrial, commercial world of her mother, her aunt and uncles, nor the autocratic and often noble class to which her cousins had aspired.

But these last twelve months, amazingly, had been the most gratifying of her life, she realised with a shock. Once she had accepted her position in the Greenwood world of business; once she had been shown how to manage that position, to fit herself into it, she had found the challenge quite exhilarating. She had never been made to buckle down to anything or face up to what she really was until Charlie's death and Drew's weakness had compelled her to it.

And she was doing it! What was more, she was doing it well! Now that Annie had returned to the mill and was implementing the scheme Tessa had devised for her and was helping the general day-to-day running of the mill's operatives; now that she had Will to give her his strong hand over the sticky patches and the shelter of his love to protect her, she had the fancy she could make as good a 'millmaster' as other women in her family had done before her.

She moved to the window and stared out across the stunningly beautiful grounds of Hadden Hall. Weekend guests were moving about the stretch of lawn which led down from the terrace to a tree-shaded stream several hundred yards away from the house. The ladies were mostly in white with flower-trimmed parasols and hats, seated beneath wide-spreading chestnut trees, taking tea at tables set with lace cloths and served by housemaids with expressionless faces. Chairs were scattered about for anyone who cared just to sit and watch, and on a flat stretch of lawn cricket stumps were being set up and several young gentlemen, one of whom was Drew, were skylarking. He was brandishing a cricket bat imploring Nicky not to be such a fool and to throw the ball but Nicky and Johnny were ignoring him, launching the ball over his head, backwards and forwards.

'Come on, chaps,' she heard him shout, his voice carrying through the open window, and when they took no notice she had the sudden dreadful feeling that he was about to fling the cricket bat down and stamp off like some small boy in a tantrum. Even from where she was standing she could see the clenching of his jaw and the astonishing flush of hot temper in his smooth brown cheek; then Nicky carelessly threw the ball in his direction, quite unaware of his alarming but fleeting danger, and the moment passed. Drew hit the ball, sending it into the far distance of the trees, his body beautiful in its grace, his beauty stunning in its masculinity. The ladies clapped in admiration and Tessa could hear the murmur of well-bred voices and well-bred laughter.

The meal that night was lengthy and intricate with a great many toasts, not as yet to the wide-eyed bride-to-be and her groom for the official announcement was not to be made until the following night, but to anything these recklessly drinking, carelessly laughing ruling classes could think of and which gave Sir Anthony an excuse to

555

order another bottle from his well-stocked cellar.

Tessa was placed on Sir Anthony's right hand where he commandeered her attention for the whole of the meal. He was said to have been something of a ladies' man in his day and though well past the age for such things, she would have thought, considered himself still to be one! He admired her dark hair which Emma had brushed until it gleamed, placing a white silk tea-rose in the heavy coil at the nape of her neck. He admired her shimmering white gown consisting of nothing but lace and seed pearls, newly designed and made for her by the young assistant to Miss Maymon, just come from Paris and, it was rumoured, so clever she was desirous of setting up in business for herself in the growing and increasingly cosmopolitan town of Crossfold. The dress clung to her, emphasising the loveliness of her high breasts, her small waist and the suppleness of her long-limbed body. The whiteness of her skin was enchanting, he told her, and the velvet-grey of her eyes unbelievable, and all the while his eyes probed the low neckline of her gown.

Once she would have thought this amusing, quite harmless, of course, and therefore not to be discouraged. She would have flirted and laughed, making every gentleman at the table long to be seated with the delicious and witty Mrs Drew Greenwood. She and Drew would have exchanged secret smiles and been highly diverted, falling into one another's arms at the end of the evening in heedless and giddy merriment which would have turned to love-making. They might drink too much of Sir Anthony's fine French champagne, dance every dance, with one another or with any of the dozens of like-minded guests, diverted by anything which kept them from the sin of boredom.

'You are a very pretty woman, Mrs Greenwood,' Johnny Taylor's elderly father told her. His eyes, still on her breasts, informed her that given the chance he had every intention of furthering their friendship and that she, as an industrialist's daughter, should consider herself honoured to receive his attentions.

'Thank you, you are most kind,' she murmured, removing her hand from where his fondled it.

'That husband of yours is a lucky young cub and I shall tell him so.'

What was there to say? 'Thank you again.' She smiled politely, realising that Drew was watching her from some way down the table, the expression on his face quite unreadable. My God, was he angry with her for rebuffing what he considered Sir Anthony's innocent advances, or because he thought she was inviting them? She was never sure these days. His eyes were cool, disinterested almost with that disdainful narrowing which he had learned from the gentlemen with whom he socialised. Then the lady beside him spoke and instantly, courteously, he turned to her and she heard his laugh ring out.

She danced with them all, doing her best to be the Tessa Greenwood they expected. She laughed and flirted, throwing back her head until her lovely hair rippled down her back and they told her it was like old times and, really, they would be very cross if she didn't accompany them on the first grouse shoot the very next week; to Squire Longworth's hunting box in Leicestershire when the season started; to Sir Anthony's castle in Scotland, his villa in Monte Carlo and indeed to every important event in their pleasure-seeking calendar.

It was the same the next day as they boated on Sir Anthony's splendid lake, picnicked under the trees of his lovely woodland, dined in his superbly panelled dining-room and danced the night away in his magnificently appointed ballroom. The announcement was made of the forthcoming marriage of his son to Miss Alicia Henderson and the champagne flowed until not one gentleman was completely sober, nor all the ladies either. Miss Henderson, being only sixteen and just out of the schoolroom was returned, Johnny's duty done, to her mama and the horseplay which the young gentlemen thought appropriate on such an occasion began in earnest.

'Come on, darling. We're going into the billiard room. Nicky has wagered that he and I can drink more champagne in sixty seconds than Johnny and Freddy and we want you to be referee.'

He took her hand, his face flushed, his eyes a quite startling blue. His dark curls tumbled over his forehead and he was excited, feverishly so, enchanted with her beauty and with the envious admiration of the men who had clustered about her all evening. She wore poppy-red in sharp contrast to the pure white of the previous evening, a long, fluted sheath which was stark and simple but extremely daring. Her breasts were almost exposed and suddenly, just as he pulled her to him to let the other fellows see that it all belonged to him, she hated herself, and she hated him.

'No, I don't think so, Drew. I'm going to bed.'

His expression was foolish and behind him his friends became quiet, sensing at that moment

558

something different about Tessa Greenwood which promised to be entertaining.

'Don't be silly, Tessa. Come on, we need your expert champagne-drinking advice. Now then, chaps, I have just had a simply splendid idea.' He turned wildly to the 'chaps' who crowded closer. 'Why don't we drink out of Tessa's slipper?' He bent down, falling on to one knee and lifted the hem of his wife's dress revealing her poppy-red satin slippers, her neatly turned ankles in their sheer white stockings and upwards to her knees and thighs. They all stared, absolutely silent now, for even they knew that this time Drew Greenwood had gone too far.

'I don't think so, Drew. Now, if you gentlemen will excuse me, I shall retire.' Tessa's voice was low, cool and contemptuous.

Leaving her husband lurching drunkenly on the floor at the feet of his friends she moved gracefully towards the stairs and went up them.

He did not come to bed that night though she lay awake listening for his stumbling footsteps. She heard laughter below her window and later the sound of wildly pounding horses' hooves on Sir Anthony's smooth lawn. There were cries from the lake around dawn and women's laughter and a male voice begged someone to 'be a good fellow and help him out of the water'.

She lay in the darkness with her eyes burning in her aching head and her body tossing restlessly, longing for Will and the sane and comforting shelter of his love which would never be wholly hers.

The Drew Greenwoods left at noon the next day. He was haggard and hollow-eyed, she serene and

559

gracious, apologising for their early departure which was unprecedented since Mr and Mrs Drew Greenwood were well known for their staying power and strong constitutions. She spoke vaguely of a family matter and her husband said nothing at all beyond the necessary courtesies. Drew's hunter was inexplicably missing and so was one of Sir Anthony Taylor's fine bays which his own niece, a Miss Victoria Bleasdale of the Northumberland Bleasdales, had ridden only the day before. Miss Bleasdale was still in her room when the Drew Greenwoods made their polite farewell.

'Now, don't you worry about that hunter of yours, Drew, my boy,' their host told him genially, taking his arm across the gravel to his carriage since his guest seemed somewhat frail. 'It will turn up in some farmer's yard and my groom will return it to your ... where is it you live? ... oh, yes ... er ... Crossfold, as soon as it does.' He smiled at Tessa, his manner implying that he fully understood the extravagance of youth, indeed had he not himself once been as rashly imprudent? No mention was made of his own missing bay, nor of his missing niece. He leaned onto the carriage for a last look at Tessa's charming bosom, then stepped back to wave a gracious hand, remarking in an aside to his son that he need not invite that drunken upstart again which was a pity, really, for his wife was most delectable.

Drew waited until they were in their bedroom before he spoke, ordering the maid from the room when she began to open her mistress's boxes.

Tessa sank down on the windowseat and stared blindly into the sun-filled garden. Her mind was cold and empty. She wished someone would tell her what to do, how to deal with the coming crisis, how to calm him, soothe him, convince him that it was all right and that she was not angry with him, that she really did not care that he had probably been unfaithful to her. She would have to care, at least about him, soon. If only he would leave her alone for a while, allow her to steady herself, to gather the resources necessary to paint a tolerant smile on her face, return the fondness, the compassionate fondness in which she held him, to her eyes, the accustomed tone which was needed in her voice. She loved him, and she always would. Still inside him was that core of sweetness he and his brother had shared. Pearce had died with his still intact but in Drew the sweetness was beginning to sour and she no longer knew how to stop it. Well, she did really, of course she did. Had she not been aware for the past twelve months of what was turning her merry, good-natured young husband, her dear cousin, into an unreasonable ... no, that was not the word ... *spiteful* and bitter man? He was afraid, of course, and he really did not know why. He only knew he felt better when she was with him, not just her physical presence but her involvement in all the giddy escapades, the foolish pranks, the recklessly defiant madness he and his well-bred friends got up to.

And last night she had refused so he had insulted her before them all. He had earned himself their frightening disapproval for though he had shown himself to be no gentleman, they were.

'Now then, madam, I would like an explanation of your atrocious behaviour this weekend ...'

'Drew, not now, darling.'

' ... when we were guests, weekend guests that

561

is, for the first time in the home of one of my dearest friends. You chose to be bloody awkward right from the start, giving Sir Anthony that glacial stare of yours from the moment he took your arm. Oh, yes, I noticed, and so did the others . . .'

'Really, Drew, you know that is not true.'

He had begun to stride about the room, unable to contain whatever it was that drove him, his movements rapid and awkward, his arms lifting convulsively with every turn. His intention was clear. He wanted to wound her; to hurt her as he had been hurt for he had made up his mind that the failure of the weekend was her fault, that, and the damned mill!

'Is it not, Tessa? It was not I who insulted Johnny's father when all he wished to do was make himself pleasant. He is an old gentleman who admires a pretty woman. There is nothing wrong in that surely? All it needed to make him happy was . . .'

'For me to fawn about him and make a fool of myself.'

'Fawn about him?' He stopped his striding to stare at her incredulously. 'Is that how you see it? Is that what you call good manners and breeding of which, I must admit, you were sadly lacking this weekend?'

'Oh, stop it, Drew. You really are making a mountain out of a molehill. Sir Anthony certainly is an old gentleman and should be past such foolishness.' Though she could feel the anger, the indignant outrage growing within her, she attempted lightness, even a smile, since she did not care for the glittering brightness of his eyes nor the hectic flush of his face and neck. 'Come and sit

562

beside me and we will order some lunch. We could go for a ride later, up to Badger's Edge and then, perhaps, an early night.' Her smile was inviting but she was prepared to do anything to calm the conflict which was in him.

'Don't try those whore's tricks with me, you slut,' he hissed.

'Drew, really ...' Her eyes had narrowed and her chin rose menacingly. 'First I am frigid and unfeeling in my treatment of that old lecher at Hadden and now I am a slut who practises ...'

'You do yourself no good when you insult my friends, Tessa. They have been splendid in their support of me since Pearce ... since ...'

'And I have not, is that what you are saying?'

' ... and I think it was not asking too much of you at least to be polite to them, particularly Sir Anthony who is no longer young. They are ... or were, though I doubt it now, extremely fond of you but after your refusal to join in the harmless fun they had planned ...'

'Don't be ridiculous, Drew. Perhaps it is harmless but do you not find it to be somewhat childish for grown men? All those "pranks" you get up to ...?'

'Which once, madam, you found enjoyable yourself.'

'Indeed, I suppose I must have done, but by God, I am twenty-three and you are twenty-four years old, Drew, and surely there is more to life than ...'

'Oh, of course, one could spend one's day in the company of those ... those *oafs* at the mill, I suppose, which you seem to find infinitely more entertaining than that of gentlemen.'

563

'It is gentlemanly, is it, to lift the skirts of one's wife and reveal her legs for a crowd of drunken, gaping simpletons to leer . . .'

'You go too far, Tessa.' He took a frenzied step towards her but her own wild and heedless temper, for so long held back, had risen to the surface.

'No, *you* do, Drew. I have done nothing of which I am ashamed. Can you say the same?'

'I hope I am a gentleman since I move in their . . .'

'Don't be so bloody pompous, and besides, I was not talking of your behaviour before I went to bed, but after.'

'We did no more than we have done a hundred times when you were with us. We gambled on . . .'

' . . . who would bed the delectable Miss Bleasdale, no doubt, and guess who it was who won? Did you drink out of her slipper, you and your playful friends, or perhaps she still wore them, if nothing else, when you all took a dawn dip in Sir Anthony's lake?'

'You bitch . . .'

'I see, I am a bitch now, but what does that make you, my fine honourable gentleman? What is the male equivalent of a bitch? Well, whatever it is you are welcome to become one because I'm tired of being your toy, your plaything, your playmate. I have dragged about this damned country with you in pursuit of . . . of *fun* . . . is that what you called it? Harmless fun. Well, I'm . . .'

'Be very careful, Tessa, please . . .'

She was too incensed to hear the sudden pleading in his voice as though he was, for perhaps only a moment, aware of how close he was to the madness which was taking him over.

564

'No, Drew, *you* be careful just for once. Take a good look at yourself and those overbred friends of yours, if you can call them "friends". Believe me, should the fancy take them, they would drop you and me like live coals and treat us as the upstarts we are. Vulgar social climbers, that is how they really see us. Common people whose money is new and very ill-bred. We have amused them, Drew, you and I and Pearce . . .'

'Don't . . . not Pearce . . . don't you dare to . . .'

'Dare what? To tell you the truth? I'm only sorry I didn't realise it earlier myself. All these years of playing the fool, wasting our lives on idiots like Nicky Longworth . . .'

'He is my friend.'

'No, he is not . . .'

'Then who . . .'

'I am, Drew, and Pearce was but . . .'

His face altered subtly before her eyes, changing shape and colour. It seemed to slip and the blood drained rapidly away from it, leaving only the brilliant and raging blue of his eyes.

'Leave Pearce out of this . . . bitch . . . bitch . . .'

He raised his arm and she threw back her head challenging, daring him to strike her, not believing he would. Her snarling anger, so long leashed, curled her lip dangerously. When he hit her the blow stunned her, snapping her head to one side, lifting and swirling her loosened hair and knocking her to her knees. She was dazed, blinded as blood flowed from a cut where his ring had caught her flesh. She did not see him raise his arm again and the second blow struck her to the floor.

When she came to he had gone.

CHAPTER THIRTY

Drew Greenwood did not attend the next day's meeting of the board of directors though his wife was there in her capacity as chairman. Strangely, she wore a close-fitting bonnet with a face veil, unlikely apparel for her elegance was now a byword in the Penfold Valley and the dark bonnet was not as fashionable as it might have been.

The meeting was held in the quite splendid board room of the new Chapman mill. A great deal of worthwhile discussion occurred amongst the directors on the excellent start the new mill had made in its first year of trading. The interest and the dozens of enquiries they had received from men in the cotton industry had been extremely gratifying. They had a full work complement with every position filled, from managers right down to piecers and scavengers. The bales of raw cotton which had been stored in rented warehouses in readiness for the new mill had been opened, blended, carded, drawn out and spun and many thousands of yards of fine cloth had been woven. Providing there was no reduction in the supply of raw cotton which came, as they all knew, from the southern states of America, they would be able to promise a fine profit by the end of the financial year. If Mrs Greenwood would care to look over the figures for July she would be able to see at a glance that what Mr Bradley had forecast at the first board meeting a year ago was already taking place.

Tessa stared through her veil at the neat rows of

566

figures put before her. Mr Bradley's words about the supply of raw cotton and its connection with America rang in her head and more to divert these astute businessmen from her own odd appearance than from any particular desire to know, she asked:

'Should we be worried then about the flow of cotton from America, in view of the possible war there?'

Will Broadbent leaned back in his chair and watched her admiringly. She had got over that first hurdle. Her own shrewdness had connected Mr Bradley's remark with some small doubt on the matter of cotton supply, and these men about the table were pleasantly surprised by Mrs Greenwood's grasp of the situation.

'Well, it's early days yet, Mrs Greenwood, but as you will have read in the newspapers there is some . . . shall we call it . . . disagreement between the northern and southern states of America. Now there appear to be many reasons why they are at odds with one another, difficult for those not involved to understand, but it seems to be more and more obvious that the cotton-growing states are certainly going to be affected. To what extent is yet to be seen. Already there has been some slowing down of supplies and we have men, agents, looking in the East and West Indies, in Egypt and India for alternative supplies, just in case, you understand.'

'Do you mean to tell me that we have committed ourselves to this new mill and the hundreds of people who work in it and now there could be difficulties in obtaining the raw cotton which keeps us trading?'

Tessa's voice was bewildered but beneath it was a

splinter of steel and Will felt his heart move with pride in her. She was no longer the uncaring, furiously riding, defiantly challenging girl with whom he had fallen in love seven years ago. She was no longer the restless, frighteningly high-spirited young woman looking for adventure anywhere it could be found, who had casually thrown his love aside for something her vigorous nature had told her was more exciting, more to the taste of Miss Tessa Harrison. Nor was she the high-flying, imprudently pleasure-seeking woman who had married Drew Greenwood when all else had failed her. Slowly, in the two years since the death of her uncle, she had lifted her head and looked about her; looked beyond her own thrill-seeking world which made fun of those who were sober and hard-working, and had been changed irrevocably by what she had seen. She had not liked what she had been forced to do, forced by some element in her nature inherited, no doubt, from her own positive mother, but by God she was doing it. And she had something else in her, though perhaps she was not fully aware of it yet: it was that she *cared*. She had carried her unstable husband around for years, guided him, distracted him from his obvious frailties, not shrinking from the responsibility he laid on her. She had defended him, become everything he needed to sustain his tenuous hold on reason. Enough for any woman, most would have thought, since he was scarcely fit to be let out alone, but now she had to take on another burden and judging by her steely manner was not to shirk its difficulties.

Mr Bradley put out a placatory hand, then withdrew it hastily since it did not do to pat the arm

568

of the woman who was, after all, his employer.

'Mrs Greenwood, a civil war in America is foreseen by no one, at least not in this country, and even if it were, would you have told us not to rebuild the mill?'

Will sat up, straightening out his long, indolent body, waiting for her answer, ready to support her should she need it.

'I really cannot answer that, Mr Bradley, but I certainly would have considered deeply the effect it might have on my operatives.'

Her operatives! Will almost smiled.

'As we have, Mrs Greenwood,' Mr Entwhistle, who brewed the finest ale in Lancashire, or so his signs said, put in, 'and I can assure you that in our opinion there is no cause for alarm.'

'You know about such things then, Mr Entwhistle?' she asked sharply. 'I believe you are a brewer.'

'That is so, Mrs Greenwood, but I am also a man who knows business and the world markets and therefore I am certainly in a position to know when I am, or when I am *not* to make a profit.'

'Of course you are, Mr Entwhistle, and I hope you will forgive my ignorance. I apologise if I appeared to be questioning your ability.'

By God, she knows how to handle them, Will exulted. First she puts their backs up with questions they are convinced she would not even understand, let alone ask, then, just as they realise the sharpness of her and are about to bristle, she smoothes them down with a soft word and a smile.

'Nevertheless, I think we should consider that we may have to go on short time, Mrs Greenwood.'

Mrs Greenwood turned politely to Mr

569

Broadbent who had spoken. Her cool, silvery-grey eyes met his through her veil with nothing in them, should they have been seen plainly, but the concerned interest one business associate gives another, nothing in them or her manner—nor his— to reveal that the last time they had been together he had made love to her naked body on his greatcoat in an abandoned hut high on Saddleworth Moor.

'At my own mill,' he continued smoothly, 'which, of course, is smaller than Chapman's and without its resources, we are already running for only four days a week. Temporarily, I hope, but rather than turn anyone off I recommended this policy. Perhaps we may discuss doing the same here, should it be necessary.'

'Indeed, Mr Broadbent, but for the moment we must endeavour to find our cotton wherever we can and perhaps by the next meeting Mr Bradley will be able to report any new market where it can be obtained. And let us hope this war in America will come to nothing though the headlines are that the Union is to be dissolved.'

'I read that report too, Mrs Greenwood.' They smiled politely at one another before turning back to other matters for discussion and for two hours Tessa Greenwood said little as she listened intently to what each member of the board had to report.

Coffee was served at eleven but Mrs Greenwood declined to drink a cup. When they stood up at the end of the meeting she reached for the bank manager's report on the financial trading of the company.

'I will take this with me if I may, Mr Bradley, to study more thoroughly.'

570

'Of course, Mrs Greenwood. Perhaps your . . . husband might care to peruse it. I am only sorry that he was not able to attend.'

'It is the twelfth of August, Mr Bradley.'

'Has that some significance?'

'Come, Mr Bradley. Grouse shooting starts today and it being such a short season my husband was eager to take advantage of it. Now, if you will excuse me, gentlemen, I have one or two things to attend to in my office.'

Will bowed with the rest of them, then, as she was about to leave the room and move along the richly carpeted hallway to her own suite of offices, his voice cut across the polite farewells.

'If I may beg a moment of your time, Mrs Greenwood?'

She turned her head a fraction, speaking over her shoulder.

'I'm afraid I cannot spare even that, Mr Broadbent. I have an employee coming to see me in five minutes regarding a matter which I intend to bring up at the next board meeting. Perhaps in a day or so, if you would care to make an appointment.'

'It really will take no more than thirty seconds, Mrs Greenwood.'

'Mr Broadbent, I . . .'

Will smiled urbanely and the gentlemen who still stood in groups about the table, looked round, surprised by the sudden tension in the room.

'I would be immensely obliged, ma'am.'

'Very well, but no more than . . .'

'Oh, indeed.'

The moment they were in her office with the door shut firmly at his back, she did her best to avoid him but his left arm held her tightly whilst his right hand lifted her veil. Across her face was a livid red weal and her right eye had a small cut in a raised bruise at its swollen corner.

'I thought so,' he hissed perilously. 'I thought there was some reason why you were wearing that bloody silly hat and veil. He did this, didn't he? That . . . that thing who calls himself a man. He hit you, the bastard, but by God he'll not do it again.'

'Will, please . . . I hit him back,' she lied.

'And is that supposed to make this more acceptable?'

'He was provoked . . .'

'Provoked! By what? Your refusal to go with him to shoot bloody grouse, I suppose, or was it your ability to take over and do what he is incapable of doing himself?'

He flung himself away from her, turning about the room in a snapping and uncontrollable spasm of torment. He was beside himself with red-hot anger, and with his own impotence at not having the right to prevent what had been done to her. And yet at the same time he was cold, forcing out each word distinctly, dangerously. His face had gone quite blank and his eyes were empty and bitter. It was as though what had happened had been her fault, something she could have prevented, by distancing herself, she supposed numbly, from what threatened her.

'He was . . . he had . . . I had led him to believe that I would . . . that there was no need for either of us to attend another board meeting . . . and then . . . we had been . . . we were guests at . . . I taunted him . . . I have been at the mill on many occasions recently, to see Annie . . . and others, which he had allowed . . .'

'Dear Christ, *allowed?*'

'It is not as it seems, Will. I should not have said . . . what I did.'

'So he struck you across the face?'

'Believe me, Will, I did not . . . I should not have . . .'

'Do you think I care about that? Do you think that because you say you . . . what was it? . . . provoked him, I can accept this as though . . . ?'

'You must.'

'*Must!*'

'It has nothing to do with you. It is between my husband and myself.' She made herself hold back from the comfort she longed to find in his arms, the comfort of having him hold her, his sympathy, his kisses and the tender concern she badly needed. She had dreaded this. She had hoped at best she could get through the meeting with no one questioning too deeply the strangeness of the dense veil she wore but she might have known that Will would see through not only the veil but her reason for wearing it. He was too aware of her, too deeply involved with Tessa Greenwood and too well acquainted with every inch of her body which only last week he had explored minutely from her hair-line to her toe-nails.'

'Is it now, and so I am to stand aside and see the woman I love, a woman whose boots he is not fit to polish, take a beating which would not look amiss on a bloody prize-fighter?'

'Don't exaggerate, Will,' she said coldly, and was alarmed when he made a violent movement towards the door, his fists clenched tightly, his face ominous and snarling. 'Where are you going?'

573

'Up to the bloody Hall, where else? That's where I'll find him, isn't it?' he wrenched at the door handle just as she reached him.

'Will, you can't, you can't. I won't let you. Can't you see it will destroy him?'

He turned, his chest heaving, his eyes bloodshot, his fists clenching and unclenching. His face was soaked with his own maddened sweat and she knew it was taking every ounce of his control not to strike her, as Drew had done, in sheer, full-blooded frustration. He breathed heavily as the agony of her last words almost felled him.

'Destroy *him?*' he whispered. *'Destroy him?* What in hell's name do you think it's doing to me?'

'You are strong . . .'

'And better able to bear your cruelty, is that it, my lass? To see you defend a man who . . . goddammit . . . you so obviously love more than me.' He turned away and crashed his fist against the sturdy frame of the door, then leaned slowly, heavily, against it, defeated, his face pressed close to the dark wood.

'Darling, please, try to understand . . .' Her voice was gentle, begging for his sympathy.

'Understand what? That I must allow him to do just whatever he pleases to you and then have you defend him for it? Jesus Christ, Tessa, what d'you think I am? Other men have suffered far worse than he has and not become the weak and irrational misfit he is. Why must you give your life, and mine, to keep him from killing himself? That is what he will do one day in his mad ride to destruction and if he does not do it himself, I swear I will do it for him.'

He turned then and with the utmost gentleness

put up a hand to her face, almost touching the livid weal which marred it. He smiled so lovingly her heart ached for him and tears blurred her eyes as he placed soft lips on her swollen cheek.

'I love you, Tessa, and despite what I said I know you love me. But he will not hurt you again. It will be the last time if he does.'

Annie found her ten minutes later staring from her window across the cheerful bustle of the mill yard, out to the high moorland which led from the outskirts of Crossfold up to the sky.

'Nay, what 'appened to thi, lass? Yer've not come off that animal o' thine, 'ave thi'?' She studied Tessa's closed face intently. 'I've summat at'ome, a potion I mek that'll tek that swellin' down in a minute. Yer can tek me ower ter Edgeclough in yer carriage an' I'll give thi' a jar.'

'Thanks, Annie.' But Annie knew Tessa had not heard what she said.

'What's up?' she said after several minutes of silence.

'Nothing.'

'Ow did yer come by that black eye?'

'I . . . fell off my mare, as you said.'

'Oh, aye, an' what did Will 'ave ter say about it?'

Tessa turned sharply, wincing as the flesh about her eyes was stretched by the movement. 'What has Will to do with it?'

'I saw 'im comin' out of 'ere no more an' ten minutes since lookin' as though 'e'd like nothin' better than to thrash the livin' daylights out o' someone. Your 'usband perhaps?'

Tessa's shoulders drooped and she sighed deeply.

'Annie, what am I to do? What the hell am I to

575

do? I can hide nothing from you so you are bound to know that Will and I are . . . well, you will know what I mean. But Drew is . . . he needs me so badly. If he should learn of our friendship, it would be the end of him and yet I can't give Will up, I can't. Dear God, what can I do?'

'Eeh, 'tis nowt ter do wi' me, lass, an' there's nowt I can say to 'elp thi'. Yer mun walk the road tha's chosen, Tessa Greenwood, an' take consequences an' all. Tha' knows that an' thi' don't need me ter tell thi'.'

Tessa sighed again then turned to smile painfully. 'You're a big help to me, Annie. I know exactly where I stand with you, if no one else.'

'What did tha' want me ter say? Thee an' Will are . . . dear ter me but I can do nowt ter 'elp either of thi'. Yer both welcome at my 'ome any time yer care ter call an' thi'll always find me there, 'appen thi' needs summat. Tha' knows that. I can say no more.'

'I know, Annie, thank you. Now then, how are you getting on with the project?'

Annie sat down in the chair opposite Tessa and shuffled the papers she held, edging them into a careful pile.

'This is't list so far. There's dozens of 'em still turnin' up at factory gates askin' fer me even after all this time. Word's got round. I've fixed 'em up wi' decent lodgin's. Mind, some of 'em 'ave children wi' 'em, but 'appen they can go ter't school while their mams are workin'.' She pulled a face irritably. 'Eeh, Tessa, I can't get mesen set in that there . . . office. It's right awkward ter me what wi' that daft beggar as calls 'imself 'ead clerk lookin' down 'is nose. Pompous devil!'

576

Annie had regained the flesh which she had lost in Manchester but she was still gaunt. Though she was Tessa's age she looked ten years older, craggy as the granite which sprouted on the moorland, and as indefatigable. There was a grimness about her which said that though she had been dealt some of life's severest blows she was still upright and always would be. She looked even more drab and colourless than previously, an over-all impression of grey, in her skin tone, in her pale eyes and her hair which was scraped back into a tiny, uncompromising knot at the back of her narrow head. Her skirt and long-sleeved bodice were also grey, charcoal-grey relieved by nothing but a narrow snow-white collar. Yet despite her austere appearance there was something in her eyes, in the way she looked directly into those of the person she addressed, which gave her hearers a feeling they could not have described. Trust perhaps. A manner which said she would never let them down. A steadfast reliability and strength on which anyone who wished could lean.

For the past eighteen months she had been what Tessa called her 'administrator'—a fancy name for 'overlooker', Annie said bluntly—in the plan which had come to her in the pin-heading factory in Earnshaw Street. At that moment when Annie had refused to leave without the other hopeless and derelict women and children with whom she had worked, the scheme had sprung, completely formed, into her mind. Annie had been compelling her, applying pressure, using their friendship which would not allow Tessa simply to leave her to her fate, to make her see what was happening in the industrial world of which she was now a part. There

577

were thousands upon thousands still suffering the degradation and poverty, the dreadful conditions of their lives in the cotton industry. Most of the cotton manufacturers took little interest in their operatives and made no attempt to improve or ease their plight. They bent their energies and capital to investment and improvement in their mills, not seeing, or if they did, not caring about the squalor around them, nor the men and women who lived and died in it to achieve the profit the masters required. Annie was realistic enough to know that Tessa could do no more than help a few of the multitude who suffered, but by God, her attitude had said on that dreadful day, Annie would make sure she did help those few she could.

Now those same women together with others who had heard of the 'plan' the great lady in Crossfold had set up to relieve women like themselves, were making their slow and often hopeless way—since some of them did not reach it—to the mill where, it was said, decent work and lodgings would be found for those in need. It was not like the poor-house, they had been told. All their lives they had fought to stay out of that since a woman might be parted from her children there and never see them again. A clean bed was available, nourishing food, a doctor where needed. But what about payment? No, the 'lady' would help there and, providing you genuinely wanted work and a decent way of life, she would not see you starve, nor your children. Mind, she knew a malingerer—and there were those, of course— when she saw one and soon sent them packing, but any woman with no man and with children to support was made welcome. She was one of them, it was said, since she had worked in a factory all her life, and had suffered as they did.

Tessa smiled, wincing again at the pain in her swollen face. 'You can deal with old Rigby, Annie, you know that, so don't complain to me about him. And you must have your own office. These strays of yours must have somewhere to find you.'

' 'Appen, but it teks some doin' fer women like them ter come up 'ere.'

'You will persuade them to it, if anyone can.'

They talked at length on the progress of the small pin-heading and pin-sheeting factory and of the other employment which was being found, not all in the mills, for Annie's workers. Some had been put into domestic work and indeed anywhere that offered a respectable life, their children admitted to the Chapman school and some, sadly, to a small grave in the churchyard. Annie was busy, her mourning for her own dead family done in private, and her new job with Mrs Drew Greenwood fulfilled some need in her which had shrivelled at Spicers. She was needed now and her gratitude to Tessa, though never voiced since that was not her way, was enormous.

'I'll be off then. I'm ter see a chap about some new fangled pin-headin' machine.'

Tessa was still smiling at Annie's dignified acceptance of her own rise to a position of authority and her evident pleasure in the work she was doing, but when she had gone she left an empty silence, a void into which Tessa's despairing thoughts slowly infiltrated. Though she tried hard to keep them centred on what Annie was doing they would keep returning to the increasingly hopeless situation between herself and Drew, between herself and this mill, and between herself and Will. She was like some favourite toy which a group of defiant children swears belongs exclusively to each one of them, played with and handled, torn and tossed from one to the other until she cared not who had her as long as she could settle peacefully somewhere. Drew was becoming harder to handle with each day, threatening unimaginable terrors if she did not stop going to that bloody mill. Yet the mill, though it had its board of directors, was claiming more of her time and, if she were honest, she was beginning to find it ... well, a challenge, she supposed, interesting and even exciting at times.

And Will. Where was her relationship with Will, so rapturously renewed, leading them both? He was on a tight rein, a self-imposed rein in his contempt and jealousy of Drew. How long before that rein snapped and when it did, what catastrophe would follow?

She turned as someone tapped lightly on her office door, not even taking the trouble to replace her bonnet and veil. Dear God, what did it matter? The story would be all over the valley by now, how the half-deranged husband of Tessa Greenwood had knocked the living daylights out of her, and each screaming, violent word, carried by the servants' grapevine, would be reported and gloated over in every household.

The door opened and Will stood on the threshold. His cravat was disarranged and his short hair stood up in tousled disorder as though he had ridden hard and at speed.

'I couldn't ...' His eyes were haunted and his strong face worked with the depth of his emotion.

'I got as far as . . . as Linthwaite but I couldn't . . .'

'Close the door, Will.' Her voice was soft but commanding for there would be curious eyes in the outer office she was certain.

'Yes.' He closed the door behind him and lifted his arms to her. When she ran into them, pressing her poor, damaged face against his chest, he crushed her to him, groaning.

'I can't bear to lose you, my darling. I must accept what we have . . . what *he* has, because I love you. Christ, it tears me apart that . . . I have to share you, but . . .'

'Yes, my love?'

'I can't promise not to . . . to protest,' he laughed weakly, 'if he hits you again, really I can't . . .'

'He won't do it again, Will.'

'How can you know that? He is violent . . .'

'No, frightened. If I can . . . allay his fears he won't . . .'

'Dear God, oh, sweet Jesus . . .' He knew exactly what she meant. They stood for several minutes, drawing strength from one another, then he put her gently from him.

'Perhaps we had better make this look like a business call, lass. Those clerks out there were somewhat alarmed when I stormed past them just now. Call in that head chap of yours and ask him to fetch in the ledgers. Weekly accounting, wages books, order books for the months of August and September, oh, and some coffee. I'm going to give you a lesson in book-keeping. Now, where is that report of Bradley's?'

When Mr Rigby brought in the ledgers Mrs Greenwood had asked for, she and Mr Broadbent were sitting a respectable three feet apart, one on

581

each side of her desk, speculating politely on the possibility of the hostilities in America being averted.

*   *   *

In November 1860 Abraham Lincoln was elected President of the United States of America but by February of the following year eleven of the southern states had seceded from the Union and Jefferson Davis was sworn in as the President of the Confederate States of America. Fort Sumter, an island off Charleston, South Carolina and in Union hands was fired on by the new Confederate troops, President Lincoln called for the mobilisation of Union forces and a state of war was declared between the northern and southern states of America. The 'Brothers War' had begun.

CHAPTER THIRTY-ONE

Chapman Manufacturing Company Ltd put all its operatives on short time in December 1861 and its largest shareholder, Mr Drew Greenwood, who had come home drunk for the third night in succession that week, was heard to remark to his wife that she could close the bloody mills for good, it was all the same to him.

In the previous month forty-nine mills in the cotton industry had closed down completely and 119 went on short time so that the wages of the millhands fell dramatically or disappeared altogether. The scarcity of cotton, which was after all the life-blood of the industry, had become critical and it was estimated that stocks of raw cotton could last only until the middle of December. There had been a skirmish, it was reported in the newspapers, at a place called Leesburg in Virginia where the northern states of America were defeated, and at Frederickstown in Missouri where this time the South was defeated. What was the cotton manufacturer of Lancashire to make of that? he asked himself as he despaired over the prospect of ever obtaining his bales of raw cotton from America again. How was he to keep his spinners and his weavers at their mules and looms? He stared hard times in the face, and if cotton was not to be shipped from America, where might he obtain it and, in the meanwhile, were his hands to starve?

'There is a rumour that Prince Albert is dead, Tessa,' her husband remarked later in the month, quite cheerfully, since it made no difference to his life, as the war in America made no difference to his life, as the short supply for cotton to his mills made no difference to his life. Tessa was disinclined to believe the report. All kinds of stories circulated among the gossip-mongering society in which Drew moved, of the nobility and their goings-on and even of royal misdemeanours, but this was surely a bad joke on someone's part? The Prince Consort was a young man of only forty-two and in the prime of his life.

But the rumour proved to be true and the nation was plunged into mourning as the bell of St Paul's began its death toll. Grief was universal, pervading every household as if each had lost a dear and respected relative. The funeral was held a week later and the whole of the country came to a halt. Shops and factories were closed, blinds were drawn and flags were flown at half-mast. The Queen, it was said, was out of her mind with grief and shock, and what was to become of them all if Her Majesty did not recover?

January 1862 came in on a wild gale of snow and wind which scarcely abated for three days leaving snow drifts of six feet and more through towns and villages and turning the Pennine moorland into an incredibly hostile stretch of unmarred beauty.

Starvation began to stare into the faces of those who had, over the last few years, come to believe that they were at least adequately provided for. Out of work and having spent what savings they had, those operatives who had been employed as spinners and weavers and in trades allied to cotton pawned their furniture, their Sunday clothes, since they could be done without, and even their bedding in order to feed themselves. By now the shortage of cotton was becoming desperate for the industry, and the *Illustrated London News* printed headlines and pictures of the plight of the Lancashire cotton towns and the great suffering of the people. Men and women were prepared to do anything rather than go on relief. One man advertised that he would shave other men, four for a halfpenny. Another took to 'chair-bottoming' and many sold newspapers, religious tracts or back numbers of penny periodicals. Groups of young girls could be seen gathered on street corners singing, some with musical instruments. They appeared shame-faced, sad and awkward, but their efforts could not last and by the end of April, just a year since the American Civil War had begun, most were thrown

584

entirely upon the Guardian and Relief Committees.

Scenes which had once been commonplace in Crossfold and which were thought to have gone forever, scenes going back to the days when the power loom took over from the domestic hand loom, throwing thousands of men from their ancient profession, returned and multiplied. Sallow-faced, half-naked women lounged about in doorways listlessly watching sickly children in half-hearted play, the two shillings per head or less each family was allowed from relief failing completely to keep them in anything but the poorest of health. They lived on bread, oatmeal and potatoes and had it not been for the tireless work of Mrs Tessa Greenwood and her equally tireless helper, Miss Beale, it was doubtful, so it was said, that they would get through this crisis.

'We have to have some kind of organisation, Annie, and the only way to achieve it, I think, is for you to devote your time to setting up a committee to make sure that those who are in need get at least one decent meal a day. Our own operatives are still able to manage, even on two-thirds of their usual income though how long that will last remains to be seen. They say there are a quarter of a million unemployed, and the cotton which is coming from India is of a poor quality—mixed with an even poorer! They have not the machines to clean away the filth which it contains. Will tells me they are forming a cotton company in Manchester with the intention of raising a million pounds to buy such machinery and send it out there but whether anything will come of it is pure speculation. And even then the price will be exorbitant. They say in

Manchester it will be no more than a stopgap measure until the war in America is over but in the meanwhile we must do what we can to alleviate the hardships of those who have depended on us. D'you know, when I was visiting some spinners who were thrown out by the Moorhouse mill there was a woman living in the most appalling conditions in one of those awful courts at the back of Jagger Lane. Everything in the house had been sold except the bed and one cooking pot. Her five children were in the last stages of malnutrition and her husband was in gaol. He had obtained some provisions for them on credit, no more than four and elevenpence halfpenny but when he was unable to pay the debt they took him away . . .'

'An' tha' got 'im out?'

'Oh, yes, and provided them with bedding, clothing, coal, flour, I believe, and other items of food to see them through until you could get round to them. Here is their name and address.'

'An, what of Chapman mills? 'Ow much longer can tha' keep on four days?'

'I bought up a cargo of cotton last week through an agent in Liverpool. It had got by the blockade out of New Orleans, don't ask me how for they say that only two out of six ships get through. The Union navy has a blockading squadron stationed off each port to prevent ships taking cotton out of the South and returning with essential supplies. Last year we imported 1,261 million pounds of cotton and this year it has fallen to less than half. Eighty per cent of it was from America, Annie, and now we shall be forced to accept the Indian, despite its poor quality.'

The two friends were sitting in Tessa's office,

both gazing out on to the strange and empty silence of the Chapmanstown mill yard. It was Friday and last night the machines and engines had been turned off and the boilers allowed to go out. They would not be switched on again until the bales of raw cotton Tessa had purchased arrived at the Chapman warehouses. Only a fifth of those employed in the cotton industry were fully employed, the rest were on short time or with no work at all, and the exact figures were stamped indelibly in the mind of Tessa Greenwood. Once she had been concerned with nothing more complicated than the number of shots it took to bring down fifty birds on the Squire's moor, with how many gowns she should order for the season's hunt balls and how many sovereigns Drew gambled away in one evening, none of which mattered in the least.

Annie seemed to find nothing unusual in the conversation and it was evident that this different aspect of Tessa Greenwood was nothing new to her. Tessa had been chairman of the board of directors of the Chapman mills for two years now, perhaps the most difficult in the history of the company since it was begun so long ago by her husband's great grandfather. In the last year she had seen so many businesses falter and fall, but not once had she turned her back on her own to return to the pleasures her husband seemingly enjoyed without her.

'I called on Mrs Poynton yesterday,' Annie said, sipping her coffee, her straight back an inch from the back of the chair on which she sat, unlike Tessa who lounged carelessly with the wide skirts of her muslin gown, a lovely shade of soft rose, in a circle

587

about her feet. She wore no bonnet and her hair was piled haphazardly into an untidy coil on the top of her head. She had tied it up herself with a wide velvet ribbon in the same colour as her dress that morning, ignoring Emma's pleas to be allowed to arrange it for her.

'I've no time, Emma, and no, I cannot stop to choose a bonnet. I must be in Crossfold by nine to meet Mr Bradley and then Miss Beale and I are to inspect that old mill in Hardacre Street to see if it is suitable for a school and a kitchen for ... Stop fussing, Emma. No, I can't be bothered with a parasol. If the sun comes out I shall ask Thomas to put up the hood on the carriage. Oh, and Emma ...'

Her voice dropped and Emma leaned forward to hear what her mistress was saying. 'Don't ... don't disturb the master. He is still sleeping and ... well, there is no need to wake him so early.'

Emma nodded respectfully, then turned to look in the direction of the closed door of the dressing-room where Mr Drew slept on most nights now. You could hear him snoring, even through the solid wood of the door. They were the snores of a man who had come home in the early hours of the morning so drunk he really should not have been in charge of that fancy cabriolet he drove. Right across the lawn, Percy said he had ploughed, and through Miss Laurel's roses, leaving a trail of destruction six feet wide and singing so loudly the whole household, including the children in the nursery, had been awakened. Laughing at nothing, he'd been, his horse and vehicle left to droop at the front step and Mr Briggs and Hibberson compelled to carry him up to his bed whilst he begged them to join in some bawdy song he and his wild friends had heard at a music hall in Manchester. He'd sleep the best part of the day, coming down to the small back parlour to sprawl before the fire, avoiding Miss Laurel and her callers in the drawing-room, his lovely blue eyes narrowed to increasingly puffy slits, his mouth hard and ill-humoured, his temper short and unpredictable and, if Miss Tessa was not there, his voice hoarse and his words offensively rude.

Where had he gone, Emma mused as she watched her mistress climb into her carriage, that handsome, good-natured, recklessly laughing young man they had once known? Him and his brother, both of them up to all kinds of pranks but with good hearts and no malice in them, merry as larks providing no one tried to harness them. And now one was dead and the other killing himself, they said, in his search for something even his wife couldn't seem to provide. All his time was spent riding to hounds, shooting grouse and pheasant, drinking brandy and claret until he could hardly see to play cards in the often-dubious company he and his friends kept.

And Miss Tessa toiling all the hours God sent in an effort to keep not only her own mills working and her own operatives from the poor house, but taking in the down-and-outs from the whole of Lancashire, it was rumoured. Her and that Annie Beale.

'Oh, and what was the outcome?' Tessa questioned Annie. 'Will she sit on our committee?'

'Aye, an' that Mrs Bayly an' all. They've promised ter speak to as many ladies as they can about the soup kitchen an' Mrs Bayly knows a Miss

Gaunt as she reckoned'd teach school fer nowt. Not just childer but any man or woman as wants ter learn. I've bin round most o't manufacturers an' though some were ready ter show me't door, I managed ter persuade 'em ter remit rents on't workers' cottages. I told 'em if you could do it so could they. Mrs Poynton says as 'ow she knows t'parson at parish church an' all them as goes ter't Sunday school, an' believe me it'll be every bairn in Crossfold an' Chapmanstown by't time I've done wi' em, will be given petticoats an' shirts, blankets an' such fer their mams, an' a bit o' brass 'as bin set aside fer the mendin' of boots. An' Doctor Salter ses as 'ow 'e'll give 'is services free to them what needs 'em.'

'Heavens, Annie, you have been busy.'

'I've nowt else ter do wi' me time.'

'No.' Tessa put a compassionate hand on her friend's arm, then smiled when it was snatched away from her. Annie would never change. As long as she had breath in her body she would use it to help anyone she thought to be in need of it. Many of the ladies of the town moved amongst the destitute cotton workers helping those they called the 'deserving poor', those they considered worthy of assistance by the measure of the respectful gratitude they displayed.

But there were others in utter poverty who were proud, who would not bow their heads for charity and they showed these same ladies the door saying they wanted no busybodies interfering in their household arrangements. And there were others, in order to get more than their entitlement of relief, who included children recently dead in their list of the needy, or who 'borrowed' children to make up

590

their family numbers and so 'diddled' another two shillings per head for each one. There were husbands who were found drunk in bed and starving children in the gutter. Annie saw them all, helped them all, sorted them into some kind of order and intended keeping them there, choose how, until the mills were opened again and woe betide *any* who fell by the wayside when she was in charge!

But they were indebted to her and to Mrs Greenwood as in increasing numbers young men and women, youths, adults who had never been to school in their lives, unemployed hands with time hanging heavy, were encouraged to attend the Working Men's Institutes. There they were taught reading, writing and simple arithmetic for they needed an occupation of some sort to fill their empty days.

Mr Will Broadbent, the largest stockholder in his own mill and therefore the worst hit, was struggling to keep open for a couple of days a week. On the days when the mill was closed, he used the silent and empty rooms to hold classes for his women operatives in sewing and the cooking of cheap and nourishing dishes, and an industrial class for his men in tailoring, boot-making and similar crafts, all of which would come in useful when the present crisis was over and they had returned to their spinning mules.

But in other parts of Lancashire out-of-work millworkers fared a great deal worse. There was widespread bitterness over the 'Labour Test' where the poor who applied for relief had to show their willingness to work. The cotton operatives disliked being classed as ordinary paupers by the Guardians and felt that more lenient rules should govern the granting of relief to decent workmen who were only temporarily unemployed through no fault of their own. They objected to the manner in which the so-called Labour Test was enforced. Men who were indoor workers, badly clothed and close to starvation, were sent out in that first bitter winter on jobs such as stone-breaking, a task which was not only cruel, they said, but often fatal. A man who had worked in a cotton mill required delicacy of touch, and his hands were singularly soft from working in high temperatures and by continual contact with oil and cotton-wool. The stone hammer blistered his flesh and the oakum many were compelled to 'pick' galled his fingers. Flesh and fingers which would soon, please God and the good sense of the people of America, be back at work in the spinning mills and the weaving sheds of Lancashire.

Discussion of the Public Works Bill began in quarters where the relief of the increasingly large numbers of the poor was of particular concern. The hot weather of that summer brought swarms of flies and rats into the alleyways and back streets which meandered through the old part of Crossfold. The cotton famine had caused whole families to move in with another in the same circumstances in order to save rent and, in the previous winter, economise on fuel. Windows had been boarded up and doors padded to retain what little heat there was. Bodies lay close together for warmth and even when the weather became kinder as spring and summer approached, they still squeezed together since they had no chance to do otherwise. Cleaning materials were low on their list of priorities as women watched their children starve and the filth, the mud and raw sewage which seeped through the uneven ground, the overflowing middens and foul pools of dung and rotting garbage became one huge, stinking cesspit. It was a breeding ground for the fevers, typhus, typhoid, scarletina and smallpox which the swarming flies and rats carried assiduously from one house to the next, from one street to the next, from one town to the next.

So what better way, the Public Works Act wanted to know, to keep idle men employed and the fevers at bay, than to put these men to the vexed problem of main sewering? The distressed cotton operatives would be asked to volunteer to do the unskilled manual labour of building not only sewers and drains but reservoirs, good roads, public parks and recreation grounds at labourers' rates of pay. The experience would strengthen their puny frames and improve their skills and without undue exertion they could earn themselves twelve shillings a week and at the same time relieve the Guardians of the task of supporting their families.

'Tis said there's sickness at back o' Jagger Lane,' Annie offered in the long silence which had fallen over the two women.

'What kind of sickness?' Tessa's voice was sharp and she returned her cup to its saucer with a clatter.

'They say tis nowt'. Doctor Salter fetched me from't school this mornin'. 'E knew I were . . . well, that I'd 'ad some sort o' fever when I were in Manchester. Reckoned as 'ow I'd survived it then I'd be in no danger now.'

'But what is it?'

'Nay, lass, don't ask me. I'm no doctor.'

'Has Doctor Salter no idea?'

' 'E ses as 'ow its bin a long time since there were an epidemic an' 'im bein' a youngish man, like, 'e's never bin in one.'

'An epidemic? Does he think . . . ?'

'It's bin nearly a year since most of 'em were in full work, Tessa, or 'ad a decent meal except what we give 'em. They're all low, in poor 'ealth, an' the first illness what comes along'll 'ave 'em before thi can say 'pickin' stick'. They'll not call't doctor since they've no brass ter pay 'im. Will ses as 'ow . . .'

'Will?' Tessa felt her heart lurch sickeningly. 'What was he doing there?'

'Nay, Tessa. Tha knows Will, or should do by now. Wherever there's trouble 'e's in't thick of it. Doctor Salter was talkin' of puttin' them what's sick in one o' them empty warehouses in Ashton Lane. Keep 'em apart from t'others until 'e knows what's up wi' 'em. Just ter be on't safe side, like. I said I'd find some women ter nurse 'em. There's a few o' my pin-headin' girls wi' nowt ter do an' they'd be glad of a bit of extra cash.'

Tessa sprang up. 'I'll come and help.'

'No, tha'll not. Will wants yer kept out of it.' Annie's face was impassive, half-turned away and Tessa smiled at the very idea of being 'kept out of it'. These were her operatives, some of them, and she was part of this working community now. Besides, Will had no control over her. If she wanted to go down and inspect the premises she damn well would. He ought to know *her* by now as well. She came and went as she pleased, or as much as she was able with Drew in the often violent moods which came over him. But certainly, despite

594

their love for one another, Will had no authority over her.

'Don't be foolish, Annie. If there is to be an epidemic of some sort in the town then those who are sick will need all the help they can get and I must see what is needed.'

'I know what's needed, lass, an' there's nowt you can do that I can't.'

'You mean because of who I am? Because I am Tessa Greenwood and not brought up to hardships as you and Will were?'

'Aye, 'appen that, but most of all because Will wants yer kept out of it.'

'Dear God, what has it to do with you or Will? I'm not a child . . .'

'Then stop actin' like one. Anyway, let's see what's to 'appen first. Get yer gone up to that 'usband o' thine an' see if there's owt' yer can be doin' fer 'im. I 'eard as 'ow 'e caused summat of a disturbance, 'im an' that merry band o' gentlemen 'e rides about with, up at Five Pigeons t'other night.'

'Oh, Lord, what over?'

Annie looked uncomfortable, fiddling in a most unusual way with the enormous reticule she carried around with her and in which she kept all the many and varied items she might need in the course of her active day. No one was quite sure what they were but she could provide anything from a clean rag to wipe a child's runny nose to a safety-pin for a torn hem, a pencil for making a quick note here and there, and even a screw of paper containing tea for some needy woman she visited and who might gain comfort from a brew.

'Nay, don't ask me. 'Tis nowt ter do wi' me,

595

Tessa.' That meant, of course, that it *had* to do with some woman, or Annie would have told her.

It was nearly three years now since Tessa had taken up the burden which she had unwillingly inherited from her mother and Charlie; more than three years since the fire in which Charlie had lost his life. She did her best to share her time between the mills and her husband, going only to Chapmans when it was absolutely necessary for a board meeting or when, as Drew's proxy, her signature was needed on some document, but now the crisis caused by the cotton famine demanded more and more of her time. Secretly she admitted to herself that she found the time she spent there increasingly absorbing and the hours passed in the company of Drew and his friends increasingly trivial.

'We are off to Nicky's for a game of croquet, my love,' he had said to her at lunch-time. 'Why not join us? Johnny and Alicia will be there and Nicky has persuaded Polly Arbuthnot to give that elderly husband of hers the slip. Afterwards we thought we'd ride into Oldham. There's a new song and supper room just been opened, or perhaps the music hall. Who knows? That is the charm of being free, don't you agree? Go wherever the fancy takes us, for that is what makes life exciting, Tessa. Come on, darling, leave those bloody awful figures. In fact, give them to me and I shall dispose of them where they belong. In the back of the fire . . .' He had snatched a sheaf of notes and figures Will had made out for her to study on the variations in trading from month to month since the new mill had begun operating.

'Don't, Drew. A lot of work has gone into those notes. Please, put them back,' she said urgently as he made a movement towards the fire. 'I know you think they are not worth bothering one's head about, any more than the mills and the operatives, but someone has to look after our interests at least until this crisis is over.'

'And then what excuse will you give, my pet? What reason will you dream up so that you might give your undivided attention to the business and not to your husband? Will it be that another catastrophe of desperate proportions will spring up to claim you, d'you think? Or will it be the fascination of making money which seems to have afflicted every member of my family, except myself and Pearce, of course? Really, Tessa, your commercial heritage is beginning to show quite dreadfully. I was only saying to Nicky last week that one can hardly believe that you are the same dashing girl who once rode out with us on more than one escapade. Adventure, that is what we were after, the three of us, you and I and Pearce . . . No . . . I mean . . . Drew. Don't I?'

His voice became uncertain and his eyes narrowed as he looked at something in the far distance of his memory. The papers dropped from his hand and she quickly retrieved them from the carpet where they fell before turning back to him. His taunting manner had disappeared. His shoulders slumped and in his face was the lost and desperate expression he had brought back from the Crimea. He shook his head wonderingly and his voice was soft when he spoke.

'Where has he gone, Tessa?' he said, in much the same way Emma had done only that morning. 'I seem to have lost him somehow.'

'Pearce?' She put her hand to him, her own face

597

as gentle as his.

'No, not Pearce, not Pearce. But ... both of us ... myself ... I cannot seem to function these days now that both of you have left me. I know I do dangerous things but I seem to have no control ...'

She moved quickly to his side, taking his hand in hers, but he turned away to look into the fire. She lifted it, a hard, horseman's hand, brown and strong, to her lips.

'You have not lost yourself, Drew, nor me. I am always here.'

'No, you are not, Tessa, and I'm afraid that ...'

'What, my darling?' In her voice was the depth of her love for him.

'That one day, when I really need you, when Johnny is with his Alicia and Nicky off on some private jaunt with a lady and I have no one, you will not be here when I look round.'

'I shall always be here, Drew, always. You know that.'

'Do I, Tessa? Do I? You were not here this morning when I awoke and called out to you.'

'No, I had to ...'

'I know. Go to the mill, or the school with that woman, or to the soup kitchen ...'

'There are so many of them, Drew, and all needing ...'

'None need you as I do, Tessa. Please come with me this afternoon. Show me ...'

'What ...?'

'That you mean what you say. That you love me still. That you are here for me now. Prove it by coming with me.'

And so she had gone dressed in her outrageous black riding coat and cream breeches, her white

598

waistcoat and tall top hat, her boots polished and her mare beneath her. She and Drew raced one another along the wild stretch of track between Greenacres and Longworth Hall and the solitary figure of the horseman who rode quietly, tiredly in the direction of Crossfold was noticed by neither of them as they shouted with delighted laughter in one another's company.

CHAPTER THIRTY-TWO

'I thought you said Will was coming with you. I wanted to speak to him about . . .'

' 'E couldn't manage it. 'E sends 'is apologies.'

'Apologies? What on earth does that mean? You and he had your meeting with Doctor Salter, I suppose?'

'Aye.'

'And . . .?'

'And what?'

'Annie, for God's sake stop playing games with me. Has the good doctor decided what is wrong with these people in the vicinity of Jagger Lane?'

'It's come so sudden, like, an' 'e's still not sure. Give it a week or two . . .'

'A week or two? But I thought it was urgent.'

'It could be 'owt, Tessa. Doctor Salter ses as 'ow 'e wants a second opinion so 'e's asked old Doctor Ellison to come an' look 'em over. Not that Doctor Ellison was too pleased ter poke 'is 'ead in them alleys at back of Jagger Lane. But 'e's 'ad more experience than Doctor Salter seein' as 'ow 'e's worked in London where such fevers are rife, they

599

say.'

'But what form does it take?' Tessa sat back in her chair and studied Annie's averted face. There was something about her reluctance to meet Tessa's eyes which was most alarming since Annie never flinched away from anyone's gaze. Just the opposite for sometimes her steady eyes seemed to probe right inside Tessa's head just where she didn't want her to see. Now she was staring out of the office window, this time at the busy yard for the cotton Tessa had purchased was at this moment being unloaded and carried swiftly to the warehouse where the bales would be opened in readiness for blending.

'Well, naturally, none of 'em are what yer might call fit. Scrawny and pale from a poor diet . . .'

'Dear Lord, I hope we can keep our own people working, Annie, and if we can't we must not allow them to fall into the state these are in. Are they all from the Moorhouse mill?'

'No, some are Abbotts. Jenkinsons've turned off 'undreds an' there's some from every mill in't valley.'

'And Jonathan Abbott refused to donate a penny last week when I cornered him at the Cloth Hall.'

'Aye, well, that's as mebbee, but them at back o' Jagger Lane'll need more'n a penny ter see 'em through. There's women wi' babies they can't feed. No milk, tha' knows. There's others've never got over the bronchitis and pneumonia they took last winter. They'll be't first ter go, Doctor Salter ses.'

'Is there nothing we can do to stop it?'

'We're doin' all we can, lass, but 'appen it'll come ter nowt though Doctor ses the symptoms are . . .'

'Yes?'

'Well, tha'll not want to 'ear what they are.'

'Annie, really. I am no genteel lady who is about to faint away at the thought of sickness, nor am I to shirk the responsibility of doing what must be done.'

'Do thi know, lass, sometimes I can't get over the change in thi'?' Annie smiled and her eyes, so pale and cool more often than not, had a softness in them, a warmth which spoke of her deep affection for this woman. 'Wheer did that 'oity-toity young madam go, the one what used ter come ter my 'ouse an' treat it as though it was 'er own? I'll 'ave a cup o' tea, Annie, if yer please, tha' used ter say, expecting' me ter stop whatever I were doin' an' brew up for thi'. Yer'd sit in't best chair an' keep me from me work, jawin' on about nowt, then, off yer'd go, ridin' like the divil on that animal o' thine, off on some foolish, wasteful jaunt wi' thy scapegrace cousins ...' She stopped suddenly, aware that she was speaking of Tessa's husband, then her face hardened. 'Nay, I'm not sorry I said that even though one is dead ...'

'Please, Annie.'

' ... an t'other's no more than a ...'

'*Annie!*'

'Right, lass, I hear thi'. I'll say no more except that tha've turned out champion, Tessa Greenwood. Now, where was I?'

'About to tell me the symptoms of this illness, you fraud, you!'

'Aye, 'appen I am. Well, they start wi' vomitin' an' a loosenin' of the bowels. They shake, Will ses, an' can't stop, an' no one really knows what it is. They say as 'ow it comes from abroad somewhere,

601

India an' such places. It seems ter live in muck an' wi' all them stinkin' sewers an' drains at the back o' Jagger Lane it's a right breedin' ground. Them as is took can't keep owt' down, an' it's a quick death, Doctor Salter says.'

'There have been deaths already?' Tessa's voice was sharp.

'Aye, a few.'

'How many?'

'Well, Will reckons . . .'

Tessa felt the first dreadful thrill of fear skim along the surface of her flesh and her stomach lurched for no accountable reason. She sprang up from her chair and reached for the parasol Emma had persuaded her to bring this morning.

'I'm going up to Ashton Lane,' she said abruptly, heading towards the door, her every instinct telling her that for some reason she must hurry. Annie stood up too and followed her, her face becoming even paler than usual, her hands reaching out and swiftly capturing Tessa's arm.

'Nay, tha' musn't, lass. Not until Doctor Salter ses tha' might.'

'So it's Doctor Salter who is keeping me away now, is it? I thought it was Will who was giving the orders on where I may or I may not go. What's going on here, Annie?' She threw off Annie's restraining hands, barely stopping in her stride, turning heads in the counting house as she stalked by the clerks at their tall desks, Annie at her heels. Neither of them had taken the time to put on a bonnet and as they reached the yard the sweltering sun struck savagely on their uncovered heads. Tessa called to the stable boy to tell Thomas to fetch round the carriage and all the while Annie was

602

reaching for her, shouting above the clamour of the yard that she was not to go, that Will would be furious, that Doctor Salter would blame her if she brought Mrs Greenwood where it really wasn't necessary for her to go. There were a dozen other good reasons why Tessa should stop right here, or better yet, get on home to her husband.

Tessa swung round to face her, still holding the pretty parasol, making no attempt to put it up to protect her white skin from the sun's rays.

'What are you trying to save me from, Annie? Why is it that suddenly I'm not allowed to visit Ashton Lane? Why can't I see for myself these people who have been struck down by something which may or may not be fever, which may or may not be scarletina, or measles? What is there that . . . that Will . . . Dear God, it's Will, isn't it? He doesn't want me to . . . to see what? Tell me what it is he doesn't want me to see?'

'Nay, lass, don't. I give 'im me word . . .'

'To do what, Annie?' All the while the terror grew and grew within her, threatening to crush her heart and freeze the blood in her veins. 'Tell me the truth, Annie. You might as well because, whatever you say, I shall go to Ashton Lane and find out. As soon as the carriage comes I mean to go there, or the infirmary, or wherever Doctor Salter and Will are, and find out whatever it is you're keeping from me.'

'Tha can't, lass. Doctor Salter won't let thi . . .'

'*Won't!* Doctor Salter has no authority over me, Annie Beale, and neither have you. See, here is the carriage. Now, will you come with me or will I go alone?'

She climbed into the carriage, nodding at

603

Thomas who helped her in, giving him instructions to drive her to the old Clegg warehouse in Ashton Lane. Annie sat beside her, saying nothing, for what was the use?

It was the stench which hit her first, the foetid, appalling air, so hot it lay thickly against her skin. It was dim in that first moment and she could not make out what it was that retched and gasped and groaned and cried out as she moved beyond the open doorway which led from the warehouse yard to the ground floor of the building.

The room was crowded with iron bedsteads, cots, even mattresses laid out on the bare floor. Some sort of attempt had been made to keep the beds separate from one another but to Tessa it seemed that it was impossible to get from one side of the room to the other without stepping on the prone figures that crowded it. There were men and women, children, tiny and silent, others writhing and vomiting, and moving from one to another was Doctor Salter and half a dozen women, some of whom she recognised from her own recently opened pin-heading factory.

'Dear, sweet Jesus,' she whispered. 'What is it . . . ?'

'Now yer 'ere, lass and thy've seen it, yer might as well know. Dr Ellison reckons it's cholera.'

'*Cholera!* Oh, dear God . . .'

'Aye.'

'But what is being done about it?'

'There's not much can be done 'cept let it run its course. They're tryin' ter keep 'em separate from . . . the rest. There's none o't suspects gone to't th'infirmary since weekend. Authorities 've bin informed an' all them 'ouses in't back o' Jagger

604

Lane, where it began, 'ave bin limewashed an' t'bodies an' all.'

'Dear God, why was I not told?'

'What good would that a' done?'

'I could have . . . helped . . .'

' 'Ow, lass? Tha' knows that 'usband o' thine wouldn't let yer come 'ere 'elpin' out. I wanted to mesen but . . . I were persuaded I could do more good in other quarters . . . as you can.'

'Where is Will, Annie?'

Annie's disjointed words dried up abruptly and she put a hand on Tessa's arm as she began to move forward into the packed mass of suffering humanity. Flies buzzed lazily over a pool of excrement which dripped on to the floor from the cot of a quiet child and Tessa knew quite definitely that the child was dead. There was vomit on the blankets which covered the shivering, sighing bodies and bluebottles gorged there, but still Tessa pressed on.

'Where is Will, Annie?' She knew if she did not find him soon, if she did not see his tall, dependable, strong and beloved figure bending over some bed she would run, screaming his name, into the warehouse yard. She could feel the panic, the horror, the dread, the awful, awful fear fill and expand her lungs until she knew they would burst. She could feel it rise in her throat, threatening to choke her. She wanted to cry out his name, shout his name at the top of her voice, but Annie had her by the arm, struggling to drag her back from the appalling, writhing misery.

'Tell me where he is, Annie.'

'No, lass, tha' can't. He asked me ter keep thi away.'

605

'Where is he, Annie? Take me to him or, by God, I'll search every bed in this place until I find him.' And Annie, perhaps with the picture in her mind of the elegant Mrs Drew Greenwood handling every stinking, shivering body in the makeshift hospital in her search for Will Broadbent, led her to him.

He had been put in a corner beneath a window which someone, with a decent attempt at cleanliness had tried to wipe over. He lay on his back, his unfocused gaze on the high ceiling. His short hair lay limply to the shape of his head and his face was grey and withered. A blanket covered him and his large hands plucked at the wool, bony somehow, the flesh already burned away, as it was from the rest of his big frame, by this disease which could kill a healthy man in twenty-four hours. He muttered and mumbled, his head turning towards her as she bent over him, though he didn't know her, then away again as he heaved convulsively in a great spasm of vomiting.

'Will . . . Will . . . Oh, Lord God . . . Will . . .' She reached for his hand and from behind Annie tried to stop her from touching him but she sank down beside his bed, oblivious to the stench which came from him, her hands smoothing his forehead and cheeks. 'Oh my dearest, what . . . ?'

'Dear God in heaven, woman, what d'you think you're doing? Get away from that man, Annie Beale, and who in hell's that . . . ? Goddammit, woman, have you no more sense than to touch that man? Oh, Mrs Greenwood, I beg your pardon, but would you come away from my patient? Do you not realise how . . . how unwell he is and how dangerous . . . ? You could take the illness with you ...'

Doctor Salter, his young face old and hard and lined, tired beyond endurance, dragged quite forcibly at her shoulder, not caring any more for the niceties of their differing social position in his desperation to get her, not only from the dying man in the bed, but from this hospital. But she struck his hand away, bending, incredibly, to place her lips on the man's brow.

'Mrs Greenwood!' This was not, of course, the time for amazement at Mrs Greenwood's behaviour, though that was incredible enough. He simply could not cope with *visitors*, for God's sake, in the midst of this catastrophe which had come upon the town of Crossfold. 'Please, Mrs Greenwood, this man needs attention ...'

She rose crisply, no hint of the soft anguish she had just displayed lingering in her decisive manner.

'Which he shall have, Doctor Salter, but not here.'

'I don't understand you, Mrs Greenwood, and I'm afraid I have not the time to stand and discuss it with you. As you can see, I am an extremely busy man.' He waved his exhausted hand in the direction of the dozens of people who lay about them awaiting his attention.

'Which I shall help to alleviate at once, Doctor Salter.'

'I cannot imagine what you mean, ma'am, so if you will excuse me.' He began to turn away but she had not yet done.

'What nursing does this man need, Doctor Salter? Is there anything special in the way of ...'

'No, ma'am. All we can do is try to make their passing a little easier ... more comfortable ...'

Her face spasmed in horror and he relented somewhat. 'Go home, Mrs Greenwood. There is nothing you or Miss Beale can do here. It will run its course, this . . . fever, and you are needed and can do so much more elsewhere. We are deeply grateful for all the help you have . . .'

'Thank you, doctor, but I have done nothing. Now, if you could find me some men . . . you have men to carry the patients in, I presume? . . . Good, then if you would be so kind as to fetch them, and my coachman . . . no . . . very well, I suppose it would not be fair to ask him to risk himself . . . some blankets which I will replace, naturally. I shall take Mr Broadbent to . . . oh, no, not to Greenacres, there are children there, but to the home of my good friend, Miss Beale. I intend to nurse Mr Broadbent myself, Doctor Salter.'

'Tha can't do this, Tessa,' Annie said, all the way back to the cottage at Edgeclough.

Her face was like stone.

'I am doing it, Annie.' She held his mumbling, tossing head in her lap, drawing the blankets more closely about his heaving shoulders though the sun's heat struck fiercely even through the carriage top which Thomas had put up.

'Tha can't do it, lass. Doctor Salter said . . .'

'I heard what he said and it appears to me that Will had just as much chance, more, of . . . of surviving in your cottage than he has in that stinking . . .'

'Tha knows what I mean, Tessa.'

'No, I don't, unless it is that you do not want us in your house. I'm sorry, Annie, I had not thought. The fever is infectious, dangerous, I suppose, and Will could bring it with him.'

608

'Now then, madam.' Annie's voice was sharp and biting. 'Don't tek that tone wi' me. Will ... an' thissen are welcome in my 'ouse whenever tha wants, illness or no. I told thi that years ago, but it's thi 'usband an' family I'm thinkin' on. Tha knows 'ow it'll look ter folk, Mrs Drew Greenwood nursin' a man who was once overlooker in 'er family's own mill. It does look a mite strange, don't tha think?'

'You'll be there, Annie, to safeguard my reputation, if that's what concerns you.'

But it was clear to Annie that Tessa was not really listening to what she was saying. She bent over the delirious man, her face no more than six inches from his foetid breath, her arms holding his head to her breast, supporting him on the carriage seat. Her face was strained and pale and her eyes enormous in her anxiety. She stroked his cheek and murmured his name, soothing him, whispering to him that they were almost there, my darling, telling him that soon he would be in a clean bed and she would give him a sip of soup, broth to keep up his strength, and soon, soon he would better. She had not the slightest notion of what she was taking on, Annie could see, believing naïvely that once they had Will away from that dreadful place, which surely had been doing him no good at all, he would begin to recover. A warm bath, a hot drink and a good night's sleep: wasn't that the remedy for all the illness Tessa Greenwood had yet seen in her life and wasn't that what she would give to her love, Will Broadbent, her attitude said? Annie knew that Drew Greenwood was away from home on one of his frequent visits to his autocratic and privileged friends. Was it shooting, fishing or just some drunken debauch which they got up to with such regular monotony? She didn't know or care. She only knew that when he came home and found his wife had taken the carriage to Edgeclough with the intention of helping to nurse Mr Will Broadbent, a director on the Chapman's own board, he was not likely to be charitable about it.

They got him out of the carriage and up the stairs to Annie's bedroom with the help of Thomas who couldn't stand by and see his mistress and her strange friend struggle with a sick man, whatever he was supposed to have.

'You must go home now, Thomas,' Mrs Greenwood said crisply, 'and tell them I shall stay here for a day or two to help Miss Beale nurse her . . . friend. Mr Broadbent has no one at his own home to . . . to look after him, you see, so we shall keep him here until he has recovered. Now then, here is a list of the things I . . . we shall need. See that I . . . we have them within the hour.'

And Thomas had driven home to Greenacres as though the devil himself sat in his carriage, declaring to the ring of fascinated servants who, thankfully, were not aware of the growing epidemic in the town, nor of Thomas's involvement with one of its sufferers, that Miss Tessa had taken leave of her senses, really she had. There would be holy war when *he* came back from his jaunt to Cheshire and found her gone!

They bathed him first with cooling water, stripping him naked on Annie's plain bed which had known the weight of no man. Together, without embarrassment, they performed the intimate task of cleansing every part of his body as he mumbled and fretted under their hands, knowing neither of them. They dressed him in a nightshirt which had

610

come from Greenacres, watching with dismay as it was stained with the thin contents of his bowels. They changed him, and the bed linen, again and again since he had no control of his bodily functions and they were both obsessed with the need to make him as comfortable as they could. The boiler in which Annie washed her own garments was never taken off the fire and on Annie's clothes-line in the strip of yard at the back of the cottage, sheets and blankets hung limp and unmoving in the humid heat.

'Tha'll 'ave ter leave 'im naked,' Annie said wearily, as she watched Tessa shake out the last dry nightshirt, ready to drag it over Will's head. ''E don't know any difference an tha's only tirin' thissen over what don't matter.'

'But the sheets?'

'Give 'em 'ere. I'll put 'em in't boiler but them's the last. Tha'll 'ave ter spread squares o' linen under 'im until them on't line's dry. We can't keep up wi' 'em, lass, an' 'e don't know.'

And it was true. With every hour which passed Will had sunk deeper and deeper into a frightening state of insensibility. His face was grey, just bare, protruding bones and deep hollows. His cracked lips parted as he dragged in a morsel of air and his breathing barely raised his chest. He no longer muttered or roamed restlessly over the bed. He no longer sweated or vomited. It was as though every drop of moisture his body contained had been wrung out of him. His flesh had gone, melting away like the wax on a candle.

Tessa knelt beside him, watching his face as she had watched it for almost twelve hours, ever since she and Annie and Thomas had manhandled him

611

up Annie's narrow staircase and on to this bed. Only twelve hours and in that time he had lost shape and form and colour with an incredible speed. Even this morning when she had first seen him at the temporary hospital he had still been Will, recognisable, and though ill and delirious a man she would know as the man she loved. Now the face on the pillow could have belonged to anyone. He appeared a skeletal stranger with a grey, mottled face, at first glance already dead, with closed sunken eyes and a ghastly slitted mouth, dry and cracked, which no woman in her right mind would dream of kissing. Even the hair on the apparition looked dead and grey, dusty where the salty sweat had dried on it.

And yet there was something left of Will, something that was just the same. Resting on the dry, cold cheek beneath the closed eyes lay the long and silky lashes she had often teased him about, a soft brown, fine, like those of a sleeping child. In her anguish at the thought that they would never raise again she showered passionate kisses on the wrecked, almost inhuman face of Will Broadbent.

'Will, stay . . . don't leave me,' she whispered. 'I cannot manage without you, Will.' The pain overwhelmed her. She had loved him since before she was seventeen; she knew that now. In the nine years which had passed they had lost one another for a while due to her own foolish yearning for something which did not really exist. But for almost three years they had been lovers again in the truest sense of the word. She had bathed in his love, blossomed and grown in it, becoming the complete and loving woman she knew herself to be. Will, strong and lusty, sweet-tempered, good-humoured.

Will, unique and irreplaceable. As she watched the disease consume him, dry him out to no more than a husk, the full devastation of what his loss would mean to her struck her a mortal blow from which she knew she would never recover. Robby had been taken from her in the most agonising way but the anguish she had known then had been nothing to what she experienced now.

She could not bear to lose him. She could not face a world without that special blend of gentleness and vitality he gave her. His ardour warmed her female body and his good-humoured wisdom cooled her wild and impulsive nature. His lively, incisive mind sharpened hers. He was positive, daring and filled with his own invincibility and she had known from the moment his amber eyes had smiled whimsically into hers that she could rely on him while he had breath in his body. Though he had laughed at the girl she was, spoken sharply, roughly, she had known instinctively that he was concerned for her, and that concern, compassion and understanding had shaped her, brought her to this moment of true and selfless love. She loved him beyond any love she had ever known. She always would.

She wanted to pray, if only she could find the words; to ask some God in whom she scarce believed not to take Will from her, and not just from her but from the world which would be the poorer without him. She wanted to, she even tried to as her tears fell on to his beloved face. But as the sun sank in the fiery furnace of the sky below the high line of the moorland and Annie moved quietly to light the candle, her tears dried up, and the words of hopeless prayer dried up.

'I won't let him die, Annie.' Her voice was like a splinter of ice. 'Dammit, I won't let him. Dear God, does he not know how much I love him?'

' 'Appen 'e don't, lass.' Annie's shadow was huge on the wall of the bedroom, moving slowly as she approached the bed.

Tessa turned to her, startled. Her own face had hollowed during the day, with deep purple fingerprints pressed beneath her eyes. She was bathed in perspiration for despite the open window the room was hot and airless and she knew she smelled sourly.

'What d'you mean? Of course he knows.'

' 'E' saw thi and thy 'usband a day or so since . . .'

'Drew . . . ?'

'Thi were up on't tops, 'e said, ridin' together like thi' 'adn't a care in t'world. Laughin', just like tha used to, you an' Master Drew, so wrapped up in one another tha didna see 'im pass thi by.'

'No . . . oh, no, Annie. No, you know that's not true.'

' 'E only knows what 'e saw, lass, an' it took the spirit from 'im. 'E must've 'ad the fever on 'im then.'

'No, I can't bear it.' She put her arms about him, lifting his heavy, lolling head from the pillow, cradling his face against her breast, rocking backwards and forwards in a frenzy of dry-eyed grief. Dear God, she had only gone with Drew to ease his wretchedness, to reassure him that despite her obligations at the mill and to the people who depended on the Greenwood family, he was still fixed deeply and irrevocably in her heart, that she loved him and always would. He was all that was left of the bright childhood he and Pearce and herself had shared. He was in her care and she would never desert him.

Even for Will!

'Will, oh, Will, my dearest love, how can I tell you what you mean to me? You are the first breath I draw each morning and my last thought at night before I sleep. I awake with you and lie down to sleep with you in my heart. I cannot bear to think of the pain I have caused you and the pain which I know I could bring you in the future, but please, please, my darling, stay with me. Love me, keep me in the safety and shelter of your love . . .'

Her anguish was almost more than Annie could bear but she stood, transfixed by the love and suffering of Tessa Greenwood, unable to leave her friend to endure that suffering alone. And yet it seemed to be an intrusion to watch it, a violation of the privacy which was a sacred thing to Annie.

But still she stood, and waited.

'Will . . . Will, listen to me . . .' Tessa bent her head and her tears flowed again, soaking into Will's lifeless hair, washing across his forehead and thick eyebrows, from her eyes to his, dewing his eyelashes. His cheek was turned to her breast, resting there in the peaceful attitude of a sleeping child, and neither woman saw the flicker of his eyelids as the tears of the woman who loved him bathed and soothed their dryness.

'Please, Will, don't let me lose you again . . . I love you so much. My need is more than I can withstand . . . without you I am useless.' Her voice was broken and desperate. 'There is no one but you in my heart . . . only you . . .' And she buried her face in his hair and held him to her as she rocked in desolate mourning.

She felt him move then, a mere stirring of his head, a tremor, but when she looked down disbelievingly into his face, his eyes, no more than dark slits, were open and aware. They were wet with tears, whether her own or his it did not matter. Her cry of joy raised Annie's bent head and when she saw the light in Will Broadbent's eyes she turned away and was torn by loud and painful weeping.

CHAPTER THIRTY-THREE

'Don't tha think tha should go 'ome, lass? Will's mekkin' good progress an' tha knows I'll look after 'im as well as tha does.'

'I can't, Annie. I simply can't bear to leave him. Not just yet. I nearly lost him, Annie, do you realise? I nearly lost him for good and I must just stay another day, or two perhaps, to make certain he really is on the mend. My . . . husband is not yet home, Thomas says . . .' Her manner was defiant as though daring Annie to remark on it. 'Just another day or two, Annie.'

'Nay, tis nowt' ter me, Tessa. Tha mun stay as long as tha pleases, tha knows that, but d'yer not think folk'll begin ter notice where Mrs Drew Greenwood 'as bin fer the last four days? Tha knows 'ow they talk.'

'Let them. Do you think I care what others say? They have always gossiped about me and my family so I am well used to it. Besides, you're so busy at the mill and with the Poor Law Guardians. You know Mrs Poynton and Mrs Bayly are excellent

616

ladies with the best intentions in the world but they don't know, as you do, what is needed and from what I read in that newspaper you brought home, things are only going to get worse. That committee really needs you, Annie. Local resources will not be able to provide for the mass of destitution which is coming. The American war is not going to end soon, as we had hoped, and relief committees will be desperately needed. So go, Annie, and let me have these few days with Will. As soon as he is able to get down the stairs I'll go home. Now show me again what I must put into that broth and then be off with you.'

It was still hot and sultry and Will had thrown back the sheet from his shrunken body when Tessa carried in the tray of delicacies she and Annie had prepared to bring his strength back. There was a bowl of steaming broth made with shin of beef and a cool egg custard with cream whipped into it. Annie had mixed up a potion of arrowroot rhubarb and honey to prevent any further onset of the debilitating diarrhoea which had drained the life from him, and linseed tea to defend the lining membrane of his stomach. Cinnamon water and syrup of poppies—all mixtures to bind to him the nourishing food which, he complained weakly, Tessa shovelled down his throat whenever he opened his mouth: veal broth, chicken broth, rice, bread pudding. Already the colour was returning to his pallid skin and the brightness to his clear brown eyes. They watched Tessa as she placed the tray upon the small pot-cupboard which stood beside the bed, following her when she moved to the window and pushed it open further in an attempt to allow in a breath of fresh air.

617

She was dressed in a plain cotton skirt and bodice of Annie's and her heavy hair was tied up in an old cotton duster from which slipping tendrils escaped to lie on her white neck. The dress was too small for she was taller than Annie and fuller in the breast. The buttons on the bodice strained to contain her swelling flesh and her nipples were blatantly outlined against the fabric.

'You look like a country lass, sweetheart, especially in bare feet. Where are your boots?'

'I've stopped wearing them in this heat. Besides, they don't quite match my outfit.' She smiled as she moved back to the bed, fussing with the sheet, pulling it up about his naked body, but he pushed her hand away weakly.

'Leave it, lass. I know it's not heavy but even that weight is too much for me and I'm so hot.'

'Well, get some of Annie's broth inside you and you'll soon get your strength back. No, lie back and allow me to feed you, if you please. Look at you. No more than a bit of old stick and a hank of hair.'

'Give me a day or two, Tessa Harrison, and I'll show you a bit of strength, in fact if you were to lean this way a little more and I was to undo one or two of those buttons ... See, already my power is returning ... look ... My God, woman, you could return a man from the dead. Look at me ...' And indeed his manhood which nestled unobtrusively in the dark curls of his pubic hair was stirring, albeit gently.

'Will Broadbent, you old devil, and here I am waiting on you hand and foot, giving you bed baths ...'

'And lovely they are, my darling. In fact I think I will continue to employ you for that purpose when

618

I return home . . .'

' . . . running here and there at your bidding . . .'

'Is that so? Then I bid you get into this bed with me. Take off that fetching costume and lie beside me.'

'Well, really, Will Broadbent, I do believe this illness of yours has been a sham. I think you have been deceiving me and I can only assume it was to get me into your bed . . .'

'Get in and I'll show you how ill I am.' But though he lifted his arms to her and his eyes glowed with his love he had not the strength to continue and fell back on the pillow, a slight sheen of sweat coating his body.

'The spirit is willing, is it not, my darling?' she whispered as she leaned over him. She kissed him tenderly, stroking his thin face with gentle hands, his throat and chest, her love for him shining like a bright candle in the dim bedroom. 'But you must be patient. Eat this broth and custard and then sleep. Another few days, my lusty lover, and then you and I will busy ourselves with such things as you have never even imagined.' She continued to kiss him, her mouth sweet and moist, her tongue parting his lips. He groaned in delight and despair.

'You're a wicked woman, Tessa Harrison, a wicked woman. You tell me to be patient and not to become aroused by all the abundant flesh which is erupting out of that . . . that thing you have on, and then you kiss me like a wanton and suggest all kinds of delights to come. You have the most beautiful breasts, d'you know that? Of course you do or you would not be displaying them to me. Oh, Tessa, Tessa, soon, my love, soon.' He grinned audaciously, his eyes telling her exactly what he would do to her soon. 'But in the meanwhile give me some of that bloody custard.'

They continued their delightful and loving diversion for another hour, lovers, enchanted with this feast of the love which they had almost lost. It had become infinitely more precious because of that danger and though Will was still weak, they were unwilling to part to allow him the restful sleep he needed to regain his strength. Tessa was content to do no more than sit beside him, to watch him sleep, to hold his hand when he awoke, to laugh softly and whisper the bewitching nonsense which lovers cherish and which she sensed was so important to him now. She could not forget what Annie had told her and though she knew she could not discard her obligation to Drew nor go back to erase the pain she had caused Will on that day on the moors, she was aware that she must treat him and his love for her with infinite care. He was made vulnerable, not just by his illness but by the threat to him inherent in her care and love for her husband. She must protect, shelter and support him until he had regained his full vigour again, as he had always sustained her.

'Sleep now, darling,' she whispered, holding his thin hand to her cheek. 'I will be here when you awake.'

'Promise me.'

'You know I will. I won't move an inch.'

*   *   *

Drew Greenwood rode with a clatter into the stable yard, dismounted and threw the reins to Walter.

620

'Nice day, Walter,' he said cheerfully. 'A bit warm but very pleasant as I came over the moor. The carriage will be along presently with my boxes. Make arrangements to have them sent up, will you?'

'Aye, sir.' Walter touched his cap before leading the bay away, turning to watch over his shoulder as his master strode across the cobbles and disappeared through the side door of the house. Well, thank God, he himself didn't work in the house, he thought, as he rubbed the horse's nose. There'd be hell to pay in about five minutes, at his guess. He stopped in the doorway of the stable, holding the bay's head, and Percy, who was applying polish to one of a number of saddles, looked up at him as though reading his mind.

'I'd not unsaddle that bay if I was you, Walter,' he said quietly.

' 'Appen tha right, Percy.'

Drew was whistling as he entered his wife's bedroom, not yet aware of the absolute silence which pervaded almost every room in the big house. Housemaids and parlourmaids, busy about their duties, stopped and looked apprehensively at one another and in the housekeeper's sitting-room Mr Briggs and Mrs Shepherd exchanged significant glances. Even the gardeners turned to look up at the opened windows as though some message was being sent through the still air.

Laurel Greenwood was pouring tea into fine china teacups ready to hand them to the maid who would pass them to her callers. It had been a most trying afternoon for each one had been bursting, positively bursting, that was the word she would have used, to discuss her sister-in-law's scandalous

621

behaviour—was she never to stop scandalising the Penfold Valley? And what would she say on the matter if they should be ill-bred enough to bring it up? She just prayed they wouldn't, though it would have been pleasant to pour out her own outrage at the way in which her sister-in-law continued to flout convention. She lifted her head to listen as her brother's quick footsteps sounded in the hall and the three ladies who were seated with her exchanged glances, vicariously thrilled to be here at this dramatic moment. Surely they were to witness one of the valley's greatest scandals since Kit Chapman had married Joss Greenwood some thirty years ago?

Only in the schoolroom did life go on just as it did every day, calmly and quietly as Laurel and Charlie Greenwood's younger children obediently learned their lessons.

The bell rang in the kitchen and poor Emma who had been backed up against a wall, her face as white as her own frilled apron, gave a small moan. Every maid there sighed in dreadful sympathy since it was not one of them who would now have to face Master Drew.

'Emma, up you go, if you please. The master has rung the bell in Mrs Greenwood's bedroom. Can you not see it?'

'Oh, please, Mr Briggs . . .'

'I'm sorry, Emma.' Even Mr Briggs pitied her for the devastation which was to fall about her ears.

'He'll kill me, Mr Briggs.'

'Don't be silly, Emma. And I'll be here . . . if needed.'

He was striding about the pretty bedroom when Emma opened the door in answer to his shout to

622

come in. A pale little mouse, she seemed, thrown into the arena with a snarling monster which turned on her the moment her head peeped round the door.

'Where is my wife, Emma?' the monster roared. 'Goddammit, it *is* Sunday so she cannot give the excuse that she's needed at the bloody mill. I go away *alone* for a bit of shooting, giving in to her insistence that the whole of the Penfold Valley would grind to a halt without her, so surely it is not too much to ask that she be here to greet me on my return?'

'No, sir, but it's . . . it's Friday, sir . . .'

'Friday! Is it?' He looked confused and an uncertain expression clouded his infuriated blue eyes and for a blessed moment Emma believed that the crisis had been averted. She even allowed herself to move an inch or two further into the room. Miss Tessa had been gone for four days and nights so surely she would be home from . . . Oh, dear Lord . . . from that cottage today and perhaps, if she were to come soon, the master might be persuaded to calm down. But she might have known it could not be so.

'Well, it makes no difference. She knew I was to return today and promised to be here when I did. Confound it, Emma, where in damnation is she?'

'I . . . I don't know, sir.'

'You don't know! Good God, woman, you're her bloody maid! Does she not tell you where she is to go?' He clapped a hand to his brow and turned to the window, staring out over the garden as though she might appear, *should* appear at any moment. 'I suppose she's fussing round those damned peasants she thinks so much about. Making them soup and egg custards and pampering them into believing that it is their right to be fed so royally. Does she never think of her own family, Emma, and what they might need?'

'I don't know, I'm sure, sir.' Emma clung to the frame of the door, ready to dart into the hallway should Master Drew make a move she did not care for. She was aware that Mr Briggs stood motionless at the foot of the stairs and would be up them at the trot should she need him. They were all of them very wary of their master's uncertain temper, sweet and cheerful one minute and running out of control the next. One day, in his remorseless ride towards destruction, he would take anybody with him who got in his way.

Drew turned sharply and the full light of the sun fell about him. He was dressed like a young lord: the finest breeches of pale cream doeskin, well cut and extremely expensive; a shirt of soft cambric, frilled at the front, and long boots called Wellingtons or Napoleons, after those two famous generals who had once worn them. He had discarded his jacket in the dull, throbbing heat of the afternoon and he was bare-headed, but for the first time Emma noticed the puffiness about his eyes, the slight slackening of the flesh beneath his jawline and the discontented droop to his well-shaped mouth. He wore a full moustache now, scorning the long Dundreary side whiskers which were the mode, saying they made him look like an old man. He was handsome still, able to turn any maiden's heart in her breast, but the look of dissipation was clearly etched in his face.

'Where is she, Emma?' he said irritably, his previous good humour completely gone. 'Is she at the mill?'

'Oh, no, sir, not today,' Emma replied then could have bitten her tongue for now she must reveal to her master where his wife was, or find some decent lie to protect her. 'At least, she ... well, I know she was ...'

'Now then, Emma, stop blethering like some old sheep. All I need to know is my wife's whereabouts and then I can go and fetch her home. Surely that is not too hard, even for you?'

'No, sir, but I can't rightly say ...'

'Is she at the blasted Relief Committee thing then? Speak up and come into the room instead of hanging about in the damned doorway.'

'Oh, sir ... please, sir ...' Emma began to weep because, really, she didn't know what to say. It was nothing to do with her and whatever she said she'd be in the wrong. She couldn't tell the master where Miss Tessa was, could she, and yet he'd not be satisfied until he had the truth.

'Now what's the matter, for God's sake? There's no need to blubber, is there? Or is there? What is it?' He strode across the room, his face pinched and suddenly suspicious and Emma shrank away from him, lifting her arm to protect herself for surely he was going to strike her. His eyes had turned the dark and stormy blue which heralded one of his wild tempers and Emma squeaked in terror as he pulled her savagely into the room. 'Where is she, dammit? You're hiding something, aren't you? Covering up for her. Where the bloody hell is she?' He shook her like a terrier shaking a rat and Emma's head flopped about on her neck and her pretty fluted cap fell to the floor.

'Oh, sir ... please, it's nothing to do with me,
625

sir . . . please . . .'

'What hasn't?' His suffused face was an inch from hers.

'She sent a message and Thomas took . . .'

Drew Greenwood became unnaturally still, his face quite expressionless but in his eyes was a look which his wife, if she had been there, would have instantly recognised. A fox has it when the pack closes in, or a deer which finally knows that he can run no more, that the hunters at his back have worn him down and he can go no further.

'Where is she, Emma?' This time his voice told her he would stand no more prevarication. He had himself under control, but only just. Something had happened whilst he was away and he was quite terrified of it even though he had no idea what it was; something he had dreaded for years, ever since he had come back from the Crimea. No matter how many times he had ridden away from her, hell-bent on danger and damning the consequences, he had always known she would be there, waiting for him, when he came back; loving him always, controlling the outrageous rashness with which he frightened even himself, but which he seemed incapable of overcoming; ready to hold him in her arms until he was steady again.

Today she was not here. Today was the day he had known would come. Today he was finally alone.

'Where is she?' he said quietly, hopelessly. 'Tell me or I'll break your bloody neck.'

*　　　　*　　　　*

They were laughing, the three of them, as they almost tumbled down the awkward stairs into

626

Annie's kitchen. Will was dressed in a clean shirt and breeches but had no shoes on his feet and Tessa had stepped on his toes with her high-heeled boots.

'Watch where you're going, woman, and don't push me, Annie. Give me a minute to get my breath, after all I *am* an invalid and this is my first time downstairs.'

'Dear God, are we to have this wail of self pity every time you move that lazy frame of yours, Will Broadbent? See, lean on me and hold on to the table . . . there, the chair is right behind you . . .'

'Christ, I had no idea I was so weak.'

'An' I'll 'ave none o' that language in my kitchen, if yer please. Now, sit thissen down, lad, an' I'll get thi a glass o' milk.'

'Confound it, not milk again, Annie. I'll have it coming out of my ears at this rate.'

'Never you mind, Will Broadbent. It'll put some o' that flesh back on thi bones an' a bit o' strength in thi legs, then 'appen th'll be able ter see to thissen. Tha'll not be leavin' 'ere fer a week or two yet so just get that down yer an' 'ave less ter say.'

'D'you mean I am to have you bullying me for another week?' But he obediently drank the milk, his eyes on Tessa, his whole demeanour, though striving to be cheerful and determinedly resigned to her going, telling her that he didn't know how he was to manage without her. His heart was in his eyes, loving her, worshipping her, begging her to stay with him, to keep them together as they had been in the last few days though his mind told him she must go. She was dressed in the gown she had worn to the makeshift hospital in Ashton Lane. Thomas was to call for her in an hour and their life

627

was to go on, hers and Will's, just as it had done before his illness. He could remember the desolation which had claimed him only a week ago when he had come across her and her husband as they roistered over the tops. He had thought her to be fickle, empty and fit for nothing but the life she led with Drew Greenwood, a woman who could play with two men and thrive on it, but now he knew the width and depth of her love for him. She had had no need to explain to him what she had been doing up there, where she had been going on that day. There was no need for disclosures between them, nor avowals of eternal love. His head and his heart were clear now and ready to absorb the full and lovely gift of her complete devotion. What they would do tomorrow, next week, or next year he did not know. She loved him. She had risked her life, her health, her marriage, her reputation for him and in future he would accept from her only what she could give him of herself. His eyes told her so and she smiled, understanding.

'I must go, my darling.'

'I know.'

'I will come as soon as I am able.'

'I know you will. Perhaps . . .' But she knelt before him placing her fingertips against his lips. He kissed them gently and Annie turned away, leaving them to their farewell. Will was looking into Tessa's face and the two women had their backs to the door when it opened, only the sudden shaft of sunlight which streamed across the kitchen telling them that someone stood in the doorway.

Annie was the first to turn and the empty glass she held fell from her fingers to shatter on the

628

stone floor. She uttered no sound but every drop of colour drained from her face, even from her lips. She put out her hand in some gesture of defence, aimed, she was aware, at Tessa and Will, the two people she loved best in the world, but the man in the doorway had eyes for no one but the couple by the fireplace. Tessa had turned, still on her knees and when Drew Greenwood lunged, whether at her or the man she had been kissing, Annie was not sure, she fell back awkwardly against the brass fender. He said nothing, her husband. He was completely silent which was the more terrifying since always before his rages had been loud and explosive, strident with his runaway temper. He kicked her to one side as she tried to scramble to her feet and his hands, strong and brown and lethal, reached for Will Broadbent's throat. They circled it, sinking deep into the loose flesh which had come with Will's illness. Drew's face was contorted, livid and snarling and his eyes were narrowed, a dark and vicious blue. Though Will put up his hands to grip his attacker's wrists he was no match for the younger, more vigorous man. He had been ill and though he was making a steady recovery, his body was weakened, frail still, his enormous strength and power melted away by the fever.

'*Drew.*' Her scream was chilling, high and filled with despair. Like some old, old woman whose age has taken her spirit and whose strength is too frail to lift her, Tessa scrabbled on the floor, reaching with desperate hands to find some purchase on her husband's steel-like legs. She could hear Will's breath choke in his closing throat then it was cut off and the silence contained nothing but Drew's frantic gasping and the drumming of Will's feet on the floor.

'Annie ...' Still she tried to lift herself, to drag Drew away but he was maddened to brute strength and nothing could break the grip of his fingers about Will's throat. She watched in absolute horror as one of Will's hands dropped slowly to the arm of the chair, then fell to hang limply beside her face.

'Hit him, Annie' she screamed, but Annie was paralysed with shock and Tessa knew, quite calmly now, that she was the only one who could stop Drew Greenwood from killing Will Broadbent. She was the only one who could save his life.

Save him for the second time in a week, she remembered thinking incredulously, then her hand found the heavy brass poker and with her strength renewed she brought it up, then down again and across Drew Greenwood's forearms. She distinctly heard the bones snap and her husband screamed before he fell away, stumbling back against the table, then back again to the doorway through which he had come.

'Tessa ...' His voice was no more than a whisper. His eyes were on her, huge and clouded, not just with pain and shock but with despair. The rage had gone and the madness, and there remained only a childish uncertainty, a need for her to tell him that she was there, as she had always been there and that he had only to hold out his arms to her and she would fly into them as she had always done.

But he couldn't lift his arms. There was something wrong with them and so she had turned to the man in the chair and was holding him instead.

Blindly he turned into the sullen heat and smoky

sunshine and began to run.

*   *   *

The men found him wandering along the track towards Badger's Edge, muttering and already feverish, his useless arms hanging limply at his side.

'Come along, Mr Drew,' Walter said gently, putting a hand on his master's shoulder since they had been told to be careful of his arms which had suffered a serious injury.

'Who is it?' his master said, swinging away wildly, then crying out with the pain of his flailing arms.

'Tis Walter, sir.'

'Walter? What are you doing up here?'

'Us 'ave come ter fetch thi 'ome, sir. Tis gettin' dark an' thi'll not be able ter see thi 'and in front of thi face afore long.'

'No, indeed. I had not noticed ... It has got dark, hasn't it?'

'Aye, sir.'

'And who is that with you?'

'Tis only Percy an' Jack, Mr Drew.'

'But where is my bay, Walter? I cannot return without my bay.'

'Er ... 'e come 'ome a while since, sir. You were throwed.'

'Never, not me, not me, eh Pearce?' and he laughed boisterously over his shoulder into the darkness.

The three men stood about him warily. He had fallen, Mrs Greenwood had said, thrown from his bay in the street outside Miss Beale's cottage in Edgeclough but had immediately regained his feet

631

and run away. It sounded daft to them but who were they to argue? There were some funny things going on these days at Greenacres what with Miss Tessa away up at that mill when not so long since she'd hated the very sight of it, same as him. And what was she doing at Annie Beale's place with Annie no better than a common mill-worker, and in the company of Mr Broadbent who had once been an overlooker?

Still, it was nowt to do with them. They were used to Mr Drew and Miss Tessa and their wild ways and had become accustomed to their strange and unconventional behaviour. Find him and bring him home, they had been told. Look in the direction of Badger's Edge or Friar's Mere for they were the most likely places he would be. And here he was, and poorly by the sound of him.

He wandered along beside them, laughing over something he seemed to hear on the still, warm air. He talked all the time incoherently, and his dead brother's name was constantly on his lips. They tried to help him, even to carry him for he kept straying off the track and was difficult to lead back, but he screamed when they touched him.

It was midnight when they met the carriage on Reddygate Way, just where the edge of town spilled out on to the moors. They managed to get him inside and home to his wife who was waiting on the steps at the front of the house.

'Darling, there you are,' they heard her say, then Hibberson and Mr Briggs were there, and old Doctor Ellison since Doctor Salter was still busy at the warehouse in Ashton Lane which was now a hospital, it was said.

Doctor Ellison strapped up his arms,

considerably surprised at the suddenness with which his patient had changed from incoherent delirium to an almost trance-like state, scarcely seeming to notice the pain he must be suffering. And the watery loosening of his bowels was not quite normal, nor the dramatic onset of vomiting. Drew Greenwood's face had become cool and withered, drawn almost, and his pulse was too faint for the doctor's liking.

'We must try to get some fluid into him, Mrs Greenwood, and do go and lie down yourself for a while . . .' His patient's wife looked none too strong herself. 'Let your servants clean up this . . .' He indicated the foul-smelling man on the bed whom his wife was trying frantically to keep clean. 'I shall remain in the house, naturally.'

As some time during the night, Tessa could not have said when exactly since she must have dozed, she found Laurel standing next to Drew's bed, her hand on his brow, her face pale and worried.

'He seems to be cooler,' she whispered when she saw Tessa's eyes on her. 'Do you think it means he is about to come out of this . . . this . . . ?' She could not seem to find the word to describe the strange state her brother was in.

'I hope so, Laurel,' Tessa said softly and though her pity for him put truth on her lips she could not help but wonder what was to happen when he did.

'Would he drink some of this lemon wine Mary Abbott sent over with her coachman? It is thought to be strengthening and the doctor said he was to have fluids.' Laurel placed the tray on which was a cut-glass jug containing a pale lemon liquid and three glasses on the bedside table.

'He seems to be sleeping and I shouldn't wake

633

him but perhaps I might try some. I'm dreadfully thirsty.'

'I might join you.' Laurel poured them each a glass of the cordial in which ice chinked and as they sipped it they watched over the mumbling, restless man on the bed. They finished the jug between them and the last thing Tessa remembered was the quiet click of the door as Laurel left the room.

The pestilence, carried in the water from which the kind Mary Abbott had brewed her refreshing lemon wine and which was to kill four of her own household began its secret and deadly work during the night.

*   *   *

It was about noon the next day when Tessa began to hallucinate. She distinctly saw her mother in the doorway, her face stern and disapproving, and behind her Charlie told Tessa that it was no use in arguing, someone must mind the mills. She stood up then, leaving the flushed and mumbling figure on the bed, and moved to the window. She was surprised to find it standing wide open since she felt so terribly hot. She really must change her dress for it was wet through with something which had soaked right into the fine cream foulard and it clung to her skin most disagreeably. She lurched back to the bed and placed a trembling hand on Drew's brow but could not make up her mind whether it felt cooler or if perhaps the extreme warmth of her own skin only made it seem so. And she felt so nauseous. She really ought to eat something, she supposed, since she was quite light-headed. When had she eaten last? She couldn't

634

remember. Perhaps if she asked Pearce who had just sat down beside Drew if he would stay with him for a while she would go down to the kitchen ... or should she ring the bell to summon Emma? No, Uncle Joss and Aunt Kit stood in the shadows and ...

It was some time later, she couldn't have said how long, when she found herself on the floor, her cheek pressed into some foul-smelling stickiness on the carpet. Lord, she felt dreadful. So hot and tired. She'd just lie here for a while and then she'd get up and give ... Who was it on the bed who tossed so fretfully? ... Pearce? ... Drew? ... She didn't care really but whoever it was would need a drink. If only Laurel would stop shrieking about the fever and God striking someone dead for bringing it into the house to threaten the children ... Who ... who were the children? ... Robert? ... Her head hurt so she could barely think ... and where was Will? Her dear Will ... she wanted Will, his arms about her to help her up and keep her steady ... Will ... Will ...

It was delightfully cool when she awoke, clean and cool. She was in her own bed and though she felt amazingly weak her mind was clear and at peace. She had memories, small and puzzling, like pieces of glass which have shattered and fallen, jumbled, and though she knew what they were, they would not fit into an exact and recognisable shape.

Her mother had been here, many times, weeping. Why? she had thought since it was not like her mother to weep, leaning over her, touching her face and smoothing her hair back from her forehead as she had never known her to do before. And Annie. She could recall awakening to find her in the chair beside the bed, in the dark of the night, the firelight playing on her dozing face, thinner than Tessa remembered her. What on earth was she doing here, she had thought, quite astonished, for Annie had so much to do on the Relief Committee and with the Poor Law Guardians.

And had she dreamed that Emma had been at her bedside, spooning some stuff, milky and sweet, into her mouth, cross with her when she refused to open her lips, begging her to try, to be a good girl and try? Emma had cried, her head on her bent arms on the side of the bed, her face tired, thin and drawn. And Dorcas. Good, sensible Dorcas had been heaping up the fire with coal though it was so hot Tessa thought she had died and gone to hell.

It was like fighting a way through cobwebs, but perhaps the sharpest, sweetest, most disturbing dream had been about Will. He had leaned over her and kissed her. Many times. Warm, comforting, safe. He had never wept like the others but bore her up to a place which delighted her; a place in which he and she had shared moments of truth and beauty. His amber-flecked eyes had smiled and his hands were strong in hers. He had spoken softly to her, bringing her peace and she had slept in the shelter of his arms.

The light from the sky beyond her window was a pale green, the clear aftermath of an evening sunset. She thought she heard the whinny of a horse and the answering call from another. She turned her head and there was Emma, a newspaper in her hand, no longer weeping as Tessa had last seen her, but calm and at peace. Tessa smiled and wondered what her maid was doing reading at her bedside, ready to tease her for it, to make her jump

636

guiltily. And where was Drew in the midst of all this tranquillity? Perhaps it was his bay she had heard a moment ago and soon he would come bursting into the bedroom, striding across the room to lounge indolently at her side, sending Emma shrieking to the kitchen.

But he did not come.

'Where is Mr Drew, Emma?' she asked, but Emma did not lift her head from her absorption in the newspaper.

'Where is Mr Drew, Emma?' she asked again, shouted, she thought, and this time Emma looked up and the most amazing thing happened. Emma stared speechlessly, her mouth open, her wide eyes beginning to leak tears. Tessa felt a small prick of exasperation for, really, there was no need to be so dramatic. It was a simple question needing only a simple answer: "He has gone up to the Hall," or "He is downstairs, shall I fetch him?" But Emma sat speechless and motionless just as though Tessa had caught her out in some dreadful act of which she was utterly ashamed.

'Miss Tessa?' she said, or rather, asked, as though she was not awfully sure. Her hand reached out vaguely in the direction of the bed.

'Of course, Emma. Who else?' The words were tart and came out of her mouth in somewhat of a croak, surprising her. She swallowed and her mouth was dry.

'Oh, Miss Tessa, darling . . .' With a great surge of apparent heartache which she could no longer contain, Emma sank down to kneel beside the bed, weeping as though her heart really was split in two. She sobbed and sobbed, her face buried in the smooth white counterpane, her neatly capped head bobbing with the intensity of her weeping.

Tessa was astounded. Surely there was no need to be quite so distraught? What on earth was the matter with the girl, for goodness' sake? Perhaps she herself was the reason for Emma's mournfulness. Had she been ill? Was that why Emma was weeping so grievously? Whatever it was Emma was dreadfully upset.

'Emma, for God's sake girl, calm yourself, and get me up.'

'Oh, Miss Tessa . . .'

'Never mind, "oh, Miss Tessa". Get me up,' she ordered. This time Emma raised her head, bemused it seemed and quite unable to do more than stare in wonderment at her mistress's face.

'Get me up, Emma, or fetch someone who can. I appear to be dreadfully weak.'

'Oh Miss Tessa, oh, lass, if you knew how we've prayed for this moment. We thought we'd lost you . . .'

'Lost me? What the devil are you talking about, girl?' Her voice was irritable and she seemed unable to manage more than a hoarse whisper.

'Miss Tessa, if you only knew . . .'

'Knew what, Emma? For heaven's sake, don't stand there blubbering. Go and fetch my husband. Oh, and I'll have some hot buttered muffins, I think, Emma. For some reason I have an enormous appetite.'

They came to tell her then that her husband was dead and had taken his sister, Laurel Greenwood, to the grave with him.

CHAPTER THIRTY-FOUR

'I cannot see him, Annie, and that is an end to it. We have nothing to say to one another.'

'Will's got plenty ter say ter thee, lass, an' 'e'll not rest while 'e's said it. Thi' can't treat 'im like this, Tessa, an' I thought thi was fair-minded enough ter see it. It's not Will's fault what 'appened.'

'No, but it's mine and I cannot just take up our ... our relationship as though nothing had occurred. I brought the cholera from Will to Drew and it killed him and not only him, but Laurel. I have made five children motherless and I will never forgive myself. Do you think I can simply go back to being the woman I was before it happened? I know it was not Will's fault that he passed the fever through me to Drew and Laurel, any more than it was the fault of the man or woman who brought it to Crossfold in the first place, but it was me, Tessa Greenwood, who carried it into this house. It was my ... my connection with Will which brought my husband to your cottage and to his ultimate death ... and ... and Laurel to hers. I am not blaming Will, nor punishing him as you seem to think. I am saying, and you must tell him, that I am no longer the woman he loved. I have nothing to give him. I want nothing from him only his acceptance of it. We are two different people now, Annie. I must look after the welfare of my nieces and nephews. I have the mills to run and the people in them who have been thrown out of work by the cotton famine need my support. They need

639

what I can give them. I have nothing left for Will.'

The words were spoken dispassionately but with a firmness and strength which left no doubt that Tessa believed exactly what she was saying. She was dressed in the deepest black of mourning, severe and unadorned. Even her hair, heavy and sliding with glossy health, was strained back from her pale face and confined in a black chenille net. She was thin still from her recent illness, her breasts, once so full and womanly, reduced to the slender proportions of an immature girl. Her grey eyes were shadowed and almost colourless, without expression as she looked out of her study window to the autumn garden beyond.

It was almost the end of October and a cold and early winter was forecast. Gone was the sullen heat of the late summer and with it the illness which had so swiftly struck the town of Crossfold. Two weeks had passed and no new cases had been reported, Annie had told her, and Doctor Salter was to close up the temporary hospital in Ashton Lane since there was no further need of it. Laurel Greenwood and, strangely, several members of the Abbott family had been the last cholera victims to die.

The trees were almost bare now. The late October sun was very bright on the magnificent gold, copper and bronze of the leaves some of which still clung to their branches. Others fell in bright, twisting spirals, covering the grass in a multi-coloured carpet. A couple of gardeners raked them vigorously and continuously, collecting them in piles ready for burning. From beyond the kitchen garden a fine thread of woodsmoke rose into the clear air and the lovely but poignant smell, proclaiming the end of summer and bleakness of winter to come, drifted through the partly opened study window.

In the far distance, way beyond the boundary wall of Greenacres, stretched the endless grandeur of the moorland. The deepest green of summer was changing to the brown of autumn. The heather which was a dense purple in July was taking on its November shades of umber, puce and sienna and above it all the pale, transparent blue of the sky reached out its loveliness as though calling to the woman who stood impassively at the window and who once would have answered with a whoop of joy. Once she would have called for her mare who now stood sadly in the stable and ridden out to meet the beauty which lay all around her.

Annie sat straight-backed in the leather chair beside the glowing fire, the comfort of it in no way tempting her to lean back and relax. It was a pleasant room, completely masculine for it had been designed over eight decades ago for James Chapman, the great-grandfather of the man who had recently been buried. Since those early days two generations of the same family had sat at the splendid desk and now it belonged to Tessa Greenwood whose husband, the fourth generation, had never entered the room unless forced to it. This was the Tessa Greenwood in whose veins no Chapman blood ran; the Tessa Greenwood whose mother had been a 'pauper brat' come from some unknown workhouse with a cartload of others nearly sixty years ago.

It was a snug and intimate room, comfortable with a log fire, the walls lined with books and sporting prints. There were rods and guns, with a chest for fishing flies and a herbarium cupboard for though neither James nor his son Barker Chapman had been sportsmen they had liked the notion of adorning their study as though they were. But mainly it was a working room with functional furniture for the keeping of papers relating to the running of Greenacres and the estate. There were several oil lamps, a drum table, a fine inkstand, winged leather chairs and beside the fire a round table with several of the latest newspapers scattered on it.

Tessa turned away from the window and moved slowly across the room, seating herself on the opposite side of the fire. Her face was expressionless. It was as though the life, the fire, the warmth had been extinguished inside her, leaving behind a passive, unfeeling shell. Still lovely, she possessed an ethereal fragility which was the direct opposite of the tempestuous, undisciplined, carelessly warm-hearted girl she once had been and inside Annie Beale something ached for the loss of that girl.

'Tis no good 'iding, lass. 'E'll get in ter see thi one way or t'other, choose how. Tha knows Will, or should by now. 'E reckons thi owes 'im at least a chance ter say 'is piece an' no matter 'ow many times 'e's turned away by them footmen o' yours, or that chap you 'ave on't gate at Chapmanstown, 'e'll find a way ter do it. 'Appen tha don't want ter see 'im again. That's thy affair an' nowt ter do wi' me but yer mun tell 'im so to 'is face.'

'I cannot see him, Annie.'

'Then tha's a coward.'

'Maybe. Does it matter?'

'It does ter Will.'

'I'm sorry but I cannot help the way I feel. What

642

Will and I had . . . did . . . was wrong. And now . . . I am paying for it, not with my own loss though that was grievous enough for I loved Drew dearly, but through what I have done to Laurel and Charlie's children. Good God, if I spend the rest of my days trying to be to them what Laurel and Charlie were, it would not be enough. I cannot forget that it was what I . . .'

'Give over, Tess. Can thi not see it couldn't be thee, or if it was tha could have fetched it from anyone in't mill, or from Ashton Lane . . . ?'

'But I didn't. It was from Will that Drew and Laurel, and myself, contracted the fever. And I was the only one to survive.'

'Dammit, lass . . .' The oath on Annie's lips was so completely out of character that Tessa turned her head sharply, tearing her haunted gaze away from the burning logs in the fireplace. Her lips parted in surprise, then the corners of her mouth lifted in a half-smile though the unequivocal expression in her eyes did not alter.

'Annie, really, whatever next! I have never heard you swear before.'

'Never mind that, my lass. Tha's enough ter make a saint swear. Can yer not see what tha's doing ter thissen? Tha's tekkin' on the blame fer summat that's not tha fault. An' not only that, tha's relishing it. Oh, aye, thi are. It meks tha feel better ter blame thissen, though God only knows why. An' yer can tekk that hoity-toity look off thi face an' listen ter me fer a minute fer I mean to 'ave me say.'

Tessa stood up without warning, ready to turn away, to ring the bell for Briggs to show her visitor out, but Annie gripped her arm fiercely.

643

'What's up, lass? Are thi afraid o't truth? No? Then sit thi down an' 'ear what I have ter say.'

'Very well, but I can assure you it will make no difference.'

'Right, then it'll do no 'arm ter listen.' Annie leaned forward earnestly, her plain and awkward face lit with the strength of her sincerity.

'I bin 'elpin' Doctor Salter clear up the 'ospital in Ashton Lane . . .'

'Dear Lord, Annie! Don't you have enough to do with the Relief Committee?'

'What I do wi' me time is my business. Now listen, lass. I 'ad a word wi't doctor an' though there's not a lot known about the cholera, from what 'e's seen this last couple o' months 'e reckons thy 'usband couldn't 'ave tekken it from Will. *Tha* did for thi were with 'im when the fever were at its worst but 'e ses Mr Greenwood must 'ave 'ad it when 'e come to't cottage. There were no way 'e could've developed it so fast and died so soon. Now I know it comes swift an' tekks 'em off swift . . . I'm sorry, lass,' she sighed as Tessa's face spasmed in pain, 'but I mun mekk yer see the sense of it.'

'And what about Laurel? Who gave it to her?'

Annie sat back uncertainly and studied the cold, unbelieving face of Tessa Greenwood and it was clear from the expression in her own eyes that she did not know how to answer the question. Laurel Greenwood was the last person on God's earth to put herself in a position which might bring her into contact with the persons who inhabited the abominable hovels at the back of Jagger Lane. As far as Annie knew she had not stirred beyond the confines of her own home ever since the dread word 'fever' had been mentioned in the town.

644

Greenacres was situated some distance from Crossfold and though she had still received callers they too lived out of town and only mixed with their own kind.

'So you see, Annie, you don't have the answers, do you?' Tessa continued sadly. 'Someone brought the fever to this house and killed my husband and sister-in-law and who could it have been but myself?'

*　　　*　　　*

Her days were full for which she thanked, not God—for how could she possibly believe in Him after what had happened to Drew, to Pearce, to Laurel and to Charlie?—but the fates which, through these very deaths, filled her days from five in the morning until midnight with the demands of her business and her new family. Though less than half of the cotton imported at the start of 1861 was now coming into the country, barely enough to keep her operatives at their machines for more than a day or so a week and sometimes not even that, yet she was at the mill on most days before the factory bell rang and did not leave until the last worker had gone. She was in constant touch with her agent in Liverpool but all that was available was low-grade cotton from India, Chile and the West Indies and every other cotton manufacturer in Lancashire was after that.

Many of her competitors had already given up, preferring to escape whilst they still had a sovereign or two in their pockets rather than lose even those. All the major ports in the southern states in America were stoppered up tighter than a cork in a bottle by squadrons of the Union navy and the flow of raw cotton which escaped the blockade had become no more than a trickle. The distress in the cotton towns was appalling. In Preston, Blackburn, Crossfold, Manchester, whole families were starving and men to whom the word 'relief' was the foulest imaginable, seeing their wives and children reduced to skin and bone, went cap in hand to claim it. Towns once filled with the cheerful clangour of clogs on cobbles, the factory bell and the bustle and noise of steam engines, became populated by wraiths who slipped along quiet, empty streets without a sound as they searched for nourishment for their empty bellies.

In an effort to draw attention to their plight, spinners and weavers, carders and piecers from all over Lancashire somehow gained the strength to march from Stalybridge to London and even, on arrival, to entertain the sympathetic London folk to a concert of brass-band music. Best brass bands in the country, the northerner proudly reckoned he had, and if it gave them at Westminster summat to think on, then the arduous march had not been wasted.

Tessa grew thinner as she shared herself amongst these people who, though they had done their best to be self-sufficient and proudly, fiercely independent, could no longer feed their own children. She and Annie bullied committees into giving further help, if not with money then in relief tickets which could be exchanged for bread and flour, for clothing and bedding, rent and firing for the weather was becoming increasingly colder. They went to every businessman in towns as far apart as Lancaster in the North to Northwich in

Cheshire; from Liverpool in the west to Leeds in Yorkshire, to beg help, financial help for distressed operatives. Lord Derby, at the Lancashire County Meetings spoke of the estimated £200,000 distributed by private charities. The landed gentry had rallied to help those in need, even Squire Longworth himself, who had been much affected by the death of his son's close friend and the bravery of his tragic widow, the once magnificent Mrs Tessa Greenwood.

And in the ever-increasing claims on her day she must find some time for the children who had fallen, with the death of their mother, into her care. She discovered that she scarcely knew them. Though they had lived together under the same roof with her ever since the eldest, Robert, was born fourteen years ago, they had been no more than diminutive figures seen walking sedately in the garden in the care of their nanny, well scrubbed and starched little ladies and gentlemen who presented themselves to their mother for an hour each evening in the drawing-room. She dimly remembered a shriek or two of natural childish laughter when their father had been alive but since then it was as though they were small ghosts, misted and silent, moving on the periphery of her disinterested mind, for what had they to do with her?

Robert and eleven-year-old Henry both attended the local grammar school, taken there each morning in the carriage by Thomas and returned the same way in the late afternoon. They were polite, respectful and serious, determined, it seemed, not to allow this tall lady in black who, amazingly, turned out to be their Aunt Tessa whom

647

both remembered as rather fun, to see their confusion. Anne and Jane who came between the boys were small replicas of their mother with her fine, red-gold hair and dainty prettiness. Even at twelve and thirteen years of age they were too taken up with their own destiny in life which, of course, was to be the wives of well-to-do and important husbands, to be much concerned with the woman who had just lost hers.

Only Joel at six years old seemed inclined to be tearful, glad of her interest in him and willing to be her friend. Nanny stood in their midst, the one totally unchanging fixture in their young lives, getting old now and not really needed but still ruling the nursery and the schoolroom where the girls and Joel spent their day.

Tessa, in those first weeks after the funeral, did her best, if not to take her place, at least to stand as substitute for Laurel but she was herself too deep in shock and despair at her loss and too overcome by guilt to do more than visit the schoolroom in the evening before dinner, to smile painfully and ask them how they were. One day, she promised herself, she would take them riding, up on to the high tops where she and her cousins had been as children, teach them to love the rich moorland as she and Pearce and Drew had done. One day when she was ... recovered—would she ever be that?— when she had put her disintegrated life together again, she would do it. Until then she did all she could to give them a sense of continuity and shelter in their shaken world.

Her grieving in private was terrible and tearing and she knew, deep inside her where no one but herself could see, that it was not for Drew that she mourned but for Will Broadbent. It was six weeks now since she had torn herself from his arms, climbing into her carriage and frantically urging Thomas to take her back to Greenacres. Six weeks since his bloodshot eyes had stared out from the waxen pallor of his face and his bruised throat had worked convulsively as he tried to speak her name.

But he was dead to her now, just as Drew was dead and she must put him away from her, put away his memory as the memory of all those who, though cherished in the heart, are gently laid to rest. She loved him still, that she admitted to herself, but that too would die and in the meanwhile she would wear her widow's weeds, for him as much as for Drew. Somehow she would survive. Somehow.

She became even thinner, like a stick she was, or a black and graceful wand and so withdrawn when she was not at her mills that it was hard to get a word from her, Emma reported tearfully to the rest of the sympathetic servants. She did not weep, not even at the double funeral to which everyone, high and low, in the county came. The Squire and his lady—how gratified Laurel would have been, she had thought—held her hand and begged her to consider their home as hers, and that as soon as her period of mourning was over she was to come and be amongst her friends again. She was an extremely rich and childless widow, the Squire said later to his wife, and might she not now be considered for their Nicky who seemed disinclined ever to settle for one of the lovely young things who had been discreetly put in his line of vision. Perhaps an older, more sophisticated woman might appeal to him. He had always been fond of Tessa and she was most presentable, mixing easily with those of their own class.

She had seen Will that day. Like an emaciated old man, his large frame was gaunt and somehow disjointed inside his loose flesh, his haunted eyes searching her out, his arm trembling in Annie's. He had tried to tell her something with those eyes, or ask her something perhaps, but she had nothing for him, then or now.

She had spent her days in her office at the mill. There had been no cotton for a week now beyond some Indian from Surat, a district in the presidency of Bombay. It was badly packed so that it was dirty, knotty, full of seeds and leaves as well as being short in staple with fibres which broke easily. Carding and spinning machinery had been damaged and at best it was suitable only for coarse cloth and not the fine quality velveteen woven in the Chapman weaving shed.

'I can get no decent cotton, Annie,' she said quietly to the woman who sat across the desk from her. 'How am I to keep them in work? How are they to live? Less than two shillings a head from the Relief Committee . . .'

'An' what tha gives 'em from tha own pocket, lass.'

'Little enough, Annie.'

'Tha's a generous woman, Tessa. To them, an' to anyone that come to thi for 'elp, so why not Will Broadbent? 'E's given thi time ter come ter terms wi' thy grief. 'E's stayed away from thi though it's caused 'im pain. Will tha not see 'im, lass? Talk to 'im?'

Tessa bent her head.

'I can't Annie.'

'Why? In the name o' God, why?'

'We have been through this so often and really I do not think I can stand much more. What is there to say to him that you have not passed on? I cannot go on trying to explain how I feel, what I know I must do, so you must just take my word for it that I know I am right. What sort of woman would I be to . . . to . . . consort with a man who, unknowingly I admit, killed my husband and sister-in-law? Through me, through me, Annie, and we cannot continue as we were before. It would be . . . indecent. No, he must get on with his life in whatever way he thinks fit and allow me to do the same.'

Her face was like a pale, translucent mask, a mask carved from pure, white marble, the lovely bone structure prominently displayed in the fineness of her skin. Her dark eyebrows slanted upwards in stark contrast like blackbird's wings, and beneath them her eyes were the silver streaked grey of the winter lake which was set in the garden at Greenacres. Only her poppy-red mouth had colour, startling and full, the mouth of a sensual woman who knows well the meaning of love. Now it was firm, her jaw clenched challengingly, her expression telling Annie that she was no longer prepared to discuss the man who had once been everything in life to her. She had gambled with the lives of others, not only her own. She had recklessly chanced her reputation, her marriage, her husband's reason, the safety of her family with what she knew to be a killing disease in her love for Will Broadbent. She had given no thought to the danger to others in her own arrogant determination to be with him, to nurse him when she had known that

651

Annie could have done it just as well. And devastation had overtaken her. Now she must pay the price.

'This is the last time I wish to hear his name mentioned, Annie. I will not change my mind. I will not see him and you must tell him so.'

'Tha mun tell 'im thaself, lass.'

'Annie, once and for all . . .'

' 'E's in t'other room.' Annie nodded her head towards the closed door of Tessa's office, her own face as pale and resolute as her friend's. Then she stood up abruptly pushing back her chair.

Tessa's face lost even its pearly whiteness, becoming ashen, almost grey, and her eyes turned to brilliant, enraged diamonds. She narrowed them like a cat which is ready to attack and her voice was no more than a sibilant hiss.

'How dare you? How dare you interfere in something which has nothing whatsoever to do with you? Who gave you the right to play God in my affairs, Annie Beale? Who gave you the right to meddle, to take it upon yourself to change, or attempt to, the direction in which my life must now go? I cannot forgive this, Annie, and I cannot forgive you. You go too far this time.'

'Tha mun see 'im. 'E needs to 'ear it from . . .'

'Annie . . . Dear God, Annie, what about *my* needs and those of my family? I thought you were my friend, that I could trust you . . .'

'Always, lass, always, so trust me in this.'

'No, no. How did he get in? I gave orders that . . .'

'I fetched 'im.'

'You had no right, no right . . .' For the first time since they told her her husband was dead Tessa's

652

face lost its white, expressionless mask and became distorted with her despair. She turned this way and that, lifting her hands to her head and gripping it savagely. She was like an animal caught in a trap which she had avoided for weeks but from which she could now find no escape. There was pain in her, desperation, fear, and yet a tiny bubble of joy formed which she did her best to quench. This would not do, it simply would not do. She must not see him. She must not. Annie was watching her compassionately, understanding, she realised it now, what it was that terrified her. She held out her hands to her beseechingly.

'Annie, please, Annie, ask him to go.'

'Nay lass, tha mun do that, not I.'

'I cannot see him. I will not. You are cruel . . .'

The door opened then and he was there. Will. Older than she remembered him, the pain and desolation he had known etched in deep lines from his nostrils to the corners of his mouth. His eyes, so clear an amber as to be almost transparent, were steady as they rested gravely on her and his mouth was clenched firmly, rigidly, as though he was desperately afraid he might speak the wrong words. This was his only chance, his expression admitted and he must make no mistake. He swallowed and she saw his Adam's apple rise convulsively in his throat. Someone, probably himself, had cut his hair and it was short and shaggy across his strong brow. He was still thin and drawn but his jacket no longer hung from his broad shoulders in awkward folds as it had done the last time she had seen him at the funeral.

'Tessa?' He spoke her name, then cleared his throat and she knew he was as afraid as she was but for a different reason. He was afraid that she would not surrender to him and she was afraid that she would.

Neither of them saw Annie slip from the room.

Her fear made her harsh.

'What is it?'

'May we not speak to one another?'

'About what?'

'Surely we have things to . . . to discuss?'

'What things?'

He moved further into the room, awkward and stiff as she had never seen him before. Will Broadbent, good humoured, positive, easy with himself and the rest of his world, was replaced by a man who was unsure, doubtful of his own wisdom in coming, afraid to alarm her with his desperate need to know that she still loved him. She must not let him see what was in her or he would not let her go.

She stepped back from him, knowing that if he touched her she would be incapable of resisting him, but he took it for a sign of rejection and his face hardened.

'Tessa, you cannot simply mean to . . . to go on as you have done since your husband died? Ignoring the past and what you and I . . .'

'Naturally,' she interrupted harshly, 'and why should I not? There are the mills and my dead sister-in-law's children who take up a great deal of my time.' She had a frail grip on herself now but it almost slipped away as she saw him wince.

'I know that. Jesus, do you think I don't know . . .' He passed a hand over his face. 'But soon . . . or sometime in the future . . . surely, when . . . when . . . Oh, sweet Christ, help me,

654

Tessa, don't let me flounder out here all alone. You know what I'm saying, what I'm asking. I love you so much ... don't ... please don't turn away from me ... let me see your face, your eyes ...'

She had her back to him now, unable to bear any more. She stared, blinded and tortured at the wood panelling of the wall, reeling with the pain of him, holding herself steady, forcing herself inch by slow inch away from the dreadful need to turn back to him, to run into his arms, to hold him, soothe him, comfort and calm his agony with a great outpouring of the love she had for him, but she knew she could not. This man was not for her. Not now. Not ever. She had killed her own husband and her husband's sister for this man and could she live with him knowing that? Could she forget it? Could she ever forgive herself? Did she want to?

'Go home, Will. There is nothing for you here.' Her voice was flat and devoid of all emotion. 'I have nothing for you and I can be nothing to you. I have work to do and have no time for ... diversions.'

She heard him gasp, then there was silence for a long while. She knew he was still there but she dared not turn to face him. She felt the great sorrowing beat of his heart inside her own breast, the pain in his head drumming into hers, the tired and weary ache of his body which was not yet returned to its full strength. Everything he suffered, she experienced too, and she prayed, again to a faceless, nameless god, for the resolution to remain where she was until he had gone. And in her heart a tiny voice, bewildered, angered, persistent, begged to know why she was doing this when all she had to do was turn about to claim the love he was offering her and which she so badly needed. But her heart could not reason. Her heart was warm and unthinking, longing to ignore the cold logic of her mind which told her she and Will Broadbent could never be the same to each other again.

'Diversion, Tessa?' he whispered at last. 'We were more than that to each other. Don't dishonour me or yourself by pretending otherwise. I have loved you truly for the past nine years and I believe you had come to love me in the same way. I came today, as I have tried to come for the past six weeks to offer you whatever you might need at this time of . . . grief in your life. I came as a friend as well as the man who loves you. You are free now— let us be truthful with one another—and when a decent interval had passed I wanted to ask you to become my wife. I can give you so much, my lass. We can give one another . . . all that we have . . . all that a man and woman . . .'

He could not go on. The tears ran silently down her face and dripped just as silently on to the black silk of her mourning gown. The absolute quiet moved on and still he stood there but she did not turn to him.

'I came to beg you, Tessa,' he said at last. 'Annie told me how you felt . . . the guilt . . . but I can see you are not to be moved.' He sounded surprised as though he had expected more of her. 'I was ready to shout and bluster. I was angry, you see, that you had not turned to me. Then I was convinced that I could . . . sweep you off your feet, I believe the expression is, that our love would overcome all obstacles. But it doesn't, does it, lass?'

'No, Will, it doesn't.' Her voice was firm and her

back which was still turned to him was the same.

'Well, then, I'll not bother you again, Tessa Greenwood. I've waited long enough, I reckon. More than any man should wait for a woman. I'll do what you suggest and make a new life for myself. You see, I want to settle, have sons, a family, and I'll not get it from you, that's clear.'

He was gone when she turned round. Only Annie was there ready to catch her as she fell in a storm of weeping into her strong arms.

CHAPTER THIRTY-FIVE

They said in the Penfold Valley that they had never seen a woman mourn the death of her husband as Tessa Greenwood mourned but then the pair of them had been close since childhood, hadn't they, along with that other cousin of hers, Drew. Greenwood's twin brother, and was it not to be expected that the loss of the one she married would affect her more than most? And then her sister-in-law going like that at the same time and them children to be seen to was enough to undermine the strongest constitution.

She'd gone a bit crazy, everyone agreed, going at all times of the day, and night too, most likely, high on the moors of Saddleworth, not always riding as one would expect but sometimes tramping in her stout boots with a weaver's shawl thrown about her head as though she had reverted to being the mill girl her own mother had once been. The gleaming stretch of Hollingworth Lake which was actually a reservoir, called the 'weavers' seaport' because it was a place where the millworkers strolled on their day off, seemed to draw her. None knew why for in the days her cousins were alive the three of them had favoured Badger's Edge and Friar's Mere. Sometimes she was seen on the little paddle-steamer which moved across the shining surface of the lake. Mr Talbot, who had designed her new mill four years back and whose wife was particularly fond of a sail on the lake, had seen her, he told Mr Bradley, standing like a figurehead in the bow of the steamer, her shawl slipping about her shoulders, her white face straining upwards to the moorland peaks which surrounded the lake and which contained, though Mr Talbot did not know it being a newcomer to the district, Badger's Edge and Friar's Mere. He had seen her lips move as though she addressed some unseen companion. It was all most spine-chilling really, his wife had remarked, not at all sure she believed him when he told her that this plainly dressed, working-clad woman was the wealthy Mrs Tessa Greenwood.

But worst of all, rumour had it, she had walked into the Five Pigeons, an inn on the moor where the Lancashire and Yorkshire roads met and where radical agitators like her own uncle had gathered in the old days, and asked the landlord for a glass of ale. Bold as you please, she had been, staring round her at the stunned and silent working men, sipping her ale as though she had as much right to be there as they. Going back to her roots, one fool said, but would a woman as rich and powerful as she want to step into the past, they derided him.

'Is there anyone here who knew Joss and Charlie Greenwood?' she had asked, sensibly enough. No one answered for forty years had gone by since they'd been there and she had laughed, shaken her head and made some remark about short memories before striding off again into the autumn afternoon.

Despite her loss and her strangeness she was tireless in her work for the relief of the Lancashire operatives and in her struggle to obtain cotton for her own millhands to spin and weave but during the spring and summer of 1863 she was often to be seen riding her dead husband's bay on the tops of the South Lancashire Pennines. Great wild thing it was and far too much for a woman to handle, they told one another. Those children of whom she was now guardian would be left completely alone if she did not take more care.

She was like a person split in two. She moved about Crossfold and Chapmanstown, watching over her own workers quite fiercely. Sitting on endless committees with that working-class friend of hers from Edgeclough she was the picture of lady-like gentility, her black mourning gown correct in every detail, stark and elegant, her black bonnet discreet and hiding the glossy darkness of her hair. She spoke quietly but her voice was heard and no one starved that she knew about. When there was cotton to be had and her mills were open she was there in her office, dealing with orders and accounts in consultation with her counting-house clerk, her managers and overlookers.

She took an interest in her factory school, even reading aloud for an heroic half-hour or so from the books which she borrowed from the Greenacres schoolroom. In the winter months she brought great cans of hot soup from the Greenacres kitchen and watched with quiet pleasurc as eager mouths sipped the tasty nourishment and big eyes, round and attentive over the rims of their mugs, became clouded with satisfaction, minds fed and bellies fed. She sat in on classes where women who were mothers of half a dozen or more spelled out 'cat' and 'mat', their own eyes as gratified as those of their children. They were shown too how to gain the maximum nourishment from the cheapest food, how to sew, not a fine seam or delicate embroidery but sensible, decent garments to keep the children warm in winter.

But there were times when she was doing none of these things, when she could find no man, no woman or child who needed her, no cotton to be carded and spun and woven, when her heart was like an empty, echoing cavern with nothing to fill it but the words she and Will Broadbent had spoken to each other. Then she would fling on her breeches and boots and jacket, tie up her hair with a scrap of ribbon and stride from the house as though the ghosts of all her past were at her heels.

'Let me saddle tha mare, Miss Tessa,' Walter begged her that first time she ordered him to get ready her husband's tall bay. 'Tha cannot mean ter ride Jupiter. 'E be too strong for thi. It tekks a man to 'andle 'im. Anyroad, 'e's not bin out of't stable since ... well, only wi' me for exercise an' 'e's full o' mischief, Miss Tessa. I reckon 'e misses ...' Walter's eyes took on a sad and musing expression for though Mr Drew had been a bugger at times Jupiter was not the only one who missed him. He shook his head and turned back to Miss Tessa who stood waiting, not as imperious and as high-handed as once she had been but determined on her own

660

way just the same.

He took her over that first time, her dead husband's bay, tearing away like a wild beast from a cage. She could do no more than hang on and let him, praying that his hooves would not find a rabbit hole or a loose rock in the dips and folds of the rough terrain; that he would not falter as he leaped across fast-flowing streams and raced along the old trackways which had been there since medieval times, constructed to carry the materials of the booming textile trade to and from manufacturers and markets. Up, up he sped, on to the crest of Saddleworth Moor which had derived its name from the saddle-shaped hill which formed it, crossing the railway line which ran from Manchester to Huddersfield. It was as though the bay, like herself, was searching for something or someone in his mad race into the middle of nowhere with the dogs she and Drew had trained to instance obedience close by his heels.

He swerved suddenly, almost unseating her. It appeared to her that he had heard a call in his own noble head for she could hear nothing but the thunder of his hooves, her own harsh breath in her throat and the high wind in her ears. She thought he would stop then for his lungs laboured and the breath from his nostrils mixed with the steam from his sweating coat, but he went on, almost tearing her arms from her shoulders. North he turned then, back across the railway track, beyond the quarry at Delph until at last they stood, gloriously free both of them, and temporarily at peace in the place known as Badger's Edge.

She was slow to dismount for it seemed the stand of rocks was too emotionally peopled by the

661

men she had loved in the past. They were all there, tall, strong, handsome, laughing up at her in the soft spring sunshine, calling to her to come and join them, to sit and dream with them as they looked out over the softly wooded valley from which no factory smoke rose today. Pearce was there, young as he had been when he had died on the battlefield of the Crimea eight years ago, and his brother, her husband Drew, older but just as merry as he and Pearce skylarked like the young colts they had once been.

There too was Robby Atherton, the man her young girl's heart had loved. He had been forbidden her for in his veins had run the same blood as hers since they had shared the same mother. Warm brown eyes, crisp golden curls lit by the sunlight, slender and fine-boned, he had that air of easy-mannered courtliness she had loved so well. Delightful and charming, but perhaps he lacked the stamina their mother had given to her, Tessa, since concerned with his own devastation he had ridden away with no thought to hers. Sadly she recognised it.

And leaning indolently against the tall, grey-pitted rock, his mouth stretched in a wide smile, his arms folded across his broad chest, his face tipped to the sun, was Will. Will Broadbent, a strong, working-class man, as her own forefathers had been, but with the sweetness and warmth of heart of a true 'gentle man'.

She bent her head and closed her eyes to shut them all out for she simply could not bear the pain of her loss of any of them and her loneliness was quite insupportable. When she opened them again she was still alone but for her dogs and the well-

662

bred, handsome horse she rode and she knew she always would be. She got down slowly and let the reins hang loose. The tired animal was not reared for endurance and had raced for over an hour to reach this familiar place where his master had once come, and she knew he would not roam.

She sat with her back to that same rock where she had sat so often before, convinced she could feel in the hollow the warmth where masculine shoulders had leaned against the granite. Where was he now, her heart asked painfully? Not Drew, not Pearce, not even Robby, but Will. No one had spoken his name to her for months ever since Mr Bradley had informed the board regretfully that Mr Broadbent had resigned from his position as managing director of Chapman Manufacturing Company Ltd and had put his shares up for sale. They were not worth a lot in today's fragile market but perhaps Mrs Greenwood herself might be interested?

She had answered mechanically that indeed she was, her heart thudding badly out of control but relieved at that moment that the anguish of seeing Will at the now monthly board meetings had been averted. She had heard, like bird twitterings from afar, the discussion and vote on who should take on the position left vacant by Mr Broadbent, and was shaken when she discovered that she was their choice.

'But ... I cannot ... really ...' she had begun to protest. Then, as their faces turned politely in her direction, her cool brain had asked why not? She had been involved in the business in one way or another almost from the day Charlie had died five years ago, and though she knew she was not yet the 'businessman' her mother or her Aunt Kit had been—indeed there was not a great deal of business to be had—she knew in that instant that she could do it. Had she anything else to do with the rest of her life, she asked herself? So she had accepted gracefully, pushing aside the memory of Will's humorous face as it had smiled at her from the shadows in the corners of the dark-panelled room.

It was high summer when she remembered her promise to herself that she would take Charlie's children, as she now called them in her own mind though she could not have said why, up to the moorland tops where she had spent so much of her childhood. They all now had ponies which the girls rode in a decorous, slightly alarmed circle about the paddock, encouraged to do so by her own example and the assurance that it was a proper occupation for a lady to be concerned with. Though they had not said as much, she knew that their minds, which were so like their mother's, saw the exercise as a step nearer to the grand husbands they hoped to win, perhaps from among the gentry with whom Aunt Tessa was acquainted.

Robert and Henry rode to school on their small roans, quite incredulously delighted with the sudden freedom their Aunt Tessa seemed to think was appropriate for them to have, though Nanny was none too pleased and said so repeatedly to Miss Gaunt in the privacy of the schoolroom. But they were bent on careers as manufacturing gentlemen, as their father had been, serious and eager to learn their lessons so that when the time came they would be ready to take up their duties at Chapmans as all the Greenwood men did. They really had no time, they explained politely to Aunt Tessa, to ride in the narrow wooded valleys, across the wooden bridges which spanned tumbling waters, up the old packways and on to the splendour of the tops. Oh, yes, they were certain it would be grand to explore the Druidical remains at Fairy Hole, the Rocking Stone, the Standing Rocks, Dovestone Wood, Badger's Edge and Friar's Mere where Aunt Tessa, Uncle Drew and the scarcely remembered Uncle Pearce had known such 'fun', but they would really rather go into the weaving shed, if she didn't mind. Mr Wilson had promised to explain to them the workings of a new loom he had seen at the London Exhibition last year. Perhaps another time, they said, looking exactly as their father, Charlie Greenwood had done, smiling but very resolute. She had not the heart to dissuade them, wondering at the same time what the ingredient was in them which had been so sadly lacking in Pearce and Drew.

Only Joel showed any interest in the hesitant invitation his aunt extended to him. She was not used to children. She did not compel them to her own preference which might, perhaps, have done them more good in the long run but gave them the choice and only Joel chose to follow her.

They took the dogs. She had Walter saddle her own mare this time for Drew's bay was too fast for the short-legged cob which Joel rode and when they reached Badger's Edge she dismounted at once, automatically striding to the edge and looking out across the deep clough as though she were alone. In the back of her mind she could hear the boy chattering as he scouted about the rocks, asking questions but apparently expecting no answer, calling up the dogs in a high, excited but unafraid voice.

'It's grand up here, Aunt Tess,' she heard him say, the only person to shorten her name. 'I can see right across the valley . . .'

'Clough,' she said mechanically, her eyes turned away from Badger's Edge, beyond Dog Hill, beyond Whitefield towards Rochdale where . . . where Will . . . But perhaps he had gone now. Perhaps he had left the world of cotton, the broad sweep of the South Pennine moorland, left Lancashire itself and gone to a place where he would not be reminded of Tessa Greenwood and the misery she had brought him. She had not asked Annie who she was quite certain would know, for she wanted . . . hoped . . . that if his name was not mentioned his presence would finally leave her and she would find some peace. One day, surely . . . sweet Jesus, one day the tearing, clawing agony of loss and guilt would ease and she would know, if not peace, then perhaps the oblivion of forgetting.

'Pardon?' the boy said beside her and his bright face smiled up expectantly into hers.

'What . . . ?'

'You said "clough".'

'Oh, yes. The valley. Well, round here we call a narrow valley such as this one, a clough.'

'Why?' She did not as yet know the inquisitive nature of a child, the eternal questions, the ever-ready word 'why?'

A small spark of interest stirred her heart and she smiled. She sat down on the sun-warmed rock and he sat obligingly next to her, his small body leaning quite amazingly against hers. His sea-green eyes, pale and just like those of his mother, were

666

trusting and hopeful and she realised that this child had received affection from no adult except Nanny since his mother had died.

'I have no idea,' she answered honestly.

'Haven't you?' He was clearly amazed that a grown-up could admit to a lack of knowledge. In his experience they knew everything and told you so frequently.

'There are quite a lot of things I can tell you, though.'

'Really?'

'Mmm. For instance, a quarry like the one in the far distance is known as a delph. The narrow bridge we crossed . . . do you remember . . .?'

'Yes.' He squirmed with delight.

' . . . that's a hebble and that clearing on the far side of the clough is a royd.' His face gazed up into hers earnestly, then turned in the direction of her pointing finger.

'Why?'

'Because we're in Lancashire.'

'But why?'

She began to laugh and instinctively her arm went about his narrow shoulders and hugged him to her. He wriggled even closer and she knew a moment of unexpected delight at the warmth and contact of her body with that of another human being. A small, defenceless human being who was looking at her as though she was as much a pleasure to him as he was to her.

'Most of the places in Lancashire came by their name because of what was done there, or sold there,' she explained, gaining great satisfaction from his rapt attention.

'Really.' His lips parted in awe and admiration

667

for this clever and very beautiful aunt of his. He had really only just noticed what a very pretty lady she was. The pale, doe-like expression in her face had gone and a flush of rose pinked her cheeks. Her eyes sparkled brilliantly, the sunlight dipping into their silvery depths, and her hair tumbled in a rich, glossy cloak about her shoulders. He could smell her breath as he looked up, his face no more than six inches from hers, and it was nice, not like Nanny or Miss Gaunt who always sucked some nasty sweets, for her throat, she said.

'Oh, yes. Have you heard of Haslingden?'

'Yes.'

'Well, that got its name from the valley of hazels where it was built. Salterhebble came from . . .'

'Bridge?'

'Yes, good boy.' She was delighted with him and his sharp memory and he wriggled again in the glow of her approval, grinning joyously. 'It was a salt-seller's bridge.'

They talked for an hour, leaning companionably back against the stone where she had leaned with this boy's cousins, for that was what they had been since Charlie and Joss Greenwood had been brothers; with her own half-brother and with Will. When they stood up to leave she felt the balm of Joel Greenwood's childish happiness soothe her, and the beginning, perhaps, of an affection they each needed from the other.

The civil war continued, meanwhile, to rage in America where thousands upon thousands of brothers died and their blood soaked into the ground of their own homeland which they defended against one another. The thin supply of cotton dried up completely and all the mills in

668

Lancashire stopped work but it was said that preparations for a great battle were being made and that soon the war would be over and all would be in work again. It was not so and 1863 became 1864 and still it went on, that war which seemed so cruel and pointless to many. Surely the slaves in the South could be freed without men killing one another over it, some said, and if the trouble was that the South wanted to leave the Union, well let them get on with it and then the rest of the world—meaning Lancashire where they did not understand what was happening—could get back to normal. Three years the war had been going on and machinery was rusting up, some of which had not been in use since the end of 1861.

The sympathies of the distressed cotton operatives for the slaves of the cotton South swung dramatically towards the northern states of America when it was made known that since the civil war was the chief cause of the hardship in Lancashire, the people would receive some of the plentiful corn which the splendid harvest had brought to northern America. In January the steamship *Hope* arrived in Liverpool with 1010 barrels of flour from the New York Produce Exchange, 11,236 barrels from the International Relief Committee and later in the month a further 1500 barrels from the Exchange. The food was distributed by the Central Relief Committee and the people of Manchester and Oldham and Burnley amongst many others went to bed with their bellies full for the first time in three years.

The starving cotton families were beginning to take a stand against the grievous suffering with which they were afflicted through no fault of their own and to which there seemed no end. They had been patient long enough, they said, and the war in America which was starving their children was nothing to do with them. Disturbances occurred in the distressed districts, the first noteworthy incident taking place during the distribution of the food sent from America. There was to be a meeting in Stevenson's Square in Manchester and it was intended that the grateful workers should march to Kersal Moor where 15,000 loaves would be given to them. The meeting took place but the operatives declined to allow political speeches to be made about their distress, no procession was formed, the loaves were seized and the operatives went home.

But something had begun that day and serious riots broke out in Stalybridge and neighbouring towns. Dissatisfaction with relief which was to be reduced yet again aroused anger in previously submissive breasts and windows were broken and machines damaged, just as in the old days when the first power looms had come to take the employment from handloom weavers. Special constables were sworn in and the Riot Act read and a company of Hussars was called out to clear the streets. The next day, despite the reading of the Riot Act and the posting of a notice forbidding crowds to assemble in the streets, a mob gathered, stones were thrown, shops invaded and sacked and twenty-nine men were arrested.

The disturbances which took place then and for several weeks afterwards brought the question of emigration to the forefront yet again. Many operatives who could afford to go or were able to obtain assistance had already sailed for America and the colonies, but those employers whose mills were still somehow limping along regarded with alarm the prospect of losing skilled spinners and weavers. What were they to do, they asked one another, when the war was over and cotton came pouring back into Lancashire, as it was bound to do, if their hands whose craft had been handed down from generation to generation and learned during long apprenticeships were no longer available? The northern states of America, where cotton mills were springing up, particularly in New England, were doing their best to attract Lancashire cotton operatives to emigrate and from May 1862 until December 1863, 60,000 persons left the country though only 14,000 of those were from Lancashire. Most of those who had professed a desire to emigrate had been carefully dissuaded from it!

'We'll get through some'ow,' Annie said stoutly as she and Tessa sat with their feet on her kitchen fender, the blast of warmth from the fire reaching up their lifted skirts. It was November and a heavy frost, earlier than usual, had lain a coverlet of white over town and moorland alike and the thoughts of the two women turned pityingly to the thousands beyond their door who had no such comfort.

'Dear God, it had better end soon,' Tessa said and Annie knew she was referring to the war.

'They say t'South'll not 'old out much longer. They've not got resources like t'North. Blockades got 'em by't throat an' their strength's dwindlin'.'

'Like those poor souls out there.'

'Aye,' Annie agreed sadly.

'I never guessed it would last as long as this, Annie, nor how it could affect people so far away. Will we ever recover, d'you think? Will we ever make up all that we have lost? Oh, not in money, but in the improvements which were beginning to come in the lives of the operatives.'

'Millmaisters weren't all as obligin' as thi family, lass.'

'Perhaps not, but a better life was bound to come.'

'An' it'll come again, you mark my words. Will said only t'other day . . .'

Annie stopped abruptly, cutting off the words on her lips as though they had burned them. She watched the soft flush caused by the warmth of the fire drain from Tessa's face as she sat up slowly in sharp, disjointed movements as though her body were suddenly stiff. She turned her head away and stared blindly into the shadows at the edge of the kitchen, then looked back at Annie. She seemed incapable of speaking though her mouth opened and closed. She stood up jerkily and began to stride about the room, her hands clasping and unclasping. Annie watched her sorrowfully. It was over a year since Will's name had been mentioned between them. Tessa had not asked about him. She and Will had both made it perfectly clear to Annie that neither of them wished to know, ever, what the other one was doing and though she stood between them, friend to both, she had respected their wishes. Now a slip of the tongue had brought Will Broadbent savagely back from the past.

'I'm sorry, lass. I didn't mean ter . . .'

Still Tessa flung herself fiercely about the kitchen, avoiding Annie's eyes, turning this way and that in her effort to escape the pain the sound of his name was causing her. Her wide black skirt brushed madly against the table, the chairs, the dresser, threatening to dislodge the crockery until finally she stood, as she had stood on that last day in her office, with her face to the whitewashed wall.

'I should have guessed,' she said at last, her voice no more than a whisper.

'Should've guessed what?'

'That you still . . . saw him.'

'I told thi a long while since that even if thi an' 'im fell out 'e were still my friend, as thi are.'

'I should have known, of course. I suppose I did know. You were always loyal.'

'I'm . . . fond of thi both. I can't choose between thi, lass. It's bin 'ard at times when tha looked as though tha'd never get over it but recently both of thi' 'ave found other . . .'

The silence fell again, hard and hurting, and Annie watched as the trembling began in Tessa's shoulders, moving her head wildly and running down her long, graceful back. She folded her arms across her breast, hugging herself tightly as she turned back into the room. Annie had never seen such despair on any face, not even on her own in the mirror when her family was torn from her in the stews of Manchester when the fever struck.

'He . . . has . . . someone . . . ?'

'Nay, lass, don't . . .'

'Don't . . . ?'

'Don't ask me ter tell thi what Will's doin'. Not now. Tha made it quite clear a year ago that tha wanted nowt' ter do wi' 'im. Get on wi' tha life, tha said to 'im, an' tha can't blame 'im when 'e 'as done.'

'Annie . . .' The shaking of her body became uncontrollable so that Annie stood up, alarmed, reaching out to the woman who surely was

673

breaking apart. She pulled her fiercely into her arms, awkward and clumsy for Tessa was six inches taller than herself, but she held her firmly, murmuring words which said nothing, stroking the smooth and glossy hair which, as Tessa wept, began to fall about her neck and shoulders.

'Annie ... I ... cannot ... bear ... it. I ... just ... cannot ... bear ... it ... without ... him ...'

'I know, love, I know.'

'What ... am ... I ... to ... do?'

'Sit thi down, lass.'

'Annie ...'

'Come on, love, sit down an' I'll give thi summat ter mekk yer feel better.'

'Annie, Annie ...'

She was quiet at last, the empty glass which had contained one of Annie's 'potions' still clasped limply beween her flaccid fingers. She stared dazedly into the heart of the glowing fire, her colour returned though her hair still fell in shining swathes about her haunted face. Annie watched her, knowing that the valerian which she had put in the elder-berry wine would make her sleep soon. But when she woke? What then? Would she want to know, demand to know what Will Broadbent was doing, where he was, and who, if there was someone, had taken her place in his life? Would she be bent on torturing herself as Annie believed women were in circumstances such as this? Well, she would cross that bridge when she came to it for there was no use in looking for aggravation when it damn soon found you on its own. In the meanwhile she would send a message to Thomas at the Dog and Gun where he waited with the carriage for his mistress, to go home. Tessa could sleep here tonight and in the morning ... well, that was tomorrow.

'Tell me about that little lad, Tessa,' she said softly at last.

'Who?'

'That there Joel tha's so fond of.'

'Annie ...'

'Nay, not if tha don't want to but I 'eard as 'ow. 'e was as able as thissen on that pony of 'is. Ginny Briggs was tellin' me only t'other day she'd seen the pair of thi racin' up ter't top o' Dog Hill an' thi was 'avin' a job ter keep up wi' 'im. What will 'e be now ... seven ... eight?'

'He's almost eight.'

'An' a likely lookin' lad. Reminds me a lot o' Charlie Greenwood.'

'Yes.' Tessa's lips lifted in a tiny smile and her unfocused eyes became soft.

Annie relaxed and let her breath ease thankfully from her lungs.

CHAPTER THIRTY-SIX

'Where shall it be today, darling? You know we won't be able to ride out for much longer, don't you, at least not far from the estate so we must make the best of these last few days. The snows will be here soon, Percy says, and that will be the end of our riding until they melt. Of course, we could go walking ...'

'Even in the snow, Aunt Tess?'

'Well, it would be difficult but it is possible.'

675

'How?'

The boy looked up into Tessa Greenwood's face and his hand which was held in hers, shook it excitedly. He danced along beside her as they went towards the stables, wide-eyed and as unsteady as a colt, small for his age, not like the tall Greenwoods a bit, but endearingly full of charm. He was the only one of Charlie's children to have captured her heart, try as she might to feel other than pity and a deep sense of responsibility for the rest. They had been too old, she had decided, too far down the path on which Laurel's upbringing had set them, knowing exactly what they wanted from life and expecting to get it, as their mother had done. Only this one was Charlie's true child, just like him as a boy, though Tessa of course was not aware of it. Sweet-tempered, generous, affectionate, he yet had a strong core of resolution in him which would not allow the others in the schoolroom to take advantage of his size and youth. There were five years dividing himself and Henry, two dead children between them, but it did not deter him despite his smallness from raising his fists in his own defence against his brothers.

He loved it when she called him 'darling' and he loved her. She didn't call his brothers and sisters 'darling'. She belonged exclusively to him now, he knew that with the selfishness of a child and he basked in her love and approval. He could scarcely remember his father but Aunt Tess kept him alive with tales of her own childhood, her two cousins, and Charlie, who was his father, of course. He loved Charlie because she did and his small world was secure and steady in her loving grasp.

Tessa smiled but on her face was that look of

676

strange sadness Joel had seen now and again though he couldn't for the life of him imagine why she was sad. Of course, he knew she worried about the American Civil War and the shortage of cotton which affected workers in the family mill, but this look had nothing to do with them.

'I can remember,' she began and his delight knew no bounds for she had such lovely 'rememberings', one year when it snowed for days. There were drifts twenty feet deep in places right up to the top of the stable door and Walter and Percy had to clear a path across the yard to get to the horses. It was Christmas . . .' She sighed and he tugged on her hand to remind her he was here for sometimes she was inclined to allow her thoughts to wander.

'Oh, yes,' she went on, ' . . . Christmas, and I wanted to take a present to someone . . .'

'What was it, Aunt Tess?'

'What, darling?' She was forgetting that as a small boy he wanted to know everything down to the smallest detail.

'The present?'

'It was a bright red knitted scarf.'

That seemed pretty unexciting to him but he wanted to know how to walk on top of the twenty-foot drifts of snow which she described. He had seen it in previous winters lying over the parkland which surrounded his home, so deep Nanny would not allow them out in it saying they would be 'swallowed up'. He waited patiently.

'How . . . splendid.' His voice was polite.

'Yes, well . . . I wanted to get to . . . Chapmanstown and the snow was so deep, too deep to walk on, so I searched in the cupboard—

677

you know, the one where we keep all the cricket bats and things . . .'

'Yes, yes . . .'

' . . . and I found two tennis bats. I had seen pictures in a book, you see, of a man who lived in Canada and walked on top of the snow and the things he had on his feet and . . .'

'Yes, what happened, Aunt Tess?'

'I walked to Chapmanstown.' Her voice had become clipped now and her eyes had gone quite funny. He didn't like it. For one awful moment he didn't like it, then she suddenly put her arm about his shoulders and pulled him to her, hugging him, and he knew it was all right again.

He sighed happily but pulled away as they turned into the stable yard. He was nearly eight now and it would not do to let the men there see him holding his aunt's hand.

'Have you decided yet?' she called out to him as they cantered up the back slope behind the house. 'Where shall it be? Friar's Mere, Dog Hill or . . .'

'Badger's Edge,' he shouted joyfully into the teeth of the biting wind, for was not that his most favourite place of all? It was where they had gone on their first ride together and though he was only a boy he sensed that it was the place she liked the best. They had sat together through the seasons with their backs to that certain rock since that day when she had first taken him out on his fat pony.

They had watched a skylark soar almost out of sight, a quivering dot in the dazzling summer sky, not lingering at the top of its flight but descending again, dropping and pausing as though it were on an invisible thread. The bird ate the tender stalks of sprouting corn and the farmers hated it, Aunt

Tess told him, but it was grand to lie in the sweet-smelling grass up on Badger's Edge and watch it dive from the sky.

They had seen the wheatear, its white patch looking like a dancing snowflake as it spun above their heads into the languid blue of the sky. There had been hedges where wild roses and honeysuckle grew as he and Aunt Tess moved up in the direction of the tops, and in autumn the sharp scent of heather and gorse and peat, the season of mists, of blackberries still warm from summer and swifts flying over his head to warmer parts than the bleak winter moorland which was to come.

But in the depths of that winter, when the moors were cruel and the weather as fickle as a woman's heart, or so Walter had told him though he was not certain of his meaning, they must stay away from Badger's Edge for if the snow should catch them up there they might not be found for days.

It was achingly cold and Aunt Tess had made him put on an extra jumper beneath his warm woollen cape. He had a scarf about his neck and wore gloves knitted by Nanny and when they reached the top they sat shoulder to shoulder for half an hour, the dogs about them, close and warm, gazing out over the steep clough and down to the glint of water which could be seen amongst the leafless trees at the bottom.

'Will we walk on the snow when it comes, Aunt Tess?' he asked presently, his gloved hand smoothing the head of the dog which rested on his knee.

'I dare say,' she replied but her eyes were far away on something he could not see and he moved impatiently. The dog stood up and wandered to the edge of the rocky cliff and Joel watched as the others rose, following with the curiosity of all animals, to investigate what the first had discovered.

'But will we have enough bats?'

'We can look if you like,' she answered vaguely.

'Perhaps Walter could make us some. If you showed him the picture of the man in Canada. He makes all kinds of things with wood and I bet if we were to ask him he could make us some, don't you? We could walk wherever we wanted to then,' he finished, the prospect of a winter shut in with his brothers and sister not a pleasing one.

'Shall we ask him then?' he said after a moment or two.

'What, darling?'

He stood up suddenly, his face reproachful. She wasn't listening to him. She'd gone off to that strange place as she did now and again and he might as well do something interesting as sit here and try to get her to talk. He loved her, really he did, but sometimes she was very irritating, especially when they were having such a good talk about those fascinating 'snow-bats' she had mentioned.

He sighed dramatically, just to let her know he was not at all pleased, then wandered across the stiff, springy turf to see what the dogs were quarrelling over. They were all milling around just as they did when they came across a rabbit hole from which the scent of the animal, safe deep in the earth, titillated their keen noses.

'What is it, Bart?' he asked, leaning into the middle of them, pushing aside two large heads to peer in the manner of small boys at anything which might interest their inquisitive minds. The dogs, big and heavy, were not disposed to be moved from the frozen carcase of the small animal—he was never to know what it was—which some large bird must have dropped and they nudged him, each one's weight four times that of his own.

His thin scream as he lost his balance brought Tessa from the sad reverie into which the talk of Christmas and snow had plunged her and as she leaped to her feet, turning her head sharply she was just in time to see him fall backwards over Badger's Edge.

*　　　*　　　*

'Mistress not back yet, Walter?' Percy asked, poking his head round the stable door. Walter was brushing the floor vigorously, his strong shoulders pumping as he propelled the stiff bristles beneath the line of horses' heads which hung over each stall. There were a dozen of them all told, inluding two pairs of matched grey carriage horses. When he stopped, turning to Percy, his late master's bay nibbled his shoulder but he pushed the handsome head to one side, leaning on the brush.

'Nay, what the bloody 'ell's the time? I'd not noticed.'

'Tis gone four an' comin' on dark.'

'She'll be in afore long, Perce. She'd tekk no chances now.' Percy was well aware that Walter meant now she had young Joel to fill the dreadful gap Mr Drew's death had left. A year ago they would have worried for she'd been wild and daft in her grief, but he'd steadied her a trcat, Mr Charlie's young 'un.

681

'Aye, 'appen yer right but she'd best mekk it quick 'cos if it don't snow soon my name's not Percy Barlow.'

'D'yer reckon?'

'Aye. Them clouds've bin bankin' up along't tops fer't last 'our. You mark my words, it'll be comin' down by full dark.'

They worked side by side, settling the animals for the night with soothing murmurs and heavy, affectionate slaps on their rumps. Thomas came in and looked about him, then moved to the carriage horses which were his responsibility, whistling through his teeth as he performed small, unnecessary jobs about the place, secretly as worried as they were, going to the door every few minutes to stare up at the rapidly darkening sky. The lamps were lit and all was cosy in the warm, horse-smelling stable. The men's work was finished for the day. All they had to do was see to Miss Tessa's mare and the lad's pony and as soon as that was done they would go to the warm comfort of the kitchen where there would be steaming mugs of Cook's strong, sweet tea, hot soup to keep them going until their supper, the comfortable laughter of their 'family', for most of the Greenwood servants had been employed at Greenacres for many years. Some, like Dorcas, had even served old Mrs Greenwood and Mrs Harrison, Miss Tessa's mother, who were both now living in the sunshine of Italy with old Mr Joss Greenwood.

There was the pitter-patter of light boots on the cobbles in the yard and holding an old shawl about her head and shoulders, Miss Tessa's maid Emma ran into the stable, her eyes searching anxiously into every corner.

'Miss Tessa's not here then?' she asked, although it was obvious her mistress was not present. Her glance fell on the empty stall which was waiting for Miss Tessa's mare and the next one to it which was also unoccupied and her eyes widened in alarm.

'Don't tell me she's not back, Perce?' She put her hand to her mouth. 'Dear Lord, she should be back by now. It's almost full dark and I felt snow on me face as I crossed the yard.'

Percy looked about him in triumph for had he not forecast this very thing? Then he remembered the seriousness of Miss Tessa's failure to return and he scowled to hide his own misgiving. There was nothing wrong, of course, for Miss Tessa knew them moors like the back of her hand and was not one to take lightly the hostile and furious changeability of the wilderness which lay about her home. She had been riding out there since she was ten years old and Percy was sure that if she had the slightest doubt that snow might be on the way she'd be headed home in an instant.

Then where the bloody hell was she?

'Where did she say she were off to, Walter?' he asked, attempting to be casual for Emma's benefit since they wanted no hysterical women on their hands at a time like this.

'Nay, don't ask me. She were askin' t'lad, seein' as 'ow it were their last ride afore ... afore the snows. Where did 'e want ter go, she said, but I didn't 'ear 'is answer.'

'Oh, my God ... oh, my God.' Emma began to moan and flap her hands and the men looked at one another over her bobbing cap. 'She's lost, Miss Tessa's lost and that little lad with her. Poor lass ... oh, my poor lass, whatever next? When's it going to end, Percy? It's one thing after another and, really, why one family should have so much heaped on them's beyond me.'

'Give over, Emma,' Percy said roughly, his own dreadful fear only just hidden. 'You'll 'ave her dead an' buried next an' 'er not gone fer more than . . .'

'When . . . when did she go?' Emma shrieked.

'Well, when did she go, Walter?'

Walter shook his head fearfully for Miss Tessa and Master Joel had been up on them moors for over three hours. It was dark now and when the four of them looked out on to the stable yard the lovely dancing snowflakes which were caught in the lamplight were thick and heavy.

*   *   *

He had landed on a small, grass-covered ledge, no more than eighteen inches wide and as far as she could judge about thirty feet down. She was never to know how it had broken his fall and in that first moment she did not even stop to wonder. He lay on his back, one of his arms hidden beneath him, the other hanging dangerously over the edge. His cape had flown out as he fell, spreading behind him, and his face was pale and unmoving against the dark cloth.

She began to scream his name and all around her small birds and animals, disturbed by the dreadful noise, became still, their hearts pounding in terror, and both horses flung up their heads, snorting, Joel's pony pawed the ground, then rolling his terrified eyes, reared up and, trailing his reins, galloped off into the gathering dusk. Her own mare, steadier than a young pony, stood for a moment but as her mistress's screams intensified, tearing the air in terror, she took fright and followed the pony along the track which led to her stable and safety.

'Oh, God ... Joel, darling, can you hear me? Oh, please, Joel, answer me ... Joel, can you hear me, darling? Joel ...' For thirty seconds Tessa Greenwood lost control and was no more than the hysterical, panic-stricken, useless female she herself had always despised. The dogs wheeled about her, confused and afraid but not leaving her, waiting for her command as they had been trained to do, but in those first moments she was out of reach to them, unable to command herself, let alone them.

Still he did not move and she took a deep breath, fighting her need to scream again, to shout for someone to come to help her, to calm her terror, to tell her what to do, to reassure her that there was no need to panic ... anything ... someone ...

But there was no one there, only Tessa Greenwood who must climb down to Joel and carry him up to safety. He was hurt, even from here she could see he was hurt ... not badly, God, please not badly ... and she must get down to him, now, now ... She had no rope, and if he should awake and move ... no, he was not dead ... *he was not dead* ... she would not *let* him be dead ... he could fall further, go over the ledge and down into ... down ... *No! No!* ... she would not let him ...

She flung off her cloak so that it would not impede her, leaving it lying carelessly on the edge and one of the dogs went to lie down on it, guarding it fiercely for it was hers. She did not look

685

down but turned her back on the depths behind her. Her gloved hands ... she should have taken her gloves off for a firmer grip on the rocks ... there was no time to turn back now. There were rocks which were deeply imbedded in the turf at the edge of the drop and with the abyss clutching at her back, dragging her down into it, she clung to them, feeling carefully for a foothold. She found one, then another, each boot planted firmly in some small crevice.

'I'm coming, darling,' she called out again and again as her fingers clawed the rough gritstone rock, glad now of her gloves for her flesh would have been torn to pieces on its sharpness, thanking the fates which had decided that Joel should not fall in the softer shale for had he done so he would have gone straight to the bottom of the clough. Her heart pounded and threatened to break out of her rib cage and she was bathed in the sweat of fear.

'Joel,' she panted, 'I'm coming, don't move, sweetheart.' Her boots slipped on a patch of wet rock and she almost went down. *Wet?* How could it be wet? And then she felt the snowflakes rest lightly on her cheek, then more on her eyelashes and she blinked despairingly. She was almost there, surely? She dare not look down, only up and the edge of the cliff was very high above her head. It was outlined against the dark grey of the sky and from the sky the dread pattern of the slowly whirling snow danced above her, coming to rest on her upturned face.

'No, God, no, not now. Haven't you done enough? Let me at least get down to him. Don't let it snow now, God.' She stared with hatred up into the malevolent heavens as she screamed out His

686

name.

She didn't know how long it was before her booted feet felt the grass which lined the narrow shelf. Even when she reached it she knew she must be careful for it was only as wide as Joel himself and she would have little room to manoeuvre. Somehow, when she had satisfied herself that he was alive . . . *and he was alive* . . . that he was not badly hurt . . . oh, why did he not cry out to her? . . . she must get him up the cliff and on to the back of her mare, yes, her mare for she was more placid than Joel's little pony. Please God, help me . . . and she began to inch her way along the couple of feet of ledge which separated her from Joel.

*   *   *

Annie was just about to leave the emptying mill yard when Mr Drew's handsome bay clattered through the opened gates. Walter was on his back, his face as white as the snow which had begun to stick between the cobbles and to the rough bricks of the factory wall. She had been in conference with Mrs Poynton and Mrs Bayly, discussing the possibility of those unemployed mill women who had become good, plain needlewomen in the three years they had been at it, making simple garments such as infants' underclothes and selling them to the good-class shops in Manchester or Oldham. There would be nothing fancy but fine cloth and well made, aimed at the middle-class mother, and if she could find a market might it not open up another avenue of work for them, even when the war was over?

She was startled when Tessa's groom loomed out

of the growing dark and was ready to be sharp with him but his words stopped hers.

'Tis Miss Tessa an't little lad.' A crowd of men had gathered about them, jostling one another to hear what Walter Hobson was saying. Must be serious for he looked as though he'd seen a bloody ghost.

Annie thought her heart would stop beating and never start again. Though she was only half-aware of it she realised at that moment the strength of the loving bond which lay between her and Tessa Greenwood and how desolate she would be to lose her.

'What . . . ?'

'I'm lookin' fer men to search . . .'

'Search? Dear God, Walter Hobson, speak up man. What's 'appened?'

'Miss Tessa, 'er an' the lad are lost on't moor. Their animals come in not ten minutes since. There's only an 'andful o' strong men at Greenacres, Mr Briggs an' old Jonathan's past it an' . . .'

'Will yer stop babblin' yer fool. Where on't moor?'

'We don't know, lass.'

'*Tha don't know!* 'Ow in God's name are thi ter find 'em then?'

'We don't know that either, lass.'

'Well, don't just stand there. Get these men organised inter groups, then ride on to t'other mills an' fetch all the men there. And on't way shout tha damned 'ead off an' tell every man tha meet ter come ter Chapmans. Able-bodied men . . . that's if there are any left,' she said bitterly, 'an' when tha've done that come right back 'ere. There's
688